W9-CFM-890

YOCONA
PUFF ADDER

YOCONA
PUFF ADDER

GERALD
INMON

TO JAN:

I SURE HAVE ENJOYED MEETING

Y'ALL.

GO WITH CHRIST,

Taylor House
Publishing
OXFORD, MISSISSIPPI

Gerald P. Inmon

Although the author and publisher have made every effort to ensure the accuracy and completeness of information contained in this book, we assume no responsibility for errors, inaccuracies, omissions, or any inconsistency herein. Any slighting of people, places, or organizations is unintentional. Although "Faction" is inspired by actual events and resemblance to real people, this book is a work of fiction.

FIRST EDITION
First printing 2006
ISBN-13: 978-0-9774864-3-4
ISBN-10: 0-9774864-3-5
LCCN: 2005909605

ATTENTION CORPORATIONS, UNIVERSITIES, COLLEGES, AND PROFESSIONAL ORGANIZATIONS: Quantity discounts are available on bulk purchases of this book for educational, gift purposes, or as premiums for increasing magazine subscriptions or renewals. Special books or book excerpts can also be created to fit specific needs. For information, please contact Patricia A. Vining, Taylor House Publishing.

Dedication

THIS BOOK IS DEDICATED to the Taylor Sisters:

Emily, my dear Schoolmarm Mother, who loved me no matter how often I screwed up and kept encouraging me to be bigger than the things that bothered me;

Aunt Kathleen, the University of Mississippi English Professor who set the example for all of us...and who was our Southern Baptists' closest thing to a Nun; and to my

Aunt Margie, the WWII Registered Nurse of the U.S. Army Medical Corps, who put up with me during some of the summers of my childhood...and even yet, has just edited this book as hard as I wrote it.

C.B.'s Auntay promises, "'At's jus' th' way it bees. Wouldn't be no Heaben a'tall if'n we wadn't gon' know one 'nother...come time to gather up yonder."

Acknowledgments

THANKS TO THE FOLLOWING individuals for their various contributions to improving this manuscript:

Dr. Frank Anderson
Mr. Larry Brown
Ms. Margarite Brown
Ms. Kaye Bryant
Dr. Allan Burns
Mr. Kevin Cozart
Ms. Emily Foster (illustrator)
Dr. David Galef
Lt. Col. Steven Gray
Ms. Kate Gunn
Mr. Barry Hannah
Ms. Emily Inmon
Mr. Michael Inmon
Ms. Patricia Inmon
Ms. Judy Jones
Mr. Randall Kenan
Ms. Jo Middleton
Ms. Jo Dale Mistilis
Dr. T. J. Ray
Ms. Darcey Steinke
Mr. Curtis Wilke

Contents

I:
Charlie Boy

AS 1954's JANUARY MORNING sun brings vapors out of the Mississippi ground, an unseasonable warmth and high humidity hang a haze over my near-sacred circle. In reverent posture, I kneel again on a smooth, bare surface of my backyard.

"Come on, God, don't stubborn-up on me now. It's half-past time you…. Excuse me, Lord. I didn't aim to talk to You that way. Please just help my taw knock that green cat-eye out of the ring. Then I'll know You're for real…and You could stop her inside there where I can finish off the rest of them by myself. Thank you, Jesus, Amen."

It's a three-foot wide grassless ring where I play and pray. With Cocoa, my favorite marble, and prayer failing me, I'm guessing some colors don't really make better shooters than others after all.

Dampness from the soil soaks through double-padded knees of well-worn, oft-washed Sears and Roebuck jeans. I think how strange it is that I can't actually smell the dirt until my pants legs pick it up and somehow bring the odor into its own.

Considering all the teachings and talk from Sunday schools past, I think I'll give this procedure for prayer another shot. I'd hate to think all that training went to waste.

"Lord, forget the marbles. Let's try something bigger and better. You know how sad and lonely I've been since my best friend moved away to Pascagoula. You've got to understand how bad I need a buddy. Please give me one good friend. Amen again."

Casting out with the confidence of conviction, I lift my head, open my eyes, and look straight forward to fish for reaffirmed faith.

"Gol-lee!" It worked, sort of, I guess…but not exactly what I was praying for.

Through the dormant grapevine and privet hedge intermingled with chicken-wire fence, a little Negro is staring at me. With his log-roller eyes and big ears, all he needs is a lantern and a fishing pole to look like one of those lawn jockey statues I've seen in front of the big houses in Holly Springs. Instead of a crew cut or haircut like everybody else's, he has an unkempt and kinky head of hair.

As a broad grin across the stranger's round face snickers into laughter, I realize this guy must think he's caught me talking to myself. My ears heat up, and I feel myself turning embarrassment red. All I can come up with is the idea of going on the attack.

"Who are you, and how old are you?"

"I'm Charlie Boy," he proudly states, "an' I'm seben."

"Charlie...Boy? What kinda name is that?"

"Good as yourn I bet. Who was you talkin' to, anyways?"

"I was just asking for a friend. My name's Scott, and I'm seven, too."

He steps forward enough to be no longer half hidden and be where I can size him up. He's a good head shorter than I am. Solid and squat, he's kind of paunchy like a bulldog...and might outweigh me, all told.

"Is Charlie Boy your God-given name?"

"Uh...well, I ain't sure what you talkin' 'bout. My Auntay calls me C.B. What you mean—God-giben?"

Hearing that he knows so little about God, I go on to explain. "It's the name on your papers from the hospital, and what's an Auntay, anyway?"

"I wadn't born at no hospital. My Auntay's th' one I stays with. An' how come you always ax two questions 'fore anyone can eben answer th' first one?"

"Had a good teacher, I reckon. My Granna's always telling me to think before I talk and how if something's worth doing a'tall, you ought to be able to kill two birds with one stone."

"My Auntay says 'at too," he claims.

"You know how to shoot marbles or not?"

"Don't look like there'd be nothin' much to it, to me."

"Come on over here then, Charlie Boy. We'll see what you got."

Abandoning the shadows of the restaurant called The Mansion, Charlie Boy crawls through the gap in the bottom of my fence and edges through a sparse spot in the privet hedge. With a bowlegged walk and holding his head up in cocky boldness, the Negro enters my yard. He's probably thinking his negotiation of the fence and hedge is something I don't do ten times a day myself.

"I got on what Auntay calls my prayer meetin' tennis shoes, with holy-soles to 'em," Charlie Boy takes up for himself.

Instead of laughing, I try to think of something funny to say back. When I draw a blank, I'm left standing, staring and no doubt looking stupid. As he reaches my marble ring, I notice he has a strange smell to him, like a mixture of barbecued potato chips and sardines. I suppose he smells like that even after he's had his bath. He's black-dark…all over. I wonder what color his thing is.

"You go first," he suggests, widening his smile.

Seeing such a full set of perfect, milk-white teeth makes me want to put my hand over my mouth when I talk. I'm not thinking I'm any better than him…just different, and right now, my choice of playmates looks like it's him or nobody.

I secure Cocoa. Her two-toned brown color suits me more than all the fancier mixtures of the latest models. She is uniquely mine and has earned her nicks and scratches from many days of intimate contact. She has a warmer and better feel than the hard and shiny newfangled marbles. No longer slippery and smooth, my taw's little miniature craters provide for good finger friction.

Putting my wrist into the motion, I shoot extra hard. Cocoa is a finesse marble, as opposed to being a power marble. She collides with a fat, gaudy-gray striped log-roller and breaks into two nearly equal parts. I don't want my newfound friend tagging me as a crybaby, but he has no idea how much Cocoa means…uh, meant to me.

Candy and rubber soldiers aside, marbles are serious business in my world. Trying to re-absorb my tears is about like trying to stop the rain before it hits the ground. Not able to calm my quivering lips, I realize I need to divert attention from my emotions. And now that my beloved Cocoa is stone-dead and no longer in the taw pool, it really doesn't matter which marble he selects.

"Go ahead on, Charlie Boy. Take you a turn," I urge. "Pick you out a shooter from the ring."

Charlie Boy grabs a blue aggie and looks up to see if his selection meets with my approval. I give him a slight nod that it's a good pick.

"We're not playing for keeps, since you're not bringing nothing to the ring," I announce.

"All right," he agrees.

He hunkers down, and I think he's about ready to shoot. Instead, he bows up and shakes his hand around with the marble in it as if he's fixing to roll dice. I've never seen such a totally non-marble-like warm-up maneuver, but I'm pleased with his honesty about marble shooting being new to him. While it gives me a seldom-felt air of confidence, it also dawns on me that I'd probably be trying to bluff him if the tables were turned. That's not such a good feeling.

The layout of black silt loam underneath us makes our targets look small. Charlie Boy's eyebrows lift. Knobby wrists stick out from shirt sleeves that are too short. His pudgy fingers fumble the marble off a bony knuckle. He laughs and breaks out in a good-natured smile. When he tries again and gets off a shot, Ol' Blue misses everything in sight. With all the agility of one of Granna's geese on ice, Charlie Boy waddles across the ring.

"Hold it!" I demand. "Gee-whiz, you can't step in the ring like that."

He looks at me as if his pride has just been destroyed.

"You have to go around," I explain.

"How come?" He lumbers back around with his shooter.

"It's just one of those things. You know, like a rule. It's probably to make sure you don't kick the marbles and ruin the game when you get behind. And you're for sure fixing to get behind. Now, go ahead and take you a third try. I'm more'n fair."

Charlie Boy's third effort is almost as clumsy as his first. Barely rolling across my personal shooting gallery, his shooter doesn't come close enough even to scare a marble.

"Shooters get to keep shooting as long as they don't miss," I inform my opponent. "Here's how it's done." I clear out about half of the marbles before missing.

"Scott, you th' best I ever seed at shootin' marbles."

Being called by my first name and given such praise from somebody I just met seems strange but good. Maybe he likes me and wants to be friends.

"Well, thank you. It comes from lots of practice."

I notice Granna Taylor looking out a window from the back room. Seeing me see her, she pretends to be straightening her red and white-checkered curtains. They're hand-sewn. Since Mom died, the Singer sewing machine has done nothing but sit, collect dust, and look black and spidery. Even though it's been seven years, Dad still won't let Granna touch some of Mom's stuff. Then, too, I think Granna just likes the old-fashioned way for doing things like sewing.

Peeking out a mid-high windowpane, she looks like the integral part of the pawn-to-king's-four chess move. She's a straight up lady, tall, thin, and small waisted for her broad shoulders. If her long silver hair weren't twisted up in such a swirly knot, it'd probably be drawn back in a bun. In a rare but memorable compliment from my grandfather, he once told her that she missed a fine chance at being a totem pole. I've also heard him say she does women well all over.

"Charlie Boy," I whisper, "act like you....uh-oh."

"What is it?"

"Act like you don't see those two grown-ups over there in the house behind you."

"Huh?" He turns and looks.

My father has joined Granna. Now they are both in a hard stare at us. Charlie Boy turns back so quickly I assume he was caught looking.

"How come I ain't 'sposed to see 'em?" he asks.

"Because I don't want Dad running you off before I can teach you how to shoot marbles."

Dad's standing there, solidly squared off, with Granna talking to him. He's holding his elbow in his hand and propping his chin with his fist. It looks as if he's guarding his own windowpanes...but his would be squares on a checkerboard. Granna won't play checkers with him or any of the other taxi drivers, and they won't play chess with her. Right now, I'm thinking the most troubling move for either of them is what to say about Charlie Boy's presence in my marble game.

"Then, don't you be a'lookin' at my Auntay," my new friend comes back.

"What?" I ask.

"Don't look, but she's standin' over yonder behind Th' Mansion rest'rant, takin' a break an' gawkin' at us like she's a mite put out fer me bein' over here."

I peer right over. Sure enough—a large, thickset colored woman is standing out back of the restaurant. Silhouetted by The Mansion's white wall, her middle sticks out like a fish-belly. Her whole body looks to be squeezed into the teal blue dress. She's got a matching hat that's shaped like a big envelope. From her stare, I agree with Charlie Boy's call that she's none too happy. I glance back at my Dad. He now appears to be laying down the law to Granna over something...and I don't doubt it's got to do with my answered prayer.

Curious about this double first name, I ask, "What are you going to do when you grow up and people are still calling you Charlie Boy?"

"That's when I'm short'nin' it an' lettin' 'em call me C.B., all right?"

"Yeah, that'll work. I'm gonna call you C.B. now. Okay?"

"Uh...all right." He grins and rolls Ol' Blue around in his hand again...blowing on it, of all things.

"And you can call me Mr. Scott."

"What kinda deal is 'at?" he snorts. "You ain't old enough to be no Mister, yet. 'Sides, you said you wanted a friend. What kinda friend'd I be if I's to be callin' you Mister while we both kids an' ever'thing?"

"I was joking you. You can call me Scott."

"'At's better."

"Listen, C.B."

"What?"

"Your Auntay's calling you."

He peeks over at her. A high-pitched and demanding voice is coming across the parking lot from The Mansion. C.B.'s Auntay stops smoothing out the wrinkles on her big white apron and motions for him to join her. He looks me square in the eyes and forms a curious expression.

"Nigger pile!" he yells.

Quicker than a flying squirrel bites, C.B. jumps in the middle of the ring and scoops up two handfuls of marbles. I watch in shock as he laughs like a turkey cackles and then plows through the hedge to dive and slide head first under the gap in the fence. Running toward The Mansion, he looks back over his shoulder with the grin that I thought I had liked...his fat and greedy fists now hoarding my marbles.

As much as I want to chase Charlie Boy down and clobber him, I don't want to reveal to my father what has just happened. There will be another day. To my surprise, it feels sorta good to find Granna's cool temperament in me instead of Dad's hot temper.

The remainder of the day moves slowly until evening sucks the sun down behind the Methodist Church. As the winter winds die for a day, the time has come when I'm glad to be home. I walk halfway around the old two-story, red brick house and climb the steps. Despite Dad's cab being parked at the curb, my front porch becomes a ship. With my yard the sea, from the double-wide white rocker, I can almost taste the salty air. I'm riding a whaler boat and hunting by harpoon, but the murmuring of a screech-owl from a nearby willow oak reminds me that I'm really in dry dock at Oxford, Mississippi.

Granna is probably still here. She generally stays with me until my father is through taxiing for the day. Since child-birthing carried Mother to the better life, Granna makes lunch and supper for Dad and me. Then she'll go to her home and tend the evening meal and other chores for Papa and herself, probably eating a little at both places instead of a lot at either.

When the dark and cold of the night team up to push me inside, I no sooner get in the front door than I hear Dad's loud and angry voice. Most times Granna doesn't confront him enough to argue back. When she does stand up to him, she's as likely as not to come out ahead. With the living room door half closed, I stop to listen in the hall. Perfecting an eavesdrop in case I am seen, I pretend to be straightening up a painting of "The Last Supper."

"What's he thinking about?" Dad's almost yelling. "This town's not ready for that...not out of my son."

"Munford...." Granna tries to slip her view in the stew.

He won't let her, as they stand face to face. "Not with no jungle-bunny. No, sir...ee," Dad goes on. "Scott's got no need to be hanging around any darkies. Not right here in the middle of town—I just can't be allowing it. There's no call for him to be associating with those no-accounts."

Figuring I've been spotted anyway and knowing I would like to contribute, I burst through the door of elderly debate. Both of my adults stiffen themselves up and look at me the way grown-ups do when they're waiting around to get as mad as possible before they lay in to you for interrupting them. Granna frowns at me and then looks back to Dad.

"Munford, we should just count our blessings that we weren't born colored. We could have been, you know?"

"Well, I couldn't have," Dad states with confidence.

I laugh...and realize I shouldn't have. Granna puts her hands on her hips and glances at me as if I should shut up before I don't help any more. I want to take my laughter back, but it's done. I feel awful. I'm thinking I've betrayed her and all of her efforts on my behalf…knowing I can always count on her to be around for me.

She puts her bad-eye stare on Dad. I'm secretly wanting her to shake her long weathered finger at him the way she sometimes does at me. She doesn't speak. She doesn't have to. Her look says it all. Coming up with an un-Dad-like look from somewhere, my father tries to play the stare game, too.

Granna breaks first. "Maybe if you'd had a brother or sister or someone to play with when you were growing up, you wouldn't be so sour on Scott having a friend."

"Gertrude…wouldn't it be somethin' if one of my taxi drivers heard this—my own mother-in-law talkin' disrespectful to me?"

Dad begins back-and-forth pacing, his speed and disposition intensifying with each other. Despite being crippled from polio, he can push elbows with the best of men. Dragging a near-dead leg, his limp includes a hop when he gets going fast. If you're not used to seeing it or you don't have too good a heart to laugh, it could be kind of funny. People stare at him when he walks. He seems not to mind when one of his so-called buddies calls him Crip, but it makes my insides kind of achy and my stomach tighten up. I just don't know what to do about it.

Granna usually stays on the opposite end of grumpiness from Dad. She'll generally lack the kind of impatience that most grown-ups have with kids. Tonight she's standing firm, uncharacteristically stern, even in silence. Her spectacles slip away from her high Chickasaw cheekbones and down to the tip of her nose. It's a nose that Papa said looks as if it were chiseled out of cypress.

Dad clears his throat, which means he's about to break through the heavy tension. "We ever let the coloreds get out of control, we're going to be in for a fix then. I can tell you that much."

Granna questions, "Do you even know where that boy's from, where he lives, or anything about him?" She leans back against the kitchen sink to wait for his answer.

"I don't have to. I'd guess he's just another little bastard that's been sired for orphanhood. That's what I'd say about him," Dad baits her. "He'll be on our charity rolls with the rest of 'em."

"Munford," she chides but pauses.

Dad takes advantage, "He probably lives in some niggerish shack not fit for a hog, and I'm sorry for him, but that's what his folks ought to been worried about." Stumbling, but not falling, Dad starts up talking again as if regaining his balance helped him decide what to say next. "With all the heathenish rites they've got going on down there in Niggertown, if they're any less civilized, they'd be eating each other like the savages they came from." He stops pacing and looks right at me.

I figure I'm about to hear the final "no." To try to divert it, I start in before I can even think of what I'm saying. "Come on, Daddy. C.B.'s not like that."

"Don't argue with me, boy. You don't be disputing my word. Of all the impudent things...."

All three of us pull out a chair from the kitchen table at the same time. If it's not an amazing family coincidence, I guess it's a sign we've taken up firm positions.

Granna is first. "I can tell you a few things about that little boy, Munford." Her face tightens up. "It's not the negra backside of town where he's from...or up on River's Hill either. He lives across from our farm at Taylor. Him, his family, and theirs before them have all been eking out an existence right there. Whether it's been dust-dry or flash-flooded, ever since there's been share-cropping on my father's land, the Mississippi Taylors have looked after our field hands...just as we've stood up for one another."

"Gertrude...."

"We've helped that family with a place to live and work and raise their kids since before I can remember." She won't let Dad slip in her lecture this time. "You go up to Yocona Cemetery, and you'll find their forebears buried just downhill from our own ancestors."

She pauses again, but Dad doesn't capitalize. "That little boy is being raised by his Aunt Belle. That's right...he's Magnolia's child, and you know about her. Belle is keeping him on no more money than she makes cooking and doing dishes at The Mansion. His name is Charles, and he has a hard row to hoe. He never knew his father and then had his mother leave him behind." Granna takes a deep breath and sits back.

"That's none of my affair," Dad grumbles. "And I can't have my boy getting such un-moral influences."

"Well, I grew up playing with his grandmother," Granna goes on, "both of us grinding meal and flour and washing our clothes at the Yocona River watermill, and I'm here to tell you—the toughness of that lot and being associated with their life hasn't hurt me one bit."

"That's debatable," Dad answers along with a low chuckle.

I'm hoping that means he's giving in a little. Granna's not letting up.

"Munford, let's get down to seeing if the coffee's gonna float the horseshoe."

"All right," Dad agrees. "Lay it in there."

Granna pulls her chair up closer to the table. My adults look as if they're fixing to deal the cards and leave me out of the hand.

"Ever since my daughter died, I've worked hard around here...helping you with meals and washing clothes and trying to keep two households going."

"Oh, Lord," Dad exclaims with a tired sigh.

"Elmer has sacrificed, too. I've been helping you and Scott when I should have been better tending to my husband. Now I'm asking you for something in return. I'd consider it a personal favor if you wouldn't interfere with my grandson playing with that young'un."

"Gertrude, you know I'm grateful for your help, but...."

"Don't 'but' me. Do you want me to keep cooking and cleaning over here?"

"You ought to know I don't hold with threats."

"That wasn't a threat, Munford. It's a promise. If you'll just give an inch and be reasonable for a change...."

"I'd hate to think this is what keeping the peace in our family has come to. The first thing you know, he'd be coming home talking like them and having thieving ways and the nigger nature."

"Munford, you know all colored people are not like that. And I wouldn't let anything like that happen. I just aim to do all I can to help those boys have good, happy lives...without being bit by your racist bug."

Granna reaches for my hand and pulls me out of my chair and over to her for a tight hug. I know for a change to stay quiet. Dad will have to have the last word. I'm not sure, but I think I see a tear in his eye.

He gets up from the table and limps toward the door. Looking back as he leaves, he announces his verdict, "We'll give it a try...but you just remember I was bad against it." Bumping the door on the way through, he mumbles, "I'm afraid it's gonna mean trouble aplenty. You'll see who's right. You can mark my word on it."

II:
Square Looks

MY HEADACHE AND FIRST Baptist's sermon and songs about Jesus let out simultaneously. I wonder if other kids are like me and if other towns are like Oxford. Bad needing to shed my Sunday clothes, I can't get home fast enough to suit me.

Before I bow to my backyard's bidding, I'll have to shovel down a moderate helping of Granna's fixings. We'll have roast beef cooked with potatoes and carrots and covered in brown gravy that's been laced with wild onions. The ever-present something green is likely to be Granna's tri-mix of collards, turnip greens, and poke. I can always count on the iced and mint-flavored sweet tea being as good as it is present.

Another mild winter afternoon allows me to pretend I'm practicing my marble shooting, when what I'm really doing is waiting, watching, hoping, and even contemplating more prayer...all that my new friend will come calling. With this Auntay of C.B.'s cooking the noon meals at The Mansion restaurant, he has a ride in from Taylor if he wants it.

I vow—when I grow up, I'll be rich enough to dine out more often than only on my birthday eating-out meal. I might even buy The Mansion, but for now I resign myself to checking periodically on whether or not C.B. is next door.

On half hours, the Presbyterian Church chimes strike to complement and not compete with the courthouse clock's top-of-the-hour signals. Each time one of them sounds off, I walk up to the winter-brown greenery that separates my world from the gravel parking lot of the restaurant and look.

If C.B. came to town, I don't know where else he could be. Granna's theory about a watched pot never boiling comes to mind, but I can't stop myself from checking again. About the fifth time over, I find C.B.

ambling from side to side. He looks like a dusty breeze working its way toward me. His walk reminds me of how I ride my bike back and forth across Thrill Hill to make the climb easier.

Retracting myself from the seasonally resting vine and hedge border, I scurry back to my marble ring and become nonchalant. Shortly, C.B. crawls under the rusty wire fence and crashes through a sparse spot in the privet hedge. He's carrying a sock with a knot tied at the top, apparently holding my marbles. Seeing me looking at it, he tries to divert my attention.

"Scott, my Auntay told me to ax you somethin', she did."

I know it's just the funny way he talks, but I picture him chasing me with an ax raised above his head as if he's fixing to chop me down for the rest of my marbles.

"What is it, Thief?"

"She must'a seen th' Cap'un watchin' us or somethin'."

"The Captain?"

"Yeah, th' boss man, you know…your dad. She told me to see'f he said anything 'bout if'n he minds me bein' over here playin' with you, an' all. What'd he say?"

"He's never been in the Army. Where do y'all get calling him Captain?"

"I don' know. What'd he say? What'd he say 'bout me a'comin' over here to play with you?"

"Oh, he said…uh, sorta, first, I need to settle a personal account with you over the marbles before that sort of thing gets out of hand. You can't be acting that way around here."

"You mean you want 'em back?"

"Dang right."

"'At ain't no problem. I got 'em all right cher in this sock, 'cept th' yeller one. Good a marble shooter as you is, you prob'ly gon' win 'em back in what Auntay calls a short order, anyways."

"The yellow one's my favorite," I claim.

"I can't help it, Scott. I give it to my little sister, an' if you knowed her like I do, you wouldn't want to be no Injun giver 'bout it neither, an' 'at ain't no lie."

"All right," I yield, "I'll trust you about that."

Looking back from where he came, C.B. says, "There's this kid gon' be over here in a minute. I want y'all to race."

"Bring him on. I'm the fastest boy fixing to be in third grade."

Upon C.B.'s whistle, a light chocolate-brown face appears through a hole in the hedge.

"Who's that? And how many more are there?"

"First, y'all race. Then we'll talk…if you still wantin' to know anything. Matter'a fact, I'll bet'cha 'at yeller marble back against another sock full of 'em."

"You're on," I accept, knowing I've got this race in the bag, or sock.

———————————

AS C.B.'s PICKING OUT his second sock full of my marbles, he consoles me, "Don' feel bad. She's a lot faster'n she looks."

Without so much as a victory snicker, my better works her way back through the hedge and under the fence. Still light-headed at the outcome of it all, I'm made to feel worse when she picks up her rag doll. To think someone who plays with a rag doll can outrun me….

C.B. gives me a look that says he's ready to hear my defense. I'm thinking the race started out as if I could slow up, but then I'm not sure what happened. Unlike C.B., who's barely on the graceful side of awkward, she sort of flowed by me. Having her bobby sox rolled down to her oxfords may have given her some kind of advantage…my just having standard tennis shoes and sox. Her short blue skirt rode up almost to her waist, and her rear looked like a puffy white, cotton heart that was upside down. It was beating every time her legs pumped back and forth. I couldn't quit watching her bottom enough to try very hard to pass her. That's probably what it was.

The best comment I can come up with is—"Who was that kid?"

"She's my half-stepsister, Miss Sippy."

"Half-step's nothing to be calling anybody who runs like that, and what kinda name is Miss Sippy, anyhow?"

"Maybe it's her God-giben name."

Payback demands I'll have to live with the remark I'd earlier made about his name.

"Ever'body says she's eighth Injun," he adds.

"The eighth Indian?"

"No, an eighth of an Injun. It come from when th' Christians an' Injuns got together some kinda way."

His explanation sounds like nonsense, but C.B. and Auntay being black as bottomland crows, I suppose it's got something to do with how Miss Sippy came by such a light shade to her.

"Are there any more of 'em?"

"I got some cousins here in town, but it's just me an' Miss Sippy stays with Auntay at Taylor."

"Well, tell her she can come back over here if she wants to."

"It's all right, Sippy. Come 'ere," he yells to her.

She hesitates.

"Come on, now. He ain't got it," C.B. reinforces.

She pretends to be looking at everything except me.

"Ain't got what?" I ask.

"Th' white bite," C.B. answers. "Don' let on nothin' to her 'bout me wagerin' her yeller marble, or it'll set her off to cryin', an' she'll tell on me. She's a pretty good sister, 'cept when she wants to be a tattletale."

With fluid ease, she slides back under the fence, cradles the rag doll under her arm as if it's a football, and jumps a low spot in the hedge.

"White bite," I'm thinking…? I try to greet her again with my eyes, but she won't have any part of it. The way she's got her head dropped, you'd think she'd lost our foot race. Seeing me staring at her doll, she starts throwing it up in the air and playing catch with it. She can pretend that she's not worried about hurting it, but I know better. I know how I feel about my late and great Cocoa splitting.

"Come on, Sippy. Let's see if you're any good at marbles," C.B. offers.

I suppose he's trying to help her feel as welcome as he's figured out he must be.

"Take 'at red marble an' use it fer ya taw." He points at it as if he owns the place.

She picks up the green marble next to the red one. I'm thinking she must be as color blind as a bat in a double-ended rainbow.

"What's a taw?" she asks in the sweetest voice I've ever heard, holding her hand over her mouth as if she doesn't want me to hear her.

"It's th' shooter," he answers, as if he hadn't just learned it himself.

Miss Sippy tries, but she isn't ready for marbles. With C.B. now ignoring her as much as possible, we play on. When she realizes she's cramping our styles, she glides over and sits under the chinaberry sling-shot tree. Hugging and talking to her rag doll, she's apologizing, I suspect, for treating it so roughly when she was showing off for me. Her pretty color matches that of the doll. It's a cocoa shade I'm thinking she must have gotten from the eight Indians.

C.B. catches me staring at her...and apparently feels the need to explain. "Th' other kids call her a high yeller. It makes her cry, but that's just th' way it bees. Dark black coloreds are gen'ly bad to let on like they better'n those 'at ain't. I know her front two top teeth's come out, but they gon' grow back. Mine done th' same thing."

"Me too," I admit and then wish I hadn't. Although I hadn't noticed her teeth, now I understand why she was holding her hand over her mouth.

C.B. misses another shot and moans over it. Fifteen minutes later, he has learned to shoot marbles reasonably well...but not before I've recovered all except the yellow one. I don't want it bad enough to make Miss Sippy cry.

As I stuff my pockets with the winnings, I think about C.B.'s being resigned to marble poverty. For a minute I consider living up to my Sunday school lessons and dividing them or at least giving up a sock full. The moment passes.

"Scott, th' reason I lost all them marbles back to you is 'cause Jesus didn't want me keepin' 'em...since on account of th' way I got 'em."

"C.B., it was my good shooting that got them back. God don't care nothing about marbles."

"Maybe you right. It ain't like I took 'em on a Sunday or nothin'."

———————

ALTHOUGH DAD DOESN'T COTTON to my friendship with C.B., I start seeing a lot of C.B. on Saturday and Sunday play days. We both have other friends, but they're for during the week and at our respective schools...mine for whites and his for coloreds. In a startling revelation, I come to realize that this friend is not a mere possession I can easily discard, but a buddy I really need.

Midway through a spring day of basketball in my backyard, I'm thirsty enough to suspect C.B. may also like a drink. With a quarter in my back pocket and a desire to be good-hearted, I decide to try on some unselfishness.

"C.B., I got two bits. Let's go over to the restaurant and get us a couple of Pepsi Colas."

"I don't wanta go Th' Mansion."

He throws up an air ball. I grab it and hold it to get his full attention. "It's Okay. I'll pay for both of us." I reach in my pocket and produce my allowance. "This quarter'll get us a Pepsi apiece with tax and all."

"Naw, I can't."

"You won't have to pay me back," I offer, thinking I can buy my way into being a hero. "Come on."

"You ain't gotta spend yo' money just 'cause you got some. Lay it up...or let me hold it fer you."

Not knowing if he meant laying up the ball or the money, I take a free throw. Dead center. When the ball comes through the net, C.B. fumbles it off his fingers and foot and then runs after it. Upon returning, he sees that I'm still puzzled and looks at me as if I'm doing something wrong here for trying to be nice to him.

"Scott, listen up. I done been told I can't go in there. An' Auntay'd skin me alive if'n I did."

"She probably just don't want you disturbing her work none. She won't care for you getting a drink, as long as she knows we've got the money for it."

"'At ain't it, Scott. I said I can't—I ain't 'llowed in there, an' I don' want a lickin' over it."

"Then let's go to the soda fountain at Blaylock's Drug Store."

"Can't go in there, either," he mumbles.

"How come?" I'm about to get irritated.

"Don't you know nothin'?"

"If you want me to understand, you've got to start making some sense."

His belly growls loudly.

"See there." I point and laugh. "Somebody in there is agreeing with me."

He manages a weak grin. "If'n you wanta squander yo' money so bad, we can go to th' fillin' station." He gives me a slantwise glance and troubled expression. "We can get a long-neck RC."

16

After his suggestion of that alternative, I realize how stupid I have been. The message has finally come through. Because he's colored, he's not allowed, and being my friend buys him nothing...not when it comes to getting him in where he can't go. I'm thinking I can see through C.B.'s eyes now.

It's hard even to imagine not being able to go in The Mansion or Blaylock's for a Pepsi. I've seen coloreds in Morgan-Lindsey, so I propose a compromise, "Let's go up to the five and ten cent store and see what the lady's got at the candy counter."

"Okay," he agrees. "Let's see'f you can go all th' way without steppin' on a sidewalk crack. Step on a crack an' break yo' Mama's back."

"My mother died while I was being born," I admit.

"An' I ain't never met my mom, so I guess 'at wadn't such a hot idear."

"You haven't ever met her?"

"Naw, but I'm gon' track her down someday," he answers in a plaintive voice.

I wonder what he'll do when he tracks her down. As we round the corner in front of the restaurant, I realize C.B. and I have lonesomeness in common. We are both motherless and in need of a good friend to make up for it.

"I'll bet you can't jump up and touch all the crossbars of the awnings between here and the store," I challenge.

"Scott, I ain't tall enough, but I bet you can't."

"Hide and watch. Since you can't jump, then you have to zigzag around all the parking meters between here and there. If you miss one, you have to leapfrog all of them on the way back."

"I ain't tall enough fer 'at neither," he admits.

"Yeah, yeah, you ain't doodley-squat. Come along then and just do the best you can."

With me thumping awnings and C.B. semi-circling parking meters, we make our way to the town Square. The Confederate soldier statue looks as if it's fixing to lead a squad of willow oaks and water oaks in a march down South Lamar. Granna says the marble man faces that direction on account of representing soldiers who would never turn their backs on the South.

"Come on. Let's cut through the courthouse. I want to show you something."

C.B. holds back. "'At ain't eben on th' way. An' we'd hafta go 'tween all them men?"

"We'll give them a wide berth. They're nothing to worry about, just a bunch of old codgers sitting and spitting. Besides, they're fun to watch."

My friend follows sheepishly. We stop a minute and watch identical twin old men playing checkers.

"I don' know how they can play 'gainst one 'nother, bein' so alike an' all," C.B. comments.

"Maybe they're not that much alike," I suggest.

"Or they must take time about winnin' without eben tryin' to," C.B. counters.

We walk on. Looming before us are two massive hardwood doors. Trying to bring the courthouse down to size for my friend, I ask, "Aren't you glad you don't have a front door like this at your house?"

"Yeah, I can see me tryin' to get through it in a hurry when Auntay's chasin' after me with a hickory switch."

"Maybe that's why they have such doors—so folks'll behave when they come to court." We enter.

"Is 'at what you wanted to show me?" he asks.

"Naw, here's something else. See how you can make the floor squeak when you walk on it just right? You hear?"

C.B. slaps his leg and over-laughs like he thinks it's extra funny.

"There's another place in the bathroom where if you jump up and down on it just right, it sounds like a bullfrog."

I look back to see if C.B. is laughing again. He's not. He's stopped in his sneaker tracks…and is looking around uneasily.

"Let's go. I want you to hear it…and I gotta pee, so follow me."

"I don't wanta." He steps back, acting as if he's watching for trouble.
"Why not?"

"I can't…an' don't be doggin' me no more 'bout it."

"You afraid I'll see your tally-whacker or something?"

"At ain't it."

"Yeah, right. Sure it's not," I agree in jest.

"You want me to prove it?" He unsnaps his pants. "I'll drop my drawers right now an' show you."

"Lordy mercy!" A white-haired old lady in a purple dress has come around the corner and bumped head-on into our private conversation.

"You boys get outta here." She wrinkles her face up and waves both of her hands in a shooing motion at us.

C.B. hightails it down the hall toward the back door. I laugh and scamper to the safety of the public toilet for men. Upon relieving myself, I discover a better escape route than the door I came in. Fearing the woman stands waiting for me outside the bathroom door, I climb out the screenless window.

C.B. is leaning against the largest old water oak tree in the courtyard. My father told me he once saw the authority hang an unlawful Negro from this same tree. Now my friend rubs his back against the tree like a mule scratching an itch.

I see the outdoor water fountain like never before. It's speaking to me through very white, three-inch tall, stenciled letters on its side: WHITES ONLY. Although the fountain's message is plain to me, I'm figuring it proclaims something different to C.B. To him it must read like a punch in the gut—NOT FOR YOUR KIND!

I understand the cruel and cowardly message that C.B.'s probably been hearing all along. Until this moment, I've never really been concerned about how the coloreds must feel. C.B.'s thirst and his need to pee and even his whole life aren't as simple as I imagined.

Although I doubt I'll ever be able to see through C.B.'s eyes as clearly as I thought I could, I do vow this day to build a strong enough friendship with him that I'll help him. Maybe we can put up a billboard or something on the side of the courthouse to help set things right, announcing NOT FAIR. If we don't paint over the writing on the water fountain, maybe we can put a dead snake in it or something. To think that a person would have to stay thirsty while in plain sight of water, forbidden water…and I know how it feels to have to hold it when there is no necessary room in sight.

It's mean and ugly the way coloreds are treated, and I'd like to make things like that better. Maybe with me being a white boy, if I were to be a real friend with a colored boy, it might help folks see things aren't fair and aren't right…and give C.B. some better hope.

III:
Bailey Woods and Mr. J.

"ANY FOOL CAN LEARN the names of things," Granna tells us. "What I want you boys to understand is how each plant and animal interacts with its surroundings. You see, plants are a lot like people—some operate in opposition to everything offered up, whereas others act as associates. There's always going to be a few that insist on remaining indifferent, but the bulk of the bunch will go one way or the other. Now, are y'all following this?"

"Say 'yeah,' C.B., so we can get out of here," I whisper. Our heads nod in agreement.

Upon dismissal we jump off the back porch of my grandmother's city house and make a beeline for Bailey Woods. It's not that we don't enjoy hearing Granna's outdoor philosophy, but we're wanting to play right now. And her being a schoolmarm for so many years, it's not fair to expect anybody to have to learn everything she lays on us. C.B. says she just knows too much.   A gully separates the Bailey Woods land belonging to Papa from that of Pen-Oake, which belongs to Mr. Jefferson. My grandfather's tract runs alongside University Avenue, a short quarter to the Ole Miss campus and the same distance from downtown Oxford and my house. Due to my living no more than a hundred yards from the town square, C.B. is forever cutting me down with comments like my being city-bred or shit-outta-luck.

Scalping settlers, massacring Indians, and re-creating other sorts of uncivil wars, we come to love Bailey Woods. In our own form of hide-and-seek, a slight nudge on C.B.'s trusting nature is usually all it takes to send my buddy blending in with the shadows. He'll be as ready to spring out with a Rebel yell as I'll be anxious to blow him away with a stick gun. Our personal patch of woods is faithfully there for us. It guides us through our first year of friendship…as if Mother Nature is a substitute for neither of us having a mother of our own.

BY SUMMER SUCH A special bond has developed between C.B. and me that there's serious talk of becoming blood brothers. We even make it to the point where each of us has a rusty-bladed pocketknife resting on his wrist.

"You go first," I dare.

"Naw, you," he counters.

"We could wait on a better day…uh, I mean, a knife, a better knife I meant, one of them ivory-handled knives that's sharper and all."

"An' more better suited fer making blood brothers," he agrees.

ON THE OCCASIONS THAT rain prevents us from being soldiers of misfortune and exploration, a particular problem persists. It's that Dad doesn't want C.B. coming inside my house. Sometimes a colored woman is paid to come in and help Granna with chores like ironing, cleaning, and even cooking, but that's somehow different. According to my father, a Confederate cousin is supposed to turn over in his grave if C.B. is ever allowed in our home. Personally, I would have thought that'd be a good thing for somebody who had to lie around in a casket all day.

Rainy weekends on my back porch are when Granna seizes the opportunity to let her old teacher ways come out of retirement. She's plenty teacher to know how to make stuff generally interesting…as long as her bird and plant books are connecting us to the outdoor world. It's when her drilling and grilling of other subjects sway over to being a smidgen too school-like that we run into trouble.

If weather lets up enough on those weekends, Granna sometimes ventures out and into our woods with us. According to her, nothing is out there without some deeper meaning to go along with it. Plants put on personalities. Animals act with attitudes. She says even the rocks have their reasons. Based on Granna's interpretations, things seem to be where they're supposed to be. They're growing or flying through right when she sees fit to use them in sharing some explanation about humanity or such.

The big message finally gets through. It's ironic that when it finally hits home is when C.B. and I are stumbling through Bailey Woods on our own. The many various plants and birds and other animals from Granna's field guides seem to discover us. We come to appreciate the out-of-doors as being fascinating in and of itself. Finding recreation that's better than play is a major turn of events in our lives.

About the time my buddy and I think we've become familiar enough with every tree and bush of Bailey Woods, a roaming sort of craving sprouts within us like a couple of spring buds. The temptation to canvass out farther than we're supposed to flowers. Despite having received repeated threats from Dad, Papa, and Granna to steer clear of Pen-Oake, it becomes entirely too enticing.

Mr. Jefferson is said to be so peculiar that I'm not even supposed to go out and talk to him when he's walking down the sidewalk in front of our house. But such constraints build on a body...and it seems as if all three of my adults, who have at least triple-warned that I'm to give this man his space, should have known that the very idea of being told to avoid him would become a desire to meet him instead.

Encroaching on the forbidden private property, we encounter its owner as he is trying to persuade a muscadine vine into paying better attention to some chicken wire he's wrapped around it. Wearing his hat and dress-up clothes, he's sporting a 'possum colored mustache and looking pretty neat. Like Papa, Mr. Jefferson is not a tall man.

C.B. boldly calls out, "Hey, Mister, we hear you a pretty good story-teller."

Mr. Jefferson looks up and answers in a gruff tone, "You calling me a liar, boy?"

I speak up and try to save us, "No, Sir, that's not what he meant."

With my buddy slumped in a rare, silent-bound state, I present my most polished explanation...with success. When I'm done, our notorious neighbor has listened with patience and warmed up to us enough to tell us a story. It's about a ghost that carried away the last two kids who came over to his place without being invited. As we're excused to go home, I can tell C.B. isn't quite as taken by this old man as I am. In spite of everything I've heard about Mr. Jefferson, I decide there is something here to like.

––––––––––

ONE OF GRANNA'S BACK porch lectures turns on us one day when she reveals she has somehow come by the knowledge that C.B. and I have been over to see Mr. Jefferson. Apparently she feels obliged to enlighten us about him and some of his strange ways.

"Boys, I know it takes y'all little trouble to persuade William to share stories from his good ol' days, but you just as well understand there's only a trace of truth in many of his claims."

"Can we go now, Granna?"

She ignores my request. "He'll let on like he still runs and rides with the hounds, but truth be known, his best days and a good chunk of his memory are long gone."

"Granna?"

"If you could bank on him being sober long enough, I wouldn't doubt his more gentle and somewhat reserved nature might show itself, but...."

"Mrs. Taylor?" C.B. starts to question her but thinks better of it.

"Yes, you may go." She nods our release.

We round the corner of the house, and I'm thinking I don't even understand her warning that C.B. and I ought to take some kind of grand salt with whatever Mr. Jefferson is feeding us in his stories. That gentleman may be one subject Granna and I am going to have trouble agreeing on.

––––––––––

PAPA'S STANDING BY THE taxi stand and talking to Dad. I hope it's not one of their quarreling-type times when I have to appear that I'm not taking sides with one of them over the other. That worry is short-lived. Right in front of Dad, as if they are together in it, Papa starts in on C.B. and me.

"I hear tell you boys have been bumping into Mr. Jefferson in some of your recent trespassing."

"Uh, yes, Sir."

Papa looks at Dad. "Munford, believe it or not, Bill said he didn't mind these young'uns dropping in on him from time to time." Papa turns back to us. "But if you boys are going to be aggravating Mr. Jefferson, there's some things you'll need to know about him."

"I'll say," Dad agrees.

I'm hoping Papa's remark about the trespassing went right on past Dad, but I'm doubting it. I'll probably have to account for it when Papa leaves. As my grandfather continues, I'm figuring he's gonna tell us the same things Granna already did.

"He's written some books and won a big award. People that don't know him like we do, they think he's famous. While folks who live in Oxford regard him as being somewhat eccentric, the rest of the world considers him a celebrated character. But he's just a tad high-flutin' and a mite too stuffy, that's all," Papa summarizes.

"He's got a permanent personality is what it is. I'm not so sure he's as harmless as Preacher Taylor seems to think, and I'll have to study on it, about y'all going over there," Dad ends the discussion.

They both may be right, I'm thinking. Even Granna called him a ree'cluse and says he's starting to shun home folks now that he's about half-known all over. But so what if he thinks he's somebody? I can overlook such grown-up traits. He makes time for me and my friend. Not counting Granna, it's a rare adult who'll treat us with very much of that. Yeah, Mr. Jefferson's plenty good enough for me.

———————

ONE DAY, C.B. AND I hear typewriter pecking through the window of Mr. Jefferson's back room. With little discussion and even less thought, we decide to see if he'd mind us interrupting him. We won't do that again.

———————

THE FOLLOWING WEEK, MR. Jefferson catches up to us in Bailey Woods. "I've got something for you boys."

"What is it?" I ask cautiously.

"This is yours, and this one is yours."

Mr. Jefferson holds his closed fists out and waits for our outstretched hands.

"Aw—right!" C.B. responds.

"Wow…a new jackknife."

"Actually, they're a couple of old Barlow knives, but *new* is not always better. These may have been swapped around the courthouse until they've about worn out every pocket that would hold them, but there's a certain quality about country cutlery."

"Thanks." I'm quickest.

"Thank you, Sir." C.B. one-ups me with his manners.

"You're welcome, and I'm counting on this making amends for my being a little short with y'all last week."

"Consider ever'thing mended," C.B. offers.

"You'd better believe it," I add and decide he has found forgiveness in a big way.

"Now, if the two of you can stop your yapping long enough, I'll tell you some interesting things about the spit-and-whittle science of sharpening…and the ancient art of honing and safe handling."

"Yes, Sir." I'm too obvious in catching up with the sirs.

"You gots it," C.B. agrees.

Mr. Jefferson sits on the ground Indian style and leans against a sourwood tree. He'll start his lecture after he gets his pipe out and stokes it up. We've been here before, waiting through his pre-smoking ceremony. I stare at his Granna-like riding pants and high-topped boots. I don't understand why anyone would want to look so much like the English dudes in the movies, but I'm glad we're approved to once again venture on the Pen-Oake property. We'll meet up with him as often as possible, as long as he's already outside.

"First off, y'all will want to ask Preacher Taylor for a whetstone like this. I'm sure Elmer can part with one that the two of you can share. Right from the get-go, I'm telling you that you can cut yourself a lot quicker with a dull knife than you can with a sharp one."

"I ain't believin' 'at," C.B. interrupts. We all three wish he hadn't.

Mr. Jefferson looks at him as if he's fixing to take his knife back. Instead, he changes the subject to something about a practice he calls selective listening. As I hear about it, I'm thinking I can get the hang of this selective listening. Then Mr. Jefferson points out that it's just for adults. He says, being kids, we're to practice a kind of listening he calls attentive, especially when he's the one talking. He's really considerate of us, pointing out things like that. For some reason, Mr. Jefferson gets up in sort of a huff, turns his back to us, and heads toward his house.

"Thanks again for the knives, Mr. Jefferson," C.B. and I call out in unison.

He doesn't speak back and may still be perturbed over C.B. for cutting his lecture short. But as far as we are concerned, Mr. Jefferson's giving us these knives has made him our friend for life. And it's not just that. There's something about him the other adults seem to be lacking. When we're out of his hearing range, we start referring to our new friend as Mr. J.

IT'S A CRISP JANUARY day in '55. As far as C.B. and I can notice from the edge of Bailey Woods, Pen-Oake is Jefferson-less, and thus clearly forbidden. Always an attracton, today it has an extra pull that's too important to ignore.

"C.B., look! That little barn's on fire."

C.B. squints and responds all too slowly, "I don' think so, but we jus' well check it out."

Upon inspection, my friend enlightens me in one of his more chastising ways. "City-boy, this here's a smokehouse, for curin' ham meat an' stuff. Looky here." He sticks his nose in a crack and takes a deep whiff. "Try it."

"Wow, that smells like hungry. I need me a corner like this at the house, as often as I gotta put my nose in—"

"See over yonder. Look at that," he interrupts.

"What is it? Where?"

"In 'at pigpen by th' big barn, I believe 'at's th' biggest hog I ever seen. Let's go take a closer look at him."

"I don't know, C.B."

"Come on, City Sally. He ain't gon' bite ya."

Negotiating steps around horse manure, I follow my buddy for a viewing that's as close as I want to go. When the big hog grunts as if he's sizing us up for a meal, C.B. informs me that it was simply asking for food. Upon my limited analysis and C.B.'s extensive interpretation for me, the fate of this hog being destined for that smokehouse becomes a riveting reality. The more I picture the poor animal being sliced into strips of bacon, the worse I feel for him. One thought leads directly to the next, until....

"Coast is clear. Let him go."

Faster than such a fat hog ought to be able to move, he heads straight into Bailey Woods.

"Look at him run," C.B. laughs. "Listen to him oink. 'At be one happy hog, roamin' free."

"Let's get outta here, too, before we get caught. Hear that squeal, C.B.? That's pig Latin for thanks, guys."

"Don't be makin' no more fun of my jokes if 'at's th' best you can do, Nin-com-poop."

SEVERAL WEEKENDS LATER, C.B. and I spot Mr. J. leaning against a post of his recently mended pigpen fence, admiring his slightly more recently recaptured hog.

"Come ahead on, C.B. Let's go tell him about the snake." I traverse a downed tree trunk and look back to see how my friend, with his shorter legs, is going to negotiate it.

"I'm a comin'. Wait up," C.B. begs as he tries to step over the log the way I did. Now straddling it with both feet off the ground, he falls back instead of forward.

"Hold up, Scott. I ain't split as high as you."

"Hey, Mr. Jefferson," I shout. "What chu doing?"

"Just holding up this post. What are you young'uns so excited about?"

"Me and C.B. wanta tell you about something." I get lined up to jump a row of lilies on the garden's edge.

"Whoa-up, there, boy. Go around my flowerbed and try to miss everything that isn't grass. I took in account partial shade versus direct sunlight, the likelihood of late spring versus early summer, how well lilies can handle dampness versus drought, and most everything else any self-respectable gardener would concern himself with...but not kids' clodhoppers."

"Yessir." Going around, I concern myself with the fear that Mr. J. may be overly moody again today. C.B., having struggled to his feet and about to catch up, starts our story ahead of me. "Mr. Jefferson, we had a copper-headed rattlin' moccasin get after us."

"You had a who, do what?"

"A big snake what blew hisself up," C.B. answers in a rush of breath.

"First I've ever heard tell of a herpetological bomb."

"Not like a 'splosion, Mr. Jefferson. Blowin' up like a balloon," C.B. clarifies.

"Yeah, he got bigger than he was and came at us. I mean...well, he hunkered down like he was ready to get after us," I explain.

"Let me make sure I understand this. You two got chased around by a legless reptile that just lay there and pouted?"

"Well, he hissed at us," I revise my statement.

"Now, we're coming up on the truth, in its more round-about way from the rear."

"We both seen him that'a way, Mr. Jefferson," C.B. supports me for a nice change.

"We sure did."

"Fellows, let's muddle over to the garden bench where I can take a seat. I've got a feeling I'll need to get comfortable before I can take any pleasure in unraveling such a misguided tangle of serpentry." Mr. J. goes for his smoking pipe. Even as he walks, he fills, tamps, lights, and puffs.

It all looks like too much work for some smoke. He dusts off the corner of his ancient wooden bench and plops down. We stand in front of him, determined to convince him that we did see what we saw. The whites of his eyes are pink. I think it's got to do with his being up all night writing. According to Granna, Mr. J.'s work is what pushes him into being pompous.

"Well, now, if both of you gentlemen witnessed him, it might have been him, and I don't suppose I should question it."

"Him, who?" we both ask.

"He doesn't generally come out of hibernation until along about mid-April, but I hear he sometimes gets active this early during the warm-up. And I'll grant you—we've been having a slight warm spell. I'll give you that."

"He, who?" C.B. asks, again.

"Yeah, Mr. Jefferson?"

"What color was he, boys?"

"Yeller," I say, at the same time C.B. says, "Brown and grey."

"And red...well, sorta reddish, you know, with black rings around him, kinda," I try to clarify such confusion.

"Now, boys, if you want me to help get us to the bottom of this, you can't be tainting the truth." Mr. J. takes a long slow draw on his pipe.

"Mr. Jefferson, C.B. doesn't ever say anything wrong unless he's mistaken."

"And here I heard you two usually blamed your significant troubles on the mere fact that you'd been caught?"

"I don't know where you heard that, Mr. Jefferson, but we was both there, an' we both seen him, an' I ain't lyin' 'bout it, neither," C.B. insists.

"There's a chance, more possible than probable, less than likely, but...that could be him," Mr. J. strings us out.

"Him, who?"

"Who you talkin' 'bout, Mr. Jefferson?" C.B.'s pushing now, and I'm getting the feeling that's what Mr. J. is wanting out of us.

After another deep breath and long pause, right when I think he's fixing to speak, the old man starts sucking his smoking pipe again. He stokes it up. I don't know why he doesn't buy one that'll stay lit. After taking an exaggerated draw, he puffs out a big doughnut-like smoke ring.

I step forward to savor the sweet smell of his Velvet brand smoking tobacco...and develop second thoughts about its being worth all the trouble it looks like it takes to smoke a pipe.

Mr. J. crosses his legs like a woman instead of the way a man does. He just sits and looks at us. I know Mr. J's not to be rushed in the middle of a story and worry that C.B. is getting too antsy since he's starting to paw the ground with his sneakers.

"Now, tell me exactly what it was that this critter did under the circumstance of meeting up with the two of you?" he finally asks.

"Raised up his front end an' puffed himself up to bigger, an' opened his mouth," C.B. offers. "An' 'at's how come I knowed it was a rattlin' snake."

"That could be him, all right," Mr. J. again teases us about who he is.

I'm getting as impatient as C.B., but I'm not going to show it.

"What'cha talkin' 'bout, Mr. Jefferson?" C.B. pushes harder.

"So, what'd y'all do?" Mr. J. asks, instead of answers.

Thinking I can speed up the tale, I help, "C.B. got a big long stick and was fixing to hit him—"

"Fixing to?" Mr. J. interrupts.

"Yessir," C.B. chimes in.

"He kinda got to moving along pretty good," I explain. "And...uh, I couldn't tell for sure what he was doing."

"C.B.?"

"Not me, th' snake...th' snake was whippin' 'round in big, loopy twists 'n turns. We couldn't tell if he was really strikin' at us or just tryin' to crawl off without goin' nowheres."

"Then, I went on one side where I could keep his attention, and C.B. got around back of him to where he...I mean where he could've whopped him with his stick, if he'd wanted to."

"Could have?"

"Yes, Sir, but he gave up," I explain.

"C.B.?"

"Naw, th' snake. He just give up," C.B. affirms.

"Boys?"

"He did. Didn't he, Scott?" C.B., who is usually ready to lead me astray, now looks to me for backup.

Mr. J. looks at me also. I know it's past time for me to come up with something that will lend more credence to our story. C.B. pulls up the belt loop of his pants like he does when he wants everybody to know he has spoken the definitive truth. Remembering how it tastes to be discounted in the middle of a true tale, I have no choice but to try to help.

"To my best recollection's details, the snake rolled over on his back and stuck his head up his...I mean, under himself, is what I meant, I mean."

"He 'ad blood comin' outta his mouth," C.B. jumps in. "An' I ain't never eben hit him. I put my stick up under him an' lifted him up, but he just hung there, like he didn't have no stiff left in him or nothin'."

"Then C.B. flopped him back over on his belly, and he rolled right back over on his back again." I demonstrate with my hands.

"And he throwed up an' crapped," C.B. adds.

"Scott did?"

"No, th' snake did. Come on, Mr. Jefferson."

Smiles all around acknowledge that we know we're being strung along, but I'm still wanting to know who Mr. J.'s talking about.

"All right. Did either of you ever hit him or do anything else to him?"

"No, Sir, I swear I didn't," I answer.

"Well, I didn't neither, too, uh…we jus' sorta left him. Then we got to wonderin' if he had killed hisself or if he was just playin' 'possum."

"So we sat there on a log and watched him awhile," I explain. "And he finally did decide to roll back over and try to crawl off."

"Try?"

"We didn't hurt him, Mr. Jefferson. We just made a run at him and scared him some more, that's all."

"An' he rolled right back over like he done before, so we just left him there a laughin', really, us…we was th' ones laughin', not th' snake."

Mr. J. takes his hat off and guides his fingers through his white hair. I'm reminded of one of those new cotton pickers driving down between rows. C.B. and I watch and wait for further reaction. He straightens his hatband, replaces his hat, and looks sternly at each of us. I can tell he's finally believing us, and I'm hopeful he's finally going to tell us who he's been talking about.

"Well, boys, I'm not sure who got the last laugh. But I'm beginning to believe it really was him that harassed you so. Did all this by any chance happen in the Yocona bottom?"

"No, Sir. It was 'tween here an' Ole Miss…below th' big horseapple tree." C.B. points northward.

"I suppose he could have strayed that far from Yocona. If a Toccopola terrapin can do it, why couldn't he?"

"Why you wanta talk to us like we can't have th' rest of th' story yet, Mr. Jefferson?" C.B. asks.

"Oh, is that what you want? I'll give you the rest of the story, if you're sure you're ready for it."

"Yessir. We ready."

"It goes like this—the Pleistocene deposits have proved that this particular serpent might inhabit an area such as the sandy clay hills of the University of Mississippi…probably when the Yocona bottom gets too much water in it."

"But, Mr. Jeff…."

"C.B., don't be asking him any more questions until he finishes." I give my friend a push, and he shoves me back.

"Boys, boys, cut that out now, and listen. If I was a betting man, I'd say what you saw was more than likely the Yocona Puff Adder...more properly named, spreading adder. Infamous were it not for yours truly, it has deep roots around these parts. I believe a fictitious county was formulated for his indigenous namesake...but I share that with you in confidentiality. It was Yoc-na-pa-tawph—something or another...and I'll expect y'all to take that tid-bit of trivia to your graves."

"Then maybe we could have him as our own private, pure and special mascot," I suggest. "Like Ole Miss has the Colonel Rebel."

C.B.'s eyes light up with question. "What you do with a mascot, Mr. Jefferson?"

"Hopefully, the University of Mississippi will figure that out by the time they need to," Mr. J. sort of answers. "With such changing times, they might best select their mascot wisely."

"Why's that, Mr. Jefferson?" I ask.

"Because, deep in the shadows of football's Southeastern Conference, we're liable to have an overwhelming desire to recruit a running back based on the merits of his speed...or in round ball, a guy who can go so vertical he can touch the top of the backboard."

"What you mean, Mr. Jefferson?" C.B. asks.

"I mean yesteryear's historic symbols and flags might well become tomorrow's albatrosses."

IV:
A Cussin' Curin'

"YOU BOYS KEEP DRUDGING around in that drainage and you'll be finding all kinds of damned snakes."

"Oh—h-h! Mr. Jeff—er—son," C.B. rebukes him for his language.

Mr. J. gets up from his bench, brushes off the seat of his pants and gives C.B. an authoritative glance without comment. The look alone says it's not a young boy's place to be questioning the world famous wordsmith's choice of expression.

"How many kinds of snakes are there, Mr. Jefferson?" I try to lessen the impact of C.B.'s scolding.

"Boys, before you get along home, there is something here I best explain. We'll call it the Pen-Oake pecking order. It's like this—because of who I am, cursing is on my literary license…and I can employ profanity at my discretion. But not just everybody is authorized to express himself in such a manner of meaningfulness. Is there any further confusion about any of this?"

"No, Sir," I respond.

C.B. nods his head back and forth and picks up a magnolia cone.

"Unlike your run-of-the-mill hollerin' cussin', that lacks color, my cursing is for emphasis. Now, I must get back to curing society's ills."

"Huh?" C.B. pushes for detail.

"I've got some writing to do. And that's more than I aimed to say all day, so it's high time you boys get back to your own rat killing."

"Rat killing?"

"Rat killin'?" C.B. echoes my echo.

"Yeah, I'll bet you boys have never been to a good rat killing, have you?"

"Naw," C.B. answers.

"No, Sir. You reckon we could?" I ask.

"I'll consider that possibility, if you don't mention any of this conversation to your grandpa."

"You mean you don' want Preacher Taylor to hear you was cussin'," C.B. summarizes what he thinks was the point.

"Or I could talk to him about how my hog might have gotten out," Mr. J. answers.

I am shocked into silence. C.B. breaks the stem of the magnolia cone like he was pulling the pin on a hand grenade. When he stiff-arm throws it and makes the usual explosion noise, I picture dozens of rats and one big hog being blown up in the air on all sides of us.

"Any more questions, boys?"

"Don' answer 'at, Scott," warns C.B. "It's prob'ly one of them trick questions."

Mr. Jefferson looks at us with his you-need-to-ease-on-off gleam. We've seen it before.

"That will be all, boys. I bid you adieu. Disperse forthwith and come again. Go aggravate Elmer for an episode, and see if he can do any better by y'all." Mr. J. ambles toward his house.

"Bye, Mr. Jefferson. Come on, C.B."

"Yeah, bye. Let's get outta here."

We work our shortest way back through Bailey Woods to Granna's. Papa is sitting in the backyard and under his soft maple shade tree. This is where he likes to prepare his sermons.

Today, Papa lays his Bible down when he sees us coming. Probably in hopes that he won't pick The Book back up and start in on us with it, C.B. quickly questions him.

"Preacher Taylor, in th' olden times, eben way 'fore you was born, was it any such a thing as a big old snake named Puff at Her...one 'at eat bullfrogs outta th' Yoc'ny bottom?"

Papa's eyebrows raise.

"He wasn't calling you old, Papa. He was just trying to say—"

"Scott, I don't need you 'splainin' what I was tryin' to say. Preacher, what we wantin' to know is—if Mr. Jefferson was horsin' around with us an' makin' all 'at up an' 'spectin' us to go for it, 'cause we seen some kinda snake, whether it was th' one what had th' worst of all snakes crossbred into her or not."

"I suspect your main problem with Mr. Jefferson is that you don't listen hard enough. Believing someone is normally a good thing, but not unless you've listened really well. And y'all simply need to learn how to listen better."

"Yessir, we hear," C.B. tries to speed us along.

Papa won't let him. "As a matter of fact, that's probably going to be y'all's main concern and biggest problem with anybody and everything for the rest of your lives."

"But, what about the snake, Papa?" I ask, scared he is fixing to get off for fifteen minutes on what the Bible probably says about listening.

Papa picks his Bible back up and points it at me. "See what I'm saying, Grandson? Here I am telling you what might be one of the most important things you're ever going to need to know, and all you want to do is ask about a snake that Mr. Jefferson has already told you about. If you'll take heed to what I'm telling you and listen well enough, then you'll know whether or not William is pulling your leg."

I hate when Papa gives me an answer that leaves me hung up. It gives me nightmares about God All-Mighty, Himself, meeting me on my day of reckoning and pointing a bumper crop sized Bible in my face and speaking in a way I don't fully understand.

"We're sorry, Papa. Go on and get done with it. You can tell us about the snake afterwards." "Yeah, we're a'list'nin'. Go to head on, Mr. Taylor."

We take our seats, me up on the chopping block and C.B. on a pile of stove wood. Papa cautions me to watch out for the ax. He still hasn't opened his Bible. I'm hoping our listening lecture doesn't cause him to bring religion into the discussion before we can get him back to the snake.

"What you need to do is direct your listening, like you sometimes do when you're talking," Papa preaches. "You know how you raise your voice and talk a little louder when you want to be sure folks hear what you're saying?"

"Yes, Sir." I try to look serious.

"Yessir," C.B. is like a tongue-tied parrot.

"Well, when someone like me or Mr. Jefferson is talking to you, that's when you need to raise your listening a little too. That way, you can get what it is they're saying. You got that?"

"Yessir, we got it good now, Mr. Taylor," C.B. chants.

"We understand it all right, Papa," I say. "Now, will you tell us about the damned snake? Oh shit! I'm sorry! It slipped. I mean…they both slipped." I give my best face for forgiveness, my expression pleading silently as I wait for my grandfather's reaction.

"C.B., go to my back porch and get me that soap and pan of wash water."

"But Papa, please. I'm sorry. It slipped I tell you. Don't, Papa. I didn't mean to. I won't say that, I mean them, no more."

"Scott, it wouldn't slip if you weren't used to talking like that when y'all are off to yourselves. Now, come here, Grandson," he instructs without the least bit of anger in his voice.

Knowing he's got a wash-basin full of punishment in his mind whether he's mad or not, I ease over, closer. My so-called friend brings the soap and water with such a sincere look I'd like to wipe it off his face with a corn shuck.

"Thank you, Charles," Papa says.

Out of my reach, C.B. steps back to observe, not willing even to glance at me. But I know he's laughing on his inside.

"Aw, come on, Papa, let me—"

Slop, slurp, slosh, slush…pish, wher, psk, tsk…ugh!

"I ought to be seeing to it you can't sit down for a week. Do you understand that?"

"Yes, Sir, I'm not going to say it any more."

"How about you, Charles? Do you need some of this today?"

"No, Sir," C.B. responds piously and retreats further to sit on the stack of wood. "I ain't cussed since…never, I promise. But I would like to ax you somethin'."

"What is it?"

"Could a feller go to Hades fer cussin' to himself…if it ain't nobody else around to be a'hearin' it?"

"Yes, yes, and yes! Sometimes I absolutely don't know from Adam's off ox if you two are ever going to get the message."

After a while of no one being able to figure out what to say next, Papa starts up again. "Scott, you sit here under this tree and think about the disgusting way you talk, while Charles tells me more about this snake."

"Yes, Sir. C.B.'ll tell you," I offer.

"No, Sir, I'd a heap rather Scott be th' one to tell you 'bout it."

"I may have to hear from both of you." Papa mumbles something about talk being bad enough to make the Lord Himself heartbroken.

I whisper to C.B., "Why is it you always want to be the one to talk until we get around somewhere you can't cuss?"

"What's that about cussing, boy?" as Papa overheard the last part of what I said.

"Nothin', Mr. Taylor," C.B. answers in his imposture of innocence. "He was…uh, mistakin' me fer my cousin. I ain't been doin' no cussin'."

"Well, Scott, if you get to confusing them again, C.B.'s cousin is the one who's not your best friend."

"Yes, Sir, Papa."

"Why don't you tell us 'bout th' snake, Mr. Taylor?" C.B. tries for distraction.

"All I can say is—you boys better be glad y'all didn't come across a timber rattler who was shedding or a cottonmouth in a dog-day mood. You might not be here now if you had. Are you listening?"

"Yes, Sir, we'll be carefuller next time. Go to head-on, Sir," C.B. pleads.

"Based on what William called it, I'd guess what you saw was really an eastern hognose snake."

"Ha ha…." C.B. almost falls off the woodpile.

"Oh no, here we go again. Come on, Papa…we want to know the truth this time," I ask.

"Tell us fer real, Preacher Taylor. We know it ain't no snake named hog nose."

"We're going to try this listening thing one more time. If either one of you interrupts me again, I will cut me a hickory switch. If I can't get through to your ears, then we'll see if maybe you can hear through your rears."

"Yes, Sir."

"Yessir."

"There is such a snake as a puff adder…in Africa. There are none around here."

"But, we seen…"

"C.B.?"

"I'm sorry," C.B. apologizes for interrupting.

I look around and make a quick inventory of any hickory trees in the backyard. Seeing no likely branches for switches, I wonder if Papa forgot about his threat.

"What we're talking about here is called a hognose snake or spread adder, as well as about fifty other names I've heard over the years. Seeing as you have been told many times not to disturb any snake at all, what did you do next?"

"We run like hell. I'm sorry, I meant...uh," C.B. stutters.

"It's too late to be sorry," Papa explains.

I pick up the pan for Papa. "Here's the soap and water."

"Sc...ott?" C.B. whines.

"Well, it's your turn, and he's going to do it anyway." I move around and climb up where C.B. was sitting on the stack of stove wood. I'm going to enjoy a prime view of this.

C.B. steps right up to take his punishment medicine.

Slop, slurp, slosh, slush...pish, wher, psk, tsk...ugh!

Other than carrying on with a slight coughing spell, C.B.'s face shows no confusion. He looks back and forth between Papa and me. I just smile at him and say a big nothing, but I'm guessing going through experiences like this together will seal our friendship like nothing else would.

"Now that you've both had a taste of foul language, do either of you boys have anything more to say about anything?"

"No, Sir, Mr. Taylor, I don't," C.B. answers. "I may not never eben talk around you again...a'tall."

"That might be all right too. How about you now, Scott? Do you have anything more to say about any of this?"

"No, Sir—ee. Not a chance. Not me. I'm afraid I might just fuck up again."

"Come here!"

"But it slipped...and I'm sorry. I'm really sorry."

"Sorry won't get it, young'un."

Slop, slurp, slosh, slush...pish, wher, psk, tsk...ugh!

V:
Dickie Birds and Chickens

"PEENT, PEENT, PEENT," GRANNA whistles a nasal call for us.

"A timber doodle," guesses C.B.

He's right. She's pleased, and I'm jealous. Other than that, it's a good day for birding Bailey Woods. The morning's cool, but nearly all of the snow is gone. The sky's going through its ever-changing yellow through pink to orange, a sky like you seldom see other than during the month of the snow in a Mississippi that seems too far north in February.

C.B. zips up his second-hand coat, and I snap together my new, Christmasy-smelling insulated jacket. I'm pleased my friend wasn't too proud to take my old coat, and I'm glad to be past my own discomfort about wearing my new one in front of him. He's not as tall as I am, so my old one still fits him.

Things might have been different if my previous best friend hadn't moved to Pascagoula. All I know is—for now, when C.B. and I are together, we hardly notice the separate and unequal parts of our lives. Any black and white problems the rest of town has with my buddy and me being close friends are Oxford's problems.

It's 1956, and our friendship has established itself beyond our respective races' expectations. As far as I can tell, Papa never did judge C.B. as any different from us, and Granna likes him. Not willing to cross too far over unfamiliar racial lines, Dad has finally yielded to a moderate toleration of my black playmate.

Over and above having someone of a contrasting culture and color I can count on, I have begun to respect C.B. as a person. The ultimate gesture of true friendship is my willingness to share Granna with him. Sometimes I even get a little put out with her for liking him so much. You wouldn't think I'd have to compete with somebody who's not her grandson.

Leading us into the late winter bird world, Granna points out a soggy area, "Look right in there, Boys."

I see the woodcock she apparently wants us to spot on our own.

"You see how she blends in with the wet leaves?" Granna asks.

I figure I'm being baited again, but I know I'll learn something by going along with her, even if it is the hard way. Her favorite teaching trick is to get me thinking about something out here before she equates it to some peculiar or particular way humans act back in people habitat.

"All right, Granna, how do we know it's a girl bird?"

Her smiling before answering tells me she's pleased that I was listening enough to pick up on a good question. She's like that.

"A female woodcock is half again the size of her mate. And that beak she's probing for worms with—it's also about that much larger than the male's. Your grandpa says her larger beak is because a female talks more than a male. But it's really on account of it being all the better to peck him with when he gets out of line."

I can mostly tell when Granna is joking or serious about things. When I'm not so sure, sometimes I ask, and sometimes I don't. While I'd hate for her to think I'm as stupid as she probably already does, I also don't want to miss anything good she has to offer. C.B.'s been stumped so many times he's finally learned to just keep quiet and let me take the fall and play the fool's role.

"Now, if you two will hold still and stop your talking, we'll likely find the male woodcock somewhere close by."

I'm thinking since Granna shared the male-pecking story with us, she may just be trying to prove some truth somewhere nearby. She usually balances things out like that.

There he is…right at the edge of the creek. He's poking around in the moist leaf litter with his small beak, just the way Granna had described. I wanta be like her when I grow up.

"See his drab-brown color and smaller stature? He resembles a snipe," she shares. "But there's no way you can mistake a snipe's flight for a woodcock's. Due to a snipe's quicker, more erratic, and low-to-ground way of flying, he's been nick-named Go-Devil by the lumberjacks who get to see him the most."

Moving away from the trickling sounds of the creek, we angle uphill. Granna is again first to spot something on the ground ahead.

"Young'uns, do y'all see that turtle shell? That's from a spotted turtle. When she died, she was probably as old as I am."

"Da...ng, Granna...."

"Watch what you say, Boy."

"How you know it wadn't a boy turtle, Ms. Taylor?" C.B. asks and probably steps right in it.

"By being as old as the turtle," she nails him and then looks at me with her eyebrows raised.

"What's 'at little yeller an' black bird there?"

"Good eye, C.B." She swings her binoculars up to make a positive identification. "That is a Kentucky warbler." She hands the glasses to my best friend. "He probably just crossed the Gulf of Mexico."

"An' th' Yoc'ny River?" C.B. asks.

Granna glances at me and shakes her head. At last, I have some satisfaction that she views C.B. and me on a different level. Maybe I'm still her favorite.

When he lowers the binoculars, she locks in on his eyes and continues. "I suppose we need to step back and get you a genuine grasp of geography before we can cultivate any real degree of admiration for Mississippi's natural heritage."

I have my turn looking through the lens. Every feather seems to come into focus.

"It's a male, of course, with those colors," Granna adds.

All this talk about boy and girl birds and different sexed turtles has me thinking of Miss Sippy. While Granna tries to heighten our interest in the wonders of the out-of-doors, I start daydreaming of touching Miss Sippy's smooth skin, to see if it would feel as silky as it looks. Instead of worrying about sharpening my forest senses, I'm more than half-curious about a different kind of birds and bees.

Most Saturdays, when C.B. comes in with Auntay, Sippy stays with a cousin in Taylor. I'd rather she would come in, as long as we don't have to run any more foot races. I like to see her laugh, so I try to be funny around her. When she flashes her white teeth across that cocoa-colored face and her brown eyes light up, she's the prettiest girl I've ever seen.

Morning-moisture clings to the vegetation. The air lends itself to the part of the forest that you can smell. We've not gone far when Granna identifies a male northern junco. A little farther and there are male and female purple finches and several house finches.

I feel like I'm being dragged behind Granna and C.B. as they trudge along. As we approach the property line between Papa's place and Pen-Oake, a yellow-billed cuckoo starts up his clucking repertoire.

"Raincrow," C.B. calls it, quoting the name Auntay's taught him for the bird.

The long gray bird, looking like a mockingbird with an extended tail, flies right down the boundary in front of us.

"Look how he seems to be pumping his wings instead of flapping them," Granna points out. "That's characteristic and helps you to be able to identify him."

"You'd think he's havin' trouble flyin'," C.B. adds in his brown-nosing way.

Steering us away from Mr. J.'s woods, Granna circles back toward her city house. C.B. looks at me with his unsatisfied expression. I think I know what he's wishing. He, too, would probably like to slip on over and see if Mr. J. is out and about. One of these days we're going to get Mr. J. and Granna together where they can philosophize each other until only one of them is left standing. That'll be a sight to hear.

C.B. breaks off a farkleberry twig covered with army green moss. After he lays it in a rare spot of snow that hasn't melted because of its shady location, we stare quietly at it. The contrasts of the winter colors are as fascinating as C.B.'s simple creativity. I appreciate both.

After Granna's identification of another assortment of songbirds, she lumps them into a category she calls common winter residents. Learning things that way is supposed to season us to some kind of grounding...or is it to ground us to some kind of seasoning? Anyway, she says we'll better understand grouping and sorting in good time.

The highlight of our hike is reached when we get to watch a great horned owl feast on a field mouse that Granna said had no business being out this time of year. With the owl ripping into the flesh of the fury little rodent, Granna simply states, "That's the way of nature." And it sounds as if our outing is closing.

My grandmother sticks her binoculars and bird book into the hand-sewn, deer-skin ditty bag that Papa made for the cause. Now I'm just hoping she's not fixing to shift to being that grandmother who makes me sit on her front porch and practice my reading to her. I hate when I have to read aloud, and the letters get all mixed up, and the words come out different from the way they really are.

She adjusts the horse-riding pants she wears for woods-walking. "Boys, do y'all even realize how privileged we were to have witnessed some of Mother Nature's finest this morning?"

"Yessum."

"Yes, ma'am."

"Good. Because it's now time you learned to hit a curve ball."

"What is it you thinkin' you know 'bout baseball, Ms. Taylor?"

"Not baseball...that was a figure of speech." She picks up our hiking pace beyond that for birding and heads us toward the house. "I intend to lay a heavy spread for Sunday dinner, and you boys can help with the fixings."

"Then we don' know nothin' 'bout no cookin'," C.B. continues to push back.

"I'll do the cooking," she responds. "What I aim for y'all to do is learn some simple, factual things about Domesticata Americana. You need to know of real-life stuff, as opposed to the sort of gup Mr. Jefferson is always babbling to y'all about."

"Granna?"

"In spite of all the beauty we have seen this morning, there is also another side of Mother Nature." She won't let me defend my Mr. J. "You got a small taste of some of the cold, hard ways of the world when you were watching that owl and his mouse. What I'm talking about here is the development of some critical values. I'd like you to contemplate how certain animals exist and others make certain sacrifices for food. Humans, for instance, have a God-given dominion over dumb animals."

"What'cha mean, Miz Taylor?"

"I'm talking about a little character-building exercise for you and your city sidekick. It's one that's hard enough to help you stand, when leaning on something less would be too soft." She looks at me.

"What C.B. said," I respond. "What do you mean, Granna?"

"We're going to prep a chicken."

"One of yo' chickens?" C.B. asks.

"Unless you think y'all can sneak one of Mr. Jefferson's. Forget I said that. I was joking. Of course, one of my chickens. What do you think...they come from the grocery store or something?"

What I really think is—when she lets comments like that slip out about Mr. J., it means she's tired of hearing C.B. and me talking so much about him. She may be a little jealous. I believe she'd rather have us talking about her than Mr. J.

As we reach the backyard, I think more about how much I really don't like chickens. A crispy-coated drumstick the way Granna fries them up is something else, but I'm doubting I can become very concerned one way or the other about how to turn a yucky-smelling, stupid-acting live chicken into a meal. But this is one of those times Granna doesn't ask for my opinion or C.B.'s.

We receive our instructions as we're led over to the city chicken pen and little coop. It's all a small version of what's at Granna Taylor's home place at Taylor, Mississippi. C.B. seems somewhat anxious for a country boy, and I'm not about to let him keep showing me up.

Beating him to the gate, I go in first. A rooster struts as if he's the ruler of the roost. I look at Granna. She shakes her head no, as if I were asking if that was the one. "No" suits me. The colorful cock looks like he's in no mood to participate.

"Grab a fryer and be done with it," instructs Granna.

C.B. enters behind me, and forgets to shut the gate. A speedy chicken slips out and changes the rules of the contest. Simply hemming up our selection in the henhouse is no longer an option. Finding ourselves chicken chasing outside the pen, the three of us head for one of Granna's flowerbeds. The air fills with petals from winter carnations before our self-chosen chicken's run is straight through Papa's early season English pea patch. Feathers fly.

"Get him, C.B.!"

"I'm tryin'."

When you're running full speed, it's hard to tell Granna's smile from her frown. On top of that, I'm not sure what's most important between catching this particular chicken or not smashing too many of a grandmother's precious snowdrop flowers. Searching for a sign but seeing nothing except a blur as I go by, I figure I may as well go with the chase. I'll probably be wrong no matter what I do.

Herding the chicken between us and then under the house, C.B. and I have managed to position ourselves with only room to crawl. After corralling our prey in a corner, I emerge with confidence peaked…and our prize tucked neatly under my arm like a feathery football. My buddy plods along behind me and promptly names our chicken, Henrietta.

With the wind blowing in the wrong direction, a quick whiff of foul fowl reminds me again how much I don't like fryers until they're fried.

As I proudly hand over our captive to my grandmother, I can almost taste the smell. The sour, sweaty, chicken-feather odor would cause me to gag if it were not for knowing that C.B. is smelling defeat behind my victory of being the one to catch the dumb bird. I never knew a chicken to have an expression, but as I hand her over to Granna, Henrietta looks like she'd just as soon stay with me.

My grandmother matter-of-factly lets go of everything except our chicken's head and neck. Hardly committed to any of this, Henrietta furiously flaps and chokingly clucks her objections. As if Granna was answering such chicken behavior in her own way, she immediately starts slinging Henrietta in a circle. Making a big blurry white ring around her own head, Granna looks as if she's about to lasso something with our chicken.

"'At's why they call it ringin' th' chicken's neck," C.B. explains.

"And probably why they call cussing fowl language," I counter.

After around a half-dozen looping swings, the bulk of Henrietta goes sailing by…to hit against the picket fence and drop to the ground. Headless, she gets up and leaves a bloody trail by running around in short circles.

C.B.'s serious demeanor goes quickly from simple skittishness into a full-fledged panic. Being his good friend brings with it the obligation to follow along. When I make an indecisive step and slow up for the blueberry bushes, I can almost feel chicken claws between my ears. I look back and see that it's just the same C.B. I was following.

Thinking our chicken, by now, has surely dropped dead, calm and quiet, I see that I'm wrong. Still headless and flapping her wings without flying, Henrietta makes a bloody trail toward us. C.B. jumps straight up in the air and hits the ground running. Knowing he appreciates the comforting presence of a buddy like me when he's being chased by a headless chicken, I come along again. When we round the corner of the house, I look back and see that Hentietta is headed back toward Granna. It's amazing how quickly you can feel better when you know your buddy is all right.

"C.B., I wonder how long she can run around without her head before she gives up and dies enough, like she's supposed to?"

"I dunno, an' I ain't in th' mood fer no chicken riddles right now."

"You're the country boy. I'd have thought you'd have seen that before."

"I'z jus' tryin' to keep you company. 'Sides, worldly pride's somethin' best kept inside…better left unspoke."

"Then let's go back and have us a look-see," I challenge.

"Well, I shore ain't scared to," C.B. accepts.

We ease back to the corner of the house and peak around. Standing with one hand on her hip and the other now holding Henrietta's finally dead feet, Granna spots us.

"Come on back, boys. It's prime time now for the plucking portion of your poultry lesson, not to mention your mm…bl…er…un…st…."

With the last part of Granna's warning trailing off without an obvious blood trail, it's almost as if she didn't intend for us to hear what she said. That always worries me when it happens. I'm pretty sure we'll find out what she said, but probably not nearly soon enough.

Within ten minutes, I'm knowing what her mumbling had to do with. Who would have thought you had to scald a chicken with boiling water, pluck the smelly wet feathers, and singe the small pin feathers off with a burning newspaper. And it's not until after all of that is done and re-done when we have the fun of gutting it.

When C.B. and I have convinced ourselves that our chicken is prepared, Granna touches it up, as if we hadn't done it totally proper. Lastly, she gets to cut it up in small pieces…and says something about Mr. Jefferson giving us knives before we were ready for them.

THE SUNDAY DINNER PLATE that Granna passes at me is a platter of fried chicken. Seeing beyond the crispy, golden crust to remember Henrietta, I hesitate. As I've paused a second too long already, Granna shakes the plate as if she's trying to get my attention with it. Still skeptical, I'm glad Dad and Papa don't know what's going on between me and Granna and in my head…and double glad C.B. isn't here to see me puzzle over my predicament.

When Granna makes a face like she's fixing to have to say something in front of Dad and Papa, I know I must eat a piece. Taking my usual-looking, but definitely different drumstick, I can almost hear my best friend's voice saying, "It ain't our fault 'at dumb chicken didn't have sense enough to cross th' road."

46

VI:
Taylor Creek Home Place

"SCOTT, YOU 'MEMBER WHAT your Granna called these little yeller an' green flowers 'at likes to grow down near th' wet?"

"Oh, yeah. That's mustard, and she calls it poor-man's pepper grass. There's some kind of way you can eat it."

"I don' know but one way to eat nothin'."

"I mean she has to do something to it first. You can't just eat it straight out."

"I oughta 'membered 'at plant. Mama Nature ain't got a lot of 'em flower 'fore February's finished. On th' other hand, I'd be wore plumb out if'n I 'membered ever'thing of hers."

"Mother Nature's or my Granna's?"

"Six uh one, half bushel of th' other."

"Dozen."

"Half, an' 'at's a fact," C.B. takes his stand and tugs at his pants. "My trousers got a way of workin' down below where my hip-bone oughta be holdin' 'em up."

"C.B., you reckon maybe I could go home with you sometime?"

"To Taylor? At Auntay's?"

"Yeah. I've got a hankering to see some country besides Bailey Woods. What do you think?"

"I can ax."

Considering our encounters around Oxford, any exploits to what should be a less-than-adventurous Taylor shouldn't be a big deal to either Auntay or Granna. Dad might present a problem, but he doesn't need to know I plan on a journey down Taylor Creek to the Yocona River.

A COUPLE OF WEEKS later, C.B. comes by my backyard home court and catches me with the round ball. "What's up?" he greets me.

"It's been a school day. What can you say?" I shoot a left-handed layup for show. "Hey, what'd your Auntay Belle say about me coming over?"

"Right off, she threw her hands up an'prayed aloud, 'Lord, be my helper'."

"Which means?"

"It means she like to come unbuttoned in th' girdle. She said I gets enough of you an' yo' stuff durin' my trips to town."

"Sounds like we need to get her and my dad together. You want to shoot some hoops?"

"Shu...er. I can see 'at happenin'."

"Shooting hoops?" I pass the basketball to C.B.

"No, gettin' yo' dad an' my Auntay to agree. What'd he say?"

"After he pitched a fit, he said he'd study on it, and I'd probably come back disreputable or...never mind, you don't wanta hear the rest."

C.B. takes a long set shot and hits the backboard's pole.

"You had it lined up right, anyway."

"You should'a told him we prob'ly couldn't of come back dis-rep-whatever-you-said, even if we knowed what it was."

I dribble out and sink a hook shot from the free-throw line and try not to look surprised.

"To tell you the rest of the truth, I fibbed...and told him Auntay Belle had already said it'd be okay with her for me to go home with you."

C.B. makes an expression of admiration. "Then we'll jus' have to keep after Auntay. I'll beg on 'til she treats us right about it. I knowed better than to push her on it right when she went an' laid across th' couch. We'll get our way. I'll have you to th' place. You jus' wait an' see."

A FEW MONTHS OF winter and C.B.'s persistence wear Auntay down. Even knowing Dad's not partial to it, she finally gives in and says she'll allow I can visit where they live. With the rains turned off, the foulest moods of March moved on to the north, and our earth thawed soft, Granna steers her Crayola-green '49 Chevrolet down the muddy ruts of the long and narrow farm road.

Auntay's place is on the backside of Papa's and Granna's farm, and I've never seen my grandparents' spread from this view. Ours seems more impressive from across the cornfield. Bright white shutters set off a southern charm I've never noticed before. I'm supposing C.B.'s view of everything in life may be a little different from mine. From this distance, even the flock of crows from Papa's pecan grove kind of clatter and cry instead of caw-cawing their usual raucous calls.

A three-strand barbed wire fence skirts the ditch along the road right-of-way. It's country-road straight but bad grown up in a good way, according to Granna. She says bushy fences do more good for wildlife than they do harm to people who like such nonsense as having their fencerows looking like they've been manicured.

A covey of quail bursts out from under the mass of weeds and better vegetation. "Look at the partridges, Scott," Granna needlessly points out.

A few singles scatter, but most of the birds hold their spread-out flight until right before they hit the ground. Like miniature airplanes needing a runway to land on-the-run, they move their tiny little legs so fast it looks as if they have landing gear instead of super quick feet. For their short height, they stand tall taxiing down several rows of barren cornfield. As they double time along in their columnar formation, they look like little soldiers, all decked out in the drab colors of uniforms.
"I wonder if a cherry-bomb dipped in glue and rolled in BB's would make a good bobwhite hand grenade for a sling-shot?"

Granna looks at me with both sides of her mouth turned down but then moves her attention back to carefully and slowly negotiating the rough road. I'm glad she doesn't have one of those little cars they're starting to bring over from the foreign countries.

Toward the Yocona River, golden-brown Johnson grass flows across the pasture as if it were ripples on water. I look down the trail-like road for a quarter mile. In its silhouette, Auntay's house appears to be waiting to leap out to take the lead in some parade of the downtrodden. A mimosa tree on the west side looks as if it's holding up the shanty.

I'm hit head-on with the stark contrast between this weather-beaten dog-trot and Granna's big and stately house. Wheras Granna's house was well built by my great-grandparents, Auntay's humble home appears to have been thrown together with discarded logs and planks. The solid footing of heart-cut, old-growth shortleaf pine I've heard bragged on doesn't sound so sturdy any more. And my former feelings of pride from hearing about how my family homesteaded the land now takes second place to my sense of embarrassment over such a difference between the houses.

A partially covered breezeway at C.B.'s must be holding everything together, barely. The bare front yard is marked by two large rip-rap rocks that must have come from the spillway at Enid or Sardis. He couldn't possibly want me to see any of this, but it's too late now.

Forgetting to use the clutch, Granna bounces the green bomb up to a jerky stop. Papa's always said the only reason he double-clutches is to make up for her driving around so much without using the clutch.

C.B. steps off the porch of warped and uneven boards to greet us. My friend is wide-eyed, but it's not as if he's trying to figure something out. It's more like a look that says he's accomplished something. Granna gives me a small sack of sandwiches and says I'm to share with C.B. Any minute, I expect a pre-warning about how to act and then her final warning.

"Remember your manners now, Scott. You weren't weaned by a wild-cat. Miss Belle is supposed to be home soon, and I want y'all to see her before you head for the woods. Act like you know's right. You hear?"

"Yes, Mam."

"We will, Ms. Taylor," C.B. adds.

Granna U-turns her Chevy in the front yard and heads for her own home place. A lonely looking post oak shades three surplus school chairs. Blocking the nearest corner of the house and not looking as if it's there for any decoration, a black cast iron pot sits…big enough to hold a boy. Realizing I'm now stuck here for the duration, my stomach sinks.

"What's that big pot for, C.B.?"

"It's a yard pot, like a water cistern, fer washin' dirty clothes."

Thank God Almighty, I think. Maybe I won't be stirred into some black magic recipe. The pot does seem poised to catch roof rain. After all, a witch wouldn't need that.

A weathered, upright two-by-four anchors a clothesline stretched to the back corner of the house. I scan the hung-out clothes hoping to see some kind of undergarments of Miss Sippy's. Everything there appears to belong to Auntay. Three teal-blue cook's uniforms sway with the early spring breeze. White stockings hang, flapping, each looking big as stovepipes. Auntay's bloomers are wide as a BB gun is long. I think I could climb up in a pair and swing as if I were in a hammock.

The ground off the porch is grass free, with a wet dirt smell. It looks as if it's been swept by a broom. I figure Sippy has been out here playing house. Why else would someone sweep the ground?

Coming up on the sagging front porch steps, I'm cautioned by C.B. "Watch where you put your foot. Don't be walkin' where th' boards is loose."

Each step looks the same to me. They squeak the same. I'm afraid it'll be too late by the time I figure out which ones are loose.

"Whose dogs?" I ask.

"Mine. They don't take to strangers right off, but don't worry—they don't bark or bite."

Before I reach the top step, a scraggly red-bone hound and an un-kempt cur of the pot-hound variety give up their territory and drop off the side of the porch. They look at me as if they've never seen a white boy…and I wonder what good they are if they don't bark or bite. Living where I do, I've never had a dog and can't anticipate ever getting one. C.B. tries to call the one named Red…and Red doesn't exactly ignore him but eases off with an intentional sort of indifference.

"Take this here stick an' scrape th' mud off'n th' bottom of your shoes," C.B. instructs me.

I sit on the porch floor and look up with caution. I'm uneasy that leaning against a honey locust porch post might bring everything down on top of us. What comes crashing down on me is reality. Around me is a drab picture of existence.

Four of the kind of ferns that grow naturally in Bailey Woods hang artificially here, in coffee cans. I believe there are more dirt daubers up under the eaves here than on Papa's woodshed. A nice spider web capturing the roof joist glistens to reflect the humidity.

A creaky sound accompanies the opening of the front door. The floor is swept as clean as the front yard. I'm met by that now familiar smell, the one reminding me of sardines and barbecued potato chips. An unlit kerosene lantern reinforces a darkness that can't quite overshadow what I'm seeing. C.B. notices me looking at the oil lamp.

"We ain't got no lights run out here. Auntay says they's jus' some things you gotta take as you find 'em." He smiles, somehow.

Although my white, middle-class life is a far cry from the aristocratic society C.B. assumes it to be, seeing this makes me think it may be so far out of his reach that it might as well be all he believes it to be. The kitchen and front room have somehow been run together and caused two corners from each to disappear. A barrel of flour occupies one of the kitchen's two remaining corners. Where a wall would have separated the two rooms, a big black wood-burning stove stands in what looks like the core of the cabin.

C.B. points at the stove. "'At's th' way we heat an' cook." With pride, he states, "I hafta keep up th' sto'wood an' kin'lin'." He takes the toe of his worn-out tennis shoe and pushes what must be Auntay's jar of snuff closer to a corroded tin can spittoon.

A spare envelope-style hat from The Mansion restaurant hangs from a nail by the door. A pair of flat black shoes try to trip me, as if they're testifying in their own way as to Auntay's difficult walk in life. Sitting by a spent sofa is a plastic-like purse of tacklebox size and shinier black than the shoes I'm glad I don't have to walk in. Faded red and no doubt well worn, a dustless Bible holds down several folded-up, teal-blue bed sheets on a small table. A sewing basket next to the sheets suggests that it's not a coincidence they're the same color as Auntay's uniforms.

The telling silence is interrupted by C.B. "Auntay an' Miss Sippy'll be along directly. We got it to ourselves fer a while. Come on an' I'll show you my room."

Quietly following C.B. to his personal space, I'm thinking I'd rather see Miss Sippy's. C.B.'s looks as if the Salvation Army has delivered all the cheap and worn-out stuff it didn't want. His bed is a small cot. In a corner is an open, makeshift closet. Clothes look like seconds and thirds, probably passed down from kin, and a couple of shirts I think used to be mine. Granna must have given them to Auntay for C.B.

The room's walls are hewed out logs, with mud mortar in between them to help hold out the weather. Around me is a real-life demonstration of why I should have that attitude of gratitude Papa preached about last Sunday. It all makes me think about the way C.B.'s getting by and making do with the ugliness of poverty.

"Don't tell Auntay yo' Granna give us 'at sack of sam'witches," C.B. suggests. "Maybe she'll do us th' same. What you wanta do while we wait on her?"

"I don't care, C.B., whatever you want. But first I've gotta take a leak. Where's the bathroom?"

"Out back."

"Huh?"

C.B. laughs and walks toward the door. I follow him and don't realize he's not joking until we step outside. His story is sealed for the truth when I see a small wooden table with a big white porcelain wash bowl and matching pitcher sitting on the back porch. It's the 1950s, and there is still no running water in this house. My friend still lives like this…and without brooding over his misfortunes. I'm again brought to wonder about the injustices of Negro life and how C.B. is not one to be defeated.

"This th' way it be with us," C.B. admits. "'At's it, right there." He makes a pistol out of his fist and first finger, and shoots the necessary house with emphasis.

A few loose chickens glean the bare backyard for insects, in what looks to be a stark struggle to survive. The privy is bordered by milkweed plants, themselves half-covered with bright yellow butterflies. It's amazing to me why flowers or insects would fight the smell to hang around here. Cupping my palm, I slide my hand through the hand-carved half-moon of the johnny's door. Pulling the worn-smooth wooden latch behind me and twisting it on its ten-penny nail pivot, I have closed one world and opened another. I need to breathe, but for the moment, I'm more concerned with not barfing.

Having lost much of the desire to be in such a technologically deficient place, I vow to hold my pee back until I can make an excuse to slip away from C.B. and find a tree somewhere. I need to hold my breath in waiting until what I think will be long enough for C.B. to assume I've used his facility. The hole is an image that won't be easily forgotten. If this is supposed to be a defining moment in my curiosity about country life, I'll secretly consider remaining a city-boy.

C.B. stands right outside. With his natural mixture of suspicion and curiosity, he was probably listening and didn't hear anything. His one-sided stance and the patting of his foot remind me of my Dad's posture as he's about to nail me over something. C.B. looks at me without saying a word, but I can tell he knows.

About the time I'm thinking silence is the best thing we have going for us, there's a car sound from around front. Hearing an automobile pulling up to and then away from the front of the house, I look at C.B.

with questioning eyes and a silent plea to divert my dilemma of trying to explain why I went but didn't *go*.

"That's Auntay an' Sippy's ride. They back," he informs me.

The explanation is no sooner out than we are descended upon from around the corner of the house. With the late afternoon sun at her back, Auntay's a massive figure of a woman. She hustles along on top of her shadow, a sight to see up so close. Pushing three hundred pounds clear out the backside, she's curved over and stooped without even bending. Her right shoulder's humped up like it was busted or something.

"Howdy, boys."

"Hello," I respond.

"Afternoon," C.B. adds.

"You boys go 'round to th' front yard fer a while. I got to see a man 'bout a dog."

I'm thinking the only dogs here are still around front. And this is the first I've heard of any man—but we do as we're told. It suits me. I'm not really wanting to hang around here or talk about anything on this side of the house.

Miss Sippy's on the front porch. "Long time, no see," she welcomes me with a wholesome spirit I wasn't expecting.

"Hi," I respond and then give her the once over.

She's neat and clean looking. Her blue-and-white-checked dress shows evidence of starch and ironing. She is definitely becoming easier to look at and lighter colored than I've been remembering her. She's about the color of the well-creamed coffee Granna sometimes lets me have. As she starts humming a tune I've never heard, I try to think of something clever to say about it, but my head stops working again. I don't know why that has to happen when I get around her.

Auntay makes her way back around front and immediately gets her chatterbox started. With the ordering up of routine domestic chores, it becomes apparent young'uns along Taylor Creek have a dutiful respect. Without much room for any kind of disagreement, bickering, or talking back, it's a love with good conduct or swift and simple justice. Kids are kept underfoot or out from under it, depending on how their adult feels at the time. In that respect, a Negro family must not be that different from a white one.

Auntay's lower gum must be packed with snuff. Her lip quivers above it. Long since robbed of any youthful pep, she waddles up steps that must be much stronger than C.B. let on. The snuff can in her uniform's hip pocket is outlined against her impressive backside like some kind of growth, but I think better of trying to say something cute. I don't think she's one for anyone to trifle with or tease. Everyone but Mr. J. calls her Auntay Belle to her face and Big Mama Belle behind her back. He calls her Auntay-Bellum all the time.

We're herded in the house and informed we'll be having dinner before escaping to explore Taylor Creek. As our head chef proceeds to cut slices from a big white slab of fatback for frying, I think what a hardy race of folks they are…eating breakfast victuals for supper.

"I wouldn't wanta put y'all out none, but if you'll fetch me up a full kettle of fresh spring water, I'll make us some sweet mint tea good as them RC colas."

When we return with Auntay's order, Sippy has changed into a loose-like dress for kitchen duty. C.B. and I take one of the split-cane-bottom chairs each and think we're going to be waited on…while I watch his stepsister scramble a bowl full of eggs. She mixes in a handful of chopped-up pasture onions, and when the eggs are done, comes up with some of those grits Auntay must have been talking about. Instead of a stick of margarine in a tray from the refrigerator, there's a hubcap-sized glob of cow's butter in the middle of a plate on the table.

When I think we're about through the meal, Auntay presents me a big tin of the iced tea and shoves another plate at me. "Here, Hon, get you a gen'rous portion of this gravy an' put it on you one of them cathead biscuits. Eat 'em up. They'll stick to ya ribs."

"Thank you, Mam. Y'all sure know how to set a table."

"If'n I had you around here fer awhile, I'd put some weight on yo' skin an' bones," Auntay declares and causes Sippy to smile.

I wish she hadn't said that in front of Sippy. I feel bad enough about being skinny, but I'm scared anything I say in my defense might be misunderstood. I'm not sure what an appropriate conversation is at this table, but I am beginning to understand why Auntay's so big around the middle.

"Mmmmmmm," C.B. proclaims and sops up his red gravy with a lop-sided biscuit. "This th' kinda eats 'at's sho' 'nuff good. An' I don' see how you can stomach 'at stuff from Munford's Grocery."

"C.B.!" Auntay chastises.

Apart from my buddy's favoritism toward everything that's Taylor, he's right about the food. Everything is tasty in a country way, a good kind of greasy. Of course, I can't admit that to him. I savor every bite I chew of what Auntay's declared is only a goodly portion of fried fatback.

C.B.'s method of eating is unique. When he puts a forkful in his mouth, he might take one bite before it goes down. It's like his upbringing in hardship has him not knowing if he'll ever get another meal. By contrast, Miss Sippy sits cutely and sips at the rim of a milk glass that used to be a jelly jar. The meal's conversation goes to talk of Granna when Sippy asks about white women treating their faces.

"You mean putting on makeup?" I ask.

"Yes."

I don't mind this. Talking to Sippy gives me an excuse to keep looking at her, with secret thoughts and youthful optimism. I hope I'm the only one who knows I'm paying her more than casual attention. Every time Sippy asks something, Auntay starts talking as if she wants to end it. But they both listen to my efforts at answers. They must want to know about white folks' things. Auntay apparently wouldn't dare ask Granna things like that outright. For a colored adult, asking so abruptly would be snooping and meddling where she doesn't belong.

Sippy finally takes Auntay's cue to hush and sit quietly. Her dark brown hair is the color of the wood of Granna's piano and curled softly around her face. Her sweet smile dimples right into that cocoa skin color of hers. She's beginning to proportion like a female, and I'm flat-out curious about the bodily differences developing between us. I hope her sidelong glances in my direction mean she likes me, too.

My eyes are momentarily drawn from Sippy when Auntay pours off some coffee from her cup into her saucer. She blows on it and then pulls her lower lip out to hold under the saucer. Next, she slurps noisily. The next time I see this will be the second time I've seen it. C.B. and Sippy are looking at me for a reaction, so I try to say something nice to Auntay.

"Granna says you're a gentle-minded lady, with beauties not seen." As soon as I've said that, I realize there could have been a better time for such a comment than right after such a slurping.

Auntay comes back pretty quick with a return compliment about Granna. "Well, some say your Grandmother's a mite stiff sometimes, but I say she knows th' Lord. I'd say most all th' Taylors gots God in they hearts."

"You can say that again," I agree a shade too fast.

Auntay cocks an unsure eye at me, but goes on, "It's likely most of 'em done reserved 'em a place in Heaben. If nothin' else, by th' way they treated their hands over th' years. Always been good to me an' my family, providin' a roof fer us ever since 'fore we was share croppers an' God sent word all men was created equal."

"Wait a minute, Auntay," C.B. interrupts. "I thought it was Abraham Lincoln said that."

"Jesus Christ, Son of God an' Holy Ghost speaks thru man sometimes, an' times is ever'thing," she explains.

"An' it's timin' that's ever'thing—not times," C.B. argues.

"Don' you be arguin' with me 'bout th' Bible, Charles. I knows th' Bible."

As plain as Auntay puts stuff and as tiresomeness as it is when Papa preaches it, I'm wondering if Auntay and Papa have Bibles that are different.

Auntay goes on, "All that timin' talk…no matter how you words it, what Psalms an' Proverbs say is—you gots to get sitch'ated to capture th' moment."

I'm practically into C.B.'s brain, worried he's fixing to say something smart-alecky, so I jump in. "Auntay Belle, how do you get situated and go about capturing the moment?"

"It's like right now—jus' 'preciate it as best you can, right when it's happenin'. You rein in yo' time, an' time' yo' reinin' in. Fer instance sake, ever' other limb on yo' family tree's been puttin' out a man of th' cloth. Praise Jesus, Amen. 'At might mean in time, it'll be hereabouts yo' turn to jine th' clergy."

"I'll be da…darn."

"Watch it, Young'un." Auntay cups her hand behind her ear and asks, "What was you 'bout to say? Don' you be lettin' yo' Christian get away from you in this house."

"Darn…I was gonna say I'll be darned."

"'At best be what you's gon' say. You not near old enough fer no mo' underscorin' than 'at."

"Same thing Mr. J. said," C.B. tries to help.

"Y'all been over there a'cussin', have you?"

"'At ain't what I meant, Auntay," C.B. clarifies, but doesn't know when to stop. "It must'a been one of them timin' things you was talkin' 'bout.

Mr. J. just warned us not to be cussin' 'fore we could get started. I mean, if we was gon' be startin' up any, but we wadn't."

"Uh huh...."

"You can go crank up Mrs. Taylor's telephone an' call Mr. J. an' ax him if that ain't so...if'n you don' believe us. Right, Scott?"

Before I can figure out what part of all that I can substantiate without incrimination, Auntay comes back, "Oh sure. I'm knowin' that old coot's gon' tell me on th' two of you."

To his credit, C.B. sees this as a good time to change the subject. "Mr. J.'s set on teachin' me an' Scott new words from his mother's tongue, like they talk in England an' all."

I'm thinking that was a mistake. This is one arena where Auntay won't be out-done. On her home turf of Taylor, she's acting as if she won't take a back seat to anybody. Being largely self-taught, there's a certain weight in what Auntay says, and when it comes to talking, she isn't timid about sharing a strength gained from the struggles in life.

I try to change the subject. "Mr. J. says he's going to build him a houseboat."

"And me an' Scott are gon' help him."

"'Fore you know it, he'll be teachin' y'all yachtin' words, like 'gee' and 'haw'," she jokes.

I'm not always sure where all her words come from. I guess it doesn't matter if she makes them up, as long as she can use them well enough to communicate. She's the kind of woman that could misconstrue a Bible story, and God All-Mighty Himself would probably let her get away with it, knowing she was just trying to help someone by it. Papa calls it interpreting.

Around Auntay, ordinary and simple things often become interesting in an extraordinary way. When it comes to laying hold of basic truths, she's got as good a handle on her own philosophy as Granna does hers. She might sometimes be a little light on being right, but it's hard for me to conceive of her ever being tee-totally wrong.

It is apparent that Sippy and C.B. have had the kind of sensitive-like childhoods that encourage them to participate in chores. Auntay starts singing a blues ballad that must be a signal for Sippy to start gathering up the dirty dishes. I assume C.B. and I are expected to do our bit to carry our own weight, in addition to having to hear the song about the perils and particulars of "Bein' Brought up by Hard Times and Not Havin' No Terms fer Pressin' Troubles."

"I wouldn't mind helping dry the dishes or something," I offer.

Without any consideration for his sister, C.B. says, "We need to get on."

"I he'p Auntay milk th' cow," Sippy mentions.

"I think that'd be pretty interesting," I offer.

C.B. gives me a visual nudge to try and shake off my curiosity.

Auntay shifts her singing into lecture, "Charles is always talkin' 'bout 'Granna told y'all this an' Mr. Jefferson told y'all that. Well, I got some things I can teach you young'uns too, if'n you willin' to listen."

"All right, Auntay, we're a'listenin'. Get on with it," C.B. comes back.

"Don' be short with me, Boy. You watch yo' smart mouth, talkin' to me like that. Where's yo' church trainin'? I'll take you back down to th' baptizin' pond an' give you another dunkin' myself, you aggrivatin' little contrarian you."

"Yessum, yessum," he's quick to agree. "What is it you want to teach us, now? We need to go."

It's so hard to keep a straight face over C.B. and Auntay's trading of words, I decide I need to concentrate on C.B.'s stepsister. She gets more interesting every time I look at her. Sippy's soft and shyly spoken innocence from the first time we met is giving way to a gentle gift of gab. Where she used to be standoffish, she is now so friendly she's almost inviting. Thinking back on how Dad first feared my friendship with C.B., called it a taboo and probably still privately detests it, I suspect if I showed up with Miss Sippy as a girlfriend, it'd kill him outright.

Auntay'll take only so much of what she calls C.B.'s jawin'. I don't know why he'd push her as far as he does, unless he's just trying to show off in front of me. I do know I'm needing to go pee like all get out. Of all times, I pick now to remember a time when C.B. was standing outside Oxford's WHITES-ONLY public toilet at the courthouse.

Auntay gets back on her make-believe stump, "Th' key to learnin' is to 'member what's so, an' I've been 'memberin' things since I'z a little bitsy girl."

"It's been a while, huh," C.B. responds, as he rolls his eyes at me.

"What is it, Auntay Belle?" I hurriedly ask, not wanting C.B. to dig himself in any deeper.

"You know what's th' best day of th' week?" she asks.

"What's the best day of the week?" I answer with the question she wants to hear asked.

"It's to...oo...day, that's when it is, an' it comes in good stead on its own. Th' aches an' pains an' blames of yesterday is spent an' went...an' today ought not have no dread of what's ahead."

"That's really good, Auntay," C.B. mocks her.

"I ain't through yet," she goes on. "You best to savor th' flavor of today in ever' way."

"What do you mean by that, Auntay?" Sippy asks in a rare contribution to the discussion.

I'm bouncing my leg up and down now so much that I know it won't be long before everybody knows I've got to pee, even Miss Sippy.

"It means we need to be 'preciatin' what life offers, 'stead'a always wantin' more of what ever'body else got."

"We'll do that, Auntay. Can we go now?" C.B. asks what I'm wanting to.

"Boys, am I botherin' y'all?" Auntay answers with a hint of humor.

"Not any a'tall." C.B. quickly rhymes and looks at me to signal visually that what she said was our release. Heading outside, he whispers to me, "Come on, we done caught up to one of them timin's ever'thing times."

"No bout-a-doubt that, Bubba," I agree, and walk a little hunched over. My blatter hurts so bad I have just about reached the limit of my endurance. "What's your favorite bush to pee on?" I ask as we leave the house behind us.

"A yucca, I reckon," he answers, "'cause they'll stick you if'n you ain't watchin'."

He tightens his belt a notch. Just thinking about that almost makes me explode.

"I favor a purple thistle. Look! There's one now. I'm gonna see if I can."

VII:
Turpentine, Souls, and Old Men's Roles

WITH HONEY LOCUST-LIMB SLINGSHOTS stuck in our back pockets, C.B. and I climb a box elder tree on the southeastern corner of my house. Auntay calls it a false-maple, and we've learned not to argue over nomenclature when Granna calls something one thing and Auntay calls it something else. I think the old ladies are in cahoots with one another and do it on purpose, to help the names stay with us. If we forget one, we're likely to remember the other. I recall Auntay saying, "Best way to 'member things is re-memory by 'sociation." Granna said something similar to that in the Queen's English.

Halfway up, I strip off a handful of its whirly-bird seeds. Throwing them out to the side is fun…watching them twist their way to the ground like miniature helicopters. C.B. sneezes and claims this tree is giving him the hay fever that Auntay says is from goldenrod and Granna assures us is really from the ragweed that's flowering at the same time as the goldenrod.

Upon climbing to the height of my two-story house, we reach the roof by walking out one limb while holding a higher one as if it's a handrail. A chinaberry tree shading the northeast corner of the house is our destination.

"I don't 'spect you to know this, bein' such a city boy, but chinaberries gots another good use to 'em 'sides fer sling-shootin'."

"And my country-hick friend is fixing to tell me what that is, right?"

"They good for keepin' th' weevils outta stored corn."

"Store-bought corn?"

"Never mind, there ain't no helpin' th' likes of some folks."

After securing two baseball caps full of ammo from the over-hanging tree, we ease back up to the eave of the house. Kneeling on sun-warmed shingles, we peek over and spot our first challenge. Practically begging to be shot at, a brand new shiny, red Corvette sits on Haney's Chevrolet lot…too much to resist. Dad says nobody'd ever pay the four thousand dollar sticker price on the window anyway. And I say if they don't want folks shooting at it, they ought not paint it so red.

After tiring of plastering such a helpless and stationary target, we begin chinaberry pelting the passing vehicles. C.B. spots Mr. J. down at the "T" of South 11th Street and University Avenue. Our mentor appears to be just standing and looking off into nowhere. Maybe he's trying to smell the magnolias again. Scurrying back down our climbing tree of two names, we hustle out to meet the old man. He's dressed up today in all of what Granna calls his ivy-league pretense.

Seeing us, Mr. J. starts his staggering kind of strolling up our street and calls out, "Well, well, if it's not the Mississippi's most motley crew. What has the county's clamorous kids been messing up recently?"

"We don't never hurt nothin', Mr. Jefferson," C.B. answers, as we fall into our places on each side of him.

"Horsefeathers! What a pair…a plaintive disclaimer if I ever heard such."

"We ain't been up to nothin', an' 'at's th' God's truth," C.B. continues to back our innocence as we help guide Mr. J. toward town.

I reach around and check my back pocket to be sure my slingshot isn't showing. Mr. J. paces our walk so as to admire the trees along the way, as if he hadn't seen them all a hundred times before.

"Extracting any more than a moderate portion of truth from y'all is about as sure as seeing the air."

"Really, Mr. Jefferson, we been good," C.B. says.

"Well then, how's Preacher Taylor?"

"Fair to middlin', I reckon," I answer.

"Whoa back, don't you think you might owe your grandpa a little more consideration than that?"

"What'chu mean, Mr. Jefferson?" C.B. tries to butt back in.

"I mean that was a powerfully quick response. I need you to first study the question and then give me the correct answer—how is he, really?"

We walk on. Mr. J. unbuttons his tweed coat like he's fixing to get serious about something. I want to give him the answer that suits him. I just don't know what to say. He's proved time and again he can see sideways around exaggerations and tell when there's enough truth somewhere to find whatever is left out somewhere else. The smarter I try to think, the more my thoughts run together. No matter what I say, I'm afraid it's still not going to be what he wants to hear.

"Aw, Papa's in pretty good health, for the shape he's in."

"What in Sam Hill does that mean? And who did you hear saying it?"

"Doc Mac Lordy's the one who said it, when Papa went to him about his bad leg."

"And...?

"And what?"

"And what else did Doctor McLarty say about Brother Taylor's leg?" Mr. J. shakes his head as if he's already not believing anything I might say.

"Oh...uh, he looked it over and told Papa that he couldn't find anything wrong with it. He said Papa needed to remember that his leg was eighty-three years old."

"Well?"

"Well, what?"

"Well, what did Elmer say to that?" Mr. J.'s voice is getting a little louder.

"He said he knew that wasn't it, 'cause his other leg was eighty-three too, and it didn't hurt."

Mr. J. smiles and picks up our walking pace. He removes a cloth sack of Velvet smoking tobacco from the breast pocket of his coat and prepares his pipe as we walk. The aroma is enough to make me want to try smoking.

"Modern medical science doesn't know any more about Elmer's leg than it does my cirrhosised liver." He blows a smoke cloud. "You boys let this be a lesson to you."

"Wha'cha talkin' 'bout, Mr. Jefferson." C.B. bravely tests him.

"That I can reduce either of you to near-honesty within only a few minutes of interrogation."

Mr. J. puts his matches and pouch of Velvet back in his coat.

"How come you don't get your tobacco in a tin can?" C.B. asks.

"You don't buy something for its container, and that's a slice of intellectual property I'll give you permission to use someday when you least expect to need it."

It's nothing new for Mr. J. to be stringing together big words and aggravating sentence puzzles for C.B. and me to have to try and cipher. Auntay calls him the living dictionary of Pen-Oake. I think he's more like a set of encyclopedias.

As we round South 11th Street onto Van Buren Avenue, I see Papa standing out in front of Gathright-Reed Drug Store. Normally a man of easygoing character, my grandfather appears to be in something of a huff. Unless it concerns sinning, Papa is gentle in his ways and slow to anger.

As we approach, Mr. J. asks, "What's wrong, Preacher? You couldn't get your free coffee this morning before the fifteen cents a cup started?"

"I've been dog bit, and that aristocrat in the store there, he won't help me."

"What do you mean he won't help you?"

"He won't sell me a bottle of turpentine to pour on my dog bite."

"You'll have to get you one of those credit cards everybody is starting to use nowadays," Mr. J. suggests.

"The money hadn't got anything to do with it. He said he wasn't a doctor and couldn't be prescribing something for what it wasn't intended for. I knew he wasn't a doctor. Now, I know he's not much of a pharmacist."

"Where's the dog, Papa? Me and C.B.'ll shoot him with our sling shots."

As if a nine-year-old's offer doesn't count for anything, Mr. J. interrupts my question. "What are you aiming to do, Brother Taylor?"

I try again to find out about the dog, but Papa still ignores me and answers Mr. J. instead.

"I believe I'll sit out here on the curb awhile and protest."

I'm thinking if Papa's gonna start talking about believing, that's when everybody'd better run.

"Maybe I'll die right here in front of Gathright-Reed," he raises his preacher voice as if it will carry through the store door.

"But, Reverend...."

"I'm not going to any doctor over a dog bite," Papa interrupts Mr. J. "It'd be different if the dog had rabies, but he doesn't. I know him and his owner and both of their mothers. It was Lovelady's dog."

"Well—" Mr. J. tries to speak, but my grandfather won't let him.

"Can you imagine how I feel, having a merchant refusing to wait on me?" Papa complains.

I look at C.B. His eyes return the memory. I recall The Mansion Restaurant, Blalock's Drug Store, the public toilet at the courthouse, and the water fountain FOR WHITES ONLY. Perhaps C.B. is remembering a dozen other times and places…and other things I would never have thought about. Sometimes I wonder if I should feel guilty just for being white.

Mr. J. places his tobacco-stained tamping-finger in the middle of his dark-rimmed glasses and pushes them further back on his nose. "I'll declare and be damned if mankind's not near doomed. I've got a notion to…. I'll tell you what, Preacher—when a man's drugstore won't sell him what he's perfectly willing to pay for, this newest nature of customer service has slipped too far."

"You don't have to tell me. It's some circle of merchants we've got," Papa shakes his head in disgust, "trying to protect me right into an infection."

"Brother Taylor, let me go in there and see if they know just who in the hell I am." Mr. J. storms through the front door while we wait.

I'm wondering how he dares to talk in cuss words around a preacher. He emerges from the drugstore with a ten-cent bottle of turpentine. Proud of his accomplishment, Mr. J. twirls the left side of his mustache to try to make it stay up and match the right side. It's lint-white now, instead of the 'possum color it once was.

Papa pours a good quarter of the bottle of turpentine on the broken skin near his ankle. A couple of pharmacists watch from the front window of the drugstore. Before the bottle is re-plugged, the store-bought, near-home remedy has the whole sidewalk smelling like the Yocona River sawmill. After tying his handkerchief in a hard knot around the wound, Preacher Papa turns to the onlookers in the window. In common with his character, he just tips his hat with dignity and says, "Good day."

Mr. J. leads us across the circular drive called The Square. Like buzzards waiting around on something to ripen, dusty trucks and shiny automobiles are parked, facing the courthouse. Reaching the two old gentlemen's favorite, good-settin' bench, C.B. and I plop down on the ground. We're out to both sides but facing them. English sparrows gather and begin to hop on the dirt beside us. They must know that bench-sitters and boys will be too busy talking and listening to cause them any harm.

Papa tries to tell us the story about a gang of outlaws headed up by a General Grant. He points out where green grass never grows because that's exactly where each of the intruders stopped and rested. Mr. J. interrupts the Preacher and claims he shouldn't be blaming everything on the Yankee aggressors or they might not come back as visitors, but Papa says that'll be all right with him. He was about to show us where the best limb was shot off Oxford's hanging tree.

A chilly breeze comes through, and Papa pulls up his collar. He says, "Look at you, William, all dressed up in the finest clothes money can buy…wool pants and a little brimmed hat so stylishly small it couldn't do battle with rain or sun either one. What's your occasion?"

"Don't be carrying on about me. You're the one all duded up in reverending clothes."

"Well, these are some of those new permanently pressed, pleat-less pants Sears is putting out now," Papa admits.

Mr. Jefferson crosses his legs and coincidentally shows off his extra-high, brown riding boots. C.B. looks at his own sneakers as if comparing them to Mr. J's leather boots. I can tell he's dreaming about growing up and having things like that someday.

Mr. J. pushes Papa. "Did you get all cleaned up like that to do business with your moralistic manual, or you just come up here to get dog bit?"

Papa ignores him. Preachers don't brag on themselves, but my grandfather is looking slick enough to stand bareheaded right alongside of God Himself. I'm noticing Mr. J's reinforced elbows. Everybody knows his coat doesn't need patching. I think it's just so it doesn't look new. He gets called out enough on showing off, as it is.

A honker announces passage of a large flock of Canadian geese flying high above. Papa uses the geese to change the subject.

"This time of year feels a lot like it sounds…with wild being in the wind and all."

"Yes, Sir," Mr. J. answers. "February will be out of here before you know it. Seems like it gets harder and harder to keep pace with the months."

Papa is lost in watching the flock of geese. Like me, he's probably thinking of where they might be headed.

"You ever noticed that, Brother Taylor?"

"What's that? Notice what, William?"

"How it gets harder with time?"

"Oh, yes," Papa answers. "But it seems like it's always in the wrong places."

"That's not bad for a little old preacher-man of gentle tongue."

"You're not big enough to be calling anybody little," Papa lets him know. "And I'll thank you to keep that kind of talk about three feet over my grandson's head, please."

"You're the one who said it. I believe that dog bite's got you a mite feisty. Was it a feist that bit you?"

"I yield," Papa gives. "You're the only man I know could drown a duck in your dry wit." "Now, Preacher, with your sly humor, you've got no call to ever yield to anybody."

"Well, that's not it a'tall," Papa states. "It's just I've taken notice that your cock-'n'-bull tripe is usually not worth turning face up on the stump."

"You've sure got a way with a few words, Reverend."

"You had to go and stick a few in there and ruin a perfectly good compliment. At least you did manage to get me my liniment."

"There's a back-handed thank you if I ever heard one. And you're quite welcome, too, Parson."

"Well, it's not like you saved my life."

"I'm beginning to wonder if that pharmacist wasn't right about you and your mongrel medicine. It's smelling more like the logging-woods than any liniment I ever smelled."

Papa doesn't answer, so Mr. J. continues. "What do you do in your spare time, Brother Taylor?"

"What's spare time?"

"Now, don't let that pine tree sap cause you to skid past the pearly gates with such exaggerations as that."

C.B. sticks his neck way out and leans forward to get a good listen.

"It must be nice to sit and peck on a typewriter all day long. How does it feel to get money without doing any real work?" Papa asks.

"I don't know so much about the money part of it, but I'm here to tell you one thing—if you sit in my typing chair, the grass'll seem greener outside the window. Truth is, I envy a man who has the individualism to work the land and preach a little on the side."

A pigeon sails over South Lamar and right up between the willow oaks. His white wings and tail feathers contrasted against a gray body make him easy to follow in flight. He lands on the short hand of the courthouse clock and starts cooing and fluffing his feathers and doing what Granna taught us is preening. I try to point it out to our adults, but they don't seem interested.

C.B. interrupts them as if to merely show me he can get their attention. "Preacher Taylor, is somethin' we can learn any better'n somethin' we already know?"

"I'd have to know the particulars on that, Charles," Papa answers. "While I think on it without the particulars, why don't y'all tell William, here, about your chicken fixing indoctrination?"

"Aw, there weren't nothing to 'at," C.B. quickly answers.

Hoping to change the subject, I add, "We just helped with one of Granna's chicken dinners, and that's all there was to that."

"Not the way I heard it," Papa prods. "What do you think, William? Reckon there was any more to it than that?"

Mr. J. stretches and leans way back on his bench, "Ah, yes, Mississippi-styled southern fried chicken—the only way to get a better piece is to be a rooster."

"What'cha mean, Mr. Jefferson?" C.B. asks, instead of his usual waiting to let me be the butt of adult jokes.

"Never mind, boys," Papa intercedes. "You don't need to be trying to understand everything William puts out until you're a little older."

Mr. J. takes Papa's cue and leaves the subject. "Preacher, how are the birds out at your place this year?"

"I'd say most of them are about wintered out. With their diet getting pretty much depleted, I suspect they're just trying to fatten themselves up and store enough energy for their migrations to Hither and Yonder, Yankeeville."

"You know I'm talking about quail, Elmer. And you know they don't leave your farm."

"Yeah, yeah, I just wanted to see if you had a funny bone left in you, maybe hid somewhere."

Behind the grownups' backs and awareness, the pigeon is repeatedly sticking his head up and down. I'm as sure Granna could explain such bird maneuvers as I am equally sure that these two men would make light of it if I did get their attention.

"How about the quail?" Mr. J. presses the Reverend.

Papa spits at the small group of English sparrows and misses.

"They ought to be coveyed-up pretty good by this time of year, as many of them as you missed last season."

"What would you think about shooting some after church Sunday?" Mr. J. asks.

"I wouldn't care to," Papa answers.

"Why not?"

"I said, I wouldn't care to."

"And I said, why not."

"Have you got chewing tobacco in your ears? I wouldn't care to means, yes, it wouldn't bother me any if we did," Papa explains.

"If that's not taking grammar to new depths.… I hope you don't say things like that from your pulpit. What would the Lord have to say about you confusing your sheep into going astray and turning to their own way because of what you pray?"

"It's not my pulpit. The Lord looks after such. And you're not any better poet than you are at shooting that left-handed double barrel of yours."

"Elmer, I've got a thought for you. With your religious vein about the past and my belief in a grand plan for humanity's future, what if there isn't a plug nickel's worth of difference between your theology and my philosophy?"

"That's not a thought. It's a question, and I'm here to answer you. There is, there's a lot of difference, William."

"But, Preacher—"

"No 'buts' to it. You best be getting ready to meet your maker. You're going to be dead a lot longer than you're going to be bird hunting…or a struggling writer."

"I've got past the struggling part of it, so much so that I'm thinking I'm needing to go bird hunting while I've still got the time."

"What's all your fame and fortune going to get you when your last covey rise comes up, in the final sunset? It's where you'll be going then that amounts to something. Nothing else counts."

"Now, I didn't come to town for a sermon, Elmer."

There's a pause.

"Well, your future's of your own making, William. I'd love for you to understand just how long forever is. It'd be more important to you than anything you'll ever write about."

This conversation is heating up a little warmer than where I'm comfortable. If they're fixing to go to arguing for real, it may be about time for C.B. and me to leave. Our pigeon flies off. C.B. looks at me and motions with a nod that we need to move along, too.

I thought there was something significant about that bird, just by the way the grownups weren't willing to consider him when I knew he needed to be observed. I'm re-hearing Auntay's words—"Seein' an' feelin' at th' same time is where we gets our best signs."

As C.B. and I excuse ourselves and get out of our old folks' hearing range, my buddy shares a deep thought. "I got a feelin' 'at ain't so good."

"What do you mean?" I ask.

"We been doin' all this hearin' from a couple of powerful smart men, an' eben they was quarrelin' over what might be 'bout as important as anything's ever gon' get."

"And?" I ask for elaboration.

"An' that don't help none decidin' what's right, 'bout th' soul an' all. Mr. J. don't seem to go past his smarts, an' me favorin' preachers much as I do…. You know what I mean?"

"Yeah, C.B., I think I do. I suppose when it comes to stuff like The Word, I'm figuring Granna and Auntay would both side more with Papa than they would with Mr. J.'s lost nature. And you don't hear anybody arguing with Auntay or Granna. That's what my intuition tells me."

"'At's jus' 'cause if you was to argue with either of them, yo' inner-tuition li'ble to get turned into outta-tuition."

"Maybe we can play it safe and hang onto both sides," I suggest.

"Sorta like gettin' tobacco an' a little tin can both?"

"I'm thinking more like making it to Christianville, but only by the skin of our teeth."

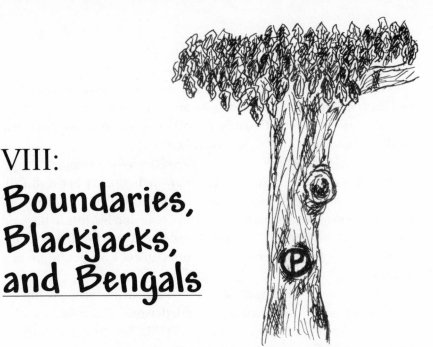

VIII:
Boundaries, Blackjacks, and Bengals

IT'S A LATE-FIFTIES, BAILEY WOODS type of fall Friday. After school, C.B. and I are walking along our creek and happen to catch up to Mr. J.

"Hey, Mr. Jefferson," I get his attention.

"What'cha doin', Mr. Jefferson?" C.B. follows suit.

"Remembering how I used to come down here and get some peace and tranquility."

"What kinda knife you got there? Let me see 'at, will ya?" C.B. asks.

Holding it up where we can better see it but not reach it, Mr. J. shows off a strange-looking knife with a hooked blade. The thick wooden handle constitutes the bulk of it.

"It's not a knife," he proclaims. "This is a scribe, made for carving."

"Fer folks 'at's courtn' to be drawin' hearts an' 'nitials on beech trees?" C.B. asks.

"Not hardly."

"Well, what then?" my buddy continues his questioning.

"It's for lumbermen to tag logs with, but I'm using it to run the property lines and get my trees lined up. After I scribe a tree, I'll come along after the sap's run and paint over my mark. Maybe it will keep some people from trespassing."

"I don' see how 'at's gon' do nothin' to keep folks away," C.B. bravely challenges him.

"Tell him, Scott."

"I don't know, neither, Mr. Jefferson."

"Then it's past time you both learned. A man maintains his property lines so his neighbors will know whose trees are whose. A body wouldn't want, accidentally or indifferently, to gather up wood or anything else that didn't belong to him, now, would he?"

C.B. frowns at the accusation, but keeps quiet for a change.

"You two could learn to respect better the boundary between Pen-Oake proper and elsewhere. Contrary to popular belief, I don't own all of Bailey Woods. Scott's grandfather, Preacher Taylor, has title to the land on that side of this line. The point that could be taken is—there is plenty of room to stay over on your family's side, unless I happen to be in a visiting mood."

As if to leave us, Mr. J. starts down the semi-visible property line.

"How we gon' know when 'at is, Mr. Jefferson?" C.B. asks.

With a lingering look over his shoulder, like he's trying to think up an answer, Mr. J. finally comments, "You'll know."

We follow, trying to walk without making noise, like Granna's taught us for better seeing birds.

Mr. J. looks back over his shoulder again. "I suppose, before the devil gets to quarrelling over my dues, there's a couple of things the two of you need to be shown. So, cut out your yapping and come along."

We follow Mr. J. to the westernmost edge of his property. It's a hill overlooking the road to Taylor, the community named after my great-great-grandfather.

"Quiet as rabbits now, boys. Don't make a sound until I tell you." Mr. J. puts his number one hush finger up to his lips and looks serious. "Right there by that big tulip poplar tree, that is where I've left a square can of yellow boundary paint." Before I can ask him why he's telling us this, he puts up his hush finger harder this time. "Do y'all see that purple Plymouth down there, pulled in the edge of the woods as if it's trying to hide?"

"Yes, Sir."

"Yessir."

"It's got a Louisiana license plate, and there's this fellow who has been here for the past two days. Look over there, now." Mr. J. points. "Do you see him hiding behind that tree?"

"Yeah."

"Yes, Sir."

"He's watching the Rebels practice their football plays with his binoculars and writing notes in a log."

"With a scribe?" C.B. asks.

"It's a different kind of log from that. Now, listen—between lunch and suppertime tomorrow, he'll probably show up again and do the same thing. He's out of sight from his car, mind you, because of this ridge we're on. If a boy were standing lookout right here and that man decided to start this way, then another boy who was over at that purple car could be signaled to ski-dattle."

"How come you tellin' us 'at, Mr. Jefferson?"

"Oh, no reason in particular."

"Huh?"

"Do I have to share all my contrary thoughts?"

"Go to head on, Mr. J., uh…I mean, Mr. Jefferson."

"All I was thinking is—it would be a real shame if someone were to take some yellow boundary-marking paint and write 'LSU SPY' on the side of a certain purple car."

"Auh…oouu," C.B. says.

I try to make eye contact with Mr. J., but he turns toward his lines.

"Boys, I'm not saying anything more about it. This conversation never happened…and I don't want any further questions. Now, come along. Let's get back on your boundary line lessons."

We follow along. Mr. J. points out the different kinds of trees, all of which Granna has already taught us. He does have a different slant on them. He tells us which ones are good for burning and which ones aren't, how some wood burns too fast or won't give off enough heat and how others pop and spark and won't split. With Mr. J., every tree has a new peculiarity about it. Granna probably knew all that, too. She just hadn't got around to telling yet or figured we weren't interested in those kinds of tree traits.

"Your early bloomers, like the maples and elms, they don't make good firewood," Mr. J. informs us.

C.B. counters, "Colored folks burns anything we can get a holt of, without payin' no never mind to what kind of wood it is or whether it's done bloomed or not."

Mr. J. looks at C.B. and shakes his head instead of speaking. C.B. sulks and stares at me, but I'm not about to take sides. Stopping by a blackjack oak, Mr. J. points to the ground. We know to sit quietly and listen. Our lecturer walks around to the side of the tree that faces my granddad's forest. After scraping off a baseball card-sized area of outer bark and exposing the manila-colored inner bark, he carves out a "P" with a circle around it he says is for the "O."

"'At ain't no post oak," C.B. states emphatically.

"It stands for Pen-Oake, the name of my place," Mr. J. enlightens us.

"Unlike firewood," he states, and stares hard at C.B., "you do have to use whatever tree you can find along your property line for marking boundaries. If a blackjack happens to be among those available, then you should always select it."

"Why's 'at?" C.B. impatiently presses our luck.

"Because you don't have to worry about the tree disappearing. Nobody is going to steal a blackjack. Some other witness tree or line tree could get used for furniture or a number of other things."

"You mean a blackjack ain't no good for nothin' but markin' boundaries?" C.B. asks.

"I'd never say that," Mr. J. comes back. "Everything and everybody, no matter what kind or color, has purposes, sometimes unfulfilled."

C.B.'s eyes light up. I think he feels Mr. J. was talking about his being a Negro but still being important because of some unknown reason.

As we move down the line, Mr. J. elaborates, "A blackjack, for instance, has good grasping-roots. It helps keep things in their place, and that's valuable for holding onto our north Mississippi soils."

Moving our lecture along again, we come to a dogwood. Mr. J. repeats his scribing procedure and starts up once more, "A dogwood is a pretty fair line tree. In addition to an occasional Crucifixion, it has all the boundary line qualities of a blackjack, except for attracting fish."

"Attractin' fish?" C.B. questions.

"Oh, yes. Ninety-nine percent of your better fish are caught by the one percent of better men who know what in the hole they're doing."

"The hole?" I question.

"That's right. The Chickasaw used to construct for themselves what modern-day fisherman call a honey hole."

"How?"

"That's what the Chickasaw used to say." Mr. J. holds his hand up for the international Indian sign, How!

"That's corny, Mr. Jefferson."

"Come to think of it, corn could also be attributed to the American Indian. I don't know how I let you boys distract me like that. Weren't we trying to discuss property lines?"

"Nossir," C.B. quickly answers. "We was talkin' 'bout fishin'."

"Well, well, deep in such thought as we were, the Indians would drop a blackjack tree or two in the deepest spot in the river. Then, they'd come back later and fish around it. Catching a mess of fish there would be almost as easy as using a potato-sack full of crushed walnuts."

"How's 'at, Mr. Jefferson?" C.B. sticks his neck way out toward our old friend for some serious listening to our new fishing instructor.

"It works because a blackjack is the one and only tree around here with such specific gravity that it will sink instead of floating off."

"Naw, I mean, what was 'at you said 'bout fishin' with crushed walnuts?" C.B. clarifies his question.

"You two are not yet responsible enough to learn about using crushed walnuts."

"Then what's pacific grabady?" C.B. asks.

"Specific gravity, and it's got to do with ratios and volumes, but for now we'd better stick with how a sunken blackjack attracts fish. It provides shade for big fish, makes escape cover for little fish, and gives somewhere for medium-sized fish to hang around and dream about worms. A conglomeration of blackjacks make a good place for all kinds of fish to float and grow and participate in the big fish to little fish ratio that distinguishes stock from quality…and to do whatever else it is they like to do."

"Like huntin' fer crushed walnuts?"

"No, no, quite the opposite, but like I told you, we are not getting in to that right yet."

"Then, what about th' acorns from blackjack oaks? Can't animals eat them? Can you crush 'em up to catch fish?" C.B. continues trying to make the connection for easy fish.

"Sort of yes to the first question, but definitely no to the second one. On a good year, a bad squirrel might do good to get a hat full of average acorns from a twenty-plus year old blackjack oak, and that's not near enough to warrant favoring such a species over much of anything else. Second answer—no, acorns are not any good for fish. Crushed walnuts don't do them any good either."

"But you said…."

"I said you two don't need to be accountable for certain things until you come to know a moderate degree of discretion, so don't hold your breath waiting on it." Mr. J. looks up at the clouds like he's fixing to get lost in his thoughts again.

We've seen him drift off like that before, so trying to get him back down to our world, I loudly agree, "Yes, Sir."

"All right then, a prerequisite for boundary line101 is to acknowledge that no man is willing to give or take more than an inch, not over his property lines. Where it is, is where it is, and any idiot knows what 'is' is. Since trees don't grow exactly on the line between ownerships, except occasionally by accident, a landowner should pick the nearest tree on each side of the line. He scribes his tree and his neighbor's, both blazes facing each other. Anyone who is worth a pinch of salt will know the boundary line goes somewhere in between the two blazes. Therein lies the tricky part. The precise location or personal situation often wavers with who is wanting to know, and why."

"How come it's to change on account of that?" C.B. asks.

"I know it doesn't sound fair, but such are the peculiarities of property lines and life. Therefore, you need to keep a vigilant eye on your trees and other things that your neighbor might think are his."

"Mr. Jefferson?" C.B. tries to get in a question.

"Trust me," Mr. J. ignores him and goes on, "if you line up trees or people right, then everything else will fall in place."

"Let's fix 'em, then," C.B. offers.

"Yeah, Mr. Jefferson, me and C.B.'ll do whatever you say."

"That's the spirit. Sometimes you boys make me plumb proud."

"What can we do, now?" I ask.

"Keep listening for the time being. You just as well understand early that around these parts, changes don't come easy, regardless of right or wrong. Tradition is one such classic example. It has never been accused of dying easily."

"I ain't seein' what's so hard 'bout lookin' fer blackjacks," C.B. argues.

"That's because you're not through listening. Virtually everything about blackjacks and such diversity in life is hard, and harder for some to accept than others, but a lot of life's lessons are tough by proportion to what they're worth."

"What'chu talkin' 'bout?"

"For instance, you could chop on this blackjack with pigheaded persistence and a pile of patience all day long, but other than getting some good exercise and being tired, all you'd have to show for your work would be an ax that looked like a sledgehammer. Your blackjack oak would still be standing there laughing at you. Some people are like that, no matter how hard you try to get through to them."

"You're not talking about us are you, Mr. Jefferson?" I ask.

"Not entirely, not at this time. And speaking of time—there is a lot here to be learned about timing, too."

"Auntay's done taught us all 'bout timin'," C.B. offers.

Mr. J. shakes his head and walks on. We follow. It's another blackjack stop…and I'm hoping C.B. was successful in diverting the lecture about time.

"At certain times, your landlines commence to take on astronomical importance," Mr. J. continues. "When a surveyor has one of those fancy doohickey things that lines up with the stars, or when your neighbor goes to cutting wood, it's times like that when folks tend to argue over their lines. Phenomenal circumstances can be carved out by proportion to the value of the land and timber. Are y'all following this?"

"Yes, Sir." *How many times have I heard Granna ask that?*

"Yessir."

"I don't want to lose you now."

"You ain't," C.B. answers. "We right here."

"All right. It's a well-known decision of Mother Nature's that the better the tree-growing soil is, the fewer blackjack oaks she allows on it. And if the trees are not properly identified as to whose are whose, let's just say—that can contribute to some monumental grown-up arguments."

"What's monda-menel mean, Mr. Jefferson?"

Mr. J. peers over his dark-rimmed spectacles at C.B. and then at me. "In cases concerning monuments, someone has usually stacked up piles of rocks to show property corners. Some corners are found and verified by our heavenly beacons." Mr. J. points up at the sun.

"Like moon rocks?" C.B. asks.

"No, not hardly. They're more like graveyard headstones. Monuments maintain boundaries and corners where our dearly beloved had long since recognized them as being. We call that the true line…until someone gets mad and simply moves the rocks and his neighbor's property line to suit himself."

"Mr. Jefferson?"

"I am as serious as a snake in a strawberry patch, and tinkering around with a man's land is right up there with kicking his dog. A fellow could get himself hanged by the neck for several weeks."

"What about th' space in th' middle, Mr. Jefferson?" C.B. asks. "'Tween th' facin' scribes?"

"'Tween?"

"Yessir, 'tween 'em."

"Oh, yes, that's what I believe you'd call the taint. It's land that really ought to be off-limits, kept as a kind of buffer for mistakes and peace-making, not to mention mankind's inadvertent contribution to wildlife habitat. Often we can do more good for animals by accident than we do on purpose."

"Why they call it a taint, Mr. Jefferson?"

"Well, I'm glad you asked that, C.B. It's sort of like your 'tween. It's not on one man's side of the line, and it 'taint' on the other man's either."

C.B. looks at me and rolls his eyes.

"Beep-beep-beep-beep-beep...beep."

"Listen, Mr. Jefferson. What kinda bird is that?" I ask.

"It's not a bird. That trilling sound is the call of a gray tree frog. You'll often hear them right before a warm rain. The Chickasaw claimed when you hear that, the frogs are praying for rain."

"That's pretty neat, Mr. Jefferson," I admit.

"Well, I just hope some day some professor doesn't come along and try to tell y'all that it's really the fore-rain's humidity or something like that bringing the beep-beep out of the tree frogs. I'm glad you can appreciate it for what it is." He points to us and to the ground again, and we sit.

"You can feel the very order of life out here, the interdependence of plants and animals with most everything else," he continues. "Look at that rotten log. It's not sitting there doing nothing. The fungus covering it up is busy breaking it down. See those little plants in the edge of the creek? They are working to purify the water and the air, and everything out here is somehow related. Isn't that something?"

"Humph...I mean, yes, Sir. Uh, it's just that sometimes you sound like my granna."

"Yessir, 'at sho' is inter'stin'," C.B. chimes in.

I could slug him for being such a brown-noser.

"Boys, I'm bad afraid there may come a time when you won't be able to walk along this little creek and hear tree frogs."

"Why's that, Mr. Jefferson?"

"Because Ole Miss and Oxford are growing together like a couple of cancers trying to mate. Multi-lane roads and shopping centers make for concrete and plastic. What's left of the working woods is sure to become threatened by the socialites."

"What's a so-sell-light, Mr. Jefferson? Is 'at th' same thing as a shoppin' center?"

"Not exactly. You'll recognize one when you first come across her. Modern technology and our so-called progress are changing the face of most everything near and dear to a man of the land."

Mr. J. goes on to tell us about the passing of peckerwood sawmills, the replacement of circular saws with band saws, the last of horse logging, and how we are losing mules to mechanical equipment.

"It's a shame what's happening to the last of our bottomland forests. Cold-hearted commercial cotton cropping is chewing up most of it. With the big-time soybean farmers sawing down and squaring off what's left, the greed barons are clearing beyond control."

"Can't we do somethin' 'bout it, Mr. Jefferson?"

"I don't know, now. It'd be a hell of a challenge for a couple of young boys. Somebody who wasn't afraid, though, might possibly have a profound effect on the very fate of it all."

"We ain't scared, Mr. Jefferson," C.B. offers.

"That's right," I agree with the challenge.

"Well, it'd be a contest leading to a life of combat. Not just anybody would be worthy of the cause. I'm not sure if you boys are cut out to be soldiers of such struggle. I'm not merely espousing a better land ethic but talking about waging war, everything from fighting fragile soils in over-logging our shortleaf pine hills to clashing with the Corps of re-engineers over their ditching and dredging of our rivers. I just don't know if y'all would ever be up to that calling."

C.B. and I glance at each other without further commitment. Mr. J. moves us toward another tree. A white-tail doe slips out of the edge of a honeysuckle patch ahead of us. Remaining silent, Mr. J., C.B., and I exchange looks among ourselves. The deer, fluffed in her fall coat, eases off without ever seeing us. We start back walking, and a yellow-shafted flicker flushes in front of us. I'm sure C.B. can identify it, from birding with Granna.

"There goes one of those white-ass dickie birds," Mr. J. says. "I believe they favor insects, but a lot of birds plant seeds with their droppings as they fly scared. I suppose the moral of that story is—when it comes to planting a forest, perhaps one old man of the big woods shouldn't push two young'uns too hard all at once."

"What's all 'at mean, Mr. Jefferson?" C.B. asks.

"It means you're dismissed now, and don't be forgetting how I 'did not' tell you boys where I left my paint bucket for tomorrow. Good day to you." Mr. J. starts toward his house.

"Bye, Mr. Jefferson."

"Bye, Mr. Jefferson."

He eases off without acknowledging our goodbyes.

"C.B."

"What?"

"I'm powerful glad Granna wasn't around to hear him give such a disrespectful name to that perfectly good yellow-shafted flicker."

"I'z sorta wishin' yo' preacher granddad had'a been, but speakin' of yellow, I don' see why we gotta wait an' see if 'at LSU tiger gon' return tomorrow. He ain't 'bout to quit watchin' football practice 'til they through fer th' day, today...an' 'at be right 'fore dark."

"We might could probably keep him from coming back tomorrow," I add.

"An' learnin' somethin' 'bout Ole Miss football he ain't got no business a'knowin'."

"You want to be the lookout or the one who gets to put the stripes on the tiger's tail?" I ask.

"'At ain't no decision a'tall. Man yo' lookout, my friend."

IX:
Lightning Bugs and Yocona Bottom Girl

NEEDING A MENTAL CHANGE and charge from five days of school, I'm ready to attack the weekend. The first Friday of my May '59 unwritten diary is marked by permission granted to camp out from Taylor. C.B. sits on the shaky top step of Auntay's front porch and waits for me with one of his not-so-predictable hounds. The big bad watchdog leaves when he sees me coming, but I know better than to be flattered. He'd probably have done the same for a burglar, if not a coon, rabbit, or deer.

Miss Sippy is swinging in an old truck tire that hangs from the shade tree. Also under the oldest post oak on the property, Auntay sits squeezed into and sticking out from both sides of some school's discarded desk chair.

As I walk into the yard with my camping roll and my new Benjamin pump-up pellet rifle, Auntay stops shelling English peas and stares with a suspicious eye.

She issues an Auntay Belle decree: "Ain't gon' be no shootin' birds 'cept fer th' sap-suckers. Now, mind what I'm a'tellin' ya."

"Why come not blackbirds?" C.B. argues.

"Y'all ain't near 'bout slick enough to slip up on no crow."

I'm dying to tell her a crow is a far caw from a blackbird, but I don't want her thinking I'm a know-it-all. She also underestimates my slipping prowess.

"God give us 'em songbirds fer more'n jus' lookin' at an' list'nin' to. They be holdin' down th' bugs fer us an'...."

"You sayin' sap-suckin' peckerwoods don't eat bugs?" C.B. interrupts to argue.

"Don't be a smarty-pants, now. I got th' faith God got all 'at leveled out, 'thout th' likes of yo' thumbs bein' on no scales. Y'all payin' nuff 'tention' to hear me?"

"Yessum," C.B. answers. He makes his caught-in-the-cookie-jar look for her sake, but sends me a rolling-of-the-eyes communiqué.

I lean my pellet rifle against the porch and commence picking cockleburs and beggar-lice off my socks and trouser legs.

"You get you a handful of cotton bolls an' roll it along yo' socks an' britches," Auntay offers. "'At'll get them things off'n ya, better'n you havin' to pick 'em."

"I'll try it." I walk over to the nearest cotton bushes...and think of how I'm starting to cotton to Miss Sippy.

Heading back with a handful of cotton and a wacky thought, I picture Auntay as some high-priced professor from the University. Being authentically experienced and not shy about sharing her observations, I'll bet there are some things she could teach the Ole Miss students, if they were smart enough to acknowledge her. I doubt the bulk of the all-white student body would consider such a grandmotherly old colored lady worth their time. Not many of them will ever have the distinct pleasure of being acquainted with Auntay and wouldn't recognize her as a wise person, valuable teacher and friend...and it's their loss.

I watch as Sippy pushes off with each back swing of the tire. She's got on her favorite pink dress with the white collar. I can't help noticing how soft and smooth her bare legs look as she points them out with each push and pulls them back in. She's probably wishing she could go camping with us, and I'm wishing it, too.

"Y'all best stay to Taylor Creek an' not get on 'at river," Auntay advises.

"Why's that?" I ask.

To my pleasant surprise, Miss Sippy answers instead of Auntay. "'Cause you stray too far down th' Yocona River an' Gut-Hook's liable to get'cha an' skin ya alive."

"Who's Gut-Hook?" I ask.

"You foolin' with me, boy? You don' know 'bout Gut-Hook?" she asks instead of answers and laughs as she reaches out with her foot to almost touch me as she swings.

C.B. butts in, "Aw, he's just an old commercial fisherman. Ain't nothin' to him, an' he ain't no concern of ourn."

Sippy comes back, "He ain't jus' no old fisherman, neither. Th' Gut-Hook's from somewheres 'round Wildcat Landin', an' he's one white man would jus' soon cut you up fer catfish bait as look at you cross-eyed, he would."

Wondering if it's Sippy or C.B. who is closer to knowing the truth, I look to Auntay for the answer. She goes on shelling peas as if there's no need to say anything right now.

Sippy continues, "He got carp lips an' field rat ears an' skin that's all crawly, an' eyes that's near 'bout all white. An' he don't take no stock in young'uns, he don't. Y'all best steer clear of him, I tell ya." She looks at me, and I feel good that she's concerned for me.

Not knowing who'll answer, I ask, "Where'd the name of Gut-Hook come from?"

Sippy is quickest. "Rumor got it he catched a man robbin' his trapline an' put th' gut hook to him, he did."

"The gut hook?" I question and scratch my head.

"Yeah. His wrong hand's a hook 'cause a alligator gar got aholt of all his fingers once't. Gut-Hook thought he was grabblin' with a granddaddy catfish. Talk is—he an' 'at gar both thought a lot of them fingers, they did. Both of 'em got to countin' on their stubborn to see 'em through, an' ever'body on th' river knowed Gut-Hook wadn't 'bout to let go, not with all his pride on th' line. After a spell, Gut-Hook wadn't holdin' onto nuthin' 'cause he didn't have nothin' to hold with. An' 'at's where th' sayin' 'bout th' big un got away come from."

Auntay finally looks up from her pan of bright green peas. "Naw, 'at ain't where th' sayin' come from, but it do say somethin' 'bout keepin' ya pride inside."

"Wait a minute," I ask. "What happened to the man who was caught in Gut-Hook's trap?"

"Gut-Hook's th' one what catched him, not one of his traps," Sippy clarifies with a grin at me. "But to answer yo' question, th' game warden said Gut-Hook stretched 'at man out on a bent willer like a beaver hide, an' he didn't get no Christian burial a'tall. An' 'at be how th' high-sheriff found him, an' knowed to arrest Gut-Hook fer seben year, he did."

Sippy stops pushing the tire swing and looks at Auntay. I'm figuring it's to get approval to go on with her tale. Auntay rearranges her snuff from her upper lip to her lower lip, which could be some kind of secret and unspoken approval for Sippy to continue.

"'Cordin' to folks 'at know, ever'thing got to crowdin' in on Gut-Hook at Parchman prison. He come near tearin' th' place down tryin' to get out of there. Then our Guv'ner, he put Gut-Hook out on a parole what banished him from th' penny'tench'y, an' he ain't neber went back yet, he didn't."

I hunt for confirmation in Auntay's stoic face, but see none.

"I ain't never paid Gut-Hook no mind," C.B. says. "He's just a old man spends all his time trappin' an' runnin' trotlines." C.B. starts patting the back of his thigh like he does when he gets antsy and wants to leave.

Trying to come up with a new subject for discussion that will keep us here with Miss Sippy awhile, I say the first thing that comes to mind. "Tell us something we need to know about girls, Miss Auntay."

"Girls?" Auntay scoffs and looks at me with a slight grin. She gathers hulls into her apron and makes an excuse instead of an answer. "Young'un, you not near ready to take on knowin' 'bout girls."

Sippy gives me a quick glance and smiles big time. C.B. curls down both sides of his mouth as if he wishes I hadn't asked anything...much less something like that. With her hand on a big hip, Auntay takes on a stance that says this is all too much to let go.

"Someday you gon' meet up with some little gal who gots a mind to be kind. 'Bout that time you'll catch on pretty fast or yo' whole world'll be turned bottom-side up an' catty whomp."

"How am I going to know when I meet the right girl?"

"Ha, ha ha...aah. 'At's li'ble to take you comin' up on th' wrong one a time or two first...ha, ha ha...aah."

"Miss Belle?"

"When th' right one come along, you'll be done figgered it out, if'n she's taken a notion fer ya to...ha, ha ha...aah."

I don't think Auntay or C.B. has a clue who I'm thinking about, and I wonder if Sippy does. She's got her head tucked down, but I can see her mouth's half-smiling. My buddy's expression indicates he has decided this might be worth learning more about, after all.

"What you talkin' 'bout, Auntay?"

She points her finger right at C.B.'s nose. "Yo' time's a'comin' too, boy...ha, ha, aah."

Sippy giggles, and her cheeks dimple in the way I love to see them do. I don't see how she could help notice the way I look at her.

Auntay carries on, "First frilly filly 'at wiggles her little tail at you…ha, ha ha…aah, I just wish I could be there to see it a'happenin'. You be tryin' to figger out which way to go—this'a way or that'a way."

"I'm getting scared, Miss Belle," I jest.

"Yeah, you terrible funny sometime," C.B. sarcastically adds.

"We be a'seein' who's funny when y'all get a bit older. You start to find favor with someone special to ya, 'at's when you be gettin' schooled on th' ways of womenfolk." She puts her pan of peas in her apron full of hulls and squeezes her bulk up and out of her desk chair. Heading toward the house, she warns, "You boys just as well mark my word on it right now—you in fer some times, sho nuff."

"Yes, ma'am."

"Yessum." C.B. jumps off the step. "Come on, Scott. We need to find us a campsite 'fore time to roost."

I grab my gear and pellet rifle, give a little half-wave at Miss Sippy, and head to the backyard. She smiles again and pushes herself higher in the tire swing.

With the minimal camping stuff rolled up in a blanket, C.B. leads the way across the first field. A flock of half-a-dozen shadows floats beneath us. We both look up. Large white birds are quietly flying for the rookery Auntay calls their heron home. As they flew over Granna's first, they no doubt got dubbed as snowy egrets.

"Dumb as a stump, them cranes," C.B. comments. "Ain't got no better brains than to be takin' cover under clouds an' pickin' through cow cakes fer food."

After that assessment, I feel almost obliged to take up for the birds. "Granna says when you see one flying with his neck pulled in like that, instead of it being stretched out, that means he's a heron and not a crane. I've been looking for cranes every since she told me that, but I hadn't seen one yet."

"I have," C.B. one-ups me.

"Where?" I challenge him. "When did you see one?"

"I don' know. Once a'fore. I disremember it right now."

Granna has prepared sack-suppers. We're to share half of each. She made me promise not to open them until suppertime but did advise that we'd be dining on Italian hors d'oeuvres and Mississippi round steak. Never having had either, I am looking forward to it.

A water snake sliding off a sycamore limb welcomes us to Taylor Creek. Next, from a half-submerged log, a turtle plops into the water for his own safety. This time of day, the green corridor that separates the cotton and the cornfield from the creek yields a May pop and morning glory fragrance.

We side-slope our way along the sapling-studded bank to stay out of the fields. It's rougher walking and a little farther, but we're not going camping to walk in fields. A pair of great blues land in the bend just ahead of us. C.B. reaches over and pats the stock of my pellet rifle.

I shake my head, no. "Let's just watch them for a while."

Walking and stalking with poise and the very definition of stealth, one of the large birds effortlessly takes a bluegill. With his snack in his long bill, the heron apparently having the better fishing skills wades out and stalks up onto a sandbar. The other bird follows, and they both stretch their wings as if to air out. They begin hopping around as if they've lost their minds...and then rub each other's neck with each other's neck. C.B. thinks the bird antics are funny, but I'm recognizing them as courting rituals...and my situation with Miss Sippy as fantasy.

Contrary to the Auntay General's direct orders about staying away from the Yocona River and Sippy's specific words of warning about Gut-Hook, we make our way through the cane break in that direction. Aimed for downstream where Taylor Creek feeds into the river, we find a thick gray haze as if it were some kind of warning we should but don't take. The creek water is the color of an acorn, and the river water a slightly darker shade, perhaps the color of an acorn's cap, or cup as Granna calls it. The marbled mixture of the two colors where the waters mix reminds me of none other than Miss Sippy.

The flow along the Yocona River is wide-open compared to that of tree-covered Taylor Creek, with its drooping black willow branches and shade. In the river everything is all spread out, as if it's suddenly exposed to the dangers of the world, with no bank-restraining bushes or small passages reserved for swifter water. I wonder if the water itself is more vulnerable to something bad...something like Gut-Hook.

A piece of the earth caves off from our path and into the river. We pass through a two-foot tall patch of poison oak. C.B. breaks off a small leaf and puts it in his mouth.

"What are you doing, Fool?"

He looks at me and pretends he has no idea what I'm talking about.

I know full well he knows what I'm questioning. "Do you know what that was you just put in your mouth?"

"Poison ivy."

"Are you trying to kill yourself off?"

"Naw, naw. Ever since I'z a little boy, come spring an' Auntay'd have me take a little bigger piece than th' year before, to keep up my amoonity from th' scratching-rash."

"Immunity, and I'll probably break out from just thinking about that."

"It ain't no use arguin'. It's a proved fact of business."

"Yeah, right."

"You want me to see can I find you a pansy leaf or somethin' mo' in line with what a city boy prob'ly needs?"

Knowing I'd merely be out-talked, I don't even answer. Fighting our way beyond a briar patch full of blackberry stickers, we come to a small swamp. A well-defined niche, instead of one that blends in and out through transitions, it's bordered by a distinct line of sandpapery leaved elms. I'm supposed to remember what kind they are by their wide-spreading crowns, as opposed to the elms that have the flat tops or the ones with the rounded crowns or the ones with the cedar-like bark. I can usually remember the name of something when Granna's associated it with something else, but I have flat-out forgot this one.

Trying to hop from vegetative high spots of unidentified cabbage-like greenery to clumps of bunch grass, I manage to keep my feet dry for all of the first two hops. Cool follows wet right in between my toes. It settles in as if to stay but to remind me that no longer having to worry about dry socks also has its advantages.

As we wade and slosh on across the slough, I contemplate the culinary potential of this unique habitat. A couple of swamp rabbits simultaneously pound out from behind both sides of a stand of cattail. I jump back. C.B. looks at me and shrugs his shoulders…at my being too startled to get off an air-powered pellet rifle shot. Unilke these big swampers, our rabbits in Bailey Woods are the smaller and less spooky cottontails.

Reaching the far border of the bog, we find high and dry ground and an animal trail available for walking along the upper berm of our river.

The deep scarlet-colored bloom of a strawberry bush catches my sight and draws me over to let my nose have a whiff. To my surprise, C.B. doesn't make some flowery wisecrack or comment about my appreciating one of nature's better perfumes.

Commotion in a muddy pool ahead of us turns out to be a pair of muskrats. The swamp rats, as C.B. calls them, appear to be swimming in a game of tag. We stand and watch until one of them sinks out of sight and the other swims downstream to disappear around the corner. Another hundred feet along the way, a pair of wood ducks swims into the near darkness. I'm figuring they're scouting out trees for a roosting site.

"C.B., have you noticed how most everything we've seen is paired off, a male with a female?"

"'At be th' way of May, Auntay say."

"I reckon you've got an answer for everything, don't you?"

"No more'n you always questionin' ever'thing."

The wood ducks flush and fly off to find a spot with two less quarrelsome boys.

"Do you ever think about growing up without ever finding a girl of your own?" I ask.

"Pacifically, I ain't shore I'm wantin' to."

"Specifically, C.B."

"Yeah, yeah." He stops to re-tie his shoe.

"Well, I don't know about you, but I don't want to grow up and be all by myself. Don't you worry about being lonesome, when everybody else'll probably have a wife?"

"I like bein' by myself," he answers, as the thick jimsonweed slows our foot travel.

The grass gets progressively taller, but I'm not worried about snakes. I'm in front, and it's my understanding that a snake always bites the second person in a line.

"Have you done got yo'self a girlfriend?" C.B. asks.

I cast a furtive glance at him before answering. "Sort of."

"Nuther'words, no," he pronounces with assurance.

"There's one I'm beginning to think is, uh...sorta special, but I haven't let her know it yet."

"How come?" He smiles. "You scared to?"

"Not really, I just don't know if I can tell her without messing things up."

"Why not?" He presses me.

I'm wondering without C.B. knowing, what rejection across the forbidden racial line would feel like. She looks more Indian than colored, anyway. Maybe it wouldn't be so sinful.

"I don't think I could even talk to her about that. If I tried to tell her anything, I'd probably just step all over my ding-a-ling. By the time I get done stumbling around, wouldn't either one of us know what I'd said."

"You or your ding-a-ling?"

"Me or her," I clarify.

"You crazy."

"All I know is—everything feels right when I'm around her."

"'Splain that," he insists, as we hike on.

"I'm not sure I can. It's kind of like...you know how, when something's funny enough, you go from laughing so hard that your eyes end up watering like they were crying. It's nuts, I tell you."

"Yeah, I'd say 'at's a big part of it. But you can get yo' head right, out here. You can get yo'self sitch'ated fer th' night an' that'll he'p ya get justified."

"What did you just say?"

"I said th' Yoc'ny Bottom gots a way of brinin' out what needs to be brought out of you."

"We'll see," I answer and figure he's got no idea it's his sister that I've got it bad for.

When my buddy announces we're where we're headed, dusk and a campsite just happen to reveal themselves.

"I'll gather th' makings fer a couple of mossy bedrolls if you'll see can you get us a one-match, driftwood fire goin'," C.B. offers.

"How come it's gotta be a one-matcher?"

"Practice."

Nightfall closes in firmly as we finish up with our agreed-upon chores. Crickets tell us it's time for supper.

"'Member what yo' Granna said 'bout sharin'," C.B. reminds me.

"I am. You do too."

There is silence while we dig the lunch sacks out of our packs. I peek in without showing off the contents of mine. C.B. does the same with his, and we each take sample bites and look at one another for responses.

"Scott, this Mis'sippi round steak we was promised seems a whole lot like rag baloney to me."

"And I hate to tell you this, but our Italian hors d'oeuvres ain't nothing more than Vienna sausages."

"We been had agin."

Doing as Granna instructed, we divide the food from both sacks. Though not what we expected, everything is appreciated, to the extent that there's nothing left for breakfast.

An already good darkness thickens and mixes with the evening haze. A bat zigzags back and forth along the edge of the river and comes so close I feel uneasy about it. As the driftwood from our campfire catches on, fireflies flirt with its sparks. I remember Mr. J. telling us that it's the sand in driftwood that causes the sparks. When even a grain of sand has someone to come courting it, I don't see why I've gotta be so left out.

"Scott, I wisht we had us a lantern to hang on a limb."

"Yeah, we'll have to get us one. I'm gonna turn in." I crawl in my bedroll, and a cool breeze sends a chill down my ribs. Drawing my legs up to my chest, I place my hands over my nipples to warm them and press my arms to my ribs for their chills. "Good night, C.B."

"Same to ya."

As the river flows into the night, several owls show up to complete our evening's sounds. Our feathered friends have brought with them a restful chorus that I hope will continue until I can drop off to sleep. The trickling sound of the Yocona River suggests the need to pee, so much that I pay the river back for making me get out of my bedroll. Between the serenading owls holding me at half-sleep and C.B.'s periodic sort of snort-type snore, I'm kept from very much meaningful slumber.

We have a standing agreement that the one who wakes up during the night assumes the responsibility of stoking what's left of the fire. Eventually, and only after getting up several times throughout the night, an all-too-vocal chuck-will's-widow helps me recognize consciousness slightly ahead of sunup. C.B. mumbles something about a whip-poor-will, but I decide it's too early to argue over which it is.

The campfire's flames have died, and its once crackling sounds and softly sporadic song have now taken on smoldering silence. Coals would probably still be good for stick-roasting most anything, if we hadn't already eaten everything last night. Wind whistling through the tree cover brings a soothing familiarity as rays of light slip through the canopy. The entire bottom fills with sounds of birds that soon out-vote the chuck-will's-widow.

"You hear that? Them's th' kinda sounds Oxford ain't never heard."

"Don't start that crap, C.B."

"You can do some good thinkin' along th' Yoc'ny."

"It's too early for one of your Mother Nature speeches. I'm not listening."

"I ain't lettin' you go back to sleep. On a mornin' like this'un, you can feel th' woods good as you can see 'em."

"Yeah, and I wanta keep my eyes closed for a while, so I can practice that...that uh, whatever you said."

Hearing him climbing out of his bedroll, I give up. After an extended stretch and a deep breath of new air, I climb out of my warm and comfortable blankets. Of all things, a yellow-shafted flicker lights on a snag about twenty yards in front of us.

"Look," C.B. points out, "there's one of them white a...."

"Don't say it," I interrupt him.

We watch as she calls to her mate. Something in woodpecker is chattered back to her. I'm thinking they were probably saying something about breakfast...or going back to bed.

Turning the red of the back of her neck toward us, she presents C.B. an all-too-irresistible target. He has grabbed my pellet rifle and nailed her with one air-powered shot before I have time to object. Ordinarily he'd brag about his accuracy, but this time he sees enough disapproval in my expression to know I don't want to hear it.

"C.B."

"What?"

"You're not shooting my pellet rifle any more if you kill another songbird for no reason."

"A flicker ain't no songbird, an' eben Auntay said we can shoot sapsuckers."

I suppose he's right, but I'm seeing it as awful unfair that some male flicker will now have to live alone...like me without Miss Sippy. When Auntay's directions and Bible misquotes start getting confusing, that's when I'm not knowing if I'm gonna understand anything, anymore.

C.B. walks over and picks up his kill. It's not fair that he is such a good shot. It's my gun, and I've had gobs more practice shooting than him. First with my BB gun and now with my pellet rifle, he's the superior marksman, steady as a dead ironwood tree...while I shake like jelly that's yet to set.

"C.B., please tell me we're not going to eat that thing for breakfast."

Stroking the yucky, wet, and smelly feathers, he looks at it with a blank stare. "Why not? I'd say a Bailey Woods kinda boundary-line bird with a white rump would have a lot more meat to it than them tadpole tails we've eat."

"I don't guess I remember either of us turning down any of them."

"Not once't we got 'em skint out an' fried up. 'Member me tellin' you how th' Yoc'ny bottom brings out what's true? Somethin' 'bout these woods 'at clears up ever'thing, an' keeps you knowin' what's important."

"You got all this preachy philosophy from murdering a poor and helpless little bird whose mate is now gonna have to live all alone?"

"Th' bottom'll talk to you, if you'll jus' listen."

He still has no idea I'm stumped over Miss Sippy.

"I'm tellin' ya, Mama Nature'll show ya th' stuff 'at you might uh thought didn't make no sense. She'll stay with you after ever'thing else has went."

Swatting at deerflies around my ears and nose, I challenge him, "How about bugs then? What kind of woods-reading do you get from insects?"

"Give me a minute to think about it."

"Oh, Lord, why'd I ask?"

"Seein's you did ax, you 'member them lightnin' bugs we was watchin' last night?"

"Yes. Why?" I ask out of habit, while I'm still secretly wondering what to do or not do about my first love.

C.B. looks at me and takes on his got'cha grin, before bursting into an uninhibited chorus—"Let Yo' Little Light Shine, Let it shine, Let it shine!"

X:
Gut-Hook Holler

THE BACKWATER OF ENID Lake is hardly moving. C.B. and I wander downstream at about the same pace as the Yocona River. The morning is dew heavy, and natural stands of blue phlox and panic grass grow like a planted garden along our path. Fog has moistened everywhere the greenery can't reach, and my brushing up against the lush vegetation has me soaked from my knees down.

Whereas I'm off from school, with Granna attending some kind of parent-teacher deal as my fill-in mother, C.B. is simply skipping colored school. I don't know what he's missing, but it's a glorious day for me not to have to think about long division and fractions.

Our first significant find of the day is a bird's nest that looks just like one Granna once proved to me belonged to a barred owl. Having seen my grandmother demonstrate it, I decide to make a bold announcement that I can do the same.

With more hope than confidence, I ask, "You wanta see me call up the owl that goes with that nest?"

"I'd haf'ta see 'at fore' I'd believe it," C.B. responds, looking at me with the doubt I anticipated.

Accumulating excess saliva in the back of my mouth and an absence of air at the top of my throat, I hoot from deep within my diaphragm, "Ouh, ouh, ouh, ah, oooo!"

While I'm thinking it sounded pretty good, in an all-too-obvious response, a hound from right down the river starts baying. C.B.'s laughter is uproarious.

"You just wait," I proclaim and hoot again.

The dog answers back. Ridicule doesn't stop. My buddy's teasing is relentless. Around the bend of button-bush and down an alder-choked path, we encounter the mournful coon dog…caught in a fox trap. If I never see it again, he has a look on his dogface like he knew answering an owl call would set him free. Displaying a grateful gleam in his eyes, he sits back and holds up the paw with a steel foot-hold trap hanging on it. C.B. and I can't help laughing.

"Look at th' human-like way he's holdin' 'at trap out fer ya to take it off'n 'im."

"Me?" I question C.B.'s jump to that conclusion.

"He ain't gon' bite you. Go ahead. Let him loose," C.B. cheers me on from a safe distance.

Securely fastened to an exposed root wad, a small chain dangles below the trapped paw. The dog doesn't appear to be in any pain. With a soft voice and slow speech, I ease up to him.

"Good dog, you're a good dog," I tell the coonhound.

Looking pitiful, my new canine friend doesn't appear to be the type that could even think about growling. The trap comes right off. He simply limps over to the berm of the riverbank about six feet away and lies down. His expression has sheer appreciation pawed all over it, and I'm thinking this dog may now want a lifetime of friendship with me.

"Listen!" C.B. says.

We hear an outboard coming up the river.

"Reckon it's Gut-Hook?" I ask.

"I dunno, but if you know what's good fer ya, you best set that trap back, in case it's his."

Not wanting to fight fate, but being all fingers, I fumble with it until it is re-set. In order to place the trap back where it was, I momentarily turn my back to my new, seemingly grateful dog friend.

"Look out!" C.B. yells.

Before the warning registers, the dog has jumped across to where I'm bent over and bitten me on the pointy part of my buttocks. Quick as I can swing around to kick at him, he scurries off toward Taylor, without any visible limp.

"I don't understand that," I mutter and rub my rear.

C.B. tries unsuccessfully to stifle a laugh.

"Shut up and tell me if it's bleeding." I turn around and pull the top of my pants partway down and the bottom of my underwear partway up.

"It's red but th' skin ain't broke. He didn't hurt nothin' but yo' feelin'."

"Speaking of feelings, why would a dog bite someone right after they'd helped him?" I ask.

"I 'spect it had to do with who he figgered 'at trap belonged to…when he seen you re-settin' it."

I don't know if I can leap to C.B.'s logic, but I know a bite of betrayal when I feel it. I'm about convinced that old-time, good Samaritan Baptist Bible stuff doesn't apply to dogs. My butt feels like I could use a dose of Gathright-Reed's turpentine dog bite remedy.

"Scott, 'at boat's gettin' pretty close."

On plane, a johnboat comes bouncing around the bend at full throttle before we can run. There is a loud pop that sounds like cheap metal breaking. The driver and seat, still sitting together, go flying out of the boat and skip across the outside of the wake. As they tumble into and under the water, I look at C.B. for his reaction. Other than being wide-eyed and open-mouthed, he's apparently uncertain about what's appropriate. The driver resurfaces yelling and waving his arm straight up in the air, as if he's shaking it at God.

At the very same time I realize there is a hook on the end of his arm in place of a hand, C.B. announces, "It's Gut-Hook!"

The boat has slowed to an idle and putters around in a tight, circular pattern. As it chugs from one side of the river to the other, I figure if Gut-Hook doesn't drown, he'll at least get run over by his own boat. Instead, he manages to hook onto the side of it and climb in. His words are much clearer from the boat. I can now hear that I was right about his talking to God.

Prior to any significant settling down, Gut-Hook looks over and sees C.B. and me on the bank, warm and dry and watching. He starts waving his hook again and yelling at us like he did at the Lord. I'm thinking the trap I just re-set and put back must belong to him, after all.

C.B. picks this moment to establish how he feels about the whole affair. Pointing at Gut-Hook and bouncing up and down in laughter, C.B.'s reaction creates a fitting time for us to depart. Appearing to be unappreciative of any humor right now, Gut-Hook starts toward us.

"Let's get outta here!" I shout.

Prior to sprinting off through the bushes and just for spite, C.B. throws a stick in my re-set trap to re-spring it. That's enough initiative for me to run in front. This being no time to be indecisive, I'm hoping the coon dog knew the best running lanes. The harder I run, the more I feel like Gut-Hook is closing in, but I'm not about to look back for fear it would impede my speed. As if to slow me down, sorrowful-looking black willows sag into both sides of the creek run. Granna's always said God manifests Himself in the out-of-doors. Not seeing any game wardens or anyone else around here to help, I'm finally ready for Jesus.

When I'm almost convinced we've put a good distance between us and the river, we run right up to it. Being forced finally to look back or swim, I select the dry choice. Seeing no sign of Gut-Hook, I am religiously born again. No longer anticipating all the ugly things in life that Gut-Hook could have done to us if he'd caught us, considerable calm seems to have come over the entire Yocona Bottom.

"I oughta knowed you'd run us in a circle 'til we got dog-tired," C.B. complains. "What we gon' do now?"

Before I can question whether our determined adversary's legendary run-ins with the law are all Sippy cracked them up to be, we hear the outboard coming up the river again.

"It sound like he's off 'bout a quarter. We got time to hide. Let's get behind them bushes an' have us a better look-see at him when he come by."

"All right," I agree.

"Man, hearin' 'at is knowin' Gut-Hook ain't right behind us. An' bein' shore he ain't fixin' to come out of them woods, 'at feels good as a toothache bein' over with."

I'm looking forward to getting a better view of this swamp celebrity. Flipping through the air and ricocheting across the top of the river in his boat seat, Gut-Hook looked half again taller than the high water marks on the trees. We scoot around behind a stand of thick smartweed, where we can peek over into the river without being seen.

"Was that the first time you've ever seen him?" I ask.

"I ain't neber needed to see him to know 'bout him. Chicken-Hawk says he ain't had both oars in th' water since he got screwed over in th' big war."

"Screwed up? You didn't tell me nothing about that before we came out here."

"I figgered it wadn't no need in it. He's 'sposed to be enough like a snake 'at he'll leave you alone if you leave him alone."

"What part of leaving him alone do you call springing his fox trap and laughing and pointing at him after he had a boat accident and near drown?"

C.B. doesn't answer, and Gut-Hook motors right in front of us. As if I can't see for myself, C.B. sizes him up for us.

"God bless A'mighty, he's bad tall. He's wide like a flyin' squirrel an' ain't got no thick to him through th' middle neither. I guess 'at's what he gets on account of bein' French an' In'jun both."

Gut-Hook passes on by, but when he gets barely upstream, he cuts the motor off and guides the momentum of his boat to drift over to our side of the river. C.B. puts a hand on my shoulder, as if he's fixing to push off to run. On my own verge of bolting, I stop breathing.

With Gut-Hook's good hand and the shortest paddle I've ever seen, he makes a well-placed stroke and turns his boat halfway around. I'm gonna be able to drive a boat that good someday. It drifts backward into the mouth of an old oxbow, where he ties up the side of the boat to a cypress knee.

As we sit tight, he throws his hip-booted legs over the side of his boat. In the height of contrast to his last entry into the river, he slides into the knee-deep water. After giving each hip boot a tug with his hook, he uses his good hand to straighten his overalls. Two traps are carefully selected from the boat. Hand-carrying those, he seems to hook a third one indiscriminately. Considering his purposeful shuffle, wading out through the underwater mud to avoid tripping over an unexposed log, Gut-Hook appears to be easy afoot. He negotiates the dead water of the slough with his head thrown back as if he were well-born or something. I consider the possibility that instead of being so maladjusted he may just like being out here by himself. I am honestly prepared to appreciate such backwater nobility.

"Scott, I'm sipherin'—it should oughta take longer fer one man with only one hand to set three beaver traps than it will fer two boys with four fast feet to inspect one boat. Don' you reckon?"

Being as Gut-Hook is obviously a man who knows his domain and how to travel through it and this is an area that's tougher walking for shorter people, I'm not so sure C.B. is right, but we ease on over for a closer look.

It's as if the smell is guarding his boat. I'd have guessed Gut-Hook had more than an admirable toleration for animal odors, being a trapper and all, and now I'm thinking he may have needed that river spill we witnessed.

Holding my nose to emphasize my evaluation, I suggest, "That smell probably helps him to be a better than average trapper."

"If'n he was any good, he wouldn't be accidentally catchin' no coon dogs," C.B. comes back.

My buddy may be right. Any self-respecting skunk would probably run for cover if he were to hear Gut-Hook's boat coming. Other than its rank odor, the boat doesn't appear to be of remarkable interest. I do notice a nice spool of trot-line cord lying in the back of the boat, by the plug and drain hole. The mischievous side of my mind takes complete control over what a good guy I normally consider myself. I'm seeing potential for the cord and plug in a way they were not meant to work together.

With Gut-Hook living a life so withdrawn into river bottom hermitage, I don't doubt he gets blamed for a multitude of sins he may not even be guilty of, but I'm also willing to believe that he has fallen foul with something somewhere else and gotten away with it. A little prank now, whether deserved or not, could be considered pay-back for what was warranted at one of those times.

"C.B., you see that plug and that cord?"

"Uh huh," he answers.

"If that plug was stuck in real lightly from the outside, instead of being securely plugged from the inside, it'd still work, sorta, for a while. Gut-Hook could still drive off, while a piece of that trot-line tied to a cypress knee could pull the plug out."

Grinning like a persimmon-puckered 'possum, C.B. reaches over into the back of the boat and pulls the plug, seals the plug-hole with the heel of his hand, and then re-inserts the plug from the outside in. I cut an appropriate length from Gut-Hook's spool of cord and tie one end to the ring on the plug and the other to the underwater part of a cypress knee behind the boat.

We opt to follow the river back upstream and hold down the risk of taking any more unwarranted, circular walks. A half-dozen woodies are disturbed into whistling their displeasure at having to leave the serenity of their riverside pool, a pool they probably think beavers came out from the backwater muck just to build for them. Minnows are skirting around in a razzle-dazzle.

"C.B., this looks like a campsite for sometime like a playin' hooky day, when we need to do some meditating."

"Yeah, I 'spect it could sho he'p a feller ferget whatever it was he needed to do without fer a while. I could start comin' down here now an' agin."

Next, we come to a little waterfall where pebbles gleam, polished by the wear of the water. My sidekick scoops up a handful of water and drinks from his palm. Leaves from a Tupelo gum tree float around in the confused current where branch water ripples into the not-so-clear river.

"We best quit dilly-dallyin' around an' get movin' on," C.B. suggests.

Mid-slope, along the river's edge, an animal trail carries us below a field that's rich with yellow and green goldenrod. From damp and slippery footing, I make a careful hurdle over a beaver run. C.B. makes it, too.

With the sounds of what's bound to be Gut-Hook's outboard motor coming up river again, we find another good hiding spot and wait. The boat and motor stop just around the corner and still out of sight from us. There is yelling again. I recognize the voice.

"Listen, Scott, listen to him holler."

"Yes, we're gonna have to start calling this bottom, Gut-Hook holler."

"He's sayin' somethin' 'bout th' boat a'takin' on water, an' hollerin' at...."

"I hope he's not one to hold a grudge," I answer.

C.B. glances toward the heavens and slowly shakes his head from side to side. "Fer Gut-Hook's sake, I'm a'hopin' God is th' One don't hold no grudges."

XI:
Two-Wheeling
Freedmen-Town

"COME ON, C.B., GIVE it a little go-juice. That's all you got to do."

"I'm tryin'."

"All you've got to remember is, it needs to move."

"You ain't wrong there," he complains. "Ever' time you let go it moves straight down on th' concrete."

"That's not what I meant. Since it has to go somewhere anyway, you just have to make it go front-ways instead of down. That's the secret to riding a bike. See to it that it goes this way instead of that way. That's the only difference between riding and falling."

Here it is nearing the end of what Mr. J. calls the fabulous fifties, and C.B. still doesn't own a bicycle. Up to now, we've been riding double on my bike…with me always getting to drive. He's normally more than happy to sit on the handlebars, back fender, crossbar, or even the seat if I agree to stand up in front of him to be where I can pedal. Coordination-wise, C.B. has never been the kind of kid who could keep a Hula-Hoop going and bounce on a pogo stick at the same time.

C.B. tries again and continues to prove only that the challenge is no minor feat, but today is going to be different. This is the day I'm determined to teach him to ride my bike.

"If you'll try it going down thrill hill, you won't even have to pedal."

"You crazy, too."

"I'm serious. The best way to learn is by coasting. All you'll have to do is steer."

"I'll keep tryin' on flat ground, thank you jus' th' same."

He sets his mouth with a grim line of determination. As he mounts the seat, I steady, and he pedals. With one hand on back of the bike seat to help hold him up and my other hand pushing on the fender, I run along behind him for all I'm worth. It brings back memory of my crippled father doing the same for me. Dad had to limp-skip to keep up. Looking back on his polio and seeing that, a kid can get to love his father. I don't know of a lot of fathers with two good legs who did as well. There may be some, but C.B. will never have the experience of a father doing it for him. He can remember me.

"Ever'thing looks differ'nt from a bicycle seat," C.B. acknowledges. "It's a kinda windy freedom, an' makes you feel like you leavin' behind what all you don't want."

He strokes the shiny chrome handlebars with a longing touch. I remember the joy that came from learning to ride, and now it's almost as good watching C.B. get the hang of it. As he curbs most of his wobbles and holds his falls to fewer, he doesn't have to thank me. What he said about life looking different is good enough.

"This is one thing Oxford has over your Taylor...lots of concrete to ride on."

"Eben if it ain't no hard-top roads in Taylor, I wisht I had a bike. Let's ride over to where Sassafras stays an' see what's goin' on there. You wanta?"

"Think it'd be all right for me?" I ask.

"You mean, 'cause you white?"

"Well...yeah, I guess."

"Don't nobody care 'bout that," he reassures me, "bein' as you jus' a kid."

"I'd better drive. You're not good enough for doubles yet."

Bicycling to the section of real estate that's affectionately referred to as Freedmen-Town by the Negroes and unaffectionately called Nigger-Town by some of the whites takes about ten minutes. It's a sub-community made up of one long hill with shotgun and shanty houses lining both sides of the dirt and sparse gravel road. Auntay's sister, Sassafras, lives in the middle of it.

When he can't satisfactorily coordinate commutes to and from Oxford and Taylor, C.B. sometimes spends nights here. I've seen this side of Oxford from a distance and even ridden through it in Dad's taxi, but two-wheeling down the middle of Freedmen-Town allows me to size up everything in a way I can almost taste the smell of cabbage cooking.

There's an aroma that's got to be a mixture of sardines and barbecued potato chips. I've smelled it before.

Whereas a few yards have bright and sparkly junk gaudily strung about, most are flowerless or weedy. Unlike the rest of Oxford, lawns here aren't manicured…but some do have the dirt-swept look of Auntay's place in Taylor. Not like the rest of my city, there are no neatly-paved, tree-lined driveways. A long-eared mutt of the city-pound variety chases us and starts a chain reaction of dog barks.

"C.B., are there any mad dogs here we need to worry about?"

"They's a few bad uns we got trained to bite white boys." He grins.

"Get off it, C.B."

"Th' bike?"

"Never mind."

"They ain't gon' bother you…not long as you with me."

"Yeah…right." With that comment, I feel like a decoy that's been brought along to attract them to me and keep them away from him.

The mainstream of contemporary society seems to have come to town and passed right on by this neighborhood. A whole different Oxford from the so-called respectable side of town, this is an area drenched in desolate poverty and drowning with despair.

It's a day a lot of folks have fled their small houses for fresher air…or whatever limits of liberty they think they can find from their front porches. I doubt if many residents in this gregarious hodge-podge of a community could hold much stock in something good ever coming their way. It's like God under-blessed them. Mothers up and down both sides of the road appear to range from the ageless to those all-too-young teenagers nursing their first of what will probably be many babies. Without any illusions, I picture a bleak future for my friend.

In contrast to everything here, I think about how fortunate I am to have such a nice game plan all laid out for me. C.B. doesn't have a life promising added privileges with age. His is a different world…and I must not look down on anything in it. Any show of pity over such a sorrowful situation would do nothing but make the indignities worse. Determined to present an attitude that says I'm at home with whatever I find, I skid to a stop in front of Sassafras' house. With more drama than necessary, C.B. sails off the handlebars.

There's not much to the house. The whole thing could use some white paint. A tiny porch holds a couple miniature milk churns with discouraged rose bushes in them…and everything else pretty much looking like a refuge of the oppressed and impoverished. The yard on one side of the house is set off from the neighbors by sad-looking cross vines. The other side blends across a small open space shared with the occupants living over there.

Sassafras comes out through the front door and greets us with a questioning look. C.B. said she was close to forty, and I say she looks every bit of it. Only about half the size of Auntay, Sister Sassy still has the family's round look to her. I don't know how Sippy escaped it, but I'm glad she did.

"You boys get on outta here." The city branch of their family tree doesn't appear to be overly-rooted with friendliness. "I ain't up to havin' no loud company now, not with no Granny Re….I mean, a headache."

I'm guessing the aggravated air about her is why she's called Sassy. C.B. had suggested that I should try to get off to a friendly footing with her. I wish he'd say that to me about his sister. I'm not sure I can see a lot of promise in either of those possibilities.

From what I know about my white world, I suspect C.B.'s colored one is frowning on us for running around together. It's not uncommon to hear some pretty ugly remarks from my 6th-grade class about my preferring to spend weekends with C.B. instead of with white kids. C.B. and I simply play through others' confused feelings and decide we don't need anyone sanctioning our friendship.

As the strangeness of Freedmen-Town wears off, it becomes easier to go over and hang around Sister Sassy's house. Slightly shaking the foundations of the antebellum South, it becomes commonplace for C.B. and me to be seen together. Taking hold of no such prejudices as most of those around us, we quietly and gradually integrate a bit of Oxford.

In addition to my becoming as bored with C.B.'s shoddy side of town as he does my snooty side of it, the distinct monotony of both Oxfords helps grow our devotion to Bailey Woods and Yocona Bottom. With the out-of-doors becoming the common ground in our friendship, an unspoken, yet unwavering loyalty to one another further develops.

There's much talk going around the University and town about the likelihood of problems with regard to desegregation. When my father starts up on the subject of my spending so much time with a colored boy, I can't feel the same shame he does. I turn a deaf ear and reason that out of sight is out of mind.

C.B. seems more interested in next year's move into the 7th grade, but I'm more worried about how not all of the Negroes of Freedmen-Town have accepted me. Chicken-Hawk is the center of my concern. Chicken, as he's sometimes called for short, is Sister Sassy's undeclared and un-husband-like live-in boyfriend. For the better part, he is plain mean and uncommonly loathsome. Despite trying to be C.B.'s main male role model, Chicken doesn't appear to have any positive qualities.

It's a spring Saturday on Sassy's little front porch when I ponder the subject with my pal. "Is it that Chicken-Hawk doesn't like me because I'm white?"

C.B. shakes his head in expressionless defense. "Chicken don't like nobody, so 'at ain't wholly it."

Wholly or not, I'm knowing every time Chicken-Hawk sees us, his personal struggles somehow become enmeshed with C.B. and me and our own affairs. Dealing with the Chicken gets old fast. Talking to him is bad enough. Although he has a bias toward higher education, he openly admits his most appreciable success was going through the "B" encyclo-pedia and learning everything from the blues to bull hockey...but he didn't say hockey.

"Scott, Chicken-Hawk's aims is by an' large higher'n his faults. He might eben like you once he catches up to his Christian love."

I don't know how he can figure that's gonna happen, considering how Chicken harbors such definite and malicious intentions toward me.

"He's jus' got to have somebody to goad," C.B. continues. "Liken him to a yellow jacket, pointin' his sting at you jus' 'cause you there."

"C.B., he's barely got good walking-around sense. I'll lay you odds— if God told him to go outside and kick our butts, he'd kick our butts on the way outside instead."

"Couldn't you jus' give'im some credit? Couldn't ya do that? Try to see past Chicken-Hawk's foolin' with us."

"C.B., how's anybody supposed to see past a six-and-a-half-foot-tall crazy man with a pock-marked face? How are you going to miss him? You ever notice how his shirts have sleeves about four inches short of his wrists? Why would anybody want to show off such girly-looking arms with thin bones and big veins? They're probably swollen on account of straining to avoid work."

When C.B. doesn't respond, I'm thinking this is about as close as he'll come to giving up on the argument. I'll shut up and see if he does, but I can't stop thinking about Chicken-Hawk. In Sassy's eyes, he's above reproach. Unless she counts his self-deception, he can do no wrong according to her. Therein lies one of our problems. With Chicken not getting his due credit for being the cause of anything bad, Sassy has come to see everything that isn't right as being the doings of C.B. and me. The truth be known—most of our worrisome woes are on account of C.B.'s shady mentor.

WITH SUMMER BUMPING UP against the end of the school year of '59, a stranger hits town. He's a *State Times* newspaper representative from Jackson. Through some fancy finagling by my father, I am hooked up for an interview. Even though Dad had already told me about it, the fat man visiting from the state capitol explains to me about a contest to see which kid around town can sign up the most subscriptions to his newspaper. The grand prize will be a new Schwinn bicycle and a $50 savings bond.

When I tell the newspaper man about my buddy, C.B., and how bad he wants a bike, Dad mentions to the *State Times* man that C.B. is colored. Since I'd already told C.B. about the contest and promised to get him entered, I now have to tell him about how it seems I got the last slot for entry in the contest and that the applications were officially closed without him.

Eager for good news, C.B. comes over the next day. "Afternoon, Scott, you get me th' innerfue 'bout winnin' th' bicycle?"

"Interview, C.B." I stall by re-tying my tennis shoes…and try again to think of how to tell my buddy the problem.

"Well, did ya?"

"No. The paper man said the slots were closed."

"What's 'at mean?"

"I don't know for sure. I can't explain something I don't really understand myself, but since they turned you down and…uh, since I got in, you can help me."

"How come you get to do it an' I don't?" he demands.

"Because of who I am, I reckon."

"What'cha mean by that?"

"C.B., I don't know…my father maybe, because of who he is."

"'Cause you got a father, you mean?"

"Naw, because he's not just anybody, but somebody...you know, somebody."

"Because he's white?"

"I don't know, C.B."

"You oughta know. He's yo' Daddy."

"I know he's white. I just don't know if that's all there is to the reason. How come everything with you has always got to be black and white?"

C.B. reaches down, unties one of my tennis shoes, and looks at me with an angry stare. "You sure you axed him 'bout me? Did he know I'z colored?"

"I asked him for you, C.B. That's all I can say. That's all I could do."

"How many colored boys did they let in th' contest, Scott?"

"None I know of."

"At's what I thought." He turns and starts to walk away.

I grab his shirtsleeve. "Wait a minute, C.B. You know none of that's my doings. Now, listen up a minute. Since I've got a bike and you don't, when I win the new one you can have my old bike."

"You swear?"

"Yeah, and it stands to my reason you ought to help instead of going up against me. We'll be more likely to win. If we don't, then...well, we're still riding double. Okay?"

With resignation, but appreciation, C.B. agrees. "I'll buy that."

"You don't have to buy it. I'll give it to you, free."

"'At wadn't what I meant, an' you knowed it."

With a business-like handshake, our deal is sealed. Before the subscription-getting contest commences, I lay personal claim to the savings bond. Sharing goes only so far, and I plan on buying a .22 rifle with the money. C.B. can shoot it, but it'll belong to me.

My buddy signs up somebody from about every fourth house in Freedmen-Town. Trying my best to get subscriptions, I visit roughly ten times the number of houses as C.B. When I'm finished with Oxford proper, I cover University housing and then some residences out in the county. Still, I secure only about half the number of new customers as C.B. Combining our subscriptions, the contest is in the saddlebag. If I'd just known the second-place kid wasn't even in the running, I sure wouldn't have knocked on all those doors and taken all those rejections.

At the official presentation for contest winners, C.B. is nowhere to be seen. I'm awarded the shiny, new red and chrome colored bike and my fifty-dollar savings bond…without my sidekick being there to share in the elation. I suppose being defiant is C.B.'s idea of a silent protest. I don't guess I can blame him for it.

The bike is like a good-fitting baseball mitt. White, streamer-laden, and molded handlebar grips feel like they were made for my hands. The pedals don't squeak like those of my old bike. Unlike my fenderless old bike, this one has fenders that should keep rainwater from splashing up on my ankles. I sail with the silence and grace of a buzzard's soar.

When Dad admires my bike, I don't think much about it, until he says he's proud of me. That, I believe, was the first time ever. It makes me happy, except for remembering the part of the affair where C.B. was excluded.

"Son," Dad says, "I expect you to take on this paper route with responsibility, now." When I don't answer, he senses reluctance. "Don't you want a little spending money?"

"I guess so, Dad…and I want to buy a .22 rifle with the savings bond I won. Okay?"

"When your little black buddy gets elected Grand Wizard of the Klan," he snorts.

"Dad? I earned it. I won that money fair and square, and I worked hard for it," I plead earnestly.

"Son…."

"Come on, Dad. Please? I won't shoot nobody with it."

"No. Not now. You're too young for the responsibility. You save that savings bond for a few years, and we'll talk about it again after you've proved yourself."

"All right, Dad." Obligating myself through rain or shine, I pledge to serve all of my new customers.

———————————

AS PROMISED, I GIVE my old bike to my friend. Dad gets a little upset that I didn't sell the old bike, but he'll get over it. Bicycle freedom and hours of fun riding together will bring much joy to both C.B. and me.

For a promise to split the profits, my friend is easily talked into helping with the paper route. Our earnings should be enough to bring with them a taste of financial independence from Dad and Granna for me, and from Auntay and Sassy for C.B.

Thinking about having people count on C.B. and me to help keep their world in check by delivering their evening news gives me a worthwhile feeling. Apart from working in Dad's grocery store, the *State Times* paper route is my first real job. In addition to playing a part in the adult world, I'm planning on doing some adult spending.

The first day of delivery comes with excitement. "Let's ride," I announce.

"Scott, I ain't felt so special since yo' Granna showed us 'at *Reader's Digest* wrote about Mr. J. complainin' over some local kids lettin' his hog out."

"Yeah, I don't know what other kids do to fill in their days…but compared to us, they hardly got a handle on their bikes."

"An' ridin' all these hills around Oxford gon' help our legs get horsestrong. I feel sorry fer anybody 'at ain't us."

"I can taste the future, C.B. With all the money we'll earn, we can make all our dreams come true."

"An' jus' think 'bout what's gon' do it fer us—a little black ink on thin white paper to be read all over."

Hearing his not-so-rhythmic riddle is supportive, but looking back at all of the many papers in my baskets, I also hear something from deep within my soul's gut praying—*Lord, them or me one needs some delivery.*

Amen, I add.

XII:
Chicken-Hawk's
Tater Eyes

TO SPEED UP PAPER deliveries, C.B. and I try splitting up. When the first couple of days of dividing our ride evolves into racing, that idea gets old and too much like work. As opposed to being in a hurry alone, we opt for the leisurely, more pleasant ride together, be it longer.

With baskets crammed full of rolled and rubber-banded newspapers at the ready for throwing, en masse rides provide opportunity for discussion and dialogue. Ideas and ideals range from impersonal philosophies to personal problems, with plenty of time to kick them all around. Numerous deliveries allow for the showing off of newspaper throws, with accuracy in the toss becoming casually competitive. Admiring good throws and laughing at each other's roof, bush, cat, and dog throws, our only worry is that we might have a window throw.

Oxford's a quiet town with scarcely a squeak of commerce. Unless you include education from the University, to find much of anything one could call manufacturing, you'd have to count the commercial growing of trees, and that's out in the county. As a result of all this, there's a nice absence of automobile traffic. Gentle hills, smoothly paved streets, and the scent of freshly mowed grass, all make biking in the white part of town ideal for a paper route. It's a wonderful place, for most of its people.

AS I COAST DOWN the hill through the Freedmen-Town leg of my paper route, C.B.'s companionship takes on an additional value…that of security. Although the rest of the residents leave us alone, Chicken-Hawk is the exception to all rules…and anything else that gets in his way.

Dust wheeling up behind us, the driving force of momentum pushes us down the long, unpaved section of road. If we don't accumulate enough speed to outrun the barking dogs, our fall-back plan is throwing newspapers at them, which sometimes causes deliveries to come up short of papers.

"You think Chicken-Hawk'll chase us today?" I ask.

"To pat us down fer money, you mean?"

"For anything? Or no reason at all?"

"I don' know."

C.B. makes the perfect paper throw and immediately starts talking, as if there wasn't anything to making such a great toss.

"Scott, you ever notice how good's jus' good, but bad's got all kinds of partic'lars 'bout it?"

"No, but I've noticed how you're the only one in the world who could come up with crap like that."

"Jus' tryin' to keep your head to workin' 'tween your ears."

There's a blurry and furious commotion ahead. A rat terrier has apparently caught a 'possum. As we approach, the little dog takes his larger prey by the throat and shakes him unmercifully. The 'possum, although twice the size of the terrier and three times as ugly, rolls over and plays dead. I feel so sorry for him, I kick his squeaky little attacker off of him. While the dog runs off, the 'possum continues to fake his expiration, I think.

C.B. proudly points to the fact that we don't see things like this in the other sections of town. Contradicting himself and his own country-comes-to-town trivia, he informs me, "I can catch me a 'possum behind Th' Mansion restaurant any time I wanta."

While I'm wondering why anyone would want to catch a 'possum, I pretend not to be impressed. He continues anyway.

"I can box-trap him where th' leftovers is thrown out 'at causes th' Chinese kids to starve to death."

I've heard that story from Granna about Chinese children starving because we throw out food, and I'm not sure I buy it.

Before the 'possum shows any signs of appreciation for what I've done, Chicken-Hawk materializes from out of the nowhere that is Freedman-Town. Nearly succumbed to the indignity of drunkenness, the

Chicken stumblingly straddles my front fender and holds my handle-bars. If he weren't so tall, I could ram his crotch. Before I can think of the next best alternative, he orders me to put the 'possum on top of the daily news in one of my bicycle baskets.

The critter's tail is not cold as I thought it'd be, and he's heavier than I expected. Chicken probably thought I'd be afraid to touch it. After warning C.B. and me that the consequences of the 'possum escaping could be seriously damaging to us, Chicken instructs us to go to Sassy's and standby for his further orders.

Fretfully waiting for our nemesis at Sassy's, C.B. tries to assure me that half the fright of dealing with Chicken-Hawk is in the wait. Although it's the other half I'm worried about, I'm pretty sure I know how a 'possum lying in a bicycle basket feels. I try to convince C.B. to consider not complying with any of the Chicken's additional innovations, but I'm assured there is nowhere to run, not with Chicken strutting down the hill at us like a fighting rooster.

Next door, five men have a yard fire burning that smells like a garbage dump. They must just like to stand around trash fires because nobody could be cold enough to need a fire in the summer. Chicken stops to visit briefly with them and then waves his long and bony hand to summon us to join them. C.B. was wrong about the wait. This is gonna be worse, distress elevating with Chicken's look at me. He picks up our captive by the tail the way he saw me do it and then rears back as if to 'possum-slap me. Instead, he slings it past me and into the fire. Everyone except Chicken steps back in disgust. He laughs and moves even closer for inspection of his fiery tribulation.

With gray fur charred and tail singed, the poor 'possum jumps up and out of the fire to leave a smoke trail into the kudzu gully behind the house. Smoldering its way under the leafy green maze and out of sight, the 'possum leaves the five men laughing. This apparently encourages Chicken enough to think they have come around to his perverse way of thinking. Fresh with their depraved endorsement, he commences with new orders for C.B. and me.

"Y'all catch ol' fireball an' bring him back, now, or you gon' wish you had of. You hear?"

"Yessir," C.B. says.

I don't make a sound and receive Chicken's mean stare again for my silence on the matter. He's probably trying to think of something else bad to do to us. As Chicken takes his control compulsion in the house to recoup, I look for some degree of wiggle room, but my buddy sees nothing except complete obedience. I argue, but C.B. is insistent.

During an all-but-gallant losing effort to re-catch the 'possum, I'm wishing I could keep an ear on the circle of men around the out-of-season and pathetic fire. Three older men sit facing the fire, one on an RC Cola case, another atop a cracker barrel, and the third on a metal folding chair turned backward. A couple of younger men, both cuddling mason jars wrapped in paper sacks, stand drunkardly swaying with their butts toward the fire.

Beyond the cardboard, rags, and scrap pallet, a green piss-oak limb is about to be enveloped by the fire. An old car tire lies ready to be rolled on the pile and reminds me of one of Granna's proverbs. It preaches about diligent men making use of what all they can find. I sure don't want to go against the Bible, but I can't see how five men given to excessive drinking this time of day could beget anything but hopelessness.

Toting a bushel basket full of Irish potatoes under each arm, Chicken-Hawk staggers out of Sassy's. "It was yo' choice not to catch 'at 'possum. Now, here, this ain't gon' take y'all but 'bout an hour. Put a stack of papers right cheer 'tween these two baskets."

When I mention that this plan will cause the second half of my paper route to be late and that I'll be short some papers, Chicken makes it perfectly clear that he simply doesn't care.

"These here is gon' be plantin' taters," he points out, and explains the details pertaining to us.

We nod in understanding, but Chicken continues with more specific instructions anyway. "Tater's gots these eyes an' 'at's what sprouts when you plant 'em. Y'all cut ever' tater up so each chunk's got a eye on it. Then wrap it in a half sheet of today's newspaper fer th' plantin'. Now, get to work."

Not one to devote my full attention to a potato, as I cut and wrap, I make the best of my time by listening to the conversations around the fire. I always enjoy listening to Papa and Mr. Jefferson when they sit around and do nothing but talk. It soon becomes apparent that this is strikingly different. Old wives' tales, stories of hoop snakes, and other assortments of superstitions and Negro folklore all come up short of what I recognize as the truth.

Talk of relief office subsistence and welfare worker assistance is hard for me to get my mind around, but I'm about to realize how standing around watching a 'possum be thrown into a fire could almost be considered entertainment. Such an existence in idleness is what C.B.'d call hurtin' fer cert'in.

A merry-go-round of unemployment must promise little cure for difficulties that appear to be so settled in they are almost comfortable. I wonder if some of these ailments affect only the poor and if they couldn't be doing something to improve their lot. Regardless of how much can rightfully be blamed on others, the inhabitants of Freedmen-Town appear to be merely waiting around for an inheritance of more poverty.

Maybe C.B. endures his situation at Sassy's to get to what he enjoys at Auntay's. As I see him smile when he reaches for the last potato piece, I know he won't accept this for his way of life. Somehow he always maintains a cheerful face and happy attitude through this sort of abuse. It's probably all his laughter and caring and grateful praise to the Lord at Taylor that helps him along.

Dad's taxi pulls up in front of the house. He's brought Sassy from where she's been janitoring on the campus. He looks at me with an expression that says I have no business being in this community other than pitching papers. When he drives off without speaking, I'm thinking I should have asked him to come over here to pluck the Chicken.

Sassy waddles her way up the dirt walk and makes her way around to the yard fire. Obviously flustered over her day's work, she greets us with an angry scowl. "What's goin' on here, dip wads?"

Looking around to make sure she's not talking to someone else, I see that Chicken and all his friends have disappeared. I know just enough to let C.B. figure out how to best answer Sassy's threatening mood.

"Chicken-Hawk said...uh, 'fore you could plant these tater chunks we...uh, had to wrap ever' one of 'em by theyselves in a half piece of newspaper."

"What?" she angrily demands that C.B. clarify.

"To...uh, keep th' dirt outta their eyes. An' we jus' finished 'em up," C.B. boasts. "They ready fer you, Sis,"

"Where is Chicken-Hawk, now?" Sassy's voice rises to what C.B. calls the pissed-off pitch.

"He musta left 'round th' back of th' house, 'bout th' time you was comin' up."

"So he did, did he?"

"Yessum...an' he said th' papers had to be today's, 'cause on account of th' signs an' ever'thing. They's four sheets out of ever' paper. We had to tear each one of 'em down th' middle where it's folded 'cause Chicken said th' whole sheet was too much, an' anything short of a half weren't enough. An' he said you'd pay me an' Scott fer 'em."

"An' you two ijets believed all this, did you?" With her hands on her big round hips, she rolls her eyes and shakes her head.

"Uh-ooh," C.B. lets out an understanding, apparently realizing what I'm now thinking. He tries to cover up. "You know how Chicken-Hawk is 'bout us believin' him, Sis. We had to do what he said."

Sister Sassy looks grim but agrees, "Yes, Charlie Boy, I'm 'fraid I do, an' when I get aholt of him, I'm gon' skin him with a dull knife."

Looking at Sassy and then at me in unspoken acknowledgment that we've been had, C.B. reaches deep into his trouser pocket. Pulling his jackknife back out, he offers, "Here, Sis, you can use my knife fer th' skinnin'."

"Y'all two's gon' hafta learn to play 'possum when th' Chicken gets to pullin' yo' funny bones thata way."

I'm not going to argue with Sister Sassy by any means, but I'm sure thinking—*yeah, that'd be a good way to get thrown in a fire.*

XIII:
Camp Meeting and Cemetery Work Day

WITH SO MUCH GOOD countryside around Taylor, C.B. claims even the acres are surrounded by acres. Within hiking distance, we have roamed the forests and fields and explored enough briar patches to uncover every place that could hide a rabbit…the entire drainage basin from Thacker Mountain on the north to Springhill on the south.

Labor Day weekend calls for closing out the summer of '60 camping, climbing trees, and wading swamps along both sides of the Yocona River. Having come to call the backwaters of Enid Lake our second home, it's not to Auntay's or Granna's surprises that we opt for converting their Taylor spreads into our bases of operation. As usual, we double up on grub by telling Auntay we're carrying on out of where she stays and Granna that we're working out from her country home.

Auntay is last to see us off. "Y'all make shore yo' final destination's where you set out fer, you hear?"

C.B. reacts, "What the Sam he…hey, hey, hoe, hoe…uh, does that mean?"

"Hoe, hoe's right, boy. What'd you 'bout say?" Auntay puts her hands on her wide hips and becomes even more intimidating.

"Nothin'. I didn't say it. I mean I didn't say nothin'."

"Th' Lord knows what yo' full meanin' was, Charles."

"I didn't say nothin'," C.B. continues to claim.

"It's bad enough if'n you's thinkin' it."

"I didn't think it, then, Auntay," C.B.'s voice trails off into his whip-poor-will-like whimper, reserved for such times.

Her look continues to scold C.B. Figuring my buddy is half again past needing a diversion, I interrupt. "Auntay Belle, what did you mean about our final destination?"

"I means if'n y'all not wantin' to 'tend th' camp meetin' with me, my own self, then you ain't got no business nowheres near Yocona Hill Cemetery fer th' meal. You don't be leavin' 'at bottom is what I means. You hear?"

"Yessum," C.B. is almost too quick to respond.

"Yes, ma'am," I add.

Being told to stay away from a church-going activity almost makes me want to go…for perhaps the first time ever. I wonder if Papa would be proud of that, not to mention God.

"Now, y'all best get on outta here 'fore you go to rubbin' on my raw state of nerves more'n you done done. I gots to go to work in a little bit."

C.B. mimics Auntay without her seeing him. As we ease away from her immediate influence, I worry that C.B.'s dubious decision-making will sway me into going along with what's normal for us, in spite of my better judgment. In doing exactly what Auntay warned us not to do, trouble's familiar signs promise just such potential.

We make preparations to roam instead of to camp out and stow our camping gear in a hideout at the briar brush patch just off State Road 328. Hiking along the Yocona River works up a tremendous need to cool down. When we reach the spring water hole, temptation is too great.

"What ya say we go skinny dippin'?" C.B. suggests.

"I will if you will," I answer without first putting enough thought behind it.

Having never seen each other in the raw, I am suddenly realizing this may not have been such a hot idea after all. Before I enter the frigid water, I'd better be sure he gets a glimpse of me being uninhibited…or better yet, not let him see me at all. Taking a peek at C.B.'s privates for the first time, I see that I was right. Despite the preceding rainless weeks and near-currentless river, a deep water hole has enough water for refuge.

The loose-like floating feeling of the nude wilderness experience is rather enjoyable, until I imagine a giant snapping turtle big enough to turn me into a girl with one bite. Experiencing the cold water soft-shrink and having my extremities turn their bluish shade of white is a combination that makes me want to drip-dry and put my clothes back on before my unfairly disproportionate buddy can see me. With C.B. at my back, I wade back in toward the banks and find the shallow river rich with every sort of creepy crawler imaginable. The above-surface world doesn't concern itself, as I knead the wet sand with my toes, but an assortment of aquatic insects scatter. Pushing over an underwater rock and sending a crawdad scurrying too fast for inspection, I wonder if they really scoot around backward. All I can ever see is a blur leaving a cloud of muddy water.

After getting back into our clothes, we continue through the flats of the hardwooded flood plains that stretch out along the river. We eventually work our way up to and through the red clay rolling hills. After the gully-cliffs, we reach the sandy ridge and hilltops of the virgin shortleaf piney woods, with its otherwise unvegetated world of an eerily dry understory. There's nothing but needles in the pine shade, at least on the surface.

Approaching the Yocona Cemetery and church-house complex, C.B. describes for me how we should anticipate homecoming at the cemetery. "There'll be singin' all 'round, with dinner on th' ground."

Arriving at the church from a gully side, it's not at all what I expected. I've never seen a House of The Lord that looked like sin could slip in under the back baseboards and infiltrate. A rusted tin roof allows for a matching steeple that would probably lend itself to a greater faith if it were a little straighter.

A nice crop of what the Yankees call Mississippi vine covers a window that will afford an outside blind. Wallowing through the kudzu weed, we climb up to a close secrecy, from which we can hide and spy on the goings-on inside.

My first peek makes it clear what I've heard about these revival weeks and Negro camp meetings. These folks have caught the spirit. Dad says Holy Roller reunions for re-religion are a colored annual equivalent to the daily repenting that Catholics have to do. But here you can get it all over with at one time, which sounds a whole lot better to me.

"You either get th' Spirit or you don't," C.B. explains their behavior. "It ain't no in between."

"Sort of like catching a cold, huh?" I offer, in fun.

My partner gives me a defensive look. "Accordin' to Auntay, who knows th' whole Bible's insides an' out, th' good news is—th' Spirit's also somethin' you can grow to know." His look turns offensive.

I'm thinking he and his Auntay don't know any more than me and my Grandfather, but when C.B. gets argumentative about his colored religion I don't like to over-push him on it, in case God might side with someone who's thinking different from me about it.

Everyone inside must be dressed in what's their Sunday best. Church music and gospel songs have set them to swaying. Tasting the spirit right through the windowpane, I think the heartfelt foot stomping on their yellow poplar floor would be contagious if I had a better place to stomp. C.B. is slapping his thigh and bobbing his head like rhythm is rocking his soul.

No one seems to be paying any attention to anyone else as they move with the spirit. The womenfolk seem to have caught the religion in a most powerful way. Ladies' arms rise while their bodies jerk.

There's leaping up in the air, bending over double in the hardwood pews, and lying on the floor. Heads bob and weave as all inhibitions must have been left at the front door. There are constant calls to "Sweet Jesus" and "Precious Lord," but the joyful noises unto the Lord sound more like wailing and moaning to me.

The black brethren don't appear to share their women's enthusiasm fully. If they weren't of the professed faith, I don't suppose they'd be here, but most of them sit passively as if they're simply going along with the spiritual program…and I think I've been there before. Eventually, congregational movement is slowed through song and music. The harmony of souls' salvation has spread throughout the rough-sawn barn-board walls…and possibly leaked a little through the window.

What Papa calls a hellfire-and-brimstone sermon erupts. From sins through sorrows to gladness and good tithing, the preacher covers it all. As the congregation drinks in the words of passion, I wonder if it will linger when the part about ten percent comes…and if it will seem like just as much in a black church as it does in a white church.

"Th' archangel gon' descend from heaben, an' th' angels will come down," the preacher promises.

Preaching reverberates from trance-like to rhythmic chant as I hear strange words that must be prophetic. There are words and ideas I've never heard, like being vexed. I wonder what that feels like, being vexed.

After the preacher repeats the part about angels coming down like he really means it, I look up to see if it's happening. Seeing nothing and seeing that so many others who are looking up are also seeing nothing, I envision dropping down from the rafters with a bed sheet tied over me. That'd send them scattering and beat the Hades out of Bible drills and having to read aloud when you're wishing you were somewhere else. I hope it's not a sin to hate Sunday school.

"C.B., I believe your Christian Methodist Black way of dealing with God's gospels helps your faith to sorta come out."

"Where do you get Christian Methodist Black?" he asks.

"Isn't that what the C.M.B. stands for on the church sign?"

"It's Colored Missionary Baptist, fool."

Miraculously, I am provided with a distraction from my embarrassment at mistaking the name of my buddy's religion. I would have thought it a pure phenomenon—Chicken-Hawk is right here inside the church. Who would have thought it? And here I thought I was going to detest and despise him utterly every chance I got. C.B. seems as pleasantly surprised to see him as I am.

"Maybe th' devil will turn him a'loose an' come out of him fer good," my buddy prays aloud.

"You may be giving the Chicken too much credit by blaming everything on the devil. Some of it is bound to be Chicken-Hawk's fault."

"'At's just his way. He don't mean nothin' by his doin's. You ought not pay him so much mind."

"Sure, we'll try not minding him next time he tells us to do something," I suggest in jest.

"Chicken's gotta have more'n a smidgen of religion in him. Come to think of it, he's always sayin', 'fer Christ's sake'."

The preacher's emotional commentary slides into prayer, and one from among his flock does not have his eyes closed. As a slight grin moves over his face, he looks around.

"Heaben help us. Sumpin's up," C.B. analyzes the situation. "Chicken-Hawk don't usually smile no more'n a snake 'at jus' eat."

The very mention of a snake at such a sacred place reminds me of Papa's stories about Christianized snakes being used by church folks way back in the country. I picture this preacher trying to handle a Yocona Puff Adder to prove his faith. I don't know why my mind has to work like this. I can almost see one crawling out from under that pulpit podium right about now and starting his puff-up procedure. Somebody would be finding or losing his religion.

With many members kneeling and all but two heads bowed, Chicken-Hawk stands up. Before I can celebrate that this might be one of those miracles where the Lord works in mysterious ways, Chicken turns toward the back of the church-house instead of the front. When Vidallia nods a non-Christian-like acknowledgment and gets herself up, they slip out the back door together.

Being Sassy's cousin and niece all rolled into one, Vidallia has always been sort of special. Chicken takes her hand, and they walk over to a '50 Ford. Such an expensive-looking car couldn't belong to either of them.

As they get in the back seat and go down and out of sight, C.B. asks, "You wanta bet they ain't prayin'?"

The car starts rocking. "Maybe it's what the Preacher meant by laying on the hands," I suggest with sacrilege.

"They gots th' spirit an' th' spirit is strong," C.B. jokes.

After about five minutes, Chicken-Hawk rolls down the window and throws something out. Next, he and Vidallia ease up to the church and wait on another prayer to close everyone's eyes again. When that happens, the two of them slip back in.

C.B. goes over to the car to see what it was that Chicken threw out. Of all things, it must have been a balloon. C.B. blows it up and ties it on the rear antenna of Chicken-Hawk's borrowed car. When C.B. returns, he explains that it oughta teach Chicken a lesson not to be trashing up the church yard with that kind of littering.

More pleading and praising up to heaven lasts on into the dark and then way past. A nocturnal kind of reverence comes from the moonlight and all the stars highlighting what's going on inside. I hope God doesn't mind our finding funny some of the carrying on we've witnessed. The sense of accomplishment does prevail. As it is well beyond time for supper, the congregation is told to go home, eat, get some rest, and return tomorrow for a cemetery workday with dinner-on-the-ground.

"Looks like it's took," C.B. sums up what I was thinking.

By believers' standards, or any other way one could call it, the revival looks to have been a resounding success. The big ditch directly downhill from us is so thick with shrouds of kudzu that C.B. suggests it will cradle us like a web and work like we're in a couple of hammocks. We try it, and I'm quickly convinced. Lying back in total comfort of such a natural bedroll will serve as good a place as any to spend the rest of this night.

When the clear night sky puts on a star show better than I've ever seen, I wonder if it's something religious. Scanning the heavenly bodies above, I can't help wondering if sleeping this close to one of God's churches might help us find better favor with Him.

"What you reckon's th' most," C.B. breaks my tranquility, "th' number of stars up there or th' number of grains of sand on th' Yoc'ny riverbank?"

"Where do you come up with crap like that?"

"Right here, man, all you gotta do's look up."

"Never mind. I'm fixing to get some sleep." I turn my back to him and hope he'll stop talking for awhile.

"Yeah, it ain't far 'til sunup. Good night."

"Same to ya."

With the tiny purple kudzu flowers quivering with the breeze and spreading their grape fragrance, it's like the night has its own natural perfume. The large leaves periodically flop around with gusts of wind, and the late night air fills with the songs of close-up crickets and the cries of far-off coyotes, as I doze off to a restful sleep.

Although it hasn't rained during the night, morning breaks heavy with dew, and I'm feeling a little heavy myself. The vine has wrapped around both of my ankles. I don't know if the darn stuff grew that much during the night or if it was C.B.'s outdoor equivalent of tying my shoestrings together.

Auntay was right about the weatherman being wrong…or either all that praying for good weather has worked. Regardless, The Lord has let some of His church-goers get started early. Others will return throughout the morning for trimming weeds, cutting grass and whatever it is they're going to be picking up around the church. With Chicken having been here, there's no telling what they're liable to find laying around the churchyard.

One thing I'm pretty sure of is that no one will be crawling through this kudzu. Lying around so late and spying on cemetery workers all morning works up an appetite. By an early noon—and since we know Auntay has to work and won't be here—I've convinced C.B. that he can go over and take more than a look-see at this dinner on the ground I've heard so much about.

After a brief absence, C.B. returns with a plate of eats. Dad's grocery store has never seen the likes of what the Negro Christians have spread out for their special occasion.

"Take this here an' I'll go back an' get me a plate," he offers.

I take the plate and try to figure out what I'm looking at. While I recognize peas, figs, sweet-potatoes, and cracklin' cornbread, I can't name the three types of mystery meat or figure out what kind of cake I have. Strong smells surround them but only add to the puzzle.

When C.B. returns with his plate, I ask, "What's this fish?"

"'At's carp…or buffalo fish."

"And this?" I poke at a strange mound.

"'At there is chitlins." He rubs his tummy and licks his lips.

"What's shitlins?"

"Chitlins, an' I ain't so shore what they are, pig parts I think. Eat 'em. They good."

"What kind of cake is this?"

"It ain't cake. It's 'simmon nut bread. Don't you know nothin'? I'm beginin' to wonder if you can tell a walnut from a hick'ry nut."

"You know better than that."

"Then what's this right here?" He asks and points to what looks like some kind of cake on his plate.

"I don't know," I admit.

"Hick'ry nut pie. See what I told you?"

"Well, what about this other meat?" I ask.

"'At's coon."

I feast on everything except one of the meats. While C.B. has managed to slip in and out of the kudzu without being seen, the legitimate guests have served themselves and selected piled rock-type headstones on which to rest their drinks and plates.

Just as everyone has commenced to fully enjoy themselves, the Chicken-Hawk comes driving through the cemetery, with the little balloon still on his back antenna. At first, only a few folks seem to notice his badge of litter. Then, when the Chicken turns around and drives back through a second time, more people apparently see it. Several of them go from just giggling to pointing at it and laughing real loud.

"He's comin' thru more'n once to signify," C.B. says.

I'm left wondering what it means to signify, but I'm thinking the Chicken is going back and forth because he's so pleased with himself about having a car. His arm's hanging out the window in a careless sort of way, as if he drives all the time. He's apparently got a bad need to be admired. The kind of attention Chicken craves doesn't normally come from walking.

The third time he drives through, his antenna decoration is prominently flapping in the breeze, and I think nearly everybody has pointed it out to each other.

C.B. surmises, "I bet th' Chicken wouldn't be so all fired proud if he knowed ever'body was makin' fun on account of th' garbage hangin' from his antenna."

XIV:
Mother Annie's
Sandlot Sanctimony

"I WISHT THEY HAD a Negro Little League," C.B. admits and stands bareheaded, looking on as I crimp the top of my new, shirt-matching blue baseball cap.

1960s' official Little League uniforms are graced with big white numbers on shirts of the various team colors. Mine's a "3" on blue. As long as everyone wears jeans, we look pretty sharp. Maybe next year we'll get uniform pants.

Accustomed to innovating, C.B. has taken a chunk of coal and improvised the number "1" on his T-shirt. I don't know how to fix my emotional struggle at being embarrassed over the richness of my life compared to his. He seems to be having less trouble with it than I do. I tell myself I'd turn my back on what's rightfully mine if I thought it would get him any closer to playing Little League ball, but I don't know if I'm being truthful.

My white friends have gone along with letting C.B. practice ball with us on non-game days. In the spirit of more compromise than brotherhood, they realize the only way to get me to go along is for them to let him come along, too. It's not that they want me all that much, but summer sandlot pick-up ball works best with a plurality of players. It's more like real baseball when you have four or five on each team.

If we were as good as C.B. is eager, I'd be playing shortstop, and my buddy'd be pitching, coaching, and umpiring all at the same time. Although neither of us is considered good enough to play the infield, enthusiasm is an attitude that does work well for us. Group attitude governing, we're locked in to the not-necessarily-prestigious positions of right and center fields. The upside of that is that we're close enough to each other to talk during the game.

From different limbs of the same sycamore tree, a couple of mock-ingbirds signal to one another. I pretend they are spectators of our major league game. This largest tree on the lot serves as our out-of-bounds marker down first base line. Cars no longer park along the dead-end street on that side of the field. Knowing grown-ups will limit their choice of parking places gives me a worthy feeling. The other side of the field is a different story. A privet hedge pretty much parallel to the third-base line regularly eats foul balls.

Nobody I know has ever met Mother Annie or knows who it is that makes her a mother. What's more important to us is that her generous front yard accommodates Sunday afternoon baseball. Her house is deep center enough not to affect the long ball. The lot lies about halfway be-tween my house and Mr. Jefferson's, if you were silly enough to walk around by way of sidewalk instead of cutting through Bailey Woods.

Rumors are running around that we might soon be losing our ballpark to what Papa called the sad fate of progress. Not that we don't believe what my grandfather says, but C.B. and I plan on double-checking at first opportunity, with our main-most non-kin confidant. Mr. J. does profess an obligation to see to it that C.B. and I are in possession of what he generally assures us is the broad truth…or maybe it was assuring us of the generally broad truth.

Everybody's got an opinion about Mr. J. Granna says he's one of the foremost thinkers around. He knows things other men don't admit to knowing. Trying to think on his level is what Auntay calls dippin' from th' deepwater gourd. Dad accuses him of looking right on past common sense but concedes that he's entitled to it for winning a Pulitzer Prize. I plan to win me one of them because I sure could do without having to worry about common sense.

Joe Billy's up to bat.

"Let's move up," C.B. suggests. "'At boy couldn't hit th' wall of a silo if'n he was standin' inside it."

"All right. Keep your eye on the ball now, if he hits it."

"I wonder how long we got 'fore th' 'dustral'zation ruins all this?"

"Industrialization, C.B."

"Yeah, yeah, if you knowed what I'z aimin' to say, how come you think you always gotta change it ever'time?"

"I don't know that. I don't know why I bother with you."

"Well, that's a first—you not knowing somethin'. Maybe me an' yo' Granna's makin' some headway with you after all."

"Right, like you're in the same category with her."

Joe Billy strikes out. John Daniel comes up to bat. We spread out and go back.

"We've gotta catch this ball, C.B. It could be the game winner."

The first pitch is hit hard and high, straight toward C.B. The ball is taking forever to reach him, and I'm thinking he's going to miss it and my teammates will blame me and hate him. He's not going to have to move a muscle to catch it…right into his borrowed glove. Game's over. C.B. has proved his value and made me proud of him.

As we are breaking up, in almost perfect timing, Mr. J. strolls into view. The only thing better would be for him to have seen my buddy's game-winning catch, or better yet—if I'd caught it in front of him. Coming from town and headed home, Mr. J's got his old hat cocked down in front like an excuse not to have to speak to most folks. C.B. and I are the exception to that mannerism. He calls us by our first names, right in front of all the other kids. It's one of those things that make him genuine and us bigheaded. He looks typically sharp, wearing his tweed jacket and gray flannel trousers.

Our special friendship with Mr. J. is not to be shared with my other teammates. Leaving them to themselves, C.B. and I non-verbally invite ourselves to tag along with Mr. J. to Pen-Oake. He knows when he gets tired of chatting with us or has to go to writing, he can easily dismiss us, to cut through the woods to Papa's.

We're barely past pop-up range from Mother Annie's backstopless home plate when C.B. starts up. "Mr. Jefferson, 'tween you an' Scott's Granna, Ms. Taylor, who you reckon's right most orften of th' time?"

"Orf…ten?"

"Yeah, happenin' time'n again."

"Oh, I know what it means," Mr. J. admits with a trace of indignation.

"Well?"

"Young man, if I can get past your pronunciation, I'll be trying to figure out what it is that makes you think either one of us is ever wrong."

"'At's easy. It's 'cause y'all don't always agree on ever'thing me an' Scott ax about, so one of you gotta be wrong sometime."

"Assuming you can ask the same question to both of us without stretching it out of proportion by the time you ask it a second time," Mr. J. prefaces his question, "who is it that seems right most often?"

"That's hard to say," I jump in, not wanting C.B. to offend my mentor or my Granna.

C.B. ignores me and answers him anyway. "I 'spect either one of y'all could outfox th' other one if you was to take a notion to, but I can also see y'all goin' 'round in circles without neither one of ya bein' willin' to holler uncle."

Mr. J. smiles without further comment, and I'm glad the discussion is over with…if C.B. will shut up about it. With me on the street bordering Mr. J.'s left and C.B. framing him on the right, we make our way toward Pen-Oake. In spite of his slight stature, the little old man has a way about him of taking up the whole sidewalk. To enjoy the well-trimmed, front-yard grass along the way better, C.B. takes his tennis shoes off and carries them. I'd like to do the same but not badly enough to look like a copycat in front of Mr. J. Shade from century-old oaks stretches out before us as we round Old Taylor Road.

"Where you been, Mr. Jefferson?" C.B. asks.

"Not that it's any of your affairs, I've been to the barber shop. I got my ears lowered a little and my boots polished a lot. If you'd go up there and let Willie teach you how you tend to folks' shoes, you could help him and make you some spending money."

"I'd rather play ball," C.B. is quick to tell him. "What'chu gon' do now?"

"Anticipating the shorter limits of my impatience, I may very well position myself to take a negligible tug on an afternoon jug."

I would have thought Mr. J.'d know by now that's just the sort of answer to spur C.B. into treading water he ought not be out in.

"Auntay says you a tol'rant an' mostly gentle man when you not lubricated, or maybe it was a gentleman when you wadn't mostly lubricated?"

Smiling once more, Mr. J. twists his mustache. I think that's one of the reasons he likes having C.B. and me around, to make him smile every now and again. As long as the conversation is already laid out, I'm thinking I might as well get in on it.

"Papa says a man can go to Hades for drinking too much," I offer.

"But Ms. Taylor said that'd be all right fer you," C.B. inserts, "'cause you one man that'd go to Hades fer a drink."

Mr. J. looks at us both in that way he does when he is fixing to respond. I can always tell.

"Boys, do you suppose either one of them could talk their devil into issuing me a round-trip ticket so I could check it out?"

An unwelcome growl comes from Miss Bessie Baker's guard dog. C.B. walks around and gets on my left.

"Where are you going, Young Man?" Mr. J. teases C.B.

"I'z jus' figerin' you walk by here ever' day an' you an' him knowed one 'nother an' y'all'd be better off settlin' this."

"I thought maybe you were just getting around there where you thought you'd have a better chance of out-running me."

"You?"

"Never mind."

The dog growls again.

"Drake, you settle down now. These boys are not going to bother you or your territory."

Mr. J.'s calling the dog by his name reassures me. C.B. gets back on the grass with hot feet from his minute on my blacktop.

"Mr. Jefferson, how come sometimes you talk so's we can't un'erstand it?" C.B. asks.

"So's? I haven't the foggiest notion what a 'so's' is."

"Mr. Jefferson?"

"Okay, let's say I can figure out what you mean...then there's a lesson here for y'all. It's called listening in context. You boys can better figure out what words mean if you'll listen in context and hear what's on both sides of what you don't understand. If that doesn't work, you might try a dictionary. You do know what a dictionary is, don't you?"

"It got pictures in it?" C.B. jokes.

Mr. J. shakes his head. "I don't know if there's a good picture of a 'so's' in there, so, maybe y'all need me to demonstrate—"

"No thanks," we interrupt in unison.

"'Bout th' last thing we needin' is another one of yo' da...duh... demonstrates," C.B. adds, almost cussing.

"But Charles...." Mr. J. teases and leaves it at that.

Walking down between the parallel rows of eastern red cedars, the three of us give up the hardtop, sidewalk, and grass lawn for Mr. J.'s gravel driveway.

"Granna sometimes gets concerned we might be bothering you, Mr. Jefferson."

"Is it anything to that?" C.B. interrupts.

I give Mr. J. a sidelong glance to preview his reaction. He sometimes doesn't answer right away...or at all.

C.B. doesn't give him an option. "Auntay and Scott's Granna both said if we get to aggravatin' you enough, we li'ble to come to find out some of yo' affections fer us was really mistook."

"Boys, there may be more to Mrs. Taylor and the Antebellum than you'll ever know, but we'll just take all this in stride…and as material for my writing."

Grapevines draped over little fence-like lattices guide us around the side of Mr. J.'s house. In his backyard, two field mice scurry into the assortment of flowers under a large scuppernong arbor. A red-tailed hawk screams his shrill call as he rides the air currents. Mr. J. says something about the hawk's perceived dominance over the world beneath him and tells us just to listen for awhile.

At the edge of the woods, a dove coos. When a crow invades his space, the bird of peace takes flight. Mr. J. waves his arm, tilts his head, and quotes, "And who will not exchange a raven for a dove?"

"Another raven, I reckon," C.B. answers…and I think it's a pretty good answer.

"It's a good thing Shakesphere didn't know the two of you," Mr. J. comments, instead of telling us who'd swap.

"Shake's fear?" C.B. repeats.

"Never mind, boys."

"Mr. Jefferson, how come it is—sometimes you talk fer a few minutes 'fore it is you get to what it is you gon' say?"

Mr. J. looks at C.B. without answering. I sense it's time to change the subject. He's about to get irritated enough to send us hiking without him.

"Dad said you keep a hogshead of 'shine hid in your barn, and I was wondering—could we see what that looks like, you reckon?"

"The very thought of that right about now is certainly an inspiration. As I recollect, there is a bottle of gift-Scotch in that shed, and I suspect it doesn't need to get any more lonesome that it probably is. Just inside the door there on the right side, there's a little willow basket. Would whichever one of you who might know his right from his left please fetch it for me. The other one of you could be so kind as to take the cup that's hanging over the spring and fill me a cup full of water. I'll be obliged."

As I go for the shed, my buddy heads for the spring and asks Mr. J., "When we gets back, will you tell us a good yarn?"

"Yarn? A yarn, he says," Mr. J. repeats C.B. and himself.

I'm not knowing if that meant yes or no, but I guess we'll find out soon enough. With missions accomplished, C.B. hands over the battered tin cup filled with water.

"Thank you, Sir Charles. I received this cup from the Royal Canadian Air Corps. Did I ever tell y'all about—"

"Here it is, Mr. Jefferson, just like you asked for," I interrupt on purpose, thinking we don't need to hear that story again.

"Much to thank you." Side-tracked for the moment, he opens the basket and removes one of two bottles.

"What was you 'bout to say?" C.B. asks.

I make a face at my buddy and quickly answer as if he was talking to me. "I was about to ask Mr. Jefferson if he'd tell us a hunting story about the old days."

"Well," Mr. J. starts out like he does a lot of his thoughts, "I suppose as long as y'all realize what I share with you is not by any stretch of your inexperienced and unlimited imaginations a yarn…then I'll tell you one."

"All right," I answer.

"An' we done heard about th' cup," C.B. answers, as if his timing did any good.

"You two would be well advised to pay close attention when I go beyond history to share grade 'A' prime slices of wisdom. It's the kind of knowledge that…."

"Yessir," C.B. interrupts.

"Yes, Sir," I add…and figure if he's gonna yell at somebody for interrupting, it might as well be both of us.

Instead of continuing, Mr. J. pours out half of the water C.B. brought him and replaces it with scotch. He tastes it, looks at both of us, and sighs with satisfaction. We sit on the ground in front of him and take up our listening posture for listening in context.

"As opposed to what I was trying to tell you about, there is the other side of a too-often-tilted scale. When the two of you talk instead of listening, you remind me of a couple of old women, talking for recreation as opposed to communication. You just as well take note—one of the differences between us and the female half of this world is their ability to talk without saying anything. You can either come to respect that difference or you can stumble through life wishing you understood what the hell was going on."

"I knows what you talkin' 'bout, Mr. Jefferson," C.B. agrees.

"'Know', C.B., not 'nose'," Mr. J. corrects him.

"Well, anyway, it's like 'fore Auntay goes to talkin' 'bout somethin', I wisht she'd first figger out how interestin' it is, so's she'd know how long to carry on about it."

"Young man, you are a virtual master of prose." Mr. J. takes another sip and then a longer one.

"Thank you…I reckon. Auntay says we done got ourselves under th' 'fluence of such a learned bookmonger we li'ble to never be th' same no more. Is it anything to bookworms, Mr. Jefferson?"

Mr. J. takes a look into his old cup instead of answering. He takes what's more like a gulp than a sip. Sometimes I don't know whether C.B. is trying to jerk him around or if such questions are serious. Nevertheless, the old man's face smooths out and looks as if it's relaxing.

Somewhere between us and the house, a fox squirrel announces his own presence. We all three trace back the falling shortleaf pine cone pieces and seeds falling from where the squirrel is eating.

"What's going on there, boys? Watch that squirrel's tail and tell me what you're seeing. What's that movement all about, with his tail?"

"It flickers every time his heart beats," I guess.

"Not bad," Mr. J. answers, "and I like the way you came up with the word 'flickers,' but that's not it. It's not the heartbeat. That movement is more of a twitch. Not everyone appreciates a good twitch, but it's one of Mother Nature's ways of telling us not to overdo anything. It could cause a predator to dive for movement, as opposed to say, a squirrel's acorn-fat, potbelly…or one full of pine seeds in this case."

C.B. and I look at each other. Mr. J. takes another drink before continuing.

"If he doesn't twitch so much that a hawk sees him, it could be the very thing that allows the tree-rat to escape instead of be eaten. Twitching is a lot like drinking—you just don't want to overindulge."

I sit in awe, and C.B. is at least silent. Mr. J. takes another long guzzle from the cup and waves his hand in a shooing motion. The squirrel scampers out of sight. After another extra-long draw off his drink, our storyteller sloshes around what's left of the mixture in little circles. It's as if he's looking for gold in the bottom of the cup.

"Now, a lizard…he can even give up his tail if a predator grabs it, but squirrels simply have not been evolving as long as the reptilians," he explains.

"Ms. Taylor says you's a mite 'centric, too," C.B. offers up, as if he's tired of hearing about lizards and squirrels.

"You mean, eccentric?" Mr. J. asks.

"'At's what I said, wadn't it?"

"Wasn't it?"

"Yessir, it was."

"Tell me when you get ready to listen—*to hear?*"

"That's what Auntay is always tellin' me—to listen here."

"I rest my damned case," Mr. J. asserts with another flourish of his hand…but this time it's like he was shooing off C.B.

"She ain't never said that," my buddy continues as if he didn't see Mr. J.'s motion.

"You may be a bigger challenge than I bargained for. What else does the Antebellum say about yours truly?"

"She don't say nothin' 'bout me. It's you she's all time talkin' about."

"Me, then, what does she say about me, for Christ's sake?"

"I don' know about the Lord, but…uh, are you shore you wanta hear this?"

Mr. J. looks as if he's about to explode, and I'm starting to squirm pretty good, my own self. Somehow, he hesitates in his impatience.

"Go ahead. I'm thick-skinned," he gives just the license C.B. is looking for.

"She said…uh, you was 'bout th' only one could fun th' Negro Little League…if you was to want to."

"Fund?"

"That's what I said—fun," C.B. emphasizes his incorrect pronunciation.

"And they call me the local color," Mr. J. mumbles mostly to himself. "Another half-cup of water please? I'll be thinking some on this funding affair for a little Negro league."

"The Negro Little League," C.B. corrects him.

I think about how neither of us should be correcting Mr. J. C.B. may have just pushed his luck too far. I sit quietly and wait, but I can almost hear Mr. J. thinking. When C.B. returns and hands over the half-cup of water, Mr. J. pours in a big slosh of Scotch from the fancy bottle. After giving the mixture a circular motion as if to stir it, he gives it an unsatisfied look. It must not be quite right. Instead of getting onto C.B. for bringing the wrong amount of water, he adds another swish of Scotch.

"Boys, we'll talk again in a day or two about this situation of Oxford not having a Negro Little League…and America's game not being

America's game after all. But now, I've got some powerful pondering to do. I can best do that if y'all go ahead and move along, now."

We say bye and head out. I look back over my six, as Mr. J. says they call your rear end in the Royal Canadian Air Force. He's having trouble screwing the Scotch bottle's top back on. He fumbles with it some more and says something to himself about how he's screwed it on good enough for the time being…and then something else about screwing it.

XV:

Pen-Oake League

AFTER MAKING OUR WAY through Bailey Woods to try to catch Mr. J. outside, C.B. and I are pleased to see him coming out of his horse barn. It's been two weeks since C.B. broached the subject with him concerning the creation of a Negro Little League.

"Good afternoon, Mr. Jefferson," C.B. greets him. "I thought uh somethin' else Auntay said 'bout you. You wanta hear it?"

"If it won't hurt too bad. Go ahead."

"She says you can do things can't nobody else get done, like helpin' us with th' ball team an' th' uniforms."

"Is that it?"

"She said you one of them self-taught sons-of…uh, guns, that wadn't born that'a way, but learned it on your own, she did."

Thinking C.B.'s effort wasn't the best way to ease a conversation into the subject of black baseball, I try to change directions. "What's something me and C.B. can be when we grow up, Mr. Jefferson?"

"Boys, we're going to have this conversation just once, so I want you to listen carefully for a change."

"Yessir."

"Yes, sir."

"Nothing of any significance has to do with what you can 'be.' What counts is what you can 'do.'"

"Wha'cha mean?" C.B. asks.

"Being an author, for instance, is nothing special. But to write…now, there is an opportunity to do something worthwhile. Think of the significance of influencing modern thought, of being able to sway the will and way of man throughout the land. Can you imagine having your work scrawled on every schoolhouse wall?"

"I think I'm gon' be a ballplayer," C.B. states proudly.

"I've been telling him he's a Negro, Mr. Jefferson."

"He is?"

"You know what I mean."

"I'm not sure that I do. Would you kindly recount your hypothesis for me?"

"How many coloreds do you think ever gonna make it to the big league?"

"There's a couple getting those big five-digit salaries as we speak, and there will be more."

"Come on, Mr. Jefferson," I argue. "Without Little League uniforms and equipment and everything…be serious."

Mr. J. walks us toward his favorite garden bench.

C.B. takes the silent stroll as a trigger to try again and share his feelings. "If coloreds was borned equals, we sho' got over it quick. What'd you decide 'bout th' Negro Little League?"

"Well, Sir," Mr. J. answers, "What do you boys know about the game of chess?"

"I'd rather play baseball," C.B. responds.

Mr. J. ignores him. "I haven't thought this through completely, but since you're already here, we'll opine under the pines."

"Huh?"

"Analyze it aloud."

"Yes, Sir," I agree.

"Yessir." C.B. says as he looks with hope.

Sitting in the middle of his favorite bench so we can't take seats on either side of him, Mr. J. strokes his mustache and looks thoughtful.

"Here's the way I see it. As the Bishop of Taylor, C.B. can slip around using the angles and maintaining the importance of color. Scott, you being the Knight of Oxford can hop around every which direction except straight…in a manner that allows you to take time about with different colors. And that, my fearless collaborators, in the game of chess and life, is what increases the Knight's value over the Bishop's."

"What's all 'at mean, Mr. Jefferson?" C.B. asks.

"It means the game of chess is a pretty accurate portrayal of humanity, regardless of how fashionable Yankee society thinks it is to claim the colors are equal. It means that Scott will have to take the lead role here."

"I ain't follerin' ya, Mr. Jefferson," C.B. admits, and I'm glad of it.

"That's all right for the time being. I'm just thinking out loud. It might just be about time somebody put something of substance into practice around here. And the two of you might be just the ones to orchestrate such an exciting social statement for ol' Ox'patch."

"You bet'cha."

"Yes, Sir, we'll do whatever you say."

"Boys, we're talking about more than baseball here. Reconciling race rights in our fair city will encompass a commitment to rising above the norm, a dedication to do away with class differences wrought with discriminatory distinctions. We'll have us an irregular festival of purification."

"Mr. Jefferson?" I start to question what he means.

"Then, can we get them uniforms?" C.B. doesn't wait for my question. "What all we got to do? How's 'at work?"

"Like a writer uses a pseudonym...."

C.B.'s face lights up with hope. "If a suit'adem's what it takes to get them suits...."

"I'm still lost," I admit, this time. "Will you talk to us so we can understand it?"

Mr. J. gets up and begins walking around nervous-like, in his little circles. "Become each other, and let black exploit white for a change."

"Not in chess talk, Mr. Jefferson, so's we can un'erstand it," C.B. practically begs.

"How about in football terms, then. Do y'all know that play where an unexpected way-back runs a double-reverse around the wrong end to find the right goal line?"

"I gots it," C.B. informs us. "You sayin' Scott oughta let on that a collection he's takin' up is a team of white kids, when it'll really go to buy uniforms fer a team of coloreds. Is that it, Mr. Jefferson?"

"Where did you get an idea like that?" Mr. J. kids, in his way of letting us know C.B. has hit on it.

"There's gotta be a better way to start up a Negro Little League than that," I protest.

"And here I thought you boys were going to be resolvers. Do you actually want to get something done or just bellyache with everybody else about the inequities and unfairness of everything in life?"

"But, Mr...."

"Now, I wouldn't want either of you consciously misleading anybody too far, but taking into consideration the greater cause, no one has to know this is for a Negro team until I decide the time is right."

"But, Mr. Jefferson," I try to jump in.

"There is no 'but' to it. One lap around the town square and you will have covered the game board of possibilities for Little League sponsorships. You'll be done with it."

"How come you can't do it?" I ask.

"I'll have to lay low…sort of like an extra pawn or card under the table…because the bank and merchants around here have already acclaimed me an instigator. They would be on the lookout for me doing something of controversial consequence."

As Mr. J. refines the plays and players, I'm the Panhandling Solicitor General and C.B. is what he calls the Sergeant-of-the-Guard. While C.B. sits outside the stores watching out for the constable, Mr. J. holds down his bench over at the courthouse. I have to do all the work…encouraging the store owners to assume naturally my request for a donation is to help my own team.

Skipping Munford's Grocery and my father's inquiring mind, I learn from everyone else around town that they are pretty good about sports…probably on account of a lot of them have kids of their own. In practically no time, I've raised enough money for the T-shirts and caps. With three double-cola soda waters and three cinnamon rolls, I lead C.B. to go and tell the chess master our good news. Mr. J. is not too happy about my buying the drinks and cinnamon rolls…even though I got one of each for him. I'll just consider C.B.'s pleasure over his to make up for Mr. J.'s sudden attitude.

OVER THE NEXT WEEK we begin to spread the word of the time and place for our big game. Billed as Oxford vs. Lafayette County, the game would be exciting enough…if that's all there was to it. With C.B. organizing the Negro team and me getting a white team lined up, players from both sides are sworn to temporary secrecy about the color of the competition.

When our big day of white boys and coloreds playing organized ball against each other finally arrives, I'm figuring the results could be both painful and pleasant. My main team-building criterion was securing boys I knew I could trust…whether they were any good at baseball or not. As I lead my team toward Mother Annie's from the north, I perceive the hint of clouds forming as only a small threat of rain. Oxford's first Negro Little League team and C.B. approach from the south, as if all was sunshiny.

More than the usual traffic seems to be passing through South 11th Street. Since Mr. J. came through with the uniforms, with my help, I'm proud to see the coloreds coming, all decked out in bright purple caps and matching T-shirts with gold numbers. C.B. looks like he must feel good and proud, too.

All meeting by the field at the same moment, we find Mother Annie's taped off with a big yellow ribbon, posted with construction site signs. Keep-out posters line the street, and a Sheriff's Deputy is parked where we normally foul balls off on the dead-end street.

C.B. and I look at each other. Everyone else is looking at us, too. There is a lot of automobile-type looking but no stopping. They seem interested but not enough to get involved.

With uneasy ballplayers from both teams probably fixing to blame me for everything bad in their lives, I'm thinking I know the best thing to do…but it's likely that a kid or two from the black team could catch me. The sheriff drives up.

"The game is not going to happen, boys," he says.

Again, everyone looks at C.B. and me. Making sure I'm loud enough for everyone to hear me, I declare, "This game is gonna happen. We can use Mr. Jefferson's pasture. Y'all come on!" I wave my arm around in a follow-me circle.

I'm feeling the sheriff looking at me as if I'm bringing shame to his town, but I'm not looking back…except enough to see if everyone is following. The march to Pen-Oake is on. I pull my belt up higher and wish I had the hipbones to hold it up. C.B. is on my left, with his team staying to his side and in the street. Mine is on my right and using the sidewalk and part of people's front yards. Neither team is in front or back, so it's not so much that Negroes are on one side and whites on the other. We're all in this together, more of a side by side…and I figure it's a good start.

It takes about five minutes to get to Mr. J.'s., with the high sheriff riding behind us—almost like a parade but different. Maybe he thinks he's herding cattle. The hot and humid day, along with excitement, has my baseball shirt sticking to my back. When we turn down the drive, I ask everyone but C.B. to wait while he and I seek out Mr. J. This being one time we're not waiting until we can catch Mr. J. already outside, my best friend and I go right up to his front door and knock. The maid comes to the door.

I start to speak…and a summer cloud bursts open. The rain intensifies before I can finish explaining myself. C.B. looks at me hard. I become determined to get pasture playing rights, even if for another day.

"But Mr. Jefferson's not home," the maid says. "He's gone."

"Gone where?" I demand, without thinking about my manners.

"He's gone to the hospital again…gone to dry out."

"But it just now started raining?" I question her. "And it hadn't rained for…."

"He's dryin' out on th' inside," she cuts me off to explain.

"Well…listen, he's already said we could play ball in his lower pasture, and I was just coming up here to tell him we were here…because he said he wanted to watch the game when the coloreds and whites got together to play each other. So we're gonna go ahead and play, and you can send him down there if he gets back in time. Okay?"

"Younguns," she says with admiration in her voice, "Mr. Jefferson…he'd be proud. But it's pourin' down an' y'all can't play in th' rain. You'll catch your death's cold…and them pretty, purple shirts those boys got on…they'll fade."

I pull my pants up again. "Ma'am, this game is happening, fading or not."

C.B. finally participates, "'Sides, it's jus' a matter of time 'fore th' colors is gon' run together."

XVI:
Ox'patch by Night

"TH' BEST SHOW IN town ain't on no screen," claims C.B. "It's durin' late show, up in th' balcony at th' Ritz."

"Bull-hockey. If you're talking about couples necking, they do that in the white section, too."

"I ain't talkin' 'bout folks in th' audience. I'm talkin' 'bout th' girls Chicken-Hawk lets in his little film room where he's runnin' th' movie projector."

"Are you kidding me?"

"Nope. I can't see a whole lot, but I sho can hear 'em. You oughta come go with me this weekend. Once't it gets dark in there, can't nobody tell you white."

With 1960s Oxford still having certain prohibitions for keeping coloreds separated from whites, the thought of seeing a new perspective from the theater is intriguing. And there's only one way to see what the big screen looks like from up there.

A WELL-ESTABLISHED ESCAPE route from home means I'm no stranger to the deserted streetlight shadows of downtown's after-evening hours. Although the squeaky, wooden stairs out back of the house slope down right by my father's bedroom window, their metal pipe handrail allows me to slide to freedom without making a sound. Halfway down I stop to listen for Dad sawing logs. If he is, I know he's not looking out the window. If I don't hear the snoring, I'll shimmy back up the banister.

When C.B.'s staying in Oxford with Sassy, his get-away situation is not quite as well-defined as mine. More than cautiously creeping out once Sassy goes to bed, there's always Chicken-Hawk for him to have to worry about. He is as likely as not to still be out carousing, so there's the possibility of meeting up with his ugly face coming in as C.B. is trying to slip out.

This is a night when everything clicks for us. As we make our way to the picture show, I enjoy feeling the late-night blacktop street still holding heat from the day's long-gone sunlight. When the late show begins, C.B. and I ease up to the balcony. I hope the upstairs moviegoers' eyes aren't yet well enough adjusted to the dark to recognize me as being white.

We hide in the back corner away from the projection room but where we can see its entrance. Shortly, the shadowy figure of a woman slips over to the little door. When the door to the henhouse opens and some light shines out, we recognize the Chicken's hen. Putting on the kind of politeness he must have seen in the movies, Chicken-Hawk extends his hand and helps Vidallia in.

Where the camera shoots out is the only place we could possibly see in. Our shadows would surely show on the movie screen if we were to stick our heads over for a look. Everybody would yell and we'd get caught...so we just take up better listening positions. Right outside the door, we'll settle for hearing what's going on...and probably coming off.

"Listen to her," C.B. whispers.

A gentle ooh...ing and ah...ing from Vidallia is almost enough to make me relax.

"Man, I thought sex was something girls just went along with on account of boys want it."

"Yeah, it sound like Vidallia likes it."

"Ooh...ah...ooh...ah...Ooh...."

I can't imagine a white girl ever carrying on like this, at least not any I know. A rat runs by, between the door and us. C.B. and I look at one another. When my buddy smiles, I sense we may be thinking up the same good idea. I remember C.B.'s bragging about his box-trapping expertise around the dumpster behind The Mansion restaurant.

"What do you think?" I ask.

"Only one thing sorta bothers me—no better'n Chicken-Hawk's been 'bout keepin' jobs, I'd really kinda hate to see him lose a good un like this."

"Have you forgot we owe him big time for the potato-eye incident?"

C.B. smiles again. "On th' other hand, an' they's always a—nother hand...."

Knowing it won't be wise to cause any more disharmony and open conflict between Chicken and us than necessary, I'm still thinking—what's due is what's due. It's simply what Mr. J. would call the overriding factor. C.B. and I agree to come back the following weekend with a well-developed plan.

———————————

UPSIDE DOWN ON ITS lid, a shoebox with our surprise inside is slid to the back corner of the little projector room. So that it can't be seen, a fishing line is run along the wall and floor trim. It's then tied to a small hole in the new top, or former bottom, of the box. C.B. shakes the whole thing pretty well and then uses a crumpled jacket we found in the room to hide it and help hold it down. Returning to the lobby, we'll wait there until Chicken-Hawk arrives.

Chicken mans his station, and the balcony lights yield to a serial before the main feature. While everyone is interested in seeing what's coming on, we slip up to our corner to wait there for any unauthorized visitor who might happen to show up at the projector room door. One of Chicken's lady friends shows. It's whom we thought. Vidallia tiptoes over to their cubbyhole getaway, and Chicken quickly lets her in. The door is shut over our loose end of the fishing line, and we ease into place to listen and attend the line sticking out from under the door.

There's a moaning and groaning that must go with habitual infidelity because we heard it once before. I want to pull the fishing line, but C.B. demands that we wait. I don't know how it could get to be a better time than this, but he's insistent.

"It's not time yet—but it'll come," he again reassures me.

Normally a soft-spoken woman, Vidallia comes to a hushed kind of ooh...ing and ah...ing, but with intensity. When she starts in on her third straight, long series of letting on like a lovesick cat, my imagination reaches its limit. C.B. looks at me with a grin that can only mean "now." My buddy gives the fishing line a hard yank. The box comes flying off its lid and hits up against the door with a loud thud. Not able to see it, I can only imagine it is startling enough to make a suddenly exposed, live jack-in-the-box go berserk enough to jump up and down looking for a place to run.

More than willing to forfeit the rest of our dime's worth of the picture show, C.B. and I run for the exits with all the other moviegoers, while Chicken-Hawk and Vidallia are both screaming. One of them must have kicked the power cord on the projector loose because the movie has stopped, but I don't think that matters. I don't believe anyone is going to be left in the theater to notice.

Milling around outside, the moving picture patrons are telling each other various versions of what they think must have gone on. Apparently the people that were downstairs were alarmed by all the commotion from those in the balcony, and the folks from the balcony were running from the ruckus that was right behind them.

"C.B.?"

"What?"

"If Chicken-Hawk sees us anywhere around here, you know he's gonna be apt to blame everything on us."

"Yeah, as unforgivin' as he is 'bout ever'thing, we jus' as well steer clear of him."

"They did get pretty loud about it, you know," I add.

"Well, I knowed all along it wadn't gon' take Vidallia very long to 'preciate a half-growed 'possum tryin' to pass hisself off as a world-record-sized rat."

XVII:
Taxi Bear

I TWIRL MY SPAGHETTI around my fork. "Dad, I ran into Mr. Jefferson this morning. He said to tell you to be expecting his call for a taxi ride this afternoon."

"Another trip to nowhere, huh, Munford?" Granna interrupts, instead of letting Dad respond. "So much for his drying out."

I hate it when she talks about Mr. J. that way, but I still pretend I'm not paying attention so I can hear more.

"You don't know that that's it, Gertrude," Dad answers.

"What else do you think it could be? He's got his own Jeep, if he was simply needing to go somewhere. What's the other difference in that and you taking him?"

"Well, if it's like usual, I'll have to go in and wait. He'll fix himself a stimulant and gather up some more for the road before we leave out."

"It's the 'leave out' part I'm worried about," she says.

"What's your problem?" Dad pushes back.

"Is that what he calls his fire water, now—a stimulant?"

"I think it's as apt to be second-run corn liquor as it is the finest of Kentucky bourbons. We *are* talking about a man who wouldn't set down a jug of rotgut to go to a good hanging."

"Munford, you're already talking like an expert. The last thing you need is a predilection for his bad habits, and I certainly hope you don't let him influence you."

"Now, you don't have to go and worry yourself about that."

"If it's not confidential, where will the two of you go?"

I'm thinking Granna has taken Dad right up to his edge and is about to go too far.

"Gertrude, you know I don't mind giving you the guts for your gossip," Dad teases.

"I won't repeat anything," Granna promises.

"I usually just drive him…all over the countryside. He talks and does what he calls his thinkin'-drinkin'. The more he drinks, the more he talks."

"And what are you doing all this time?"

"I mostly just sweat through my toleration for the man. I'm well aware of what drinking's done to him. He could have really been somebody meaningful if it wasn't for that stuff."

"Does he pay you like he's supposed to and when he's supposed to?"

"Now, Mother-in-law, don't you be concerning yourself with things that's none of your affair. You're about to go beyond the essentials for mere mudslinging."

"I should have known any mention of money would put you over the top."

"And you sure know how to kill a conversation."

As Dad is right about the talking being over, I think about how his two-toned blue '57 Chevy taxi station wagon has its back jury-rigged. It's a boxed-in storage compartment for carrying lots of cargo without knocking out the windows. Just once I'd like to see what's in those chests the Ole Miss students bring to college…from the bus station, the train depot, and from Southern Airways.

Finishing lunch and being excused from the table, I look outside and find C.B. Having pondered the taxicab's modification, I share an inspiration…that we might tie our afternoon schedule to the upcoming trip Mr. J. and Dad are planning.

"Sound like a good plan to me," C.B. agrees. "Ain't no tellin' what all we might hear from hiding back there durin' one of them rides."

OXFORD'S TAXI STAND IS a little office on the northwest corner of my house. Several taxi drivers outside the dispatcher's window are pitching pennies. They keep a stack of washers on the windowsill. If Papa happens up South 11th Street, they'll switch, not wanting the Preacher to catch them gambling.

The high-wave radio blurts out a personal dispatch for Dad. It's the one we've been waiting on. C.B. and I sprint down University Avenue to

Granna's city house, from where we cut through our Bailey Woods short-cut to Pen-Oake. By the time we run up to the back of the barn and peek around the corner, Dad has already driven up to the end of the estate's clay brick sidewalk. Supposing Dad is inside with Mr. Jefferson, our opportunity appears to be as I'd envisioned it.

We ease around to the backside of the cab. The car door creaks loudly as I open it, so I close it back behind us with a steady slowness. After positioning ourselves inside the homemade, plywood storage compartment, I see that vision is as limited as I had anticipated. With the lid completely down it looks like taking in any scenery is going to have to wait for the paying customer.

"You reckon we might oughta forget this idear and get outta here?"

Before I can answer C.B., I hear a noise from outside. We are now in for the ride. Car doors open, seats squeak and bounce, and each man must be wiggling into comfort. Lifting the lid ever so slightly, I peak out and see that Mr. J. is sitting in the back seat and on the opposite side from Dad. I put my index finger over my lips and signal in the semi-dark that I don't even want to hear a whisper.

"Munford, being as I'm having a bourbon for the road, I should be gentleman enough to offer you a little nip."

"You know I don't drink…and you'd be a lot better off if you wouldn't neither," Dad lectures.

"Wouldn't neither, huh?" Mr. J. repeats, for some reason.

The starter kicks the engine in, and the car rolls forward. My eyes have grown accustomed to the limited light enough that I can now read C.B.'s expressions.

"Well, it's like this, Munford. Indulging the ardent spirits once a day helps to keep the doctor away, not to mention loosening you up enough to let the nurses play."

"You're just blowing smoke out your butt now," Dad responds.

C.B. giggles with his hand over his mouth.

"Munford, I'm guessing you don't know the third thing about being a medicinal drinker."

"Yeah, yeah…I'm sure you'd frown on a body that was to sip socially, wouldn't you?"

"Cheers." Mr. J. holds up his cup. "Here's to good health and your Methodist message."

"I'm Presbyterian, William."

"Now there's a testimony, with your father-in-law being the Baptist preacher at Taylor. Do you suppose either of those particular religion's gods would begrudge you having a little persimmon beer with me if you were just needing to wet your whistle sometimes?"

"It's all the same God, and there's nothing wrong with my health that needs a drink."

"I'm not so sure of that. If you were to get yourself a little tipsy, it might counterbalance your one-sided walk, with that polio-limp of yours."

"At least I'm not crippled in my mind," Dad nails him.

I don't know how anyone can be so hateful and so hurtful toward my Dad, especially a man I usually admire. C.B. starts to whisper, but I press my finger to my lips again. I shake my head, no.

"Just tell me where it is you wanta go, before you pass out," Dad asks in a demanding sort of question.

"Munford, haven't you ever wanted to go just any-old-where, instead of having to go somewhere?"

"What kind of answer is that?"

"Drive. I'll tell you when we get there. You ought to know by now it doesn't matter. You drive, and I'll drink. And try to keep your car between the ditches for a change."

Mr. J. rattles on, boring at first, but getting funnier as the ride goes along. He says something about a good book, and Dad tells him that there's already a Good Book. Mr. J. gets a big laugh out of that. The more my father tries to participate in the conversation, the more Mr. J. teases him. Seeing the back of Dad's ears, I can imagine him getting red-faced to match. The further we get into the ride, the louder Mr. Jefferson becomes. I suppose since we're all riding on Mr. J.'s six bits, Dad has decided to sit quietly and simply let his anger simmer.

"Let's go to Yocona, Munford."

"I should've known."

I'm feeling the same aggravation as Dad. State Highway 334 to Yocona is split long-ways, right down the middle of the road. One side is concrete, and the other side is gravel. Everybody drives on the half that's concrete until they meet oncoming traffic. The folks driving on the wrong side are supposed to scoot over on hills and curves or when meeting someone with the right-of-way.

"Of all the fool places we could go, why there? You want to wear out my tires, having me go back and forth over the edge of the concrete?"

"I'm financing this trip. You just do the driving and leave the observations and inspirations to me."

"Are you going to buy me some new tires when I have a blow out?"

"I'm not asking you to go back and forth between the gravel and the pavement. That's your call, Munford. You can stay on the right side of the road for all I care."

"That's about what I thought. You and your wild ideas are about as crazy as your wild tales about wild women."

C.B. looks at me. I shake my head no again, afraid he'll speak too loudly if he speaks at all. Mr. J. says something back about some Royal women being disloyal in another Oxford, where everybody drives on the left-hand side of the road. I'm not understanding everything I hear, but when Dad responds as if he doesn't believe it, I listen harder. There's gossip about women I know from town. I've never heard adults talk like this, much less my father.

A gnat flies in my nose. Somehow, without making noise, I manage to breathe. I don't know why such things as a bug at a time like that always have to happen to me. If I don't sneeze, I'll be lucky.

"Munford, I'll be having a stiff shot of that supplemental 'shine we brought along, now, before the night air sets in."

"Yeah, yeah, any excuse for a toast, huh?"

"Where is the jar?"

"It's right here." Dad reaches down and under his seat, causing the car to swerve.

Mr. Jefferson seizes the opportunity. "Where'd you get your driver's license…the roller-rink?"

"You just keep it up, and you'll be walking home, or staggering I should say." Dad hands him the jar.

"Thank you, Sir."

"I'm not saying you're welcome because I don't see why you think it does you any good."

"Well, you're wrong. When I loosen up a little, I get creative a lot. I call it my contained deliberation." Mr. J. takes a drink. "Aw—yes, while this is special, even your ordinary re-run of the mill belly wash can often contribute to floating with the smooth flow of innovation."

"I think I finally understand all that garbling, William. It's like fertilizing a garden."

"Now, Munford…."

"It's sort of like that old saying—you are what you eat, but in your case, it's more like you think according to how much you drink."

"Are you insinuating there's a ghost writer in my Mason jars?"

"From what I hear of your writing, you probably need a little hotty toddy before you can interpret your own potty from what you wrote the day before."

"Have you ever read any of my books, Munford?"

Dad doesn't answer, so Mr. J. continues. "I'm quite certain if you'd take a little snort of this and read a sample from my work, they'd both do you a world of good."

"Yeah, to help me understand what you write." Dad laughs as he's getting at Mr. J. for a change.

"Driver, I'm beginning to worry about your disposition."

"My disposition? If that isn't the kettle calling the pot covered with smut...." C.B. starts to whisper.

"Shu...uh," I cut him off again.

"Here, try this." Mr. J. sticks his jar across the top of the front seat.

"I told you—I'm a good Presbyterian who was married to an even better Baptist...and I don't want any of your devil water messing with that. You understand?"

"Yeah. Let's go to the river."

"The Yocona, I assume...since we're practically to Toccopola?"

"No. The Little Tallahatchie."

"How did I know that?"

"Probably because your subconscious is tired of seeing all this cut-over brush and these little pine plantings. We need to find some big oaks. There's a good turn-around. Pull in right there and stop a minute. I'm having a hankering to piss."

The thought hits me that C.B. and I are going to be in huge trouble if we have to pee...or worse. When Dad stops, Mr. J. sets his jar on the floorboard and steps out of the car.

"I won't tell your father-in-law if you take a little taste of my drink while I'm taking care of business." Looking back over his shoulder and through the open window, he continues, "See if you can get this thing pointed in the right direction."

"I'm afraid you'll have to do that on your own," Dad jokingly insinuates what Mr. J. could have been talking about.

"The car, Munford...I was referring to the car."

I'm about to burst with laughter…while I don't think C.B. got it or heard it.

After getting back in the car, Mr. J. secures his drink and shouts, "Tallyho! And away we go. I wish we were looking for the little red som-bitch now."

"Humph," Dad exclaims.

"Munford, have you ever been on a good fox hunt…or a bad one for that matter? No, of course you haven't. So I'll tell you—it's a lot like responsible drinking or irresponsible sex."

"I can't wait to hear this," Dad encourages him for a change.

"There's a point you want to savor…at the pinnacle. You don't want to violate that zenith. If you're really good, you can hold everything right there. Do you understand that, about being at the right spot at the right time and knowing not to go beyond that point?"

"Like you knowing your way around a bottle?" Dad asks.

"Now, you see…there's one of those myths about me—knowing my way around a bottle. The truth is, I would hardly ever go past one."

The taxi gives up the periodic hard surface for full-time gravel, and worse yet, it's a bad wash-boarded road. I assume we're now headed north to the river. When C.B. farts, I want to say "pokes" and hit him in the arm, but we've got to be quiet…and now I've got to try not to breathe any more than necessary. Realizing how cramped up I'm getting to be in this box, I wonder how long this trip may take. C.B.'s wiggling way too much, and I'm thinking how good it would feel to get out and stretch.

"Set off toward Bakersfield," Mr. J. orders.

"The boat landing?"

"Yeah, I'll show you something about the Corps of Re-Engineers, and what they're doing to the Little Tallahatchie River."

Dad doesn't answer again.

"With what they call their channelization project, they have flat-out performed an abortion on a river. Do you know what I mean by an abortion, Munford?"

"They're keeping it from having a lot of little rivers?" Dad guesses.

"That's just what I need—a smart-aleck chauffeur."

"You don't pay me enough to call me your chauffeur."

"I've been aiming to talk to you about that, Munford. I prefer that today's ride go on my tab."

"Tabs are for bars, not cabs and cars."

"That's more than half good, Munford. You might say it was a P.U., about two-thirds of a pun. But with numbers like that, maybe you'd better stick to being a skinflint taxi driver and let me be the world-renowned author."

"If you're supposed to be so hot at reading and writing, how come you aren't any better at arithmetic…least ways good enough to pay what you owe?"

I don't know if it's the way Mr. J. is talking to Dad or if there's something about the movement of a car without being able to see out, but something is making me nauseous.

"I'll tell you what I will do, Munford—I'll sign a copy of my next book for you. All you have to do is hang on to it, and someday it'll be worth a hell of a lot more than your damned cab fares. What do you say to that?"

"I'd say it's not fair, but it'd be a sight better than more of your indefinite credit on a bank account that's no a'count. I'd also say if you don't straighten up your affairs, those draft checks on your acclaim to fame are gonna get you a reputation."

"I'm more worried that I might not cultivate one. A man in my business needs to make a lasting impression…sort of like Noah did in your Bible. I'm thinking of building me a houseboat to put on Sardis Lake."

"The bottom of it, more than likely," Dad says.

"Somewhere between humanity and eternity there is a big stretch of water…and I may just be the one who can connect the two for readers. Instead of taking these taxi rides and all of your abuse, I could—"

"Float around the lake and drink," Dad finishes up, but I don't think it will stop him.

It seems like the gravel road is coming up through the floorboards. The bottom of this box is not nearly as soft as a car seat. I think we're hitting every bump between Toccopola and the Little Tallahatchie River.

"Munford, do you ever think about this kudzu vine they're bringing in here?"

"I got better things to occupy my mind with."

"It's going to come back to bite us right square in the ass someday. Our government's got no business trying to make natural what's not. Plants around here have spent centuries learning to live with one another…and now we have these invaders coming in here from somewhere else and changing how they've all gotten along with one another."

"So, you're saying plants are like people, except maybe for the booze?"

"Mankind should be so predictable. We could get a lot from plants."

"Corn, especially, huh?" Dad jokes.

"You take those plants right there by that turnout…the ones with the pretty purple berries. They're American beautyberry. Like a lot of people, you know exactly when you can count on them and when you can't. Their dazzling fruit display will be with us until well into November. Then there's other plants and people…where you just never know."

I can't see it, but I can sure picture the plant Mr. J.'s talking about. Granna calls it French mulberry. I try to imagine it's familiar smell, but all I can come up with is the college students' dirty laundry odor of Dad's storage compartment…and C.B.

"Jumpin' Jehovah! Look at that! Would you look at that?"

"Is that what I think it is?" Dad responds. "I'll be…."

As the car eases to a stop, C.B. and I look at each other. The whites of his eyes show out in the dark almost like lights. I've got to see what they're so excited about. Without lifting the lid too high, I peek through the crack.

"It's a bear…sure as hell," Mr. J. announces.

"Damned if it isn't," Dad acknowledges.

Risking being caught, I lift the lid on our compartment four or five inches high. A real live black bear stands broadside, about a football field away.

"He hadn't seen us yet, Munford. Turn off the motor. The sound of Baker's Creek feeding into the river must have drowned out the noise from the car."

"The road's more dirt than gravel. That's how we slipped up on him," Dad gives his opinion.

"Have you got a gun?" Mr. J. asks.

"I got an old 44:40 Winchester under the seat, but I doubt it would even reach that far."

"Get it, before he steps behind that honeysuckle patch."

"That's close to a hundred yards. The bullet would drop two or three feet at that range."

"Hellfire, shoot over his head. Trajectory doesn't mean anything to a bear. How many chances like this are you going to get?"

Mr. J. leans over the front seat as Dad retrieves his carbine.

"I really don't think I ought to do this, William."

"What's the matter with you? You'll never have a shot like this again."

Dad sticks the lever-action rifle out the window and steadies his left arm on the door. He takes aim. His right elbow slowly raises. He breathes in deeply and part way back out. He can't hold it long enough. Gasping for another breath, he admits, "I can't stop shaking."

"Give me the gun," Mr. J. offers.

"No, no, I can do it."

My father tries again. His right elbow slowly comes up once more. Breathing stops again. His right arm is almost parallel to the ground as the point of the right elbow looks for a place to rest. It finds one…coming down squarely on the car horn. A sharp honk sends everyone jumping. The bear takes off at a startling lope.

"Shoot! Look at that sucker go, right down the creek. You're going to have to shoot him on the run, now. Shoot him. Go ahead. Shoot the sum'bitch."

BANG!

The bear rolls head over heels, but immediately stands upright like a man. With his two front paws, he grabs his right back foot and hops around in a circle on his other hind foot.

"Look at that. You must have hit him in the foot, Munford. Look what he's doing. Hell's bells, put him out of his misery. Shoot again."

"My gun's jammed."

The bear drops back down to three of his all-fours.

"There he goes. You better drop him before he gets out of sight. He's getting away, damn-it."

Dad fumbles with his gun but can't make it work.

"Look at him hobble, favoring that hind foot. You crippled him. Now he's going to have to limp around like you."

There's silence…until Dad asks, "How'd you get to be so hateful? Do you practice it?"

"Let's go see what kind of blood trail he left." Mr. J. is too excited to answer Dad.

The men get out of the car and plow through the briars, Dad cripple-hopping right along behind Mr. J. After splashing right through Baker's Creek, they start inspecting for fresh blood. Within about five minutes, they head back.

Dad opens the car door and remarks, "I shouldn't have shot him."

Mr. J. ignores him and carries on his own conversation. "I guess they don't leave much of a blood trail when you shoot them in the foot. He'll probably cross on that sand bar below where the road hits the river…unless being lame, he'd prefer to swim. Drive on over there and let's see what we can find. The wet sand ought to make for a good set of tracks."

Again, the men are out of the vehicle for only about five minutes before they're back.

"Quit your bellyaching, Munford. We'd have probably found more if you hadn't got to favoring that limp of yours and walked us around in a big circle."

Dad ignores Mr. J. for his own opinion. "As sparse as the grass was, if there was more than a trace of blood, we'd have seen it."

"Munford, I love these rides. Truth is so much better than fiction. Not many men around these parts could even dream up a bear walking around with three toes less than he's supposed to have…and that bear track sure reveals one unique imprint from the right hind foot. If you haven't made that gimpy foot become hereditary, maybe my writing can at least make it become legendary. Forever and after, a bear track with only two toes…shall bare the mark of redneck riflemanship."

"Bear the mark? Are you just naturally double-tongued, or does that dribble only come out when you've had too much to drink?"

"Driver, I'll have to give you your due credit. You've also given a whole new meaning to the tradition of hunting horns. For years untold, cow horns have been used for calling the dogs, but honking your car horn to warn your prey that the chase is about to commence…that's downright sporting of you."

Dad remains defenseless. C.B. shifts his position. I give him a shake of my head that says, "Don't move so much or they'll hear us."

"Munford, did you notice how much that bear acted like a human when you shot him? If you had hit him in the chest, he'd have probably crossed his front paws right over the bullet hole like a Jap."

"What would you know about shooting Japs?"

"Hey, everybody didn't have one-legged polio preventing them from participating in the big one."

"Well, how come you don't start talking about your war experiences until you're looking at the bottom of about two of those Mason jars?"

"As a blatter of fact, and contrary to bop-lar po-lief, you'll never see me ineb…inebri…inebriated," Mr. J. exaggerates his stuttering, I think.

"Or haul you home hung over, huh?" Dad adds.

"You should be honored I called you to come along on my trip. I don't have a whole lot of drinking partners."

"Doesn't that tell you volumes, if not gallons?"

"Keep it up, Munford, and you can watch your tip get dull."

"Yeah, right, like you're even gonna pay what you already owe for these rides, Mr. Big Shot Writer."

"Speaking of a shot, Man, you're a crack shot with that little rifle of yours. Ol' Teddy's got nothing on you, shooting your first bear's foot half off. Maybe I could write a sequel about a steady-bear, one toe at a time being absolved of big game mortality."

"I've about had enough of your lip," Dad warns.

"All right, Munford. You're right. We've immortalized enough bears for one day. We probably need to do some less serious riding now. Do you hear Memphis calling?"

C.B. and I look at each other with similarly worried faces.

"No, I sure don't," Dad answers.

"First, let's make a run by the Coontown bootlegger's."

We ride in silence, and I assume Dad's not answering him means we're going to Memphis, by way of the bootlegger's.

"I do hope he can fend for himself. You reckon he'll make it, being wounded?" Dad asks.

"Ol' Two-toes? Yeah, he'll be okay, unless he starves to death trying to rob corn-cribs with half his paw shot off."

"You're the most spiteful man God ever made, if He's even the one that made you."

"I suspect Mr. Crookedness-a-foot is studying that sandbar as we speak, trying to figure out such an odd set of tracks as you left, dragging that lame leg of yours around."

"William—"

"Yep, you're one hell of a shot, Munford. Next time that bear tangles with Blue or a better dog, he'll probably have to box him, having nothing but a nub."

"As few bear as we've got left, it was probably illegal even shooting at him," Dad says. "You shouldn't have insisted I do it."

"Hellfire, I didn't think you'd hit him. Besides that, I well know how to handle that young game warden if he comes up on us."

"You're blowing smoke again."

"No, Munford, I'll swear—I'm more than willing to vouch unequivocally for you. We'll just honestly admit that you didn't aim to hit the bear in the toe."

"What's that got to do with anything?" Dad asks, but I'm knowing Mr. J. is setting him up.

"I'll claim you were aiming to aim right between his eyes. When I get through with the warden, he'll know that bear was putting his paw up to shield his eyes from the spotlight when you happened to pull the trigger."

"Thanks a heap," Dad says. "It's good to know I can count on you."

C.B.'s head is down in his lap to try to keep from laughing aloud, and he's bouncing up and down so hard I'm afraid he's going to give away our hiding spot. Mr. Jefferson holds up a Mason jar in each hand and looks at their liquid levels. He takes a sip from each, and then pours some from one into the other. He holds them up for another look and twists his wrists outward to make what's left of the 'shine gather up in the bottom of each jar.

Clearing his throat as if swallowing now hurts, Mr. J. toasts one jar to the other and asks, "What do you boys think about all this?"

After no more than three seconds of dead silence, C.B. responds, "How'd you know we was back here?"

Silence comes again…anything but dead this time. Dad pulls the car over to the side of the road and stops.

"Actually," Mr. J. answers C.B., "I was talking to these two clear-glass quart country tumblers. But now that we know you boys are back there, the more relevant question becomes—what do we do with you?"

I sit in painful quiet with a large hollow in my stomach. The whites of C.B.'s eyes are glued to me, but I'm more worried about how to help myself. I hear his breathing and feel my heart pounding.

Pulling back out on the road, Dad speaks, "You boys just stay in my cargo box for the time being. Use your time to think about what you've done. I'll figure what to do with you by the time I get you home, if I take you home."

Shortly, Mr. J. starts up, "Seems like we got us a couple of regular freeloaders back there, Munford. Stowaways. Snoops. That's what they are. Moved in on us like a clan…regular snoops, like a family of Snoopes."

It's such a long, quiet ride back to Oxford, I'm thinking Mr. J.'s gone to sleep. When we finally approach Pen-Oake, Dad speaks up.

"William, we're home, and I appreciate you tolerating those boys the way you do."

"Humph," Mr. J. answers, sort of. "Think nothing of it. See if you can keep from running over any of my private drive signs, and try to miss some of the potholes I dug in my driveway."   "Holes that you dug?"

Dad questions, and stops short of the red-brick circular drive with its parallel rows of big cedar trees…and the potholes.

"Yeah, I had to do something to stop sightseeing snoops from bothering me so much."

In spite of Mr. J.'s words being sleepy and slow, I'm thinking they are not helping our case. He gets out without arguing over Dad stopping instead of dodging where he's dug in his driveway.

"Much to thank you, Munford. I'll have that book signed for you by our next ride. Or you can put my share of our trip on my running ticket…after you deduct a discount for the boys." As the famous author staggers toward his front porch, he glances back over his shoulder with a wink for C.B. and me.

Dad says to us, "I don't know how that man could ever amount to anything. Now, you boys come out from back of there. We're fixing to have us a serious talking to before we settle up. I'm talking about something you can spend the rest of your lives trying to forget."

We climb out of the storage box and into the back seat. Dad starts driving too fast for being in town.

"We're sorry, Dad," I try to ease the tension.

"Sorry is just not going to get it this time, Son. We've got to come up with an appropriate punishment for snooping where you know you've got no business being. You tell me what you think would be lasting enough to do any good. What?"

"I don't know, but we're really, really sorry. And we won't never do it again. I don't know what it is, Dad…you take a kid that's always doing stuff bad, and he'll get away with it every time. But the first time me and C.B do something wrong we get caught."

"Well, now that you have entirely missed the point, let's give your negra friend a shot at it. What about you, Charlie Boy? What do you think we ought to do about all of this?"

"Uh…well, Sir, I reckon if you was to let us go, me an' Scott…uh, we could sorta forget all them stories we overheard 'bout th' wild women an' ever'thing."

The taxi swerves over and bounces off the curb and then to an abrupt halt.

"Get out," Dad yells. "Walk from here, both of you…out!"

XVIII:
Farmerless Watermelons

"THERE'S A LOT TO be said for being your own man," Dad lectures me, "not having a boss to report to…not worrying about pleasing anyone but yourself. Grocering and taxiing has worked well for me, without some high-powered education." He walks back to the rear of the store.

The not-so-bad side of working in Munford's Grocery is that it keeps me out of the summer sun. The downsides are having to do things like dusting enough canned goods to have a smoker's chest. I don't care too much for sweeping that powdery green stuff Dad throws on the floor either. He says the detergent-like material holds down dust and picks up dirt, but I have a feeling it's really just to make sure I don't skip a square foot of sweeping. I think I'm about to wear out the hardwood slats from over-sweeping.

Father's assessment of my generation is something along the lines of it's going to pot. Apparently he is wanting to etch his devotion to the store into my character. Trying even harder than usual to get me interested in the family business, he claims my fate is written in concrete cursive. Silently and secretly I vow to defy merchantship and accept any alternative other than being a groceryman. I especially wonder if there isn't something in the woods that would help keep the ever-present grocery gene from dominating my destiny's direction.

On a typical summer Saturday most Lafayette County roads lead to Oxford's heart, The Square. Four faces of the oversized clock atop the courthouse watch families come from every direction to the focal point of the truck-farming business. It's market day, and country folks come to the county seat to trade.

Along about dusk on Fridays, many of the pickups filled with fresh vegetables begin to arrive. These country traders come an evening early to stake out the best parking spaces around The Square. Social activities go on until after dark, renewing acquaintances and having everyone catch up on their gossip. Men stand around or sit underneath the willow oaks they mistakenly call pin oaks. Yarns and pocketknives are traded, only to be brought back the next week for updating and re-swapping, respectively.

The men sleep in their trucks so they'll be ready to sell early on Saturday. That's the day they'll peddle their produce, most anything they can do without. Whatever they can grow, beg, borrow, or steal...it all becomes fair game to barter, swap, or sell.

By midday, wives and kids of the vendors have come to town. It's usually late morning when the other country people make it in and afternoon by the time the affluent city folks come out. Then the shopping really picks up, although the good stuff is already gone, swapped among the farmers.

In one respect, Saturday on The Square is a big change from Oxford's usual business day. It's one day and one place where color and creed don't seem to matter too much. Everyone depends on everyone else...and that outweighs a lot of the so-called social situations that some people worry about.

I wonder what the colored families do for a restroom when they spend all day in town. With the coloreds not being allowed in the courthouse restroom, I don't see how the problem can be so ignored by the small shops and full-blown stores alike. I never hear of any complaints...or solutions. They must have some place to go somewhere.

Businesses of all kinds form the perimeter around The Square, but there's only one grocery store. As fate would fancy my fanny, Munford's Grocery belongs to my father. It was Dad's father's before him and his father's before him. While I'm told I will have to go to college, I'm also instructed not to let it make me too big for my britches to return to the business of my roots.

Sometimes I envy C.B.'s having nothing he's expected to live up to. For me, it's like there's this particular rung on a ladder that's hanging high over my head, and I am expected to climb up to it. Thinking I'd rather be most anything than a grocer, I'll be double-dunked if I'm going to yield easily.

Munford's Grocery has to compete with all the truck farmers selling everything that can be grown locally: sweet corn and field corn, new 'taters, okra, collard and mustard greens, tomatoes, squash, peppers, and some less common stuff. Dad's always looking for some kind of edge on the competition.

I live in constant fear that we'll start up a delivery service when he thinks I'm old enough to handle it. For the time being, I've stamped enough prices on boxed and canned stock to memorize the cost of everything from Carter's Little Liver Pills to the various odd ounces' worth of hoop cheese. Compared to the new supermarket down University Avenue, Munford's is a meager little store. According to Dad, the big chain store with the creed for greed has taken most of our white trade.

Since my grandfather has developed a solid clientele from the Negro community, colored people still provide us with what Granna calls our bread and butter. It's more than a bit ironic because Dad likes for the Negroes to know their place and keep to their respective position in his society. For him, of all people, to have the most integrated store in Oxford is an issue in segregation that's an emotional dilemma for me. Being younger than the purchasing public, but the one who is waiting on them in our service business, I feel a peculiar uneasiness when even the older Negroes call me Mister or Sir.

No matter what the client's color, we take only hard cash, no credit. Truck farmers often come in the store and promise to pay for penny-ante purchases at the end of the day or for large purchases with next fall's money. Dad says he's learned the hard way always to tell them his motto is strictly cash and carry. That motto is written on pencils…and the taxi drivers tease us about selling them instead of giving them away as advertising.

The only part of working in Munford's store that I enjoy involves making change and mingling with the customers. Many of the Mammies, as Dad calls the larger colored ladies, keep their change pouches down between their big breasts. I can't help staring as they dig their money out of those amazing bosoms. They'll usually turn their back to the counter, but the big mirror right behind them doesn't reflect much modesty.

Immediately to the east of Munford's Grocery is the Lafayette County Welfare Department warehouse. Like the truck farmers around the Square, that is competition. As if the capitalist, corporate giant Kroger store isn't bad enough, now there's our own government with its commodity cheese and powdered milk. Although it's supposed to be free and for people who are broke, Dad claims it still somehow competes with us.

Papa, who preaches instead of grocering, says if Big Brother were to come to town with a pocket full of money, the post office would probably move out to some obscure location just to spend the money. Not far from my grandfather's joke is what's happening for real with the Welfare Department. We're told that our city fathers have accumulated so much money from those who pay taxes that they've decided they'll build a new welfare warehouse.

When the new building is established on the other side of town, the historic one next door to Munford's Grocery is demolished. As the last of the bricks come down, all the rats decide they would just as soon live in our store. They eat right through the wood to get in. Considering the concurrent destruction of rat habitat next door and our absolutely overwhelming hoop-cheese smell, I can't blame them. Dad, however, has never been one to consider my good and basic logic or side with rodents on any account.

In my best effort to help, I try to share an above-average brainstorm I've derived from a story Mr. J. told C.B. and me about rat killings. Dad looks at me without speaking, until I get to the part about having to build a fire in his store to make enough smoke to run the rats around for me to shoot at. I'm guessing I should have said we'd let C.B. shoot them in the head instead of my just shooting at them…but anyway, that discussion is over.

Dad is in the back preparing the store for closing when C.B. comes in. My buddy sits down behind the counter without Dad having seen him. Dad, being about to quit work for the day, is happy enough to have found his second wind. As he often does, he expresses this going-home level of excitement through song. He loudly sings one of his favorite closing-up-the-store songs:
"Oo…oh…Some folks say that a nigger won't steal,
but I caught one in my cornfield…."

If I could crawl under the counter to escape my embarrassment, I'd do it.
"I'm outta here," C.B. whispers.
"Aw, C.B., he doesn't mean anything by that."
"I do," my friend answers back.

With Dad now out of sight in our private restroom, C.B. slips out. Promising to wait around the corner for me to get off work, C.B. remains a fiercely loyal companion to me. Such incidents with my father make me that much more determined to prove my friendship to C.B. every chance I get.

When I meet up with C.B., I share how Mr. J.'s good rat-killing idea was almost a go. Now, it's not even in the running. We get to talking about Dad's aggravation over his business competition, and C.B. comes up with a somewhat considerate thought. Since my father is disadvantaged and handicapped by being crippled, and even in spite of his recent singing about coloreds, C.B. says those who compete with Dad shouldn't be allowed so much peace and tranquility as to have advantages over him.

"We'll figger out somethin'," C.B. promises.

"Ox'patch by night's always a good time to do something," I suggest in hopes of adding to C.B.'s plan.

"You gots it…I'll see ya tonight, then…same time, same place as last time."

———————————

BY THE TIME OUR courthouse clock tolls the summer Friday midnight hour, C.B. and I have already gone to bed, slipped back out, and met up with each other. Our wait in the alley behind Grundy's restaurant is not long. With its groaning and churning sounds, one of the wonders of the 60s rolls up South Lamar. Controlling hordes of insects along its way, what we call the fog machine leaves a cloud of white mist.

Slipping into the fog bank of DDT without the driver seeing us, we walk right along behind the city truck, concealed by the sea of chemical haze from any truck farmers who might happen to still be up. As the cool, moist vapors sprayed to control mosquitoes envelope my hot face, I am only slightly aware of the unpleasant smell.

Nearing the watermelon farmers' trucks, C.B. and I walk and talk with experienced confidence. In a midnight requisition by as much feel as sight, we each select the fruit of our choice. The original proprietors of the crops sleep, as we simply file back in line behind the city escort.

"This sho' beats grubbin' to get grub," C.B. points out the obvious.

Hoping he won't get any more philosophical than that, I don't answer. After swallowing and breathing more than enough poison to keep bugs out of our noses and ears for life, we break out of the circle that's The Square and sprint down Van Buren Avenue.

"Like yo' father's cash an' carry motto, ours can be—strictly gas an' carry," C.B. mocks us…almost like the taxi drivers do.

I nod as C.B. laughs over his own sarcasm about the motto. South of the Presbyterian Church, we come to the old, dilapidated warehouse called the gin. Its large wooden doors are chained in their middle about head-high, which allows easy crawl-in entry. It's done by pushing one bottom, middle corner while pulling the other one…and then holding them apart for each other.

Cotton bales are now stored inside what once was part of an active gin. On such an off-work weekend as this, the old gin often becomes our special and secret hideout. A virtual maze for climbing and jumping from cotton bale to cotton bale, it's also a good place to lie around and talk about such subjects as girls, what we're going to do when we grow up, and the other challenges of life.

A full moon shines through the barred windows at the top of the building, so a mellow light illuminates our private watermelon cutting. Sitting cross-legged on a bale of cotton in our private place, C.B. flourishes his jackknife. Readying himself for feasting, the corners of his mouth rise as he slices through the big, borrowed fruit to the bursting sound that could only come with melon ripeness.

"Um-m-mm," he murmurs. "Mine's a good'un," he says as he slurps.

"I hope I've picked a good one."

"You didn't pick nothin'," he surprises me. "City boys like you select yo' melons."

Trying to ignore him, I break it open and see that it looks perfect. Carving out the heart and tasting the dripping, fragrant sweetness, I announce, "Not bad."

C.B. laughs and insinuates with his expression that he realizes I was purposely underrating it.

"What took you so long picking your watermelon when I selected such a good one, country hick?"

"I had to thump a few of 'em fer ripeness," he answers.

"I thought maybe you had gone to haggling with the farmer over which one to steal."

"'At's all right. I got me one with so much water in it, it musta been planted in th' spring."

"That's not funny," I comment and savor another big section.

"Prob'ly 'cause you don't get it." He spits a seed at me.

"I got it. It just wasn't funny." With the choice center of my melon's first half almost gone, I use my fingers to separate enough of the seeds to find the remaining best bites.

C.B. pulls a handful of cotton from a bale and wipes his perspiring forehead and juice-covered hands with it. "While we settin' here eatin' free watermelon, what you reckon ever'body else our age be doin'?" He tries to stick the cotton plug back where he got it.

"I don't know, but I feel sorry for folks who aren't us. And I have thought of something else."

"Is it somethin' gon' get me in trouble?"

"Not in the least."

"How 'bout in th' most?"

"I was just thinking, C.B. You know...this sure looks like it'd be a better place for rats than my Dad's store."

"I thought we was 'sposed to be worried 'bout his competition. These cotton farmers ain't hurtin' yo' dad's business. But if'n you want a real idear...."

"What?"

"Them rats...now they might could do some good fer yo' Dad if they was over to Kroger's."

"Aw...right, you want to?"

"Nothin' to it but to do it. I can live-trap a crate full with a cheese trail...an' we can tote 'em over there th' same night we catch 'em."

"How can we get them inside Kroger's?"

"'At ain't no problem there. We'll figger 'at out when th' time come...with all them vents and things around there." C.B. lifts half his melon to his mouth and sucks the juice.

"Yep...we're gonna have us a rat-catching," I agree, slurping down the last bite of my sugary sweet melon. "I don't believe anyone could figure out a better plan than that, even if it was you that thought of it."

"Aw, yeah, if I had a little time...."

"How? Do it. Prove it," I challenge him. "How could it be any better, man? A rat releasing in Kroger's...how could anyone ever beat that?"

C.B. searches the old cotton warehouse with a look of genuine interest and then turns to me. "What if we was to somehow figger out a way to lay it all on Chicken-Hawk?"

I roll my eyes in defeat, as we both laugh too loud for being in most hideouts.

XIX:
Chimney Swifts of Rivers' Hill

"THIRTY-SEVEN FIFTY?" I question, complaining to my dad. "How come they call it a fifty dollar savings bond if that's all it's worth?"

"Because it will be worth fifty bucks when it matures," he explains.

"And I probably won't need it half as bad by then."

"Welcome to the world of high finances, Son."

If I were looking for a hard lesson in grown-up economics, I'd have gone out to the campus. All I wanted was a cinnamon roll and a Pepsi. With Munford's Grocery being customerless, I suppose this is as good a time as I'll find to hit my father up with the big question.

"Dad, I've kept it long enough. I want to cash it in. Even if it isn't worth fifty dollars, it's enough to buy the .22 rifle I want."

"Not no, but hell no! You're not buying a .22."

"But that's not fair. I earned that money. I won it from the prescription-getting contest, and it's mine."

"Sub...scription, Son. It's subscription." Dad opens a cinnamon roll for us to share, instead of letting me have a whole one.

"Come on, Dad...."

"Thunderation, boy, a .22 will shoot a mile. You could kill somebody way off and not even know it."

"I'll be careful. I'll never shoot unless there's a bank of dirt behind where I'm aiming...or some trees or something. I need that gun." In a pleading pause, I engulf my half of the sweet treat.

Dad nibbles on his. "I'm proud of you for winning the contest, Son, but I know best."

"Please, Dad. I worked hard to earn that money. I wouldn't have even entered the contest if...."

"Look, Son, I know it took spunk, but.... I'll tell you what—if you think you have to have a gun, I'll let you get a .410 shotgun."

"All ri...i...i...ight!"

"Maybe you won't kill yourself or someone else with one of them."

"Thanks, Dad." He's not much on hugging, but I give him a quick one and run before he reconsiders or puts me to work.

Appropriate study of hunting and fishing magazines at Parks Barber Shop gives me a brainstorm. After several unsuccessful visits to view the guns at the bait shop, I find the gun I want at Western Auto. It's a Savage Model 24 over-and-under. The under part is a .410 shotgun to keep Dad happy, and the over part is a .22 rifle for him not to know about.

"'AT BE TH' DEVIL'S lie if I ever heared it...buyin' 'at gun agin yo' dad's will."

"Get off it, C.B. You're always coming up with something stupid about the devil. Why would God have let me win the savings bond if He didn't want me to have my .22?"

"When you gon' buy it?"

"We've got to turn some paper route profit to go with cashing in the savings bond."

"How much you lackin'?"

"Around ten. I need a total of about fifty bucks. Knowing my gun is sitting up there at Western Auto with strangers handling it...that makes everything seem to be in slow motion. It's going to be a tough wait."

IT'S ONLY IN A weak moment I'd consider a plan that involved Chicken-Hawk. C.B. assures me it will be for our best...and I'm liable to lose the whole thing if I don't go along to get along. The Chicken claims if I let him hold my thirty-seven dollars and fifty cents over the weekend, he'll show enough interest in it to return fifty dollars to me the following Monday morning. Since it's the first time Chicken-Hawk's ever talked to us in a whispery voice instead of his usual yelly one and it's such a rare thing to see him so pleasant...and because I'm taking my health into consideration, I'm afraid I'm an easy mark. Maybe it'll not only get me my gun earlier than I could otherwise but also help my standing with Chicken's disposition.

The weekend comes and goes. Monday morning shows, but Chicken-Hawk doesn't. It's not until the third weekend later when C.B. brings over the explanation as to how Chicken lost his interest in my money. It had to do with some bull not coming to market, and that's as far as he got before his original explanation degenerated into something C.B. couldn't follow.

"An' th' Chicken, he says yo' bond money also got caught up amongst the crapshootin' on Rivers' Hill."

Rivers' Hill is a section of the county just outside of town that used to be a lot like Freedmen-Town. Now, everybody has moved, and the only things still standing are some lonely-looking chimneys left from house fires. Dad says black panthers hang out there, but I don't see why they'd come that close to town, especially since Chicken claims the site as his own for craps or cards whenever he is of a mind to.

When the opportunity arises, and if the Chicken ever feels up to explaining, I'll want to hear his account of how I'm going to get my money back. For now, he and C.B. may think this is the end of it. But it isn't. I vow to C.B. that I will get my money or get even with Chicken. Neither one of them realize just how mad I am.

———

NORMALLY WHEN C.B. AND I finish delivering the daily papers to our regular customers, we go uptown and sell any extras the paper man may have given us that day. If we don't sell them, we won't be charged for them. All we have to do is cut the date off the front page of each paper and return it. Considering how much it would help with our finances, I come up with the idea of selling, and maybe even delivering, some papers with their dates torn off.

"Jesus be watchin' 'at sorta stuff," C.B. protests. "An' it ain't worth goin' to hell over."

"All right, all right...don't hit me with your Bible. We'll think of something else."

Sometimes I think a "B" is the Lord's middle initial—Jesus be watching this, and Jesus be watching that...Jesus B. Christ.

When the time comes to collect from my customers for a month's worth of paper deliveries, the first fifty dollars is promptly spent on the acquisition of my new Savage Model 24. As future collections come in, C.B. and I spend most of it on shells and cartridges...before Chicken-Hawk has a chance to hear I'm in the money again.

We shoot so many hundreds of .22 cartridges that I hear the crack of the rifle in my sleep. By blasting a few .410 shotgun shells, we can be honest when we talk to my dad about shooting my new shotgun. It's a good thing for my ears and my pocketbook that it's not the bang of a shotgun I'm hearing as often as the .22. Dad didn't know best after all.

As with my BB gun and then with my pellet rifle, C.B. is the better marksman and puts me to shame with my new rifle. The .22 is such a natural for him that unless the wind messes him up, he can hit about anything in range. On windless days, he experiments shooting above things that are out of range, letting the bullet drop.

Mr. J. tells us about a man he saw at the carnival who could light matches by shooting the top of them. When C.B. gets the hang of it, incredible is the only way to describe some of his more than remarkable shots. As good as he is with open sights, I figure nothing within view would be safe if he had one of those telescopic sights.

Once in a while I can accidentally break one of the matches but can't ever light one, no matter how hard I try or how much I shoot. In fact, the harder I try to aim to hit something, the more I shake. It's like my handwriting. Practice does not make perfect, no matter what the teachers say. I know from practicing my signature a hundred times in detention hall. It didn't get one iota better.

When C.B. and I go back to our customers in Freedmen-Town who couldn't pay their bill the first time, we don't do any better collecting from them the second time. A lot of the people who said yes to C.B.'s sales pitch aren't staying in those particular houses any longer. Many are said to have moved to Chicago or Memphis to find work. Some are in jail. I'm thinking the ones working can send some money for their bill. Everybody we talk to says they'll tell them, but all I'm getting so far is a good lesson about ignorance without bliss...another one of those areas the teachers were wrong about.

We pedal and pitch another month away. None of the non-payers send any money. Dad and the *State Times* paper man are none too happy about my not coming up with the monthly payment when it's due. It's a good thing I already have my new bike and .410/.22. My second month's returns come out about as profit-free as the first's. As the red paint on my bike and my feeling of responsibility to make deliveries wear off, C.B.'s bike starts sounding like a wheelbarrow looking for grease.

In the kind of punishment that is music to my ears, the *State Times* man says he's not sending me any more papers. Surprisingly, Dad doesn't seem to mind. I think he was getting tired of the short and fat man from Jackson calling him so often. Through our sudden financial instability, to the extent we can afford bullets, C.B. continues to hone his accuracy. My shooting still doesn't improve, but I do enjoy trying.

Neither the state of Mississippi nor our respective schools' policies recognize ground hogs for their special day. Granna says it's just as well because we don't have enough ground hogs around here to make a good shadow if they all came out at once. Therefore, C.B. and I develop our own way to celebrate what we declare a skip-school holiday…shooting rats with the .22 half of my Model 24 at the city garbage dump.

While I plink around with tin cans and more stationary targets, C.B. learns to hit running rats and loves to show off his natural ability. When I share my frustration with Mr. J. about how C.B., instead of me, has gone from good to expert with my new .22, Mr. J. tells me about something called rat-shot. He says even I can hit a rat every now and again if I use it. It checks out to be like a miniature shot shell, with tiny little pellets instead of one bullet. Right when I'm thinking it's working well for me, C.B. gets the idea he can use rat shot to hit bottles and cans I throw in the air for him.

STILL HARBORING A BAD need to get back at Chicken-Hawk for swindling me, I have a near-religious experience. It's an idea that has materialized right before me, without even having to hunt for it. An opportunity-like plan on how I might get my money back has presented itself.

Since Chicken-Hawk is so fond of betting and so far from being Irish that we won't have to worry about luck, we'll take advantage. To Chicken's ugly ears, I am sure the sound of a ratshot going off would not distinguish itself from that of a regular .22 rifle shot. And if Chicken's buddies are witnessing, perhaps even the craps crowd has enough standards to honor a lost wager.

It must be with spiritual overtones that I am sensing this Saturday afternoon is bringing a fresh game of gambling to Rivers' Hill. When Chicken-Hawk appears, C.B. and I emerge from our own hiding place. Presenting our proposition, I'm thinking two losses in a row will be about right to sucker him in. C.B. has agreed to miss twice...two times.

"I'll bet y'all five dollars C.B. can strike two out of three matches from shots at fifteen feet away. Three shots. Two lit matches. What do you say?"

"Set up yo' matches, Little Bitch. I be glad to take yo' money," Chicken laughs with a sneer.

Carrying out our plan with perfection, C.B. purposely strikes only one of the three matches. There's hearty laughter from Chicken and all his buddies as he takes my five dollars. We repeat the process and the results. There is more scornful laughter...and I'm ten dollars in the red, as C.B. ejects his last spent cartridge. We stand around and continue to take more verbal abuse than anyone ought to have to tolerate.

When my buddy gives me the nod that he has slipped in a rat shot without anyone else seeing or knowing the difference, I proclaim, "He's really better at shooting moving targets."

Laughter and hooting become ridicule. It's late afternoon and the chimney swifts are coming home to circle the old chimneys. Flying in a closer and closer circle, by the time they're ready to enter the chimney, they're flying in a tight and predictable pattern. What Chicken and his flock don't know is—for three evenings in a row, we have been at other old chimneys, where C.B. has practiced shooting flying chimney swifts with .22 rat shot.

The birds are in their glide-path...and the time is right. Chicken and company are more than surprised to see me lay three twenties on their craps blanket. To my surprise, it's Chicken who comes through for us and curbs his buddies' suspicions.

"It's all right. 'At white boy's got him a paper route." As if it would make a difference to Chicken or his friends, he informs them, "Th' money ain't stole."

Trying to look unsure of myself, I proclaim, "C.B. can take just one shot with the .22 and uh…hit one of those birds…on the fly."

"With th' .22?" one of Chicken's buddies asks through his laughter.

"With the .22," I answer. "You can tell from the sound it won't be the .410."

They quickly huddle and pitch in their contributions. When they've matched my sixty and lay it on the blanket, the bet is on. C.B. eases over to a chimney. I position myself right by the money. My marksman selects a chimney swift from the group and watches him circle. The flight pattern establishes itself, and C.B. locks in on it. Clearly recognizing the moment, he slowly raises my rifle. Watching the money, I hear the familiar cocking sound of the Model 24's steel hammer.

Chicken elbows his nearest buddy and whispers some know-it-all comment. The whole flock cackles like hens. C.B. takes his exaggerated breath and a half…and holds it. I can hear my heart beating as my buddy swings the barrel with the flight of the birds. He squeezes the trigger. At the crack of the .22 rat shot, C.B.'s bird folds and drops to the ground…with feathers floating down after it.

"All right!" I exclaim and quickly scoop up the bills in my baseball cap and place it securely on my head.

"But…." Chicken starts to say something.

"I'd rather be lucky than skillful any day," I cut him off and start down Rivers' Hill before he can give his good friends any bad ideas about not letting us leave with the money.

"Wait a minute, boys," one of Chicken's friends calls out.

C.B., already in front of me, doesn't answer.

Picking up my walking pace almost to a run, I can't resist responding loudly and back over my shoulder, "The shotgun part of this Model 24 is still loaded, if anybody wants to learn to dance."

Before the crap shooters can give organizational thought to serious chase, C.B. and I are at the bottom of Rivers' Hill with a congregation of the general public to protect us.

"What if th' Chicken had come after us when you axed yo' question 'bout learnin' to dance?" C.B. asks.

"He'd have probably stood there doing the twist…and you'd have accidentally shot him in the foot."

XX:
End of an Era

C.B. AND I ARE supposed to be camping in Bailey Woods, but summer is about to offer an oh-so-southern heritage that we're not even going to consider missing…at Ole Miss. Sitting quietly on the edge of the University's Confederate Cemetery, I look over at the gymnasium and comment, "There's a great-looking bunch of gals for camp this summer."

"Any colored?" C.B. asks.

"Get real."

"So much fer it bein' th' top of th' crop, then."

In a good way, the old brick gym reeks of a unique kind of rebel history that has little to do with its scores of Southeastern Conference basketball contests and rivalries. From several dozen high schools, mostly in the South, the finest of their young ladies have arrived on campus for cheerleader camp.

"I don't think they're bashful as they were last year," I insinuate, hoping C.B. might believe I'd had some encounter that he could be jealous about.

"Like you been foolin' with 'em enough to know 'at," he challenges my pretended observation.

"Well, I know when I get a smile back from one of them," I try again to lead him on.

Actually, I'm wondering if I could even handle a real experience with a girl without too much embarrassment. Except for the seemingly shameful struggle of self-discovery that comes with puberty, I don't know how much longer I can ignore my physical and emotional changes.

"Scott, we li'ble to get struck down by lightnin' if'n we go th'u with this. An' I got me th' feelin' we ought not."

"Come on." I give him a playful shove. "Don't be chicken."

"Let's leave Chicken outta this," he jokes.

Despite C.B.'s skepticism, the realization that girls are genuinely something more than just soft guys is weighing heavily on my fantasies. I need to find out more about what's inflating such passion. A better view of the contoured lines and bulging blouses, if not what's under them, should be a pre-teen rite of passage.

With the cheerleaders still in the Ole Miss Grove and late afternoon approaching, we turn curiosity into action. Making our way through a service entrance and into the people-free gym, we find sleeping cots placed about ten feet apart. They're on all four sides of each other and so many that they cover the out-of-bounds area as well as the playing court.

"See here, C.B." I point to our opportunity...roll-up style wooden bleachers framing both sides and ends of the gym. "This is what I was telling you about. Come on."

On such special occasions as when the building is being converted into sleeping quarters, the bleachers' 1 x 10-inch maplewood seats are pushed back flush against the wall, folded accordion-like into triangles. As the bleacher section is rolled back, the bottom seat stays aligned with the hardwood floor and leaves one row available for sitting. From its end, this wooden wedge-complex has just enough space, allure, and temptation for us to slip in behind it and hide...for peeking.

Once under it all, we find ourselves on all fours...but in position to appreciate a crawl space that runs the entire length of the floor. This kind of crawling makes me appreciate the double-padded knees of my Levis. With his lesser jeans, C.B. will just have to tough it out.

Eye level to a couple of crawlers with curious notions, a slight span between the slats forming the bottom row provides our secret vantage point. Several rolled up tumbling mats will hide us in case the college cheerleaders who help run the camp happen to shine a flashlight in here. Once that's no longer a threat, we'll have a virtual free-for-crawl...all-ie, all-ie, all in safe.

As we stretch out and wait for the girls to enter the gym, I unwrap and offer to share a half-melted Butterfinger appropriated from Dad's store. C.B. accepts and removes his bubble gum to stick under the seat with dozens of other dabs of discarded chews, all hanging there like the bats in Thacker cave. I detect the pungent smell of dirty sneakers and sweaty shorts coming from nearby locker rooms. The small vent fans near the roof are not enough to circulate the stale air trapped under here.

The thought of getting caught creeps across my Christian conscience. Whereas C.B. would probably get off Civil War free, I'd be made to parade around with my trousers at half-mast in my school…and clamped in a laughing stock at First Baptist.

On the other hand, I'm also thinking it'd be unnatural not to take advantage of this opportunity. Anyone who wouldn't enjoy looking at these girls is the oddball who needs to be locked up. As long as we can keep from getting caught, everything will be all right.

A black widow spider descends between us on its fly-fishing line. C.B. looks at me without speaking. We watch until it reaches the floor, where my buddy promptly squashes it with the heel of his tennis shoe…and still doesn't speak.

With daydreams of deflowering chastity, I fantasize about the girls that annually invade this time and place. I don't even pretend to understand the sanctity of young womanhood. It seems like all of female adolescence is coming of age right here in front me. Maybe it's all about to open up for two boys trying to cut their own pubic teeth. It may no longer be as private or personal as my imagination has had it for what seems like forever.

Daylight dims, but my partner in crime continues to shine in the dark. When evening tries to push through the seemingly worthless little window fan openings near the top of the gym, the artificial lighting fights it off. I had thought surely the girls would be here by now.

Finally, the big doors swing open…accompanied by girls' giggles and teenaged voices with bursts of laughter. The commotion comes closer.

"Hold down your whispering now," I suggest. "Let's give them about five minutes to settle in. If nobody's checked back here by then, it oughta be safe enough to come out from under these mats."

"I'm goin' now…an' seein' what I can see."

"Wait up, then. If you won't listen to reason, I might as well see, too." We scoot up.

The big room floods with high school cheerleaders…rusty blondes, sunlight-bright red heads, beautiful brunettes, dark-haired damsels, and girls of most every flavor imaginable.

"There must be a acre of 'em here," C.B. says.

My eyes bounce from one end of the gym to the other. Knowing all these cute little uniforms are about to come off brings an erotic excitement I've only simulated before.

"If this gets much better, I'm not gonna be able to take it."

"It's a'gonna...an' I'm 'bout'a bust, now," he answers.

"Burst," I correct.

"Speakin' of bust...look'a there...er."

He mumbles something that was probably too crude for most folks to want him to repeat. I'm really more interested in what the girls are saying. There's so much talk swirling around I can't make sense of anything I do hear. Teams are apparently organized in rows perpendicular to our crawl route...meaning we can get almost intimately close to a pretty girl from any of over a dozen distant towns.

"Wo-ooh! Look'a there, Scott. This ain't hap'nin'."

A girl near us slips out of her top.

"Yeah, it is."

She reaches around behind herself and unfastens her skin-colored little brassiere. It slides off, and I know peeling a ripe peach will never be the same. I want to scream.

"Wow!" C.B. offers.

"She's beautiful."

I've been wrong about a bit of mystery and something left to the imagination being better than the real thing. She slips a T-shirt over her head, and I want to be under there with her.   C.B.'s word choice may have been right after all—I wanta bust. If I could just cup my hands around....

"What you reckon it'd feel like to handle them things?" he asks.

"Good, I guess. I mean—like knockers. Soft...or hard. I don't know. Hush, I just wanta watch."

Another uniform comes off...and another. It seems all of girlhood is undressing at one time. Most of the silky-looking little tops and bottoms match the colors of the cheerleader uniforms...bras and panties of every color in the springwoods. I want to appreciate every school and color and everything that's being uncovered. There is not a plain old pair of white, cotton drawers in sight.

"It's enough to make you swell up," my crude partner in sorta-sex admits.

"And blow up," I add.

There's so much to see I can't decide where to look. I wonder what it must feel like to be a girl...and be so different in their private places. Why don't they stop and undress one at a time so I won't miss anything?

This is not fair…that I can't take them all in. My peripheral awareness is being pulled by glimpses of girls everywhere. I could see more if I'd look at fewer, but I can't help glancing from side to side.

"It looks like they're all gonna sleep naked underneath their nighties and T-shirts," I point out.

"What was you 'spectin', fool?"

"I don't know. They're tearing me up."

A close cheerleader shyly slips out of her outfit and into a little pull-over, all done so modestly I get only a peek. Another one doesn't remove her skimpy little garment until she's first put on her sleeper, as if she's teasing me. That's really not fair. I want to see better…and up closer. Caressing the bleachers, I run my hand along the cool wood and imagine the smooth and warm sensation of fondling a girl. I want to rub up against one for real…and touch where she's never been touched. A girl slides her hands underneath her top and rubs herself where I want to be touching and have never touched.

"Look at that, C.B."

"Boy, howdy…she's beggin' me to come squeeze them boobies."

"Squeeze, my foot…she's wanting my massage."

"Squeeze yo' own foot. She's a'needin' my strokin' an' pattin' an' pawin'."

She wouldn't be sitting there so uninhibited and protruding that proudly if she didn't want all the other girls to admire what she's developed. I crawl over for a closer inspection. C.B. follows like he's afraid I'll see something he won't. She pulls her sleeper over herself. For all her pomp and pride, a tall girl behind her is prettier.

"Maybe I'm gon' grow taller by th' time I'm in high school," C.B. hopes aloud.

"Lights out in five minutes!" a grownup lady's voice blurts out from a bullhorn and shatters the mood.

"Where did that old battle-ax come from?" I ask myself, as much as I'm asking C.B. "Doesn't she know I need the light to see? Why does she have to ruin this? It may never get this good again." I try to speed up my looking. "C.B."

"Huh?"

"These girls are awesome."

"You ain't just a'whistlin' Dixie," he responds.

"I'm sneaking a Brownie box camera in here next time. Look at that blonde doll. She's taking her top off." I'm having trouble breathing.

"Look'a there, Scott."

I'd crawl down our corridor for a clearer, close-up view but don't want to risk missing someone somewhere else.

"That one there is sort of tapered and pointy," I share.

She's a bonafide Belle of the South, right before my bulging eyes.

"Plumb proportioned," C.B. whispers back.

I'm not about to let him have the last word. "The kinda good I could graze along."

"Dazzlin'," C.B. apparently accepts my description challenge for cheerleaders.

"They're sculptured and stimulating," I answer, reaching for something unique to say.

"Knockouts," he answers. "An' gots legs 'at go all th' way up."

"Gorgeously arousing, I tell you."

"Holy moly…look how round…look-ie yonder…at th' shape of them things, Scott. Woo-oh, they nice, ain't they?"

"Easy to look at. I'd settle for just bumping up against that girl."

"Or keepin' abreast of her," he gets in a good one.

"She's endowed and bestowed with sum…mm…kind of stuff, C.B."

"God's eben give her hair th' color of broom sedge."

"Don't be talking about God at a time like this."

"Yeah, we ought not be here," C.B. unnecessarily goes beyond agreeing…enough to make me give up and let him have the last word.

I'm thinking this grand place oughta be preserved as some kinda shrine or something. Instead of it being set aside, I've heard the opposite is in the wind. All in the name of progress, ailing structures around the campus are starting to undergo renovation. One fine basketball day, the Rebels will have a nice new coliseum…and such an opportunity for the introductory course to Birds and the Bees 101 will be history. If anybody knew how much I'm gonna miss this…. The end of this era ought to be marked with little pastel-colored bras hanging from the rafters…waving goodbye like flags in the wind.

Without my regard for pre-nostalgia, my buddy starts up again, "Someday ever' guy on campus gon' be sniffin' along behind that one's tail. She's sort of shapely in a bony way. You know what I mean?"

Whispering isn't easy when breathing is so heavy. "She's the kind of bony that makes me wanta pick her up and hug her. If she's not a future Miss America, I'm…."

"How long we got 'til th' lights go off?" C.B. interrupts.

"Time's about up I'd say. Look at that short gal over there."

"I bet she'd be ever' bit of five foot tall lyin' down."

"C.B., that's belittling her. You need to be more respectful of such fine young ladies. Where's your church training?"

"I thought we wadn't gon' mention religion while we here."

"But, I'm serious," I tease. "You and me sneaking into this world...we're liable to be held accountable."

"Scott, I done told you, now."

"But Reverend, we could be screwing up our souls for good."

"It prob'ly ain't but one way we can make all this right."

"How's that?" I ask.

"We'll need to grow up to be two of them woman-doctors. Then it be like we done all this fer our studies an' it would'a been legal an' ever'thing." He grins as if in anticipation of such a possibility.

"You're an idiot. And I'm gonna zero in on my favorite girl before the lights go off."

"I gots th' eyes fer whichever one I happen to be lookin' at."

They all look so good it's hard for me to pick a favorite...real hard.

"See 'at one right there...th' one with red hair, an' cupped up rear end, an' full-meated, sorta hammy like a good cut?"

"Yeah, I do."

C.B's reddish selection looks kind of cat-like to me. With those fiery locks, I'll bet she has the green eyes of a carrottop I know at my school. Those freckles look as if they continue across her everywhere. I wish I could get close enough to see if they're camouflaging the texture of her skin. She could let me touch her with my swelling innocence. I'd like to see if she's smooth or not.

Will viewing a girl in a sweater ever be as good as it once was? Maybe that's the dark and down side to being a man of the world. I am feeling a little tarnished from the cheating aspect of this sensational exploit...but continue lying here all splayed out, pressing down my front like a dog dragging himself across the lawn. While I'm already watching something I'm not supposed to be seeing and thinking forbidden thoughts...I'm also wondering if they have bleachers like this in the showers.

Gym-mother returns. She's coming toward our hiding spot...too close for any more whispering. Of all times, the dust is getting to me, and I'm afraid I'm about to sneeze. The fears of being caught return quickly. I manage to hold my breath and keep from sneezing. She walks over and hits the lights.

As the dangers of being caught peter out in the darkness, fantastic silhouettes give rise to an irreverent independence…the familiar and always before now private sensuality.

With a throbbing pulse and tabooed thoughts of woolly-bugger utopia, I ask, "C.B., have you uh…ever thought about playing with yourself?"

"It come over me now an' agin."

"How about more now than again?"

"I will if you will," he dares.

I lean over on my side and shamelessly slide a hand inside my pants. My leg muscles go tense. Imagination supplements grandiose allusions for as many possibilities as lie before me…as many as a thirteen-year old can make up.

C.B. takes something out of his pocket.

"What's that?" I ask.

"A snuff can."

"What's in it?"

"Nuthin'."

"Nothing, thunder. What have you got there?"

"It ain't nuthin' fer white boys."

"Is it soap?"

"No, it ain't soap."

"What then?"

"You promise not to laugh?"

"C.B., I'm your best friend."

"'At ain't what I axed."

"All right, I won't laugh."

"You swear?"

"Yeah."

"Then say it—say you swear to God you won't laugh."

"All right already. I swear to God I won't laugh. Now, what have you got there?"

"Miracle Grow."

"What?"

"It works on tomatoes, don't it?"

"You're nuts."

"Them too, maybe."

XXI:
Death Angels
and Herbwomen

"WATCH THIS. I BETCHA I can hit closer to them field larks than you can." C.B. grabs a dirt clod from Papa's plowed field and chunks it straight on.

Crumbling and peppering the ground a good ten feet short, his toss of topsoil scares the birds away with his challenge.

"Well, that's nearer than you came to calling them by the correct name," I tease. "They're meadowlarks."

"'At may be what y'all call 'em in Oxford, but they field larks in Taylor," he argues.

Staring at us as we approach, Granna is standing in her backdoor with her fists planted firmly on her waist. I figure she's going to jump C.B. for harassing Mother Nature with his dirt bomb. As we near, I can tell there's something more than that bothering her. Lines draw her mouth down at the corners, and the rest of her face spells grief.

"What's the matter, Granna?" I ask.

"It's Mr. Jefferson, boys. He's not coming back from Byhalia this time...ever."

My knees go weak, and my stomach feels as if a dust devil just whorled through and sucked out all my air.

"He passed?" C.B. questions her and looks at me with his big solemn eyes.

"I'm sorry, boys. The Good Lord giveth and the Good Lord taketh away. In the year of our Lord and 1962, the Death Angel rode right up on him."

"I 'spect he was ridin' up on a jumpin'-horse, Mrs. Taylor." C.B. tries to be literary, knowing how much Mr. J. liked horses.

"Or a fox-hunting horse," I add.

"For all we know, it might have been from one of those electric typewriters they've come out with, but I suspect it was probably a result of the kind of drinking William did. He left something for y'all...in his books."

I try to hide my disappointment. I was thinking we were fixing to get new pocketknives or guns or something more than words in books that we'd be expected to read.

"Do y'all remember the last thing Mr. Jefferson told you?" Granna asks.

"Yessum," C.B. answers. "He said he was bankin' on one of us bein' a resolver and th' other one bein' a clabber-ater, an' he 'spected...."

"Suspected."

"He susp...pected us to take time 'bout who was which."

"Collaborators and resolvers, huh?"

"Yes, ma'am," I verify C.B.'s remembrance.

"That sounds like he knew he might not be seeing y'all again."

"Naw, he'z jus' figgerin' how we might could come up with what we was a'needin', whenever 'at was."

"Charles...."

"Mam?"

"Scott...."

"Ma'am?"

"Now that your mentor has run his race and been called to his final summons, I want you both to know I'm still here for you. If you ever need someone to talk to about anything...."

"That's not hardly the same, Granna," I offer and immediately realize I should have chosen better words.

"Well, you're welcome just the same," she gently replies and turns to go in.

Dumbfounded, C.B. and I stand in the backyard, neither of us knowing what to say to the other. I can't quite grasp the idea of no more Mr. J. I haven't had anyone whom I personally know up close to die.

"I don't understand him dying like that, C.B." I shake my head in denial.

"It's misunderstandable. Ain't no rind or reason'."

"Rhyme nor reason," I correct him.

"'At's what I said, wadn't it? Lordy mercy, you picky."

Granna sticks her head back out the door. "Scott, supper will be ready in a few minutes. C.B., you need to get on back to Belle's. She'll be looking to feed you."

Neither Granna nor I do much talking during supper. I don't feel so good and don't ask for a second helping of blackberry pie.

IT'S MID-SATURDAY IN MID-JULY as the big black Cadillac hearse with Mr. Jefferson and his funeral procession circle the courthouse. Dad and I watch through the big plate glass window from Munford's Grocery. My father is the only merchant on The Square not closing down business for a few moments of silence to honor the famous author.

We just stare at the motorcade in silent respect. I wanted to go to the funeral, but Dad said William Jefferson preferred it private, just for his family. I suspect my father's refusal to close the store and unwillingness to let me attend the service had to do with jealousy from my admiring Mr. J. so openly and often. I'd like to talk to Dad about it, but I wouldn't even know how to start.

THE FOLLOWING WEEKEND I'M to meet C.B. at Auntay's. As I approach, Sippy uncharacteristically slides out of the front porch swing and starts for the door. She staggers and struggles to get inside. I hear her shut herself in her room.

"What's wrong with Miss Sippy?" I ask.

"She just dizzy, a little slurry-like. She'll be aw'right," C.B. tries to explain away her stumbles.

I don't push the matter. It's obvious that he doesn't want to talk about his sister. I can't discuss her with him anyway…not the way I'm beginning to think about her. No one, including Sippy, is aware of how the years of knowing her have developed my feelings for her. From the way she has recently been trying to hang around and over-laugh and toss her head at everything I say, I think maybe she likes me too.

C.B. is quieter than usual as we head for the river.

"What's going on," I ask.

"Scott, I been thinkin' a lot 'bout Mr. J.'s dying. You?"

"Yeah…I mean, yesterday, and a lot over the last week. I'm…yeah, I've been thinking about him. Why?"

"What you think 'bout his odds of gettin' to th' grove of glory up yonder?"

"Aw, shit, C.B., why do you…."

"What you reckon done happen with him when he got to 'at gap in th' fence…th' one 'tween life an' death?"

"I don't know."

"'Least ways I taught him what 'tween means. It ain't gon' slip up on him."

"C.B., I know you've got some pretty strong ideas about all that, but I'm just not sure about anything."

"Auntay says when conviction come up complicated, 'at's when what you gots to do is lean on faith."

"Maybe that'd work for her…and Papa and Granna and maybe even Dad, but I suspect Mr. J. would say something like, 'Boys, I'm having some difficulty shaking my uncertainty…and uh, I haven't fully resolved all of my misgivings about death and the possibility of a next life'."

"Until now," C.B. points out. "An' I can tell you another thing— bein' a big shot down here, it ain't gon' buy him nothin' up there." He looks up to the clouds and at whatever else might be up there.

Resorting to my father's favorite rule for me, the one on brevity, I decide to shut up about the subject, in hopes that C.B. will as well.

YET ANOTHER WEEKEND IN Taylor, and C.B.'s family is again on their porch. C.B. is sitting in a rocker. The double swing is holding Auntay, who is shelling peas, and Sippy, who is just leaning against Auntay's ample side and looking spent.

At fourteen, Miss Sippy's become a girl that anybody would appreciate looking at. She's found more height than her brother. With skin the color of a new fawn's hair, a chin dimple that makes her look perpetually happy, and a body in the perfect proportion of sexy, she is enough to make me forget all other girls. I'm knowing these feelings are going to become more difficult in time, but I can't worry about that now. I'm busy enough wondering if anyone, including my secret love, has noticed how awkward and clumsy I have become when I'm around her.

Like last week, when Sippy sees me, she gets up and goes for the door. She's tipsy again and walking zigzaggy. She stumbles and quickly catches herself before disappearing into the house. Auntay and C.B. glance at each other without speaking. I'm left standing helpless and puzzled. "What's going on?" I ask. "Something's wrong with Miss Sippy."

No answer.

"Auntay Belle?"

"It's th' conversion condition," she responds.

"What's that?" I ask and kneel on the porch steps.

"Don't you know nothin' 'at ain't white?" C.B. blurts out.

"Don't get uppity, boy," Auntay scolds him. She throws a handful of shelled peas in the pan, and then answers me. "Her health's fallin' off...is what it is."

"Does it hurt?"

"We gon' take her to see a doctor...sorta," C.B. adds without answering.

"How can you sorta see a doctor?" I ask.

"A sorta doctor at th' free clinic. We ain't got no money fer a real doctor."

"Charles," Auntay reprimands again, "you know better'n to be talkin' our concerns in front of other folks." Giving out a deep sigh, she gathers up the pan of peas and sack of shells and stomps through the door.

"I gots to go, too, Scott," C.B. informs me and eases inside to leave me in a way he's never done before.

I guess there is nothing left to do except return to Granna's and try to catch a ride back to Oxford...and try not to think about the way Sippy's hazel, fawn-like eyes dance and stay lit up. I can almost hear her, how her speech has seasoned into what Granna calls a good southern style.

THE THIRD WEEKEND OF spring, C.B. and I meet at Taylor's depot. With the sun warm and sky full of a vivid blue, it's a day made for being outside. Each of us balancing on a railroad track, my country counter-part and I make our way toward the river crossing. There's nothing but hiking on our agenda.

The smell of locust blossoms hovers over measured steps. Right through the thin soles of my tennis shoes, I can feel the sun's heat on the track. Conscious of the possibility of falling and knocking my teeth out, I am careful to place each foot exactly in front of the other. My buddy trudges along with reckless abandon, not even acknowledging the possi-bility of doing the forever-dreaded splits.

"C.B., what did the doctor at the Health Department say about Miss Sippy?"

He stretches the front of his T-shirt neck and wipes his eyes. I think he's crying, so I try not to look at him.

"Th' doctor, he said she been stricken…sick as sin."

I hear the choke in his voice. "What do you mean?" I slow my walk. "What's wrong with her?"

With hurt all over his expression, C.B. answers, "My little sister's come down with a spell of sickly cell."

I stare across to the other track. "The what?"

"Th' sickly cell, that's what."

"What's that?"

"Somethin' white folks don't gotta worry 'bout."

"Why do you say crap like that?"

"'Cause it's true. It only 'fects th' colored."

Disoriented into silent bewilderment, I stop talking, but C.B.'s tears don't. He looks away to try to keep me from seeing them.

Taylor's old, abandoned schoolhouse looms on a hill straight across State Road 328 from the tracks. Windows and pieces of windows hang like dares, seemingly perfect targets for railroad lava rocks. Needing to break something, I pick up a good throwing rock and heave it in anger. The distance is too far. Worry over Sippy's troubles are building right on top of my romantic conflicts. Frustration is bringing on rage and the possibility I could lose my love before I find her.

"Can't no doctors fix her, an' it ain't nothin' can be done 'bout what Sippy got," he murmurs. "She got her a ill 'at ain't got no pill." He wipes his eyes on his sleeve.

"You mean…she's not going to die, is she?"

"Could, if'n it gets worser. An' she shore ain't gettin' no better. Prob'ly ain't no whole lots of folks eben worried 'bout it, since it don't hit white."

"Get off it, C.B."

"Well, I'm tellin' you true. You think they woulda give up like 'at if she'd been a little white girl?"

As both of us have thrown several rocks without hearing glass, we settle for moving on down the tracks. I start to ask, "What's she...we...."

"Yeah...she, we, he, hell...who gon' help Miss Sippy with a sickly cell ain't got no cure?" C.B. picks up another lava rock and hurls it at a stray house cat but misses. "Can't nobody seem to do nothin' 'bout it...uncurable, th' doctor called it."

"Incurable," I try to correct him.

"Un!"

"Okay, C.B., 'un.' Is that all they said? There has to be something somebody can do, isn't there?"

"Not 'cordin' to 'at doctor. He says all we can do is watch her hurt. She sufferin' worser ever'day, an' 'at be 'bout th' size of it...while he sets in his fancy office gettin' his high pay check an' drivin' his big car."

After coming to where the tracks cross a kudzu-clad gorge, we sit on a couple of railroad ties.

"Granna says kudzu can grow a foot a night." Our feet swing out and over the fearless green vine below.

"At least," he agrees, but quickly gets back on subject. "Sippy's gettin' bad stove-up, Scott. She's run down puny."

"C.B., what are we gonna...?"

"We takin' it hard, but I can tell you what we ain't gon' do. We ain't givin' up. Coloreds got they own ways."

"What are you talking about?" I ask, wondering why this talk keeps going the way of black and white differences.

"Castin' out unclean spirits is what I'm talkin' 'bout."

This seems like a good time to simply go along and not say anything. We usually honor our unspoken agreement to avoid the cultural contrasts in our lives that could be related to racial problems, but he looks at me and stares, waiting on me to say something.

"How is that done?" I reluctantly ask.

"Doin' most anything 'at might help...putting a loaf of bread an' plate of salt on th' night stand by th' bedstead, a lucky jumpin' cricket in th' treatin' room, eben a whisky an' castor oil tonic fer th' fever vapors."

"Well…that's good, C.B."

"'At ain't all. Auntay's put th' word out—our public doctor done give up on Sippy. Since we on our own fer our own kind, 'at be th' message what's gon' fetch up herbwomen from ever'where 'round."

"What's a herbwoman?"

"Fer th' luva Pete." He sighs and rolls his eyes at my ignorance. "She be kinda like a middle-wife."

"A midwife?"

"Like th' woman fer birthin' babies, 'cept she knows 'bout curin' 'cautions."

"Like what?"

"Poultices like them made with fish skins an' grapes, an' pine top tea, violet leaf an' leek soup, dandelion salad an' spirit stuff to run off spells."

The last thing C.B. needs is a lack of faith. Knowing my doubts would only discourage hope, I don't comment. I'll ask Granna later if there's any good to all this natural materials medicine. Glum and quiet for awhile, we continue walking the tracks on to the creek crossing. It's a good place to think, sit, and throw rocks at turtles' heads as they pop up now and then through the brown water.

———————————

ANOTHER WEEK GOES BY before I manage to get back to Taylor…more confused than ever over my mixed-up feelings for Sippy but thinking I've grown to love everything I do know about her. Auntay's front porch looks as if it's having a meeting of the Circle of Queen of Sheba Missionary Society. I'd guess all the commotion could be a colored quilting bee, but I don't see any quilts…just a lot of colored women. C.B. spots me walking across the dusty field between Granna's home place and there. He comes out half way for a greeting meeting…as I have a horrible thought.

"What's going on?" I ask. "Miss Sippy didn't…?"

"Naw, it's them herbwomen I told you 'bout…come from all over, they did. Brung their trade secrets. We gon' try ever' curin' they got…whether they work or not."

"Good deal," I respond, not knowing what else to say, feeling his pain, and not wanting to show doubt or fear. I wish I could have my best friend's hope. "Where all did these women come from, C.B.?"

"Scattered here an' yonder. Th' lady on th' end there, she come down from Pea Ridge. Her name is Much. Much brung a collard leaf concoction of some kind and said fer it to do any good, you have to hold your breath when you take it. I smelled it an' I figger couldn't nobody take it without holdin' their breath."

He points toward two fat women who must be twins. "Them two be sisters—Cotton Cake from Coffeeville an' Cotton Boll from Dog Town. They come to read th' signs."

"What'd they say?"

"Said I'd growed three inches since they seen me."

"The signs, C.B.? What did they say about the signs?"

"Oh, yeah…uh, they said one way or 'tuther, th' signs tells most ever'thing 'bout what's gon' happen to folks sufferin'."

"C.B., listen carefully. What did their signs say about Miss Sippy?"

"I dunno—them women prob'ly don' know what they talkin' 'bout, no ways."

Giving up on getting anything worthwhile out of a conversation with C.B., I amble over to where I can assess things for myself. Big bodies of overeaters strain the benches and chairs. I'd say the porch itself is in jeopardy. Answers don't appear to be in the sweetgum tea leaves.

I spot Sippy. She's looking so sick it makes me achy. My love is being held by a herbwoman who's humming a soft lullaby that's probably gonna put everyone to sleep…and I don't want to be in that number. Even the swing is creaking spooky-like. This time, I wouldn't blame Sippy if she did get up and run inside, but she tries to smile at me. When C.B. whispers something for my ears only, I have to ask him to repeat it.

"If'n her heart beat ain't proper, it could be on account she's scared of all these old women."

"You got that right," I respond. I can feel the discomfort and disappointment ooze off the old house like woodborers coming out to play.

A young colored woman drives up in a black Studebaker. I'm surprised. It seems much too new and nice for a Negro to have. This girl-woman, who couldn't have been a herbwoman for long, is a faster talker than Auntay and claims to know every herb in Hatchie Hollow.

"We 'preciate you comin', Child," Auntay greets her. "We'll thank you fer any he'p. We gon' go 'long with all of ever'body's cures. Can't take no chance th' one we don't use might be th' one what'll do Sippy th' most good."

Instead of giving us her assurances and telling us more about her doctoring ways and all their effectiveness, this young lady starts up entirely too loud about the tough stuff. As if we didn't know, she informs us of Sippy's downcast look and how her skin is too dry and her hair is too thin.

I'm figuring my secret love shouldn't be hearing how bad she looks. It would make her feel even worse. Auntay looks as if she's about to decide the same way I do concerning this herbwoman. In an uninhibited irreverence, the stranger rattles on, right in front of Sippy. When something is said about Miss Sippy facing grave odds and being gravely ill, that's when Auntay has apparently heard and had enough.

"We ain't gon' be hearin' no more talk 'bout th' grave," Auntay expresses with her own straightforward power of persuasion. "You get in yo' hearse-color car an' hit th' road on outta here. An' if you be comin' back 'round here with 'at kinda talk, I'll give you a thrashin' to make you beg fer yo' own partin'."

With an all-too-defiant expression, the young woman leaves. Auntay looks at C.B. and me as if we're about to be put on a cookie sheet in her oven. As I start to leave, C.B. grabs my arm to stop me.

"Auntay, we was wantin' to know if'n we could help th' herbwomen gather up needs."

"'Good idear," Auntay responds.

Upon repeating C.B.'s offer to those on the porch, Auntay looks to the herbwomen for their prescription requests.

The herbwoman from Holly Springs goes first. "We be needin' th' kinda grease to rub on Sippy 'at come only from slow cookin' down a buzzard."

"Ain't no problem," C.B. promises.

With no one else speaking up, Auntay asks, "You boys gon' set around here an' sulk all day or what?"

Destination one turkey vulture or silver vulture, whichever comes first, C.B. and I depart and head for Granna's to get my gun.

"Scott, I can't stand it much longer...seein' my little sister sufferin' so."

As his eyes fill with tears, I put my hand on his shoulder.

"She can't eben keep what she eats inside her, throwin' up all th' time."

Not knowing how to respond to that, I don't even try. After picking up my Model 24, we cross the harrowed field, fight through a patch of young pine, and come out on the lee edge of Papa's number three pasture.

Looking the area over, C.B. comments, "I ain't never made a buzzard blind."

"Just put up some brush to hide you and my gun under. I'll go stretch out in the wide open like I'm lying there dead."

The cool of the ground feels good to my butt and shoulders and on the back of my head. The cotton-white clouds change their forms against a bright blue sky. Traveling east, they continually shape themselves like anything I can imagine, except for answers to my questions. Looking up to Heaven, I think about prayer and Sippy's fate...and my life without her.

> *Dear Lord All-Mighty, please help Miss Sippy get better if You*
> *don't have to have her in the afterlife right yet. She's so gentle and*
> *pure. You know she doesn't deserve any of this. Let her keep on*
> *lighting up my world, God. Amen.*

As I lie motionless, there's so much silence I can almost hear myself thinking. I hear C.B. sniffling. The sun's afternoon rays and the fact that I'm lying back team up to dry my eyes. A shadow glides over.

"Crack!" comes the piercing sound of my .22 and C.B.'s shot. A big black bundle of feathers flops toward earth and crashes in the Johnson grass on the edge of the field. The vulture's wattly red head is quickly covered with his own puke...and smells so ungodly I can't see it as the answer to prayer.

"This thing is so gross I'd just as soon have to carry a skunk," I state, as I hold it out at arm's length.

"Best not give them herbwomen no idears," C.B. replies.

We start for Auntay's yard pot for a buzzard boiling. Pleased with our dogged perseverance, I remind C.B. of Mr. J.'s old saying about a bird in hand. Rounding the side of the house with trophy in tow, I see that the place is still humming with herbwomen. Even more have shown up.

Auntay takes our quarry and gives us each a clean feed sack. My first inclination is to thank God we're not going to have to gut and clean the buzzard. My second thought is that we are probably fixing to be sent on a snipe hunt. I'm relieved to be informed the sacks are for gathering healing materials. We're told to find a cup of the little red fruits from a partridge berry plant, a handful of fresh roots from bulbous buttercups, some striplings of devil's club bark, a cap-full of horse chestnuts, and enough peach tree leaves for a poultice from them.

Armed with these new orders and knowing where to fill most of the yet-to-be conjured-up cleansers, we take to the countryside to comb the woods and fields. A goatsucker tones up his call...and sounds more like he's dealing in black magic than regular bird talk. C.B. smashes a mosquito feasting on his arm and wipes the blood on the back of his pants leg...and I think about how much one of the herbwomen looked like what I always thought a witch doctor would.

"Miss Sippy's been hurtin' miserable," C.B. opens up and lets me know just how rough it's gotten for her. "She be moanin' 'bout cramps an' pains all night long, settin' up an' sufferin', goin' back an' forth 'tween chills an' th' fever."

"I'm sorry, C.B. I don't know what to say. I don't know how any of this could be the Lord's will being done. What's the sense in having my.... I mean, Miss Sippy, hurting like this?"

C.B. looks at me like he may have known what I almost said.

I continue, "If there's a God in heaven, how come He doesn't help her?"

"I can't answer 'at, but I know she's got to have somethin' to soothe her ailin'." C.B. dries his eyes with his sleeve again. "You know how we always hearin' 'bout God working through man? If'n things gets bad enough, it might be time I stopped Miss Sippy's hurtin' my own self, since nothin' else will."

"Yeah, maybe some of this stuff we've been sent after is gonna help."

"'At ain't what I'm talkin' 'bout, Scott."

I pretend like I don't completely follow him and decide to talk instead of giving him a chance to explain what he really meant. "You're the one always talking about showing some faith. There has to be a cure somewhere. If not at the hospital, in the woods. We'll keep looking until we find it."

Within less than two hours of searching, we've found everything we were supposed to...but still no answers. Upon our return many of the herbwomen are busy with miracle recipes that apparently didn't need our ingredients. Eager to see our products join the preparations of the makings already in the works, we proudly present the various plants and parts we have to contribute.

In addition to the possibly potent plants comprising Mother Nature's own pharmaceuticals, we hear promises that may help the patient find her own healing. There are mending berries, rejuvenating roots, healing teas from leaves, and plasters said to draw poison out of Sippy's liver. The healers have brought pears, plums, apples, and other fixin' fruits, but when doctoring talk starts up that involves using leeches, my knees go weak.

"It's time for me to go to Granna's Taylor house. I've got to catch a ride back to Oxford."

AFTER SUMMER'S COME AND gone, I'm again locked into my school mode of merely surviving from one weekend to the next. Monday through Friday penitentiary-like school days have a way of making the biggest part of the week seem like a waste.

Coming home from a typically less-than-exciting weekday, I'm greeted by Granna's troubled look. As our eyes meet, I remember the day she told me of Mr. J.'s demise. Something is indeed bad wrong…big time.

"Miss Sippy has died," she states.

My breath is gone.

Granna continues, "Her funeral is tomorrow, but your father has made his ruling, that you don't need to miss another day of school."

"But, Granna…."

"He says you'd be out of place and have no business being the only white at a colored funeral. Since this was a colored kind of disease that doesn't affect whites, he is afraid we may not be welcome to attend the services. You know your father when he puts his good foot down. This just as well be the end of it, Scott."

Instead of the end of the discussion, it's almost as if Granna knows…like she's really talking about it being the end of my affections for my girlfriend. I can't remember being this upset with my father for saying no about something. He will never understand what I feel inside and how much I hurt. Being one who thinks of coloreds as people to avoid, except as buying customers, he doesn't realize how much I need to go to Sippy's last good-by.

THE DAY OF MISS Sippy's funeral is cloudy and dreary. Sitting in junior high homeroom, I'm wishing I could get to Taylor for the services. Turning toward hopelessness, I face the window to hide my tears. Sniffy breathing rises and falls until it's hard for me to keep my breath.

With my dear, sweet Sippy no doubt laid out in a southern yellow pine coffin, I should be there. Thinking about the colored preaching and praying I'll miss missing for the first time since the camp meeting, I can picture the keening and wailing up to heaven. I can almost see C.B. crying and hear Auntay singing her chorus of "Yes, Lord...Sweet Jesus...Precious Lamb."

Our study hall teacher offers her room full of students the option of going to the library. Unable to sit anywhere, I pretend to be going there and head out behind the school, into Bailey Woods. If I can't go to the funeral, I'll have my own private good-by.

Half-way between Pen-Oake and Granna's city house, I find a good crying log. A screech-owl immediately breaks through my bawling as he whistles his quavering whine and sobs a descending series of notes. It sounds like he's calling for his own lost mate. My tears fall. Another familiar feathered friend makes his presence known. Big leathery green leaves of a magnolia tree hide the mourning dove as I listen to the sad *Coo...oo* call.

I can't see the little owl or the dove, but between the three of us, we have our own philharmonic-like forest blues in a Bailey Woods kind of wake. With chin on chest, I further break down and cry too loud for being where no one can hear me. I try to rub away my self-pity and sadness. It doesn't work for either.

A vulture-shaped shadow glides across the forest floor. Knowing what it is, I don't have to look up. Even without seeing it, I'm wondering why the black thing with its black silhouette must come through here right now, reminding me of the herbwomen's failed attempts and our helplessness.

"How do things like this happen?" I ask myself. "Is this some kind of natural court of injustice where my sorrow is going to be compounded? Even Mother Nature is coming in the form of questions I can't shake…like, might Miss Sippy have somehow been saved if she'd been a little white girl?"

XXII:
Weekend Warriors and Civil War II

"DO YOU MEAN TO tell *me* that the good residents of Mississippi will not allow the National Guard to camp on their property?"

"That's about the size of it, Mr. President. Out-of-state troops down there are considered the enemy."

"If that is not arrogance...." President Kennedy reacts. "Here we are in the age of automation, and instead of being concerned with providing jobs, those segregationists are worried that a man of the wrong skin color might get an education."

"It's not that simple, Sir."

"Like hell it isn't. This is 1962. I want you to go down there and buy a sufficient parcel of land right up against the University. By God, when it's the property of the United States of America, federalized National Guard troops will not have to ask anyone for permission to camp there." "But, Mr. President...."

"Don't 'but' me. I'm the President. Do it! Do it yesterday."

THE CHANCERY CLERK AT the courthouse claims the government bought the land to have a place to locate a U.S. Forest Service Research Lab. Nevertheless, the newly acquired federal property south of the campus now has a military police battalion bivouacked on it.

Although October is normally a great time for camping out, this particular tent city looks a little out of place for my hometown. This is a

Sunday that's far too exciting for Baptist Training Union. I intend to see what's going on at the campus. I hope no one from Bible study will bump into Dad or Granna tomorrow and ask where I was during Church.

Armed with the United States Constitution, Oxford's own local troop of the Mississippi National Guard is among those units federalized…and worse yet, ordered to occupy its own Ole Miss. The invasion is to help handle protestors and assist a black student with his enrollment in the all-white University of Mississippi.

Whereas some family members get monthly National Guard checks, some don't. That second some see resistance as their obligation to save the South. In a few cases the conflict is pitting brothers against brothers and fathers against sons. It's a news-making, history-breaking integration.

Most of the students don't appear to present a whole lot of danger to anyone…but neither do they welcome James Mason. Still numb from hotty toddies, a lot of students and alumni from the party crowd are continuously filtering in from yesterday's football game in Jackson. Many local residents and curious onlooker students are simply attracted to the excitement of raising hell. For the most part, it's the strangers and out-of-towners who are reacting with the most emotional outrage.

With attitudes and customs of pre-sixties Oxford being slow to recognize civil rights over states' rights, it is all met with mixed emotions. Civil rights confrontation over forced integration has our university community humming like a nest of irritated yellow jackets. Radicals from all groups are gearing up for a second Civil War.

As I walk through the campus, I remember something Mr. J. once said about his days in the Royal Canadian Air Corps…about always trying to occupy the high ground. With that in mind I head for the height of the YMCA Building, where I'll have a safe view from which to look down on everyone else.

U.S. Marshals have encircled the front of the University's Lyceum Building. The National Guard gathers next to the tree-lined road called the Circle in support of the Federal Marshals. A swarm of students and others are surrounding the soldiers and becoming more and more mob-like. As the atmosphere appears to be changing from peacefully curious rabble to Rebel-rousing, I wonder if the show of Yankee-like force might soon be whistling Dixie, but the sun goes down and streetlights come on.

In what may be shaping up to be a battle of bigotry, Mr. J. would be proud of me for staying out of it. I see a bottle being thrown. Hostility heightens. Books, shoes, and anything available for throwing are now sailing toward the authorities. Fights break out between the Guard and the multitude of students and other instigators. The overall situation has degenerated into lawlessness. I have a riot below me.

A Molotov cocktail is heaved through the air. As marshals fire tear gas into the crowd, bricks from the biology building construction site are being removed one at a time. Streetlights and outside building lights are knocked out. A military jeep's windshield is smashed to smithereens. A civilian car is turned over and set afire.

The troops stand their ground. Those protestors who are not detained and taken into the Lyceum's basement run in all directions. The original crowd of bystanders and participant rioters are replaced by new arrivals.

With everyone coughing, rubbing their eyes, or even vomiting, smoke spreads from fires to mix with the tear gas. I wonder if I'll need a gas mask at my elevation. A newsman folds up the legs of his big camera and staggers away with the crowd. From the eerie-looking scene below me, a tear gas cloud lifts to my third-story layer of air. My eyes begin to water and sting.

"Pow!" comes the unmistakable sound of a high-powered rifle. Straight across the mob from me, on top of the chemistry building, I see a man with a rifle. The thought occurs to me that I could be mistaken for a sniper and shot...by the authorities or agitators. From atop the "Y" roof, I'm practically flying down three sets of stairs, out the back door, and sprinting for home. As many times as I've run through The Grove, this is the first time I've ever been scared to look back over my shoulder.

Still fearing the summertime soldiers or worse, I'm at last happy to be walking into the safety of my house...prepared to pretend I've had a typical Sunday evening doing sword drills with my Bible. Dad is sitting in front of the TV and snoring through a documentary on the idea of nuclear reactors for some kind of energy. A special news bulletin interrupts and wakes him up. It tells of a riot at the University of Mississippi and promises to have details by the ten o'clock news.

"So much for states' rights," Dad says. "The federal government has no business meddling in matters of the state. That's nothing more than a little campus controversy."

I don't know if he's talking to me or the TV or to himself, but between now and ten, I'll stay quiet and try to figure out on my own what I was witnessing on the campus. I'm thinking I can see beyond the colors and come to terms with a black man wanting to go to a white school, but I'm not even sure that's what everyone was protesting. If it were more in defiance of a federalized Guard coming in here and taking over, that may be something else altogether.

When it's time for the late night news, Dad and I are both glued to the TV set. Scared he's liable to see me on the roof of the YMCA, I am prepared to emphasize the fact that those letters stand for Young Men's Christian Association…and it is Sunday.

Bedtime boob-tube news is not flattering in talking about our doing our part to sustain the long-standing custom of segregation. According to the national media, a showdown between federal and local governments has left a riot-torn campus. Two people are reported to be left dead and scores of civilians and officers injured. Approximately two hundred folks have been arrested. As the national, nightly news signs off, it says upward of twenty thousand federal troops are being activated.

"Television's got no call exaggerating about all this," Dad says. "It's time for you to go to bed and not be exposed to such foolishness."

"Good night, Dad."

With sounds from groups of people spilling through the neighborhood, sleep is slow to come. The excitement of turmoil is still running down University Avenue, less than a mile from the campus and a hundred yards from my house.

A WEEK AFTER THE small war and what many are calling the latest battle in the last chapter of the War between the States, Dad is anxious to have me avoid the University. For that reason he's happy to cart me off to Taylor and drop me off for a fall campout.

Wasting no time turning his '61 Plymouth taxi back toward Oxford, my father leaves me at Granna's home place and out of harm's way. With my grandmother gone to a quilting in Harmontown and Papa preaching a revival at Bay Springs, there's nothing to hold me here.

I grab my gun and head across the field to the humble abode that belongs to Miss Belle and where Charlie Boy lives. A black-and-tan hound unofficially greets me and stretches out to turn himself up for a tummy rub. I give him just enough to get a tail wag of appreciation.

"Hey, dog, you been hanging around here guarding the house from any front porch repairmen?"

C.B. hears me and yells to come in. Waiting by the potbellied stove, he has his winter camping gear ready to go. With our adults thinking we'll be spending the weekend along Taylor Creek, we hike halfway back to Oxford, to Thacker Mountain fire tower.

The gate to the chainlink fence around the bottom of the tower is locked but presents no problem to climbing. Except for the recently thawed frost on their surface, the steps up to the catwalk are practically an invitation.

"Hold on to 'at handrail good," C.B. warns. "I 'spect these steps is slicker'n snail slime."

As we cautiously work our way to the top, I'm figuring this must be what should be called the ear-popping, nose-bleed section of Mississippi. Nowhere but from up here could the horizon look so wide. This is a world that only airplane pilots and forest rangers usually get to experience.

"I bet we higher'n th' courthouse," C.B. says.

"Maybe even the Presbyterian Church steeple," I counter.

As we expected, the man who tends the lookout didn't lock all the windows. Easy entry is afforded by the catwalk around the outside of the elevated cabin. The inside of the little metal cubbyhole smells like Rum and Maple pipe tobacco.

The sunset sort of slides into a dark orange. Oxford's street and house lights begin popping on. The sky fills with so many stars, the sight of it all is worth having to sleep on the cold floor of the highest hideout in Lafayette County. As the moon comes up, I stare, spellbound.

"What'cha bring to eat?" C.B. breaks upper nature's special silence.

Instead of answering, I open up a sack of junk food that found its way here from Dad's store. Chowing down on Butterfingers, cinnamon rolls, and assorted cookies and chips, we eat until there is nothing left for breakfast.

The steel hotel of the heights fast feels like a refrigerator. C.B. announces, "I think I'm gon' turn in early to get warm." Unrolling his bedroll, he says, "Good night."

"See you in the morning," I respond, laying out my sleeping bag on the opposite side of C.B. from the fire finder that occupies the middle of the cabin.

C.B. is asleep in nothing flat, and his snoring soon puts me out as well. Waking in the middle of the night, I normally would get up and go pee. This night I opt to hold it in order to help retain my body heat. Before daybreak I wake again, about to burst. Stepping out onto the tower's walkway not a minute too soon, I let her spew…an eerie, moonlit stream with its own cloud of steam, unbroken almost all the way down.

With the faint gray of a usual dawn, the post oak tree below our tower becomes active with squirrel play. Although most hardwoods are losing their leaves at this time, this species is one of the last to let go. The brown, shriveled-up leaves try to hide the fluffy-tails from C.B.'s .22 prowess, but my buddy sees no obstacles.

We grab our belongings, renegotiate the steps downward, and re-climb the fence. After gathering up C.B.'s squirrel harvest, I'll have to put up with his bragging. He proudly points out that he has used the tops of the five squirrel heads for targets, so as not to mess up th' eatin' meat.

Since walking back home always seems longer than heading out somewhere, we decide to hitchhike back to Taylor and meet with luck…in the form of a nice university night-watchman on his way home. Knowing Auntay would be gone to work when we got back, C.B. has previously gained permission to ride to town with us when Dad comes to get me. His Aunt Sassy will let her favorite nephew spend the night at her place.

Granna and Papa are gone somewhere again. There's some home-made vegetable soup and crackling cornbread left on the stove. Not worrying with warming either, I dish up two bowls of the soup and serve up two big chunks of cornbread to go with them.

Dad and his taxi show right on schedule. "Time's money, and we're wastin' it. Come on, boys."

"Look what we got," C.B. shows off our squirrels.

Dad hands me the car keys and tells me to put our small game in the taxi's trunk and lock my gun in Granna's house. As is usually the case when C.B. and Dad share the same space, our ride to town is not very talkative.

When we reach the intersection of Highways 6 and 7 on the outskirts of Oxford, a roadblock is set up and manned by two military police guardsmen. The remainder of a squad of soldiers is gathered around a military jeep, as if telling stories and not being very interested in whether we enter federal occupancy.

Dad says something more or less to himself about moral turpitude and the outright, overt friction of an entourage of outsiders persecuting the South. I'm not sure he even understood it himself. He may have been repeating something he heard one of his drivers say.

With the Plymouth stopped and the window rolled down, Dad gives a sarcastic kind of salute.

"Mornin', General."

Instead of acknowledging Dad's friendliness, the corporal demands our car keys.

"Where are you gentlemen from?" Dad asks, as he complies.

"Illinois," he says.

"Ohio," says the private next to him.

The private takes the keys from the corporal and looks in the trunk of the taxi...to find five dead squirrels.

"Sergeant," he calls out, "I think we've got one here."

Dad cracks a smile, and I feel better. I thought we were in trouble. A sergeant walks over and takes a look in the trunk for himself.

"Get out," he orders us and turns back to bark out orders for his men.

As they come over and give him their attention, Dad asks, "What's the problem here, soldiers?"

"Just do as you're told, sir. We need to do a more thorough search of your vehicle," the sergeant explains.

The three of us get out. C.B., turning his scared shade of gray-black, moves with me to the side of the highway. Dad limps to the rear of the car...dragging his bad leg with more drama than usual.

"Stand right over there with those boys and stay out of the way," the sergeant orders Dad.

"But...."

"And keep your mouth shut."

There's a face-off, with neither Dad nor the sergeant budging. It doesn't normally take my father this long to tire of being polite, but this time a squad of soldiers descend on the situation. Badly outnumbered, Dad hobbles over to join us, again pretending it's more of a struggle for him to walk than it really is.

A guardsman searches the front of the taxi. While he's looking under the dash and front seat, another man looks beneath and behind the back seat. A soldier lifts the hood. Sarge does a more thorough search of the trunk and comes out with nothing but a puzzled look. He orders his smallest guardsman to crawl up under the vehicle and search.

After a re-look and hard inspection all around and under the taxi, our sergeant confronts us again, with his arms folded across his chest and standing at a safer distance from Dad than he did the first time. "I give up, mister. Where's your gun?"

"Gun?" Dad repeats in a questioning voice and stands in silence as if he's surprised to hear they were searching for a gun.

"State your business in town," the sergeant continues.

Before Dad answers, there's a third question.

"And what are you doing with that colored boy?"

"Wait a minute," Dad insists. "What was that about a gun?"

"Yes, a gun. How did you get the squirrels without a gun?"

Dad limps over to lean on the trunk of the taxi. C.B. and I follow. Dad looks down at the squirrels and sighs, "So that's what this is all about…y'all are down here to help out the game wardens stop us from using our coloreds to squirrel hunt?"

"Look, mister…."

"Well, I'll tell you about the squirrels," Dad says. "I don't know how you Yankees do it up there where y'all are from, but down here it's like this—that there white boy puts salt on their tails an' then th' little nigger runs 'em down."

"I should've known we'd come across some smart aleck, redneck white supremacist," the sergeant remarks.

"If you've done gone to calling names, I believe you have taken up enough of my time, young man," Dad tells him and yanks the keys out of his hand.

Sarge stares without speaking as Dad limps to the driver's door of the cab. C.B. and I climb in the other side with me in the front and C.B. in the back seat.

"Tell me somethin'—If y'all are so big on mixing the races, how come you don't have any colored soldiers in your unit?" Dad asks out the window.

Instead of answering, the sergeant slams our trunk lid down and then informs us, "You are free to go."

"Yeah, we are," Dad answers. "If I don't get th' little nigger back pretty soon, his owners are liable to cut off another one of his toes to keep him from running away so often. An', worse yet, slowin' him down like that won't do a damned thing for his ability to catch squirrels."

C.B. doesn't know whether to laugh or cry...nor do I. Driving to our house, Dad surprises me with his good nature. Perhaps his jerking the northern guardsmen around was what put him in the moment. It's the first time he's ever been this pleasant around C.B.

"Before y'all skin those squirrels, you best remember what happened to that chicken when Gertrude cut its head off."

"Come on, Dad," I remark, with little defense.

"If one of them squirrels gets up an' runs around headless, I 'spect I'll be leavin'," C.B. offers a mutual mood. When Dad and C.B. laugh together, it may be for the first time ever.

As my father and his taxi are dispatched to a call, C.B. and I are left with another warning. "Y'all best continue to steer clear of the campus. You hear?"

"You skin 'em, an' I'll gut 'em," C.B. offers.

"Let's just share the load on everything and see who can do the best job," I counter.

"Who gon' judge?"

"We'll let the squirrels."

C.B. looks at me and says, "I ain't near 'bout ready fer no more animal riddles.

———————

WITH SEVERAL WEEKS OF civil rights settling in around Oxford, snow comes to town...along with C.B.

"What'cha wanta do today, Scott?"

"I don't know. We could always agitate the Weekend Warriors."

"You got somethin' special in mind?"

"With all this snow and the Guard having those open door jeeps...."

"Yeah, we can chunk snowballs at 'em from up on th' roof line 'round th' square."

"You got part of the plan," I inform him. "We also need to go borrow a screwdriver and some wire from Dad's workshop."

"Why come?"

"You'll see."

Two blocks north of my house, we enter the little alley beside Gathright Reed's drugstore. With wire and screwdriver in hand, I point at the vertical rain gutter. C.B. still wants me to explain.

"We'll leave it leaning up against the roof so that we're the only ones who'll know it's got to be held against the wall to climb."

I shimmy up, and C.B. holds it tight against the wall as I climb back down...unscrewing a half dozen sections on the way. Sneaking down Harrison Avenue to the back of Grundy's restaurant, we round South Lamar where there's a set of stairs against the outside wall of Blaylock's drugstore. A window accessed from the upstairs porch leads us onto the top of the building, leaving tracks in the snow.

Once on the roof, the whole series of stores that covers the west half of the south side of The Square is a snow-covered flat. There's a ready supply of snow for making ammunition. The tar-paper roof makes a neat, crunchy sound as we walk on it. I guess it's from being half frozen and the other half being buckled up and brittle from old age.

"We gots th' best view around by takin' th' high ground," he rhymes.

"It's the only way to deal with the National Guard," I answer, reminded I'm not the only one who tries to remember everything Mr. J. told us. "We're gonna have to lead each jeep a different distance based on its speed. It'll be just like having to shoot in front of a bottle I'm throwing across the garbage dump for you."

"Look who's tellin' who how to shoot," he points out and exaggerates his laugh. "Let's roll a bunch of snowballs. We li'ble to be needin' a reserve fer th' reserves...an' we don't wanta start flingin' 'em an' find out we ain't got enough."

"Good idea," I admit. "We've gotta be ready for rush."

"Rush like in a hurry, or rush like bein' charged?"

"Both," I answer and remember a third kind of rush the college kids talk about...and the fact that I never did understand what they meant.

Smoke billows or puffs from most every chimney and vertical heating pipe on the horizon. A shrill wind ricochets off the roof. My eyes water, and the drops try to freeze. As our piles of snowballs are completed, a slow moving jeep rounds The Square from the west.

C.B. challenges, "Watch this'un." His toss sends a snowball right through the open door to splatter on the seat beside the driver.

"Not bad, but watch me." I rear back to throw hard. A guardsman in a second army-green jeep looks up to see me.

The soldier yells in his radio until his three-jeep convoy slides to an icy stop. The weekend warriors bail out and head toward our building. As they look for a way to the roof from the building's front, we pelt them unmercifully. When they round the corner, they'll see our snow tracks on the steps.

Set up by the ledge over the Gathright Reed's drugstore alley, our second supply of snowballs is at hand. It's merely a matter of time now before reservesville will be coming up across the roof of Blaylock's drugstore. It's as if we both have a pharmacy sponsoring us.

"You ready, C.B.?"

"You jus' be shore you holdin' 'at rain gutter-pipe real tight while I'm climbin' down."

"And you for me…I don't wanta be stuck up here with the Guard."

The first soldier appears. "Over here, Cap'un!" C.B. shouts through a wide grin.

The lead guardsman runs toward us. Others file out the door behind him. Sounding more like a stampede than a squad, they approach our secretly encrusted layer of snow and ice harboring the exceptionally slick spot.

"Now!" C.B. yells, as the lead soldier steps on the slick spot.

We throw. The soldier tries to slow down but lands on his butt. The men behind him run into each other. As we exhaust our supply of snowballs, the big pile up of soldiers is sliding across the ice. C.B. yells something to them about southern hospitality.

While I tightly hold together the disconnected drainpipe and gutter, C.B. slides down to the alleyway. Then, he for me. With the whole drainage system now carefully leaning against the wall, it falsely looks very much supported and securely connected. The first guardsman sizes it up for climbing down, and we run for the end of the alley.

When we round the corner of the alley and Harrison Avenue, I hear sounds that are reminiscent of a sheet-metal barn caving in. From their roof, the crisp winter air is filled with cussing and moaning…in a Yankee accent. Soldiers are still shouting as we near the second corner at Elliot's lumber company. About to think we're home free, we run almost head-on into an Army jeep rounding that corner. The cold, reddening face of the sergeant we encountered with our squirrels at the roadblock is unmistakable.

Although I draw my usual blank, my buddy comes through like the champ he can be at times like this. "Ossifers, Ossifers! Come quick! This away! There's a soldier 'round th' corner, down 'at alley. An' he needs yo' help. We was comin' after you. This away. Come on. Hurry! Hurry!" C.B. runs a couple of steps back toward the alley and signals with an arm swing for them to follow.

A lieutenant looks at me. Instinctively, I point at the alley and take a couple of steps in its direction. Both soldiers bail out of the jeep and run down the alley to check on their man.

C.B. reaches in his coat pocket. "Here's a little somethin' they can 'member us by," he says, laying five squirrel tails on the driver's seat of the jeep.

THE NEXT NEWSPAPER ISSUE of the *Oxford Eagle* tells about a National Guardsman getting banged up by something heavy someone threw on him…from atop a downtown building.

When I share the misinformation from the article with C.B., he responds with his protesting nature. "We didn't throw nothin' heavy on nobody. I'd a'thought th' Weekly Wiper could get th' news 'bout a simple ass-bustin' a little more accurate than 'at."

"Yeah, I don't know what the deal is, C.B."

"I reckon 'at jus' bees th' way of th' news business on a slow news day."

XXIII:
Rebeldumb's
Misintegration

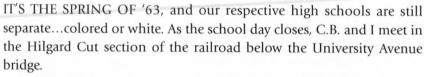

IT'S THE SPRING OF '63, and our respective high schools are still separate…colored or white. As the school day closes, C.B. and I meet in the Hilgard Cut section of the railroad below the University Avenue bridge.

We'll walk together to our fifty-five cents-an-hour jobs at the Student Union Grill on the Ole Miss campus. I'll sling hash and make change. C.B. will have to sweep, mop, bus tables, and wash dishes, but both of us have to put up with the high and haughty college students' attitudes.

"How's it hanging?" I greet C.B., as he ends his hike on the kudzu-bordered ties of the tracks.

"Oh, it's 'bout like same as always, I reckon. I'm jus' really, really…okay. You?"

"Yeah, I know what you mean. High school's a bitch." I put my hand on his shoulder to get him to stop. "I wanta show you something. Look what I've got in my pocket."

"What you doin' with 'at thing? Let me see it." His eyes widen.

I hand over the little .25 caliber Saturday night special. "Be careful with it. It's loaded. Books won it at the carnival and sold it to me for fifteen bucks. He threw in a half box of shells. Pretty good deal, huh?"

C.B. fondles my new pocket pistol's off-white, fake pearl handgrip. He half cocks the hammer and spins the shiny little cylinder as you see the cowboys do in the movies.

"Take it back. You best hide it under th' bridge 'til we get off'n work."

"No, no. See how it fits right in here? You didn't know I had it until I told you."

"You better not be takin' 'at gun to work, Fool."

"Nobody's gonna know I've got it."

We scramble halfway up the hill above the tracks to a prime mulberry tree, heavy with fruit. Knowing we'll have to leave somewhere short of contentment, we pick and eat only the most accessible of the rich, dark red berries. After a couple of minutes of grazing, we climb the rest of the way up the steep slope and then meander across the soft, weedless lawn of the Ole Miss Grove. C.B. continues to badger me about my pistol.

I try to change the subject. "Hear that, C.B.?"

"I know. It's a mockingbird, an' it sound mo' like a cardinal than a cardinal do."

"That's where he gets his name," I explain, as if C.B. didn't already know it. Spotting our state bird, I comment, "I'll bet I could hit him with this pistol."

"You do an' I'll know you crazier'n I done thought you was."

As we walk, I watch to see what the bird is doing on the ground in addition to singing. After a couple of his small steps, the gray mocker stretches his wings and rotates them so that their cupped undersides face behind him. It's as if he's giving a slow-motion forearm to what's in front of him. He does it several times.

"What's 'e doin', you reckon?" C.B. asks. "Jus' stretchin'?"

Thrilled that we've come up on one of those rare moments in life, when I think I know something that C.B. openly admits he doesn't, I eagerly share what Granna happened to have told me. "He's flashing those big bright, white patches on the front of his wings to scare up insects out of the grass. If you watch him long enough, you'll see him grab one."

We cross University Avenue and enter the Circle, with its manicured turf equaling that of the Grove's.

"You best enjoy watchin' birds an' smellin' this fresh-cut grass while you can," my buddy says.

"Why's that?"

"'Cause you ain't gon' be seein' nothin' but concrete 'n smellin' nothin' 'cept prisoner poots when they throw yo' dumb butt in jail fer havin' 'at gun on th' campus."

"Get off it, will you?"

He grabs my arm and jerks me to a halt in mid-step. "Scott, I ain't gon' let you go no further. Let's go back under th' bridge an' hide 'at thing."

"I bought it to keep it right here in my pocket, and that's what I aim to do with it." Twisting out of his grip, I continue with my back to him.

He tackles me. In fun I grab him around the neck and knuckle his head. Playfully wrestling free, I pretend to think he is kidding around more than being serious. Before I realize what's happening, he's tripped me again and is rolling over on top of me.

As my nose is plowing through grass and wild onion, I hear a college boy call out, "Come on, Scott, you gonna let a colored boy get the best of you?"

I have the feeling C.B. is not about to let up. One of us needs an out. More students gather to watch. Soon, everyone's egging me on. No one is cheering for my best friend. I get my head loose and manage to slip out from under his hold.

After we're both quickly up and faced off, C.B. circles like a fighting cock needing to prove the pecking order. The ring of spectators grows to include college girls. Everyone is white. One of the group makes an ugly racial remark. It's repeated by a copycat student and then becomes a disrespectful chant from the entire group. I consider running but know I can't.

C.B. charges and drives his head into my belly. We wrestle rougher than ever before. I don't want this to go any further, but I don't know what to do to stop it. I have to stand tough, or I'll be humiliated in front of all these same college students that I'll have to see every day in The Grill.

Struggling for the crowd's sake, I whisper into C.B.'s thick neck, "We gotta quit this and get to work."

"Then holler, uncle," he offers harshly.

I'm considering whispering it, but C.B. repeats his demand loud enough for everyone to hear. Being in a headlock with my face toward the ground, I see a long shadow that's not ours. I recognize it as that of the Confederate soldier statue...the very one I thought was supposed to be guarding the entrance to the Grove against this sort of thing.

My response to C.B.'s offer is colored by my idea of this monument's history. "When Gut-Hook takes up ballet."

I wrestle on, harder yet. There's got to be something short of surrender that will stop this. C.B. and I have always practiced cooperation over competition. Why's my best buddy doing this to me?

"Fight that nigga with more vigga," an excited student yells out, mocking President Kennedy's New England accent, but with words that would never have come from Washington. I recognize my shame for making such a stubborn stand to impress the kind of spectators who would say something like that. I need somehow to turn this conflict into support for C.B. I don't want to see his feelings hurt. If he weren't getting the best of this wrestling, I'd feel more sorry for him.

Campus Security drives up.

"There's the cops, C.B." My message is urgent. "Let's get out of here."

C.B. releases my head, and I take my arms from around his waist. We run. The patrolmen are a couple of officers who stop in The Grill every day for their coffee and doughnuts. They're more interested in talking to the girls than worrying about C.B. and me. Panting from our wrestling and running, we slow to a jog…and then a walk.

Unlike me, when we reach the center of University Circle, C.B. doesn't appear to be hurting for air. I'm knowing talk of the scuffle would be awkward. Apparently not taking any more kindly to what just happened than I do, he doesn't look at me.

Three flags grace the center of the Ole Miss Circle. On one side of the Stars and Stripes is the Rebel battle flag. In a pride I dimly understand, but deeply feel, it stands out, causing a swelling up from within my southern soul.

"Let's stop here a minute, C.B."

We sit on the flagpoles' curb-like border while I re-tie my tennis shoes…as an excuse to rest. Looking from the Confederate banner to my best friend and then back to the flying symbol of southern unity, I have the belated realization that my buddy has no share in those feelings. He doesn't appear to have even noticed it and probably wouldn't consider it a symbol of his South.

"I suppose we both sort of got called out, more or less," I offer, trying to break the tension.

"Scott, you ever think about how things are other places?"

"Like where?"

"Places 'sides Oxford an' Mis'sippy."

"No, they're probably about like your Auntay says.…"

"Six of one or half-dozen of t'other," he finishes, somehow knowing which one of her quotes I was going to refer to. "But I ain't so sure 'bout it," he continues. "I'm talkin' 'bout stuff like fightin' fer th' future instead of continuin' th' past."

"What the heck have they been telling you over there at Separate School?"

"Oxford Training School is 'bout lots more'n learnin' coloreds how to be polite an' work with their hands, if 'at's what you was thinkin'."

"Y'all may study some English and math, but I guarantee you it's not as hard as being a sophomore at University High," I argue.

C.B. picks a tiny white spring beauty from the flowerbed around the flagpoles. He holds it up to his nose and sniffs. Giving me his sideways glance, he comments, "Like another thing Auntay's always saying, or singin'—Th' black bee gots to make th' comb 'fore th' yellow bee can make th' honey."

"Don't tell me you're going to start bitching about not being white."

"Scott, th' word is, negra. If you can't say it right, then say, colored. Even darky would be better'n, not white."

"You're not gonna go and get uppity on me, are you?" I joke.

"I ain't. It's just 'at...uh, well, what if you was colored? You could have been, you know."

"Not according to my Dad."

C.B. doesn't react to my attempt at humor, as another old joke dies. As I'm wondering how I could answer him, a couple of coeds prance by. We gawk. Another college girl in a short skirt and sleeveless blouse flaunts her shapely body parts as she comes almost too close. Beyond practical reach, a bare-shouldered coed displays her legs in short shorts. The University Circle is swarming with coeds, their bosoms jiggling above flat bellies and long, thin legs. Puberty is tough here. It's near intimidating.

When two sorority sisters bend over as if they're looking for a four-leaf clover, I take the broad view and comment, "C.B., if they lean over any further in those miniskirts, they're liable to get bread instead of clover."

"Bread?"

"Bred...like being bred...screwed."

"Yeah...builds strong bodies eight ways, an' I be th' bread man."

"Sure you would, C.B. I can just hear you now, yelling for me to come help because some college girl has aholt of you."

"Shee...it."

"It wouldn't take long for you to learn your place." As soon as I said that, I wished I hadn't.

C.B. looks at me with an expression like I might as well have quoted some Klanish pledge for segregation. With his forehead wrinkling and his eyes lifting, he's appearing thoughtful enough to be hurting.

"Maybe my place is to help figger out how to set things better...care my load an' he'p make some changes 'round here."

"I'm listening, my friend," I answer in half-apology.

"It's jus' 'at when somethin's good fer you, it ain't nes'sarily good fer me."

"I don't know how to change that, C.B. If I was smart enough to come up with answers to those kind of questions...hell, there probably wouldn't be anybody that'd listen anyway."

"If somethin's good fer one, it oughta be good fer all," he continues.

With hoots and hollers from its riders to those walking, a black T-bird makes the loop around the Circle.

"C.B., I don't know what you want me to say."

"'At ain't never stopped you 'fore."

There's nothing I can say. We both know there are long, hard rows left to hoe in the fields of human rights. It's my southern society that has to deal with them.

"Well, none of this racial stuff is my fault."

"Fault? It ain't 'bout fault." He gets up, walks over to pick a nearby dogwood bloom, and looks at me. Sitting back down with it, he runs his fingers along the darkened indentations that Papa told us represent the nail-scarred hands of Christ. "I ain't talkin' 'bout blame, Scott. An' ever'thing ain't about you."

"I know that, C.B., but I just want you to know how many times I've been called a nigger-lover because we're friends."

"Don't be tryin' to lay no guilt on me 'bout that," his voice rises, and he stands, indicating it's time to get on to work.

"I've got it, C.B., you can be the first negra football player at Ole Miss. Then, everybody'll treat you white."

"I don' want white. I'll settle fer right. But I jus' might do what you said. Maybe I can pick my way right on through this cotton college with th' national guard followin' me 'round to class like they doin' fer James Mason. All them fed'ral marshals, they could block fer me when I run th' ball in practice, an' chauffeur me to class, an' 'range dates fer me with Miss America."

"All right, C.B., I get the point. I don't know what I'd do if I were you. Maybe I'd sign up for a hitch in the Marines or something."

I pick up a magnolia cone and break the stem off as if it were a hand grenade pin. "Three, two, one," I count, and heave the cone grenade over in hook-shot fashion. With my toss and explosion sound effects, a robin is frightened into sudden flight. "If you were to go in the military first, they might even send you to school. Then you could go some place where it wouldn't matter if you were a negra or not."

"'At's real good, Scott. You full of great ideas. I can leave my own home an' risk gettin' my ass blowed off so's if I come back a'tall, I can live in somebody else's somewhere else."

"I could think about you every time they played that song, 'Blowin' in the Wind.'" Another attempt at humor crashes and burns.

"Thanks a heap, college boy. An' while I'll be defendin' yo' freedom, all you'll have to worry 'bout is holdin' on to yo' big-shot college dee…ferral an' figgerin' out which one of them banks to get you a student loan from."

"What about defending my virginity from all these college girls?"

"You just ain't gon' be serious, is you?"

"What do you want me to say, C.B.?"

"I dunno," he sighs.

A gray squirrel scampers across the velvety turf grass in front of us. She leaps up to stick to the side of an old monarch of a white oak tree. Even with her paw pads muffling the sounds of her claws, there is enough of an echoing alarm from the large loose flakes of bark to send other squirrels bouncing from tree to tree. I wish we had time to stay and watch their gymnastics.

"You know…I ain't got ever'thing all laid out fer my future like you do. Fact is, I ain't got jack squat I can be countin' on."

The honking of a car horn brings us to yield, and me to an opportunity not to answer C.B. A little red convertible Corvette zooms around the Circle in front of us. It's a two-seater with three girls hanging out the sides and over the open top. They're laughing and calling out to some turtle-necked, frat-looking boys. One girl has the longest and blondest hair I've ever seen. In spite of C.B.'s challenges, I can't help wondering if all of this will ever be for me…if it will ever be my turn.

As we cross the street, a white college professor pulls up and parks his Volkswagen bus. He gets out with his necktie and briefcase and passes by an old colored man who's trimming the grass along the curb. Neither of them speak. I wonder if they even see one another or care what they are missing from not knowing each other…like C.B. and I know each other.

"They in different worlds, ain't they?" C.B. offers.

I just look without answering. It's too spooky how he sometimes reads my mind.

"Scott."

"What?"

"Soon's I get outta high school, while you goin' to college, I prob'ly will have to go into th' service of some kind."

"I don't know about the future, but right now you're fixing to have the satisfaction of watching me have to serve the only negra student at Ole Miss."

"Right on. Ain't life grand?"

"Seriously, C.B., I want you to pay attention to something. Every time Ol' James comes in the Grill, the other waiters get busy doing something else or go back to the kitchen. I'm the only one that ever waits on him. Have you ever noticed that?"

"'Ain't nothin' old 'bout him, an' you better believe I seen them bastards. I can see through 'at kinda white thinkin'."

"Not counting my superb fish sandwiches, I wonder if young James has anything in his whole day to make what he puts himself through worthwhile."

"Not old and not young…just James." C.B. gets his serious look again. "An' maybe he ain't doin' it fer hisself. Could be Mister Mason's goin' through all this so others after him will have things better."

"Like what?"

"Like goin' to school. If ever'where else can have coloreds an' whites studyin' together, why come Mis'sippy's gotta act like it's war times?"

I can't think of an answer, so I walk in silence.

C.B. doesn't let up. "'Sides, I done integrated this fiddle-fart campus…at Th' Grill, workin' side by side with th' likes of you. An' ain't nobody made no fed'ral case out of that. I ain't got no FBI or bodyguards…less'n you undercover national guard."

"The only thing I want to get undercover with is the first one of these college girls I can talk into it."

"I oughta knowed that."

As we walk pass the library, the same two Ole Miss policemen who broke up our crowd drive by. The driver waves at us as if nothing's happened. I'm guessing that's a sign he still expects free coffee and doughnuts.

"Dad says Mason hadn't got a snowball's prayer in Hades of making it through deer season, anyway."

"What?"

"Before some KKK'er do him in."

"What's a KKK'er? A fraternity boy?"

"Are you shittin' me, C.B.? What do y'all talk about around the supper table...or anywhere else?"

"It ain't Greek, 'at's fer sure. Now, what do it stand fer?"

"The Klu Klux Klan."

"Oh, yeah...I know 'bout th' bunch of white folks makin' trouble fer coloreds whether they out of line or not."

"According to Dad, once the Klan gets after Ole Miss's first negra student, then all the secret service men guarding him won't do a whole lot of good. It'd be too simple to shoot him."

"It might not be easy as you think," C.B. argues, "not with one of them fed'ral marshals on both sides of him."

"Wouldn't be nothing to it. They'd be standing there looking at each other and wondering what happened, after it was all over with but the crying."

"I wouldn't bet on it," C.B. continues to argue. He pulls his belt up and tightens it a notch. "You talkin' 'bout plum serious sin when you talkin' killin'."

"It'd be easy as mud puppy pie."

"'At's jus' yo' butterfly mouth makin' trails yo' catapillar tail couldn't crawl across, much less down."

"All right then, smarty pants, I tell you what I'll do...."

"Crap'n fall back in it, prob'ly," he responds.

"Make your fun now, but watch and I'll prove how easy it would be to segregate Ole Miss again...if I had the notion to."

"What you talkin' 'bout, Fool?"

"I'm gonna show you how easy it'd be to shoot James Mason, if I was of the crazy mind and half sense of one of those white wizards." I pat my pistol like the head of a pet.

"Scott…."

"You just listen, and I'll tell you what to watch for."

"You crazy."

"Mason will come in, and I'll walk right up to the counter and take his order like I always do. But, then you just watch me. Here's what's going to happen—"

"You done lost yo' mind?"

"When I slide his order up on the counter top, you listen real hard. I'm going to slip my hand in my pocket and wrap it around my little pistol. Then I'll cough, and right then…that's when you'll hear what it is that I want you to be able to tell me you heard. That'll settle this argument."

"Prob'ly be you whinin' when them marshals arrest you an' haul yo' mule-stubborn butt off to th' funny farm."

"The only thing keeping me from changing the course of history will be my good nature. You'll see how easy it could have been my gun going off instead of me coughing."

C.B. makes his puffy-cheeked expression and shakes his head. We clock in for work at exactly 3:30. The Grill is not yet hopping. Most of the students must be in class, shooting pool or whatever else it is that they do. C.B. and I put on our starched white aprons and begin our respective jobs. The greasy smell of fried food lingers in wire baskets behind my counter.

At a quarter after four with his federally-funded entourage of two U.S. Marshals, the first black man ever enrolled at Ole Miss eases through the door. James Mason comes to his usual spot on the customer side of the counter…a place where no other Negro before him has ever ventured. His two bodyguards put their elbows up on the counter and look at me as if they're daring me to say something about such Yankee manners…and I'm tempted.

I can sense that the two protectors are acutely aware of a tension and uncomfortable presence the three of them have created by just being in the room. While most of the students steal glances at their fellow student, no one rushes over to say "hello." Some get up from their tables and leave. Others, not about to be run off, stay and stare at the dark intruder.

Both of the rednecks working the counter with me make a big show of walking out back for a cigarette break. On the way through the door, one of them loudly says, "It ain't no big thing." The other one says, "They could send Jimmy out here to play."

The most notorious student at the University of Mississippi wipes sweat from his forehead with the back of his sleeve. For some reason that I'm not understanding, I don't look directly into his eyes. The quiet, little, big man on campus places his order...to go. It's always to go...back to Baxter dorm. I suppose he figures trying to eat with the white students would be pushing things too far. Maybe he's just doing what's necessary, without flaunting racism in anyone's face.

Preparing the usual order of two fish sandwiches, I think about all the Negroes that have cooked for white folks over the years...and wonder how often some of them might have considered doing something peculiar to the food. From about ten feet away, C.B. splashes soapy water and fumbles the dishes more than usual.

Completing James Mason's order, I sack the sandwiches and start for the counter. Now is the time. Slipping my right hand in my pants pocket, I reach out with my left hand to present the order. With a coughing distraction, I pull back the hammer of my carnival pistol. The cold, short click resonates, as my cough didn't exactly cover it with my timing. C.B.'s face fades to the gray black that I expected. He acknowledges with a nod that he has heard the cocking of my gun.

I look at the bodyguards to see if they too might have heard the steel-sounding snap through the muffled fabric of my pants. The Fed closest to C.B. does indeed have a startled expression and looks as if he is about to grab me. Looking at his partner and then back to me, he starts to speak as he slides his hand under his coat toward his own pistol. The startling split second is interrupted as extra loud music suddenly blares from the jukebox.

The TV tune music from a comedy detective series is recognized as ironic by all. It so matches the Feds' black suits, dark glasses, and exaggerated bodyguard demeanor that the humor is too much. The two hired guns, C.B., the students and I, all have difficulty holding back laughs. Even James Mason recognizes the moment of the music and displays an ever-so-slight grin.

Apparently the bodyguard's curiosity about the click of my gun's hammer was sufficiently sidetracked. I cough again and un-cock the pistol. Jerking my hand out of my pocket, I flip out a napkin within three inches of James Mason's heart. Almost poking him in the ribs with it, I cough again. C.B. drops a dish and mumbles something about the good Lord looking after fools. Having proved my boast to C.B., I now have the strange feeling I am one of the few people on the civil rights scene ever to have held integration's life or death in my pocket. It was all at my discretion for a moment in time.

Flanked by his fidgety federal agents, my customer pays with the correct change. I look straight in his face this time. There is no personal connection, not even after sort of saving his life. I am disappointed to see only a lonely, unsmiling expression. The civil rights hero of many, if not to me, simply takes his sack of fish sandwiches, his nervous twitch, and his bodyguards, and turns toward the door.

A sorority girl approaches the Grill's glass door from the inside hall as James reaches it from our side. As a gentleman of any color would, he opens the door and steps back to hold it for the young lady. Also in the customary and meek manner of a black man of the times, he does not look directly at the white girl, much less speak to her.

I'm expecting the girl to give him a simple "thank you" for holding the door, instead she flips him a dime. Dixie suddenly blares out from the jukebox speakers. Students laugh and giggle as if something clever has been accomplished. The fraternity boy controlling the music machine grins at the debutante who is obviously in on the setup. As Mr. James Mason steps through the door and the students continue laughing, I look at C.B. He is looking hard at the frat-rat and his smart-ass girlfriend.

Holding his hand out to me, but only pretending, I hope, to be wanting my pistol, C.B. says, "Give me 'at thing!"

XXIV:
Little Tallahatchie De-Rivering

"MAN, LOOK AT HOW th' deer been workin' over this greenbriar," C.B. points out.

"Yeah, they've been hitting it pretty hard." I walk on, pretending I'd already noticed the deer browse and sign.

The spring of '63 finds me in need of a good measure of mental peace from still dealing with the deaths of Mr. J. and Miss Sippy. To make the majority of each week tolerable, I look forward to weekend escapes to the river with hooks and a bait seine. Since our early excursions to Bailey Woods, C.B. and I have appreciated the serenity that refuge from the rest of society brings us.

From the woodlands along Taylor Creek, the Yocona River, and the bottomlands of Enid Lake, we are now being drawn toward the deeper forests along the Little Tallahatchie bottom and its Sardis Lake backwaters. C.B. points out wild boar signs, where they have been rooting around and leaving tracks and scat.

The Little Tallahatchie River runs pretty much from east to west. Although its headwaters drain land well to the northeast, the portion we're coming to know best is that which separates Marshall and Lafayette Counties. Upstream from where the Army Corps of Engineers dammed the river to build Sardis Lake, this part of the heavily-wooded floodplain forest is an area unspoiled by roads. By the flight of the crow it runs fifteen miles from Etta to Abbeville…Mississippi towns that respectively hit double and triple figures on the population scale.

There's a natural strength to be derived from the solitude that reigns from ridge to ridge. It's like visits re-charge the soul. Our explorations are entrenched on the south side of the river for the most part. As if they were set aside just for C.B. and me, numerous oxbow sloughs, meander scrolls, floodplain lakes, and a myriad of wet meadows have been left behind by the river's wandering back and forth.

C.B. and I make our way downstream from our drop-off at the Highway 30 river crossing. For us, it starts the vast, wild stretch of rich bottomland forest, symbolic of southern waterways. It's a floodplain forest that's been defined for hundreds of years by the buttress-based cypresses and ancient green ashes and gums.

We pause to watch a funny whirling current caused by something under the water's surface. The river is gurgling.

"Start of spring's th' best time of year, th' way I figger it," C.B. comments. "Th' changin' of th' seasons is what I like to see."

"There's too much dad-blamed school this time of year," I grumble.

"Always th' pesti'mist," he criticizes.

"Pessimist, C.B. The word is pessimist. And no, I'm not one. I just happen to like fall best, is all."

"How come?"

"Opposite of what you said, I reckon. Change doesn't come before you know it, especially in the bottom."

The river is more turbid than usual. A previous rain that was farther to the east has slightly increased the flow. The old and massive sweetgum trees we walk by are nothing short of living sculptures, exemplifying the artwork of God Himself. The smaller of the trunks reminds me of the pillars on porches of antebellum homes. Egg masses from salamanders decorate shallow and stagnant puddles from previous river overflows.

Parting waist-high wire grass as we continue downstream, C.B. comments, "Looks like all th' creeks in north Mis'sippi used to come together in here."

"What do you mean, used to?" I ask.

"I mean 'fore th' gov'ment's big ditch got to stealin' most of th' Little Tallahatchie's water. If it wadn't fer Puskus an' Cypress Creeks comin' in here, this place would be dry as a popcorn fart."

"C.B., I'm glad I brought you along. Nobody else in the entire new world would have put it quite like that."

"You jus' tryin' to sound like Mr. J. now."

"And to think, I could have been missing such treasures of the Taylor tongue."

We trudge through smartweed, spike sedge and a rare plant Granna and her books haven't taught me yet. For the swamp privet and red maple, spring has already sprung. Other plants will follow suit, more like dress in some cases, and burst out of winter with their little buds succumbing to a different but similar natural schedule.

Wooded swamps and still-water pools lie along side of the natural levee. Some are so nearly permanent that pondweed and duckweed cover their surfaces like army blankets. Musical love-grunts with frog croaks and choruses echo across their crusty tops.

"You ever notice how th' river wets th' air so your nose can feel what it's a'smellin'?" C.B. asks, as we wade through standing backwater.

"I'll go you one better than that. Sometimes when I get to thinking about it real hard, I can taste the gritty silt in my mouth before I even take a drink of river water."

"You smell 'at fishy river odor?" C.B. asks, pretending to ignore my comment by going me one better.

It's the undeniable aroma of a bream bed. Instead of answering him, I suggest, "Let's track it down and seine it. We can get enough bait to do the whole trotline in one drag."

"I don' know. I 'member yo' Granna tellin' us how yo' cherry bomb idea would mess up th' spawnin'. I 'spect pullin' a net through the nest wouldn't do 'em no whole lot of good neither."

"You've probably stumbled on being right. For fish future sake, we'll skip it," I retract my idea.

As quickly as the sweet smell of perch perfume captured my attention, it blows away with the breeze. The predominant odor is that of mud and decaying aquatic vegetation when we come to the pin oak flat where the Tippah and Little Tallahatchie Rivers come together. This was Mr. J.'s favorite campsite when he used to hunt the river.

Recalling Mr. J.'s tales makes me feel as if he's not completely gone, but the best of storytelling may be extinct. I remember talk of when time was…when virgin woods housed hordes of passenger pigeons, when ivory-billed woodpeckers were still with us, and of a time when black bear commonly roamed the bottom.

"Dark's not far off. If we gon' have any lines to run in th' mornin', we best split up," C.B. suggests. "You wanta set hooks or tend to camp chores?"

I hold my fist out in a quick challenge of the "paper covers rock but scissors cuts paper" game. After three shakes, rock breaks scissors to determine I get to put out bank hooks, and C.B. will be counted on to make a good camp. He'll get us a fire going and round up some natural grub, less the grubs, I hope. Normally we'd work together collecting the makings for a wildlife and wild plant smorgasbord supper, but time is too short today.

"Try not to burn up the swamp while I'm gone," I tease my buddy.

"You jus' worry 'bout findin' yo' way back 'fore dark-thirty. I don't wanta hafta come searchin' fer you."

"That'll be the day."

"I don' know 'bout that. We so far back in here, th' wild hog trails eben look lost."

"If I couldn't follow the river back to camp, well...."

Pulling my dead-grass-brown hunting hat firmly down to the tops of my ears, I work back upstream to a nice little honey hole around the bend we just passed. An overhanging limb is available where I can tie off a set of hook as soon as I come up with some bait. For that, I unroll our six-foot seine and scoop it just off the edge of the bank. A second and harder try is along the bottom of an inlet at the junction where an unnamed tributary creek comes into the old river.

Pay dirt! With my index finger and thumb, I carefully grasp the middle of a chapped rear-red crawdad caught in the netting. The mud bug's pinchers can't reach me as I pull and twist. When he lets go of the net, I hook him loosely under the scales near the end of his tail. In hopes he'll summon up the granddaddy catfish of the century, I tie the loose end of his new fishing line to my overhanging limb. He will tantalizingly swim around in about a two-foot circle.

After setting my second rig with a bluegill and third with a warmouth, I turn my seine upside-down, stretch it tight, and shake it. The elongated fleshy fruits of a water Tupelo tree fall out. The purple seeds, having somehow floated into the currentless cove are like water's equivalent to the cockleburs. They travel.

Before I come to a good place for a fourth set, my attention is drawn to the gray bark of a water elm. Granna's book calls it a planer-tree. I don't recall her or her book saying anything about it being such a proper place to perch. I feel the need to lean back, take a load off, and overlook the river, without worrying about setting out hooks right now. Instead, I have some heavy thinking that needs doing.

Brushing aside this tree's prickly, nut-like fruits, I wiggle my hams comfortably down into the cool, soft sand. Finding such easy comfort, I do believe I've come upon the time and place to reflect seriously on the matter of the special people around me dying.

Talk to me, river. Speak from your river-heart. Go below the depth of your dignified silence but stay above your river rhetoric. Tell me—why does life get so screwed up in the end with death? Mr. J.'s, with his tremendous past...and Miss Sippy's being without a future? Just what the hell is going on with my people, world?

Waiting on the river to answer, I hear something from high above instead. It's an eerie hum from way up in the upper canopies where the mighty bottomland trees flower. The noisy bees are soon drowned out by the bird sounds from a spring migration that has swung into full flight. A flock of crows makes its annoying presence known. Even they will soon be pairing off...while I can only mourn for the Miss Sippy that I'll never have for my very own.

"Whoo, whoo, whoo, whoo...oo," comes a distinctly recognizable human owl call.

Hearing the crows respond to C.B.'s imitation, I know what my buddy and the crows are up to. I hoot back. They respond again. C.B. whoo-whoos again. The duel is on. The crows, thinking their flock is now ganging up on a pair of owls, now become berserk, fluttering down from every direction. I hear the sharp crack of the .22 rifle, three times. In the matter of about a minute, the crow calls are gone. I'd give good odds there are three fewer of the feathery varmints left to raid farmers' corn crops.

As the Little Tallahatchie River bottom settles down again, ripples on the surface of the river become the predominant activity to watch. They're such a comforting presence, I could spend countless hours sitting on the sandy banks and just watching, in hopes the water would wash my troubles downstream. With respect to the number of bank sets C.B. will be expecting from me, I'm just not up to it.

"Yelp, yelp, yelp...cluck, cluck."

I recognize the seductive series of sounds that comprise a wild turkey hen's mating call. Although I can't see her, I can visualize her flipping over leaves and eating almost everything she finds. All the while, she'll pretend to be uninterested in some nearby gobbler, yet she's the one who called him. Listening for the male and not hearing him, I'm tempted to gobble. Maybe he's out there somewhere and doesn't appreciate what he could have. Perhaps he's had two or three hens already and isn't worried about this one's affections. It could be they'll join up when he's rested up…but none of that will help to address my questions on a more true love.

I move along to find the next feeder creek that needs a hook set in it. A cream-colored sandbar demands inspection. I wonder where such places were when I used to play with toys like rubber men. The water current has caused symmetrical undulations in the sand, but periodic protrusions in the sand interrupt the pattern. A closer look reveals they are caused by mussels. Half a hat full, steamed over river water and smoked by a driftwood fire might go well with whatever C.B. has found for our supper.

Upriver about a hundred yards, I come upon another spot with all the right set hook characteristics. A drag with my seine just off the bank produces a nice shellcracker for bait. The variety of fish within the river is so great I never know what to expect from one pull of the net to the next. Another cove up, a small sucker of some sort makes himself available for hiding a hook. Then a near-perfect sitting-log suggests I need another break.

On the way over to sit down for more and better meditation, I bump a snag with the heel of my hand. Answering back, a flying squirrel sails from it to a hollow black gum. He scurries up to a hole and out of sight before I can enjoy seeing enough of him.

By the time I'm settled, a young raccoon sleepily climbs out of a hollow sycamore that leans out over the river. Another young coon follows. And another. Roughhousing by the first two youngsters disturbs a decaying limb that's covered with some kind of fungus. A dusty cloud of yellow-green spores is released as the third coon walks through. He sneezes and shakes his head in an uncanny likeness to the way a human would.

Mother coon appears on the upper stream bank. She must have called the younger ones without my noticing it or heard them and returned from wherever she was. With squirrel-like agility, she balances her way along an exposed root system and then ambles along the wavy scallops in the mud. Spotting me, she suddenly starts to display a fake, busted leg drag. It's bound to be an attempt to lead me away from her young…and I wish for my late mentor's interpretation.

If Mr. J. were here, he could use his intellectual artistry to explain what I think I recognize as Mother Nature, her very self. Seeing the motherly coon preaching from her heart, in such a real live, outdoor story, Mr. J.'d probably pull out some morals about honor, compassion, and selflessness, or at least a willingness to sacrifice. He would have translated all this into some tall thought that might help me deal with Sippy taking my heart to her grave.

A gust of wind works its way through the trees, bringing with it a sulfur odor. I know it's just swamp gas and rotting leaves, but I'm equally certain Mr. J. would have tied the scent to some obscure idea about his universal truths…perhaps something about mankind's inner heart. Missing his counsel and wishing I hadn't taken the old man for granted when he was alive, I turn again to the river to look for my lesson on humanity…if not inhumanity.

Come on, river, answer my questions. The tree saplings along your banks have learned to bend with the wind instead of snapping. How might I handle my circumstances? Your wetland trees send out their drooping, aerial branches to adapt better in the face of flooding. How can I pay heed to such woods-laws in my own environment? Fess up, river, damn you…before the Corps dams you again.

Something's making a wake. It's swimming with what appears to be a twig periscoping up out of the water. I'm thinking it's a beaver. He's probably carrying a willow branch or cottonwood limb or some other tasty-barked stick snack to his food supply storage area. As it comes closer, I see differently. What I thought to be a stick is a pair of ears, sticking straight up in the air.

Like it's nothing new to her, the swamp rabbit dog paddles downstream, listening for danger or just not wanting to get her ears wet. If a rabbit can move her legs like that to paddle, I wonder why in Sam Hill she can't walk instead of having to hop. If someone were to get too close to her litter, I'll bet she'd display some kind of mangled hurt-hop comparable to the mother coon's busted leg act. Would God's maternal Master Plan have her swim with a sidestroke? Most anything would make more sense than letting my mother and Miss Sippy die.

Long since debarked by river wear, a tree branch bounces up and down in the murky water, as if it's keeping time with the current. Paying little to no attention to it, the rabbit swims by and then makes a quarter turn. She paddles in a beeline diagonally across the river to a wide, shallow stretch with a sandbar. By selecting the low spot and gentle slope, she's able to negotiate a bank that doesn't have to be climbed with feet or hands that grab. Her approach to life is so different from that of the coon's, not better, not worse, just different. I suppose different is sometimes good. Miss Sippy was different.

I've got to get up and move. Working my way farther upstream, I manage to find several more fish-promising sites and put out as many live-baited hooks. Trying to squeeze in one more set before dark, I stumble upon a stand of some non-poisonous mushrooms. Plucking enough for a mess, I figure they will nicely complement the mussels. If C.B. has come up with something, we'll be in good shape for supper.

The unmistakable flapping sound of wild turkeys going to roost hints strongly that darkness is close and I should head back toward camp. Dodging trees in the fading light, I'm drawn through fast-closing woods until I see the slight orange glow from my campmate's cooking fire. While C.B. stands rubbing his back against an ironwood tree, tree shadows dance and flicker in sync with the fire's lapping at the air.

"I wuz beginnin' to think I'z fixin' to have to come after you."

"Well, I had to have me a serious set-to on the bank of the river, where I could do a little listening in context."

"You get ever'thing worked out?"

"No, C.B., I didn't. It seemed like my heart wouldn't let my head think. You know what I mean?"

"Yep, hurtin's th' loudest thing I been hearin', too," he shares.

"I did figure out one thing. Those folks who get so worried about the little stuff…they just hadn't had anything big happen to them, yet. I heard you shoot. Are we going to be eating three-crow casserole this evening with stone stew?"

"I done put th' crow heads on set hooks down stream, but supper's waitin'. We got boiled tuber-roots from arrowhead plants an' sweet shad-bush juneberries fer desert. What you got there, in your hat?"

"Mushrooms on top and mussels underneath." I hand them over. "That coffee ready?"

"Yeah, but it's a mite strong fer a city boy." He walks over to his pack and digs out a tin cup. "I'll pour it half full 'til you bless it, like the men do their wine in th' movies 'fore their wives taste it."

"And Dad said you had plantation manners." As I take a sip, C.B. waits for my reaction. "Not too bad, for yours. I suspect it'd float a number four split-shot."

"If'n these woodland delicacies of yores ain't too chewy when we get done cookin' 'em, they might actually be…barely better tastin' than nothin'." He dumps the contents of my hat in his skillet and separates out the mussels for shelling. "You put out a passel of bank lines, did you?"

"Uh…well, not enough to suit you, I'm sure."

He gives me a hard stare. "You have trouble grubbin' up bait?"

"Nope, it had more to do with that sitting and listening I was telling you about." I sip coffee and watch him open mussels with the knife Mr. J. gave him.

While supper starts in serene solitude, we are pleasantly interrupted by a barred owl serenade. We know when they are good enough to be left to themselves and not commented on. The natural music intensifies into sounding like the birds are laughing back and forth. Perhaps they think it was funny the way we mocked them for the crows' mistake.

"Them folks in Oxford that can't hear th' owls carryin' on like this…they jus' gettin' by, man."

"They probably got their own thing, C.B., whatever it is. Is that a one-match fire? Now, be honest."

"Only kind I know how to make, ain't it?"

"Yeah, right," I sarcastically agree.

By the time we finish C.B.'s course of supper, our owls tire of their joking. The mollusk and mushroom course looks ready now. I hope the fire's curative crackling will help it all go down.

"How about these mussels?" I ask, as I demonstrate their…chewability.

"You want th' truth, Scott?"

"Wouldn't know if I could handle it coming from you, but give it a shot."

"They taste 'bout like rubber."

"Better than last time we had some, huh?"

Mother Nature's evening sounds soon work their sedative spell. C.B. gives up before me and crawls in his bedroll. As the soothing powers of nightfall continue to communicate with me, C.B. slips into a deep sleep. While he starts up the kind of snoring that comes only with clean living, according to Papa, I can't sleep. I keep thinking about Sippy and her loneliness…and my lonesomeness.

Nearby sloughs hum with thirsty mosquitoes. We have enough breeze, fire, and smoke to keep them somewhat at bay. Late night swamp sounds are unique in a river bottom. This is a place where the last of the real black panthers are said to own the night. I wonder if they've all gone now…gone the way of Mr. J. and my Miss Sippy.

In the morning, C.B. gets up and pokes around in what's left of our fire with a stick. We're both too excited about what our set-lines might have on them to take the time to worry with breakfast. The last thing I remember of being conscious last night was the lonely howling of a pack of coyotes on the Marshall County side of the river. I clear my head, tune in my woods-ears, and appreciate the bottomland birds' melody of first daylight.

After breaking camp and checking C.B.'s three crow-head sets, we find ourselves having caught one turtle and no fish. Working our way upstream to my sets, C.B. points out undercut banks, fallen trees, coves, and other prime locations where I should have hung hooks. Next time, I'm making camp.

We'll run our lines as we're hiking toward where Dad is to pick us up. It's on Cypress Creek upstream about a mile from where it joins the Little Tallahatchie River. A lot of people fish off the bridge from River-side Road, but superstitions and cottonmouths keep most of them from straying very far.

"Look at that!" C.B. points out.

As we are approaching my third set, the willow limb that's an integral part of the rig is being jerked back and forth. It's aggressively pulled down underwater. C.B. pulls at the line, and it doesn't want to come up. Barging in the muddy river up to his waist, he runs a hand from the limb down the line and under the surface. His eyes light up.

"Yoww…ee! All ri…ight! Holy mackerel!"

A big swirl wrinkles the water's surface right in front of C.B. My buddy gets his hand in the gills as I see the huge catfish's head. With C.B. trying unsuccessfully to hoist our catch out of the water, the big fish flaps its tail and causes another swirl. He rolls over and takes C.B. under with him. They come up, both spitting and coughing but still holding on to one another.

"I'm gon' need some he'p, here," C.B. splutters and continues to wrestle.

"You're doing all right. Just go along with whatever he wants to do...and don't let go."

"Scott!"

"All right, already." Laughing, I wade in and manage to work our camp rope through the fish's mouth and out a gill.

Between the three of us, we manage to swim to the bank where two of us pull the third one out of the water.

"He must be every bit of two feet long and weigh all of twenty pounds," I proclaim.

"We done caught ol' granddad," C.B. adds. "We gon' need to dunk him once in awhile on th' way home, to keep him alive."

"Dang right. If he's alive when we get him to the bait shop, he'll weigh more." I picture the head game warden certifying us with a new state record.

"'Stead of cuttin' cross country or takin' our walkin' trail to th' Cypress Creek bridge, we best walk th' edge of th' river, an' then th' creek, so's we can keep big daddy wet."

As we lug our trophy upstream, checking the rest of our bank lines produces only a few small fish, all of which we let go. Toting our big fish through the corridor of shrub habitat along the bank turns out to be a whole lot like work. It may be good nesting sites for songbirds, but it's not so good for human walking. The thick vegetation soon persuades us to wade the river and swim our fish behind us.

"'Member, ever'body ain't as fond of snakes as you is," C.B. whines.

"I'm going first...and it's just an old saying that snakes always bite the second one in a line. What's that racket, C.B.?"

A loud mechanical noise is interrupting the tranquility of the flood plain beyond my herpetology lecture.

"Sound like th' start-up noise fer a bulldozer."

"Surely they're not gonna log out our bottom? Mr. J. said this was all set aside for holding flood water and for hunting and camping in."

"They could still log it an' grow th' trees back...unless they was clearin' th' land fer cotton or pasture or somethin'. Sounds like it's on th' canal, next to th' old river. Let's check it out an' have us a look-see." C.B. wades over to the far edge of the river and ties up our monster cat to a cypress knee.

"Maybe that's just a big machine fixing to re-ream out the Corps' big ditch to try to keep it open."

When we make our way over to inspect the noise, we find that the heavy equipment is indeed digging machinery and not a logging dozer. Up close, the U.S. Army Corps of Engineers stenciled on the side of the giant track-hoe is as intimidating as the machine and the noise.

"This ain't th' canal," C.B. points out. "They must be tryin' to connect up th' canal to th' old riverbed…to get Cypress and Puskus Creeks' water in their ditch, too."

"Why would they do that?" I ask.

"I ain't sure I understand all I see 'bout this," C.B. admits. "If they tryin' to suck what little water Cypress Creek had goin' in here and out of th' bottom…this look like th' way to do it, sure 'nuff."

"C.B., I think I've been around enough death lately to know it when I hear it."

"What chu mean?"

"That heavy machinery noise—that's the sound of our old river dying for good this time." Standing and staring at the monstrous machine, I continue, "Yesterday the river talked to me. Today, I can even feel how it feels."

"They gon' dry up ever'thing, an' do away with all th' duck tater an' coontail. They gotta know some wildlife needs th' wet. After they done ruined th' river, why would they wanta do this to th' creek?"

"Maybe when they mess something up, they want to be sure they do it proper."

"'Fore this whole bottom gets completely screwed up, somebody needs to be doin' some serious soul searchin'. Causin' our rivers to go dry oughta be right down there with sins agin' God an' a whole flock of angels. I done seen too much of this. Let's get outta here."

I hear an outboard motor pull in and stop on the creek where we left our catch.

"'At sounds a mite too close to our fish fer my comfort," C.B. suggests.

By running, we're almost back when the motor starts up again. When we get to within sight of the spot, we see the perpetrator. It's Gut-Hook. He kicks his Mercury in gear and twists the throttle. Looking back at us with his yellow-toothed grin and laughing, he rounds the bend…with our fish. C.B. shakes his fist at him, as I remember someone on the Yocona River once doing that to us.

"Scott."

"What?"

"I'm 'memberin' how Mr. J. used to tease us 'bout th' big'un always gettin' away…an' what a old story it was ever' time somebody come up with somethin' like 'at."

"Yeah, I know what you're saying. We'd just as well keep quiet about our fish being near three feet long and thirty pounds."

"'At be best. Ain't nobody'd believe it no ways. An' I'm quite shore 'at cat was clos'ter to four foot long an' forty pounds."

XXV:
Maybe It's Memphis

I WATCH FROM THE front porch swing as my best buddy, with his long strides, practically bounces up the South 11th Street city sidewalk. His pudgy appearance having grown lean, I'm reminded how C.B. and some things have changed…and how he and some things haven't. It doesn't seem like that long since C.B. wouldn't have dared come anywhere except to the back door. According to early 60s TV, the civil rights movement has won big victories all across the rest of the country, but acceptance of change in certain Mississippi circles has come slowly.

A spring breeze works its way through the bright yellow line of daffodils along the front curb as C.B. traipses right up between the tall, straight trunks of the willow oaks leading to my porch. He looks serious about whatever it is that's on his mind today.

"Hey, C.B, what's up?"

"Scott, I gotta talk to ya'." He plops down in the wicker rocker. "I know where my mom is. A gov'ment man of some kind come to our place wavin' some papers in Auntay's face 'til she got mad enough to tell him…an' I overheard 'em."

"Yeah?" I stop the squeaking and creaking of my swing.

"She ain't in Chicago no more. She's in Memphis…performin'."

"No kidding?"

"It's some kinda Broadway Playhouse like th' Opry. She's dancin' with some sorta orchestra or somethin' like 'at."

"That's something," I comment, for lack of knowing what else to say.

"I can almost see her tippy-toein' 'round in some of them stretchy-tight pants gettin' standin' ovations an' such." His face lifts with anticipation. "Fer th' first time since ever, it makes me a little proud of her. You know?"

Knowing C.B. to stay pretty much on the stubborn side of determination, I think I can anticipate what's coming next. When C.B. was young, he shared a very private ambition with me that one day he would track down his mother and meet her.

Years of questioning, as to the whereabouts of his mother have revealed little. Auntay Belle fed him the consistent but unfulfilling story that a Negro trying to get good work in those days had to go to Chicago.

"You 'member how I always said I'd find my Mama someday?"

"Yeah, I do, C.B."

"Well, it's time to make good on 'at promise I made to myself. I done thought it over, an' I says to myself, 'Self, I'm a'gon' talk to her, 'thout her knowin' who I am'."

"Golly…uh," I stutter and grope for a better response. I'd sort of like to know myself if there is a better reason than to find work…for a mother to leave a child to be raised by her sister.

"I just wanta see what kinda person she be…an' maybe learn a little something 'bout Magnolia an' her life. You in or out?"

"Uh…sure, C.B." I push my porch swing in a skeptical shove and wonder if this particular pilgrimage should be one that calls for caution. "When?" I ask with hesitation.

"Ain't no better time than th' present. She liable to hafta get back up to Chicago or somewheres else. We outta school fer Good Friday. Th' Easter long weekend'll be perfect to meet Mama."

"You planning on riding the hemorrhoid express and leaving the driving to them?"

"I'z thinkin' we'd hitchhike." He rocks his chair faster and anticipates my response.

"Uh…." I start to speak before I know what I'm about to say.

"Don't go gettin' hummin'bird thoughts on me, now. You ain't gon' be backin' around, is you?"

"Naw, I'll go with you, C.B. You just have to promise me one thing— we won't go up there and shame ourselves."

"What you talkin' 'bout?"

"For instance, you leave your deer antler smoking pipe in Taylor. If you pull that thing out of your pocket while we're in Memphis, they'll think we're country for sure."

"Yeah, yeah, for instance sake…." C.B. waves his hand to dismiss my concern. "You all time worryin' 'bout what other folks think."

"It counts. Someday you'll see how much it matters."

"'At junk don't 'mount to a half-can of coyote crap, but I'm glad you goin' with me. 'At's what matters."

"Seriously, C.B., if you wear your jeans and tennies we won't be able to get into anywhere that's nice enough for show business. Have you got some khaki-pants and loafers or something?"

C.B. nods in recognition that I'm right. "I might could sneak my church pants out th' house without Auntay knowin' we goin'."

"That'll work. Wear your best shirt, too. And put on some aftershave. You don't want to be smelling like a butter bean fart when you meet your mother."

"We gon' need to dip into our firewood fund an' take 'bout five dollar' apiece."

"Ten," I suggest, "in case we need it."

"I just wanta see my mama's face." A long sigh follows. His lips tremble, and the corners of his mouth turn down. "I need to talk to her up close. I'm gon' look in her heart 'fore she figgers out who I am." He swallows hard.

"What will you say to her?"

"I ain't shore, but I'll know what when th' time come. I'll find her an' then I'll know. Faith don't fail. 'Member? You 'member how many times Auntay's done told us 'at."

"Over and over, C.B. I just hope she's right."

"She gen'ly is."

AS WITH MOST OF our plans that should have involved adult consent, a campout is spelled out in lieu of approval. By now everyone expects C.B. and me to head to the Little Tallahatchie River every chance we get. Permission to camp comes easy.

Good Friday arrives, and Granna deposits us at our usual Abbeville drop-off point for camping in the river bottom. The Pathetic Plymouth, as we've dubbed it, turns around at the big iron bridge. As it comes back by, C.B. and I head to a cross-vine thicket to shield our change into apparel fit for Memphis. Other clothes and camping gear will be stashed behind a considerable stand of cane and covered with an armload of smartweed for safekeeping.

"'Em Pawpaw flowers smellin' right. Th' custard apples be ready," C.B. points out.

"You know it," I acknowledge. "Let's do it."

We each pick two of the large pawpaw fruits, one for a pocket and the other for eating now. Weatherwoman Auntay has assured us that we'll have seasonal weather for the Holy Week weekend. The cold is out of the ground for the year.

"If we gon' jump th' log train, we best get goin'."

"Let's do it."

"Hoboin' to th' main most junction in Holly Springs ought not be no problem."

We hoof it about a mile south to the Illinois Central railway stop and Abbeville switchyard. From previous times placing pennies on top of nickels and then on the tracks, we're familiar with the area. A neat conversation piece can be made for six cents. When the train smashes them together, that's where Auntay says the old wives' tale about the sixth cent came from. Granna says Auntay's got a sixth scent about such sayings. I just wish I had enough sense to realize when they get in cahoots with one another to play such word games.

A railroad car is being topped off with timber. The majority of the cars are set up for hauling long logs, but a few flatbeds of pulpwood break up the pattern. As if fate were providing for C.B., which it usually does, a couple of empty boxcars display hobo capability. A rusty, ground-level water tank next to the tracks will provide a good place to hide and wait.

Selection of a northbound train is straightforward. The only train on the only tracks happens to be pointed north. After no more than ten minutes, the huge locomotive starts to jolt couplings and chug forward. Several carloads of massive oak and hickory logs roll by us. I can feel the ground shake under what Auntay calls the big iron horse.

"Seein' all them big trees goin' by that'a way...it makes me think of a funeral possession," C.B. observes.

"Yeah, we might oughta salute or something," I half-joke.

Out of respect for the old trees, C.B. does salute. I follow suit. When the empty boxcars approach, we run alongside. I jump on and climb in with no difficulty. C.B. manages to get his top half in. In near panic, I reach over his back to grab his belt and help him pull himself in.

"All aboard!" I yell, in a feeble attempt to pretend I wasn't scared half-to-death. He was close to falling underneath the train and losing both legs. As if my pulling on his pants turned him into a soprano, he says thanks in a jokingly high-pitched voice.

My eyes quickly adjust to the darkness of the inside of the car. I'm glad to see there are no tramps in here with us. Except for the cobwebs in the corner, we're empty. Hearing the heavy breathing of giant engines, I can almost feel the power of the pull. Bucking and jerking smooth out, and the rattling of the rails and steel wheels fade to a slight vibration.

As our train settles in to a roll with momentum, I stick my head out and see that we are leaving train smoke hanging low over Abbeville. Looking to the front, alongside the train's centipede-like body, I see the bridge again coming in sight. A piercing train whistle startles me. It must be signaling our approach to the river-road crossing.

"We should'a brought some stogies, Scott." C.B. settles down to sit on the boxcar's floor and hang his legs out the door.

"This probably isn't a smoking car."

"You ain't got th' brains of a tree toad on a telephone pole."

I join him in sitting on the floor. As the train continues to pick up speed, I decide simply to watch the passing scenery and let the fruitless conversation go.

"I jus' hope th' engineer knows to stop this thing at Holly Springs."

"He will," I try to assure us both.

As the train crosses the river, we both look down through the trestle. Ripples and eddies indicate there's more current than usual.

"Looks like the river's gonna overflow with floodwater," I mutter.

"Yep, th' backwater flow's done got to foamin' on top."

I'm thinking I'll have to let C.B. have the last word if I want any peace.

"Look at that! See it?" I point.

"It's just a beaver."

"Like heck it is. Look closer. See the way his tail's going back and forth? Beavers don't swim like that, and it's too big to be a muskrat. That's a river otter."

"I'll be dipped. You right. Ain't that somethin'?"

"Me being right or that being an otter?"

"Either…or both."

Holding onto the big metal sliding door that's temporarily fixed open, I stick my head out and feel the wind. We pass through our own smoke trail as the bluish-gray horizon funnels toward us. A hot steel smell from around the wheels makes me hope nothing is wrong with our train. Down the side of the cars toward the back, a set of sunlit rails look as if they are being strung out as we go.

Trees near the track race by as if they were the clickity-clack sounds I'm hearing. A countless number of trees must be required for a railroad. The half-buried sum of all the ties looks as staggering as their alignment.

Leaving the big cypress and gum that will soon have water lapping up against their swollen bases, we next pass fields in various stages of preparation and planting. Cotton appears to be trying to escape the flat land and take over the gently rolling hills. Dogwoods, wild azaleas, and red buckeyes blurrily show off their blooms. Outdoor colors in the false movement of railroad scenery flaunt their unique beauty like modern art that's smeared over the countryside. There's something about dangling your feet from a boxcar doorway that makes you feel you're good at distance spitting.

"Ain't it somethin' how a train sounds so lonely when you hear it from a distance, but when you be right here with it, ever'thing seem all right?"

I'm tempted, but I know not to answer C.B.'s philosophy unless I happen to feel like arguing. The Holly Springs depot slows our train from its rumbling to the proper deboarding speed we need. Off easily, and on the run, we size up our new situation. On another set of tracks, a cattle train is being coupled to three engines. Near the top of each car there's a gap about the same width we need in order to crawl through.

In another one of those not-so-rare moments of life when things seem to unfold for C.B. right when he needs them to, a pile of railroad ties looks to be the perfect hiding place. Half covered with sweet smelling honeysuckle, our stack of ties is wholly saturated with a creosote odor.

Sooner than I expected, the cattle train starts jerking forward one car at a time, toward Memphis. As our pre-selected car comes by, the train's speed and timing look about right and all else seems safe enough.

"Come on, C.B."

We run out from behind the ties and sprint along beside the train. I set the example and leap onto the side, my hands clinging to the cattle car's cold metal slats. My feet feel and poke for foot rests. I could climb a few slats using my hands only. Looking back for my sidekick, I see that he has secured a grasp as well. He looks like a fox squirrel pinned to the side of a hundred-year-old shortleaf pine on the first windy day of squirrel season.

We work our way along the side and climb to the gap above the top rail. With some difficulty, we manage to snake our butts through. There's a raised hayloft in the front third of the cattle car. The main floor is occupied by the livestock, and the strong stink of cow manure competes with the flowery spring fragrance from fresh-cut hay.

We watch in silence as a praying mantis crawls on a hay bale in front of us. It looks straw-like after every stop. A sweat bee lights near it…perhaps too near it. Lying back in the hay is much more comfortable than riding in a boxcar, but it does take away from enjoying the view. I guess compromise is a big part of hoboing.

"Zap!" The bee is history, and our praying mantis nonchalantly walks over to the backside of the hay and out of sight.

When I remember Granna telling me about how a she-walking-stick treats her mate, I remember where we're going…and about C.B.'s mom and how she left her only son.

"I tell you what, C.B.—as soon as this train slows down enough, we'd better jump off."

"You mean, you don't want no cowboys catchin' us?"

"Sin City, Memphis, is liable to have some folks worse than any cowboys."

"Whatever," C.B. agrees not to argue for a change.

Rusty blackhaw exhibits its blooms along the rails. Houses and farm lots speed by with wide and rural landscapes. I don't know if we're in Mississippi or Tennessee, but there are an awful lot of barns…barns of every size, old and new, and many heavy with hay.

"Long as we so close an' come this fur, what you say we go see what th' Mis'sippi River looks like." C.B. suggests.

"You got it. Good idea."

As we encounter numerous big buildings, I figure Memphis must be coming close. Factories, warehouses, and everything else in sight tell me that de-boarding may not be as easy as it was in Holly Springs. The train slows, and I realize we're already approaching the railroad station switchyard. Section hands are working on both sides of the tracks, so we do need to hit the ground on the run. I look for a safe place to land. We don't need any twisted ankles.

"C.B., when you jump, be sure and clear the ends of the railroad ties."

"Don't you worry 'bout me."

Leaving the train like a plane, we land mostly as planned. Rolling in the loose lava rocks was extra, but nothing feels broken. Scratches and scrapes will have to be ignored until a later inspection. The main thing now is—my knees and elbows are still with me.

C.B. bounces up like a champ, and we're on the getaway. After the initial look-back, I'm satisfied, until we reach the edge of the woods and look back again. In hot pursuit of us, a big, ugly man is waving a foot-long flashlight and yelling. Just when I think we don't need it, an eight-foot high chainlink fence is in our way.

On a dead run we spring halfway up the fence and scramble toward its top. I'm quickest and easily over the three strands of barbed wire on top. C.B. barely clears it as the railroad dick reaches the fence and swings his flashlight in billy-club fashion, hitting nothing but fence.

"You guys just as well hold up," he threatens. "I got a good look at you. Just wait right there." The bulldog-like man's double chin sort of sags with his cheeks.

Since he's so out of breath and probably too fat to climb the fence, much less negotiate the three strands of barbed wire, I'm seriously considering stopping to explain some things to him. C.B., always quicker about coming up with the right words at the right time, says something inconsiderate about the man's mother. The RR man gets really strong wrinkles around his eyebrows and squints and presses his lips together all at the same time. So we sprint from our side of the fence to the highway.

Assuming the standard, thumbs-up hitch-hiking posture, we are passed by only three cars before we hit pay dirt. Car four is a two-door Nash Rambler, colored like the skies seen from Thacker fire tower. C.B. climbs in the back, and I jump in the front. We introduce ourselves and tell where we're headed.

"Oh, yeah," says the driver, "I know where that club is. That's down in the red-light district."

"Where's 'at?" C.B. asks.

The driver smiles and looks at us both, like we should know without him having to tell us.

"It's on Winchester. As a matter of fact, I'm going right by there, and I'll drop you guys off at the front door."

"That's mighty white of you, Mister," I thank him.

"Say what?" C.B. questions from the back seat.

The driver laughs.

"Sorry, C.B., it was just a figure of speech."

"Then you best be re-figgerin'," he threatens.

The driver gets an even bigger kick out of our exchange.

"Where is it you boys are from?" he inquires with that same grin he gave about our not knowing where the red-light district was.

"Oxford."

"This your first time to Memphis?"

"'Tis fer me," C.B. answers.

"I guess you guys are pretty thinly peopled down there compared to this, huh?" he asks and lights a cigarette.

"Yes, sir," C.B. again answers. "Mis'sippi ain't never seen th' likes of this kinda traffic."

"I know what you mean. Some days I feel like a rat in a maze."

"'At's plumb depressin', Mister," C.B. offers with his talent for ending a conversation.

Sight-seeing, I make an effort to take in everything worthwhile. C.B.'s gawking on both sides of the wide streets, too, perhaps even harder than I am. Before I tire of the new views, our ride pulls up to the front of a theater kind of building.

"There it is, boys."

C.B. sizes it up and says, "Maybe this ain't gon' be so bad after all."

I see it differently and think this may not be as fancy a theater as we imagined. Some colored men who don't look like they've dressed for Memphis are standing outside. One man is wearing purple trousers with big bellbottoms, and I know I never saw pants like that before, even at Ole Miss. A neon marquee blinks on and off, "Drinks Reasonable," "Drinks Reasonable," "Drinks Reasonable," over and over.

We thank our driver, and he eases off with that same wide grin of his again. I hope he's smiling because he feels good about giving us a lift…and not because of where he has just deposited us.

"Scott, what if this club's fer coloreds only? You might not can eben get in there with me. You liable to hafta wait outside."

"No way, man. Big city folks outside Mississippi are not like that about integration. This is Memphis. Besides, I'm not too scared to try."

"Naw, you ain't got sense enough to be scared. Come on, then."

At the door and as tall as the door, a glossy black Negro stands with his arms crossed on his chest. At nearly seven feet tall, he towers over us, so big around he looks as if he missed a good chance at being Siamese twins. A stupid looking little golfing-type hat sits on his big head and sort of goes with his squashed nose as if he used to be a boxer. I don't think I'll be mentioning that to him. Although it looks like there's shoulder pads and a bulletproof vest under his orange jumpsuit, I've got a feeling it's all him under there.

"No cover for no cover!" he barks in our faces. "Come right in."

I'm kinda relieved and kinda not, being allowed inside. I'm lying about not being scared. It's looking more and more like a grownup establishment. If C.B.'s mom is dancing here, she must be a go-go girl like I've heard talked about at the barbershop.

"They must be takin' a break," C.B. suggests, obviously not yet sharing my impression of the place.

We ease up to the front for the best seats. Six men, four colored, two white, and all a lot older than we are, are sitting in the first row below the stage. The smell of cigarettes and beer outweighs any and all other odors. A waitress who looks too old to be wearing a miniskirt comes over. We don't push our luck by trying to get something to drink. I stare at her legs until she smiles at me.

The backdrop scenery of the center platform is that of a mountain brook. A fake waterfall is rigged to recycle the same water over and over. It's more like spewing than trickling. Off to the side are a bunch of out-of-place and off-site plastic shrubs that probably wouldn't live in the South if they were real, much less in this dim light.

"'At's a fur cry from th' Little Tallahatchie river bottom," C.B. points out.

"You reckon they'll let us camp here?" I joke.

The music starts up. A beautiful, young blonde girl in a gold bikini with a red, see-through cape dances onto the stage…and now I'm knowing there's not going to be any Opry-type ballet around here. See-through fabric clings to her enticing curves as her body pulsates with the lights and the music. She picks up a lava-lamp, waves it around, and rubs her hands all over it like it feels different from one place to the next. After dancing over to directly in front of me, she sets the lamp down and commences to run her hands all over herself the way she did the lamp.

"I'm not so sure these are all nice girls," I whisper to C.B.

"You jus' now figgerin' out they ain't your high-nosed sorority bitchletts from th' campus?" he responds with more than a hint of disappointment in his voice.

When the dancer makes eye contact with me, she makes an obscene gesture. I'm sure I'm turning red...and that my buddy is grasping the reality of the situation, if his mother is working here.

As the song ends and the first dancer fades away, a slower tune starts. Another pretty lady comes out through a doorway fringed with long strands of beads. Right away, I think she likes me. In rhythm with the music, she struts in a suggestive way. It's like she's connected to the beats.

Dancing directly in front of me, she touches herself...and I would follow her anywhere. What would it feel like for my hands to be doing what she's doing with hers? She dances on down the stage to be in front on an old man. I don't understand why she'd do that. He gets out a dollar bill and sticks it in the elastic of her drawers.

"Did you see the way she was looking at me, C.B.?"

"She'z prob'ly feelin' sorry fer you."

I want her back in front of me alone, noticing me alone. She brings her long blonde hair around to cover up her thinly clad breasts...and drops her bikini top to the floor.

"We should'a brung twenty bucks a piece, instead of ten," C.B. comments.

"I'm just hoping someone comes through that door and a big gust of wind blows her hair out of the way."

I'm thinking surely everyone knows this is the first time we've ever been anywhere like this. We're not old enough to be seeing this woman's top half naked. I'm scared we're fixing to get kicked out. She dances back over to me. My adolescence ends. I lean back and try to appear nonchalant but still peek for all I'm worth. I glance briefly at C.B. to see if he's also playing peep-pie through my girl's golden but in-the-way, hair. Of course he is.

"You're not going to see anything like this at the Ritz or Lyric," I whisper.

"Not 'less'n maybe you could see in th' projector room," C.B. agrees.

My sexy temptress fumbles with the side of her bikini bottom. I try to swallow and can't. When I lick my dry lips, she licks hers. She shows her bare legs and their calf muscles' dimpled seductiveness. She dances from flirtation to rolling her bikini panties down. When she steps out of them, I have to make a conscious effort to keep my breath going. An incredibly lucky little lacy thing is right up against her, with nothing but a tennis shoe string holding it up. When the song ends, she's gone as quickly as she had appeared. I'm wanting to go back there and find her.

As the music begins again, another dancer slips out from behind the dark shadows. She's a black-haired white lady who has such a light complexion she's probably part ghost. To highlight her washed-out look, she's wearing white-tinted stockings and a white silk see-through robe. She has a skunk-stripe colored bikini under her wrap.

Instead of going up on the stage, the ghostly skunk-lady dances over to me. I'm beginning to feel pretty good about always being first. She puts her arm around my back, touching her barely covered breasts up against my shoulder. I lean in toward her…and I've never felt anything so soft.

"How do you like these?" she asks as she pulls out a strand of what are no doubt fake pearls from real cleavage.

"I'm not sure what you're asking about me liking," I manage to answer cleverly.

She makes laughing-eye contact with me, and I gulp all too obviously. Not able to think of anything else to say, I stare at her like a dummy with my mouth open. The harder I try to think of something to say, the more I think of how her complexion is too pale for her to have hair so jet black.

"What's the matter?" she asks with the most tender of voices. "You bashful or something?"

I double swallow, knowing I'm going to be scarcely able to talk. "You're uh, beautiful…everywhere, I mean uh, all over…even, I mean especially your color."

She smiles again and continues to let me stare hard through her transparent nightie…real close. I can see almost everything, as she hides just enough to raise my imagination.

"What are you thinking about, sweetheart?" she asks.

I'm really thinking about my strong desire to touch her all over, but I know I should say something more appropriate. I start talking without knowing what will come out.

"Not much to those little panties, is it?"

She giggles and shakes her wrists, showing off how they are gemmed with plastic pearl bracelets. She comes closer, and I smell the combined flavors of all the fruits I've ever known. When she puts a warm finger under my chin and touches me gently, I hope she feels my slight whisker stubs.

"What you think about a poke?" she asks.

In all my timid modesty, I'm glad she's trying to keep the conversation going, but I'm a little uncomfortable about why she'd ask such a strange question.

"Are you talking about the guy that runs the Catholic Church?"

She shakes her head and moves down the narrow stage. I watch with awe as she swings her hips with such an undulating walk. It's like a cat stalking a cardinal. The thought occurs to me that they may not have any colored girls working here. I hope C.B. doesn't find his mother like this.

I turn to him and ask, "You think you'll know her if you see her?"

"I'll know."

A coppery, cocoa-colored woman with the body of a Sears and Roebuck underwear model comes out of the bead-covered wing. She has a familiar pigeon-toed walk. Cloaked in a sheer, black wrap-around with a long scarf, she sashays over to me instead of to the stage. Her outfit is a sensuous, see-through, with no bikini top. Dark nipples show through in a game of peek-a-boo with the folds of her scarf.

With the alarm going off in the back of my mind that we could be looking at C.B.'s mother, I turn away. I don't want him to see me gawking at her, but there's no place else to pretend to be looking…only at this flirty, floozy Chickasaw-looking woman with a bead and feather choker around her neck. As she leans over, as if to whisper in my ear, she blows in it. Feeling her warm and moist breath, I detect a second alarm. It's that unmistakable scent I've so often compared to a mixture of barbecued potato chips and sardines.

Too quiet for C.B. to hear, she whispers to me in a soft and sexy voice. "How'd you like to tip th' one an' only Memphis Magnolia for my dance, Hon?"

My face flushes. I think my heart and breathing have stopped. "Uh, ma'am, I…uh, really wasn't here when you must have danced. And…uh, I'd like to tip you anyway, but I don't have th' money."

"Done spent your allowance?" she whispers back. Putting on no further airs, she walks around behind me and on the other side of C.B.

I wish now I'd said something smart enough to have kept her by me and away from him. Turning a chair around backward and straddling it, she sets it and herself right up against him. Thinking I don't need to hear this, I try to get up and leave. C.B. puts a trembling hand on my arm and pulls me back toward my chair.

"You lookin' awful blue for such a young fella," she tells him.

"'Bout as blue as a feller can get, I 'spect," C.B. answers in a strained voice.

"I know how to make you feel better. You wanta be not so sad, Sweet Cakes?" She slips her hand on the inside of his leg, just above his knee. "How's about lettin' Mama 'Nolia get ta' better know ya'?"

"'At might be all right," he replies.

"Honey, I'll show you some love like you'll never forget…all for only $20.25."

"An' twenty-five cents?" he questions.

"Laundry, Darlin'. Them sheets hafta be done, too. They ain't gon' do themselves. They ain't that much like little boys."

"You sayin' some little boys have to do fer themselves?"

"You oughta know 'at better'n me."

"'An th' twenty bucks, then…'at's fer what you call love?"

"All right, Precious, you one of them big thinkers an' fast learners, too, huh?" She strokes his cheek with one hand as the other moves up the inside of his thigh.

"Not really. I'm sorta slow to come to some conclusions," a tone of harshness slipping into C.B.'s voice.

"What'chu mean, Angel?" she asks.

"I'm meanin' you got some peculiar ideas 'bout love bein' on an' off, like maybe th' money is all you'd be inter'sted in…you might say."

"Sweet Thing, you might say whatever you wanta say 'bout th' way I know how to love, an' I won't eben charge you extra. You ready to learn 'bout love? What you say?"

"I dunno what to say. I done without fer so long."

"Honey-chile, now you ain't that old. You must not of ever had none a'tall. Is 'at it?" She strokes his leg.

"Uh...." He puts his hand on hers to stop her from going too far.

"'At's it, idn't it? You never had no good lovin' in all yo' livin', have you? It's all right. 'At's somethin' we can do together."

"You know a lot about livin' 'thout love, do you, Lady?"

"Son, Son, just thinkin' 'bout me gettin' to be yo' first is excitin'. I'll show you how much you really don't know 'bout what 'tis you'd like to know more about 'fore you get too confused 'bout th' whole thing. The hole thing—you catch that?"

Instead of laughing at her lame joke, C.B.'s face remains frozen.

"Don't you get it? Didn't you follow me?" she asks.

"I've had some trouble followin' after you."

"Come on then. What you think?"

"Well, it's hard...."

"I bet it is." She tries to slide her other hand further up C.B.'s leg.

He stops her hand again, and his voice trembles. "I was about to say it's hard to say what I think. I'm havin' a tough time tryin' to figger out how to tell you what I do know. It might be you th' one hadn't followed me...a'tall."

"I'm hearin' you, Hon. I'll he'p out. If this is really yo' first sweet brown sugar, I'll take it on as my job to teach you how it's done right. Easy does it...."

"Well...."

"I'm better'n well, Darlin'. Somebody here don't understand just who it is he's talkin' to. I'm not just one of these ordinary gals."

C.B. turns from her and asks me loud enough for her to hear, too, "You got a quarter?"

"That's more like it," she expresses her pleasure.

I remember the red, fingernail-polished quarter I learned to keep in my wallet from listening to the Boy Scouts talk about being prepared for special occasions and emergencies. Wanting to remind C.B. that this is not what the Scout manual had in mind, I dig out that quarter. C.B. takes it and gives it a long, hard spin on the stage in front of us. The three of us watch in silence as it spins around and around and finally settles...on tails.

"Aw...ll right," she exclaims as she again slides a hand well up on C.B.'s leg. "See there, Young'un—tails. That's gotta be what they call one of them omens, right there. Yo' fate's in my hands now, not to mention what else is fixin' to be."

C.B. just looks at her without speaking.

"You go over yonder to that barkeep an' ax him fer us a bottle of North Mississippi Strawberry Wine. Pay him th' twenty big ones and the quarter. There's gon' be a key taped to th' bottom of th' bottle. It'll have a room number on it, and I'll be in there waitin' like you never believed."

C.B. stands and turns to look at the barkeep. Then he looks back down at her. My throat closes up, and my eyes start to water. When I make the mistake of trying to wipe my cheeks with my shirtsleeve, C.B. and Magnolia look right into my teary eyes.

With a puzzled expression, she looks up to C.B. He gives her nothing but his coldest stare. She looks back at me and sees another tear rolling down my cheek. Turning back to C.B., her mouth drops open. She holds her hands to her face and shakes her head slowly, in what must be the revelation of maternity. Her big brown eyes gather tears, and her head drops.

C.B. motions for me to get up and follow him. With a nod and the same blurry eyes I've seen on a crippled dove, C.B. looks down at the Memphis Magnolia. She lifts her head slightly to look out from under her shame with a tentative gesture to touch him.

"I tell you what…." he starts to say something. Then he picks up the quarter and flips it to her.

She instinctively catches it, but slaps it down like a hot horseshoe on the stage in front of us.

"Ma'am," C.B. speaks in a brittle tone, "you just keep this special quarter in remembrance of me. 'At way you can always an' forever have you a good reminder—'at around Taylor, Mis'sippi, this two bits be 'bout all yo' memory's ever gon' mean."

XXVI:

Degree Decree or Melee?

IT'S THE LAST YEAR of high school for C.B. and me. I'm supposed to graduate from Oxford High and C.B. from Oxford Training School, the colored one...newly upgraded to equal but separate. As the Vietnam war looms large, neither of us has firm plans for the next year.

Promised I'll earn a few get-out-of-detention hall credits for it, I volunteer to sit through a recruitment presentation by a cross-state recruiter...from archrival Mississippi State University.

"Forestry might be a field you'd be interested in," the retired professor suggests, "or wildlife management."

Although I came prepared to view our visitor with suspicion, I'm hearing an unexpected turn of talk. On mental point like a bird dog, I'm all ears...and even remember Mr. Jefferson once making reference to a forestry school as something I might do with my life. I can't speak for my high school classmates, but I've not gone wrong listening to Mr. J.

The more I hear, the more interesting I'm finding this counsel and offering. No one else around here has ever talked to me with such optimism and positive affirmation. There's someone on staff who's called the guidance counselor, but so far as I know he just spends all his time dealing with unruly kids.

No sooner than our special guest leaves for Starkville, my study hall coach asserts, "I'll bet a kid could go all the way through Oxford High School and graduate without ever opening a book."

While I'm sitting here contemplating that statement as a belated challenge, Coach continues, "And we'll know for sure by the end of the semester, when we see if Scott makes it."

Being made to feel like a real chump in front of the whole class, I'm set off to thinking—it might be time to get somewhat serious about my future. Trying to remember exactly what it was Mr. J. told C.B. and me about the forestry school several years ago, I recall his talk having had something to do with the seeds of education and planting a couple of acorns. He could say things that sometimes ended up with a strange twist. I may never read all his books, but a lot of people seem to think they're pretty good.

There's a lot coming at me right now. I don't know if it's my trying to convince myself this is fate…or if I'm being manipulated by a flimflam man from State. To spend the rest of my life in a field of work that I might possibly enjoy…that does sound like a plan. Going to State would give me a chance to escape the clubbish atmosphere I don't like here at Ole Miss.

With the school part of the day over, I walk into my Munford's Grocery and greet my father before heading straight for a chocolate milk and cinnamon roll.

"You been working hard today, have you?" Dad asks sarcastically.

"Yes, sir," I answer, pretending to be serious.

I know he's not going to tell me I can't have a drink and something to eat, but I also know we have to go through this daily ritual. As much as anything else, it's probably for lack of having something more meaningful to say. It's not as if we don't care for each other, but I've never been able to talk to him the way I can with Granna. Since my mother died before I even knew her, Granna has been there for me, helping Dad and Papa tolerate me.

Understanding from birth that everyone from Oxford who is white is expected to go to college, I blurt out my plan. "Dad, this fall, after I graduate from high school, I want to go to school at State."

"Boy, sometimes you don't have sense enough to fill a space."

"But, Dad…."

"You can get a good education right here in this town. It'd be foolish to go off to Cow College." He folds the newspaper and slams it down, as though to end the conversation. "And too expensive."

"It's the forestry school, Dad. That's where it is."

"It was that damned Bill Jefferson who put that burr under your saddle, wasn't it? That's the trouble with writers—they can still aggravate you from ten feet under."

"But it's what I've always wanted to do," I argue, without admitting he's right about Mr. J. being the one who first suggested I consider forestry.

"When you finish filling your gut, get this floor swept."

"Yes, sir."

Dad once let out that he wished he'd had the money to finish beyond his two years of college. He said if he had, he wouldn't have to be working two jobs today. I suppose it's double tiring on a crippled man having to run both a grocery business and a taxicab company. With childhood polio badly damaging one leg, Dad has had things tough his whole life through.

As my father limps up to the front to wait for customers to come in, I try to enjoy the good side of my mindless task of sweeping. That is, it frees up my thinking about things besides work itself…and I wonder if I shouldn't just do something like this for a living. Although most of my schoolmates have been dreaming of professions, I'm knowing I'd be called a lot of things before anyone ever got around to calling me college material.

There's an unwritten Oxford decree that says—it doesn't matter what you do with your life, as long as you do it with a degree. It's the curse of living in a college town. With my entire high school graduating class seemingly pressured to live up to the standards of an affluent society, the expectations of higher education are even laid on me.

My colored friend and his classmates don't have that kind of stress on them. C.B.'s the one who should have to go to college. He has no special trouble reading, and he's sharper than a rusty tack when it comes to ciphering. Had he been allowed a background at my school, I'll bet he'd be getting a scholarship, but any consideration of Oxford High School becoming desegregated is somewhere off into the future.

A customer comes in and slaps two dimes down on the counter to buy a nineteen-cent pack of Kools and two boxes of matches. I'm knowing Dad and I are both wanting a smoke, but neither of us will smoke in front of the other one. Dad's trying to set a good example in front of me, and I'm preventing myself from getting the tar beaten out of me.

"Damnation, Son, going off down there a hundred miles away would be about the most dim-witted an idea as anything you could come up with."

I silently sweep and wonder if Dad's not more right than he knows. Maybe I ought not even go to any college. It's a given that I wasn't born under any mathematical stars, and when I try to read, I see enough letters in their reverse sequence to keep me from squaring anything away. A lot of sentences are long enough to let my mind wander before I can make much sense out of them, but here I stand with a Dad ready to try to figure out how to pay my way through college.

C.B. doesn't know what he's going to do either…if anything. As the rest of the world is fast changing, white Oxford is satisfied not to question its status quo. By virtue of doing nothing, it is really being selective about whom and what it ignores. Oxford town has watched closely what is happening at the University. Instead of setting an example with appropriate action, it is only the difficulties and perplexities of integration that so many see…in the form of warnings.

With the University causing as much confusion as clarification, our city fathers and our school board continue living across the proverbial tracks from the well-ingrained racial divide. Campus protests rally for this and against that. The fields of higher education are fertile ground for desegregation…and de facto segregation.

Dad is always coming up with something Presbyterian to say about the students and their ideas. There're such things as Vietnam war protests and peace rallies, women's rights and wrongs, and atrocities like abortions. The way some of the students talk and dress reflects the radical side of what they copy from their TVs…boys wearing tight-fitting pants with floral print shirts, and girls displaying themselves braless under their tops and in short shorts with fishnet stockings. I'm thinking this phenomenon of a sexual revolution is something being enjoyed by everyone but me.

When finishing my sweeping interrupts my daydreaming, Dad stands ready with new orders. "All right, Son, get the feather duster and start at the top of each shelf. Dust down from the top and do them all. You hear?"

"Yes, sir."

Like a captain calling on himself to steer his ship, Dad again moves to the front of the store. When I'm finished dusting, I'll no doubt have just enough time to stamp prices on the newly arrived canned goods. While Dad's trying to tell me The University of Mississippi is right here to help me get a diploma so I can amount to something, I'm knowing he'd really be bent out of shape if he knew I may not be admitted to any university.

The C.A.T., that's A.C.T. to everyone but me, deals with being college entrance qualified or not acceptable. It is said to be difficult enough, but

I'm fearful it may also be unwittingly designed to keep dyslexics like me a good arm's length from university level studies.

Graduating from dusting to stamping cans and putting them on shelves, I start to visualize Army life…opposed to having a college kind of career. It probably wouldn't be so bad if it weren't for the fighting in Vietnam. To hear the nightly news tell it, casualties are escalating beyond all reasonable or expected odds for the fighting men…one of which I might be. So many American lives are being sacrificed that something will soon have to change.

"Don't be all day about it, boy," Dad encourages.

"Yes, sir," I acknowledge but go quickly back to my thoughts about the so-called military police action that's said to be the result of a corporate boondoggle. Granna says there's a special place in hell for lawyers and politicians who use fancy words to hide what they don't want to come right out and say. She says if we had a real leader, he'd lead…and declare war, and more young men would be willing to go. Then we could win and be done with it.

C.B.'s Auntay has the most encouraging slant on war…saying that a soldier dying in defense of this great nation would have one last chance to get his soul saved. That's an opportunity called Purgatory, and I think it's like being led to a trough of Holy Water. You can drink up or decide to be in an eternal need of a dousing.

Our politicians' latest brainstorm involves the deadly serious consideration of instituting a lottery for the military draft. While it all puts the fear of God in me, I don't know what to say or do or believe. Mr. J. was the only one I knew who said he'd been in a real war…and Dad says he was prone to exaggeration on the subject. The Vietnam I see on the boob tube every night looks to me like it would get really old really fast.

"When you're done stamping the stock and putting it up where it belongs, you can go," Dad offers.

"Yes, sir." I almost fondle the last can of potted meat…so happy to be about to get off grocery duty.

AS IF THE COLLEGE entrance exam was not a monumental challenge of sufficient concern, in and of its own, my heartless homeroom teacher/

coach finds a way to make my low score even more humiliating. All my previously humbled pride is so outdone it is put to shame. My ranking on the stupid scale is posted right up there on the chalkboard for one and all to pass judgment on. The only way I can make myself feel the least bit better is by telling myself that I can take the test again, but my teacher is still going to be a sorry S.O.B. for being so insensitive as to put my test score on display.

With another school day behind us, C.B. and I meet up at Dad's store. "Dad, we're thinking we need to find somewhere to work this summer that will pay better than The University Grill."

"Or Munford's Grocery," Dad adds...which is music to my ears. Saying nothing about the latest in C.B.'s colored fashion, my father looks without patronage at my friend's black T-shirt and Afro bushy hairdo.

I'm sure C.B. is about to graduate with flying colors from Oxford Training School. Everyone who didn't see my test score posted on the chalkboard, including Dad, still assumes I'll be going to college in the fall. If I even manage to slip through the system at Oxford High, it'll probably be because they don't want to have me around next year. I'll take it.

"I know something you boys can do this summer," Dad offers.

As uneasy as I am about any employment ideas he might have in mind, I'm equally ready to trade off the grocery store for most anything.

"What is it, Dad?"

"I picked up on something at my last Blue Stocking meeting."

C.B. raises his attention to my dad and then looks at me with a more troubling than questioning expression.

"State Highway 6 is being moved to bypass Oxford. If y'all hightail it down to the employment office, you can get at the head of the labor line. Beat the crowd and get you a good paying job with the Highway Department."

More concerned about avoiding Dad's grocery store and the University's Student Union Grill than about what I might be getting myself into, I recognize my cue to escape. "I'm game, Dad...and I'm gone."

"Good luck," he offers.

C.B. and I head for the government office. As per usual, when I don't know something, my buddy is all questions.

"Did you know 'bout any of this 'fore now?"

"Sort of...I've heard Dad talk about the highway relocation."

"What's a blue stockin' meetin'?"

"It's nothing like the Klan, if that's what you're thinking."

"What, then?"

"It's just a men's club at the Presbyterian Church. They hold with some particular notions about idle hands and the devil's workshop…and that kind of stuff."

"Th' Presbyterians musta took 'at from th' Baptist Bible. I've heared Auntay talk 'at'a way. Now, fore I get myself into somethin' I'll wisht I hadn't'a, I need to hear more 'bout this highway a'movin'."

"You heard everything I did, C.B."

A couple of jailbirds in their black-and-white-striped uniforms are sweeping the street next to the curbs. C.B. and I look hard at each other. Visualizing myself doing that kind of work suddenly gives me the same kind of concern C.B. must have been worrying about all along.

"Come on, Scott, don't 'spect me to go into this highway thing blind. You bound to know mo' 'bout this deal than you lettin' on."

"Well, to hear Dad tell it, there's two things it's got to do with it. One is—a bunch of feebleminded folks voted consciously to screw things up by cutting down enough city trees to make room for four lanes of pavement to funnel the traffic right on past town. Dad says nobody's gonna be stopping to trade at Munford's Grocery…or anywhere else around the Square. That's the thanks merchants like him and their fathers before them get for serving their customers all those years…a royal screwing."

"What's th' other thing?" C.B. asks, as if the first thing was no major concern to him.

"You're not gonna believe it."

"Probably not, but go to head on."

"It's got to do with getting government money…and until they can get everything more evenly leveled out, they're talking about busing some colored people to the white school and some white people to the colored school…even if they have to go right past the closest school to them and end up on the other side of town."

"Like I'm gon' be believin' 'at."

"I knew you wouldn't believe me. That's why I wasn't gonna say anything."

"Well, why would anybody in their right mind believe such as 'at?"

"C.B., I don't know that…I don't even know what I think I know about it."

"I could'a told you 'at," he comes back.

The lady at the employment office takes down our basic information and asks me if I'm sure I want to work with them. She bore down on pronouncing *them*. I tell her, "Yes." She never even questions C.B. We're instructed to report to work Saturday week, at eight o'clock in the morning…at the junction of South Lamar and the new right-of-way for the relocation and four-laning of Highway 6.

Leaving the government office, C.B. looks at me with an expression I interpret as saying, "We done stepped in it now."

"It's bound to beat grocering or having to serve and clean up after college students at The Grill," I respond.

"I'm still thinkin' of them new busin' rules you'z talkin' 'bout. If'n ever'body went to th' closest school to 'em, 'at'd be another good reason fer mixin' folks. But what you said 'bout longer busin'…'at don't make no sense. Ever'body be getting' th' short end of th' stick."

I pick up a twig, break it off, and try to hand the short end to C.B.

"No, no…eben if it is true, you an' me's done grad…ge…ated high school an' got ourselves past 'at kinda nonsense. Ain't nothin' left to do now 'cept enjoy workin' in th' heat of th' hot summer sun on th' highway, an' bein' glad we not in school…or Vietnam."

I give him a high-five but say nothing…knowing there's a little more to it than that for me. My efforts at taking the C.A.T. have turned into a three-step process. The pressure of waiting to hear from my third try includes being told in so many big words that another failed attempt to pass the college entrance exam will close all doors to the institution of higher learning that houses the forestry school.

XXVII:
The Black and White of It

WITH OUR RESPECTIVE HIGH schools being nevermore for me and C.B., summer has at long last set in. Showing up at the job site for our first day of taking on the highway department, I easily spot the head honcho. He's white and standing with his hands on his hips, while everyone else is black and working. This is one boss man who doesn't appear to have pushed away many bowls of beans.

"Morning, sir. Are you Mr. Morganstern?" I inquire.

"Yep." He looks us over, as if to size us up and see if we meet his personal standards…which is a tad humiliating coming from a guy whose head is shaped like a bowling ball with big ears for handles.

"We're looking for work," I inform him.

"Boys, you have found it."

After writing down our names, he starts up with a lecture that sounds like he took lessons from my Dad.

"You can start right here. This is called a tamp. Here's how you run it. Watch. You pick it up and put it down, simply tamping down the corners and edges of fresh-laid sod until it looks like it grew there. Then you move on to the next spot that needs to look natural. Think you can do it?"

"Yes, Sir."

"Yessir."

"Then have at it. You're on the clock. Take this tamp and that one over there and go to work. All I wanta see outta y'all is assholes and elbows."

"Yessir."

"Yes, sir."

"There's a water cooler under the new overpass. But don't be hanging around there all day, talking instead of working. I don't mind a man stopping for water once in awhile. In this heat, if you don't take on enough water, you'll likely pass out on me."

"Thank you," I answer.

"Oh, you're quite welcome," he answers in a voice that insinuates we won't last.

With the summer sun sapping our energy, tamping turns out to be a tiring job, but nothing C.B. and I can't handle. It's enough like sweeping in that it leaves my mind free to think about other things besides work. This happens to be a time when some things in my mind need sorting out. All of the other workers are either laying sod or driving trucks. We are the only tampers.

By midmorning, we still haven't taken a rest. C.B. may be trying to prove how tough he is, but I'm simply showing him I'm as stubborn as anybody. Boss man Morganstern announces a mandatory fifteen-minute water break. Everyone heads toward the half-constructed overpass.

I'm the closest, so I'm the first one to arrive in the rare shade. Going for the big Igloo water cooler, I discover one Vienna sausage can that is apparently used as the community drinking cup. Before I can figure out the sanitary thing to do, nine Negroes are standing in a circle around me. All eyes are on me and the public cup on top of the cooler.

For a white person to drink from the same container a colored has used is something that is not done in these parts…and going without water is not an option. In that I've already picked up the tin can, everyone's expressions and stares will continue until I get myself out of this dilemma. The unwritten and yet unbroken rule of separation means nothing to me, having grown up using the family gourd on Auntay's back porch. Since C.B. and I are the only ones who know that, I make a larger production than necessary out of rinsing the cup out. I drink and stagger back from the cooler, pretending I'm going to pass out. Everyone gawks at me, so I go for my fake, painful dying routine.

"Now, by golly," C.B. seizes the opportunity to make sure everyone gets it. "Th' University of Ole Miss ain't th' only place 'round here 'at's been inte'graded."

Through emotionally teary eyes, I see that one and all are finally brought to a heartfelt laughter. A short but exaggerated round of clapping and cheering tells me that from this moment on, I'll be treated as a part of the work force team…if not accepted as an equal.

AS CONVERSATION HELPS WORKDAYS go by, I hear details about the colored world that I'm not sure even C.B. knew before now.

"Did you ever take the college entrance exam, C.B.?" I ask.

"You still worryin' 'bout that thing?"

"Yes, and I still haven't heard from my last try. Now, answer me. Did you ever take it?"

"Naw."

I'm not sure whom it's a reflection on, but C.B. has always claimed he was smarter than most of his teachers at Oxford Training School. Rumor has it that one of the main criteria for teaching there is to be in attendance more often than your students.

"Why don't you check it out, C.B.? Score good enough on it, and you might be eligible for a scholarship or something."

"Yeah, right," he answers with sarcasm.

After a week of relentless aggravation from me, C.B. tracks down his former agricultural Vo Tech teacher to explore the possibilities of taking the A.C.T. The main-most teacher, as C.B. calls him, explains the reason they don't give the test to Negroes. According to him, they don't want them to be disappointed at not making a good enough score to go on with any further education.

ONE MORNING, A THIRD of the way through summer, I proudly greet C.B. by pulling an envelope from my right rear pocket. "I made it."

"Aw…right!" he responds knowingly. "You finally passed it?"

"You bet ya', I did." I raise my arm in triumph. "Three's a charm. I kicked the A.C.T.'s ass this time."

"What'd you make?"

"I got me a 15."

"By th' skin of yo' teeth, huh?" he grins.

"That's all right. I passed. I'm going to State an' gonna major in wild-life management at the forestry school."

"Good fer you," C.B. says in a tone of resignation. "You get yo' lily-white-assed college ree'ferral to go with it?"

"Deferral, C.B. And, no, not yet. First I'll have to get an acceptance letter from Mississippi State. A score as low as mine won't allow for any competition, so I'm thinking it'll depend on how many slots they've got to fill. I may ask Papa to lean on our congressman a little."

"I oughta figgered as much."

I've never detected so much jealously in C.B.

"You ain't aspirin' to rise high'ern your natural station or nothin' like 'at, is you?"

"Come on, C.B. Don't be that way. You know ever since I was old enough to take to Granna's brainwashing, she's been drumming the notion into me that I had to go to college."

"Ain't no 'ifs,' 'ands,' or 'buts' 'bout that. All them big 'spectations laid on you, you can't be lettin' nobody down."

"That's right."

"Won't be long 'fore you'll be one of them distinguished draft dodgers." More fiercely than usual, he begins our morning's work of tamping down sod.

"Get off it, C.B. It's not like that, and you know it."

"I know it's gon' be a damn shame when you go down yonder and flunk out."

"C.B.?"

"What?"

"You don't understand anything about…being white."

"You figgered 'at out all by yourself, did you?" he snorts with a scorn.

"Man, I thought you'd be proud for me. What do you want out of me?"

"I dunno, Scott. I don't rightly know. But you sho' right 'bout one thing—It would be different if you was black. And it's *black*, now. Not colored."

With that remark, I'm thinking he must have heard this black talk from some of these new coloreds he's been working with. I guess from now on, I'll have to start watching my colors. For the remainder of the day, we work with very little conversation between us. I tamp harder than usual.

258

Compared to the others on our near-chain-gang labor force, C.B. and I hold up well. Boss man Morganstern even compliments us on doing a good job. Due to the hard work, the sun, and folks' frequent letters from their draft boards, the highway department has a pretty high rate of employee turnover. As new laborers, always black, show up and ask to be put to work, I wonder what my white friends from school are doing this summer…or if it's me that's missing something they know about—that I don't.

One day the smallest two of a group of new employees are given our tamps. C.B. is glad to get rid of his and tries to tell me we're being promoted. Not knowing how the sod-laying thing is going to work out, I'm reluctant to give my tamp up. Tamping one-foot square, four-inch thick sod clods was something we could do to the satisfaction of our boss. From working for my Dad, I know what it's like to have a boss that's hard to please.

A few days after adapting to our new jobs, the boss comes over and asks if I can drive a truck. The appeal of driving that two-and-a-half-ton truck instead of having to handle squares of dirt and grass is too much to resist. It's too good an opportunity to tell him the truth. It'd ruin an exciting prospect.

"Yes, sir. I drive the chicken truck back home on the farm all the time."

C.B. looks at me and almost breaks up. The only reason he doesn't give me away is because Morganstern has his back to him.

"Then I want you to accompany our next driver to the sod field," Morganstern says. "If you prove to him you can drive, that'll be good enough for me."

Growing up next door to Haney's Chevrolet lot, I have sat behind steering wheels for untold evenings and pretended I was driving. I'd push in clutches and shift the gears…and I do know which gears are where and how to find reverse. I've just never done it with a motor running and the truck moving. Under Dad's training for about a year, I have been learning to drive his automatic transmission Chevy. Who's to say I couldn't drive a big truck with a manual transmission? I've watched others shift their sticks. With a little on-the-job training and a lot of encouragement from my trainer, I'll learn to drive one of the flatbeds.

Going to and from the sod field in Water Valley presents no problem. The hard part of my new assignment is in trying to back the truck behind a forward moving tractor, so that the conveyor can operate over the center of my truck bed…with the tractor and truck moving along in unison. While all this happens, the two men standing on the back of my truck to catch and stack the squares of sod can easily be knocked five feet to the ground…if I don't keep everything lined up.

When I describe the whole deal to C.B., he can't believe how some of the drivers stand on the running boards and look back as they steer with their left hand and use their right hand on the dash-operated throttle.

"Don't look at me like that, C.B. You'd have lied too if Morganstern would have offered you the job."

He stares at me with eyes full of jealous anger. "I'd just like to know if he thinks bein' white would make you a better truck driver than anybody else."

"Don't try to make me feel guilty for being white."

"You just don' get it, do ya'?"

BY MIDSUMMER THE HIGHWAY 6 bypass is sodded. We're all asked if we'd like to move to Meridian, Mississippi, to sod up and down a new interstate highway they are building down there. With a little over a month still separating me from trying my hand at college books, it sounds like a good plan. C.B. likes it as well.

On the day before we're to leave, Auntay asks us to sit on the porch with her for a spell. I'm expecting her usual outhouse philosophy on how we'd better behave. It soon becomes apparent that there's something else…and it's really bothering her. Her eyes are puffed up as if she's been crying. She's about to lay something heavy on us. It's not like her to talk this soft unless something big's coming down.

"What's going on, Miss Belle?" I anxiously ask.

She settles her wide bottom in a chair that's too small and then complains about one of them. "You done grown too 'phisticated to call me Auntay?"

"No, ma'am. I was just trying to be respectful."

"Well, I declare."

C.B. and I both stand almost at attention. His impatience takes over, "You lookin' like th' sun ain't shinin' in yo' back door no more. What you wanta tell us, Auntay?"

Hearing C.B. repeating words she knows he's heard her sing, she tries to grin. Her slight smile is gone as quickly as the effort was made.

"It's news 'bout Chicken-Hawk, boys."

"He been kilt?" C.B. presses fearfully for the rest of the story.

"Dunno fer sure. He been listed…missin' in action." She doesn't have any more details…just the cold hard fact that Chicken is unaccounted for in Vietnam.

The Chicken didn't read well or think too fast, so it's likely the Army did the only logical thing they could have done with him…and made him into a grunt. He was probably just another number on the missing list…maybe left over there and finished forever. It's like being slipped the green weenie was his destiny.

Chicken-Hawk's questionable status, to my thinking, makes for a strange and jumbled up feeling. He was a bully and a braggart, a petty tyrant whose torment of me was likely a reflection of his rage against all whites. As my old nemesis, I despised him…but I didn't wish him dead. He and C.B. had some kind of bond that I never did understand. Maybe he's just lost. That wouldn't be so bad.

WITH OXFORD'S CITY LIMITS in our rearview mirror, we grind gears and chug the big sod truck down Highway 7 south. Morgenstern would have a cow if he knew I was letting C.B. drive. Perhaps driving will help my buddy get his mind off the Chicken. If he wrecks, we'll both have to go to Vietnam to get away from the financial responsibility. My transistor radio hangs from the dash and blares away.

"Scott, all I can 'member th' Chicken ever wantin' outta life was a little respect…an' maybe just to get out of Niggertown with a dab of dignity."

I'm thinking—it could be…the Chicken accomplished all those things. I doubt he would have ever gotten any more respect or dignity than maybe someday having his name put on a big memorial somewhere. People could see it and note how he gave his all for his country.

While I was more into worrying about C.B. burning up the clutch than paying any attention to the scenery, we passed the Yocona River. Upstream from our beloved Enid Dam, a song with some telling lyrics comes on. It's something like—"driving a Chevy on a levee on the day that I die." C.B. pulls over on the road shoulder and stops without speaking. He gets out and takes a few quick steps around in a small circle before getting back in to continue.

"I'm okay," he says. "We'll go now. I'll be...best I can." A big tear rolls down his shiny black cheek, leaving a streaky, salty-looking track.

I assume the words to the music caused C.B.'s reaction. His getting out and walking around may have somehow been to release something...but I know he's still thinking about Chicken.

"C.B., if you do get your butt drafted, you'll probably enjoy getting out of Mississippi and seeing some of the world."

The truck swerves as C.B. wipes his eyes on his sleeve. "Yeah, at least I'd be gettin' gone."

"That's right. There's no telling what all you can get into. You might find some of that greener grass Mr. J. told us of...or some of that love Chicken was always lying about."

"Now, 'at could happen. 'Cordin' to...uh, 'cordin' to th' Chicken-Hawk, there's women what hang around Fort Polk on paydays that know how to he'p you spend your money."

"And I probably won't be able to find a college girl that'll give me so much as the time of day."

"If you did, you'd likely be hollerin' fer me to come help. I can hear you now, 'Help, C.B., help me, what do I do next?'"

"She-ee-it!"

We don't ride in silence long before C.B. starts up again. "Those Gooks prob'ly hadn't eben made th' bullet what's got my name on it."

"To hear the TV tell it, they don't make their own ammo. The Communists keep them supplied."

"There you go, right there—them Commies prob'ly don't eben know how to spell C.B. in Russian."

"Chinese."

"I thought you said...."

"Never mind, C.B. I don't really know any more about it than you do."

"Well, Chicken knows...or knew. He said sometime he couldn't tell who needed shootin' at and who didn't. How you gon' fight a war like that...when you can't tell who's a Com'nist and who ain't? 'Cordin' to

Chicken, you jus' gotta shoot in there an' whoever don't crawl off…they count as what's called *confirmed*."

"I guess it's not all black or white…I mean, you know what I mean."

"Sorta, I do, Scott." He pulls over to the shoulder of the highway again. "I think you best drive fer a while, now. I got me some serious ponderin' to try an' figger out."

XXVIII: Chip Ghost and the Klan

A SIREN SCREAMS ABOVE the hum of our 350 V-8 sod truck.

"I be dipped," C.B. exclaims and pulls the 2 ½-ton flatbed Ford to the right-hand side of the downtown street.

A Meridian city policeman swaggers up to the driver's side of our door-less cab. "Let me see yo' license, boy," he demands.

"Mr. Patrolman, sir," I interrupt, "I'm teaching him to drive. We're on the way to Enterprise from Oxford. He's supposed to be ready to take his test and get his license there," I lie.

"Was I talkin' to you?" the officer asks. "There's a right way and a wro—"

A radio call breaks through the policeman's lecture. Apparently he's being dispatched to a domestic squabble that's turned into something of an emergency.

"Y'all lucked out this time, 'cause I've gotta go." He looks at me. "If you got a license, I want the two of you trading places right now. And if I catch either one of you in Meridian again yo' butt's gon' be a garden an' I'm gon' be th' plow. You hear me?"

"Yessir."

"Yes, sir. Thank you."

As I pull out in the traffic, C.B. comments, "This place looks mo' like Memphis than it do Oxford."

"Yeah, there's too many folks here."

"'Least ways two too many. I'd just as soon figger out a way to go 'round Meridian, Mis'sippi, on th' way back."

A relatively uneventful trip for the remainder of the way brings us to where the Chunky River crosses paths with the right-of-way clearing for construction of Interstate 59. The boss man is standing with his hands on his big hips as we drive up.

"I know when y'all left, and I know what time it is now. If I catch you speeding again, you're gonna be laying sod, and I'll be finding me a new driver. You got that?"

"Yes, sir." I hang my head and take the rap for our speeding. Even though C.B. was driving most of the way, I figure it would be worse on both of us if I revealed enough of the truth to defend myself.

Before we left Oxford, Mr. Morganstern explained that arrangements had been made for the blacks to be put up at a boardinghouse. For five dollars a night, coming right out of their paychecks, my co-workers are to be furnished rooms, setup breakfasts, supper meals, and a place to bathe. They'll have to buy their own noon meals but will be provided daily transportation to a filling station where there's an attached café.

According to the boss, the boardinghouse is not the kind of place a white boy can stay. I'm informed that if I agree to keep an eye on the equipment, sleep in my truck, and bathe in the river, I can double as a night watchman and be paid what's called the "differential."

Twenty-five percent over and above my regular pay and an obvious lack of alternatives for lodging are more than enough to sway me into taking the offer. Although I'll have the same lunch deal as the rest of the crew, my first and third meals of each day will have to be scrounged up.

"C.B., I don't really want to stay out here by myself."

"I can't help it. I got to go with th' others."

"No, you don't."

"It's best," he insists and climbs on the back of a truck everyone refers to as the work-wagon.

As I watch him ride off toward a hot meal, I think how lucky I am for having brought fishing line and hooks from home. I figure I can catch my supper right out of the river. For the first thirty minutes, I try every fishing bait from fresh dug earthworms to creek bank grasshoppers, all to no avail.

Just when I'm about to give up, my line starts upstream. It's hard to set the hook when your fishing pole is a limb that's been cut off. The resistance of whatever it is that's on the other end of my line doesn't feel quite right. The amount of give is as if I'm pulling against a dead weight.

It could be a turtle. I'm also remembering a Yocona River oxbow grennel's tug. It felt like this. They, too, try to stay on the bottom and slowly pull instead of running. If it's not a turtle, that's what I'll bet I'm about to land for my supper…a stinking cotton fish.

Substituting myself for a drag, I walk up the creek with the line to prevent it from breaking. As my surprise wears down, I manage to horse it up on the edge of the bank. It's a far cry from a catfish supper…or a turtle or even a grennel. It's an eel. I wonder if such a slimy-looking thing as this could possibly be edible. If C.B. were here, we'd at least try it.

Living off the land isn't so much fun when you're doing it by yourself. The more I look at this thing, the more I lose my appetite. Figuring C.B.'s eating a hot meal right about now, I make a vow that where we eat lunch tomorrow I'll pick up an extra can of Vienna sausage or lunch meat or something along that shelf to save for my supper. Maybe I'll do sweet rolls for breakfasts.

State vehicles and construction company equipment are all circled up in what I call my wagon train. In the center of everything, I place my truck seat on the ground. From the knees down, I'll have to hang off, but my head, back, and butt will have a good bed. With a cheery little fire crackling as my companion and so many stars to gaze at, accommodations could be worse.

Late night brings a family of four skunks. As they inspect my camp, I decide not to bother them. Happily for me, they must have made the same decision…not to bother me. The remainder of my first evening camping is about as empty as going hungry. Doing without supper and breakfast is something I won't let happen again. Morning bathing in Chunky River is coldly exciting.

The first half of the day's work turns out to be identical to what we did in Oxford, delivering and laying sod where the earth has been worked over. When time for lunch comes, we're all loaded up on a flatbed, and Mr. Morganstern drives us to Enterprise.

"How'd your morning go, C.B.?" I ask.

"All right, I reckon. Yours?"

"Good. What you figure we'll have for lunch?"

"Supposed to be hot plate lunches," one of C.B.'s new friends intrudes on our conversation.

"Butt end of th' Baptist bird, prob'ly," C.B. guesses.

266

Probably for my sake, the boss demonstrates how to drive ten miles an hour. The rest of the crew likes it because it's time they don't have to work. As a driver, I like work.

When we arrive in Enterprise, the blacks line up outside a small café window, through which they can order their meals. As is the custom, white folks go inside where there are two six-foot tall electric fans and four big tables at which to sit and eat. The blacks have to sit out on the curb and eat with flies bothering them…in hundred-degree heat.

From a side door, a house cat is being fed scraps. I wonder if C.B. and the others will equate their treatment to that of the animal…or if they have grown so used to this sort of thing that the comparison doesn't occur to them. I wonder how long those inside will simply look the other way, pretending they don't notice.

If I weren't so dirty from unloading sod off my truck, perhaps the segregation here wouldn't be so bothersome to me. Being aware that I'm the only white person on the crew is but a part of what I feel. By all standards except my skin color, I should stay out here with the black laborers. We workers have all been handling the same dirt. With the exception of me, the men going inside are foremen and big shots. None of them are mere laborers except for me.

I could enter but might be run out for being so filthy. On the other hand, if I sit out on the curb with the blacks, the white folks inside will not like it and will likely let me know about it. Part of me wants to sit outside on the curb and eat with my crew. I want to continue to be accepted by them, but this is looking like an ugly scene no matter where I go. The choice would be easier if I were a black…or at least the choice would already have been made for me.

C.B. looks at me, and I can tell he's waiting to see what I'll decide. My so-called buddy did choose to go with the other blacks and sleep at the boardinghouse. He could have chosen to stay with me and camp out. He'll probably get to go out gallivanting around at night without taking me. With a sideways glance, I admire the shade and the cooler, more comfortable place to sit and eat on the inside. I am a truck driver…and that's more than being a laborer.

Without making a conscious decision, my words just come out. "I'll see you after lunch, C.B."

He looks at me like my decision was what he knew I would do all along…and that sort of hurts. I'm thinking I've made the right decision, as electric fans cool my sweaty, dirty self. Regret for my sweltering fellow workers stays with me…as I get ready to fill up with a lunch of farm-fresh vegetables and country-fried steak. A quart-sized glass of sweet and minted iced tea will help wash down the guilt I feel about the less than mixed-up rules on segregation…not to mention the feeling that I just stabbed my best friend in the back.

Behind the glassed-in counter, a sawed-off shotgun stands propped up in plain view. It's a clear statement that no one should challenge the overall racial arrangement of things…not at this time and not in this place. While the rest of the country is bringing attention to integration through sit-ins, me doing a sit-out here would have done no good. It would have no doubt only branded me as a communist conspirator. Infiltrating Enterprise, Mississippi, with even the slightest suggestion of a civil rights movement would likely been met by a heavy hand of the local law.

As the workday passes and quitting time approaches, the black laborers become increasingly excited about something. C.B., not being his normal, sociable self around me, goes off with his new friends. I return to my camp, left to only imagine what's happening with my friend and what I'm not a part of.

IN THE DAYS THAT follow, C.B. and company make a habit of coming to work talking about their adventures with girls from the nights before. They talk about females in ways I have only fantasized about. While I'd like to think the crew is merely putting on to try to get a rise out of me, it becomes apparent that there's a degree of truth in some of their talk. For the second time this summer, I'm realizing I'm being left out of something special. Again, I wonder if things wouldn't be better for me if I were black.

My nights are so boring it's good that the skunk family has become regular visitors. I depend on its members like imaginary sheep jumping a little skunk-fence until I fall asleep, but on my ninth night of camping out and counting, a horde of human visitors invade…as if right out of the heart of Dixie. With no apparent veil of segregationist secrecy, Mr. Morganstern is among those who have come…all decked out in white robes and little pointy hoods. Unlike what I expected from having seen them on TV, their hats don't include masks.

In a circle of brotherhood around me, the Imperial Wizard of the Confederate Gray Knights of the KKK introduces himself and takes charge. I'm announced to one and all as their visitor, even though I thought this was my wagon train. They call me "mister" and each other "sir," to the point of phony exaggeration. In a credo of white supremacy, they promise this and threaten that. I'm sure their dress and actions are meant to be enticing…as their cheap talk about niggers intensifies. From my life-long friendship with C.B., I know blacks' insides are the same as mine.

Two weeks from tonight, there will be a planning meeting at the Church of the Holy Pentecostal Ghost, a white church between Rose Hill and Enterprise. The primary precepts of the Lauderdale County Klan will be discussed. The agenda will also take up how and when to deal with a black church. What becomes clear now is that they are considering blowing the CMB Church off the face of Rose Hill. The Wizard, himself, offers me a personal invitation.

"You wanta run with th' big dogs, Scott?" Morganstern whispers reinforcement to the Imperial Invitation.

"I'll try to make the meeting," I lie.

Thinking about the way I have always felt for the life of Negroes, I figure about the last thing they need is a bunch of guys hiding under white bed linen and giving them a harder time than they've already got. It will take more than the doctrine I'm hearing here to impress me into enlisting. I can't buy into this, despite being hurt over how my best buddy seems to have abandoned me for his new running mates.

Well after I've tired of their talk, they finally finish their rambling account of the Klan manifesto and ease off as sneakily as they had arrived.

Unlike my typical nightlife of star-gazing and skunk watching, workdays pass quickly. With little more than hard labor being of much interest in the day, I'd probably do booze by night if I could do it without the day-after headache. I'd consider infiltrating the Klan and pretending to be going along just to have something to do, if they weren't so sick and hateful.

Catching me away from his other employees one day, Work Supervisor Morganstern reminds me of the upcoming KKK meeting. Instead of coming right out and asking me to go with him, he simply quizzes me over how I feel about them and their principles. I put him off by telling him I'm giving them some serious thought…without letting him know what an asinine bunch I really think they are.

By the hardest I persuade C.B. to relinquish an evening from his boardinghouse routine in order to camp one night with me. While sharing with him the disgusting talk and actions of the KKK at their recent meeting, an idea as plain as black and white comes. It's almost as if Mr. J. is talking to me from his grave…as the family of skunks comes rancidly prissing along.

"Sit still," I instruct. "We don't need to disturb them. I've been seeing them almost every night. They won't bother us if we just sit still."

As they eventually lose interest in our camp and saunter away, C.B. asks, "Scott, you 'member 'at world record rat we snuck in th' Ritz?"

"And Chicken-Hawk's reaction to it," I respond.

"An' Sassy's," C.B. laughs. "You say these polecats come regular?"

I look at C.B., and he smiles back. I declare, "Let's do it. As Mr. J. might have said, if we were merely to sniff around and scratch underneath the surface of possibilities, we'd probably stumble on something that would help cure the ills of that secret society."

"'Cept he'd'a said it better'n 'at."

I'm thinking this could be the very opportunity I need to get back in C.B.'s good graces.

"What'cha reckon would be best to 'tract 'em to a trap?" he asks.

"I noticed a house cat being fed outside the door at the restaurant."

"Yeah, whatever scraps they throwin' out th' door. 'At oughta be good enough," he agrees.

The next day I take it upon myself to do the preliminary leg work and check out where the Klan will formulate the details of their plan. One look at the abbreviation on the sign of the Church of the Holy Pentecostal Ghost and my imagination goes to work. I promptly dub it as The Chip Ghost's.

With the front door and the rear door both opening to the outside, wedges could be placed under them to prevent any Halloween-like bigots on the inside from opening the doors. If each of the three windows on the two sides of the church was nailed in place from the outside, the jerks on the inside would not be able to jerk the windows open. I can feel fate smiling as the perfect plan materializes.

AS THE TIME FOR me to try my hand at college draws near, C.B. decides to return to Oxford when I do. We strategically schedule the departure date from our summer jobs to coincide with the day the Klan is to have their meeting at the Chip Ghost's. The night before our last day, we position our box-trap crate on a highway department tarp and bait it with the café's house cat food scraps. Then we hide and wait.

When the mother skunk and her three half-grown kittens make their nightly visit, they head for the food scraps and begin to chow down. At the appropriate time, C.B. pulls the business end of the strategic string, and our propped-up crate drops with a tripping success. The skunks, standing on the tarp, are now enclosed by the crate. After running over to pull the canvas up and over the top, C.B. quickly ties it. Leaving the smell of a trail of skunk perfume behind, we manage to transport the crate to the bed of a Landcaster Construction Company pickup.

"They'll get better into th' spirit of things after a night of airin' out in th' peace an' dark," C.B. comments.

Our captives and their covered cage are delivered to a wooded holding site. It's a honeysuckle thicket about fifty yards downwind from the little white church where the Klan will meet.

For our last day of work the boss man brings a watermelon. He says the juicy surprise is in lieu of a going away party for C.B. and me. At the end of the workday, as we say our goodbyes, Morganstern whispers to me, "Scott, you keep the faith now. Get involved up there in North Mississippi."

"Yes, sir." I shake his hand in fake assurance.

Pretending to be walking to the bus stop, C.B. and I make our way to the Chip Ghost's. The honeysuckle patch seems calm enough. Apparently, the smell hasn't shifted enough to let the proverbial polecats out of the bag…and our plan is still on "go."

With a hammer and some nails that were sort of borrowed from C.B.'s segregated boardinghouse, we secure the church windows. Each is left with an opening of about four inches so as not to draw suspicion…or allow anyone to crawl out. Having nothing to do now but wait for the Klan, we take up a good hiding place and commence to talk.

There's a lot said about our summer but few ideas about uncertain futures. C.B., who wonders where all his wages went, has no firm plans other than to take one day at a time. He says he'll go home and consider staying on with the state highway department if they've got work there.

Since he won't be getting a college deferral, I expect him to be drafted before long.

"'Cordin' to what ever'body say, I can work durin' th' spring an' summer enough to draw unemployment durin' th' fall an' winter. If th' state'll work me 'at away, I might go fer it."

Without my answering, he goes on to explain the way someone from the state will help him determine how long he would have to work each year in order to fit into the system. Drawing the maximum amount of unemployment for the minimum amount of time spent working seems to be the number one goal of such a deal. I think it's more like a lack of ambition than a choice among limited opportunities.

I don't suppose the highway department mentioned that in addition to hard work this arrangement would lock their workers into a perpetual minimum-wage world. Some of these employees may like waiting around and doing nothing between work, but I'm doubting C.B. can be happy that way.

"I don't know, C.B.," I grumble uneasily. "I wish I knew enough to say…but I'm afraid my argument about your plans wouldn't even burst your bubble."

"I figger I can get on a loggin' crew an' work th' fall an' winter on th' sly. I hear tell—if'n I get paid cash 'stead of by check, it won't mess up what they call unemployment. If'n 'at don' work out, they's always th' cotton gins at Taylor an' Oxford. They'll get to rollin' 'long 'bout September through November, 'fore we start back huntin'."

I'm glad to hear his comment about continuing to hunt with me. After C.B. had spent so much time with the other blacks on our crew, I was afraid we'd drifted too far apart to still be planning hunts together. Darkness takes over, and we doze off for a spell. On schedule, the Klan shows up and occupies the Chip Ghost's.

C.B., with the clearer head, says, "Let's give 'em another fifteen minutes. We wanta be sure it ain't no more of 'em comin' 'at could drive up on us."

No one else shows during the extra time. As if it were our signal to attack, the KKK begins a fervent recitation of their cloud-white creed. Stooping to slip past the windows on the side of the church, I work my way around to the front door. After placing the wedge under the door so it won't open, I crawl back around to the rear exit to join C.B. and our four furry potential Klan members.

As the KKK garbles in unison, Top Ghost quotes some notion that they are superior to niggers. Hearing this, C.B. joins me in an expression of disgust. As his nod to me says "now," I know we're right about where we need to be, exactly when we need to be here. In fact, our timing is as good as it's going to get for persuading this bunch to see reason.

Carefully untying the tarp and lifting the crate, we swing the peacefully covered contents for a one, two, three sling. I quietly open the church's back door and then grasp the crate with both hands to help C.B. swing the crate for a good toss. On the count of three we fling the black-and-white fur balls as far as they will sail. C.B. slams the church door shut, and I quickly slide our wedge under it.

Making fast tracks away from the church and the yelling Klansmen, we're soon through the woods to a large, creek-cooled can of tomato juice we'd left waiting for washing off skunk scent. Since we were lucky enough not to get squirted, we drink the tomato juice and wash ourselves with straight soap and water.

"Leave th' can fer fisherman," C.B. suggests. "It'll be good fer holdin' worms."

We speed-walk to Enterprise. C.B. hides behind the enormous leaves of a multiple-stemmed umbrella magnolia tree across the highway from the bus stop. I run over and buy our tickets. Assuming the Klan doesn't somehow bust out, air out, and beat the 9:20 evening bus going north, we'll run over and board at the last second.

"We probably done 'at group of goons a favor," C.B. states.

"How you figure that?" I ask.

"Whoever heard of bombin' a church? Man, they was on a collision course with th' law."

"I hope we didn't prevent that," I respond , laughing.

As the unmistakable sound of spewing air brakes claims my attention, our ride comes in sight. I soon recognize the other squeaking bus sounds and smell the diesel fuel and fumes. With no Klan in sight, we sprint across the road. The bus door opens. I grab the handrail and take two steps at a time. C.B. climbs in after me. We are barely ahead of the compressed air sounds of the door closing behind us.

About a dozen folks are scattered throughout the bus. All of them are white, but none look like any of the bunch from the Klan. We give our tickets to the driver, and I throw my gear on a seat about four rows from the front. I climb over my bag to plop down next to the window, but C.B. stops in the aisle. I point to the vacant seat right across the middle of the bus from me and my bag. He stands, looking at me as if I've got his seat or something. I'm thinking surely he doesn't want to sit right up against me in this heat…not when we've got all this room to spread out. He still doesn't say anything.

"Throw your bag over there in that seat and sit next to it," I suggest. "That way we'll both have a window."

In spite of my spelling it out for him, C.B. continues to stand in silence. He looks at the bus driver, then back to me.

"What's the matter?" I probe.

Again, C.B. looks back at the driver. I look up front to see why. The bus driver is shaking his head back and forth, answering "no" to a question that I didn't realize C.B.'s eyes and expression must have been asking. The unspoken seating rules for riding this bus are being visually explained to my friend.

Memories come back to make me recall the stenciled WHITES ONLY letters on the Lafayette County Courthouse water fountain, and I can now read the unwritten regulations, posted as if in black and white…all over the faces of the passengers.

Before I can figure out what to say, C.B. speaks up. "I 'spect I best go back a little further."

He walks to the back of the bus and sits down with his sad and disgusted frown. Taking up my gear, I move through the spellbound silence to the back of the bus to join him is his frustration. I don't say anything. I figure he knows what I'm thinking.

"Scott, 'fore you go off to college an' I get drafted…you know what we need to do?"

"Oh yeah, and we'll do it, too."

"Do what?" he asks.

"Next time this bus comes through Oxford, we'll turn some of those little black-and-white furry fellows loose on it."

"Man, it's plumb spooky th' way yo' mind works."

XXIX:
Fancy French Boutique

"MORNIN', MIZ TAYLOR. I brung 'at quart of chow-chow I vowed I'd put up fer you, home-growed an' handmade."

"I sure do appreciate that, Belle." Granna invites Auntay into the screened back porch. "I hear tell it's been tight finding jar lids this year."

"Well, I'm gon' tell you somethin' 'bout them jar lids," Auntay offers. "I got my own idear 'bout what's really goin' on there."

"Pull up that rocker and take a load off, Belle."

"I wisht I could stay a spell, Miz Taylor. I thank you kindly, but I gots to get back to work. I told 'em I wouldn't be gone but a few minutes."

"You've got my curiosity up now. What were you about to say on the shortage of jar lids?"

"A gov'ment 'spirasy is what it is. Ever'body lettin' on how they can't get no lids…an' th' whole time them companies got too many jars is what 'tis."

"You could be on to something there. Anyway, I surely can't thank you enough for the chow-chow. I've been known to go get a spoonful and eat it straight, without even putting it on black-eyed peas or butter beans or anything."

"It goes pretty good on crackers. I seen where Mister Scott's home from school. Zat just fer th' weekend?"

"Yes, he claims he really likes it at State, but he hardly misses a weekend coming home."

"'At's good. I'd be powerful proud of that. I'll see you later, Miz Taylor." Auntay turns and heads back toward the restaurant.

"Bye, Belle, and thanks again."

WALKING AROUND THE SQUARE, I'm trying to see how Oxford has fared during my first year of college.

"Honk!" comes a sharp blast from a vehicle.

I turn to see if someone's trying to get my attention. Sure enough, it's C.B. in a '54 Ford pickup. He mocks turning his steering wheel pretending to be about to run over me. In an exaggerated escape, I jump farther than necessary. He stops, bails out, and extends his handshake, pumping my arm for all I'm worth. Like a well-rooted bois d'arc tree, he stands with a firm grip.

"All…ll…right, C.B., how long you had the wheels?"

"I got my truck right after you left fer school. You flunked out yet?"

"I'm hanging in there by the skin of my teeth, C.B. How are you doing?"

"I 'spect I'll have to do. Wouldn't nobody listen if I'z to complain."

"I would," I offer.

"Yeah, but I ain't gon' give you th' satisfaction. Come on an' get in. We'll cruise th' campus an' check out th' chicks while we catch up."

"I wish I could check one out and then take her back after the weekend to turn her in."

The squeaking and rattling of the truck door reminds me of Mr. J.'s old jeep. To find room to sit, I push aside a collection of paraphernalia ranging from a chewing tobacco pack to the Holy Bible. A white-tailed deer scrotum hangs from the rearview mirror by a piece of homemade rawhide.

"Tell me 'bout th' forestry school," C.B. insists. "Is it all you thought it was gon' be?" He revs up the motor. "Or is it turnin' out to be more like another one of Mr. J.'s tall tales?"

We pull away from the curb in front of the Post Office, and I'm trying to think how to answer. "Let's put it this way—when I get done, I'm going to know more about the woods than anybody," I brag.

"Anybody 'cept me, maybe."

"Get real," I argue.

"I'm serious as a snake skinnin' hisself in dog days. I donno 'bout yo' big college, but ever since I been workin' th' loggin'-woods, a day don't go by 'at I ain't learned somethin'."

"You still have to get in the last word, don't you?" I ask.

"Naw. You can have it…long as it's—'yeah, you right.'"

We pass by my old elementary school on Jackson Avenue…and I remember sneaking C.B. in through a window one Saturday so he could see what the inside of a school for whites looked like.

"Is th' book-learnin' part of it hard?" he asks.

"To tell you the truth, it's pretty tough. Sometimes I'm not so sure I'm cut out of college cloth."

"You'll do all right long as you 'member Auntay's advice 'bout a' acorn havin' to hold his ground 'fore he can make a tree."

We round the corner by the Episcopal Church and then pass First Baptist. I look down Tyler Avenue to see Dad's Presbyterian Church before turning onto University avenue by the Methodist Church. I'm wondering if God is trying to tell me something by pointing out all these churches…or is it just Oxford?

The contrast with the city comes quickly, as halter-topped coeds grace the sidewalk leading to and from the campus. Long and gorgeous legs are displayed in shorts that are not much in the way of material. I'm beginning to wonder if Dad may have been right about where I should be educated.

"You steerin' clear of gals with legs like them?" C.B. asks.

"It's more like they're staying away from me."

"Been keepin' off to yourself, huh?"

"Pretty much, C.B. What have you been doing?"

"'Sides workin' th' loggin'-woods, I been studyin', too…Th' Good Book."

"Oh, Lord!" I respond.

"'At's what you best be sayin'. You get too proud, an' yo' life gon' end up'n shame."

We pass Papa's city house, perhaps the one other place in town besides all those churches, where my "Oh, Lord" exclamation would not have been tolerated.

"Ever'thing bees in Th' Good Book," C.B. preaches. "An' Th' Word 'cordin' to Proverbs is—you gotta get meek to get wise. We wouldn't want yo' head gettin' no bigger'n your heart. 'At last bit ain't part of it. I jus' threw it in."

We pass the Catholic Church, and I'm wondering if I'm getting religiously paranoid, with C.B. and God both ganging up on me. As we cross Hiliard Cut, a flock of pigeons flies out from under the University

Bridge. I visualize a duck hawk nailing one in mid-air, but it doesn't happen, and the pigeons live to fly another day.

"You ain't doin' nothin' down there to cause us no shame, is you?"

"No, C.B., I'm not doing that."

We make the circle around the Grove and the Loop…and I want to date every girl I see.

"You wanta ride out to th' river bridge an' drown some minnows?" he asks.

"We might as well. I suspect I'd have better luck fishing than hooking up with one of these girls. Drop by Dad's store, and I'll ask him to tell Granna not to expect me home for supper."

"Still a Granna's boy, huh?"

"It's called respect, C.B."

In a quick stop at the bait shop, C.B. hits them up for three-dozen free minnows. "I still he'p 'em 'round here by bringin' in crawdads ever' now an' agin, so's I get free bait whenever I need it."

Riding out of town and taking in the sights, we get further than I would have ever thought without C.B. speaking.

"C.B., I don't think you're as talkative as you used to be."

He glances at me as if ready to open up. "'At's one of them things th' loggin' woods an' th' Good Book done taught me. It's a heap harder to put yo' foot in yo' mouth when you keep it shut. Now, tell me 'bout yo' forestry school. 'At's what I'm waitin' to hear 'bout."

"I'm not sure you want me to."

"Oh, yeah, I do."

"Well, I went away to what I thought was going to be something like a trade school. Man, was I wrong! Except for engineering, the School of Forestry flunks out a higher percentage of students than any other department on campus."

We pass Avent's Dairy. C.B. and I look at each other without saying a word. I know we are both remembering raiding the milk truck for free ice-cream sandwiches or push-ups on hot summer nights. We could stop and buy one now, but I doubt it'd taste the same as one sneaked out of the truck.

"So you feared you ain't gon' make your grades?"

"I don't know, C.B. I'm doing my best. You might say I'm in scholastic shock."

"Jus' keep yo' neck to th' yoke, as Auntay likes to say."

"You're still an Auntay's boy, huh?"

C.B. laughs.

"There's more to it than just keeping on. It's hard. The forestry school claims the second lowest cumulative grade point average on campus, and that's not necessarily a reflection on the kind of people attracted to the program. It's got more to do with the relative degree of difficulty of the forestry discipline compared to the university's other fields of study."

C.B. snorts a scornful laugh. "Man, you already talkin' like one of them professors yo'self."

Ahead, the driver of a farm tractor signals to turn left. As we pass him anyway, I grab the dash in fear.

"I'z lookin' out fer him turnin'," C.B. insists.

"You haven't heard from the draft board yet, have you?" I ask.

"Naw, but I'm 'spectin' to most any time."

We ride quietly for a few miles.

C.B. again urges me to elaborate on everything that's college. "What was th' first thing 'at happened to you when you got down there?"

"They gathered us all up in a big auditorium, and some Dean came to talk."

"An'?"

"And I figured he was going to welcome everybody and tell us how glad he was to see us, but he ruined that notion in a hurry."

"How's 'at?"

"He said for everybody to look at the person sitting on their left and then at the person sitting on their right...and that statistically, for me to graduate, both of those persons would have to flunk out or quit."

"Dang."

"Yeah. He went on to tell us that the forestry school had some courses that would cull out any students who weren't serious."

"It's a wonder you didn't tuck yo' tail 'tween your legs an' come on home right then."

Steering with his left hand, C.B. fumbles around with his right until he finds a little tin container. Single-handedly removing the top, he puts a pinch of comfort between his lower lip and his gum.

"Is that a habit you picked up working the logging woods?" I ask.

"Yeah. You want some?"

"Not hardly," I respond.

The snuff dipping starts me thinking about C.B.'s situation…loving a life in the out-of-doors and getting to work the woods the way he always wanted to. Considering the benefits of the secluded, near-solitary life of a woods-worker, that's not bad. I'd like to feel good for him instead of being jealous, but Labor Day will find me hanging by an academic thread and frustrated at having to return to college after the weekend…instead of looking forward to another week in the woods.

C.B. hits the horn to honk at a buzzard on the side of Highway 7. Temporarily leaving his road kill, the black vulture flies to the nearest tree.

"Tell me 'bout th' girls, Scott."

"There's not many. It's not like Ole Miss. Thank goodness, Mississippi State College for Women is about thirty minutes away. You might say those girls have a distinctly appetizing appeal."

"Naw, I wouldn't'a said that, but I think I'm knowin' what you meanin'."

"Let's just say they have the superior flavor of the south."

"How would you know?"

"Because visiting 'State' boys will be boys, and the 'W' girls are glad they are."

"Yeah, right. Like you got first-hand experience with that…."

"Well…hand experience anyway."

"'At's 'bout what I thought."

Passing through Abbeville, I remember the good times we've had near here. When we reach the river, C.B. pulls off the highway and onto the shoulder next to the bridge. In the unnatural channel that's been reamed out, muddy water funnels downstream.

"'Spite of what they done to our river, this would be a' awful good place fer a boat landin'," C.B. points out in a condescending voice.

"Yeah, it would."

"Th' deep woods of th' bottom's changed a lot since we been visitin' 'em. With th' re-routin' of th' 'riginal river into th' Corps canal, our old stompin' grounds is 'bout dried up. Look at all 'at sand an' mud th' manmade ditch is carryin' to th' lake. An' all them flood control measures…they 'parently didn't do no whole lot of controllin' of nothin'. A big flood killed a heap of th' timber."

"Yeah, with this much mud going downstream, the Mississippi River itself's got to fill up before long."

"An' New Orleans." C.B. tries for the last word.

"And the Gulf," I one-up him, in agreement.

We select a couple of suitable places to perch on the bank and think to ourselves. Upon getting his bait rigged up, C.B. begins to bob his minnow around in search for just the right spot. Looking at the near-ruined river, I picture Paul Bunyan carrying a giant shovel instead of an axe. I visualize him walking toward the bottom with Babe…and her back loaded down with super-sized forms and stacks of paperwork for Paul to have to fill out before he can begin to try to remove sediment from the oversized ditch. Thinking about the way I'm thinking, I wonder if too much college per square foot of forest is warping my world…and bruising my brain beyond repair.

"You ever think 'bout all th' reasons fer water?" C.B. asks.

"The uses, you mean?"

"You want me to kick yo' butt from Start'ville to Finish'ville?"

"I'd say there are hundreds of purposes for water."

"Thousands, more like it," he says, and pulls a small mud cat out of the river. "'Fore th' gov'ment straightened th' Little Tallahatchie River out fer us, we use' to could catch first-class crappie outta here."

"Yeah, you remember the two-and-a-half pounder I caught?"

"Yo' underdrawers pulled up too high. It was more like a pound an' a half. Now, tell me 'bout th' other students."

"You wouldn't believe the crap some of them come up with, C.B."

"Le' me hear it," he insists.

"All right. My roommate told me I needed to cut the labels out of the back of my underwear."

"Huh?"

"Yeah, if I expected to be invited to join a fraternity, the frat rats needed to think my clothes came from somewhere expensive."

"You should'a jus' tol' 'em you got yo' drawers from a fancy French boutique…'at one named *Jay-say Pay-nay*."

XXX:
Forest-tree 101, Wildlife Sex Ed, and Loggin' Woods Legends

BY LATE SUMMER OF '67 I'd dealt with several significant deaths, but pneumonia claiming Granna is a major turning point in my life. With my beloved grandmother who raised me now gone, I am suddenly an adult…whether I'm ready for it or not.

Without Granna being in my grandfather's existence, he loses interest in almost everything. He stops caring and gives up. After weeks of not dealing with it, Papa's hurt is getting worse instead of better. As it begins to affect his health, what's coming next is obvious. By fall my grandfather joins his wife. Although the doctors say he died of old age, I think it was more of a lack of any desire to live.

The grief and emptiness following the deaths of my grandparents are only slightly lessened by my belief that they are where they always believed they'd go after death. For me the best way I know to carry on in this life is with diversion. Home for weekends, I still take to the bottom with my lifelong friend. Away at college, I throw myself into matters concerning the conservation of wildlife.

IN LATE DECEMBER C.B. and I time an excursion deep into the heart of the Upper Sardis Wildlife Management Area to coincide with the peak of the white-tailed deer rut. Sitting together so we can catch up on conversation, we're sort of deer hunting. About fifteen miles northeast of Oxford, we are on top of an old sawdust pile where C.B. has made a blind-type stand.

It's Saturday afternoon, and fresh scrapes are all around us. Since a certain big buck has marked his territory here, there's a good chance he'll come around checking for doe visitation...if he's deaf enough not to hear us whispering.

"What you learned most lately 'bout th' woods?" C.B. questions my college education.

"Forestry in one short lesson, huh?" I delay while trying to think of how best to reply.

"It ain't like I'm gon' be'a goin' myself," he pushes.

"Truthfully, I figure I'm learning just enough to appreciate how much I really don't know and may never fully understand."

"Come on, now. I hope you can do better'n 'at...fer all th' tuition money yo' dad's spendin' on higher education'. What's th' main most important thing they learnin' ya?" he pushes, without giving me a minute to think.

"I'd say one of the most important elements in good forestry is proper timing. That's the key to a lot of it."

"I 'spect I can 'bide by 'at. It'd hold true fer most ever'thing in life. Now be 'pacific to th' woods."

"Specific. Not pacific."

"Yeah, yeah, quit 'voidin' th' question." He's sensing my insecurity.

"A....never mind. If you wanta talk local forestry, I guess it's laid out pretty clear-cut."

"At's what I'z afraid you was gon' learn." He throws his hands up in the air.

"Do you want me to say what you want to hear, or do you want the basic and irrefutable facts? And if you keep throwing your arms around like that, you're gonna scare off Ol' Rocking Chair Head."

"Feed me yo' truth then, College Boy."

"Okay, on these sandy hills, reforestation is most generally synonymous with the holier-than-thou loblolly pine."

"An' I figger I'm knowin' what soma-nonna-mous means."

"Synonymous."

"Am I gon' hafta kick yo' butt?"

"Loblolly will grow to be economically mature sawtimber by the time it's about forty years old," I bring us back on subject. "It ought to be a hundred feet tall by then. The same doesn't hold true for hardwoods."

"Whoa, Nelly. Finish up talkin' 'bout th' pine first. Then I'm gon' ax 'bout th' hardwoods…if'n they's any of 'em left by then."

His comment cuts to the quick.

"Are you sure you want to hear this, C.B.?"

"I ain't shore I wanta hear yo' answers, but I'm inner'sted in what you s'posed to learned."

"We can start thinning pine for pulpwood as early as about thirteen years old for making paper and helping the trees that you leave standing to grow better. Every five or ten years after that, we can thin it to get small sawlogs for lumber and again help the residual stand."

"An' then?"

"Well, when the trees turn forty, they start begging their owners to be clear-cut for the big money and to make it easier to start over."

"Gotta be more to it."

"Well, prescribed fire is important."

"Th' Indians knowed 'at 'thout goin' to no college."

"Burned on about a three-to-five year cycle beginning at about age fifteen, pine sites can get to be pretty good wildlife habitat."

"What 'bout th' ground nestin' birds 'at starts early…like quail an' turkey an' woodcock?"

"That's all got to be considered and worked in. There's a two-page computer printout full of things you have to take into account."

"Yeah, right…an' I reckon yo' computer gon' help put th' fire out when you done let it get away from you?"

"As a matter of fact, it will."

"She-ee-it!"

"I'm serious, C.B. It tells you where and how best to attack a fire and how long it'll take to put it out with various work forces."

"I ain't shore I'm believin' all 'at.

A deer appears in the skid trail leading to our log landing. It's a doe. C.B. and I look at each other and acknowledge without further words that we both have seen her. Another doe comes out behind her…and another. As yet another one comes out, those in front ease along the edge of the clearing.

"They browsin' on greenbriar," C.B. whispers. "An' honeysuckle."

As more come out of the woods, I start counting. Nine doe and there's still no buck. All at the same time, nine deer stop and look back to where they left the woods. Sporting an average-sized six or eight point rack of antlers, a medium-size buck steps out in the open.

C.B. and I have agreed we'll shoot nothing smaller than an eight point with at least a 14 to 16 inch spread. Since this deer is borderline, we decide to let him come closer so we can better size him up. A doe squats to pee. The young buck runs over to her and sniffs the ground where she peed. As he starts to smell her, she scampers off about thirty yards. He goes toward her.

"Crash, crunch!" Ol' Rocking Chair Head prances out of the woods. Junior looks back…and decides to go right on past the doe he had started toward.

"You think you can hit him, or you reckon I'd better shoot?" C.B. whispers.

"Let's watch for a minute," I whisper back.

Ol' Rock practically parades to the doe that Junior thought he'd have his way with. She stands at the ready. Ol' Rock mounts her. In all of about five seconds, it's over.

"Slam bam, thank you, ma'am," C.B. whispers.

"Maybe he didn't like it," I respond.

Another doe squats and pees. Junior looks hard but continues to stand at the edge of the woods. Ol' Rock runs over. She takes a few steps forward and then stops. He follows and mounts her, too…for no more than four or five seconds.

"Can you believe that?" I whisper.

After the deer graze and browse for a couple of minutes, another doe squats to pee. Without stopping to sniff the ground or her, Ol' Rock's on her. In no more than five seconds he's through again. The pattern continues with another doe. Ol' Rock is relentless. Within a total of not more than fifteen minutes he has mounted six of the nine does. There will have to be a better day for Junior.

I ask, "Would you have ever thought…?"

"Not in a hundred years," C.B. interrupts. "But I wanta be a big buck in my next life."

All deer except the dominant one ease over to the far side of the log landing and fade into the woods. Still having a good shot at the one we've waited on, I offer C.B. the shot as the big buck approaches the woods.

"After what we seen him up to…I ain't got th' heart fer it," C.B. whispers through a smile.

"And think how big he'll be next year," I add, as the huge buck steps to safety.

"'Sides, you still gotta tell me 'bout them hardwoods."

"Your good sites are reserved for growing hardwoods," I answer, "and unlike the pines, they shouldn't have fire anywhere around them."

"How's Miss'sippi State figger a good site from a pine site?"

"You have to consider the soils and exposure to the sun and water and such. It's usually the bottoms and the north and east facing slopes that are good enough sites for hardwoods."

"I still don't see why we can't have more of 'em, 'fore they all cut out. You need to make yo' college education worth th' while an' do somethin' 'bout it. "

"Trying to grow hardwoods on poor sites is a waste of time and space. How much people favor hardwood over pine doesn't change the site index."

C.B. fakes a yawn, as if he's not listening.

"Think about it, C.B. Even on a pretty good site, it takes two or three times as long to grow hardwoods as pines. The hardwoods would have to be worth two or three times as much money as the pine for the economics of it to pay off."

"I oughta knowed college would taint yo' view to a shade of dollar-bill green. Is 'at all it is to it?" he asks.

"No, there's a lot more to it than that."

"What?"

"Uh…well, you see that green stuff on the side of this ash tree?"

"Yeah, moss."

"It isn't moss. We may have always lumped it in with moss, but it's a lichen. It isn't a plant or an animal. What do you think about that?"

"I ain't impressed—I can think of lots of things 'at ain't plant or animal."

"Name one."

"'At rock right there. Th' air. Th' water. Yo' university-level stupid'ty."

"I was talking about something that's alive. None of those things are alive."

"'Cept maybe th' stupid'ty. It seems to be 'live an' well 'round here."

"Be serious, C.B."

"All right...then, I say it's a plant."

"It isn't. A lichen is a combination of fungus and alga and a bunch of other stuff."

"What difference do it make?"

"Do you like to breathe? They're important for cleaning the air. There's all kinds of things like that going on out here...stuff we've never given a second thought to."

"Speak fer yo'self. 'Cordin' to th' choker-man on my loggin' crew, th' Chickasaw'd boil it down to get dye fer colorin' their outfits an' blankets. An' th' herbwomen make tea an' salve an' perfume outta 'at kinda moss. I don't reckon yo' college professors ever give you 'at deep a view of it, did they?"

"With you around why the hell did I think I needed to go to college?"

"I wondered 'at, too. An' I'll tell you somethin' else—Auntay uses 'at moss to make a medicine th' doctors eben named after her...Auntay-by-a-dicks."

"Antibiotics?"

"Not accordin' to her. 'Course, she's also th' one what claimed you goin' off to college was gon' give you a broader wingspan."

"C.B.?"

"What?"

"None of that makes lichen a moss...and Auntay didn't discover antibiotics."

"An' I ain't so sure I'm believin' what Mr. J. used to always say...'bout th' more you really un'erstand somethin', th' better you gon' be able to tolerate them 'at differs with you."

"Give me a break, C.B."

"You been doin' any huntin' while you off down there?"

"Sort of," I answer.

"How do you sorta hunt? Never mind. Don't answer 'at. Come to think of it, knowin' how well you shoot, I think I know what you mean."

"Would you believe, on the second day of deer season, when I skipped hunting to go back to class, my major professor jumped all over me? Instead of appreciating a wildlife major for coming back to class on the second day, he was all bent out of shape for my missing the day before."

C.B. stands to stretch and stare.

"That's not the half of it," I continue. "We've got forestry and wildlife majors who don't even hunt or know the woods enough to tell a food plant from a weed."

"You mean it?"

"When we were studying fur bearers, my mammalogy Prof brought a Conibar to class...and there wasn't a half-dozen of us in the whole room who knew how to set it."

"You lyin'."

"No, man. Some of those students are from so deep in the city they've never even seen a beaver, much less know how to set a trap. A university is in a zone of its own, I tell ya."

"Sho sounds like it."

"Now, you tell me about being a woods-worker." I stand, thinking if he's going to risk scaring off deer, I might as well get my stretching done at the same time.

"Woods-workin' is all 'bout chains an' cables an' logs an' sawdust, but it ain't always no bed of thornless roses. Sometime it's hard enough to sweat th' curl outta my hair. It'll make you poor in more'n one way...bein' a feller from daylight to dark."

"I always thought you were a fella."

"A tree feller, Fool...th' man what cuts down th' trees. An' it's bad dangerous...an' li'ble to leave you with nothin' but a stump."

Picturing C.B. sitting on a tree stump with another kind of stump for a leg, I try to make light of it. "So you are the fellow who's a feller that fells trees and makes stumps?"

"Do you do yo' professors 'at away when they tryin' to teach you somethin'?"

"No, I was just picking. Go ahead and tell me the rest of your story."

"It ain't no story. Workin' th' woods is gon' be my life."

We both sit back down and squirm until we're again in comfortable positions.

"All my friends 'cept you have done moved to Chicago an' took on good payin' jobs. I'd rather keep goin' to th' woods, fer less money. They's plenty of good work out there. Work can't hide from th' man what ain't scared of it...an' I'm lovin' th' outdoors much as we always did."

"You've nailed it, C.B. Being happy doing what you do is what it's all about."

"You makin' any good friends at school?" he asks.

"Not friends like you. I have the distinct impression not many of my classmates have ever eaten frog legs cooked over a riverbank fire."

"At's a shame. How 'bout th' professors? How they treatin' you?"

"With no respect. One day when I was doing a little too much yackety-yack trying to answer an instructor's question, he called me a Roads Scholar...right in front of the whole class."

"Called you a what?"

"There's this beer joint between State and the 'W' that's named The Crossroads...called The Roads for short. A lot of the students hang out there to eat barbecue and guzzle suds instead of studying."

"He skin your bark a little, did he?"

"You bet he did," I admit. "Now you tell me what's your favorite thing about working in the woods?"

"Aw, man...'at'd hafta be th' draught horses. They somethin' else, Scott. Th' way they heave an' pull on them logs an' 'bide by th' logger's voice commands...ain't nothin' like it. When they get to strainin' an' pullin', an' them muscles in their shoulders start to bulgin' out, an' them veins in their necks get to swellin'...it's somethin' to see all right—a thing of beauty."

"Yeah?"

"An' they got such sure steps.... I wisht Mr. Jefferson could see 'em...much as he loved horses."

"I'll bet he has seen them, C.B."

"State College teachin' you anything 'bout horse-loggin'?"

"Like how to replace them with a rubber-tired skidder?" I sarcastically answer...but know in my heart that the technology of tractors is unfortunately inevitable.

"No, like how to tie a timber hitch or set a choker."

"C.B., you just as well stand aside and let the rest of the world go by."

"'At's what I thought. You don't know, do you?"

"That's not the sort of thing they teach at forestry school."

"Man, I'm beginnin' to wonder if we eben gon' be workin' in th' same woods when you get out of school."

I'd never admit it, but I know I'm missing out on a wonderful era that C.B. is soaking up. Although it would be easy to quit school and go to work in the woods, I know it wouldn't feel good to hurt my dad by dropping out. I can almost hear his lecture about not eating at harvest because I didn't plow in the cold.

"I'll admit there's some practical stuff they don't teach in college, but...."

"It sho seems 'at away to me," he's too quick to agree.

"There's some things you can show me...all right?" I try to hand him the homemade rope sling from my rifle.

"What?" He doesn't reach out for it.

"Are you going to show me or not?" I shake the rope at him.

"Show you what?" He pretends he doesn't know.

"Will you please show me how to tie a timber hitch, Oh Great Lumberjack of the Southern Forests?"

"I'll study on it. 'Fore I open up th' college of th' loggin' woods, I might need a little of yo' dad's tuition money." He stands up again and stretches with his new superiority.

Only after I make a face at him does he demonstrate his ability to tie the knot. A whiff of doe-in-heat buck lure reminds me that I'll soon have to return to campus...with the citified smells of soapy scents and collegiate odors of colognes. I'll have to settle for envisioning myself basking in the aroma of crushed pine needles, leather harnesses, and the other forest fragrances from horse-logging operations.

"Y'all learn how to figger tree volume by Doyle rule?" He's smelling blood now.

"Uh...I think we were exposed to it, but I don't remember the exact numbers," I bluff, knowing he's dying to prove how little I'm learning in college compared to his experiences with loggers.

"Lotta good it done ya, then...if'n you don' 'member." Pointing at the same small ash, C.B. sprouts, "12 minus 4 give 8, square to 64, divide by 16 give 4, time one 12-foot log, come to 48 board feet. How 'bout dem apples, Joe College?"

"Not bad. You had me going until you got to the part about getting apples from an ash tree."

"Hard to take, ain't it?" he presses on.

"How do I know that's the correct answer?" I challenge.

"I reckon you'll just have to trust me on it, since you 'parently ain't learned no more 'bout tree volumes than you have knots."

Again I sit in silence, knowing only that I didn't come home from academia this weekend to have my nose rubbed in my deficiencies. I'm already worried enough that what I'm supposed to be learning isn't the kind of practical knowledge that will help me a whole lot when I get out of school. I'll go to my deathbed wondering what good it does to know Leaf the Lucky was Eric the Red's son, when I don't even know or care who Eric the Red was.

"Have you got any regrets, C.B.?"

"Yep, I do. When you cuttin' trees all day long an' don't hear nothin' but that chainsaw, you get to list'nin to your heart. Ever' time I hear th' crack an' crash 'at comes with fellin' a tree, I wonder if it's th' right thing to be doin' right then an' right there. I know we gotta cut trees, but I'm always wonderin' if'n it's goin' on where it needs to an' when it should. You know what I mean?"

"C.B., maybe you ought to be a lawyer. You could be the world's first black logger-lawyer, hugging trees instead of harvesting them."

"I don't think so."

"Instead of running around planting trees like Johnny Appleseed, you can put signs on bathroom doors—Don't use toilet paper. Save a tree. For whites only."

"What was 'at last part thown in there fer?"

"I don't know. It just sort of came out with the other," I admit.

"I reckon 'at be another lesson they don't teach in college good as they do out in th' world."

"What's that?" I ask with reluctance but knowing I deserve whatever I get back.

"'At a fella needs to put his mind in gear 'fore he puts his mouth in motion."

He sits back down, and I realize there's a lot of truth in what C.B.'s been saying. My college education has a ways to go, considering I can still get such a good lesson from the logging woods.

XXXI:
Greener Grass...Sorta

AS OPPOSED TO JUST the usual homework assignments on top of more homework assignments, my major adviser at the School of Forestry drops something good on me. He says he can line me up for a summer job as a technician with the U.S. Forest Service.

While my suddenly favorite professor tends other business, I'm left alone in his office to fill out the required paperwork for seasonal employment. On his desk I notice several more copies of the federal government's three-page application form. In consideration for my buddy back in Oxford, completing my application isn't all I do.

Heading back to the dorm with an extra application package, I mentally work out how I can left-handedly forge a made-up advisor's signature. With C.B.'s name as applicant, the documents will suggest that he is a student from the all-black college at Holly Springs.

HOME FROM COLLEGE FOR another weekend, I wait at Oxford's Georgia Pacific plant for C.B. to return from his work in the woods. At approximately 5:00 P.M. he arrives and greets me with an offer to share a pocket full of scalybarks. As I let down the tailgate of his truck, he retrieves a pair of pliers and a hammer, the hammer I think I recognize as being borrowed from a boarding house outside Meridian.

"C.B., I've got something to pass by you. I've found out I can get us summer jobs with the U.S. Forest Service."

"What's this 'us'? You got a frog in ya pocket?"

He lays out the nuts on the tailgate between us.

"Better than that. I've got you a slot in what the federal government calls their seasonal employee placement program."

"Say what?" He bursts open a hickory nut and devours the edible part.

"The Forest Service is willing to work us all summer right up until school starts back in the fall. Then we'll get laid off."

"Did I hear 'at frog agin?" He cups his hand to his ear in an exaggerated gesture.

"No. What do you mean?"

"How come I'd have to get laid off fer you to go back to school?"

"Because it's just a seasonal job. But it might be a foot in the door for you. Who knows? If you get to know some folks and do a good job, you might get a deal and stay on permanent."

Looking thoughtfully, he questions, "Seem like to me they might oughta need people year 'round. What kinda deal'd you say it was?"

"It's called a quota, and it's a target that's got something to do with the government trying to hire a certain number of blacks."

"Bull!" comes his disgusted response.

A startled blue jay flies off instead of waiting for discarded nut meat.

"Really, C.B."

"Like I'm gon' be believin' they tryin' to help me 'cause I'm black."

I laugh, crack a scalybark in half, and savor the rich, unique taste of the inner nut.

"'Bout like I'm gon' believe you makin' yo' grades down at State," he continues.

"Seriously, I've…uh, already filled out an application for you and sent it in. You ought to get something in the mail next semester, toward summer."

C.B. shields the sun's glare with a handful of nuts as he looks at me. "You swear?"

"Yeah…and uh, you're a biology student from Rust College."

Cracking the choice nuts first, in the event we don't eat them all, we take turns trading off the hammer and pliers.

"If'n I'm gon' get hired by lyin' 'bout bein' a student, how come you didn't just have me goin' to Ole Miss?" He looks at me in a questioning manner, but in jest.

"I don't know. You don't look like the country-club type."

He sweeps nut shells off the tailgate with the back of his hand as if he's brushing away the obstacles that might stand in our way. "If you ain't done got me in another one of yo' bamboozles, I reckon I 'preciate you thinkin' 'bout me."

"Aw...right!"

———————

ANXIOUSLY WAITING TO HEAR from the Forest Service makes my second semester seem longer than the first. The fall hunting season being intermingled with first semester might also have had something to do with how fast that one went by. I still make it home on most weekends, but nothing is the same without Granna and Papa and Mr. Jefferson...and Miss Sippy.

I try to spend some time with Dad in the store, but spring is mostly for C.B. and me to fish and turkey hunt together. Finally, just a couple of weeks before the start of summer vacation, we receive our temporary job offers, from the Bankhead National Forest in north Alabama. After I've slipped off up there for a weekend of scouting out potential living accommodations, I'm reluctant to share my findings with C.B.

Again hanging around Oxford's plywood mill on a Friday afternoon, I wave from the tailgate of C.B.'s truck as his pulpwood truck rolls into sight. C.B. grins his usual acknowledgment. Having made his workweek, he may have been looking forward to relaxing, but he couldn't need a summer break from pulpwooding as much as I need one from college.

Dreading next week's exams is something I'd like to drown out by being excited about the weekend's possibilities. C.B. comes over and pulls a store-bought roll of twist from his back pocket. Knowing I'll shake my head in disgust, he still offers up a chew.

"I visited the Bankhead last weekend," I inform him, "trying to find us a place to stay."

"You learn anything?"

"We'll leave for Alabama as soon as my last final takes me, after next week."

C.B. spits on a winding column of black ants. They break formation and scatter.

"A place to stay?" he repeats.

"That ant trail probably goes between their feeding ground and their nest. Your second-hand tobacco juice has just screwed up everything in their whole routine. You get it…hole routine?"

C.B. looks at me uneasily. "Scott?"

"What?"

"I axed you 'bout where we was gon' stay." His eyes harden.

"Well, it's sort of like when you and I were working highway construction, down below Meridian."

"What you mean by sorta like?" He wipes tobacco juice off his mouth with his shirtsleeve and heads toward a red maple shade tree.

I follow. "Like when I camped out with the vehicles at the work site? We'll have to find you something like that, some place close to work."

"Find me something?"

"Yeah…uh, there's a little logging community at Grayson, and they have this boardinghouse where I can sleep…and eat…and shower."

"You lily-white mother…." He sits down with his back against the tree.

I opt to stand in the shade and face him. "Come on, C.B. That's just for the nighttime. We'll be working together during the day. I did it for you in Meridian. It's just the opposite of the way we did it working down there."

"Oh, good…then you mean I'll be drivin' th' truck, an' you'll have to do th' grunt work?" Sarcasm drips from his voice.

"That's not what I meant."

"College colorin' you kinda bigoty, ain't it?"

"No, and you know none of that's my choosing. That's just the way things are right now…over there."

"Well then, maybe we can change some things over there, in Al…a…bam…a."

"Good deal. Let's just go over there and do whatever we have to do."

"Scott, we may not eben be talkin' 'bout th' same thing."

"We've been that way all our lives, and it hadn't stopped us from having a good time yet, has it?"

"Right-on, brother." He raises his fist in mock salute.

"You start talking that crap over there, and you're liable to get us both lynched," I half-jokingly warn.

"An we li'ble to get over yonder an' you gon' hafta decide 'bout what really matters. We in th' sixties, now."

"C.B., let's just go do the best we can and play the rest by ear. I guarantee if we work hard, things will work out…like always."

"An' I'm s'posed to feel better 'bout that…thinkin' things might work out like yo' idear of what's usual?"

WITH THE NORTH ALABAMA hills being noted for its bootlegging, our working for the government doesn't exactly help us fit in. No one appears to be overly anxious to help with housing arrangements for C.B., whom they call the "Colored Boy." As much as I like the logging community of Grayson, the housing prospects for my buddy turn out to be zero. So, like the National Guard troops had to do during the Ole Miss race riots, C.B. settles for a place on federal property to camp.

A fenced-in area for storage of discarded materials on the backside of the work center is what the Forest Service calls its boneyard. Storing his gear in his own truck, C.B.'s able to stretch out in a surplus government rig that's waiting to be auctioned off. When the dew is heavy, such sleeping is substantially better than camping out under the stars. A rocky creek has spring water rippling downhill behind the enclosure. The air temperature is the deciding factor on how often he bathes.

The Forest Service tells us we'll have to buy our own steel-toed leather boots, but the dry goods store in Haleyville, Alabama, tells us in so many unspoken words that C.B. is the wrong color to establish a line of credit. With the store owner's son grinning in the background, I buy two pair of boots in my name. It turns the young merchant's smile into a frown.

Typical workdays start with us shut in the back of a work-wagon truck for slow, sweaty-smelly travel to a work site in the forest. Eight laborers share the crowded space away from any breeze or view. One of the reasons I wanted this job was to get to see some new country. Since the truck has only one small window in the back door letting in a token amount of air and light, I'm not seeing much.

This morning all I can see is the tired and prematurely old faces of forest laborers. The only reason I even know we've reached the forest is because the truck slows to travel over a woods road. I think I can feel every vibration. Not being able to see outside reminds me of when I was a youngster and not tall enough to see over the door and out the window of Dad's taxi. Sitting on my heels wouldn't do any good in the work-wagon.

As an insect chorus welcomes us, I try substituting sounds for sight. By this time of year most of the best bird singing is over, but I can still hear the jays of blue jays and the caws of the crows. Being in such a prisoner-like setting, even those calls are comforting evidence that we are indeed being taken to the woods and not to some jail to be locked away. The paddy wagon rattles, bumps, and bounces over rough terrain as most of the laborers sleep.

With a sudden honking of the truck horn, I look to an old and experienced laborer for an explanation. Assuming we are nowhere near other traffic, I can't imagine what we are honking at.

"We flushed a wild turkey," the old man in the know tells me. "Would you believe we plant seeds on the way to the work site with our truck horn? When a wild turkey is honked at as he flies up in front of the truck, he leaves us with a turkey-dropping deposit. It's full of the seeds from whatever he's been eating."

The Forest Service must think having windows along the sides of this thing would make it too susceptible to tree limbs while driving through woods roads. I'm cramped up enough to give a mole claustrophobia and can't see squat and won't be able to until I get let out of the truck for work. If I ever get in a position to have people working for me, I'll treat them better than this.

Timber stand improvement by chainsaw is hard labor anytime, but it's especially tough in the southern summertime. Arranged like a chain gang, we work walking through the woods in a grid pattern without missing a spot. Working downhill puts my face and hands a little further from where I expect timber rattlers and copperheads to be, but I think my back won't appreciate that by the end of the day. If I could start low and work uphill, I wouldn't have to bend as much or as often. Cutting down small trees or girdling the bases of some larger ones favors the better trees over the poorer ones, but that doesn't occupy my mind enough to make me stop worrying about the likelihood of flunking out of school. With my grades already on the edge, courses are said to get tougher with each new semester. Meanwhile, C.B. is enjoying the summer and is not any more concerned with tomorrow's future than he is interested in yesterday's history.

Mid-morning, our foreman announces that the entire line of laborers is to stop and take a breather. So that we don't waste any time and are sure to earn our wages, the saw boss has us sharpen our chainsaws during the break. I suspect there are places in government service where money is wasted, but out here isn't one of them.

Pointing out to C.B. that I've found a good sitting stump, I brag, "This looks like a good spot to sit and...."

"I don't think...."

"Dad-gum-it!"

"I'z tryin' to warn you," C.B. boasts. "I'd'a thought they'd'a taught you college boys better'n to set on a fresh-cut pine stump." He turns his hard hat upside down and places it on the ground for his seat.

"If that wasn't a class act," I admit with sarcasm. Yielding to C.B.'s idea of sitting in a hard hat, I try it.

My butt is not shaped quite right to balance comfortably in it. As I try to wiggle into a tolerable position, I realize I'm now probably spreading the pine stump's gummy sap from my britches to the inside of my hat.

"Scott."

"What?"

"You still allergic to poison ivy?" C.B. looks to my left.

"Yeah, but this isn't poison ivy. It's got three leaves, but it's a viney pea called trailing wildbean. If you time it right, you can see the little purple and rose-colored flowers on it."

"Yeah...right."

"Here's another one I've learned at school. This yellow flower is a touch-me-not. Watch what happens when you barely bump this little capsule. See how it explodes and expels its seeds? That's where it gets its name."

"'At's called jewelweed in th' loggin' woods. It grows in seeps an' tells th' road-man not to be layin' out no roads there. Loggers don't care nothin' 'bout no spittin' seeds. They more in'ersted in bein' able to drive cross there 'thout gettin' themselves good an' stuck."

"Well, it's a touch-me-not," I insist.

"I'll tell you something else a good woodsman would know," he says. "Th' watery sap in jewelweed is good fer th' poison ivy itch, so you best be gettin' a handful to take with you."

SUMMER IS SHORT, WITH August in the piney woods bringing something that's enough to keep any man honest. During dog days work is more like toil, and the heat seems hotter…both of them more intense than usual. Barely before the climate and copperheads get the best of us, C.B. and I are moved to become a two-man team for insect and disease control. As the I & D crew, we are to spend the tail end of our summer chasing southern pine beetles across the National Forests of Alabama.

After cutting down infested Shortleaf, Loblolly, and Virginia pines of all diameters and heights, we de-limb them, buck them into small enough logs to be rolled over, and saturate all their sides with a pesticide mixture of diesel fuel and benzene hexachloride. The chemical we call BHC is said to work on the nervous system of the insects by making them literally jump themselves to death. I'm left to wonder what it's doing for my health. Enough of the BHC mixture soaks right through leather and underneath the steel-toed covering of our boots to keep our feet and toes cooled.

As the rest of the world wonders about the hidden dangers of pesticides, C.B. and I are more interested in out-working the other crews in the forest. Since nobody's bought us any rubber boots or gloves, I'm thinking the safety precautions and health hazards aren't really serious. Because the Forest Service has apparently assured itself that our steel-protected toes are secure from chemical containers and trees being dropped on them, surely there is no further concern for our safety. We're well-trained on the lethal doses and toxicity levels of the poison required to be potent on the tree-damaging bugs of current concern.

MAIL CALL AT THE Black Warrior work center is an exciting event for some folks. C.B. and I rarely get mail, but after this hard day's work, C.B.'s name is called. As if the letter is top secret, he says good evening to me and heads toward the boneyard with his prize. I stand and look at his back as he walks away, opening it and reading as he walks. I'm hardly believing he isn't going to let me see who sent him a letter. Stopped in his tracks, he turns and comes back.

"Lay it on me. I see you're about to pop with something to share."

Waving the envelope like a sword, he announces, "I got me some news."

"I see that. Is it Chicken? Did they find him?"

"Naw, it ain't 'bout Chicken. It's a letter come from th' President, hisself."

"President of what?" I ask.

"These here United States. It says, Congratulations, yore friends an' family have selected you...."

"Are you kidding me?"

"Naw, Man, my friends an' family.... Ain't that somethin'? I 'member meetin' my mother only once, an' I ain't never eben seen my father but th' President of America is tellin' me I'm 'sposed to believe they've selected me fer th' military draft."

"Let me see that thing."

"Here you go. Have you a look-see fer yoreself. I'm good as gone."

I look at the letter and return it, not thinking of anything appropriate to say.

"I gotta go get inspected th' 13th of May...prob'ly be on a Friday, th' way my luck's runnin'."

"Are you going to try to get out of it?"

Instead of answering, C.B. just looks at me.

"Why don't you come unglued when the doctor sticks his finger up your butt?"

"I'll prob'ly do that whether I want to or not. An' Chicken-Hawk said they got ever'thing like 'at covered, some kinda way."

"Well, you could turn around real quick and kiss the doctor."

"They'd prob'ly just promote me to officer."

"Dang, dang, double dang, C.B. What are you gonna do?"

"Ain't nothin' to it but to do it." He lets down the tailgate of his personal rig and sits over to one side, leaving me ample room to join him. "I knowed it was comin', an' I aim to do my duty. When th' flood water gets to your feet, 'at's when you gotta start holdin' yo' head high. I got a couple of RCs coolin' in th' creek. You want one?" he offers.

"No thanks."

"If they send me back from Vietnam in a box, I want you to plant my butt on that bluff overlookin' Graham's put-in to th' Little Tallahatchie River. Okay?"

"Don't go and get yourself prematurely fitted for a halo…or I'm liable to sprinkle your ashes in the Ole Miss library for spite."

"How'd you like to be hain'ted fer th' rest of yo' days?" he threatens.

"If I had to go to the library to bump into your ghost, I doubt he's gonna be bothering me a whole lot."

ONE EVENING AFTER A solid day of wallowing around in our pesticide mix, the air temperature lends itself to a bath for the Forest Service resident camper. Gathering his usual pile of soap, towel, and other necessities, C.B. makes his way to the stream behind the boneyard. About the time he places the last of his clothes on a rock in the middle of the stream with his other belongings, he discovers he's not alone. As the three rednecks come out of hiding, C.B. recognizes the store owner's son, from where I bought our boots.

Wielding a baseball bat type of club, one of the good ol' boys demands, "Come 'er, boy. Gather up some dead limbs. We fixin' to have us a fire and burn your clothes. Don't say a word or you'll be in there with 'em."

At their direction and as they laugh and continue to harass him, C.B., still in the raw, prepares the fire.

"Now, wade back out there and get your clothes," their leader instructs.

C.B. complies. Approaching the bank with his bundle of personal belongings in his arms, he slowly slides a hand in the middle of the clothes…to retrieve my little pocket pistol named James.

"Now, gentlemen," C.B. instructs, pointing the pistol at the boy with the bat, "each of you will kindly remove your pants and leave them where you stand. Then step over next to that cedar." Without argument, the good ol' boys go along.

After placing their pants in the fire, C.B. looks directly at the store owner's son and says, "Y'all best return to th' dry goods store in Haleyville now. You'll need to take a better boot inventory than you had th' last time I'z in there…'fore I change my mind 'bout lettin' you go. Now, get."

TOWARD THE END OF June, we're returning to the compound from another day in the forest and someone is waiting. He's a Forest Service employee out of the regional office…from personnel management. He says he has come specifically to talk to C.B. Figuring I'm hip-deep in the trumped-up application and bogus appointment, I feel like I need to hear what's going on. Slipping around behind a vehicle where I can eavesdrop, I wonder what the penalty is for forging signatures on a federal application for seasonal employment.

"Charles," he says to C.B., "I'm Mr. Fryer. I'm from Atlanta, and I'm here to help."

"I ain't never turned down none of that," C.B. assures him.

Mr. Fryer continues, "If you'll sign up for permanent employment with the Forest Service, we would like to follow up financially for the continuation of your college education. I'm here to offer you an official internship with the U.S. Department of Agriculture. Charles, we are prepared to pay for the rest of your education and guarantee you a position with the federal government upon your graduation."

"Wow!" C.B. responds before becoming uncharacteristically quiet.

I'm about to swallow my tongue. On one hand, I think it's about time C.B. caught a break. On the other hand, I'm more than a little jealous. I'm the one going to forestry school, and C.B.'s the one getting a non-competitive employment offer. Based on my skin color, I doubt I'll be receiving a similar proposition.

"I 'preciate it, sir," C.B. says politely, "but after this summer, I'm slated to go to graduate school at…uh, th' University of Saigon."

"Oh, really?" the man comes right back. "That will be fine, as long as you are majoring in a field of study related to forestry. What is to be your major emphasis of study?"

C.B. fumbles for words. "I'm gon' study a different kind of woods. It's got to do with he'pin' stomp out com'nism."

Still not getting the message, Mr. Fryer gives C.B. his call card and assures him, "That'll be good. You just complete this paperwork and get me the signatures it asks for from your school. Return it to me, personally," he emphasizes. "It must come through me because it involves a federal target I...uh, administer."

When Mr. Fryer leaves, I approach C.B. and his paperwork. "Why didn't you jerk him around some more? You could have had that sucker swallowing the whole hook, line, and second hand spark plug. I'd have given him a taste of the Forest Service personnel policy on multiple abuse to take back to Atlanta."

"I could'a played him out a little more line 'fore I let him get away, but I didn't want to have to dig th' hook out of his gut."

"Seriously, C.B., if we work this right, you might can go to college...free. If we can get you registered at Rust College, we might can get the draft thing deferred. Being a minority can work for you for a change. Let's make this higher education thing happen or at least fish around for some possibilities."

"Scott, you not listenin' either. I all but told 'at brain sturgeon what kinda *target* I'm fixin' to be. He couldn't hear nothin' past his quota fer hirin' a black. My letter from th' President's done laid my future right out fer me...in spite of yo' best shenanigans an' all Mr. Fryer's illusions."

"I'm talking deferral here, C.B."

"Don't de...fur...al me. I'll be takin' my higher schoolin' where th' Chicken-Hawk done his...in Tiger Land, at Fort Polk, Lou...easy...ana. You an' yo' man from Hot...lan'a jus' as well combine all y'all's college educations together an' see'f 'tween th' two of ya, y'all can un'erstand that th' only kinda target I'm fixin' to be is one what's got a bull's eye on it."

XXXII:
First Kill vs.
College Deferral

IN THE MIDST OF a late-60s summer camp, things are shaping up for an all-too-characteristic week at the Mississippi State University Forestry School. With morning classes now a memory and afternoon field data finally collected, I'll soon not be appreciating evening lab work.

This is the time of day when my fellow classmates are glad to be away from the snakes, briars, poison ivy, and other aggravating particulars that are a part of working in the woods. While my counterparts consider our night exercise a welcome break from field work's flocks of no-see-'ems, mosquitoes, chiggers, ticks, and yellow jackets, I'm more concerned with something else. It's the reams of tedious and time-consuming sheets of regression analysis problems we now have to face.

As opposed to my paperwork predicament, the night often finds my mind wondering about my buddy, C.B. I suppose he's having to deal with hordes of whatever various kinds of insects are buzzing around in Vietnam. I'll bet his exterior is turning leather tough. I can only imagine his situation. I hope he's made some good friends to help watch his back.

To the extent we can help each other or innovate enough to get away with it, my study group at Starkville shares or has shared our workloads. When such team efforts are completed and papers are ready to turn in, we're all usually ready to turn in as well, but tonight something loony is drawing me out under the moon, on the tar-papered roof of the dormitory. While I'm in my private place, I hope the friends who weren't impressed with my contribution to our homework will think I have a hot date.

The far-away sky makes a kind of connection. One star stands out. I can't identify it by name, but I wonder if C.B. can see it from where he is. I'm curious as to what it is he's thinking about…and how often, if ever, he gets to spend a night under a roof. It's hard to believe this same star can shed light on our totally incomparable existences halfway around the world from one another. C.B. must be hearing the rumble of war while I hear nothing but the star's silence.

Nightly updates from TV newscasts and casters leave me confused as to whether or not our half million U.S. soldiers serving in Vietnam are doing anybody any good. Do the heavy and mounting losses of American servicemen's lives really buy us something?

While I fear for C.B. and assume he's going through hell, I'd like to think our military leaders have an entire chain of command seeing after his best interests. I have my doubts but still wonder if the spilling and splattering of blood might be something I could better handle than having to face organic chemistry and cell physiology. I may soon find out…if I flunk out of college.

IN VIETNAM C.B.'S OUTFIT is made up of everybody from non-repentant repeat-sinners to born-again sinners. The good news is—they can count on each other. Maybe it's because they don't have anything else, but the men come first. Nothing else is as important. The unaffiliated unit, code-named NTK, is of platoon size and is set up to carry out specific acts of sabotage or not-so-specific clandestine operations, whichever order first comes down from higher up. All of its soldiers, except for one, are recruited from the most elite units of the various branches of the U.S. Armed Forces. Assigned as their sniper, C.B.'s superior marksmanship is his pass.

Wearing tiger stripes instead of the standard issue jungle fatigues, these warriors feel they are the "best of the best and above the rest." It's also a chorus of the farewell toast they chant in unison when one of them "buys the farm"…as they casually refer to the act of dying.

When not soldiering in the arena of covert activities, they are likely to spend their time causing the kind of mayhem that comes with search-and-destroy missions, ambushes, and night patrols.

One of their more frequent routines is what they call "humping the bush." In such, they might be out in the jungle for a week at a time…in search for Dinks, as the foes are disdainfully called.

When the men gripe, everything is blamed on Washington. Derogatory talk about the various branches of service or their unconventional joint-unit is not tolerated. There's not a lot of open feeling about mutual concern before leaving the relative safety of rolled concertina wire fences. It's a different story, however, when an air-taxi lifts off to drop the men of the NTK unit deep in the boonies. Displays of emotions are evident when the guys hit the bush. That's when they are together in a way that sincerity and the spirit of true brotherhood set in.

Strangely enough, C.B.'s best two military friends are what he jokingly calls foreigners. Sharing tough times and trying experiences with both soldiers helps him survive. The one called "Feet" is a Specialist-5 Medic from Newport, Rhode Island. He calls himself a New Englander instead of a Yankee, but from the way Feet talks C.B. knows better.

Feet got his nickname from bragging about being named All-State in Soccer. Unimpressed at first, C.B.'s thinking if a soccer ball ever rolled into north Mississippi it would likely be used for a dodge ball or kick ball…and Rhode Island is probably not as big as Lafayette County. Then one boring morning, Feet shows off his soccer skills and demonstrates his claim to fame by repeatedly kicking a little bean bag about the size of a lemon up in the air. He keeps it going without letting it hit the ground by relying only on his feet. Seeing this, C.B. decides the nickname is well-earned and here to stay.

Feet didn't have to come to 'Nam. Since his brother was killed here, Feet could have gotten out of it. He could have been stationed somewhere else. All he had to do was ask, but he says he came because of his brother. Since you can't tell one Viet Cong from another, he says he'll waste as many as he can…and hope the one who killed his brother is in the bunch.

C.B. calls his other good friend "Hay," short for "Hay Sues." Not able to stomach anything that close to being sacrilegious, C.B. is not about to call him Jesus as his nametag reads. Hay, a Spec-4 walkie-talkie radio operator, claims he's Puerto Rican by roots. He also says he comes from a borough in New York City's west side that he calls Hell's Kitchen.

One of the reasons C.B. likes Hay is because he carries a little copy of the New Testament in his back pocket. He doesn't read it but says having it up against his rear will protect him…according to his grandmother who raised him. Hay is fond of singing, "Put your hand in the hand of the man who calmed the sea." It all reminds C.B. of his Auntay and an upbringing around Taylor.

Rumor has it that Hay was given a choice between some jail time and enlisting to learn a trade. Most of the soldiers keep their distance from the radio technician about like they do their sniper. The static and noise of the radio could give away your location and get you eliminated. C.B. is yet to understand why they are equally shy of being around him and his special weapon.

MEANWHILE, SUMMER CAMP'S concentration on the technical aspects of forestry is, for the most part, turning out to be a welcome reprieve from the rigors of common college. Since I can't get lucky enough to have to worry about catching the clap, my main problems concern professors and tests. There are slight struggles with upper classmen as to the pecking order in the forestry school's student community but nothing of real concern.

Fretting over running out of Chesterfields before getting back to campus from the school forest can hardly compare to what C.B. and his new soldier buddies are probably worrying about. Rumors have it that draftees and enlisted personnel are merely pawns of officers who are more interested in their ambitions than their men's welfare. Hearing that, I can't help visualizing my buddy as nothing more than the American equivalent of a Chinese checker in some South Vietnamese officer's promotion ladder. I suspect the underling soldiers like C.B. are simply trying to cover their own selves.

Knowing the way C.B. has approached most things in his life, I wouldn't put it past him to be gung-ho about whatever he's gotten himself into. Perhaps by now he's a war dog. He could be all but daring death daily…in a place where too many men are said to be succumbing to senseless slaughter.

As social and political frustrations over the war intensify all over campus, my thoughts merely confuse each other more than anything else. Could it turn out to be C.B.'s destiny to die and rot in that jungle so the Vietnamese can have their free elections...when they probably wouldn't have any better voter turn-out than we do in the States?

Between exploring the school forest and trying to find a girl that will have anything to do with me, I'm not much of a student or a date. I stay busy trying to experience college life in every way from panty raids to forest inventory plane flights. While the panties promote nothing beyond weak promises, aerial views of Mississippi's timber reveal a renewable resource that seems likely never to run out. Trees look like toy pick-up sticks from such a perspective. They grow and get cut and grow back and get cut again, and life goes on...as I dream about lacy negligees.

I wonder what it is that's at stake in Vietnam. I haven't heard a lot of answers as to just what it is C.B. is fighting for over there. No doubt he is well suited for soldiering, but I just can't see how any of it is going to help stop communism.

It's a bright sunny day during my forest site evaluation lab. I'm sitting on the loblolly pine forest floor. I dreamily watch a single file of ants and imagine Army regiment...with its own divisions of rows and columns and other order. I'll bet C.B.'s disgusted about all the various grades of soldiers and the officers of the military, especially since most of them outrank him.

I notice one ant in particular who is packing a piece of food three times his own size. He is the C.B. ant beyond a shadow of doubt...the way my buddy used to pack grub to the woods. I watch him successfully carry his burden to the top of the anthill and then pull the crumb in behind him as he disappears. Maybe my buddy's knowledge of the outdoor world will somehow help him get through whatever it is he's having to face across what they call the "pond."

C.B. HAS SEEN BIG changes since being an inductee. For troops in the bush everything is different. There is no segregation of officers the way there is in the rear echelon...no aggravations with the military hierarchy. Everyone in the NTK platoon works together...to stay alive. Circumstances of time and place transcend the boundaries of rank. Experience and reality give license to need over protocol...and green lieutenants who don't listen to their more experienced platoon sergeants don't last very long.

This is a fighting force where skin color doesn't matter…white for black…black for white…or brown or yellow. Members of the NTK unit are a fraternity where brothers might have to die for each other. Bullets in the bush have no interest in nationalities or color. Prejudices will have to wait for peacetime. Body bags don't come customized. Extra small through extra large and private through general, one size and style fits all.

During his third week in-country, C.B. finds himself in a tree that reminds him of a bay magnolia back home. In the middle of nowhere, he's guarding a landing zone called an LZ for short. In 'Nam everything is abbreviated or called something else besides it proper name. For all practical purposes, C.B. is by himself. The closest member of his platoon has lookout duties of his own, a click away…the distance they call a kilometer.

As often as C.B. has sat like this in a deer stand, it's not the same. There are good reasons to be scared of everything here. Death is likely to happen to anyone who doesn't stay alert. On a given day, the end could happen to anyone who simply draws the wrong straw. C.B. is even fearful that an American helicopter might mistake him for a Viet Cong.

There's movement in the tall-bladed grass at the edge of the meadow-like LZ. The vegetation isn't moving anywhere else, so it can't be the wind. Looking through the scope of his special sniper's rifle, C.B. makes his first sighting. Easing along the flat terrain below, a little brown man carries an AK-47. He is clad in the black, silky pajamas and wears the classic straw hat with the pointed top. There is no question that this is an enemy soldier.

C.B. fondles his prized weapon. As if on their own accord, the crosshairs of C.B.'s scope find the Viet Cong's ear. C.B. sets the hair trigger. His mouth goes dry, and his gut knots up. Fearing that he may be too tense for this, he hesitates. Normally as steady as steel, there is a pulsing throb in his trigger finger. His heart beats hard and fast.

It's unlikely that this V.C. is by himself. C.B. realizes he should shoot before others might come into view and spot him shooting. Resting his finger on the trigger guard he does not know what's stopping him from shooting. If he misses the shot, this V.C. may determine his location. He'd be a sitting target, stuck in a tree with no way to go but down.

Carrying his AK-47 at-ready, the Viet Cong comes closer. He turns and again shows his head from the side. The crosshairs once more rest on the ear of C.B.'s first human target. All hesitation must end here. C.B. now knows when he touches the trigger, he will have his first kill. For both men everything or nothing more in life lies beyond this point. In a frozen, minute-long second in eternity, the obligation to kill has come. C.B. fires. The enemy drops hard...like a wet sack of potatoes, slipping from life's careless grasp. Smooth, brown skin illuminated in the riflescope is covered with dark red blood. All the myths and tall tales of jungle warfare that C.B. has been hearing can now be passed on...for real.

The small vegetative opening that was made for helicopters is filled with new questions. Are there more Viet Cong out there? Are they in spider holes? Is there an entire network of tunnels all around the opening with yet another enemy soldier hiding like some kind of Indonesian mongoose?

A fifteen-minute wait seems like an hour as C.B. scans the country-side for signs of movement. He sees none. There are no other Zips or Gooks, as C.B. now feels he must call them. In a numb daze he sits motionless for another fifteen minutes, watching and waiting.

"*Silence is golden,*" C.B. hums softly to himself.

Finally, C.B. reaches in his pack and retrieves his rifle sling. Attaching it to his weapon and hanging it over his neck and around his shoulder, he climbs down from the leathery-leaved tree that no longer has any resemblance to anything in Mississippi. Cautiously and slowly, he walks toward his kill. Having heard about soldiers who wet themselves in the excitement of their first contact, he reaches down to feel himself. His pants are dry...and he's almost disappointed. He focuses and tries to concentrate on everything around him. His heart pounds as he nears the motionless body. The platoon sergeant's warning comes to memory—that if a soldier takes a good look in the face of his first kill, he can never, ever, get that image out of his mind.

"Don't do it," C.B. reminds himself. Believing that the face might stay in daydreams and bring on nightmares, he refuses to look at it.

Charley Cong lies in a puddle of his own body fluids at the exit to his earth. C.B. removes a knife from the sheath held around his kill's waist. The crude sheath and rope of sea grass can stay. The knife will be a war trophy to send home to Taylor, Mississippi.

After securing the soldier's AK-47, he carefully checks for other things as he's supposed to. Finding nothing else, he turns to go back to his post. Almost looking back, he remembers again what was said about seeing.

"Who needs it? Ain't no use to creatin' ghosts fer a future with a forever 'at could be too long."

The rest of the day seems like a week. As it nears its end, darkness threatens to push through the jungle from the DMZ. Although a helicopter is supposed to evacuate C.B., a couple of problems may complicate plan A. The downpour of a tropical monsoon is threatening. Egg-beaters can't fly in such stuff. Secondly, although they have lights, using them makes a chopper too easy a target.

God is great. As if an answer to prayer, the threatening rain is slow in arriving, and just as the last of light is about to disappear, the welcome chopping sound from rotors is so very good to hear. This particular bird is from C.B.'s home unit, the Army's Screaming Eagles Division. They are pleased with the opportunity to return to camp with a "confirmed" kill.

C.B. escorts a cowboy of a crew chief over to help retrieve the Viet Cong. An M-60 door-gunner also tags along. He doesn't look to be more than 18 years old. C.B. knows the young man is not supposed to leave the ship...and wonders if it's more out of disrespect for rules and authority or just plain stupidity.

They reach the dead soldier, and the gunner says something irreverent about there being one less Gook in the land of the soon-to-be lamed and maimed. The M-60 jockey sticks his finger in a pool of Victor Charley's blood...and uses it for his own face-paint camouflage.

As the three of them drag the dead soldier to the chopper, C.B. wonders if the young door gunner has killed so often that he just can't feel it any more. Heavy breaths are drawn as they toss the V.C. in the helicopter. It's as if he were nothing more than a sack of 13-13-13. The door-gunner sticks his finger in the V.C.'s bullet hole for more blood...as if he's teasingly taking a second dose of death.

With this new burden of death bouncing around from his head to his heart, a wave of nausea passes over C.B., but he'll be fine once he's back at Camp Eagle near Phu Bai...waiting for his next assignment. There he'll get his head straight...and think about having only 240 days and a wake-up left to go.

As the Huey lifts off, the crew chief starts singing what all U.S. soldiers in-country jokingly call the national anthem of Vietnam. Everyone on the bird joins in singing, *We gotta get out of this place...if it's the last thing we ever do.*

XXXIII:
Humping the Bush and More College

C.B. IS A GOOD SOLDIER...teachable, disciplined, and mistakenly under the impression he is or will be trained for everything he'll need to know. He's exactly what the junior-grade graduates fresh out of R.O.T.C. need as they practice giving sometimes senseless orders.

From the first contact every mission is three-fold...to survive, to be there for the other soldiers in your unit, and lastly to accomplish your assigned objective. Once you've proven your mettle in the bush, your fellow soldiers count on it.

Even as special as the NTK platoon is, they still receive some more standard or normal assignments. Despite C.B.'s perfection at his unique tradecraft, he often has to fill in for non-sniper slots. It's strange and unbefitting that such a good sniper is not valued any more than to be assigned menial tasks with their own risks, but the military way of doing things frequently negates logic.

Told he can get a pair of wings on his uniform by volunteering to take on some routine mercy missions, C.B. hovers over harm's way. Hanging out the open door of a UH-1 with an M-60, on-the-job-training comes easy. Firing short bursts of rounds for target practice is fun until practice is over and shooting is at soldiers who shoot back.

Guns are guns to the inexperienced young officer in charge of assignments. A true marksman like C.B. is just another grunt to a ninety-day wonder who sees the war only through the rattling of his typewriter from the safety of a quonset hut at Headquarters. The excitement is out someone else's window.

On the early end of a year tour of duty in 'Nam, time seems to stop. Looking ahead at such a year makes it seem like forever…and forever is exactly what it turns out to be for some. On a patrol north of Cam Lo, booby-traps claim two members of the NTK platoon. It's along the Demarcation Line that's ironically called the Demilitarized Zone (DMZ). The Sergeant they call Top had warned his soldiers not to get close to one another in friendship or distance. A buddy can be there one minute and be gone the next. These were young men that C.B. was just getting to know. They were friendships that could have lasted a lifetime, and in a way they did. They just got blown short.

MEANWHILE, IN MY FIRST senior year at the university, I'm learning about forest roads and skid trails. Exhausted from a full field day of surveying, I sit against a redvine-draped dogwood. Now that I've got my own wheels for my personal ride back to campus, I can wait around until the other students leave…to enjoy fully my intrigue with the forest.

Meditating in Mother Nature's solitude, I watch a bat. He drinks and feeds as he flies parallel to and down among water-filled ruts left from the tire tracks of a logging truck. While my professors and the loggers curse such seeps and wet spots that trucks have to contend with, the bat knows an area rich with opportunity when he sees it. The muddied-up paths so hated by the forest engineers are thick with mosquitoes and loved by the bats.

If I were smart enough to be a forestry professor, I'd give my students the whole picture. Unfortunately for me and my hypothetical students, that won't happen. Because of such things as calculus, with its transposed numbers dyslexically woven throughout, I'll be doing well if I just get by being a student. Dad's always accused me of being the one in our family to inherit the blame gene and claim everything is always someone else's fault, but I can't help the way those numbers and letters keep jumping around when I calculate or read.

Forestry in the upper-level classes turns out to be much more enjoyable than the earlier courses. Instead of having to struggle with what seems like stupid questions on more stupid homework assignments and the stupidest tests, I am now mentally saturated with the practical stuff…like more than anybody should ever have to know about the Southeast's holier-than-thou, southern yellow pine bushes. Beyond such as that, I get a taste of several other so-called lesser forest types and enjoy learning about my beloved cypress and gum complex.

C.B. IS HAVING HIS own experience…with Asian trees. He's stepped into a whole new world. The larger of his vegetation ranges from un-named monarchs of the deep jungle to rubber tree plantations alongside of farm crops. Even the simple can be complicated in Vietnam. A nipa palm is not a peculiar plant until it has somehow sprouted a sniper's platform, customized with camouflage.

Chances and ways to die are endless, and the V.C. know them all. This is a place where even dried cakes of elephant droppings that you want to kick can hide booby-trapped death. The enemy along both sides of the Laotian border are so clever about inventing ways to kill that Top makes his men count their feet every morning before they start the day. While C.B. tries to make every step as purposeful as if walking barefoot around broken glass, Feet makes a tired old joke about his nickname probably being his fate.

Every man has to handle his own mind games as best he can. With the exception of snipers, soldiers normally don't have time for the kind of thought that multiplies their worries. Too much thinking and fretting for too long can magnify things that shouldn't have been problems. That could get you killed if you're not careful. In the bush good reflexes are better than intelligence.

On a day when the unit's sniper is just another grunt, C.B. pushes his naive confidence. Volunteering to take a turn as point man, he's lead-ing a reconnaissance patrol in the A Shau Valley. Jungle combat is close. The foliage is such that what's really needed is a bulldozer to go out ahead of them.

A shift in the weather makes for a sudden surge of alertness. Increased awareness is a good thing, but better visibility could be a two-way bayo-net. In conditions not as foggy as they were only moments ago, the patrol proceeds with caution. The terrain and vegetation change. They now have to negotiate head-high elephant grass. Since Feet is taller than C.B., he volunteers to take the lead…an unexpected offering from a medic. Each one spaces out the way he has been trained and—

"Boom!" The explosion sounds like lightning hitting C.B.'s turtle shell helmet. Sounds of horror reverberate throughout the platoon.

Flying debris settles over the aftermath. C.B. determines he's not hurt and realizes the fallen soldier is Feet. Having stepped on a land mine, Feet lies still, unconscious…and gone from the left knee down. All eyes are drawn in dismay to the bleeding stump where there was once a leg.

Soldiers stand in place as they get up from where they've dived. There's muttering and cussing and wondering what to do next amid fear of finding another booby trap. Top tells his men to freeze. With cautious steps he works his way toward his soldier.

Reaching his wounded man without setting off another charge, Top lifts Feet's head and calls his name. No avail. Top shakes him. Feet opens his eyes to semi-consciousness. Dazed and no doubt in shock, Feet reaches inside his medical kit with grim determination. Hay goes forward and takes over for Top, helping Feet help himself with his own first aid. The NTK platoon watches their wounded medic stop his own nub of a leg from bleeding…and then meticulously place the unused parts of his medical kit back in its pack.

"Mucho macho," Hay says of his friend.

C.B. goes to his Lord in a sigh of prayer relief. *"There, but fer Yo' grace. An' please don't be runnin' outta no mo' grace, God. Amen."*

An airlift called a dust-off is radio requested. While they wait, they try to comfort Feet with lies about how everything will be all right. When the chopper arrives and Feet punches his ticket home, the men all bid their comrade an almost jealous farewell but carefully call him "Doc" instead of his other nickname.

A foot of distance one way or the other could have made all the difference. For Feet, of all people, to lose a foot…it's just one of those things that's too real to have happened. It's a perverted sense of war that would string along soldiers like puppets in such a horrible play of death and destruction.

In a blunt declaration Top sums it all up. "There's gotta be some Buddha'cratic son-of-a-bitch over here pulling th' strings."

C.B. wonders if Top's not right.

Instead of going straight up and then out, the Medevac chopper leaves by barely clearing the treetops. Small arms fire is drawn from the V.C. as the Medevac clears. A Cobra gunship drops down from out of nowhere, and Hell's havoc rains on those that were harassing Feet's ride home. "God's th' onli'est one 'sposed to get vengeance," Auntay used to quote from one of her memory verses. But for Feet's foot, even Auntay ought to understand how damned good it feels to see that Cobra get some payback.

TAKING A VERSE, IF not a whole book out of the Bible belt, my campus and its town are within a dry county. The University's official position on beer and better booze is that no one on campus drinks. If the authorities don't see anyone drinking, then there is no drinking. The administration is glad to look the other way and remain clean while students swim in their private sea of spirits.

Most male students worry only that they'll flunk out and find themselves drafted. So far, there are no females in the forestry school...or any being drafted.

Hours drag during some classes and dry up during others. A course like Forest Economics can make you sleepy even on the way to it. Although I really want to land that advanced degree in Wildlife Management, a legitimate concern over the possibility of my not making the cut for admission to grad school has developed.

Getting my draft deferral extended would be comforting. On the other hand, I suspect Scientific Reading in German is a bitch compared to the fun I'd probably have learning to fly a helicopter. I suppose speculation is easy. Once I got to 'Nam and had to confront actual death, a lot of my ideas would probably change.

Truth be known, I don't know if I could handle my own moral questions about what may or may not be going on over there. If communism is as bad as we've been led to believe, it seems to me we could let nature run her course. Wouldn't it devour itself and crumble on its own? I don't understand how the horrendous havoc I see on TV could be helping to increase world stability. Stereoscopically mapping out the vegetative cover types in the school forest, I'm being spoiled by getting to use the latest infrared imagery from NASA. Here I am with technology that could read a co-ed's panty lines from a satellite while I doubt that C.B. has even the most basic of aerial photo support. He probably doesn't even have a pair of those neat aviator sunglasses. It seems as if they're worn by the entire stateside military from the National Guard to the Columbus Air Base fly-boys.

IN C.B.'S WORLD WHAT is cherished is a rainproof topo map covering his area of operation. The accuracy in sizing up an area of interest and concern can hold the key to life or death for the entire platoon. Regardless of the ambiguity of the big picture, the wages of this war are site specific for the individual warrior. Correct evaluations and calculations are counted on to cover your rear. With little wiggle-room and zero chance to run in fear, the NTK Platoon's analysis of a situation must be done with dependability.

AS OUR COUNTRY BECOMES more and more traumatized over the war, the news media reports an increasing number of college students turning onto drugs and dropping out of society. I don't see any of that in the forestry program. The university as a whole has a few dissenters who carry signs and wear beads and earrings. Mississippi State just doesn't lend itself to the civil disobedience that TV finds on other college campuses.

To me flower-power means I have memorized the scientific names of forty-eleven dozen spermatophytes that I'll be able to identify on a taxonomy class final. The pot-smoking hippies will never realize how much sweat, toil, and true commitment it takes to exist in the real world of environmental academia. Being a forestry major who spends as much time as possible in the woods, I don't worry as much about fashions as a lot of college students do. Hell no, they won't go. With their bell-bottoms and frat-rat designer-cut styles, I doubt many of them could stand one night in the Little Tallahatchie bottom, much less in C.B.'s Vietnam.

A typical weekend finds most of the pseudo-superior college students more into suds than any other activity. They are carded and refused beer sales until someone in the group is successful. Most follow sports like the southern religions they believe them to be.

I'll spend October weekends squirrel hunting and plinking around with a well-worn Savage .22/.410 over and under. I suppose anyone who's anyone would tote a twelve gauge, but there is something about a first gun, the way it fits your hands…especially one that's gone through the good times mine has. I wonder what kind of weapon C.B. is carrying and caring for now. Whatever it is, I'll bet he meticulously cleans it and probably has to in order to count on its keeping him alive.

WHEN C.B.'S NOT CHERISHING his sniper's rifle, he could be doing most anything. Today he's packing an over and under of his own made by General Motors. Having an M-79 grenade launcher on the bottom and a fully automatic M-16 rifle on the top, it looks like an assault rifle with the small end of a fly rod tube attached to its underneath.

There's movement through the brush…orange stripes. What the hell? It's a tiger! Right before God and C.B.'s eyes, in all of its beauty and wonder, it's a real, live wild tiger. The orange stripes are as orange as the black ones are black. If Scott could see this, he thinks…. What a rug that would….

Not aware of C.B.'s presence, the monstrous cat lurks out of the shadows and stops on the stream bank. The wind is carrying C.B.'s scent away from the tiger and thus prevents his detection. It would be easy to flip the weapon on rock and roll and fill this beautiful animal with lead. It'd be equally easy to let the poof from the grenade launcher which precedes the explosion of the grenade announce to the awesome specimen that his time as a tiger is up. He looks so powerful…with those sinewy shoulders.

Remembering another time and halfway around the world, when he purposely missed a mourning dove sitting on a telephone line over Taylor Creek, C.B. decides to let the tiger live. "Go on, little kitty. Go along yo' way an' eat you a Gook a day. Maybe 'at'll he'p me get th' hell back to th' U.S. of A."

The tiger leaves without ever even seeing C.B. A tree frog chorus breaks the silence. There's a fog of moist clouds. C.B. wishes for something else to drown out the memory of recent firefights. The overcast is pushing nightfall ahead of itself, but even if the weather breaks, the jungle canopy will prohibit good star watching. Good memories are important to a soldier at times like this. On those few nights when you can see the vastness of the heavens, you feel small and insignificant…and scared to face what you know you'll soon have to face.

Back at various base camps and between missions, C.B. witnesses waves of U.S. regular troops being processed in. Still treated like grunts in basic training, the cherries are kept too busy for any of them to be asking the hard questions…the ones when officers seem to be having an increasingly vague understanding of their own answers.

There is a significant downside to the need-to-know rule. When you have to go where you're told and do what you're told without question, that's a sure-fire way to keep morale in the pits. If no one appears sure of what's going on, everyone ends up lacking confidence.

Everything has to be explained to the "frigging new guys" to help keep them alive. In-country terminology demonstrates to the FNGs just how little they know. It's for their own good that they learn the lingo so as to avoid costly mistakes. In situations involving dilemmas, listening and paying attention can save lives. The FNGs in the less elite units than C.B.'s NTK platoon are young and inexperienced. They often aren't even shown enough respect to be talked to as adults. It's ironic. C.B. knows their adulthood will come quickly…or not at all.

I WISH C.B. WOULD write me. I feel like a mule wearing blinders, for I know so little about the real Vietnam situation. What I believe I understand is mostly derived from TV and the newspapers. The political leaders who support the war talk about things like "doing for your country," but I'm needing to know if what C.B. and the others are doing over there is really helping. Surely there is something more than ritual performance driving these bloodbaths.

While American ground troops are dying in the line of duty, could it be that our hawkish defense industry is preoccupied with making money? Is it worried more about its own self-preservation than it is about Vietnam? Are we too scared of starting another world war to summon up some firepower that's more soldier-safe, like missiles? Is there a silent conspiracy slithering somewhere under the surface of our democracy that says military solutions can be the answer to civil squabbles? Will killing all the communists even bring about democracy? Who's going to be left do any self-determining? Should this be someone else's war?

I hear so many contradictory opinions and news reports about Congressional mismanagement that I don't know if C.B.'s being in Vietnam is patriotic or stupid. I remember someone really close to me once saying that our leaders should let the troops fight right and end the war with our military might.

Are we getting any positive results from the so-called Vietnamization or the Geneva Accords or the Tonkin Gulf Resolution or Paris Peace Negotiations or from anything else that's supposed to stop Soviet advances? Are we caught in the middle without having considered location? Is some kind of Asiatic political force herding us right between China and Russia?

C.B.'S WORRIES ARE NOT theoretical. His concerns are for real. He lives it…and knows a side of Vietnam that the media doesn't know or discuss and can't share. It's the courage of the enemy. America doesn't hear about an opponent with a profound sense of pride and place. There's a special strength that comes to soldiers who care and believe about a homeland they value as worth defending.

The individual enemy soldier has a reliance on traditions and experiences from the past. He has a proven honor as old as the tropics. C.B.'s come to respect the Viet Cong guerrillas' innate ferocity and bravery…almost as deep as he hates them for possessing it.

Although it's said that V.C. could just as easily stand for viscous combat as for Viet Cong, there's another two parts to that story. In addition to the likelihood of doped-up aggression from whacky weed or the white, powdery stuff, our South Vietnamese allies are united by their blatant corruptness. It's a murderous and scary war.

It's hard to erase individuals from the debate…when there's more squatting in the background, ready to slide right in and take the place of every one you kill. C.B. constantly reminds himself that his main conviction is doing what he needs to do to stay alive. Motives become important when hope for a future is questionable. If your next step can get you blown away, there is some incentive for not taking it, unless staying in place presents even worse odds.

A twenty-four hour day is shaping up to be one of those with long nights when there is too much time to think. Offering the Rain-Buddhas a week's pay for a jar of White Rose petroleum jelly has C.B. hearing nothing back from his prayer but a distant rumbling that may or may not be Buddha's response. There's still no jar of much-needed salve for a raw rear.

Wind-splayed drops of moisture from the South China Sea meet up with those of the Indian Ocean for the kind of weather that is continuous, the two of them making for a monsoon season that blows all the way across the Island. When the Australian winds are added, C.B. has a storm called a typhoon, again so intense he can't tell if a noise is thunder or some war-type explosion in the distance. It's another of many times that lend themselves to good prayer and genuine, fervent promises to God.

After several weeks of nonstop rain, a day shows up with a sky that only weeps. A hard rain, slowly letting up, peppers C.B.'s poncho from all directions. It would probably be refreshing if he weren't already numb. C.B. promises himself that if he makes it out alive, he'll get rich by inventing a poncho that actually keeps you dry. You wouldn't think you could be cold when temperatures hang around 100 degrees, but wet nipples make for cold ribs during tropical nights. They in turn spread the chills. Army issue ponchos only funnel the water into unexpected leaks and eventually down the crack of your butt.

Tales and talk from other soldiers grow more pessimistic with each passing day. Accumulating numbers for kill reports seem to sometimes take precedence over NTK's combat strategy. The story goes and grows that some senior officers may be more concerned with facilitating their own promotions than getting those under their command home alive. Beyond just counting the days left in-country, C.B. even tries to figure how many he'll have to spend in what they call Indian territory.

To try to pass the time C.B. thinks back to his upbringing. He recalls Mr. J. once saying something about soldiers being susceptible to politicians once their mothers can no longer protect them. Maybe that's what's needed now, he thinks—some kind of Mothers to Win the War organization. They could march around the courthouse in Oxford, Mississippi, chanting, "Bring home our sons."

With a deep sigh and a dark twist of humor, C.B. painfully says aloud to himself, "Maybe th' Memphis Belle could lead a parade ridin' on back of a convertible…protestin' th' war and wavin' at her customers."

XXXIV:
The Valley of the Shadow

AFTER A HALF-DAY HELPING to identify and measure trees during an advanced forest mensuration lab, I come up on a personal conclusion. It has become obvious enough to me that I may as well admit I'm better suited to extrapolating volumes and prescribing hypothetical timber sales than I am at making small talk with a dozen other forester trainees.

Solemnly swearing to myself that I'll never be a politician, I watch as the others head for their bus ride back to campus. They understand that I want to hang around and admire trees without human influence. I'd just as soon not have to contend with certain blowhard student personalities or expose myself to the unnecessary smells of indiscrete natural gases and discrete alcohol sweat. When an alternative is the pleasant aromas of the school forest's greenery of board feet and bushes, it's not even close. If my preference to the boondocks makes me anti-social, so be it.

Dealing with stings of insects, gashes from briars, rashes from poisonous plants and other forest lab challenges doesn't bother me. It's the indoor classes that suck. While they all start out with enough interest to get you hooked, some kind of institutional shift soon takes over.

Warm water fisheries management is great as long as we're talking about large-mouth lunkers and their bluegill prey, but when the shift clicks in, I discover there's a portion of the pond that's all about statistical methods and procedures. Halfway through white-tailed deer studies, a scary academic similarity about population dynamics unfolds. Other courses continue the pattern which I come to call my minor problem.

While C.B. is probably mired in constant crap for real, I wonder if there's some great river or hallowed bottom in Vietnam worth his fighting for…and if we will ever again get to fish and hunt together. Assuming my buddy has it tough, I try to visualize what it's like for him over there. What will he be up against this week? What will the Army have him doing? Are things as bad as they are portrayed on TV? Is my best friend in daily fear? Are he and many of the thousands of other young soldiers over there going to live beyond their teenage years?

It's ironic to think that I, of all people, am pigeonholed in a socially scholastic category of young people. Safe and sound in the world of academia, I can keep my military draft deferral only as long as I'm able to perch precariously out on the semi-literary limb that may or may not lead to admission into graduate school.

Although my transcript constantly shows me near the bottom rung of the performance ladder, fellow forestry students keep me going by reminding me that my common sense is up there with the rest of them. One educatee tries taking an umbrella to the woods. An out-of-state scholar attempts to lay out a timber stand by poking a stick in the ground and placing a roll of kite string on it. He was planning to walk through the woods while pulling the loose end of the string…instead of tying the loose end to a tree and unrolling the spool as he walked.

I hope C.B. isn't surrounded by highly educated officers who lack common sense. Surely our leaders in Vietnam are figuring out the best way to win the war…and it will be over before I have to go. All across the country there's news of growing protests against the fighting. People are looking for those that they can blame and hate for the war. Many folks are coming to perceive the conflict as immoral and unjust.

TV news showed an angry Democratic convention in Chicago. There were sit-ins by peaceniks and demonstrations by anti-war protestors. Despite the efforts of police security, the political speeches were almost drowned out by the noise of the mob. Sometimes I think the war would be stopped cold turkey if our hippies advocated prolonging it instead of protesting it.

Having been honored as "Bull of the Woods" at Mississippi State's forestry conclave, I am to lead our forestry club in the competition at the next level…the Association of Southern Forestry Clubs' event hosted by Virginia Polytechnic Institute. Before our bus reaches V.P.I., we hear a news flash on the radio about another university. Kent State students who were protesting the war have been fired on…by the National Guard.

Hearing that several students were killed, I remember the second civil war in Oxford. During the forced integration of Ole Miss I was never concerned with what the guardsmen probably thought of us. As C.B. and I pelted the soldiers with snowballs from atop the buildings around Oxford's Square, it never dawned on me that they might have had real bullets. I guess Kent State's questions and my country's answers weren't too well thought through either.

During my first day of conclave competition at V.P.I., I'm proud to secure first place in timber cruising for the M.S.U. contingent. The next day I come in just out of the money in the pole-climbing event. Our team, unfortunately, doesn't score well enough to place. Busing back to Starkville from Blacksburg, I begin to think about so many good men that were not entered in the competition because of Vietnam.

While C.B. is probably worried about getting wasted for real, I feel guilty for thinking I'm wasting away trying to digest subject matter like forest history and policy theory. Indoor classes eat away at my mornings. Each course gobbles up an hour a day for two or three days a week...but it's not Vietnam.

WHEN THE MEN IN 'Nam see one of their own die, they lose a part of themselves they know they'll never again see. With Feet having taken an early ride home, Hay assumes the role of being C.B.'s best buddy in the bush...as well as becoming the platoon's new jokester. When C.B.'s not assigned sniping duties and there's a call for the buddy-system, he attaches himself to Hay. They learn to trust each others' instincts...in a connection that can come only from enduring together what they are having to face.

As their friendship grows, C.B. tries to talk Hay into giving up New York City to live in Mississippi...if they get out alive. Instead of agreeing, Hay says something in Spanish that sounds negative and then struts off singing his slightly revised lyrics to a popular song—"I fought th' law and, th' law *run.*"

On a day that finds the NTK Platoon searching a hamlet for evidence of the former presence of V.C., the locals can only insist that there are no Viet Cong here now. While filtering through the grass-and-cane hootch belonging to the Community Leader, C.B. comes across a Bible. Opening it to see if it has scribbled writing all over its margins the way Auntay's

Bible does, he discovers this Bible has had its center cut out…to hide a collection of dog tags.

When C.B. shows the war trophies to Top, a soldier standing next to him shouts, "Burn th' village!"

Agreeing, Top waves his hand toward the cluster of hooches and orders, "Torch it."

"Time to loot and pillage," rhymes the platoon's self-appointed poet laureate. He waits for someone else to make up the next verse.

As if Top hadn't already done so, and largely lacking the sounds of soul to participate in such poetry, the white lieutenant orders, "Grease it."

"Burn, baby, burn," C.B. catches himself cheering…and then remembers a portion of something that Mr. J. once said.

His comment had something to do with soldiers coming up on their moral capability. It must have meant the hell and horror of war can sometimes control the meanest of your thoughts and actions. As he's thinking there must be a way for people to settle things without bringing out the worst in them, the V.C. Community Leader is dealt with. And these are memories that C.B. knows he will have to live with.

For the month of August the soldier from Taylor scores the most confirmed kills in his platoon. Even though the NTK is referred to as "unattached," C.B.'s home unit of the 101st Airborne Division honors him as their Battalion-level Soldier of the Month. Either by coincidence or programmed timing, "Specialist Sniper" is to go before the board to determine whether he makes Buck Sergeant.

As the Old Man preps him for his appearance, C.B. is told they'll probably start off with some easy questions, something like asking him his age and I.Q. However, when the time comes, things look different from the way Top described them.

An NCO with big arms, rolled up sleeves, and tattoos asks the first question. "Spec Four, without using your hands, tell me how you tie a necktie."

Thanks to all those times Auntay made him wear a tie to church, C.B. is able to stumble through the answer.

"What does the 'Cong' in Viet Cong mean?" another board member asks.

"Communist," C.B. answers correctly.

A couple of spit-and-shined officers take over and bombard him with a series of similar gimmies. C.B. answers correctly and builds his confidence. Sensing the end of the interview coming, he's already thinking about getting his hard stripes and how strange it will feel to be called the dreaded five-letter name…Sarge.

"Why are you in Vietnam, Soldier?" a polished monster of a Master Sergeant asks.

C.B. knows he's supposed to say something patriotic about freedom from communism but a special truth that's more important than protocol surrounds him like a spirit and takes over. In case anyone on the promotion board doesn't know it, it's time they did.

"I'm fightin' to help my brothers in th' NTK platoon get home alive…an' hopefully in one piece."

Scary silence follows for a long moment. C.B. wonders if he has blown the interview. A lifer with campaign stripes all over his uniform resumes the questioning.

"Let's talk about your unit's call sign. What does that acronym stand for?"

"I don't understand the question," C.B. admits and worries for a second time straight that he won't make the grade of E-5.

"The NTK abbreviation—what do those letters stand for?"

"Oh…uh, I'm not sure," C.B. answers.

The interrogator watches his comrades' reactions and then locks in on C.B. "That's all right, soldier. Sometimes it's safer not to know. It may be that the NTK unit is on a *need to know* basis."

The vote for promotion is unanimous. C.B.'s new Buck Sergeant stripes mean he will receive a pay raise and be on a lot less duty rosters when in base camps. He's presented an engraved Zippo cigarette lighter with his home unit's Screaming Eagle insignia on one side and a rather pertinent poem on the other. After reading it to himself, he sees that everyone is waiting for a reaction. He doesn't comment about the poem…and just nods a skeptical "thank you."

A three-day pass to visit the in-country R&R Center of his choice comes with C.B.'s latest recognitions. He's thinking any place with a rolled barbed-wire perimeter and having nothing worse than enemy sapper attacks or nightly incoming mortar to worry about would be a nice change. Having heard what a great place Vung Tau is, he makes it his selection.

Looking down from a helicopter without his hands being on an M-60, an M-16, or his special rifle brings a naked feeling, but the isolated little outpost on the South China seacoast is beautiful. As the Huey lands, C.B. is thinking that this is a place he would like to hide out for the duration of the war. Stepping out of the aircraft, he tastes nothing except the salty air of the sea and is pleased not to be greeted by the smell of diesel fuel burning human excrement. Whereas you'd expect to find that at a regular base camp, here he smells nothing but helicopter exhaust.

Perpetuating the living history of yesterday's world, a Vietnamese carries on a thousand-year-old tradition right outside the concertina wire. Even knowing war makes for a near-winless labor, he plows on…using a water buffalo. This country has no time or room for despair.

C.B. wonders if we ought to be doing something to preserve this way of life instead of blowing it to hell and back. He recalls another of Auntay's sayings from the Bible. It was something about nothing topping the courage of a noble fool.

The water buffalo swats flies away with his tail, and the Vietnamese wipes his own sweaty face on a black, silky-looking sleeve. If he were dressed this way in the bush, that alone could be enough to get the little brown man eliminated. Maybe preoccupation with a farm animal is one of the criteria used here for distinguishing ally from foe. What else could be telling anyone that this man is not a V.C. who needs to be killed?

The new Buck Sergeant is checked into what will be his quarters of three days for the strange and almost forgotten experiences of lying on a cot and sleeping with no weapon. Not taking long to feel claustrophobic, C.B. strolls outside and over for a closer look through the perimeter fence. Wearing their pointed and saucer-shaped straw hats, a group of Mamasans, as Vietnamese women are called, are apparently using nothing more than the sun's heat to dry rice. The rice is simply laid out on what looks like larger, upside down versions of the woven cane hats.

There is a young lady in the bunch that C.B. wouldn't mind looking at in a much more personal way. He tries to get her to come over to the fence and talk, but she only smiles at his efforts. She may not speak English, but the more he looks at her, the more he thinks he'd like to teach her all she needs to know. He'd like to take her back to America and hold her little copper body up against his until his last Mississippi sun has set.

On the inside of the compound, a boy san, as the young boys are called, is selling pineapples. C.B. pays the youngster a dong and gets back a couple of piasters in the exchange. From the young boy's expression C.B. figures he has been screwed on the purchase but doesn't much care. He's too awestruck by a child of no more than seven or eight years of age having such grownup ways as to be already cheating his customer.

The lad skillfully prepares C.B.'s pineapple with a razor sharp machete. He spins the big fruit on a stick with one hand and cuts off a perfect spiral of its exterior with the other…the discarded portion having all the little black pointy spikes that must be seeds. Witnessing such a preparation was worth the money, and a pineapple has never tasted so good.

When C.B. looks up from the flat and sandy coastal paradise, he gazes directly into the hills. He would appreciate the mountainous profile and beyond, if he could look without seeing what he knows is really there. He makes a conscious effort to try not to remember. He's here now, and this is a place where he's supposed to relax. The last thing he needs to do is to think about what he's left behind…and what he has to go back to.

Periodic blasts of incoming continue to remind him of what he doesn't want to be reminded of. He remembers Feet. Since a foot got Feet a ticket home, C.B. looks down at his own left foot…and thinks about his little toe and quietly says to himself, "Don't even think about it."

C.B. spends most of his three-day stay lying on his cot, waiting for meals and re-living what he had hoped he would be able to keep from thinking about. Several times a day he prays…and then dozes off, only to have bad dreams. He awakes…and thinks…and eats and sleeps, hoping it's not a sign of future sleep.

The seven confirmed kills, which earned him his three-day pass, are frightening remembrances. They are horrors that haunt C.B. at every closure of his eyelids. His first kill is the worst visitor of the unwanted memories. The first one felt and still feels so different from the others. The V.C. was a short little man to have cast such a long shadow back to where C.B. was. There is no doubt he was enemy…wearing black pajamas and carrying an AK-47. He would have killed the first American that stepped out of a chopper at the LZ. It was all his choice to die for Uncle Ho. One hope is that he was too young to have had a wife and children.

The bible of Vietnam has its own golden rule. You either do it or have it done to you. Some religious hymn of forgiveness should have come to mind as C.B. touched the hair trigger of his special sniper's rifle. Instead, as his bullet entered the V.C.'s eardrum, he was subconsciously preparing to hum, "Silence is golden."

What has happened? Why should he worry about the Gook's family and friends now…when he didn't then? How can there be such guilt in a country where killing is the necessary evil for survival? The three-day R&R is up…and C.B. is anything but rested, relaxed, or recuperated.

As he waits at the heliport for a ride back to his unit, a soldier hands him an old newspaper. "Check out the anti-Americans protesting the war."

The paper tells of the sad fate of a student protest at the all-black Jackson State College…in Mississippi. Several students there have been killed by police gunfire…while trying to make their opinions heard about not supporting the war over here. C.B. looks at the other soldier and doesn't mention being from Mississippi, perhaps being ashamed of it.

A Vietnamese girl screams. Two soldiers stand and watch as she is being roughly shaken by a third. The grunt who showed C.B. the newspaper casually walks back inside the dispatcher's hanger, as if he doesn't want to see any more. C.B. gawks, instead.

The girl is slugged in the stomach, just as if she were a man hit by another man. She looks over at C.B. as if she's asking for help. He thinks he recognizes her from three days ago…as the China doll that he'd fallen in love with through the rolled barbed-wire perimeter fence.

Yelling for them to stop, C.B. runs toward the three soldiers. Not knowing how he'll deal with his moment for heroism doesn't phase him. All he is thinking of is rescuing her and somehow taking her home. Closing in, he sees that the three soldiers are an Army Captain, a First Sergeant, and an ARVN officer of some sort and rank he can't identify.

Quick to acknowledge C.B.'s concern, the NCO steps forward to explain that the girl was caught setting the Soviet equivalent of a U.S. claymore mine just outside the perimeter…on a trail where American soldiers patrol on daily sweeps. After being bluntly informed that the ARVN interpreter who hit her is simply interrogating one of their own in the way the South Vietnamese do, C.B. is ordered to return to where he was waiting for his ride.

He obeys, shakes his head in disbelief, and thinks of the contrast between this reality and the love he could have given this young girl as the mother of his children. They could have lived in Taylor, Mississippi, happily, ever aft—

"Pow!"

C.B. executes a rolling turn on the tarmac, instinctively ducking at the unmistakable sound of a .45 caliber pistol. The ARVN has shot her in the head, killing her.

Again recognizing C.B.'s reaction, the First Sergeant repeats his order, "Go on back to where you belong, soldier."

Emotions shattered and reflexes spent, C.B. complies. While the soldiers disappear with their "confirmed kill," he'll quietly wait outside the quonset hut for his ride. A mailbox sits awkwardly by the heliport terminal. Postage is free to soldiers.

Wishing he had better penmanship, C.B. writes only a quick note to send home to Auntay. She wouldn't believe what he has just witnessed...nor does he want to tell it. Instead, he simply sticks a picture of himself and his new hard stripes in the envelope. It shows him wearing his boonie hat, but neither she nor anyone she shows it to will be able to tell from the picture what constitutes the seven strange-looking things strung on his hat's lanyard.

The other soldier who is waiting for his UH-1 air-taxi ride comes out of the hanger as C.B. seals his envelope. The fellow passenger doesn't mention the shot. C.B. doesn't either. They just glance at each other. C.B. writes "FREE APO San Francisco" where a stamp would go for anyone not lucky enough to enjoy the privilege of being in 'Nam. After he deposits his letter in the mailbox, his commuter comrade offers up a cigar to help with their "hurry up and wait."

"Thank you," C.B. accepts appreciatively and flicks his new lighter to life.

He puffs on the smoky-stale stogie until an orange glow appears. For only a short moment the aroma takes his memory off the mayhem and misery of the kind of dehumanizing warfare he is coming to know all too well. He thinks about home...and me and stealing cigars at Munford's Grocery.

Too soon his thoughts go back to the kind of fighting that probably thrives only in Vietnam. It must be giving some soldiers in the higher-up command some kind of perverse pleasure. Must our leaders continue with the war to keep from admitting they may have been wrong? Will nobody in control acknowledge that we may be screwing-up? Couldn't that idea come to the top of a list of possible options?

A tear traces a salty path down C.B.'s cheek. The words blur as his eyes fill with more tears. He re-reads the little poem inscribed on the lighter that his country gave him for becoming a Buck Sergeant and earning his three-day R&R—"*101st Airborne Division—Yea though I walk through the valley of the shadow of death, I will fear no evil, for I am the meanest son-of-a-bitch in the valley.*"

XXXV:
Jesus Saves
...Some

WHEN THE WHITE HOUSE, the House of Representatives, and the Senate tire of squabbling, politics permits a decision—U.S. fighting men will not be authorized to enter Cambodia...not even in hot pursuit of an enemy who does. According to Washington, D.C., a five-kilometer-wide boundary will prevent our soldiers from straying into forbidden territory.

In layover of Vietnamese sorts, C.B. lies on the ground near Long Xuyen. The safest two-thirds of the tour so far has been spent waiting. Looking forward to what they call a pony ride, the NTK Platoon waits at an unofficial Landing Zone. As opposed to the standard Army Slick they call a Huey, today's taxi is a large and ugly Air Force helicopter referred to as the Jolly Green Giant.

The five-click, buffer direction from the beltway is translated rather loosely within circles of military intelligence. It facilitates a dawn insertion into Cambodia by approximately five kilometers for C.B. and the other pawns in the NTK platoon. Not far inland from the Gulf, C.B. and company are to hump it on a 45-degree bearing. The terrain is not exactly the Ho Chi Minh highway, but navigating north and east will guide them parallel to the border...supposedly.

"Where there's a will, there's a jungle warfare way," the platoon pessimist complains.

Top answers with a tired old non-commissioned, military cliché having to do with his soldier's alternatives.

"Keep the noise down," L.T. orders, helping Top be in control of field maneuvers.

There're no more cynical comments and no more jungle jingles. The seriousness of the mission takes shape. The NTK Operatives, as they like to call themselves, are to set up at a strategic location and be prepared for their prey to come soldiering by. If, after a period of time known only to Top and L.T., no contact is made with the unfriendlies, then a diagonal sweep is to be executed...taking out enemy forces along the way. Based on the disputable accuracy of enemy status reports, between where the coastline and the Vietnam and Cambodia borders meet and some new ambush site that Top knows about, life is likely to become interesting.

The first half of the hike is scary but uneventful. Somber clouds hover heavily over the path-like trail that's said to be a major infiltration route through an otherwise dense jungle extending all the way from the coast. The platoon eases through the jungle-like vegetation to an area where they will set up another "hurry up and wait" ambush.

Approaching a small clearing in the vegetation, the NTK soldiers are stunned at what they see. Recoiling in horror and in the midst of death, C.B. counts over thirty human bodies apparently left to rot with their nauseous stench of decay. The odor is overpowering. In the presence of so many stiff and putrid corpses nothing can be said or done to lessen the gruesomeness of the part of the war they've come across.

A soldier tries making a dark joke. No one laughs. C.B. wonders if the abundance of bodies marks the so-called strategic location that Top was keeping under his helmet. It's apparently not, as the NTK Platoon moves on.

They are soon setting up positions for an ambush. To serve his platoon more as a lookout than as a sniper, C.B. is directed to a tree. The trance-like semi-focus that's common to ordinary soldiers can get a sniper or man on guard duty killed. A good guard stays somewhere between alert and more alert. Anything less could give the whole platoon a bad day.

A sniper fills the one role in the whole platoon in which his reflexes don't have to stay ahead of his brain to keep him alive, but time is the one thing in 'Nam that doesn't seem to die young. You have to wait for it and then take whatever it brings with it, the killing and eventually...one hopes the healing. Illusions sometimes overshadow reality. An ardent battle of will is required to fight off misery and helplessness.

Having to sit in a tree for hours upon hours brings a perilous kind of monotony. When a person's mind is free to wander in isolation and wonder in loneliness, that's how boredom becomes exhausting. Perhaps that's one of the reasons very smart people aren't sent to war as often as ordinary folks. When there's nothing else to do except feel sorry for yourself, the almost standard bliss of ignorance can be a bounty of blessing.

A snake slithers through its habitat below. When there is nothing other than thinking to release your pent-up energy, such periodic interruptions can help to keep you from losing your sanity. Resembling a common garter snake, it is dark and has stripes of vivid yellow. C.B. remembers his in-country orientation lecture. The Green Beret was lying on purpose, to drive home the point that all snakes in 'Nam were to be left alone. The super-soldier with the funny green hat was himself funny. He claimed that Southeast Asia has 150 species of snakes and that 149 of them are deadly poisonous. "The other one," he said, "eats you whole."

As the little Asian snake with the possible "big" bite wiggles into the grass to disappear, C.B. recalls the whopping of a Yocona Puff Adder. He can almost taste the soapy suds Preacher Taylor used to wash the cuss word out of his overly excited mouth. He'll enjoy telling me the Green Beret's snake story…if he can just live long enough to get back to Mississippi.

Oceans apart from the reality of combat, instructions are issued for soldiers to yell "dung li" three times before shooting. Even the more ridiculous orders from Washington must have some hidden practical value. If you're busy thinking about how stupid some of them are, then that could help keep you awake and alert when you need to be. Of course, in the bush the Vietnamese equivalent of "halt" yelled three times would translate into certain disaster…in any language.

C.B remembers back to his beloved logging woods and the futility of voice commands given to a mule who has stubborned up. He thinks about me and wonders if the leaders in college are as far removed from the real world as his wanta-be generals seem to be from this war.

In addition to weariness, the weather is another warrior to be fought and fended off. Like referees in an athletic contest who appear to be on the opposing team, the elements elect to favor Charlie Cong's game plan. When downpours drench you through to the bone and there's nothing to do but endure, it makes for long, wet nights. When the torrential rain won't let up, the extra weight of a wet poncho on the shoulders can even be a comforting warmth.

Normally soothing enough to stifle any ability to stay awake, an orchestra of jungle tree frogs teams up with a choir of Indonesian insects for a croaking, beeping, and clicking kind of harmony. When darkness deepens to the point he can't see, C.B. climbs down to join his comrades. He won't draw a turn at guard duty for at least four hours. Being on the move might increase vulnerability, so his first prayer is to thank God that they're staying put tonight.

Sleep comes soon and brings dreams of the fireflies of home. They all too quickly take on the appearance of tracer bullets in a night firefight. The horrifying dream wakens C.B. in a cold sweat. He quickly calms himself enough to realize he's really had a pretty good day. A good day in the bush is one when the North Vietnamese force didn't show and nobody in the platoon got himself or one of his buddies killed.

The rain has stopped. Perhaps the monsoon season is yielding. Morning air seems naked without rain and breathes differently.

The time has come to move out. NTK platoon doesn't go far before they come to a river that has to be crossed. With swollen and numb fingers, C.B. proudly holds his special sniper's rifle above his head and wades waist deep through the sluggishness of the water. The gumbo-like mud of the undersurface tries unsuccessfully to keep his boots. They'll have to be laced tighter at another time, maybe the first time they stop to rest. For now, he has to cover the other soldiers as they cross the river with their various types of weapons.

The excessively muddy water appears to be too—no, it isn't…. A minnow-type small fry darts across the surface of the water in an apparent effort to escape some Asian predator-fish. The Yocona and Little Tallahatchie Rivers are here for a brief few seconds. It's so similar to home and yet so different…and so very far away.

The land of green and mean doesn't admit to knowing winter, except for being that time of the year with the heaviest rains. With teeth clattering and knees trembling, the platoon is back on the move, warming up and drying out.

There's movement ahead. The point man sticks up his hand. The platoon freezes in place. With each soldier at his ready fire position, a shadowy haze reveals itself…as a monkey. Unanimous sighs of relief express the good fortune that no one was fired upon…or opened up on the monkey. Such a mistake as unnecessary noise could give away the platoon's location and cost lives.

Cautiously, they continue on, with Hay taking his turn as point man. Less than four clicks from the monkey sighting, he decides to take a short cut on an easy-looking route. It's more or less a trail and goes in the same general direction as the correct bearing.

"Ca...boom!"

A forty-foot blaze of fire shoots straight up around Hay.

Pandemonium breaks out. Small arms fire erupts, and the constant popping sound of rifle fire filters through the explosion still ringing in C.B.'s ears. Shots seem to be coming from everywhere. Soldiers scream as they are hit. C.B. crawls to thicker cover and looks for a target at the same time.

In a matter of a minute that seems more like ten, a hostile location is pinpointed. The American soldier closest to it tosses a well-placed grenade. It ends that enemy's existence. The bulk of the shooting tapers off...and was apparently from the NTK platoon. If there were any V.C. shooting besides the one just eliminated, the survivors have managed to flee through the thick jungled understory to their next ambush site. It's a kind of leapfrog or following in front that's used by both sides and allows for a fighting that won't go away.

As much as all the men would like to hear their lieutenant call in for air support, they know it can't be done. The roar of a jet won't be responding here because it's a jungle warfare that's just up too close.

Hay, history now, took the bulk of the land mine's charge. He buffered others from being hit by the blast. He'd like knowing that. Two other men were hit with AK-47 fire but neither is critical. As first aid is administered to the wounded soldiers, C.B. looks at the bright red blood all over the busted-up body of his buddy. He wonders why it would happen to the best of them and how Hay's death could make a difference in Vietnam or anywhere else.

A medevac chopper is radioed to come after Hay's remains and the wounded soldiers. A secluded spot of semi-safety for a temporary LZ is swept and checked for the possibility of mines. Additional pieces of Hay are spotted. C.B., crying, finds his late best buddy's left arm severed from the elbow down...with its hand clutching the little Bible he was known to carry.

As the helicopter arrives and two body bags are thrown out, bile rises in C.B's throat. While the two men who were wounded are helped aboard, C.B. walks around dragging one of the plastic body bags like a cotton sack. Like a rolled up rug, the V.C. who was killed by the grenade is tossed in the aircraft. C.B. is ordered to give up the hunt for more pieces of Hay and to load what's been found on the chopper.

As the Huey departs, someone starts humming. More out of respect than sacrilegious sarcasm, the rest of the unique unit joins in whistling or singing, "Put your hand in the hand...." They'll save their customary farewell chant for a toast when they can come up with some beer that probably won't be cooler than lukewarm.

The clamoring parts in C.B's silence now are questions. Why did death select Hay from among them? Is it all chance or luck? Did he just happen to be hand-carrying his little New Testament? Were he and God communicating with each other? How could he once have been so alive and full of life...to now be so dead and so gone? Is this part of the Big Plan that Hay's grandmother was so sure about...and Auntay and Preacher Taylor?

"Shake it off and move out," Top orders as he notices that C.B. is still unsuccessful at holding back tears.

C.B. knows he has to pull himself together in order to be able to continue with the caution that's needed. He'll carry on, even with the only thing for certain being confusion. Knowing that everything would be so much more comforting if God would just give some kind of sign, C.B. goes to prayer.

"Lord, a good sign'd sho' be a little somethin' to let us know You heared us singin' an' hummin' an' whistlin'...an' didn't take no offense."

XXXVI:
R&R in the Grove

TAKING ONE VERY QUESTIONABLE and measured step at a time, the NTKs rely on their platoon sergeant's compass to lead them south and east. As the soldiers move slowly and cautiously downhill on their last leg through the jungle and toward the flat coast, their goal soon becomes more to reach their destination than to search and destroy. Top has assured his men that a temporary refuge from the war is not far ahead.

When they reach the delta and cross a saline marsh full of wading birds, C.B. wonders if Scott's Granna knows their names. Walking through the soup-like quagmire tells him why such birds are almost weightless and have long legs and big feet.

Over an estuary that's probably too salty to grow rice the sun is going down red. Fading sunlight plays games with the dense foliage. C.B. could enjoy its being so pretty if flashes of memory concerning the two wounded soldiers, the enemy casualty, and the loss of Hay weren't busy preserving the ugliness of such close death. If that weren't written in blood red, the striking beauty of these bogs and the expanse of where the big water merges with them could be fully appreciated.

What Top's called The Grove has marsh on three sides and the sea on its fourth. As the NTK platoon reaches the sea, they angle back to enter a narrow and winding corridor. It's formed by a nearly impenetrable maze of mangrove trees that appear to be The Grove. C.B. follows Top closely as they negotiate the aerial roots off to each side of the strange trees.

A tired platoon comes next, wading between the limbs and roots and negotiating whatever doesn't protrude from the semi-salt water. The corridor-like channel is having one of its two daily, river-like encounters with the South China Sea's tide. Since the sea tides are coming up, the rising waters cause a current to push at the backs of the soldiers. As they wade along, slight waves lap at their buttocks and then at their waists. They are almost carried without gravity.

Later in the day, receding action of the tide will cause the current to go back out the same corridor. It's as if the sea is breathing through a river of life…inhaling and exhaling in order to stay vibrant. The salty water tries to wash out the sweat stains from everyone's jungle fatigues. Although the whitish lines under the arms and around the necks of the fatigues don't yield, the soldiers and their clothes get a good soaking. C.B.'s body feels clean, and he looks forward to his skin having the sandpapery texture that Top says it will when it dries out.

A soothing sound whistles through the lush foliage of the mangroves. The sea breeze brings with it the smell of saltwater. An aquatic challenge leads the soldiers' wetland foray to the inside edge of the lagoon. The mangrove trees will serve as their site for a temporary base camp above the water. In the seemingly safe fortress, C.B. takes time to pray. It's a simple prayer. He asks that tomorrow can be a day that's not so full of death as was today.

"These water trees keep their leaves all year long, like needle-leaved evergreens do back in the world," Top points out. "Ain't that something?"

"You must not ever seen a Mis'sippy magnolia," C.B. comments, instead of remembering that no one is supposed to out-tale the top sergeant who doesn't like being shown up.

Top doesn't answer. He and Gut-Hook could probably identify with one another. According to rumor, Gut-Hook was in a war of his own once upon a time. It's doubtful Gut-Hook talks in rhymes, but then Top's not very good at it either.

The Grove is a special place, like an island without land. Unlike the rest of this country, the hideout has seen more peace over the last several hundred years than it has fighting. It offers a temporary reprieve from the horrifying atrocities of a war that seems to be going wrong. Leeches, tsetse flies, red ants, and other such aggravations are kept out of harm's way by government-issue hammocks with built-in mosquito netting.

Regardless of the comfort of hammocks, soon after the soldiers of NTK close their eyes and try to sleep, they'll be visited by the shocking scenes of killing over and over again. They recap previous narrow escapes when somebody was trying to kill them. They remember near disasters and wonder if those experiences can help keep them alive a little bit longer. Even part of a day here will be nice. For these men, it's a rarity when the rest of a day is more than a maybe.

The almost aquatic R&R center within the bush is a natural enclave of safety and insulates the platoon from the war. At the edge of the warm sea, this is such a sanctuary that time here can actually be counted on. For a precious while, these soldiers can hang their heavy rucksacks on branches and drape their jungle hammocks above the water. Even one hundred percent bone-soaking weather won't keep the weary soldiers from finally falling asleep. All they have to do is stay under the hammock's little canvas roof. The Grove will keep the enemy at bay for the remainder of the day.

In the seclusion of their sanctuary soldiers carry out various individual and personal rituals. A G.I. blows stress from the day's events into an olive drab air mattress. One soldier gets doped up. Another gets doped out. Another soldier hangs his soiled fatigues, dirty socks, and underwear on a limb to be rain-washed and sea-air dried. One writes home, and one swaps out a battery in his radio. Yet another cleans his M-60.

Even within such a close-knit unit as the NTK Platoon, this is a time and place where each man lives inside his deepest unspoken thoughts. Relationships and co-responsibilities give way to the small but important amounts of privacy that the Grove offers. Glad to be free from the threat of danger, C.B. maneuvers into a comfortable position in his jungle hammock and has a time with a poor man's lady.

Before long, the Montagnard scout they call Yard has somehow caught a cormorant. He uses a parachute cord to cinch up one of the bird's legs to the aerial root of a mangrove tree. It must be for safekeeping. The scout's secret reason will probably come out…about time the cormorant is eaten for breakfast.

Although it's impossible to relinquish complete control of the senses, sheer tiredness and the need for sleep eventually win the battle over unknown fears. Muscles float in the ecstasy of relaxation for a great change. Top said they could rest here without accountability. Requisites for staying alive a few clicks away are not needed to keep you from getting killed here. Not having to dread a shift on guard duty is almost too good to be true.

It's not easy suddenly to stop paying at least some attention when not too far from here even the slightest sounds would be cause for immediate concern. When listening becomes such an entrenched part of survival, it's involuntary. You can't just convince yourself everything is okay. Even if exhausted eyes are finally free from the continuous searching for movement, the constant rumbling in distant mountains is a reminder of the recent ear-splitting explosions.

Silence itself would probably be too intense, but a little inner stillness and quiet might give the heart and soul a bit of much-needed rest. Knowing with certainty there are several believers back home who are trying to pray him safely home, C.B. thinks about God…and Auntay and Bible verses. Realizing they are there…that's a big help. Bruised senses and a muddled mind are a tad more bearable because of it. He remembers something about "trouble-weary ways durin' changin' days" but can't come up with the rest of it. Auntay Belle could. She could probably tell you the chapter and verse number where it could be found.

C.B. tries a prayer but can't help worrying about what God may have thought of him sending Hay's little Bible back in the body bag instead of keeping it. Shadows take strange shapes, but time escapes, and C.B. drops off to sleep. Awakening with a need to pee, a quiet struggle ensues between the stupidity of trying to pee out of the hammock and probably falling in the water below or getting out and properly peeing.

The inevitable light of day is about to float in like the sea's fog bank. Sun-up can hardly come soon enough when you're having to do guard duty, but when you're granted deep sleep the dawn comes too soon. C.B. rubs his face and scratches his chin. Feeling the stubble, he makes himself a promise that if he ever gets out of the military, he'll grow a beard long enough for it to stop itching.

In lieu of having to eat government issue for breakfast, C.B. makes use of youth's Yocona River experiences and searches for some natural nutrition. A harvest of small but numerous land crabs from the aerial roots of the mangroves appears to be Mother Nature's answer for the bulk of a wildlife buffet. The Grove teems with fish the right size for anything from bait to hors d'oeuvres. Upon gathering a variety of natural makings, C.B. feels as if he's almost home…until he sees someone who may be.

Yard has tied a non-slipping loop around the cormorant's neck and sent him fishing on the other end of a length of parachute cord. The loop around the fish eater's neck prevents the bird from swallowing its prey…and allows for retrieval. Still holding his sardine-like catch, the bird stands ready to give it up like a sword swallower. He does it repeat-edly until Yard doesn't have to eat American c-rats or cormorant.

C.B.'s land crabs turn out to be good eats, but Yard's breakfast exper-tise has aroused concern. Yard, who is supposed to be a mountain man, appears to know more about living off the lowlands than might be ex-pected. It's hard enough to tell who's V.C. and who isn't, without having someone from within to worry about. Vows are made that eyes are to be kept on their scout. In the bush your ally is guilty until proven innocent.

The next time Yard claims some sacred direction or spiritual obedi-ence as to where to go or not go, Top will decide if he's in-the-know. Is he a scout who squats ready to betray them when the time to take a stand comes? Montagnards are supposed to hate the V.C. The soldiers of the NTK platoon, for their own safety, must be suspicious of any non-American…especially Yard.

Swells bellow up from the sea winds. The tide has turned during the night, reversing the current in the corridor. This will aid the platoon's departure from the mangroves. It's enough to prove to C.B. that God is on America's side in this war.

Regardless of having many more questions than answers, NTK has to obey its orders…via Top, via L.T., via who knows who from who knows where. Maybe orders are better than choices unless you're being shot at right then. Maybe busy is better. Sometimes you think, but at other times it's best to act on instinct and training. The wrong move at the wrong time or during the wrong circumstances could get you in trouble. A lot of things seem contradictory, but there's no room for emotional sawdust…not in 'Nam.

There's always a premium on time just before the troops have to move out. The morale of the men would go sky-high if they could have just one more day in The Grove, but it's not to happen. Another day of rest could make soldiers more keenly alert when it was time to leave. That might improve their odds of staying alive. Whoever sends these orders down should consider it.

C.B. is thinking that this is a day he will give total focus to the missio—

"Ro…arr…arr!" A large cargo plane approaching extremely low in-terrupts his thought.

It's The United States of America spraying a defoliate right on top of the vegetative camouflage of her unacknowledged unit. Most soldiers don't know this particular chemical, but C.B does. From working in the

National Forests of Alabama, he is more than familiar with its pungent and nauseous spicy smell. Dog days, southern pine beetles, and being saturated in a similar smelly herbicide…it all comes back. He also remembers this smell from when he arrived in country at Cam Rhan Bay. He and another cherry had helped inventory and unload numerous black 55-gallon drums…with orange stripes around them.

In a poor but semi-poetic beat, Top announces,

"Nothin' like two-foe-five-tee,

to stink up yo' sweat an' pee.

An' there ain't no delay,

when th' ranch hands spray.

Move it out, Ladies."

"Have a nice day, Sarge," a soldier mocks his NCO.

"Make love and not war," another not-so-clever poetmonger participates in the pre-mission prattle.

Failing to think him funny, Top makes a firm fist with his big right hand. Shaking it at him, he tries one last rhyme to tell everyone it's time:

"Do what I say,

An' you might live through th' day."

To avoid th' red-crossed helico-peters,

Put 'em on rock an' roll, Señoritas."

And the M-16s are clicked on fully automatic.

XXXVII:
The Steep Steps of the 101st

"LORD, LET THIS PLANE get outta shootin' range, quick, Lord, Jesus. Amen."

It's a grand and glorious feeling…simply sitting in his freedom bird. The anticipation of leaving Vietnam stirs up the most welcome feelings imaginable. C.B.'d assumed the 727 would be loaded with as many soldiers as it could hold, but this one is special. It's a Medevac that's sharing extra space with a few men like him who were lucky enough to have escaped physical injury. To varying degrees, all the passengers have been mentally wounded.

Hospital smells remembered from Miss Sippy's sickness fill the plane. From the radio area comes an electronic scent, similar to something burning. C.B. recalls sniffing the air in the bush to try to detect V.C. cigarette smoke…and wonders how long it will take him to stop thinking about such. The smells of war are some of many things he'll try to leave behind. There are haunting thoughts of how military strategy sometimes displayed ignorance as repulsive as any odor.

Although some missions were important, many seemed senseless. Pieces of the jungle were often gained at great expense, only to be lost and re-gained and re-lost over the days that followed. The weight of memories is heavy, especially those linked with the men who didn't make it out. War or war policy wouldn't have flinched at sacrificing C.B.'s life for a number. To think, he could have been used in some egotistically political boast….

Escaping 'Nam, and doing it whole, should bring nothing but joy and thankfulness. No one should have a guilty conscience for simply living. With scrambled emotions, C.B. prays a short prayer of thanks that he isn't one of the soldiers toward the back of the aircraft. His ride is so well deserved he shouldn't have to be apologetic to anyone. Still, there's a nagging feeling of guilt in sharing what is such a happy trip for him with those who are so messed-up and blown-up. Everyone is settling in as best he can.

As the plane starts down the runway, most men have their heads bowed. Lowering his own head, C.B. feels as if he should take his seatbelt off and kneel. He doesn't know if he should be giving thanks for making it through alive or begging for a safe flight home...or if God even keeps tabs on such prayer motives. Having made it through machine gun fire, mortars, trip wires, grenades, bungi-sticks, and countless other V.C. instruments of death and damage, C.B. is at long last headed home. Other than the engines, there is dead silence as the plane picks up speed.

Seconds from becoming airborne, time ends all debate, and C.B. again goes to a repeat prayer. *"Please, Lord, give us a quick lift off."*

Finally, when the plane finishes its rumbling run and its wheels leave the ground, a roar of relief is let out by all the able passengers. C.B.'s tour of combat duty is over. As visible waves of heat roll over the wing, C.B. mutters to himself, *"Now* it stops raining." Remembering long rains that came in sheets instead of drops, he looks forward to a place with shorter, less-intense rains.

The plane finishes its climb and levels out above the clouds. C.B. doesn't have the need to take a farewell look at the landscape below. He knows the cursed little country of constant war would look beautiful from a distance. It'd have to be seen up close to realize how badly it's been blown to waste by visitors and countrymen alike.

In the sad and bitter contest with seemingly no winners, perhaps it was the war itself that came out on top. What was really lost was the tragic loss of almost countless lives of men on both sides. Looking to the back of the plane, C.B. sees the wounded warriors and wonders if they could see any sense to it all. If so, what would body parts from maimed and crippled G.I.'s be worth? Long after the ground and water are no longer visible, some passengers still stare out their windows. Their faces reflect relief at being alive, but there is something else. It looks like grief, despair, and uncertainty. What's bothering them may be more about the uncertainty lying ahead. Will they be able to leave the cruelty of killing behind? Will the horrible memory of incidents involving death and casualties keep reappearing and continue to live with them? If so, for how long?

Leaving his military occupational skill back in the jungle, C.B. will be released from his Army obligation within a day. It's called an early-out, even when there's nothing early about the past year he's had. The senior trip for Oxford Training School's sharp-shooting sniper is finished...and being the master of his special skill, there is no job waiting at home.

He closes tired eyes to try and rest but sees bright lights flashing in his darkness. His subconscious mind takes on a jumpy, three-dimensional existence. When, for a year straight, you've needed to stay alert to stay alive, it's hard suddenly to let go and relax. It's like trying to sleep next to something too loud...when you can't turn down the volume.

A soldier lucky enough to be whole in body gets up and puts a folded wheelchair next to his seat for a place to stretch out his legs. A paramedic dressed in blood-stained scrubs comes down the aisle and tells him to return the wheelchair to where it was.

"Shove off, bitch!" the soldier argues.

The paramedic looks at his patients. One has no legs. One has one leg. Others have only pieces of legs. Staring back at the offender who has his two good legs stretched out like a slob, he pulls the wheelchair out from under him. Taking offense, the soldier jumps up but is immediately descended upon. Three nearby soldiers push, pull, and knock him back down. With no words spoken, the paramedic puts the wheelchair back in its stack.

After a time-consuming, thirty-minute fuel stop in Hawaii, they are back in the air. When C.B. finally manages to sleep, he dreams hard and relives times spent with those who paid the highest price. He awakes and continues to think about how each of them got wasted.

The year-long awaited ride descends into Fort Dix, New Jersey. Upon touching down, the entire aircraft is filled with cheers similar to those when they left Vietnam. The Flying Tiger plane takes its military time taxiing in to the military hanger. When the plane opens its doors, a spit-and-polished NCO enters. He's decorated with a blue-and-white rifle badge, indicating he's done his time in the infantry.

"Welcome back to the world, men," the NCO, with his chest full of enough assorted ribbons to demand respect, greets one and all.

There's another round of cheering. Next, a cadre of medics come on board to carry or roll out the wounded soldiers. When that's accomplished, those who are able to get up on their own are ready for their turn. When they're instructed to grab their gear and fall in formation outside, C.B. can't believe such an elementary and humiliating move.

Instead of allowing for a well-deserved trot to the nearest grass to kiss the ground of the United States of America and letting them be happy about making it back, the Army again treats its own like nothing more than grunts in basic training. The Vietnam veterans are ordered to spread out and put all personal belongings ten feet in front of them for inspection.

C.B. places his duffle bag and super-sized, fake jam box forward. Since there is no credible justification or reasonable excuse for bringing an illegal fully-automatic weapon into this country, C.B. has dismantled his AK-47 war trophy and hidden it in the radio casing.

"Dump your bags," instructs the NCO in-charge.

C.B. has visions of being led off to the stockade in handcuffs. The sick feeling in his stomach worsens.

To serve as inspectors under the NCO's direction, a squad of virgin-to-war, pseudo-soldiers buzz around and among the piles of personal stuff scattered about. Like a yellow jacket from a disturbed nest, a Spec-4 soul brother settles on C.B.'s belongings. He sets the jam box to the side and says something about looking at it in a minute.

The "looking at it in a minute" comment echoes in C.B.'s mind. His heart sinks as he wonders if he'll qualify for some kind of thinking-impaired benefit for the rest of his life…in Leavenworth.

Filtering through what's been emptied on the tarmac, the Spec-4 spies C.B.'s prized, deer antler smoking pipe. Kneeling directly over it, he begins to push underwear and other personal belongings around. C.B. tries to watch him without being seen watching. As half-expected, the Spec-4 slips the pipe into the leg pocket of his fatigues. Thinking that no one has seen him steal it, he immediately makes a big production out of telling C.B. to gather up his gear and stuff everything back in his duffle bag…while he looks at the jam box.

"Sergeant!" C.B. yells, elated at having an opportunity to derail inspection of his jam box.

With a questioning expression, the nearby NCO in-charge looks at C.B. The Spec-4 has stopped in mid-stride.

C.B. continues, "I caught this som'bitch red-handed tryin' to steal my smokin' pipe."

The Spec-4 jumps back and quickly makes the pipe drop from his pants on the concrete. He picks it up and pretends to have been just looking at it. The NCO comes over to analyze the situation between the two soldiers more closely. The Spec-4 insists that he was inspecting the pipe for dope and not trying to steal it.

C.B. argues, "You don't inspect nothin' by puttin' it in your pocket."

"I didn't have it in my pocket," the Spec 4 lies.

"He's lyin' like a dog," C.B. protests to the NCO.

The NCO stares at his man and then turns to C.B. Obviously reluctant, the NCO explains, "It looks like it's your word against his. What can I do?"

C.B. hesitates and then shakes his head up and down. Everyone is watching and listening.

Again, the NCO asks C.B., "What would you expect?"

C.B. stares at the combat infantry badge on the NCO's uniform and then at the lack of anything on the Spec-4's chest. His eyes are drawn back to the NCO's blue-and-white rifle badge and then to the patch from the 101st Airborne Division on the NCO's shoulder. The NCO sees C.B. looking at his Screaming Eagle patch, the insignia that they both proudly wear. C.B. senses unit camaraderie and that the NCO is waiting patiently for the *correct* answer.

"Sarge," C.B. responds, "if you'll take you 'bout a five minute pee break, we'll settle up amongst ourselves."

The NCO again looks at his own man and then back at C.B. All the other soldiers are watching and waiting for something to be done about C.B.'s complaint.

"At ease," the NCO's announcement is made in such a commanding voice that all can hear. "I'll be back in five." He turns toward the terminal.

In a long, hard year, the Spec-4's jaw is the closest target this sharpshooter has had. C.B. drops his left shoulder hard and quick as he pivots at the waist to get his full body weight behind the force of a right lead. The Spec-4 lands flat on the concrete. He rolls over and assumes a crouching posture, looking too much like he's taking on a position from which to charge. Picturing the Spec-4's chin as a football, C.B. kicks hard with follow-through. This time the Spec-4 is out cold. Instead of taking five, like he'd said he would, the NCO is immediately back.

In the expected hush among the soldiers, he orders two of his other inspectors to cut the Spec-4 insignia off of the unconscious man's uniform. "Now carry this Private First Class to sick bay and tell them he fell down a flight of stairs...over at the 101st."

When the cheering and clapping from both the returning soldiers and the inspectors stops, the NCO announces, "Men on this side of the pond are gonna have to face it—those that's walked th' walk ain't gon' be takin' no crap off them who haven't."

C.B. gives a slight nod of otherwise unspoken appreciation to the NCO and retrieves his fake jam box type AK-47 gun case as if it had already been inspected. When he begins cramming his personal gear back in his duffle bag, the NCO turns to attend his other duties. Standing at ease in such a soldier-like stance, C.B. might as well be at attention...waiting for inspection completion of all the gear belonging to the other soldiers.

The men are moved indoors to spend one more night in the Army. Morning comes, and they are processed out without any significant form of debriefing. There is a joke of a re-up talk but for the most part it's over. Simply and suddenly, these warrior soldiers are turned loose in a world that is not ready for war-worn veterans...not for men who have grown accustomed to such steep stairs as those of the 101st.

XXXVIII:
The Real
World...Homecoming

ON C.B.'S FIRST MORNING back in the United States of America, it would be quite an understatement to say the young buck sergeant is happy to be out of tiger-striped jungle fatigues. Issued new Class A's just to wear home, C.B. knows all too well that once the dress uniform comes off, things will be different. Already, almost everything makes it seem as if he's in a whole new world.

As with the change of clothes, the remaining procedures for mustering out of the Army are completed quickly. Three other black Vietnam veterans join C.B. at the same time he leaves the main gate of Fort Dix.

C.B. takes the lead by raising his hand to flag down their ride. "Taxi!" he yells, as if the driver wasn't pulling up to them anyway.

"Where to, boys?"

"Take us to the real world," one of the soldiers tells the cabby.

"Airport—and hurry," another young man specifies as he opens the door of the nearly worn out '65 Plymouth.

"Just get us the hell away from here," the third says.

Outranking all three, C.B. slides in beside the driver, as the others climb in the back seat…knowing it's the opposite way from the military's. "What'll it cost apiece, bein' it's four of us?"

"It's six dollars each," says the driver. He pulls his orange cab into the traffic. "But if you guys are in a hurry, for an extra five each I'll take the turnpike. I'm not supposed to do that, but I'll risk getting in trouble for the extra twenty bucks. What do you boys say?" The driver's unsympathetic smile and poor effort at a sincere expression fail truth's simplest test of self-evidence.

"I say we waste this mother….and take his car for lying to us," one of the men retorts.

Tension fills the cab. The driver looks uneasily at C.B.

A soldier who had witnessed C.B. facilitate the Spec 4 thief being demoted to PFC asks C.B., "What you say, Bro? We gonna let our first experience back in the world be getting screwed by this honky cab driver? Is that gonna be whitey's thanks for what we've done?"

C.B. coughs and leans over toward the driver. He hesitates instead of passing judgment. The cab narrowly misses sideswiping a baby-blue Falcon. The driver glances in his rearview mirror at the others and then back across at C.B. again. C.B. lets his chauffeur sweat. The Plymouth again sways out of its lane as the cab driver turns to the sergeant sitting next to him.

"Let him live," C.B. announces. "I'll pay th' extra twenty, an' we won't tip him nothin'. My best friend's old man drives a cab back home. It ain't no picnic, neither. As Mr. J. used to say, "Munford's at th' beck an' call of ever som'bitch what's got th' price of a cab fare'."

"Who's Mr. Jay?" a fellow rider asks.

"He's an old man I knowed growin' up…wrote some books when he wadn't huntin'. He won some big reward from th' other side of th' world…not where we was, but th' other, other side. Eben got himself invited to a dinner party at th' White House to celebrate his prize. Turned 'em down flat. He said it was just too damned far to go fer supper."

At the International Airport for civilians, only the soldier from Mississippi says thanks to their cabby. The driver says nothing in return but appears to be relieved at delivering his passengers and living to tell about it. C.B. finds where he's to catch his plane and then seeks out a phone.

"Hello," I answer the ringing.

The operator interrupts, "That will be eighty-five cents please, for the first three minutes."

I hear the phone being fed and then a voice I think I know.

"Scott?"

"C.B.? Is that you?"

"Yeah. I made it back, man. I'm alive. 'Nam is history."

"All right!" I exclaim. "Where are you calling from?"

"Philadelphia."

"Mississippi?"

"Huh?"

"Never mind, C.B., I wasn't thinking."

"Y'all landin' jet planes in Philadelphia, Mis'sippi, now, are ya?"

"Naw, not yet, anyway." We both laugh. "Uh...what's up? When will you be home?"

"Well, that's why I'm'a callin'. I'll be flyin' into Memphis at 15:20...I mean 3:20 this afternoon. I was wonderin' if you could come get me so I ain't gotta take th' bus...or jump th' cattle train agin?"

"You know it, buddy. I'll be there waiting on you."

"Great. I'll be comin' in on Braniff 1124."

"It's good to hear your voice, man. Are you...uh, shot up or any-thing?"

"Naw. I'm all right."

"Super. Anything special you want me to have for you when I pick you up?"

"If'n you can bring along Miss Ole Miss, that'd be right good. If she ain't willin', you might have us a six-pack of Falstaff iced down real cold."

"You got it, C.B."

"You made forester yet?" he asks.

"I'm still working on it."

"Don't tell Auntay I'm back—I wanta walk in an' surprise her. I reckon she still ain't got a phone, huh?"

"Far as I know, she doesn't."

"I'll see you at twenty minutes after three, Scott."

———————————

TOTING A RADIO AS big as a moderate suitcase, C.B. comes down the corridor. He appears to be nervous about something, preoccupied with looking at the shuffling crowd.

"Put her there," he greets me with an extended hand, but in a softer whisper than I've ever heard from him. I wonder if he's been wounded in the throat.

"Put her there, hell! I want a hug."

"Can we do 'at 'thout folks lookin' at us like we was funny or somethin'?"

"Screw 'em, C.B. It's good to see you." I throw my long arms around his solid body in a fierce embrace that feels as if I'm hugging a rock. "You're looking mighty good…different."

"I don't know 'bout good, but I 'spect I'm sho nuf different."

"Well, welcome back, C.B. If you weren't already black, I'd swear you had a suntan. What's first?"

"I been studyin' on that fer a year now—what I'd do if I made it back. An' I got th' answer. While we in Memphis anyways, I wanta go to 'at boat place. You 'member th' canoe we seen th' time we visited you-know-who at th' Roxx Off-Playhouse? I'm aimin' to buy it. I bad need to spend me some time on th' rivers…all of 'em. I may eben introduce myself to ol' Gut-Hook hisself."

"Sounds like a plan," I answer.

"Then, after we get my canoe tied on top of yo' car, I just wanta go home. I need to taste some of Auntay's cookin'…maybe some real eggs 'at ain't powdered. An' then I be needin' to see me a Mis-a-damned-sippi sunset."

"We're out of here," I announce.

"I gotta get my duffle bag first," he says.

Proceeding to the baggage claim, C.B. asks me all about when I last saw his Auntay and then about my Dad and how we're all getting along. I assure him everyone and everything is okay.

"That's a hell of a radio you got there."

"I'll tell you 'bout it later."

"I want to hear about everything, C.B."

"I ain't so shore you do. Good Lord Ah'Mighty!" he exclaims as he gawks at a girl's legs. "Don't tell me they dressing like that now days."

"They're called hot pants."

"I reckon I see how they got that name," he comments.

Remarkably soon, his duffle bag comes through the carousel.

When I offer to take the giant jam box, he stops me. "No, no, I got to tote this. You can take th' duffle bag."

"Why?"

"I'll show you when th' time's right."

We work our way through the crowd and into the parking lot to find Dad's black '63 Chevy. Instead of properly checking out and paying, I decide to show off and drive over the curb. When I scrape the muffler, I realize I'm lucky I didn't knock it off.

"Here, tear up this Tennessee parking stub." I hand C.B. the unpaid parking pass. "We don't have time for paperwork when there's canoe shopping to be done."

"Whatever," C.B. agrees and rips the piece of paper in half.

"What was it like, C.B.?" I ask. "Tell me about everything."

He says nothing.

I try again, "Were you in the 101st the whole time?"

After another pretty good pause, he answers. "I kept my Screamin' Eagle 'filiation, but I'z mixed in with some others 'sides th' Army." His weak voice softens even more. "But...."

"What'd you do? Did you get shot or have to kill somebody?"

Again, he pauses before saying anything. "When they seen me shoot, right off they sent me to sniper school. I got my job 'at away."

"And?"

"An' it was a tough, lonesome, risky job I wouldn't of wished on nobody." His voice trails off again.

"Auntay showed me the picture you sent her."

"Yeah, I'd just made sergeant," he proudly boasts.

Another moment of silence follows. We work our way through the Memphis traffic. I'm not sure what stopped him from talking. Maybe it was my maneuvering in the congestion. He's watching everything closely.

After I find Bronson's sporting goods store, C.B. pays $222.00 cash for an 18' long, aluminum Grumman canoe. With his purchase hanging over both ends of what I thought was already a long car, we must be quite a picture on the road.

"Reach over in the back seat there and get us a couple of cold ones from that cooler," I suggest.

He pops a top and hands me the open Falstaff. "I reckon church keys is things of th' past, huh?"

"You haven't been gone that long. But yeah, they're all pop-tops now. Don't let me expose you to too much too fast."

"Scott, what few of these things I had the past year, I been takin' like water...warm." He opens the other beer for himself.

"Warm?"

"Yeah, it's been a while since I seen a 'frigerator."

We touch cans for a silent toast and then take long, appreciative swallows.

"So you made sergeant did you? That's good, C.B."

"They offered me staff sergeant if I'd sign up fer four more years. I had me a re-up talk at Fort Dix this very mornin' 'bout it."

"What'd you say? Is re-upping the big news you didn't want to tell me about until you first talked to Auntay?"

"Naw, it ain't. An' I told 'em 'at was one of them N.N.T.K. things."

"What do you mean?"

"'At's just what th' officer givin' th' talk axed. He said he wanted to know what did I mean by N.N.T.K. I told him it meant I didn't have no need to know 'bout his re-enlistment talk, so he just as well keep it to hisself."

"What'd he say to that?"

"Said I ought not be talkin' to no officer 'at away. Then I axed him if he'd ever been to th' 'Nam. When he said 'no,' I told him we'd talk again when he had. I saluted him an' left 'fore he said another word."

"It's a wonder you're not wearing one of those little white jackets with the sleeves tied in back."

"I'd do 'at 'fore I'd re-up fer another hitch."

We pass the "Welcome to Mississippi" highway sign and C.B. sticks his head out the window and breathes deeply. "This Mis'sippi air sho tastes good."

I continue trying to question him for details. His reluctant answers still come too slow for reasonable discussion. By the time we reach Holly Springs and turn south I have taken the hint that this is not the time to try to grill my best friend for information about Vietnam.

"I'll tell you what I'd like to hear 'bout," C.B. says.

"What's that?"

"I'd like to hear 'bout yo' forestry schoolin'. You take any time fer makin' grades or you 'bout to flunk out?"

"Sorta...both."

"I guess some sorority sister done got yo' cherry, huh?"

"Ah, man, those girls...actually, they don't have much to do with forestry majors. When you're out in the woods all the time, you hadn't got a shot at stuff like that. Besides, they like boys with money up their butts...so they can set around on it all afternoon, I guess."

"You get to come in ever' night, don't you?"

356

"Yeah, but when we come in from forest labs we have to do the paperwork. When doing statistical analyses there's not much time for girls, and not many girls are willing to join in on field trips with cottonmouths and timber rattlers."

"Scott, you ever heard of a two-step?"

"I don't guess you're talking about the dance are you?"

"Not after th' second step. It's a snake."

"I want you to tell me about it, C.B. I want to hear it all."

"I don't 'spect I can do 'at justice." He looks out the window and pauses again, before slowly and quietly continuing. "Not without you bein' able to smell it an' taste it an' hear it…you'd have to be there where you could feel it to ever really understand."

"C.B., you're not mad at me for getting out of having to go to Vietnam are you?"

He pauses again. "Naw, man. I'm proud fer ya. I'd say it was just one of them natural orders Mr. Jefferson was always tellin' us 'bout. What he'd call th' scheme of things musta pushed me to 'Nam an' you to college. Looks like we both survivin' 'em. If it'd been th' other way around, we might not of."

"Tell me about it, C.B. Tell me everything."

"Maybe later. Right now I wanta know th' truth 'bout them college girls. I know you too good to believe you ain't tried somethin'."

We pass Wall Doxey State Park, and I glance at C.B. He shakes his head, no. Neither of us says a word. I drive on instead of stopping. I assume he's too anxious to get home instead of sitting and drinking beer and talking at the park.

"You wanta drive," I offer.

"Naw. You doin' all right. Th' females, Scott…tell me you ain't at least been to 'at girl's school they call th' W. You bound to been over there smellin' th' bicycle seats or somethin'."

"All right, I guess there's one girl that's sorta special, but I can't tell you any more about her than you're able to explain Vietnam to me. There's just something about her, that's all. Sometimes I can't think about anybody or anything else. Then, other times I want to choke her. She tears me up when I'm away from her, but when I get around her, I can't even think straight."

"'At mite he'p you," he jokes.

"She's a nice girl though," I come back.

"Lord-a-mighty, 'at says it all. I done heard more'n I need to 'bout this."

"What about you, C.B.? Any girls?"

"I'll tell you 'bout it in a day or two…after I talk to Auntay."

Such a non-reply doesn't seem much stranger than his other answers have been. I was worried about C.B.'s self-confidence and adventuresomeness getting him killed. For all I know, they may have been the very traits that kept him alive. All I really know of the war are the media accounts…and I'm not sure I can believe them.

"Did you have any close calls, C.B.?"

"With girls?"

"No, with getting your ass blown off."

A deer darts across the road. It's a doe. I slow down to keep from running over her.

"First one of them I seen in a while," he says. "I ain't shore I'll ever shoot another one."

I suppose C.B. could be putting on a show to appear mysterious. On the other hand, if he's been dealing daily with life-and-death experiences, maybe it's done something to him.

"Close calls, C.B.?" I persist.

"There was some times it looked like it weren't gon' be no tomorrow. Then, some days…you just felt that'a way from sunup 'til sundown."

We drive along in silence. For the time being, I decide not to push him. C.B. and I have never had trouble talking to each other. This is an unusual feeling. I don't like it, but I don't know what to say. A log truck passes a pulpwood truck, and I pass them both.

"You going back to the logging-woods to work?" I ask.

"I reckon."

"C.B., I'm glad you're home. I was afraid you'd come back in a body bag."

"Well, I didn't," he proudly states.

"They say about 50,000 Americans have already been killed over there."

"All I know's—it's over fer me."

"Thank God, C.B."

"Yeah…I seen th' kinda death 'at makes you wanta 'preciate what little life you got left. When you been dealin' with as much hate an' horror as I have, you figger out—it's time to commence lookin' fer somethin' good…in ever' day an' in ever' way."

He pauses again. This time I try waiting for him to continue. He finishes off his beer and pops another top. When he looks at me to see if I'm ready, I just shake my head.

Finally realizing that waiting on him to talk is not going to work, I ask, "What was a typical day like over there, C.B.?"

He takes a deep breath and then a short series of gulps. "There ain't no tellin' nobody 'bout it. You wouldn't believe it, anyway. I…uh, I made it back."

"Try me," I insist. "What did your soldiering involve?"

"It jus' ain't no way…an' it didn't mean nothin'." C.B.'s voice breaks up. "You couldn't understand less'n you was there." He looks away from me, like he's not wanting me to see his face.

I'm thinking he is going to hush up again, but he goes on.

"Lot of a sniper's time is a kinda one-man thing. Other'n 'at, I can't begin to tell you nothin'. 'At's all I wanta say 'bout it right now."

His self-imposed silence about the whole thing may be speaking louder than answers could. I should have known he'd be a better soldier than he is a storyteller. While I was praying he'd come home at peace, he may be glad enough just to be home in one piece…alive and with all his parts working. I hope he isn't seeing bad memories down the road.

As we approach our old wading grounds, C.B. speaks up, "Pull over there 'fore you cross th' bridge. Let's take in th' river fer a few minutes. I wanta look at it an' think like I ain't never thought. Maybe we can hear us a bull-bat when th' summer sun cools down. 'Memberin' stuff like 'at is what kept me goin' sometimes."

I pull over when we get to the trestle and the car bridge parallel to it. C.B. gets out and walks the railroad ties over the water.

"We'll christian our canoe some other time," he says.

"Christen," I correct.

"Yeah, yeah, whatever."

Halfway across the Little Tallahatchie, he sits down on the end of a tie and hangs his feet off. He mumbles, seemingly more to himself than for me to hear, "I guess I shoulda seen what state Philadelphia was in. 'Least I knowed it weren't Mis'sippi."

Hearing him talk to himself instead of to me, I decide to let him have some space…and quiet. For the time being I'll give up on getting him to open up.

After he sits in his silence for a few minutes, he gets up and walks to the car. I follow along like a faithful puppy. He opens his duffle bag and pulls out his boonie-hat. It must be the same one I saw in the picture. The strange-looking lanyard I'd seen in the photo is now tied around it as a hatband. It looks as if he's strung his hat strap with what appears to be dried peter-peppers like Auntay Belle used to have in her garden.

Without speaking, C.B. walks halfway back out and over the water, this time on the car bridge. Again, I follow along without question. He looks down at the water below us. I'm thinking he's fixing finally to start talking. Instead, he takes out his pocketknife and cuts the odd-looking hatband from his hat. After putting the boonie-hat on his head, he takes whatever he removed and throws it off the Little Tallahatchie bridge.

"What was that, C.B.?"

He stares at me with a look I've never seen.

"What was it?"

"It don't mean nothin'," he finally answers.

We watch whatever it was float toward Sardis Lake. Since he has never hesitated to talk to me before today, I try again.

"Come on, C.B., tell me what that was."

With a cold stare that cuts clean through me this time, he repeats in his new, soft, whispery voice, "It don't mean nothin'. Now, let's go see if'n you can find Taylor, Mis'sippi, Pecker-head."

IXL:
Mayling and Little Scott

IT'S A RARE NON-SUNDAY when the doors to Munford's Grocery are closed to customers. Since this is a week I don't have to be back in school until Tuesday, Dad's decided the extra day is a good time to help him with his most dreaded annual task. Although the store is signed, "Closed for Inventory," we're purposefully locked inside with what constitutes a considerable challenge for two...especially when one doesn't put his heart in it.

C.B. knocks on the big glass door. He'd said he'd drop by and tell us the big news he wouldn't let out until after he'd talked to Auntay. Dad, who hasn't seen him since he returned from Vietnam, lets him in.

"Welcome back, C.B." Dad even shakes his hand.

"Thank you, sir," C.B. responds in the quiet voice he brought back from his war experience.

With a cracked voice of his own, Dad says, "We're glad to have you back alive and not lamed."

My father mentioning someone not being lamed is a jarring commentary. Mr. J. had claimed my dad had some kind of guilty feeling over his polio keeping him out of WWII when most of his friends had to go fight. C.B. comes right over where I'm sitting on a stool to count and record the various canned goods on a shelf directly in front of me.

"You pregnant?" I joke, before he gets a word out. "Is that the big secret?"

Dad is pretending not to be listening, but his ears are pointed straight at us, like a swamp rabbit's do at a pack of beagles.

"Sorta," C.B. answers.

"How can you be sort of pregnant? You either are or you aren't." Devoting my full attention to C.B.'s mystery, I have an excuse to stop my pencil and pad for a minute.

"Scott, I got a wife comin' from Vietnam...a Vietnamese."

"Wow!"

"An' she's pregnant."

Pretending to be straightening up merchandise, Dad eases a little closer to us.

"For real?" I ask.

"Yep. I've paid for her papers, an' she's comin' from Saigon. Her name is Mayling. She'll be here in a few days."

"Well, congratulations...I guess."

"Thanks."

"Is it your baby?" Dad interrupts with a little smile.

"Yes, sir." C.B. answers firmly and looks him straight in the eyes until Dad turns away.

"When's it due?" I ask, trying to draw attention away from such a rude question my father asked.

"'Bout five or six months. I'll catch y'all later. I gotta run."

"Well, let me know when I can come meet Mayling," I say, for lack of being able to think of anything else appropriate.

"You got it." C.B. lets himself out, and Dad locks the door behind him.

Not wanting to hear Dad make some derogatory comment, I excuse myself to the restroom for a cigarette. The whose baby question was enough. Dad may never understand, and a lot has changed since C.B. and I became friends. With the passage of the Civil Rights Act, my friend can go places he could never have gone before...even in Oxford. He can do things he was never allowed to do. If the Mansion Restaurant hadn't burned down, I'll bet he'd traipse right in and have a sit-down meal right across from our white city fathers.

AS I PULL DAD'S '63 black Impala SS into Auntay's front yard, it must be C.B.'s wife who is sitting in the creaky porch swing. A bracken fern flows from a crooked-neck gourd hanging on one side of her. A weatherworn lard bucket holding a long, leathery, and glossy-green-leaved bull-tongue plant sits on her other side. She looks as if she's in a 3-D picture frame, the first Vietnamese I've ever seen…maybe the first one Lafayette County has seen.

Mayling is young and pretty. Even pregnant, she's tiny…and swings where I last saw my childhood love. She has the same fawn-like color as did Miss Sippy. Unlike Sippy's dark brown curls, Mayling's long, black hair is smooth and straight.

I get out of the car and approach, trying to think of what to say. I suspect Mayling, with probable memories of being napalmed and bombed, has seen enough death and devastation that she wouldn't be too affected by the porch swing's history. In fact, I doubt Taylor, Mississippi, could drop a whole lot of anything on her that would shock her.

She smiles and speaks first, "You Charles' number one friend," sounding more like she's making a statement than asking a question.

"That's me. I'm pleased to meet you. I'm Scott, and you must be Mayling?"

She laughs, and I feel stupid for stating the obvious. C.B. comes out the front door in time to prevent me from having to try and make more small talk.

"You met Mouse?" C.B. asks as he beams with a joy like I've never known.

"Yes. Mayling and I were just getting to know each other," I answer.

She smiles again, and I'm thinking C.B. has chosen well. As his wife talks of her adjustments to this new life, I am surprised how well she speaks English. I can tell she didn't learn it from C.B.

"She's more'n smart, Mouse is," he goes on.

She glows with pride as he speaks so approvingly of her. He offers that Mayling and Auntay have become good friends and that he wants his wife and me to do the same.

When she stays on the porch and lets C.B. and me walk to the river without her, I'm thinking how smart it is for her to give us our space. He says she's a natural when it comes to learning how to skin rabbits and squirrels and do similar things a good wife should know about. The more I hear about her, the more I wonder if she might have a sister we can send for.

After C.B. and I get off to ourselves, he tells me the story of how he met his wife. Her mother had tried to sell Mayling's personal services to him for a quickie, for 150 piasters…an amount he says is equivalent to about two American dollars. C.B. paid the money and then talked Mayling into letting him sneak her over to an American-run orphanage to escape a life of prostitution. There she became a valued helper, taking care of babies for room and board.

Throughout C.B.'s year-long tour, he had checked on Mayling when he got the chance. As she grew and learned to speak better English, she also flowered…so much that he came to love her. When he felt her love returned in full measure, he says his life changed. He promised if she'd stay there and wait for him instead of going back to her pimp-mom, he would bring her to America. Year-end combat pay was more than sufficient to make Mayling an honest woman and get her processed and U.S.A. bound.

In Taylor, Mississippi, Auntay is pleased to have C.B. and his wife staying with her. Until they can get a place of their own, C.B.'s old bedroom is now his and Mayling's. Sippy's room will be the baby's. Through some federal funding program, the old house has had a major fix-up, including getting running water.

With the opportunities integration has brought, it would be a shame if my friend ignores his new-to-be-found possibilities…like attending forestry school on the G.I. bill. As much as C.B. likes being out in the woods, I'm afraid he's only interested in going back with another logging crew.

FOR ME, RETURNING TO college seems lonelier than usual…thinking about C.B. having someone so special of his very own. A periodic date at State or the "W" usually frustrates as much as helps.

On weekends when I make it home, I usually check in with C.B. and Mouse. From my view, it looks as though C.B. and Mayling's affection for each other runs so deep a child has to be born just to help hold all the growing love. The flirtation, glances at each other, and nuzzling all continue right on through a pregnancy that my buddy says has been a breeze. While he claims he hasn't felt a thing, Mayling says it's amazing what a woman will go through for a baby.

Even in her late stage of being with child, Mayling works at the Big Yank blue jean factory in Water Valley, about the same distance from Taylor as is Oxford. During her car pool commute, she listens to the trials and gossip of a widow and two divorcees. She is told what a good man she has in C.B.

TURKEY DAY OF 1973 brings a long-enough weekend for me to make the trip home from school. Instead of deer hunting on Thanksgiving day like you're supposed to, I'm awakened in the early morning by a phone call from the hospital.

C.B. and Mayling have a son. He's a fine boy with ten fingers and ten toes and all the other parts perfect. They name him Scott. Mouse says they'll call him Little Scott, but for now C.B. is referring to him as Super Baby…and realizing him as the cherished gift he is.

Parenthood suits C.B. and Mayling. Little Scott has made even better what I thought was already a strong and enduring bond of love. They're fascinated with the triangular strength between mother, father, and child. It's a parental love added right on top of spousal endearment.

A COUPLE OF YEARS pass quickly. Being around the two and a half of them and hearing their sweet talk has shown me just how contagious happiness can be when people are in love. There is such an outpouring of support shown for one another. I'm only imagining how great it must be to have so much fervor and passion between a man and a woman…and their child.

C.B. stays on with his logging-crew and woods work. With my old running buddy having a family of his own, time doesn't treat our hanging out together the way it used to. Family is number one when C.B.'s off the job and number one in his heart and mind when he's working.

Grad school consumes the parts of me that aren't tied up with my assistantship work to pay for it. Except for hunting together during the holidays, C.B. and I don't see much of each other. I'll also occasionally skip a Monday or Friday to make for a long weekend.

At just over two years of age, Little Scott is getting to the point where he can run around and try to tag along with us. He's a happy and friendly little boy. He'll laugh and hold out his arms to me when I appear. He hugs my neck and bestows puckered kisses. When he calls me Big Scott, my heart is his for the taking.

C.B. and I figure in another year or two we can take my Godson with us to the river, camping and fishing. I'm not only crazy about the kid, but I just know he'll learn to love the outdoors the way we do. We'll have another running buddy. There has to be a grand plan beyond Taylor, Mississippi, for this very special boy. In him I think I'm seeing God's work at its best.

WHEN I ARRIVE FOR Little Scott's third birthday party, he runs to me as usual but stumbles and falls on the smooth path.

"Whoa, boy," I say, picking him up. "You're moving too fast!" I set him back on his feet and look over at C.B. There's a serious face staring back.

"'At ain't it, Scott."

"What do you mean?"

"He been doin' too much wabblin' an' fallin'. It's been goin' on fer th' past couple of weeks. An' his talkin' 'at's been so smart, it ain't so plain no more. Mouse an' Auntay an' me fixin' to take him to see a doctor."

I immediately think of Miss Sippy's disease and hope Little Scott doesn't have that. Despite our immediate worries, we celebrate his birthday. Overjoyed with all his presents, he especially likes the Little Tyke Camping Outfit from me. Full of cake and ice cream, my precious little namesake eventually tires out from the excitement and falls asleep.

TRIPS TO DOCTORS DON'T stop the storm clouds from gathering. There are falls and more falls...and they are more often. Little Scott has an increased slurring of words. After visits to specialists in Memphis, St.

Louis, and New Orleans, C.B. and Mayling are finally told that Little Scott probably has a rare brain disease called adreno-leukodystrophy. If it is the correct diagnosis, the disease is projected to shorten his life expectancy...to only one or two more years.

According to the doctors, he will become immobile, deaf, blind, and eventually die of pneumonia. The experts offer no hope. They suggest there is no need to make any more appointments and there's nothing that can be done to stop his deterioration. The entire medical community has given up.

Remembering going through an all-too-similar death with Miss Sippy, I'm wondering when it's going to be some other family's turn. How often can medical help stop at the edge of life to offer a prognosis without help? How much is one family expected to take and still believe in anything? It's hard to pray that C.B. and the Mouse will find the strength for patience, since praying for Little Scott doesn't seem to work. Acceptance is not a possibility...yet nothing else works.

Over the next two years I visit with Little Scott as often as I can. He's always glad to see me, but nothing stops the progression of problems and his decline. He's gone from having trouble eating and drinking to having only limited soft foods and liquids...and finally a feeding tube. We watch him lose his speech and ability to walk, talk, see, and hear. As the doctors have warned, we helplessly witness his having difficulty breathing.

As death approaches, day by day, we all make promises to The Almighty and beg for Little Scott's sake. There are prayers from the black churches and white churches and everyone who knows Little Scott and claims to know God. Mayling becomes a Christian and joins Auntay's and C.B.'s church but doesn't completely discard Buddha...just in case.

When I look for assurance of hope and see nothing, the nothing is devastating. Trying to comfort each other, C.B. and I make the effort to discuss religion and God and prayer...and I just hope C.B. isn't feeling as deserted and God-forsaken as I am. As there appears to be no miracle answer for Little Scott's recovery, the question cries out from my heart, Why?

In the late stages of Little Scott's disease, grief is overwhelming. Tears drown out words. C.B. drops down on his knees to pray aloud. I hear him offer to trade places with Little Scott. As he begs God to allow it, I know C.B. loves his son more than life itself. I wonder how God could seemingly look the other way. When C.B. gets up to walk and his child still can't, something in me doubts praying and trusting.

DRIVING BACK TO STARKVILLE for my work at State, I realize I may have just heard Little Scott make the last intelligible sentence I'll ever hear from him. Barely able to say the words of a prayer I spoke aloud with him, he repeated, *Dear God, Please help my bobo get well, Amen.*

Having no more religion than enough to be confused, I begin to wonder if Little Scott's date with death won't be our fault…for not having deep enough faith to go along with our prayers. According to my Grandfather's preaching, God Himself ought to know all about a parent's love for that parent's only Begotten Son.

Leaving C.B. in an almost unbearable situation, I worry that the deepest of all philosophical debate has become too blurry…theological mysteries are so muddied that meditation might yield to premeditation. Merciful help might be a better answer of love than the no hope our medical community has left with us.

A compassionate society should not prevent C.B. from doing anything in his power to help end Little Scott's pain and misery. Why does our judicial heritage continue to claim that every moment of life is precious? Court systems ought to have to deal with long and sleepless nights, unnecessary and fruitless treatments, and prescribed drugs that no longer help. Laws, unfortunately cannot understand the difference between sustaining life and prolonging its end. Policy is immune to the lengthy torture involved with some death.

I can only begin to imagine C.B.'s hurt…knowing his son is uncomfortable and on his deathbed. I don't think Miss Sippy ever reached the point when C.B. had to do what he said he was prepared to do, but if that suffering point comes, where Little Scott needs relief and can't speak for himself, his father will be there for him. For a father who loves his son as much as C.B. does, assuming that Little Scott is not suffering may not be enough.

AS THEY SIT IN the swing on Auntay's front porch, C.B. holds his son in his arms. He knows there is little time left for his precious boy. Little Scott's small body is locked stiff and cool, while his breaths are shallow, rapid, and uneven.

Mayling is in the rocking chair next to them and reaches over to caress her son's face. It's a trial of deepest sorrow when all you can do is wait and watch your greatest love suffer his death. It's a hurt that is worse than if you were in pain yourself.

C.B. ponders God's commandment that says, Thou shalt not kill. *"God, help my boy, please,"* he prays. *"If You ain't gon' let me have th' answer I want, 'least ways respond some kinda way, will You?"*

There is a rumbling in the heavens. Little Scott lets out a long, quavering but restful breath of air. C.B. and Mayling look at each other...and wait. No other breath follows. Mayling gives up a soft moan of pain and slowly moves from her rocker to join them in the swing. Embraced in a sad release no one else could understand, they sit in silence...hugging Little Scott and stroking his hair and forehead.

Minutes pass, and tears fall quietly without anyone speaking. Finally, in a choked voice, C.B. says softly, "Auntay'll be home soon. She be knowin' what to do next."

XL:
Air Corps' Redneck Fish Facilitator

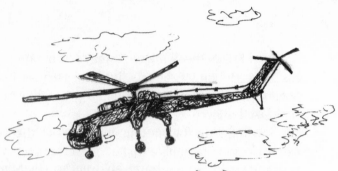

HOME FROM GRAD SCHOOL for the weekend, I'm hanging around the old homestead at Taylor. The place has been mine since my grand-parents left for the Great Beyond. From across the field I can see that C.B. has finally come home after what was probably a long and hard day's work in the logging-woods. We've agreed to meet and pick some black-berries to go with our catching-up talk.

C.B. kisses Mayling and leaves her on the porch to crack pecans and pick out the meat. Since the juicy black drupelets we're after run the length of the old fencerow, we'll start our berry picking right in front of Auntay's house and work toward the main road.

"They clustered pretty close this year," C.B. points out.

Where we've picked along the fencerow looks like a deer's browse line in reverse—the berries we would have had to bend over to pick are the ones remaining untouched.

"We'll leave enough of 'em fer seed," he goes on. "You 'member Mr. J. an' yo' Grandpa talkin' 'bout not shootin' th' birds down too far fer seed?"

"Yeah. I just hope it works for blackberries better than it did for the quail."

"You s'posed to be studyin' 'at stuff. What's th' problem with 'em?"

"In addition to loss of habitat, I think the bobwhite's big problem is that there's getting to be too many critters that like to eat them."

"Whatever 'tis, th' birds is 'bout gone."

"Ouch!" I quickly pull my hand back after sticking it on a briar.

C.B. laughs and then shares his blackberry thoughts. "Th' berries 'round head-high tall is th' ones meant fer folks to eat anyways."

"How do you figure that?"

"'Cause they taste th' best. Auntay calls 'em dewberries."

"Dewberry is a different species," I enlighten him, "and none of these are dewberries."

"You coulda stayed home an' went to Ole Miss if all you was gon' learn is arguin'."

"C.B., you'll never change."

"Not if I can he'p it. Ain't you 'bout done with school yet, anyway? Seem like you been goin' fer ever."

"Graduate school's not all I've been doing. I've been working, too...on my assistantship. But, I'm powerful close to finishing...I think. And I'm not about to work on any doctor's degree. Assuming I can land a job, I'm going to grab my master's and run."

"You finished up studyin' th' Tombigbee River?"

"Sort of. The grant from NASA and the Corps of Engineers is still paying my salary, but the work's about over."

"Well?"

"Well, what?"

"How's what they doin' to th' river lookin'?" he persists.

"You could have gone all day without asking that. It's as if the Corps didn't learn a thing from screwing up the Little Tallahatchie River. The Tenn-Tom Waterway is supposed to be for navigation, whereas the Little Tallahatchie was for flood control. I've got a feeling both projects were mainly for making jobs."

"Where all th' Teen-Tom run?"

"The canal will go from Tennessee clear to the coast...all the way down the edge of the state."

"I thought we done had a river does 'at...called th' Mis'sippi."

"Apparently they don't count unless the Corps builds them."

Indicating that I'm picking a little too close to where C.B. is, he puts a stick in my pail. "Why didn't yo' study stop it?" he asks.

I remove the stick and throw it at him. "Our assignment at State was just to help do a small part of the larger environmental impact statement."

"In other words they had done decided what they was gon' do 'fore yo' useless study...an' th' whole thing was a lot like another one of yo' chicken an' egg kinda riddles?"

"You're hitting in the vicinity of the nail, carpenter. We were supposed to determine if it would be beneficial enough. The problem is—they don't want to hear that it might not be."

"I know you better'n to believe you didn't try somethin' underhanded. Go ahead an' tell me th' rest of th' story. When it comes to hearin' 'bout yo' shenanigans, my ears is long past bein' a couple of virgins."

"Since you were in on most of them," I add to his comment.

"Go to head on," he pushes.

"Well, not that it did any good…there were a couple of rare fish that we tried to get them to give some consideration to…a snail darter and a paddlefish."

"No wonder it didn't do no good."

"Don't let the names fool you. They're both on the government's endangered species list."

"An'?"

"And the government is mandated by law to protect them. The Corps is supposed to keep from doing anything that would harm them or put them in jeopardy of becoming extinct."

"Es'stink like channelizin' a river stinks?" he comments in a question-like manner.

"You're getting some of the picture. They've got a federal court over at Aberdeen, just like the one in Oxford. To make a long story short, I went over there several times and found myself out of the loop with no one really caring to listen."

"What about yo' professors? Wouldn't th' Court listen to them?"

"Not as much as they did to the Corps. They don't like to hear about downsides to pork projects…and this one is projected to bring big bucks to the states involved."

"I 'spect it'll be bringin' trash an' mud an' ever'thing else we don't want that floats downstream, too. Ain't there no laws to protect nothin'?"

"Good question…bad answer. The federal government has a new regulation, but they've also got a new body of bureaucrats to rule over it."

"What'chu talkin' 'bout?"

"It's sort of like if you were to put Gut-Hook in charge of river patrol. A group of four or five geniuses comprise what's called 'The God Squad.' They've been authorized to override and push aside any regulations that might get in the way of whatever 'they' consider logical…and the infamous *they* isn't so infamous any more."

"You makin' all 'at up."

"C.B., I swear. They determine among themselves when the public good outweighs the environmental bad."

"So, th' Big Ditch is got th' go-ahead, huh?"

"In spite of all hell and the highest predicted waters," I answer. "They are set on doing the same sort of thing to the Tombigbee that they did to our Little Tallahatchie and Yocona."

"Same screwin'-up, huh? I bet the Injuns coulda come up with better names fer them rivers if they'd knowed what th' Corps was plannin' on doin' to 'em."

"Where'd that thought come from?" I ask.

"You ain't never heared th' story 'bout th' little Injun kid named 'Two Coyotes Friggin'?"

"I hesitate to ask."

"When his daddy come out of the tepee after he was born…he'd said he was gon' name him after th' first thing he seen."

"Good grief."

"Anyway, it's th' same screwin'-up…. She—ee—it!" He stops picking berries and talking to stomp a tiny copperhead to death.

"Yeah, the same screwing-up except, instead of wasting millions of dollars on it, this one is going for billions…numbers too big for anybody's calculators but the Corps'. You may think I'm lying, C.B., but I'm not even exaggerating. If there's one thing I've learned in seven years of college, it's that the government's facts are more screwed up than anybody but maybe you could make up."

"Yep, yep, yep," he agrees, "and some day they could be tryin' to pump th' water outta th' Mis'sippi Delta."

"With the kind of money and foolishness the Corps is given to run with, they're also liable to try that. Can Mayling make a cobbler out of these berries?"

"'Less'n it's cooked with rice, we'll have to get Auntay to show her how th' first time."

We head back toward the house.

"Scott, I wouldn't mind seein' some of that."

"Rice cobbler blackberries?"

"Naw, th' Tombigbee 'fore it's de-rivered an' screwed up like all our rivers is."

"You're on. The first weekend we can put it all together, let's canoe down a part of the rare and endangered river…and we'll paddle one of its un-federally twisted tributaries.

IN COLUMBUS WHERE HIGHWAY 82 crosses the Tombigbee River, we leave C.B.'s vehicle as our pick-up pickup. With the canoe on top of Dad's car, we drive to where Tibbee Creek goes under Alternate Highway 45, just south of West Point, Mississippi. A daybreak launch puts us instantly into the wilderness-like bottom with scenery like stretches of the *old* Little Tallahatchie River's unchannelized parts.

Perfect weather starts out as our escort. Two hours downstream and in the middle of nearly nowhere, the sky clouds over and we're soaked. Auntay's unwritten almanac had warned us about a late summer rain.

"Let's pull over up there and stretch," I suggest, thinking we've been having a contest to see who can go the longest without having to pee.

C.B. steps out in a half-foot of water. "Ow…oh! I been snake-bit."

A short, fat cottonmouth slithers into deeper water. The squared-off shape of the back of his head leaves no doubt as to positive identification. C.B. has been struck just above his ankle.

"Looks like you gon' get to be my blood brother, after all," comes the needless wise crack.

I pass on mentioning how lucky C.B. is he didn't get bit a couple of other places. After cutting the wound, I suck the blood and spit it out as fast as I taste it. Saving our drinking water, I rinse my mouth out with creek water…upstream. Seemingly calm for the circumstances, C.B. ties his headband into a tourniquet between his foot and knee, above the bite. I promptly pee in the river, while C.B. claims he doesn't have to go. I figure he went in his pants when he got bit.

It's critical to get him to a hospital as soon as possible. As remote as this country is, there's no leaving the river, especially when C.B. would have to walk on a snake-bit foot. I'd give out trying to paddle back upstream so there's really no choice but to continue on downstream. I'm afraid any way I go is going to take too long.

"C.B., you need to rest so your blood won't pump any faster than necessary. I'll paddle downstream for all I'm worth."

"You li'ble to hafta paddle harder'n 'at fer me to keep this foot."

Within an hour, blisters have formed on all sides of the bite…as they have on my fingers from paddling. C.B. complains about a stinging sensation and says the rest of his foot is getting numb. It's rapidly swelling and blending from black into purple. He starts talking about everything from Vietnam to losing Little Scott. I paddle, and he talks about stuff he has never told me about. His confusion becomes delirium.

"Th' Air Force got a helicopter they call th' Jolly Green Giant. You oughta see 'at friggin' thing when it goes to shootin'. Just thinkin' 'bout it gettin' off reminds me of Mouse."

By the time we reach where Tibbee Creek pours into the Tombigbee River, C.B.'s ankle is badly swollen. The big river is so wide here, paddling a canoe wouldn't be any fun under good conditions. With a strong wind in my face, the current that's flowing with me doesn't help as much as I was hoping for. I was counting on finding cabins and security lights and people and cars and help. Instead, I see nothing but more wilderness as my buddy drops into a semiconscious daze. Daylight's about gone. My heart pounds double-time as I become scared for C.B.'s life. Lightning starts up. Under other circumstances, anyone would pull over and get out of an aluminum canoe, but I'm afraid C.B. will die if I can't soon get him some anti-venom. I loosen his tourniquet for another few moments.

In another hour we make it to where we'd left C.B.'s pickup at Bob's beer joint. After running the canoe up on a shoal along the bank, I quickly climb up to the honky-tonk. Knowing I need help with getting C.B. up the bank, I go straight for the first possibility I see, which is three guys on bar stools. At the opportunity for heroism, they offer to help to get my friend to the hospital. With no time to waste questioning my choice of helpers, I'll work with the volunteers. When the four of us manage to drag C.B. up the hill, one of the good Samaritans suggests using their Dodge wagon as our ambulance. Without thinking it through, I accept. Once we've loaded C.B. in the back of their station wagon, I just jump in the back seat by myself. I've lost reason enough to know I should be taking C.B.'s truck.

Throwing gravel, we spin out of Bob's Beer Joint and head across the river. Better sizing up the situation, now that it's too late to select another option, I can tell from the smell we have a new problem. There appears to be a half-drunk driving us.

The half-drunk's drunk friend in the middle makes an observation. "Yo' friend's a nigger."

"Shut up, Flywheel," says the driver.

A seemingly not-so-drunk has taken shotgun in the seating arrangement. He speaks in spite of half-drunk's order, "Hell, we ain't got no need to be in a hurry—the poor snakes' probably done dead by now after bitin' a nigger."

As bad as things already appear, talk in the car gets uglier and meaner. Before I can think of anything diplomatic to say, Flywheel pulls out a pistol. My heart and innards join up. He whispers something across to our half-drunk driver and then to the not-so-drunk on his right. We turn off onto a gravel road that I don't believe is going to any hospital. Our driver announces that we are going to their hunting camp…where they will operate on C.B.'s leg.

No amount of begging seems to help. This thing may be as racial as it is alcoholic. Just southeast of Columbus, we stop long enough for the not-so-drunk to get out and unlock a gate. We drive through, and he locks it back behind us. My already helpless feeling worsens, and we go west on a dirt road toward the same river I've been trying to leave for three quarters of a day. It occurs to me that the further along this goes on, the worse it may get…and the less likely I'm going to have a chance to do anything about it.

Thinking about the situations C.B. must have faced during a combat tour of 'Nam, I'm wishing he were conscious to help with this. While his near-coma status makes him no help, at least he doesn't have to worry about what's going on.

When they stop the car, I'll jump out on the shotgun side and try to disable the redneck with the pistol. Then I'll worry about the other two. The fact that I'm sitting behind the half-drunk driver puts me on the wrong side. I slide over under the pretense of wanting to beg the not-so-drunk to take us to the hospital.

As the Dodge bounces and bumps to an abrupt halt in front of a cabin, I'm told to get out and bring my friend with me. Flywheel hands the gun to the not-so-drunk…and I figure God must be smiling on me. I make sure I'm out in time to be ready for the new pistol packer's first move. He leans over to get out. I cling onto my door for leverage and support. With his head and neck suddenly exposed, his chin juts out like it was sitting up on a kicking-tee. Zeroing in on his lumpy Adam's apple, my perfectly placed and timed kick sends him bouncing on the ground.

Before I can see where the pistol landed, the other two rednecks are running around from the driver's side. When they are half-way around, I jump in the front seat and slam the doors and hit the lock. The keys are still in the ignition...thank God. As one of the good ol' boys finds the pistol, the car engine catches up to the starter. I floor the accelerator and pop the clutch, throwing up a trail of dirt and dust.

I hear a shot that must have missed clean. The sound of broken glass accompanies a second shot. We round a corner and are out of sight from a third shot, as the spraying of glass settles all over the inside of the car.

I drive into the locked gate hard enough to take it down. Surprised my radiator's not spewing out steam and water, I'm headed into Columbus with C.B. Still out like a burnt wick, he hasn't known a thing since the last time I loosened his tourniquet...which probably needs doing again. I'm hoping his unconsciousness has slowed down his heart rate. When the gravel road turns to pavement, I loosen the tourniquet. Before I pull back out on the road, I notice a sheriff's department decal on the window of the wagon. Looking in the glove compartment, I find a portable blue light. I think about using it but decide against it. If the car belongs to a constable or deputy sheriff with the legal right to a gun, I don't know whom I can trust. I'll have to assume the local law enforcement officials might take sides with their own and arrest me for stealing the car.

Approaching the city and fearing the civilian hospital might result in some connection to the locals, I drive for the Columbus Air Force Base. They are bound to have a hospital. Running several red lights on the way, I'm planning what to do when I reach the Guard Station. Making a rolling stop at their open gate, I yell out the window, "Snakebite. We need an escort to the Base Hospital. This is a Vietnam vet, and he's about to die. Please help us."

The Military Police Guard looks in the car, sees C.B., and quickly orders us, "Take a right at the second turn. By the time you get there, an MP truck will have caught you to show you the rest of the way."

Our MP escorts us to the emergency room doors of the Base hospital. There we are met by two medics. The guard must have radioed ahead.

C.B. is promptly admitted, and finally I'm told he will be staying overnight. I make a phone call to Mayling.

Praying I'm not lying, I assure her that C.B. is all right regardless of the situation…and that we'll be home tomorrow.

The same MP who had seemed so nice before now interrogates me to the max. After hearing the particulars of my story, he loosens up considerably and arranges to get me a ride back to the Highway 82 river crossing where I retrieve C.B.'s pickup. Upon returning to the Base, I'm allowed to sleep in the truck cab, outside the gate by the Guard Station.

In the morning I'm properly processed back onto the base as a visitor, where I find C.B. alive and coherent. The Air Force doctor says C.B. shouldn't lose his foot and, over time, may fully recover. We won't know for sure until after several weeks of watching him try to heal.

Surprisingly, a medic on duty knows C.B. from 'Nam. After quite a reunion, I'm glad for them and jealous at the same time. C.B.'s buddy gets our story from him up until the part where C.B. had passed out and didn't know what was going on. From that point in the story, C.B. assures his medic buddy from 'Nam that he can believe anything I tell him about what happened.

After taking it all in, the medic advises, "The best thing for you guys to do is let the vehicle you stole disappear. I can make that station wagon vanish if that's what you decide…and I'm pretty sure you'll be better off going home and forgetting the whole thing."

C.B. gives me a quick glance. I'm worrying that the local court system might not help, if it is staffed with some of their homegrown boys.

With no discussion C.B. responds, "It don't mean nothin'."

This apparently translates as some kind of answer that they both understand from 'Nam. The medic makes a telephone call. Then I'm directed to bring our borrowed get-away car and follow his tech sergeant friend. We proceed to an airstrip where I'm told to leave the vehicle and get in his Air Force truck for a ride back.

"Should I leave the keys in the ignition?" I ask.

"It don't mean nothin'," he answers…and I'm beginning to get the hang of this Vietnam talk.

I toss the keys through the window and onto the Dodge wagon's seat and ask, "What's going on?"

He points up in the air and behind us. As we drive away, I look back over my shoulder to see a giant mosquito-looking helicopter hovering down over the loaner-car we just left.

"That's called a Sky-Crane. It's designed for air-lifting whatever needs moving...or removing."

"Where's he going to take it?" I ask.

"Well now, it's like this," the tech sergeant answers, "Captain Clark is flying that big eggbeater. He happens to be a fellow fisherman who appreciates the value of strategically placed fish cover. There aren't many holes in the Tombigbee River deep enough, but we know of one place where Tibbee Creek comes into the Tombigbee River, and it's fixing to be even deeper when the Corps of Engineers floods the bottom for their lake. It's got something to do with a lock and dam and barge traffic." He thinks he's informing someone who's not in the loop.

"But doesn't somebody keep track of.... I mean.... Are you telling me the Air Force doesn't watch what's going on closer than to let y'all do stuff like this with equipment like that?"

"Let's just say—if anybody in the military wants to see that car again, they'll need the Navy's best scuba gear. And by the way, I lost the paperwork on last night's interview with you. The official incident report at the hospital says you guys drove your buddy's pickup in here, and it wasn't nothing but a snakebite from a fishing trip. You understand what I'm saying?"

"Yes, sir," I thank him.

"I'm not a 'sir.' I have to work for a living. I'm just the tech sergeant who coordinates flight operations and has a fishing buddy chopper pilot who doesn't complain if his ten million dollar aircraft does some community service work...wildlife habitat improvement turning a piece of junked tin into good fish structure."

XLI:
Beloved
Briar Patch

SINCE THE LATE SIXTIES saw an extraordinary number of young adults catching themselves up in the environmental movement, the preferred forestry-related jobs have become scarce due to competition. Now that the seventies and the age of affirmative action are here, a white male landing one of the better ones is about as likely as stumbling on an east-facing slope dedicated to management of quality southern hardwoods.

As my former fellow forestry students, with their comfortable Cs and even Bs and better, turn into my competitors for employment, matters become complicated. Maintaining an attitude over my first five years of college that anything over a D was a waste hasn't done me any good. Although I thoroughly enjoyed helping turkeys gobble with a call and helping fish swim with monofilamented lures, it was the other students who laid hold to all the extracurricular clubs, fraternities, and other organizations that would be impressive to any potential employers.

A favorite professor accused me of having a philosophy based on hunting and fishing my way through undergrad school. For a long time I considered it a compliment but have now realized my knowledge of camping won't hold a Coleman lantern to leadership experiences the better students can brag about on their resumes.

Being a wildlife management major with a master's, I am stereotyped as a grad student environmentalist. Graduates in the other fields of forestry are widely considered the "wise users," the ones the corporate world courts and caters to for their conservationists. In trying to find a future with much of a paycheck, it's now very clear to me that I must be innovative if I am to get a leg up on my competitors.

As graduation time ticks toward nothing but uncertainties, I mull over a four-page application for permanent employment with the U.S. Forest Service. I notice something that could possibly give me a shot at landing a job. It's ironic how such a little box could be so big. It's only one space over from the one I should be checking. If I put an "X" over the box instead of the checkmark it asks to be put in it, I could claim my daydreaming caused me to cross out the one that was not applicable. If I need any supporting evidence to convince the authorities I'm dyslexic, I could interchange a couple of letters in a few other strategic places.

As I give thought to the big decision about the little box, I walk with my unsealed envelope to the campus post office. My application is complete and ready to mail except for that one mark. I'll have to decide about it one way or the other when I reach the mail drop.

The people in Washington, D.C., who will be receiving my application will see that it was mailed from Mississippi. Maybe they'll be thinking I'm black. A skin-deep skew on a little paperwork might just level the playing field for a change. They probably need someone to teach them not to use such a broad brush. Everyone knows they have a colored perception about everybody down here.

The words above the mail slot read stamped-out-of-town, and the dark hole below them speaks to me. They both suggest how impersonal, uncaring, and matter-of-factly my application will be treated. I make my tainted mark that seals the deal, indicating which race they need to think I am. Discreetly kissing the envelope for good luck, I deposit it with the U.S. mail.

UPON FINISHING MY LAST final exam, I'm out the forestry building's doors. Skipping down its steps like a kid with new tennis shoes, I have conquered higher education. With the kind of freedom that one can only know by experiencing it, I quote to myself C.B.'s civil rights hero— "I'm free at last—thank God All-Mighty, I'm free at last."

Fighting and fudging every step of the way through forestry school and the graduate program in wildlife management, I've finished what was required of me. Whether I'll find work or not, the degrees bring a fulfilling completeness and satisfaction. Never being overburdened with scholarly skills anyway, I will remain comfortable with my common sense. I'll maintain my wonderstruck curiosity about nature, which will keep me learning about the things I care about.

Once you've seen a kingsnake eat a copperhead and you realize most city folks haven't seen it and probably won't ever see it, then you feel special. You can know not to kill kingsnakes whether you're "smart" or not. When you see a flycatcher feeding her young the tiny insects that she has to catch on the fly and you think about how many it takes, then you've had a privileged sort of experience. You develop an understanding that puts your own role under Mother Nature into perspective. It doesn't allow you to worry about stuff that you can't do anything about.

It's my understanding that the university gives you a fake diploma at graduation ceremony and that the real one is mailed to you. There are a lot of things I'd rather be doing than walking through commencement for a symbolic piece of paper. At the time others walk, I'll be hand grabbling in what's left of the Little Tallahatchie River with my buddy C.B.

IN SPITE OF THE U.S. Army Corps of Engineers going ahead with their rape and abortion of our river, we spot a likely fish hole. My sidekick proceeds with his feely, grabby technique while I sit and watch with a critical eye.

He has come a long way with his grabbling skills after half-learning to swim by half-drowning a few times. With tremendous moral support and encouragement from the bank, I tell him two halves ought to make a whole, but he says it's more like there's a hole in the water. If he didn't love it so much, I wouldn't keep letting him be the one to get to grasp what can't be seen under the water.

Although we've never had much appreciation for the Corps of Engineers, C.B.'s tour in Vietnam has left him with the impression that he owes Uncle Sam no slack when it comes to giving our federal government credit for having good intentions. In college I was taught that it's fashionable to allow that our duly elected representation deserves the benefit of my doubts.

Regardless of all the "ifs," "ands," and "buts" and whatever reasons the Corps cling to, this river was re-engineered to the point there's hardly a honey hole left deep enough to hold a good catfish. Finding nothing here but his fill of feeling around under the water's surface, C.B. suggests we walk the bank upstream and look for a better spot in what's left of the old river.

"How come you ain't got you a river-rat girl to come out here an' keep us a campfire goin'?"

"I'm not sure God didn't run out of clay before He got around to creating one that'd dedicate her brown gravy to bullfrog thighs," I answer.

"You might be right."

"How come Mayling doesn't ever tag along?"

"I think I'd rather have her workin' at th' blue jean factory an' takin' care of things at th' house."

While C.B. sizes up fishing possibilities at a new site, a nearby blackgum is descended upon by a flock of cedar waxwings. Two-dozen strong, the handsome birds display their beautiful, army-greenish colors as they hop from twig to twig and compete with each other for the tree's purple drupes. All of a sudden, at the same instant, they all decide to all fly away. It reminds me that I'm out of school and jobless.

It's hard to be indifferent about waiting for an answer from my job application. My subconscious keeps whispering that I'm now the most well-instructed and highly educated fool in the forest. C.B., fishless, interrupts my musing and looks at me for a suggestion.

"As long as you're already wet, you could wade over there and get us some of those scuppernongs."

As C.B. agrees to shuffle across the river to the natural treats, I resume my private thoughts. If I ever do even hear from the government, it will probably amount to nothing more than some sort of bureaucratic double talk that says no. I ought just to forget about the Forest Service and start looking for something else. I think of the grapes left unpicked and how they will undergo their summer shrivel…wasting away like the consequences of my not finding employment. Why do I keep clogging up my mind with such negative thoughts about my future?

There are plenty of rivers and backwoods to explore. The time of year is right for wade-fishing for bass in the old river's pools. As we enjoy the strong, natural grape taste of the scuppernongs, we sit on the bank and watch the ripples calm that C.B. has made coming through the water.

A bobwhite quail scurries out of the grass and down to the water. And another. And another. The procession keeps up until ten neatly-trimmed birds sporting their duff and white-trimmed colors stand side by side at the river's edge. It seems that they need to hold their heads straight up in the air to swallow water. They look like feathered pistons as they alternately bob their heads up and down to dip their beaks. The fact that every other bird does it at the same split second probably has to do with watching for each other's rears for predators…and some in-born instinct to protect each other.

I don't see why I couldn't be part of a finely tuned machine such as that of Mother Nature instead of being an unemployed square peg looking at round holes in the forestry job market. C.B. stares at the quail without comment. Such silent moods and blank expressions scare me into thinking he's having bad memories of some kind. I wonder if he's being reminded of something in Vietnam…or of Little Scott. The birds all fly at once. Like the cedar waxwings, they have somehow communicated in a split second to all act together. Finishing our juicy ripe fruits, we head for home and curse the Corps for our lack of fishing success.

Dad walks out on the front porch as if he's looking for me. I'm worried about such uncanny timing.

He knows I've never been punctual much past my procrastination…and he has no reason to be expecting me now.

"Scott, you're here just in time. Come on in, quick. You have a long distance phone call from Atlanta. It's a man with the Forest Service."

This is the big one, I'm thinking. I've got to keep my cool now. It's bound to be the word I've been hoping for. I've been told my whole life through that timing is everything. This is my time…my turn. C.B. follows me in. I take the phone and hold it tight against my stomach so the party on the other end can't hear.

"Dad…uh, can you give me some space here, please?"

"Sure," he replies. "Come on, C.B. You can tell me about the big fish y'all always manage to let get away."

"Dad…let him stay, please."

"Suit yourself." Dad limps out fast…as if I've hurt his feelings.

When the door is closed, I explain my plan to C.B. "Please don't overdo it. This has gotta be fate…being lucky enough to get this call while you're here. It's a sign. If it wasn't, it wouldn't have worked out like this."

"Yeah, yeah…I oughta knowed it."

"No reflex answers. Slow your tongue down. Think about the questions before you say anything. Just be yourself…less your usual sarcasm. Hold the phone where I can hear, too. If they ask something you're not sure of, cover the mouthpiece and let me whisper my best guess to you. Okay?"

"Whatever," he agrees.

"C.B., please don't ruin this for me." I hand him the phone.

LOOKING OVER THE FORMAL job offer in writing for the umpteenth time, I relive C.B.'s telephone interview…while I'm the one being flown to Washington, D.C., for my professional orientation and hiring indoctrination. It would be good to think my hard-earned master's degree is responsible, but I don't have to dig too deep within myself to know a smidgen of application process creativity had more to do with it.

On the leg from Memphis to Atlanta, I enjoy a Bloody Mary and do my share of gawking at the stewardesses' legs. An hour layover is good for a margarita. I'll be ready to cross the Mason-Dixon line with a slight buzz. The Atlanta to D.C. flight's drink numbs my senses and dulls my guilt for using C.B.'s color to help find my future. I'm merely trying to even up the unfair hiring policy…a kind of re-affirmative reaction.

As the plane descends on D.C., a blanket of wet, heather-gray smog has socked in the city. It would be about my luck to make it finally to the Capitol City and not see squat. The cost of the taxi from the airport is a shock. For fifteen dollars Dad would have taken a passenger to Tupelo and back. The traffic, buildings, and people are sights to see for this country boy…and the cabby must have seen me coming.

I'm surprised how soon we pull up in front of the Auditors Building on 14th and Independence Avenue. In spite of the fifteen-dollar fee and my two-dollar tip, the taxi driver leaves without even saying thanks. Not realizing the different time zone would rob me of an hour, I pull in at the appointed time instead of having an extra hour to find my composure.

Although I wasn't expecting a forest, neither did I consider the world of Washington would be such a complete concrete jungle. The U.S. Forest Service headquarters building turns out to be an old refurbished jail.

It's a cement fortress with insignificant shrubbery and zero green to be seen. Inside, a soft light flickers on the tile-covered floor.

I visualize past prisoners trying to entertain themselves by watching the rays of sunlight coming through numerous tiny barred windows from high above. I suppose that's what the high-paid government big shots now do…for hours on end. The whole building is likely filled with forest supervisor wanta-bees, willing to do time here to get their shot at supervisordom.

I am directed through a rat-like maze of partitioned cubicles and come to a long hall. It's more like two rows of converted cells. Everyone's position on the pecking order must be naggingly reflected by whether they occupy an open box-like individual space or a real office where the previous thugs and crooks dwelled. Swirling somewhere in the middle of the Agriculture Department's food chain, the bulk of the Forest Service work force seems to be doing time here.

As my footsteps echo down the hall, I find the sad-looking space to which I've been directed. Announcing myself and proudly proclaiming where I'm from and what I'm doing here, I have the personnel officer's attention.

"B…bu…but, you're white!" he astutely observes.

"Last time I checked," I respond.

"We…uh, were uh, expecting you to be…uh, an Afro-American."

"Well…I'm sorry to half-disappoint y'all."

"Half? Y'all?" he repeats in a tone that belittles my speech.

"Yes…half meaning I am an American and y'all referring to whoever it is here who thinks skin color has any role in this age of equality for all."

"Uh…that's not it. It's just that…." He stammers and checks over the application. "We thought you…coming from Mississippi and all…."

"Well, suh, I got some assumptions 'bout Yankees too, but I'm hopin' y'all don't live up to 'em."

"Touché!" He half smiles in acknowledgment of what he must think I was making a joke about.

"Contrary to popular belief, everyone in Mississippi is not black."

"I guess not. For the time being, take this orientation package and proceed down the hall to the next-to-last office on the left…until I can figure out how to deal with this."

"Deal with what?" I pretend not to understand his dilemma.

"You just go ahead and let me worry about it," he answers.

I take the folder and quickly exit…thinking—*bingo!* This may be the foot in the door I need. For the length of the big-house hall, every step further away from this personnel officer is more comfortable…and more likely to be harder for anyone to admit a mistake.

"Dead man walking," I can almost hear the inmates jeering at me as I pass. Envisioning myself on my last walk to the gallows, I stay carefully close to the center. I sense hands and arms reaching out through bars and trying to grab me.

Joining those in the next-to-last office on the left, I notice they don't exactly look like any foresters I'm used to seeing. Doubting I'll ever blend into this crowd, I find a seat in the back of the room. Until I arrived, the twenty-some-odd recruits of various denominations and persuasions were lacking representation by one group…that of a male Caucasian.

A fairly attractive older lady comes in and takes the podium. After sharing the virtues of public service in a most pleasant and welcoming way, she singles me out and summons me to come along with her. I'd like to think this segregation is separating me out as a likely forester from the probable culls left back in the room, but I'm feeling more like I'm dead meat on the side of a highway.

I'm escorted to a former cellblock manned by a higher-up personnel officer than the first. Mr. Personality lets silence work the room…as I become even surer I know what this meeting is all about.

"Scott," he opens up, "there appears to have been some form of mistake with your application."

"What do you mean, sir?" I ask, trying to look surprised.

While his voice came with the full authority of his position, he's again working the silence like a partner in an interrogation of me. Refusing to speak first, I think so hard I hurt…and wonder if his smooth-speak purposefully used the operative word, "form."

"Right here, where there are three blocks on this form you filled out, you were supposed to have checked one of the three. The one beside Colored has an X over it…instead of the one that says Caucasian being checked."

"Let me see that thing," I demand, in surprised innocence. "Well, I'll be…. Look here. Sir, if you look real close you can see where someone has erased the check mark in the Caucasian box. Look at this. It's been changed. Somebody's jerking you around. You got some employees up here playing practical jokes on you, do you?"

"No, I do not. And indeed, someone certainly is trying to jerk someone around."

"Wait a minute. You're not trying to say that I was only being considered because y'all thought I was black, are you?"

"I am not trying to say anything. It just so happens that I was on detail in Atlanta to help do the hiring when I called and made the job offer, and I am remembering that it was an Afro-American I talked with...."

"What phone call?" I ask. "I got a letter."

Silence takes over again.

"What's going on, here?" I take charge. "If I'd known things with the Forest Service were this screwed up, I might not have come up here in the first place."

"Young man, there has obviously been a mistake...and we'll need you to sign this form. We'll straighten out this misunderstanding."

"Look, mister, I don't know how many colored foresters with master's degrees in wildlife management you think you've talked to, but Mississippi State hasn't ever even had one to enroll. It's not that they couldn't—they're just not interested. Y'all need to understand that. I've come to Washington with my job offer in writing, so I don't reckon I'll be signing any more of your forms."

"But..." he tries to interrupt.

"You can 'but' all you want," I assert with a frown, "but I'm here now, and I'm going back down that hall to finish my orientation."

His mouth drops open. Before he can figure out what to say, I quickly step out the door. Hurrying back down the hall at a get-away pace, I can almost hear the applause from all the long-gone inmates of the penitentiary's past. I mumble under my breath to the mis-uses and abuses of affirmative action, "And I'm the one with a Farce Service appointment."

When I return to where the fresh recruits are, they are enjoying a break from orientation. Some step toward restrooms and others to the water fountains. Some just stand around. I slip outside with the smokers to catch some second-hand smoked air and stretch for some relief of any other kind I can find.

Having sized up the workspace and situation in that building, I make a mental note that I never want to let them transfer me to this reformatory-like setting…or be put in jail. Next to the busy street and between the building and the sidewalk, a three-tree row of gray sugarberry provides momentary habitat to a small flight of warblers. It's easy to equate myself with the flocking birds…as I know they too are looking forward to making a southern journey. I picture myself trying to molt and grow new feathers before making my flight into the federal work force…as the birds will gather with their cohorts to do their migratory thing.

As we return from break, what really stands out for me is how the other recruits here don't look like the kind of foresters that could have even made it through Mississippi State. We're told we'll have to undergo a one-year probationary period. That reality hits me hard. Certainly they have ample ways of getting shed of employees they don't want and could have their pay back. Maybe I don't look like the others because I shouldn't be here with them.

Will my dyslexia hinder me at work as much as it haunted me in school? My self-confidence slips as I wonder if I have acquired all the knowledge I'll need for the job. Am I ready to assume the responsibilities of a professional forester? I know I can handle the woods work, but can I take out of my college classrooms what I've learned or should have learned…and now apply it in the real world?

Tension mounts and everyone's excitement peaks as assignments for duty stations are about to be made. It's explained that new foresters are not often sent to duty stations near their hometowns because the Service is striving to develop well-rounded employees. We're told federal foresters need to acquire experiences from various regions and that we're all expected to develop a broad background. That way, it's explained, the few who rise to management positions will be better prepared.

All through my university-level studies I was thinking that the better a forester knew his forest, the better a forester he would make. I think of the great variety of wildlife and how closely it's tied to habitats that resource managers must be familiar with in order to manage properly…and how government personnel policy ignores that. Something in me is saying that the Forest Service is afraid someone working near his home might get so familiar with local loggers that he might not put the taxpayers' best interests ahead of any other temptations that might arise.

Fellow recruit-mates remind me of nestlings trying to best their siblings in opening their mouths so as to get the adults' attention. Raised hands are acknowledged and then the special requests ignored. I'll settle for anywhere. As far off assignments are made, there is one glaring exception. There is but one assignment where the employee is not being relocated halfway across the nation from his home. Only one forest and one recruit will cost the Service zero moving expenses. That forest is Mississippi's Holly Springs National Forest...and the new forester is me. The Holly Springs N.F. is considered by the majority in Department of Agriculture circles as a not-so-desirable post. They probably don't want to make any unnecessary investment in me...like moving expenses.

With everyone else receiving placements long distances from homes and schools, my assignment sounds like retaliation for what they think could have been submission of a bogus job application. Perhaps I deserve it. The worry of a year-long probationary period comes to me again. If they wish to thin me from their plantation, the new Caucasian forester in the most predominantly black city of the Forest Service system could be pronounced unworthy.

Winning the first battle may not win me the war. On the other hand, if Washington, D.C.'s smart personnel didn't learn anything from the story of Br'er Rabbit and his beloved briar patch...I may just be better off than I think.

XLII:
Farce Service

A FORTY-FIVE MINUTE COMMUTE from Oxford to the Holly Springs National Forest each morning gives me ample time to worry about being fired and blackballed from further and future federal employment. I decide to tread lightly. The unit I'm reporting to may know of my hiring controversy…and stand ready to can me.

As days, weeks, and then months go by without any mention of the unusual uncertainties surrounding my assignment into professional work-life, I manage to settle in somewhat. Eventually I decide I wouldn't be exposed to such a costly and intensive year of training if plans included dismissing me as soon as my probationary period ends.

Doing what I've always wanted to do to make a living turns out to be fun. Gullible enough to go along with whatever I'm told, I come to have confidence in forest service, if not the Forest Service.

MEANWHILE, MY GOOD BUDDY, C.B., is pulpwooding away in the neighboring pines, not concerned by the fact that the bulk of the money growing on the young trees is going to the old companies. Working his hide raw for just enough money barely to get by, he logs himself further and further in debt but doesn't seem outwardly to worry about his circumstances.

Cutting down Loblolly that was planted as recently as his own birth, C.B.'s content to struggle below mid-level of the big corporations and small pine alike. I fear he is sawing his way closer and closer to a life without much of a future. He is not yet willing to concede that his woods-work labor will never allow him adequately to provide for Mayling's growing desires.

ACCUMULATING A YEAR OF work under my belt without any complaints from management, my traineeship closes out successfully. Fate flops an opportunity in my lap when I'm delegated the responsibility of training and supervising a new forestry technician. The selection of the individual is not mine to make, but since I will be the incumbent's immediate supervisor, I am instructed to evaluate the applications and make a recommendation.

Quickly absorbing more about personnel management than I ever wanted to, I learn that in the paperwork process the selecting officers use an interesting spread of numbers for a rating system. The procedure apparently first allows for a favored candidate to be segregated with a group of preferred candidates. Then a more specific favoring separates those by about the same distance as "what you know" is from "whom you know."

As I search through the stack of applications, I do not find among the prospects the sincere conservationist I feel is needed. Even though the deadline for submitting an application is at the end of the workday, I believe that the best candidate for this job may have just enough time to put his name in the hard hat.

The individual I'm thinking of is someone who has a good southern work ethic and can be counted on, trusted, and respected. If there were an evaluation criterion having to do with common sense, he'd max out. This prospective new employee is well suited for the particular demands of working out in the elements. He possesses good woodsmanship, and I know him to have an in-depth relationship with the living woods.

The successful applicant should certainly be someone whose word is always true and who has never slacked from accepting responsibility. My compass needle consistently points toward the magnetic acquaintance who's been building a bond with me since childhood. Flying in the face of other applicants who have two-year forestry tech degrees, my stereoscope keeps magnifying a candidate who has only a high school education. He does have five points' worth of the veteran's preference.

He can also check the "correct" ethnic box to be segregated into the affirmative action application stack.

My supervisor doesn't need to know the connection between my choice of candidates and me. It's merely coincidental that my nominee needs a change he can throw himself into to help him deal with having lost his son. I won't have to convince myself I'm recommending him in good conscience.

With the risk of a consequential dose of creativity accompanying my friend's application package, his numbers are manipulated almost dyslexically. From a deep pond of eligible candidates, C.B. can suddenly wade into the shallow pool called the "short list."

AS AUNTAY'S FIELD CORN browns up and the river bottom's highbush blueberries bloom, C.B. enters my work place. Irony and I have given him the better job. He's working in the woods while I'm too often tied to my desk. I'm a bit jealous and can't help it. It's a bit of a blow to my preferences.

Neither of us admits to being worried about any kind of supervisor and subordinate conflict, not beyond something short-lived. When what's customary needs a little adjusting, we both have an inclination to round whatever corners we can't completely cut…in order actually to help the public we're paid to serve. C.B. sometimes goes a step further and reminds me of an offsite baldcypress that's out of its natural habitat but doing quite well in spite of high and dry ground.

With his hard-earned experiences from the logging-woods, my buddy comes to the job with a woodsman's soul. Operating within the realms of administering timber sales and stand improvement contracts, C.B. develops into a technician who interacts well with even the most seasoned of loggers. He has a way of showing tough men that they count for something more than just being tough. Even the rougher ones respond with accomplishment when they realize he sees them and their role as important.

Without worrying about meeting others' expectations of him, C.B. gains cooperation and compliance by simply dealing from the heart. It's a gift. Watching schools me in lessons beyond those my college training had to offer. Whereas I often catch myself trying to impress others, he remains happy within himself by being his true self.

We, of course, make our share of mistakes. Mine mostly concern the mundane details of office operations. C.B.'s involve field procedures that are supposed to be strictly followed. I repeatedly remind him that he should try not to get into any more trouble than necessary and wish he'd better grasp the concept of a probationary period. We both learn that out where the real work takes place, being a good public servant often means bending and stretching official rules and regulations.

AS SWELTERING SUMMER DAYS stretch my imagination about how to make work life more interesting, C.B. comes up with a great suggestion. "Scott, why don't we sponsor us a fishin' derby fer th' kids at th' Retardation Center?"

"Great idea. Let me make some calls and see what we can and can't do."

The first thing I learn is that volunteers from outside the agency are fantastic. It's folks within the agency who bring most of the challenges to the table. There are too many red-tapists who are more interested in telling why something can't be done than in helping figure out a way to do something.

When I try to explain from all my Forest Service Manuals and pass on directions from above, Tech C.B. says something about my credibility being about the same as a prostitute trying to preach. Although the analogy may be appropriate, I have no choice but to continue sharing the latest Forest Service policy with him.

"There's a freeze on buying such things as soft drinks, hot dogs, and buns, C.B."

"'At ain't no problem. I'll talk businesses into donatin' what all we need."

"That's a problem, too. I'm obligated to inform you that federal employees are prohibited from soliciting free goods and services...no matter what the use or how good the cause."

C.B. stands and stares as if what I have said is complicated double talk he can see right through. He leaves without saying another word, as if I'm the problem.

I'M SITTING AT MY desk when C.B. returns from town with enough hot dogs, buns, and soft drinks for two hundred kids.

"I wish I didn't have to ask this, but what's the story here?"

He stands almost at attention. "You 'member Mr. J. talkin' 'bout buyin' them neat little tin cans just to get th' Velvet smokin' tobacco that's inside 'em?" He hands me a receipt that he has signed. "Ain't nothin' in yo' manuals says we can't be buyin' containers an' sacks is it?"

"C.B., you've got our necks stretched out about as far as they can go."

He takes a seat across from me, his wide grin saying he's rather pleased with himself. "Th' soda water an' buns just happen to come in 'em...is all. Th' hotdogs, they was one of them coincidences you always talkin' 'bout."

"Sure it was," I sarcastically agree.

"Really, Scott, I happened by Stephens an' Tatum Grocery, an' th' clerk come right out an' said th' Bryan Meat Company had a bunch of hotdogs they was willin'...I mean, wantin'...to put in th' back of th' gov'ment truck. You wouldn't of had me arguin' none with no merchant over that. You know how them grocery men can be sometime."

"Yeah, I know. What's this on the ticket about you buying a livestock water trough with range funds?"

"You didn't aim fer me to buy no cooler, did you?"

"C.B., this is a farce."

"With all th' 'propriate Farce Service paperwork. Now, sign it, please."

"I'm going to sign this, but I'll swear—if we get caught, I'm claiming I didn't know anything about your details. I'm not about to do thirty days in the electric chair on account of you. You got that?"

"Yes, sir." His exaggerated salute almost makes me laugh.

"Don't give me that 'sir' crap, C.B." I put on a serious expression but barely manage to hold my straight face. "You need to realize that falsification of records and fiscal irregularities are not to be taken lightly."

"I tell you what—after we've had them kids from th' mental hospital out in th' heat of th' sun fer half a day, you see if you think any of 'em's takin' their cold soda pops lightly."

"You just don't get the message, do you?"

"Scott," he offers in an exasperated but deliberate voice, "when one of 'em faints, I hope you can find th' right accountin' code in time to give 'em some first aid."

"Whatever you say, C.B. Don't let me get in your way," I submit, with a groan.

"Thank you."

"Why should it matter what our rules and regulations say?"

"What matters is whether or not you can push them papers far enough to give these special kids at least one good day, one day of fun fer 'em…that's all. Th' rest of it don't mean nothin'. I don't know how yo' sense of proportion got so out of whack."

C.B. PERSONALLY CHECKS OUT the Puskus Recreation Area to see what needs to be done prior to what he is calling our disadvantaged's event. There are only a few recreationists visiting the lake when his Senior Citizen crew polices up the grounds.

Suddenly a little girl screams. She's jumping straight up and down, flailing her arms, and yelling. Her dad is on a nearby fishing pier, but C.B. is closer and races over. She points at a really big snake right in front of her.

C.B. pulls the girl away and steps back. The father catches up to them and tries to calm his daughter while C.B. looks over the snake. All coiled up in a deadly diamondback posture, it's unidentifiable. The dad doesn't want to leave any room for argument and insists C.B. get a sizable stick and beat the reptile. C.B. complies but unwillingly. Seeing that the beaten snake is not a threat, the man and his daughter slow their yelling and crying and leave.

Upon stretching the snake out in the bed of the Forest Service pickup, C.B. realizes it might be a pet boa. Fearing someone might identify it and charge him with violating some kind of federal snake protection statute, he decides to toss it over the side of the first gully he can drive by.

Just as a good gully outside the recreation area presents itself, the boa constrictor regains consciousness.

Assuming the snake will not be in a very friendly mood upon seeing C.B. again, a new plan seems to be called for. With C.B.'s snake forsaking formula gone fuzzy, guilt and confusion guide the grass snake-green colored government rig toward the veterinarian's. Unfortunately, at the clinic, the snake refuses to go along with any serpent repair by dying for real…except in print.

When the local weekly-wiper shares its scoop with the *Commercial Appeal* newspaper from Memphis, the proverbial waste is in the breeze. As the airs of gossip flow freely, front-page headlines read—"Forest Ranger Saves Little Girl by Turning the Timber on Whip-snake."

Phone calls and letters to the editor follow. Between the printed lines, the truth slithers out—Prized Pet Destroyed. Being lumped in with automatic snake killers who destruct first and ask questions later is not the kind of public controversy the Forest Service wants. Being no better than we are at avoiding turmoil, C.B. and I are directed to keep a low profile in hopes the story stops brewing.

Associated Press, by reprinting their version of the serpent circus, crawls out from under the classifieds and puts us squarely in the comics…all across the nation's newspapers. Upper management continues to insist the best way to handle being the laughing stock of the country is to do nothing. It's my understanding they have vast experience of both.

Locally, we focus all-out public relations efforts on our up-coming fishing rodeo for special kids. We'll have snake guards at every likely location. The big day comes, and boys and girls who don't normally have a whole lot of happiness and pleasure in their daily lives do for a day. Life is beautiful as they laugh and smile. Most all the children catch fish, and sizes don't matter. The day turns out to be the best workday any of the people helping ever had. Everyone is such a winner that I'm thinking surely the snake saga is finally over.

––––––––––

WEATHER PREDICTIONS FOR THE following weekend indicate ideal prescribed burning conditions. Saturday's plans are made to ignite the perimeter of a one thousand acre tract north of Highway 30 and have the fire burn in toward itself.

Near the turnoff on the highway, where we'll go north to get to the site, we stop at a little country store. Forestry technicians pile out of the six-pack vehicle to buy their lunch supplies on government overtime. Apparently never having seen the way we are all dressed in our fire-retardant clothes, the gray-haired little old lady running the store looks at us with open-mouthed curiosity. With everyone wearing the bright yellow shirts and dull green pants, we must look like a team, if nothing else.

Sardines, viennas, crackers, and cheese are our choices for carryout. Most everyone will drink water to save their money. I'm the first to come back out to the truck. As it re-fills with employees, I count heads. C.B., alone, remains in the store. A few moments later he comes out, laughing aloud.

Curious what's so funny, I ask, "All right, C.B., what's going on? I can tell when you've been up to no good."

"I'z just answerin' th' lady's questions…that's all."

"C.B.?"

"What?" he asks with his false look of innocence.

"What questions, C.B.? What was so funny?"

"Well, she said she ain't never seen nuthin' like th' bunch of us, all dressed to match and ever'thing, like we was ghost-busters or somethin'."

"And?" I warily push for the rest of the story.

"I told her we was th' Farce Service an' we was on a mission to serve."

"And?"

"An' I axed her if'n she'd seen th' newspaper 'bout th' Forest Ranger savin' th' little girl from th' big snake."

"And?"

"An' she said she'd seen it." He laughs again behind his smile.

"C.B., what did you tell her?"

"Oh…I told her we didn't really want no rumors spread 'bout no Yocona Puff Adders, but…."

"But what?" I almost yell.

"But we'd found a whole den of 'em, an' we was headed back to get 'em."

to believe she's toying with me. When we stop for a breather, the clouds break open. We are caught in a cool, soaking rain on an otherwise hot summer day. Augusta's white cotton blouse is drenched. While her cruiser's vest covers her back, its open front allows her blouse to show off the lacy pattern of her bra and the two perfect little bulges beneath it. The wet cloth clings to her lovely, lemon-size breasts as if it were wrapped individually around each of them.

When she starts to slip off the rain-heavy cruiser's vest, I'm wondering if Augusta's doing it to give me a better view. She smiles at having caught me staring at her. Rather than the vest coming off, it rolls and wads up along the top of the shoulders. In all my chivalry and with nothing but gentlemanly intentions, I step right up to help her remove it, lifting and pulling the vest over her shoulders. The top button of her saturated blouse has worked itself undone. I'm in a subconscious state of mind. Without thinking I reach to re-button her blouse. Before I can think to pull my hands back, it occurs to me that I should have ignored it or simply told her about it…but it's too late.

Apparently thinking I was reaching to unbutton her blouse instead of re-buttoning it, Augusta reaches for the top button on my shirt. Rain falls heavier as if to signal something…or drown out what's happening. My willingness has no qualms as she continues with my buttons. The moment is seductive, and the realization that I may have precipitated Augusta's come-on is quickly put out of my mind. Everything is all about her now and how far she will go.

I undo her remaining buttons. Exposed cleavage between dainty mounds presents tiny beads of moisture that I want to taste. Hardening and rising nipples show off intriguing outlines right through the silky bra as these lovely boobies defy restraint. The thin white brassiere does not hide what I assume have been Augusta's private possessions until now.

Her warm green eyes look into mine, and I feel my face flush red. She's an opportunity I'm obligated to experience for all those who have never had it. I tell myself this college girl thinks she wants this as much I do. Personnel management and their big ideas of social engineering should have taken this sort of situation into consideration. Maybe they addressed such a scenario in some student handbook of instruction that I should have read.

Her hands slide around the small of her own back to unfasten her bra. She impatiently fumbles with the fastener, finally releasing herself and any inhibitions she might have had. I fondle her with my fingers and grope her with my hands, palming and squeezing what I am about to experience even better. She arches her back to present her perfectly matched breasts. As if I needed help in knowing what to do next, she holds my neck and pulls my face to her erect, pinkish-beige nipples the size of quarters.

Fondling one nipple with my forefinger and thumb, I kiss the sparkling beads of cool rainwater that encircle the other tantalizing titty. Wide-eyed, I look up and into the face of the girl who sort of initiated this. Life will never be the same for me. While I'm trying to figure out what to do next, she gently guides us to kneeling positions on the forest's floor of pine needles. Scared I don't know exactly how I'm to react now, I go back to a breast while I try to plan my move. Augusta takes charge.

Facing one another, we sit and untie each other's logging boots. I clumsily toss her clodhoppers in a patch of pink lady-slippers and briefly think of Cinderella. My pre-forestress peels off her blue jeans like a candy wrapper. I flounder with my own clothes…and she slowly slides herself out of her silky white panties in an erotic dance preceding total nudity. I know I now must do the same, or she'll do it for me.

Awkwardly exposed in a worked up embarrassment, I'm suddenly the object of an episode that's become hers. Taking the coward's way out, I close my eyes and try to pull her to me. She won't go for it. Taking comfort in my distress, she somehow knows I will be tasting the forbidden fruit for the first time. Her passion wins out, as she takes me her way. We ride the waves of the shortleaf pine duff until we simultaneously yield to the ultimate relaxation.

Augusta kisses me around my eyes, as turn about plays and persists. Having entered the worldliness that I've previously taken for granted, guilt cries silently over the rape of my supervisory responsibilities. Could I be in the wrong…the way she asserted herself? Surely there's two-way accountability in such a consensual manner of sex.

The rain stops, and Augusta starts…wanting to do it all again. The natural world around us sings out that this is the way things were meant to be. I close my eyes this time with the intention of keeping them closed. I hear and see a mockingbird of sorts. In my personal darkness there is a beautiful creature, now becoming one with the forest and me. She's not been hesitant to spread and bare her white wing patches and demonstrate slow wing beats of passion. Flicking her long slender tail feathers from side to side, I wonder if she feels as though she needs to take flight. Physical exhaustion closes in again. We experience a second, long gasp of perfectly timed, bursting fulfillment together. She mocks my excitement and mimics my call for climax. We two have become like one and the same.

When I open my eyes, Augusta picks a heart-shaped leaf from the moonseed vine next to us and hands it to me with a teasing gesture, "You have won my heart."

Knowing her, I assume she's waiting for me to embarrass myself with some corny effort at a romantic answer. I think but still draw blank poetic connections. Her waiting smile tells me to say something. Most anything that doesn't totally lack romance might do. I notice the dark red berries of the plant where she picked her leaf. Picking one and handing it to her, I try desperately to come up with something to say along with it but have only helped her to put me on the spot.

"A berry for your cherry?" I finally blurt out.

She puts her hands on her naked hips and bests me, "Your banal blurbs will not suffice for sweet words, so try harder or admit I'm smarter." Continuing her chit-chat and chatter, she brushes back her bangs and exposes a face reflecting the glow of womanhood. "What did you think about during that last, most intense moment, Scott?"

"Oh, Augusta.... Not now, not yet. Let's just be quiet for awhile."

"But, Scott, I really want to know."

"I don't know...uh, a mockingbird, I guess."

"A what?" she questions.

"Yeah—a mockingbird...that's what I thought of."

"Would you explain that to me, please?" She again puts her hands on her hips, in that cute way.

"I'm not sure. I don't know that I can explain. I just figured telling you the truth wouldn't hurt."

"Try me," she demands, pouting.

"Come on, Augusta."

"You come on. Try."

"All right.... Being in the midst of the brush and hearing your song of satisfaction, you simulated the very voice of all that is wonderful in the world of our outdoors. I submit that you are clearly one of the greater parts of nature's perfection."

"That's good, Scott. But what part is that?" she pushes.

"You know, Augusta...."

"No, I don't. Continue."

"Well, that's probably why it's called a 'piece'—a guy can't ever get enough."

"Why did I even ask?" she comes back. "Since you haven't got a clue, let me tell you something. In the unlikely event you're ever in this position again, a girl wants to hear that she's the best that's ever been...and there will never be anyone like her. You get the idea?"

"But that's exactly what I was trying to say."

As she continues to talk and talk some more and even more after that, I begin to daydream about my upbringing. I'd been warned about the temptation of falling from grace. I had been preached to, time and again as a youngster. I was supposed to know to be on guard for the girl who was sure to come along and offer the sinful sample. Perhaps Adam's apple was really something else that Eve offered up. My teachings from the Good Book were too hard to deal with when Augusta came to me in the garden without so much as a fig leaf. The serpent of olden times might as well have been a Yocona Puff Adder.

Still rambling pointlessly on whatever it is she's talking about, my workmate waves her hand in front of my face. Apparently thinking I wasn't paying her enough attention, she asks, "Now, Romeo, what do you have to say about that?"

"Absolutely," I agree. "Okay, all right, already."

"And?" She shoves for something more definitive.

As I have no idea what she's asking about, I stay general, "And...you are simply augustaable, my Dear Augusta."

"Which means?" She won't let up.

"Meaning simply, that...uh," I bend down and kiss her tit, "that you have such a great nipple, I was wondering if you might like to try for a triple?"

"Not in this lifetime, jerk."

XLIV:
Tech Techniques and Southern Watercress Re-Leaf

"WHAT'S 'EM MEXICANS DOIN' plantin' pine here?" C.B. clamors, as he points to the location on a map he's brought into my office.

"Good morning, and how are you doing this fine day?" I change the subject, giving myself a few seconds to gather my answer.

"Not so good…if we gon' re-pine ever'where was hardwood." He taps his finger hard and repeatedly on the paper. "Many squirrels as you and I took outta there…an' we doin' this to it?" He leans over my desk as if he's about to head butt me.

"It'll make good deer and quail habitat," I offer as consolation.

"Fer 'bout five year is all…'til it closes in. Then a hoot owl'd hafta pack a lunch to go thru there."

"C.B., this is just one stand, and when it's thinned and burned and we get some sunlight on that forest floor…it'll be so full of wildlife food plants you'll be the very one wanting to hunt there."

"Yo' squirrelly gov'ment talk is leavin' out th' squirrels." He sits down in my visitor's chair, his look saying he's not buying my explanation. "An' it don't do no good arguin' with yourself 'bout what you already know's right."

"C.B., we have to cut the timber before the trees get to falling apart."

"Yeah, but what I don't know is why we not bringin' back more hardwood than we are. They's plenty of honest-to-goodness pine sites fer th' pine. That was a good hardwood stand come off'n there."

"C.B.?"

"Don't 'C.B.' me. You need to let go of what all it is you can do 'bout this. What we gon' plant in this stand over here?" He points to another spot on the map slated for harvest.

"Soybeans?" I joke.

"Scott, I'm serious. Mr. J.'s prob'ly rollin' over in his basswood box."

I'm thinking C.B. could have gone all day without throwing Mr. J. at me. It's a wonder he hasn't quoted something of Auntay's.

He pulls up his snake gaiters and tucks in the bottom of his pants legs. "Auntay'd say to weigh it in 'n solve it. It's done got time to draw up tight what it is you gon' stand fer." He gets up and walks toward the door but stops and looks back. "You 'member 'bout Mr. J.'s levelin' th' playin' field? We be needin' to do 'at fer th' hardwoods."

"The Forest Service already does that," I answer. "It's called a clear-cut."

"You ain't gon' wisecrack yo' way out of it." He leaves mumbling, "We can do better'n this."

Leaving me with an office full of guilt in my head, he goes out without my answering. I hope he doesn't really think in the name of my own ambition that I'm going along with an agency gone bad. I don't suppose I could have convinced him some wars are won by first losing a battle or two. I don't guess he'd see that periodically bending with the wind might help a forester get to a better position of influence, where he could then make more significant changes. I couldn't presume it'd be useful telling him that a manager with the big picture might know something he doesn't.

I tell myself something else might be more important than letting everything ride on making a particular point each time something's not going my way. C.B. will soon be long gone and out in the woods with the fun jobs. Everything will seem as simple as a spring to him. I'll be the one with piles of decisions stacking up. It will look to him as if I'm compromising my very soul each time his personal beliefs clash with what I'm thinking I understand.

ANOTHER MORNING C.B. COMES in and asks, "How much a desk jockey like you get paid to set in here an' sleep?"

"I wasn't sleeping. I was closing my eyes to think real hard."

"'Bout what?"

"I'm trying to figure out how we're gonna deal with those beaver dams at Bagley Bottoms since we can't blow them."

"Who says we can't blow 'em?"

"The Forest Service has come out with a moratorium on the purchase of dynamite and blasting caps right when we need them."

"'At ain't no problem. I'll take care of that at my level of 'thoridy."

"C.B.?"

"Th' obvious ain't neber too much fer th' man what knows what needs doin'," he answers as he steps out.

I'm knowing he's not going to buy into the no-buying directive. My interpretation of our rules and regulations are sometimes a mere annoyance to C.B. If he doesn't agree with them, they're only troublesome and tiresome, not to be taken seriously.

Being the professional, I am expected to espouse my agency's theoretical ideology. As a technician, C.B.'s job is to get things done. Because of the position I'm in, I sometimes have to follow directives that appear to be nonsense to someone in the field who doesn't see my constraints.

Although C.B.'s man-on-the-ground perspective may see different solutions to the same problems I see, we both come up with the same love-hate relationship for our agency. His continuing to do things his way hasn't yet tested our friendship, despite the many differences between C.B. and me and often the Forest Service. What he often sees as clear as good water could be the same thing that'd leave me standing with both feet in something more akin to mud.

A few days later C.B. returns from the Lafayette County Co-op and hands me a sales slip. Knowing he's developed a knack for getting around bothersome orders at every turn, I reluctantly read. He has signed off on the purchase of fertilizer and applicators instead of dynamite and blasting caps.

A SPELL OF DRY WEATHER and the resulting low humidity brings with it an exceptionally high fire danger. It's so great that our Regional Forester in Atlanta sends out a mandate ordering the suspension of all prescribed burning. State forestry departments across the southeastern United States also recognize the danger and decide not to issue burning permits. A window of opportunity I'd been looking through now appears slammed shut.

Knowing how seriously I take my wildlife habitat improvement and how much we really need to prepare a bare ground seedbed for sewing Jap millet before the early season waterfowl arrive, my forestry technician makes a unilateral determination. He has decided that no duck he's likely ever to meet will be particularly interested in whether we are able to obtain a burning permit from the state. I happen to be standing around the corner from the phone when C.B. calls the Mississippi Forestry Commission office.

"We got some garbage down th' hill from Bagley tower gettin' rank an' needin' to go today," he tells them. "If 'n y'all see any smoke over there don't get concerned. It ain't gon' be no 'scribed fire or wildfire or nothin'. We be standin' right there with it—how's yo' son doin' in school this year? He playin' football?" he quickly changes the subject.

I don't know whether to choke him or sit back and admit that he just may have developed into the best forestry tech a wildlife biologist could find.

OUTSIDE MY OFFICE WINDOW in a competing sort of frenzy, a ruby-throated hummingbird and a monarch butterfly are feeding from the orange-red horn-shaped flowers of a trumpet creeper. Just as the hummer and flapper prepare for their future flights, Augusta will soon be making her preparations for returning to college. In fact, this will be her last day to be at my beck and forest *service*.

A rotten trellis beyond my window serves as termite fodder and as support for the aerial roots of a cow-itch vine. Not willing to go too far from its support, the vine begs for something else to climb. Maybe it's looking for something new and exciting to cling to. Augusta will probably be like that. When she returns to school she'll be finding some stand-up college boy at her Yankee university to take my place. I'll become a mere memory to her. I wonder if she'll even miss our botanical bedrooms in the bottomlands of blue waxweed.

As appealing as she was on the day I met her, Augusta shows up with that special bounce in her step. We waste no time heading for the truck to drive to the woods for our last day in the field together. I guess she's been powdering her tail or whatever it is she does to make me grow so impatient…but I still don't want to see the summer end.

Like Augusta's read my mind, she shares her intentions. "What do you say we have one last little fling?"

"Wooh…oh back, Nelly," I interrupt. "Haven't I taught you anything? You don't ever want to use the word 'little' when you talk to a guy about his fling."

"All right, since this is our last awesome fling together…."

"That's better," I cut her off again. "And I thought you'd never suggest it."

"And you haven't learned the first thing about romance," she comes back.

"What are you talking about? I'm trying to initiate foreplay sooner…is all."

"Some folks just don't ever get the message," she scolds.

"But I'm serious. I'm even agreeable to you accosting me in this truck while I'm driving to the field…hint, hint."

"Nice try, but no thanks."

"I don't know why not. That'd be about the most romantic thing you could do for me."

"Since my return to school will make this our last time together, why don't you come up with a place that will be sentimentally memorable?" she challenges and looks at me for a response.

"My dear, all of our encounters have been so memorable to me that anywhere with you will be a special place."

Her stare says that I'm still on the spot…without a spot.

"Augusta, in earnest, I remember how special you were at my favorite overlook above the river, for our first time. How could you think I'd ever forget the second time, on the sun-warmed boulder in Yocona bottom? How about the time on the cool and moist half-decayed log of that old landing? What about the bed of cushiony sphagnum moss at the minnow ponds, the cold floor of the back of my pickup, the rough-cut boards of the fishing pier at Puskus and then again under the picnic table when the rain came? It was a special forest *service* to me up in the Denmark fire tower…and during our post-western detail, after-hour encounter on the Forest Supervisor's desk. Can't you see that you would be memorable to me right here right now…in this truck as I drive?"

I look at her for agreement, but she sits and gives her secretive smile. She's no doubt waiting for me to suggest somewhere offering a more lasting impression for her.

"All right, I know of somewhere way back in the Little Tallahatchie River bottom where the Corps and the Forest Service haven't even dreamed of…not the way we're talking about using it."

"Tell me about it."

"My camp rope won't stretch around the oldest of the hardwoods. There are virgin cypress trees like ancient towers. It's between the old river and the new canal. You'll have to be willing to hike half a day in and the other half out."

"Sounds good, but it wouldn't give us enough time for what I've got in mind," she teases.

"All…ll ri…ight! All righty then…uh, well, another part of the outdoor world that hasn't held your sweet, bare backside is coming to mind. How about a swamp."

"Works for me, " she's quick to answer.

I almost wreck turning my truck toward the nearest slough I can think of. "You're serious?"

"As serious as a beaver." She throws a fetching smile.

"Augusta," I sigh, "I'm going to miss your puns."

"Then come…see me at school sometimes," she adds and grins again.

"What's with this obsession about a different place today?"

"Let's call it getting your bearings before doing any baring," she answers.

"I'm thinking it's who's present and not the places that make for memorable experiences."

She looks at me with her happy face. "Yeah, yeah, I won't forget you either, Don Juan of the dandelions…not if your swamp turns out to be the slightest slosh romantic."

"Augusta, I remember everything from the way we reacted to each other's touch for the first time to last week when we used the fronds of a sensitive fern to tickle each other. I recall how the virgin-white flowers of wild carrots matched your lacy little underthings the time we laid in the loosestrife of the new highway right-of-way. What could be more romantic than slowly undressing you under the stars and in the elusive light of the moon?"

She looks over at me through those long lashes and gives me an approving pat above the knee...but that's all.

"Don't stop now," I beg.

"Be patient."

"I'll be the patient. You be the doctor," I continue to plead but to no avail.

Pulling off the logging road, I park about ten feet from the edge of a secluded slough carved out from West Cypress Creek's old and better days. Augusta's out of the vehicle by the time I turn off the engine. When I get around to her side of the vehicle, she's already three quarters naked. I think how strange it is that she was talking about me not being romantic. I'd even like to have some rare moments of quiet, but I know better.

She chats on and on and places her panties in her boots. When she sits erect to roll her socks down and off I sense her all-too-quick mood change. She slides herself into the water like a mink. She spins smoothly and swimmingly over onto her back and has never looked better. My desire to experience her has never been so uncontrollable.

After I finish undressing myself, I crawl toward the slough, feeling the sun's warmth on my bare buttocks. She stares as I ease into the cool water to join her. With everything of mine except my head and rear now under the water's surface, Augusta slaps me hard on my butt.

"Yeah, you keep your precious little tush submerged so I can't pay you back," I tease.

We engage in a play wrestling match which turns into a slippery embrace. Aquatic undulations ripple throughout the otherwise calm water until the slough owns us. With Augusta gasping and oohing and aahing, all the swamp-like forces of nature come together. In sheer ecstasy, we should be lying still and quiet. It's not to be...not with Chatty Gabby's continual gibberish.

"Scott, to make this kind of experience complete—"

"This kind of experience?" I question.

"In a swamp," she explains, "all we need is for a snake to come slithering through here."

"Yeah," I answer, thinking I might summon up myself into another memorable peak. "There's always the ol' Yocona Puff Adder."

"I should've known I could count on you to get totally un-romantic on m.... Uh, ah...oh...ouu. Scott...Scott."

"Shh," I tell her. "Shh...."

"Don't shh me. Open up to me. Tell me, Scott, how much do you like me now? Tell me while we do this. Talk to me. Now...now...Scott," she asks, without giving me a chance to answer if I wanted to. "Tell me what you're thinking. Tell me now...ah...oh...ouu.... Tell me exactly what you are thinking about right this second."

"This," I answer pulling up a handful of coontail from the water beside Augusta's head. "It's good like water cress. Here, try it. Really, it's best when you taste a big mouthful."

XLV:
Pot Cop, Kraut, and Soldiers Past

BEYOND NARROW SPECIALTIES, PROFESSIONALS in the U.S. Forest Service sometimes show little regard for the big picture. Instead of coordination for conservation and cooperating with each other for the benefit of all, we are as apt to rob each other's work force of personnel. It's not at all surprising that Uncle Sam's latest affirmative action initiative is flirting with my number one forestry technician.

As a permanent employee of my agency for several years now, C.B. has become nothing short of a workaholic. When you have someone as talented as C.B. is, you need to hang onto him. In the process of becoming a proficient timber marker and good wildlife biology technician, he has accumulated an impressive collection of good performance ratings.

With the exhaustion of Little Scott's insurance coverage, medical bills are hanging heavy on C.B.'s shoulders. He owes his soul to the Forest Service credit union and could use a job with higher pay. When a law enforcement career path comes courting, he leans on a lesson from losing Little Scott…about keeping his attention on things he *can* influence.

Part of me says to discourage him. The other part knows a new and exciting mental challenge might do him a world of good. The wood-fiber wolves in authority have pushed their annual quotas and big numbers of board feet sold until we've hardly had time for our spam and tomato sandwich picnics in the woods. Perhaps I haven't done enough to make C.B.'s current job rewarding.

The Forest Service is slowly changing. All through the 70s a new perspective on public forests has been evolving. As the general populace is becoming more aware of and more involved in the environmental movement, non-timber resources, such as forest recreation, are coming into their own. With this loosening up of the old-line forest guard, C.B. and the other grass-rooters in the outfit are tempted to consider new careers. That temptation, plus the opportunity for him and Mayling to meet their debts, is too great.

C.B. goes for the newly-created job but stays within the chain of command that includes me. The reorganization means I, too, am going to have to learn about law enforcement. Whereas we once thought we were going to be able to escape to the woods and manage resources, we are now forced to become people-oriented. This new philosophy is a foreign concept to the outfit and a whole new stump to jump for C.B. and me. A recreation-avid public is actually being invited to utilize its national forests. The park-like resources of public woodlands are now to be emphasized rather than kept tucked away as best-kept secrets. In this new way of interacting with the public, the Forest Service discovers the second half of its name.

I'm sent to a week-long training session at the Glynco Law Enforcement Academy in Georgia, where I'm exposed to the manager's expanded view of what C.B. will face on the ground. After attending an advanced course in federal copsmanship, C.B. returns to the Holly Springs National Forest well trained. As the agency's new law enforcement officer, called an LEO, he has a distinct walk with a cocky swagger…and a pistol to tote on his belt.

Word comes that the Level IV LEO from Mississippi had remarkable accuracy on the shooting range and left legendary marks. There was also mention of the shoot-no-shoot scenarios of the video exercises and C.B.'s eagerness to blow away all suspicious characters. I can only hope he will not have some kind of a Vietnam carryover response that will cause problems.

We are directed, in no uncertain terms, to continue keeping a low profile when it comes to law enforcement. Unfortunately, C.B. discovers that people problems don't go away just because upper management wants them to. My LEO's new-blue eye can't afford to observe the world around him from Washington's perspective. He tells me that to try and do his job "their" way would get him killed.

By mid-summer the novelty of being a para-cop supervisor without adequate support from above has worn off. C.B.'s real-life experiences are seemingly different from our supposedly well-thought-out policies. And my authority is turning out to be different from my capability.

FROM WHAT STARTED OUT as a typical day's work, C.B. returns to the office overly excited.

"Scott, you 'member how we stumbled on them moonshine stills when we was workin' Alabama?" He leans on my desk.

"Don't tell me...."

"Naw, but it's somethin' 'at might be as bad an' could get worst, 'lessen we nip it in th' bud."

"What are you talking about?" I stop hen-pecking on my computer and give C.B. my full attention.

"I come up on somethin' I ain't heard since I'z overseas—automatic weapon fire."

"On the Forest?"

"Right over my head." He sprawls in the chair by my desk and mops the sweat from his face with an army-green bandanna. "'Long th' powerline 'bove Hickory Flat."

"Are you serious?" I ask.

"I 'spect they was just shootin' to warn me to stay away from th' crop."

"The crop?"

"Their pot patch," he clarifies.

"You saw it?"

"Oh, yeah."

"I'll call the drug authorities, and we'll let the D.E.A. do their thing, whatever that is or isn't. This is definitely one of those low-profile things we've been instructed not to get directly involved with."

"Yeah...right," he answers with enough sarcasm to validate my own skepticism.

"C.B., just pretend like you didn't see anything. There's nothing more we can do about it."

"Scott, I'm knowin' there's things we can't do nothin' 'bout, but this ain't one of 'em."

Assuming he's referring to our helplessness and struggles with the disease that took Little Scott, I decide to tread lightly. "What would you propose that we do?"

"Burn 'em," he suggests.

"The state will do that after they pull it and take publicity pictures."

"I wadn't talkin' 'bout burnin' th' pot."

"Give me a break"

"Scott, you need to hear what I'm sayin'—my .38 is out-gunned."

"Load your shotgun with number four buckshot."

He looks at me like that answer isn't going to cut it.

"If you're concerned with being out-gunned…then that's just another good reason for you to steer clear of the whole thing. We're supposed to let the specialists handle such as that."

"You still ain't listenin'. I hereby an' officially request an automatic weapon."

"It's not that easy, C.B."

"Yeah, it is."

"The truth is—I don't know what kind of authorization that would take or if it's even possible."

"'Til you find out fer me, don't go lookin' under my jeep seat. What you don't know ain't gon' hurt neither one of us."

"C.B., you're gonna get me fired one of these days."

"'Least ways, you ain't bein' fired at." He eases out.

Pretending that what I don't know isn't mentally hurting me, I go back to typing on my idiot terminal.

THREE WEEKS LATER C.B. sticks his head in my office door with his daily greeting. "You heard back from my weapon's request?"

"Yeah. There's no easy way to tell you this, but the Department has turned us down. No automatic weapon."

"Am I 'sposed to be surprised?" he responds and looks at me as if I'm part of the establishment.

"No, I don't suppose so, but don't forget where we both get our checks."

"Well, thanks fer tryin'. I'm now havin' to make weekly reports of new spots to th' state drug enforcement officers. It's getting' 'at bad."

"I did try, C.B. And you're welcome. Has the state pulled the latest plants you told them about?"

"Yep. They prob'ly havin' a big circle-jerk down wind of a marijuana fire right now."

"C.B., if you wouldn't be so cynical...."

"What?"

"Maybe we'd get invited."

———————————

BY THE TIME OVERALL Forest Service law enforcement hierarchy develops into knowing about half what it's doing, C.B. has managed to get his cop's legs solidly under him. I'm glad I'm merely on the sideline. With law enforcement here to stay, some of the officers seem to do a little too much people-pushing. Some do a lot too much strutting with their new-found authority. I remember Granna saying we should be careful what we wish for.

As the LEO's and special agents become increasingly independent, many of them forget much of what they ever knew about natural resources management. Growing up as close to the hills and hollows as C.B. did, I don't expect him to be one of those who strays too far from Mother Nature's slant on things.

A higher-up official decides C.B. is a good candidate to participate in a pilot project...to become half of a Forest Service K-9 unit. In spite of Mayling's skepticism, C.B. agrees. Sent to Texas for training, he and a German Shepherd are to bond.

With political correctness out the window and profiling now able to trump stereotyping, the dog's name is Kraut. Looking much like a timber wolf, Kraut is a beautiful and massive specimen. His dark brown coat is tinted black along his back and his face. His legs and belly are a dirty blonde. Despite his German heritage voice commands for him are all in Russian. I'm told that is so no one other than C.B. can try to control him. You want to pet this dog, but you don't.

In time Kraut learns to tolerate the Mouse and me. Still, no one other than C.B. can order him around. Always close by his master's side, Kraut uses his eyes to follow every move of C.B.'s. It's a look with apparent devotion if not pure love. For a long time Mayling patiently puts up with her husband's obsession with his new pet.

A one-man dog living with a man and a woman would probably work better if the dog and master relationship wasn't so close…and closed. Mayling becomes less fond of the Forest Service than she once was. Eventually, I think I'm seeing too much jealousy entering the picture.

ON A ROUTINE FIRST-YEAR survival inspection of a loblolly pine plantation, one of our forestry technicians comes across a half-dozen marijuana plants. The report that they're interspersed throughout the stand comes as no great surprise. What's different is what C.B. decides to do.

After verifying the plants are indeed what the tech said they are, C.B. goes for a little more personal approach than simply letting the Narcs pull it, picture it, and burn it. He sets up a stakeout of sorts. Realizing such a procedure requires too much time, he adapts his approach to observing the patch systematically. Figuring the owners periodically water the plants around dusk, he schedules his watches at that time on various days, increasing the frequency of inspections as the plants approach maturity and their harvest date.

Not expecting to catch anyone during the heat of midday, C.B. stops by to check the site for signs of recent activity. Instead of having his canine partner at his usual heel, C.B. lets him run ahead for some cherished exercise. The dog runs out of view. Being a take-down partner and not so much a drug dog, Kraut doesn't know wild-grown Mary Jane from any other plant he'd like to pee on.

A terrible series of whining yelps sends Krauts's master running. He charges forward with his service revolver drawn from under his belt. Someone has strung the area with fishhooks. Advancing with caution, C.B. dodges dangling fishhooks to find his partner hung up in a terrible way.

Automatic weapon fire opens up. C.B. dives for the dirt and low-crawls behind a cluster of farkleberry. Knowing his pistol is no match for the flurry of firepower whizzing over his head, he makes a run for his jeep through the sparse vegetation. Bullets continue to rip through the woods.

Upon retrieving his AK-47 and radio calling for back-up, he hears the last of the shooting. There are also no more hurtful howls or painful whimperings from Kraut. Locked and loaded, C.B. is not about to wait on the local law enforcement he has called. Slipping from tree to tree, he works his way back to the site. The bad guys have left…and left a horrible message.

Kraut is hanging limp and silent, riddled with bullets holes. C.B. untangles the lines and cuts Kraut's body loose. Knowing his dog may have just saved his life by giving up his own, C.B. carries his partner's bloody remains toward the jeep. He meets two state drug enforcement agents dispatched to the incident. There is quick talk of C.B.'s helping them process the crime scene. He informs them he will tend to his dog instead.

"I'll bring y'all a written statement first thing in th' mornin'," he offers.

The state officers think they know what C.B. is going through. They think they recognize the trauma surrounding the situation. They can understand how much a man can love a dog. They can understand the flashbacks of a war gone bad, when so much blood and shooting brings back memories of other limp bodies. But there is something more than all that.

C.B. is having one of his private discussions with God. It's about how the two of them lost their only sons. It's not until the officers have been there that they could even begin to feel what C.B. feels and only God understands.

XLVI:
Black Texas
and Mississippi Gravel

THERE'S NO DISCUSSION ABOUT getting another dog. C.B. is far too devastated over the loss of Kraut to think of a replacement right now. Accepting a new Kraut would be about as unlikely as trying to replace Little Scott. And the Service is not about ready to go through that kind of expense so soon after their experiment with the first one.

Instead of taking the hemp farmers' clear warning message to back off, C.B. vows to crack down on them with all his might. In time he becomes more and more successful at finding the outlaws' illegal green growth. As C.B.'s reputation grows, he becomes well-known all over north Mississippi as the black pot cop who wears a cowboy hat and drives a puke-green government vehicle.

While monitoring a citizen's band radio conversation one day, I over-hear some thugs make a threat on the life of the black federal agent who wears the Forest Service uniform. They refer to the officer as Black Texas. Threats intensify. Our leaders in higher management finally get the message that crawling back into our low-profile law enforcement shell will not work. A determination is made that C.B. is to be transferred for his own safety. From Old Taylor to New England, C.B. is expected to uproot his family and accept an offer to move to Middlebury, Vermont.

In the still of a Mississippi summer night, C.B. and Mayling sit and consider their possibilities. Knowing he'd probably be the first black on that National Forest, C.B. pictures himself trying to blend in with all that snow. If Auntay would consent to move with them, acceptance of the offer would be more likely.

Window glass is shattered and sprayed all over the floor as gunfire erupts. Bullets pepper the front of the house. Mayling screams and dives under the table as C.B. grabs Auntay and pulls her to the floor. With Mayling still yelling, C.B. looks at her to see if she's been hit. She appears to be unhurt.

Black Texas looks out where the window used to be just in time to see a dark van heading toward uptown Taylor. Almost as suddenly as the terror of the noise and flying glass had come, it is gone. C.B.'s thought of pursuit is negated when he sees that Auntay is lying motionless. Carefully checking her over for blood or bullet holes, he finds nothing. Thinking she's fainted, he shakes her by the shoulders. No response. He checks for breathing and a pulse. There's neither. Auntay has had a heart attack.

"Call fer a' am'lance," C.B. tells Mayling, as he starts administering the CPR he learned from the Army.

Emergency personnel arrive from Oxford. After twenty-five minutes of unsuccessful resuscitation efforts by C.B., he lies back, exhausted and out of the E.M.T.'s way. A paramedic assesses the situation and explains his conclusion.

"I'm sorry. Due to the victim's advanced age and the time elapsed, there is no need continuing emergency breathing."

C.B. stands up and stares down at Auntay. In a tone of reverent agreement, he whispers, "She had a good life."

Still frightened, Mayling cuddles herself in the corner of the couch. The paramedics place Auntay's body on their stretcher and then into the ambulance. C.B. knows they'll take her to the funeral home for coloreds...where she will be subjected to Oxford's segregation for the last time.

———

IN A CELEBRATION WORTHY of her, Miss Belle would have enjoyed this funeral. Maybe she is enjoying it. Nearly the entire black community from Taylor has come to Auntay's last farewell. There are relatives from all over with cousins to the forty-eleventh degree. When C.B. insists that I sit with him and Mayling, I feel proud to be an honorary son. The Memphis Magnolia may or may not have gotten the word that her sister has passed, but she hasn't shown up.

The service is long. Several black preachers testify as to Auntay's faith and good works. The sound of wailing and keening mourners rises and falls. Finally, a choir of singers give fervent voice loud enough to alert all of Heaven that Auntay is coming. There is a murmuring background of "Praise God," "Sweet Jesus," "Have Mercy," "Yes Jesus, Blessed Lord," along with loud "Amens."

To the sounds of laughter and reminiscence, a feast follows the burial. As the last of the guests and well-wishers leave, C.B., Mayling and I adjourn to what is now C.B.'s place...on the backside of what will someday be my farm. We sit on the porch and talk late into the night. When I shake C.B.'s hand to leave, he squeezes my grip extra hard.

"I got me a good feelin' 'bout Auntay now. She be holdin' Little Scott an' both of 'em bein' happy...more'n it's ever been fer 'em."

On my drive back to Oxford I think over C.B.'s life. By this time I figure he's dealt with death in more ways and places than anybody should have to, but this one still shakes his world. Auntay was his rock and foundation. When his own mother abandoned him, she was the one who stepped forward and accepted the responsibility of raising him. She validated what he learned and anchored his reality.

DETERMINED TO FIND, CATCH, and punish those in the drive-by shooting, C.B. turns down the Forest Service offer for his job transfer. To my surprise, what was first thought to be a mandatory reassignment suddenly becomes optional. I'm told minorities in this agency are too hard to come by to be forcing any of them to do much of anything they don't want to do.

Pulling the AK-47 out from underneath the seat of his Cherokee, C.B. fondles and strokes the automatic rifle's barrel. He remembers a friend in Vietnam making a pledge to revenge his brother's being killed over there. C.B.'s plan is to find and eliminate every pot-grower on the forest. Assuming the shooters responsible for Auntay's heart attack will be among the bunch of growers, his retaliation will come from burning them all.

EXTREMELY EARLY ONE SATURDAY morning when marijuana growers least expect a government employee to be on duty, C.B. decides to log some overtime. A dark van is parked in the vicinity of a patch of pot C.B. has been watching…a dark van like the one he remembers from the night of the shooting that scared Auntay to death. Two suspicious-looking characters are in a hurry to leave. One of the two tosses a five-gallon plastic water jug in the vehicle, and they climb in.

C.B. turns his vehicle around and flips on its blue light. Instead of stopping, the suspects speed off. A high-speed chase ensues. C.B. closes in. With one hand on the steering wheel, he uses his other hand and radio requests for backup on the law enforcement agency frequency.

"Any available agents, I—" There is static…and quiet.

The Jeep Cherokee slides through the loose gravel at the Chickasaw Ridge junction. Reaching the outside edge of the curve with too much momentum, C.B. has lost control. The wheels drop in the ditch, and the vehicle flips. Landing on its top left side and crashing into a large cow oak, the roof and door of the driver's side is crushed.

While the dark van continued on, our recreation crew of senior citizens is first to drive up on the accident scene. The work leader of the Happy Pappies radios me, with a shaky and most unhappy voice and story. After I summon an ambulance, I head out Highway 6 east of Oxford. My stomach hollows as I'm passed by an emergency vehicle, its lights and sirens flashing and blaring.

When I arrive at the wreck, I'm told C.B. is alive but unconscious. I want to help, but there is nothing I can do. Emergency personnel check C.B.'s vital signs and prepare him for transport. Demonstrating EMT proficiency, they are quickly headed to the emergency room with him. Left standing there with my heart still pounding furiously, I try talking calmly to my older American work crew. There is nothing now that the seniors can do, so I send them on their way. Waiting for a wrecker, I have the site to myself. After recovering C.B.'s illegal, non-issue AK-47 and securing it under my seat, I get his service issue shotgun and pistol to be turned in. The communist-made automatic rifle will be saved for C.B.

Once the wrecker arrives and removes the demolished vehicle, I leave for the hospital. Again, there is nothing I can do but wait in the emergency room. They do not have a prognosis, but C.B.'s condition is said to have stabilized. Mayling has already been called by hospital personnel. She arrives weeping and shaking uncontrollably. I take her in my arms, and she mumbles in Vietnamese, perhaps reflecting old fears with new terror. We're in the wait-and-see period.

At long last a doctor comes to the waiting room. The news is not good. We are told there are several critical problems. Diagnosis includes a serious head trauma and a spinal cord injury that may not lend itself to an operation or healing. C.B. has no lower body movement.

Two days later our worst fears concerning the prognosis are confirmed. The accident has left my best friend of well over twenty years paralyzed from the waist down. His eyes are open, but he isn't responding to us. He doesn't react to our words or tears and can't respond to Mayling's caressing. I stand by, helpless in my own pain.

Within the week, it's determined that C.B.'s head injury has brought on a type of dementia that's similar to Alzheimer's disease. The doctor says it's progressive, which I find out really means degenerative. It's a brain trauma like a psychiatric disorder that affects all aspects of his thinking, perceiving, and remembering. When it happens at an early age as it has for C.B., the problems usually advance more rapidly than they do for an older person.

C.B. will have to remain in the hospital for at least one more week. Mayling and I visit him daily. In time, and with slurred speech, C.B. starts to try communicating. It's a challenge to figure out what he means to say, but it's effective enough to reveal whether he's in or out of depression at a given moment. Usually his words don't make sense, and he often repeats himself.

Over time I learn to communicate with him to a small degree, but Mayling doesn't seem to understand how to deal with the situation. One thing I discover is that it's best not to correct him when he says something wrong. The only effective technique in dealing with him is to provide psychological support…no matter how incorrect he may be about something. I either try to guide him away from a subject or quietly agree with him and ask him to tell me more about whatever it is he thinks he's talking about. He usually forgets by then.

As I help take C.B. to his home, I think how lucky he is to have a wife who will remain dedicated to him. The Mouse will have to comfort him and be his constant aide now that the hospital stay has ended. We're told the familiar and more comfortable surroundings might help his memory. After a month at home he gains enough upper body strength to be able to move around a little in his wheelchair…but his memory hasn't improved. Day-to-day realities prove he can't be left without someone to watch him and help. Mayling, having to fulfill his every need, is awakened by him at all hours during the night for total care. For the five ten-hour days per week when she's working at the factory, she pays one of Auntay's cousins to stay with him.

I continue to visit as often as possible, and C.B. gradually improves his communication skills with me. Mayling doesn't do as well with him. I come to the conclusion that his ability to reason may not have declined as much as his recall and memory. As I think back on it, this is exactly what the medical community told me would happen. C.B. sometimes knows what he is talking about, but it's very likely to be gone by the next moment. He'll have zero recall from only a minute before.

I have to keep reminding myself that C.B. has no apparent concept of time. He lives in the present...seeing everything at once. There is no before and will be no after. There is only the now, and talking in sound bites is emotionally draining. With long-term memory coming and going, and short-term memory on again and off again, a sixty-second discussion is about the best we can do. I try to tell myself he may be better off in the state of mind he's in rather than being constantly aware of his situation.

MAYLING OVERHEARS ONE OF the women at the blue jean factory gossiping. The woman says God let all of Mayling's troubles happen to her as punishment for marrying a black man. Not knowing the appropriate reaction to such small-town Mississippi talk, the little Vietnamese woman keeps her thoughts to herself and her own culture. From then on she will split her time between prayer with Jesus and meditation with Buddha.

There's a change in the Mouse. Her caring for C.B. has taken her marriage from one extreme to another. Where she was once passive, she's now exhibiting independence. In the space of a year the love between them that I thought was so special it was almost spiritual is now sliding. What I thought was a part of holy vows is now slipping on shaky grounds. I try to be supportive and encourage Mayling, but she simply doesn't have the concern for C.B. that she used to have.

The more I see, the more I find hard to understand. When Mayling connects with a Vietnamese community in Memphis, her care and time with C.B. grow less and less. Despite all he has done for her, she decides she's not up to coping with an invalid. She makes up her mind to desert. With Auntay gone and the Mouse splitting, there is only one realistic option for C.B.

Since his injury was Forest Service work-related, the cost and eligibility requirements for Oxford's nursing home are covered by the federal government. On the day I help the Mouse take her husband to what becomes the Golden Olden Care Center to me, I pray it's one of those times when C.B. doesn't comprehend what's going on around him. He doesn't know that Mayling is planning to leave him...or where we're taking him.

When we get him out of the truck and into his wheelchair, he looks around wildly and gives an anguished groan. He begins to cry. I think he must recognize the front of the care center where we've brought him. Mayling doesn't help any, as she begins weeping too.

I try to reassure C.B. cheerily, but I haven't felt so helpless since I held Little Scott for the last time and knew he would probably die before I saw him again. Even in C.B.'s fog of confusion, I think if I said anything besides just telling him this is best for him, he could feel my deceit. My words would be false and hollow if I tried to say much more than I've already said.

Once checked in and settled, C.B.'s awareness proves to be short-lived. Almost on cue, he retreats into a seemingly safe and certainly limited world. When he seems to have some degree of peace and appears content, I figure it's time to leave. I promise C.B. and myself I'll make a habit of stopping by as often as possible on my way home from work. I suspect Mayling will soon leave, too...and probably won't be visiting very often.

On my way out of Golden Olden, I see that most of the residents are gathered in the lobby. Maybe they're preparing to eat, but I suppose it's quality time whenever they are out of their rooms. Looking at the clientele here gives one perspective. C.B. will be the only resident young enough to be considered middle-aged. Some of these folks are living so long it's rude.

VISITING AT THE NURSING home is tougher than I thought. I keep my promise and stop by every chance I get, but it's hard seeing my best buddy having to sit his time away…with the frail, elderly, and impaired. With little to no hope for recovery, everyone around him is a companion in waiting. They're waiting for nothing but the end, and he's probably got longer to wait than the rest of them.

Every time I think about the visits being tough on me, I feel a wave of guilt. C.B.'s the one hurting. Considering what's best for him in the long run, this is the only option. It's best for everyone involved. There's no worry about his safety or well-being here. I watch for any misconduct or suspicious behavior, though I'm probably not here enough to pick up on it if it happens.

This is a place where racism could very easily raise its ugly head and go either way. Prejudice from blunt and tactless residents toward the workers could cause a problem. The staff must certainly have to be on guard to prevent any payback from the aides toward the residents. I've seen no evidence of such feelings or actions. Perhaps overshadowed by the struggles of people needing each other, equality is easier here. Maybe that's been the key to the lifelong friendship C.B. and I have shared. If people would recognize their need and dependence on each other, this could be the answer to many of today's problems…such as bigotry.

Just as C.B.'s world is the same every day, my visits to see him are starting to seem the same. In a language I can understand, he is always wanting to go home, forever telling me, "I gotta go." Anxious and agitated, he'll rock his upper body back and forth as if that might help him get somewhere. I know he can't help it, but it's a test of my patience when he loses interest in our conversations. He might be having a good time one moment and appear miserable the next. Both times he'll be just sitting there with nowhere to go or nothing to do.

I've learned to appreciate the small pleasures like seeing C.B. smile. Eating ice cream usually does it. Other than that, if my buddy looks happy, I tell myself he's reliving the times we had trying not to grow up. Perhaps it's a good thing we made such memories. Maybe in his recalling of them, they'll be better the second time around.

Conversations are like a trip through an hour-glass every few moments. As C.B. leads, we go from one world to another, whatever his inclination. I hope his mental camp outs are without mosquitoes, his bait-casting without backlashes, and his stolen watermelons without seeds. As hard as I used to try to get him to open up and talk about Vietnam and his experiences there, he never would. Now he starts telling me an interesting war story but never finishes it…and there's no chance he'll finish it later. As I might have guessed, C.B. is fond of asking, "When we gon' eat?" He never asks what we're going to have to eat. It's not soul food, but the meals are nutritional, and he does enjoy them.

For the most part, I think he is treated with dignity by all the nurses and aides who care for him. The staff at Golden Olden check on him periodically but not all have the same degree of knowledge about dealing with conditions like C.B.'s. I try discussing treatment options with C.B.'s doctor…everything from drug therapies to rehabilitative experimental trials.

I'm warned that I am trying to get C.B. back, something that is probably not possible. It does seem as if I am the only one who sees my friend as a normal person with a disease. That's problematic for me because it's a difference in perspective that makes dealing with his condition easier on others than it is on me. I'm convinced there's something I'm coming to understand better than all the health care professionals. Since they never knew C.B. the way he used to be, they can't begin to experience the loss that I do. When they first met him, he was the way he is now. The workers here see him as that person, but I can't accept that this shell of a body is my long-time friend…not having known him the way I did.

I become increasingly aggravated with myself as it gradually appears that I cannot enhance his well-being or improve the quality of his life. For me, it's a mixture of guilt and anger that I have trouble learning to deal with. By C.B.'s second autumn in the nursing home, I have accepted his fate.

Mayling has developed her own strategy to cope. Her way seems without compassion. Once she finds out there is not any money in it for her, she surrenders her power of attorney to the nursing home. When she withdraws completely and doesn't even visit him any more, I hate her for it.

MONTHS GO BY…THEN a year….
"Afternoon, C.B.," I greet my buddy.

"Ah...y...ee," he says.

"Has that good-looking, red-headed nurse with the freckles that look like they'd go clear across her knockers been in here bathing you today? I wish I could get her to do that to me."

"Ah...y...ee."

"Yeah, when she starts in on you with that warm bath cloth, I'll bet the old Yocona Puff Adder thinks about coming out of hibernation."

"Ah...y...ee," he answers again.

I shut the door, slide a rubber wedge under it, place my jacket at the foot of the door to cover the air crack, and open the window. "Here, I brought us a couple more cigars today."

"Ah...y...ee."

"Yes, they're laced with some medicinal supercharger from the Ole Miss farm for experimental painlessness."

"Ah...y...ee."

"You'd better believe it, buddy. It might be the same stuff indirectly responsible for getting you in here, but as sure as you've got a pot to pee in, a little mind altering puffing on this kind of pot and you'll be taking a trip right back out of here."

"Ah...y...ee."

"Yep, I know it's a bit ironic, but if it takes a little medical marijuana to help bring you some satisfaction, so be...ees it, as you and Auntay used to say. If they'd let you have your rabbit tobacco and grape vine around here, we might not have to resort to this...then again, we might. You know...this is one of only a couple of places in the entire nation where your old buddy can take care of you like this...and I couldn't do it if I didn't have a good friend tending the university crop."

"Ah...y...ee."

"And I've been thinking about something else for your pleasure. As big as the University of Mississippi is on their experiments, it might just be that the Medical School would team up with Golden Olden on another little experiment. I don't reckon it could hurt to ask them...or axe 'em as you'd say. I'm gonna see if they won't let you have a pet in here. What would you say about having a little German Shepherd puppy?"

"Ah...y...ee."

"Ah...y...ee it is, then. We'll name him...Sauerkraut. Maybe you can teach him to fetch your slippers or your pee can...and to bite anybody from the Corps of Engineers."

XLVII:
Puerto ...Where?

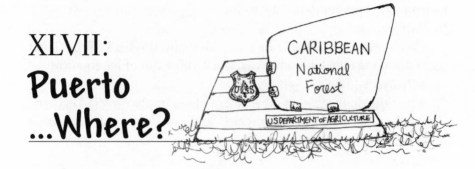

I WELL REMEMBER THE time, almost like a decade ago was yesterday....

"Germany is far ahead of the United States in forest management and research," my major advisor in graduate school preached.

"But Doc, Spanish is supposed to be the easiest foreign language for a Gringo like me, and I've already had two years of it in high school," I argued.

"This is why you have an advisor—there's a wealth of knowledge in German forestry publications and literature. Spanish is about the last course you ought to take," he insisted.

It would have broken my first Forest Meister's heart if he'd known that about the last thing I was considering in fulfilling my foreign language requirement was how it might somehow be useful in a forestry and wildlife management career. Based a little on his counsel and advice, and a lot on his threats, I gave up looking for the easy way out and fought through four semesters of German.

SO HERE I AM in the late seventies, on the way to my new assignment as Supervisory Resident Field Officer at the Caribbean National Forest. I'm wondering if any Puerto Ricans will speak German. Being raised on Southern English, harassed with high school Spanish, and intimidated by college German, I'm barely fluent in anything. With Puerto Ricans speaking their form of English called Spanglish or varying their native tongue by their infamous provincialisms, my efforts to communicate will likely be as humorous as they are helpful.

On the initial 747 flight from Miami to San Juan, I try desperately to focus on my Spanish correspondence course, but a child on the seat in front of me reminds me of Little Scott…and all the things I had looked forward to doing with him and C.B. I try not to go down the "if only" path, but the sharp memories keep pain alive. I can't help but think of all the twists and turns leading to the loss of Little Scott.

Was I negligent in the way I handled the pesticides in Alabama? Did the pesticide pass the problem to C.B.'s son because C.B. came home every night with his leather boots and feet soaked from the BHC. And why didn't he have a proper place to wash? If I ever have a child, will my exposure to that chemical also cause him to inherit a premature death?

Haunted by the trauma of my godson's death and now by C.B.'s debilitating accident, the best way of dealing with my agony may be throwing myself into my work. I hope this new assignment will help me escape my self-pity. Since both problems may have been directly related to Forest Service work, it would be an ironically perverted twist of fate if it turned out that my professional work took my mind off what's bothering me.

I picture myself surrounded by the lush rainforest where I'm headed. I'll have my trusty camera at hand and be ready to wear out my new *Birds of the Caribbean* field guide. An air pocket bumps the jet and brings my mind from the imaginary photograph into the present. For the remainder of my flight I study the forest plan I'm told I'll have the responsibility of revising…once I fully understand my mission.

After a smooth landing and quick departure from the plane, I'm greeted by a seaweed-smelling breeze blowing across the tarmac. Having read about the trade winds here, I take deep pleasure in experiencing for real what I've first learned from a book. Whereas most of the plane's passengers are probably attracted to the sandy beaches and beautiful blue-green water, I'll be heading for the hills.

"The Hilton in San Juan, por favor," I hail the taxi publico driver, in my best reverse Spanglish. As the driver leaves the International Airport, I feel encouraged at having successfully communicated in my third foreign language. So far, Puerto Rico looks like traffic, condos, and buildings.

At the hotel I step out of the cab and set my suitcase down on the curb. By placing my briefcase on the roof of the taxi, I have my hands free to negotiate my wallet. Remembering all the years my dad drove a cab, I'm generous enough to include a three-dollar tip in squaring away the tab. After returning my wallet to my pocket, I turn my back on the cab for about one second to pick up my suitcase. When I turn again and reach up to grab my briefcase, I see it going down the busy street on top of the cab.

Since there's a lot of traffic and several red lights in sight, I decide to try to catch the cab. Setting my suitcase back down, I run until the first light changes and my taxi stops. Nabbing my briefcase and securing the runaway papers, I start to be proud of myself. Pride is short-lived, as I see a pack of natives looking on and laughing at the stupid Americano. As if that weren't humiliating enough, when I glance back up the road, I see a small child trying to run off with my heavy suitcase.

Cradling my briefcase like a football, I charge back against the grain of the traffic. After managing to catch the underage thief, I shake him by his shoulders and try to think of what to say…and how to say it in Puerto Rican. Everyone on the street is staring at me as if I'm the one who has done something wrong. The miniature hooligan wiggles in my grasp. Unable to free himself, he looks around as if summoning help. When it occurs to me that the locals may be about ready to jump me for some kind of international child abuse, I try the little nino's English.

"If you don't change your ways, you'll wind up in jail or worse." Still holding the young boy's shoulders, I give him my most sincere and affectionate stare. "And you'll go to hell, too." Keeping my eyes glued on the handsome face of the boy and judging him to be about seven or eight years old, I ask, "Su comprehende?"

Fully expecting him to plead, "No habla English," he stares back with boldness and protests with bravado, "Damn *Americano*—I'm only six years old!"

AFTER SUPPER I DECIDE to spend my first night in the motel studying the brochures and other propaganda related to my new assignment. It doesn't work. I can't concentrate for thinking about the little boy. I keep thinking how much the youngster who took a liking to my suitcase resembled Little Scott. Sleep is no better. I drift in and out of nightmare and sleep, fretting about how it was that we came to lose C.B.'s son.

Work will surely give me a degree of temporary relief. My first morning on the island I am delivered by a Forest Service driver to the office of The Institute of Tropical Forestry, in the nearby city of Rio Piedras. My new boss promptly orients me on paper and plastic maps. The Caribbean National Forest, called El Yunque by the locals, sounds fascinating.

After introducing me to the rest of his staff, the Forest Supervisor takes me around the corner to a small café. I'm bought a shot-glass size cup of coffee and a sandwich called a media noche. The small, hot sandwich is laced with different kinds of cheeses and meats and is very good. I think it strange the way they smash the sandwich flat as they heat it. When I experience their coffee, I no longer have to think what strange is. Latin-American formality or not, I watch amazed as my new boss pours sugar into the tiny cup and stirs and pours and continues to stir and pour until I'm thinking his concoction is now syrup and will have to be eaten with his spoon. Strong is too weak a word for this coffee.

We escape to the forest for the afternoon. My ranger station is on the edge of the small community of Sabana. It's on the east end of the island, about twenty miles from San Juan. I'm told it takes almost two hours to reach it when the traffic is at its peak…and that's something I'll have to see to believe. According to my boss, there is a kind of Yo primero or "me first" power play among the drivers here. I'm supposing the laid-back attitude that I've heard so much about does not hold true when drivers are behind the wheels of their automobiles.

The rainforest is unbelievably beautiful. Clad in saturating clouds, it's a primeval wilderness of wet greens beyond my wildest imagination. I'm told many of the two million or so Hispanics within jogging distance of the forest are afraid of it, for reasons ranging from bonafide bandits to imaginary UFOs.

After I'm escorted to my office, the mandatory introductions of my main staff are completed in a stiff and overly formal manner. After I'm given the keys to my vehicle, mi Jefe returns to Rio Piedras alone. Surprised to be left to search for my own quarters, I'm thinking maybe it's some kind of test to see if I sink or swim.

The northern edge of the forest is bordered by another small community called Colinas del Yunque. Two-bedroom, one-bath, flat-topped stucco houses rent for twice the $150.00 a month they would bring in the states. I make offers on a couple of houses that have "Para alguiler" signs advertising their availability for rent. Turned down the same number of times, I wonder if it's discrimination.

Am I to assume that this could have something to do with my being an Americano? Have I just tasted what C.B. has had to swallow all his life…growing up in white Mississippi?

XLVIII:
Department of No Response

FROM THE ROOM ADJOINING my office, timber tech Gerardo grunts a less-than-enthusiastic acknowledgment of my presence, "Good Morning."

"Buenos Dios," I answer.

Don Gerardo is overcome with laughter and ambles through my door. In his broken English, he informs me that if I continue to say "Dios" instead of "dias," I will be greeting everyone with, "good God" instead of the "good day" I mean to convey.

It's my first actual workday at the Caribbean National Forest, and I'm overwhelmed by the number of forest workers I'm introduced to. There are more than I'll ever be able to remember, much less adequately supervise. A good part of the day is spent in round table getting-to-know-you meetings with the first level supervisors of El Yunque work force. I would like to think they feel comfortable with me. I like everyone I've met today, but I'd guess they are still sizing up their new boss.

The next morning at my ranger station, a perfectly proportioned direct descendent of the Tanio Indians grinds coffee beans in the corner of our reception area. She is so beautiful, with her satiny, golden skin, and precious body, that I wonder if she's been positioned here to impress me. No one should look as good as this girl…and I can only hope the coffee tastes as great as it smells.

Determined to hit the field running, I'll save trying to get to know the coffee grinder lady for another time. Yesterday I warned my number-one timber management assistant to be prepared today to accompany me on an outing for tropical forest inventory and analysis.

"Don Gerardo, I will appreciate your candor in helping me learn your language."

He chuckles at me, probably remembering yesterday's "Good God" greeting. I force a smile and assume there's no way around these ice-breaking exercises. I feel like I've just fallen off the turnip boat.

"No problema," he answers, matter-of-factly.

"You can really help in teaching me Spanish just by not pulling your punches. Tu entiendo?"

"Si, como no. Pero…you'll need me for more than simply being your translator." He rubs his bald head and beams with importance. "I was uh…eh tay, como se dici…born and raised among the orchids and bromeliads of the Caribbean. While you may have only seen their pictures in your books, I know a thousand tropical plants."

Figuring there's probably about as much fact as braggadocio in what Don G. has proclaimed, I can only imagine what else he's thinking. Behind his second language and ahead of my tropical experience, I'd guess he's wanting to call me a young whippersnapper who knows little over jack-squat. Although I'll find the big bucks in my salary, I fear my academic learning is going to be pretty lame compared to Don G.'s experience-based knowledge and touch-and-feel kind of familiarity with the rainforest.

When we step outside, my assistant tells me the sun has made what will likely be a short appearance. Bright light on the wet vegetation brings out an awesome array of vivid to pale greens. No farther away than my office window is a garden paradise. Coqui frogs croon in chorus.

As beautiful as all the different shades of green are, they are still just green. Even though it's October, this land seems to be slighting the seasons. A green stalk of bananas beginning to yellow is all it takes to remind me of the leafy contrasts of fall colors in the Yocona bottom. A coconut palm by my Jeep reminds me of the acorns that must be falling at home. Wild persimmons must be ripening in my southern haunts around Taylor, Mississippi, right about now. The early frosts are special times in my memory. There are special places where C.B. and I won't get to re-visit or bow hunt for deer with Little Scott.

My main forest tech volunteers to drive us through the forest that apparently knows no dormant dirt. When it's just the two of us, I start to mention the girl back at my office, but realize I shouldn't say anything about her in front of my new employee. I don't want to act that young and immature around someone of such a different generation and culture, especially since I'm his supervisor. He could be her uncle or something.

A few miles from the ranger station, Don Gerardo stops at a roadside stand. I'm thinking this is just like the forestry techs in the States—stopping at the first convenience store they drive by on their way to the woods. Why be prepared when you can shop on Uncle Sam's time? My new partner with the old habit says we are stopping so I can experience some of the local culture and taste some foods that I've probably never seen or heard of.

The most obvious presence here is a small boy who has a bad case of the jerks. He's sitting on a milk crate out back of the makeshift shack behind the food stand. His shoulders are bouncing up and down while his neck is jerking. He appears to be about twelve years old and shudders constantly…as if he's possessed by spasms. Don G. doesn't mention him, so I just acknowledge to myself, "There, but for the grace of God, sit I."

Brewing up some kind of a concoction, a little brown gentleman stands behind his counter. During complimentary cups of the semi-medicinal potion, he and Don G. share lengthy conversation in muy rapido Spanish. A land-crab taco later, I'm seeing how easy it would be to view the clock with a sense of indifference. I think I'm getting the idea of what being on Puerto Rican time means. Maybe my contribution to this culture will be in demonstrating the value of organizing time to accomplish goals better. Then again, maybe before I go trying to change centuries of tradition, I'd better just try to get by.

With his constant chattering, Don G. pulls our Jeep back onto the narrow and winding mountain road. I can't fully appreciate the view because of the scary way in which my driver negotiates the curvy single lane hardtop up the mountain. My new supervisor had warned me about Don G.'s unique persona being a blend of genius and stubbornness. As we steadily climb a continuous succession of curves that almost meet themselves, I recall the story. Don G.'s thirty-five-year career has produced only one reportable traffic accident. It seems that on the incident report he claimed the steamroller he ran into was speeding.

After a scenic and all-too-short drive, we park by a stream crossing. I explain that every hundred meters we'll stop to "put in a plot," which means inventorying the rainforest from that point. We continue on foot with every step uphill. It's not raining at this exact minute, so Don G. and I start out dry, knowing that will change during our trek.

After loping out at a brisk pace I'm sure is not normal for Don G., he stops...on the pretense of wanting to show me how to make a drinking cup from a palm frond. As we drink from a pool of clear rainwater, I appreciate how well our make-do cups work. I think of the contrast from all the times C.B. and I sipped the gritty brown water of a Mississippi stream from our cupped hands.

We've made it up the mountain about as far as I thought we'd get before Don G. is out of breath and needs an excuse for a rest. When we're finished drinking, he takes his pocketknife and cuts off a couple of small stalks of bamboo. Demonstrating how to separate the shoots from the stalks, he shares and shows how to eat the shoots. As I sample the surprisingly tender but near-tasteless treats, I listen to a short lecture on the merits of bamboo.

We settle into another steady and unrelenting crawl up through thick grasses, vines, and flowers, the like of which temperate forests have never dreamed of. I had the foresight to dress in jungle fatigues and army surplus Vietnam boots, both designed to dry out quickly. Don G. sports a good-looking pair of light-weight, green, Browning boots that he must have ordered from the States. His extra-wide khaki pants and a guayabera are really too nice for this kind of work...and starting to show patches of sweat all over.

My new assistant is probably trying to make me think he takes this kind of outing everyday. What I'm thinking is that he's paying the price for enjoying half a century of the rum-punch life. I'm determined to demonstrate that there is nothing he and his solid-set self can do to wear me down.

Even though we're between plots, we pause again...this time for him to show me how to harvest and eat palm hearts. Better than the bamboo shoots and just as tender, these have a vanilla amaretto-like taste. If chilled and served with vinegar and oil, they would no doubt be gourmet fare. I make a mental note that I'll try adding some to one of my artichoke heart and anchovy omelets some day.

As we near another thousand-foot increase in elevation, I notice a gradual change in the vegetation. After checking my pocket altimeter for a reading, I indicate our location to show the forest-type transition on my topo map. Each new plot's record of what we find continues to prove what Don G. had told me about his being good at plant identification. To make up for it, on our hike between plots I'll show him the kind of tough that he can only wish for himself. I wonder how long he can follow a stride that bounces his big belly. Another hour's worth of hiking, climbing, and putting in inventory plots should see my helper paying for muy pinas coladas from his past.

Perspiration is rolling from Don G.'s forehead to his mustache. Air is huffing and puffing from his lungs. I've finally worn him down, along with his superior airs about himself, I hope. Not wanting to have to try lugging such a big lug off the mountain, I go over the procedures for CPR in my mind. If need be, I suppose I could roll him down.

As quickly as Don G. identifies the trees, I look them up for verification. It's clear that we have left the Tabanuco forest and entered the Palo Colorado forest. Recognizing a true ecological phenomenon, I try to share a bit of knowledge remembered from my college studies.

"Don Gerardo, this Palo Colorado is the exact same species of a tree called a Titi at home. Would you believe that in the coastal lowlands of south Mississippi it never makes a big enough tree to amount to anything? Yet, look at it here. On the mountainside, of all places, it's become as monstrous as a redwood. Isn't that amazing?"

Don G. doesn't seem impressed. He probably doesn't believe me, so I decide to ignore the ignorer. Again I check the elevation with my pocket instrument. At this point I draw the forest-type stand line on my map. Knowing the distances and number of plots on our particular bearing, I can orient the map and know our location in relation to the bridge where we left the jeep and started our plot line.

After working our way up through every shade and subtle blend of God's greens that a rainforest could possibly grow, Don G. pulls another stall. This time he plucks a tiny orchid from the mossy bark of a Granadillo tree trunk. Holding it up to me, he proclaims, "Do you see this orchid? Only about two percent of the orchid people have ever seen this species in the wild."

"Orchid people?" I question.

"Si, you know—the people who specialize in orchids."

Thinking what a neat color slide and story that would make for some civic club presentation back in the States, I fumble through my pack for my camera. When Don G. throws the flower over his shoulder, I watch helplessly as it gets caught in the up-draft and then floats out and down for about two plots below us…where I'm sure it will be lost in the thick of the brush.

I hope there will be other opportunities for pictures…and other stories as good as that one. Trying to catch a moment for my own breath, I slowly stow my camera back in my pack. Don G. is too busy gasping for his air to detect that I'm breathing hard enough to feel a slight discomfort. Somehow, from somewhere down in his big diaphragm, he starts another conversation.

"Someday the Forest Service is going to make a backpack with a strap that doesn't eat into your shoulders."

There is movement in the upper foliage of a Guava tree. An endemic Puerto Rican lizard cuckoo chases a medium-sized lizard in a corkscrew-like game of deadly tag-around-the-tree. With what seems like an additional layer of vegetation up there, it's almost as if there's another world…like a forest on top of a forest. I wouldn't doubt that the lizard is a species that's found nowhere else in the entire world except right here, just like the cuckoo.

C.B. may have seen this sort of vegetation in Vietnam, but I doubt he had the time or inclination to appreciate it…not while dodging bullets. I wish the herbwomen around Taylor, Mississippi, could witness this diversity of plant species. If they had the privilege and opportunity I have in seeing all this themselves, they could probably find a cure for those who are hurting…if not for cancer. It's too bad the medical researchers won't better investigate what nature has hidden away here.

What my field guide calls a Puerto Rican Todi graces our presence. Looking like a hummingbird, but not said to be one, his size, shape, bill, ruby-colored throat, bright yellow belly, and astro-turf green back all make me think he missed a mighty good chance at being a hummingbird. Don G. assures me he is quite common here.

Over time our humidity changes from sticky-dry to moist-wet and then on to wet-wet. Every ten or so minutes a rain starts and stops as if trying to decide what to do. Bone-soaked, we work on, my lead pencil never hesitating on my trusty Rite-in-the-Rain paper.

"Don Gerardo, do you like jerky?"

"Si, bueno."

I dig through my pack again. "Here. Try some of this. I made it myself."

"Gracias…bien, bien." He takes a cautious nibble. "This is very good. I would be happy for you to show me how to make it."

"Well, first you'd have to get the venison."

"Venison? What is that?" he asks.

"You know—deer," I answer.

"Ugh! Cono! carajo!" He spits out what's in his mouth.

"What's the matter?"

"Deer meat? Ugh! Disgusto!"

"Lo siento mucho," I apologize, laughing as I get up to lead the way.

The terrain is so steep it's almost straight up in front of my face. It takes a total body effort to keep moving. Grabbing small trees, I pull them toward me with my hands while I push my feet against the thick grasses, fighting each step. Don G. is crawling nearly snail-like behind me. When he complains that he could select better spots to stop and record information, I share a graduate-level rendition of unbiased statistical design. My comments about someone else's random sampling theory don't appear to impress him.

We're approaching enough elevation to make a flatlander like me dizzy. Trees are stunted. Their short height doesn't matter because they're growing at a high enough altitude to intercept clouds without being tall. It's a phenomenon causing more runoff than rainfall...according to the literature. Remembering that it gets about two degrees cooler per thousand feet increase in elevation, I feel a sudden chill around my ribs.

Somewhere above us I hear the Puerto Rican Parrot, federally "listed as endangered." When Don G. returns my look, I offer, "I suppose we have little chance of seeing him, huh?"

"I doubt we will."

"He's probably 'endangered' from crashing into the trees during such overcast up here," I joke.

Don G. doesn't laugh. I hope he realizes I was not criticizing his world. In fact, I'm amazed at the cloud-wrapped sky of the sunless rainforest. If there were any sun, I'll bet the clouds would be connected to the shadows. Even up here approaching the top, cool and clear drinking water is found almost any place you can look. My tired companion now shows me how to fold the leaves from a Yagrumo tree for my second lesson about making natural drinking cups.

I notice a strange palm tree. There have been several palms along the way. That's expected because the vegetative type just below the Dwarf Forest is supposed to be the Sierra palm type. But the odd thing here is— this one big tree is not the usual, straight, long-boled, and no-limbed tree that fits my picture of palms. Three-quarters of the way up, this one is atypically forked…like a giant sixteen-inch diameter slingshot.

"Don Gerardo, have you ever seen a forked palm?"

"No. That's a first."

He offers no further comment so I decide this will be a good time to try and sound professor-ish.

"It's probably a chromosomal mutation," I proclaim and think about how that kind of observation can only come from seven years of college.

When Don G. doesn't respond, I can almost hear one of my old forestry profs talking from back when we'd see something he wanted to teach his students about. "What have we got here, boys? What does this tell you? Where are we now?" We'd mock him when he turned his back, but we all loved him.

When we encounter a second forked palm, I look around for others but see none. Since the fog has come down around my ankles instead of lifting, I can see only about halfway up through the over-hanging vegetation. I don't know what's up there where I can't see.

"La Culebra!" Don G. calls out.

"Holy sh…!"

A seven-foot-long Puerto Rican boa constrictor slithers out from under the greenery about fifteen feet in front of us…with two heads. It stops its crawl and coils around itself to look back at us with one head. The other one just sort of hangs there. I'm thinking it needs to be in a freak show at some carnival.

"I've never seen a snake with two heads," Don G. offers.

Despite the hair on the back of my neck sticking straight out, I pretend to be nonchalant. Instead of being my elated and excited self, I professionally point out, "The Puerto Rican boa is on a federal registry of endangered species…even with one head."

Neither Don G. nor the rare snake makes a move. Regardless of pretenses, I'm knowing this is a special moment in time for all three of us. Understanding it to be non-poisonous, I close in for an even closer inspection. After respectful observation, I have the feeling that simply noticing such a strange creature in passing is not enough. I contemplate the consequences of capture under the guise of scientific snake study. I think about all the laws and about how to and how not to treat endangered species…whether they are strange or not. There may be some exception for a federal biologist and his commonwealth conservation officer. I settle for snapping a half-dozen pictures and leaving my encounter with one of Mother Nature's oddities.

The taxpayers footing my salary would likely want me to finish the forest inventory. As we continue the climb, our plots don't reveal any more crotched palms or screwed-up snakes. Well over two hours from our vehicle, we're still probably not over a mile from where we started, due mainly to the slow going on steep terrain.

I have a burst of energy when the top of our mountain comes in sight. The temperature is a good eight degrees cooler than where my alarm went off this morning...at sea level. Marveling at everything I see, I appreciate the tremendous privilege of merely being here. Don G. lumbers along in the lush vegetation as if it's only a chore to him. On what looks like the top of the world to me, we take a break and sit in the cool and wet grasses among the tree ferns. The cloud coverage breaks for a minute and gives us an incredible glimpse of the navy blue ocean about four thousand feet below.

As Don Gerardo pulls out a plastic sack of fried plantain slices, he reminds me of a big toad eyeing a fly. His lunch doesn't look like much to me, but then I think he could miss a few meals and not be hurt by it. He probably doesn't think a whole lot of my peanut butter sandwich either. Our lunchtime vista socks in, and the landscape and ocean disappear as quickly as they had come.

According to my plan, our predetermined route will eventually loop us back down to the river crossing where I hope no one has stolen the jeep. With the morning now under my new tropical web-belt and me soon to be literally on the downhill side of the day's work, I'm feeling what's probably more confidence than competence.

"Tell me more of what I'll need to know about your forest," I try to engage my assistant.

"You have a lot to learn, my friend," Don Gerardo says, "and it will come only in time."

"Aqui...por favor...ahora?" I show off my best Spanish.

"Do you know the reasons for our tremendous variety of plants?" he asks.

Without giving him time to tell me, I share my book knowledge. "I understand the northeasterly trade winds come in here off the ocean at sea level and are suddenly forced up to the top of the mountain. That creates a sort of sponge-like effect, dumping about 250 inches of rain a year up here. Who would have ever pictured a wetland up at the top of a hill? It's almost contradictory."

Instead of responding, Don G. takes another bite of his back-pack plantains.

"Then," I continue, "with the moisture dropped out, the lee side of the island stays dry about as often as the windward side gets wet. That makes for the plant diversity that comes with five distinct ecological life zones right here within walking distance. Gerardo, that's as many as there are in all of the United States. Is that unreal or what?"

"Yes, I know." Don G. pretends not to be impressed.

Sure he knows it, I'm thinking. I wonder if he also noticed I called him Gerardo for the first time, instead of Don Gerardo. I don't know if it's the exact same as leaving off the "sir" or "mister" in English, but it's my guess that it's pretty close.

Our line of plots back down the mountain is almost as fascinating as it was on our trip up. We encounter a pearly-eyed thrasher, which Don G. informs me is the nemesis of Puerto Rican parrot eggs. The next bird we come across is a smooth-billed ani, which I'm told is mistakenly called a black parrot by amateur Americano bird watchers. The ani has the body of a crow but a long tail and a beak like a hawk.

I feel I'm a part of the rainforest itself, with the dampness and my skin one and the same. I'm guessing Don G. has sweated more on my first field day out than he has any time in the past several years. I can almost hear his bones creaking as we approach our ride, but he must feel good…having kept up. I picture his wife rubbing some sort of Latin liniment all over his heavy-duty body in hopes that he can perform tonight and still walk tomorrow…and wonder if she has a sister for me.

My assistant again volunteers to drive. On the winding road back down toward the ranger station, I reflect on the day's inventory of the Caribbean National Forest. In addition to the local food and Don G.'s rum-punch driving, I've survived the environs and feel that I should no longer be considered a turista. Old Chris Columbus conquering islands has nothing on me.

As we re-enter the neighborhood where we had visited on the way out this morning, Don G. sees a relative standing beside an enterprise that's almost identical to the one where we stopped earlier. An enthusiastic wave from the proprietor induces another stop…to let me taste Puerto Rican afternoon culture, I suppose. The two men take pride in proving that when they speak the native tongue, it's much too jumbled and fast for me to follow.

Our money is no good at this establishment. Knowing acceptance of a free gift is a federal no-no, I remind myself that this is also a strange culture to me. The last thing I need to do is break tradition wide open on my first field day…and I didn't get fired this morning. Turning down a local's double-rum punch would probably not be good for international relations. Instead, I'm treated to a shaved ice with pineapple flavoring…and then a coconut flavored one. It's as if I'm some kid they don't want to lead astray with their alcohol.

As Don G. goes for his second double-rum punch, I try giving him a diplomatic hint in their language. I hope I said something akin to announcing that I would be the designated driver when we have to leave shortly. Both men laugh, so I may have only thought I said something appropriate. The next time I want to be serious, I'll know to speak in English.

Giving up on being a part of their conversation or even understanding their speed-jabbering, I mosey toward the counter. I'll pretend I'm interested in looking over the merchandise. This is not the first time I've wondered if this assignment is going to let me experience what C.B. felt like…being the minority in most crowds.

Glancing out the back window of the shanty, I see a strange-looking child. He has a head about three times the size it should be to match his little body. Like the little boy from this morning, this child also appears to be about twelve years old.

"There again…but for the Grace of God go I."

I don't mean to stare, but two in a row translates into something sort of spooky. Am I in a land of the afflicted? As it is true for my visions of Little Scott, freeing my mind of the sad image of these unfortunate children's predicaments will be hard. Undeserved impairments like these are impossible to understand…and they have a way of working on my mind and my religion.

Managing to herd Don G. to the Cherokee, I jump in the driver's seat before he says anything. After I pull our vehicle back onto the road, I ask, "Don Gerardo, what's the story about the child behind the shack?"

"That's something you're going to have to get used to here," he answers. "The mentally retarded in Puerto Rico are not provided for the way they are en el Estados Unidos. Even our Policia let them sit undisturbed along the busy streets of downtown San Juan."

I don't know if it's the emotional subject or the rum-loosened tongue of my assistant, but something is leading him in an easy-going and soft-spoken manner.

"I enjoyed spending the day en el Bosque with you, Scott. I have not been back to that part of the forest since the early 60s when your Army was aqui."

"What was our Army doing here?" I ask, emphasizing that it is no more my Army than it is his.

"Oh, they were testing some defoliant to see if it would work well enough to be used in Vietnam."

As I think over his comment, a horrible thought hits me. The only forked palms were in that same small sub-watershed with the bewildering boa.

"Where exactly was that...where they tested the herbicide, Don Gerardo?"

"Actually, it was right about where we saw La Culebra," he answers and questions my question with his look at me.

My terrible feeling turns worse, and I share aloud, "Deformations in nature are usually trying to tell us something is out of balance."

Don G. does nothing to indicate he understands my thesis. "Don Gerardo...the screwed up trees...the mal-formed snake...Holy mackerel...surely to God this area is not straight downhill and in the same watershed from....?"

I screech the jeep to a halt on the narrow shoulder of the steep road. Thrown into the dash, Don G. clutches the door and yells something in rapidly sobering Spanish that I can't translate. I rip through my gear searching for the paperwork. Finding the map, I line up my protractor with the locations.

"Oh, my God! Gerardo...the children...the kid with the jerks...and the one with the big head...."

"Que?" Don Gerardo asks.

"Don Gerardo, don't you see? Lord, have mercy...they are about the right ages to have inheri...."

Don G.'s hands now cling to the seat beside him. He pushes up as if being higher will help him better understand. His puzzled expression and tan skin color turn a shade of Puerto Rican pale.

"This map shows the road curving so that first establishment is directly below the other…and both of them are straight downhill from the sub-watershed where you said the herbicide experiment took place."

"This should not have happened, Scott." Don G. shakes his head.

"I'm ashamed to tell you I was thinking the two little boys' problems were the result of some enclave of in-breeding or something like that. Considering the boa and his condition and the messed-up tree, I'm now suspecting a horrendous atrocity of a different nature. Mankind's technology sometimes betrays us. These abnormalities may be linked to the lingering ills of 2-4-5-T."

Don G. stares without comment.

"It's the recently banned poison that was used in Vietnam…called Agent Orange."

"Jesus Christo!" he exclaims. "Que es…what are we going to do?" He looks at me with his puzzled face.

"We need to think this through…and figure out what an appropriate reaction might be," I answer. "Hitting the panic button before we consider some alternatives or getting everybody stirred up may not be for the best."

I've got a feeling Don G. is not going to sit on this information for very long. So that he doesn't perceive my comment as my resolve, I decide to try to explain what I meant…as I think through it myself.

"We may very well need to get the public involved, but if that turns out to be the case, it should be at the right time. Proper timing could be everything. We don't want to mess up what might be our best option."

"Scott, what are you thinking?"

"I'm not sure. This is an environmental catastrophe, but it may also reflect environmental racism at its worst. These issues are governmental…and we might need to enlist the right people to help."

"Que?"

"An Americano expression says—it's not what you know but who you know. We can get more done better if we don't prematurely alert the improper authorities. Right now, we've just got to think this through."

I pull the jeep back out onto the road. It's hard to keep us on the side of the mountain. Don G. notices I'm all over the road and asks if I want him to drive. Even after his rum punches, it may be a good idea. I pull over and we exchange places.

"Scott, how can they have done this to my people? We can't let them get away with this."

"It's not your people, Don Gerardo. It's our people. And it's not them. It's us."

"Someone here didn't care. No concern was shown for las criaturas y las plantas...la tierra, el agua y el aire."

"Don Gerardo, our government may have done something short-sighted, not even realizing that there might be serious consequences. They may have just acted in ignorance. Surely what they did was not done in malice. They could have underestimated, misunderstood, and been careless. Then again, a cover-up would be nothing but greed."

"Scott?"

"Maybe we need to figure out how to be resolvers and not simply complainers. Mr. J. taught me that."

"I don't know about your Mr. Jay, but screwing up my only island es muy dangerous."

"I agree. It's outrageous, Don Gerardo, and nobody is going to get away with anything. But let's stop talking about 'they.' Let's figure out what we can do. I'll think out loud if you'll hold off on your accusations long enough, okay?"

"Dios mio, I can't get a word in as it is."

"Por favor, Don Gerardo."

"Si, como no."

"When such havoc is caused on planet earth, it's too much to let go. It's one thing to attack boll weevils and noxious weeds and indiscriminately kill millions of birds, but when our Department of Defense's spraying results in debilitating deformities to our children, something's got to give. Somebody will pay. We have to figure out who and how...and when."

"How about compensation to the families?" he asks.

"I'm not sure, Don Gerardo. Industry may need to make amends for some basic irresponsibility but so does our technologically-damned society. Corporate America is so rich that hitting it in the wallet might not be enough of an answer. They'd probably just write it off as the cost of doing business and pass it on to their customers...who are us."

"Somebody needs a kick in the ass," Don G. oversimplifies. "The way things were done here needs to change."

"Now you're getting it," I say, hoping that agreeing will at least momentarily quiet him. "Our job is not only about caring for the land but also stopping crimes against it."

Don G. sits, probably thinking he knows what I'm thinking...but he couldn't. I've constantly wondered if C.B.'s exposure to benzene hexachloride in Alabama or Agent Orange in Vietnam or both resulted in little Scott's disease and death...herbicidal homicide...genetic genocide...every "cide" but our side.

"How many chemicals like this do they have?" Don G. asks.

"Thousands. There are literally thousands of registered pesticide products. That alone ought to be screaming overkill."

"They should have a skull and crossbones on those safety labels we hear so much talk about," he says.

"The question is—how can we effect a change in the almighty money-driven policies?"

"No se," Don G. admits.

Continuing to think out loud, I pray, "Lord, just give me some kind of sign, please God."

"S q u a k—squelch—squ-ak," our radio comes to life. "This is FS 1. Can anyone on the CNF read me?"

"Don Gerardo, who is that?"

"Yo no se. He said FS 1. You don't suppose it's...?"

"No, no...hell no. Somebody's just screwing with us. They're trying to make a fool out of the new guy. That's all right. I'll go along with it. Give me that mike."

"Aqui, pero..." Don G. tries to warn me as I take the mike.

"10-4, this is Sabana Uno, Que es eso?"

"Good afternoon. This is the Chief. I'm flying back to D.C. from a meeting in the Virgin Islands. I thought I'd check out the Forest Service frequency from up here and also see how you guys are doing down there. Over?"

"Not too damned good. I'll call you by telephone when you get back to your office," I answer.

Silence takes over for about ten seconds.

"FS 1 clear."

"Sabana Uno clear!"

"Scott," Don G. says, "I'm not so sure that was someone playing a joke. I think maybe it really was the Chief of the Forest Service."

"I know it was, Don Gerardo."

"Jesus Christo! You're loco. Do you know that? You get a chance to talk to the Chief and you swear at him, on the radio…in front of Jesus and all of heaven. You're a classic…a bloody continental classic in everything you do."

"Well, thank you."

"That was not a compliment. What did you do to get sent to Puerto Rico, anyway?"

"That's a long story…for another time," I answer. "It's got to do with my being a little too vocal against a policy that was converting too much hardwood to pine. A buddy that you remind me of got me involved with it."

"I don't know anything about any of that, but I do know you can't be jerking the Chief of the Forest Service around…not if you want any kind of a career."

"Career? Don Gerardo, you may need to talk to somebody that's got one of them damned things."

"Dios Mio!"

"Besides, I asked for some kind of sign…and right off, I got one. You heard the whole thing. Now, please, let me think."

"It's a little late for that, Lone Ranger."

"Por favor, Tonto."

"Si, como no."

We make our way back toward the ranger station with very little conversation. I do persuade Don G. to promise me that he won't let out our discovery until we have talked again.

––––––––––––

IT'S A DAY LATER when Don G. comes in my office and sits down. "Buenos dias."

"Bien. Y tu?"

"What did you decide, Scott?"

"That for the time being we need to focus on the Farce Service, as my good friend used to call it."

Don G. stares at me with an empty look. I wish I could tell him of the almost unbearable loss of little Scott to me and C.B. I know that I can't do that without crying, and I don't want to do that in front of him.

"Don Gerardo, nothing is going to bring back normality for those already affected. I know from personal experience that their families need to move on with their lives instead of fretting over their loved ones' past ills. I think we should target the future. The past is history."

Only his eyes speak…and I don't like what I see them saying. He continues to stare at me with a disappointed expression, as if I now represent the unidentifiable "they" that he's been hating. He just stares that stare. I've seen C.B. do it…and I hated it then, too.

"Don Gerardo, it's hard to zero in on one fault. When that experiment was tried, I'm sure it was perceived as a worthy idea. It wasn't anything malicious. But when implemented and in the long run, it just came out all wrong."

He continues to look dissatisfied…and I can almost see C.B. giving me that same stare. He'd push me into doing things I didn't want to do but usually knew I should.

Don Gerardo starts to speak, but I stop him by holding my hand up. "I sent the Chief a fax this morning. Okay?"

We are interrupted by the phone ringing. My secretary tells me who is on the other end.

"Buenos dias, Chief. This is Sabana One…and, uh, I assume you got my fax this morning?"

"Yes," comes a grumpy and short answer from the landline.

"Concerning what I stumbled on yesterday, sir, we have a tremendous opportunity for your skillful collaboration with the Puerto Rican people…at a time when we really do not need a class-action law suit from a couple of million Hispanics who receive their water from the forest…not at the very time when the U.S. and Puerto Rico are trying to decide upon statehood versus some other legal status for the Commonwealth."

I pause, but there's nothing but a clearing of the throat on the line, so I capitalize and continue. "Final closure on this whole affair would be possible by the implementation of the four action items identified on my fax." I pause again but not long enough to be interrupted. "First, Forest Service-wide, there needs to be an immediate and permanent moratorium on all aerial spraying of pesticides."

He clears his throat, so I continue, "Second, we need to make permanent full-time federal employees out of each of the forest workers I listed. I have come to find out that they have been put out to labor and then laid off, over and over, every year for their whole lives. These people have families and needs just like you and me. Leaving them with no health or retirement benefits is no way to treat good employees. It's not like there is a season here when they can't work or aren't needed."

The Chief clears his throat again, as if he wants to speak. Before he can, I continue.

"Third, on all National Forests in the Southern Region, there needs to be no more net gain of pine acres over hardwood acres due to conversions. And lastly, when my tour is up here, I'll need to be transferred back to the Holly Springs National Forest in Mississippi. That's all it will take, sir…and they're calling for me out on the Forest. I have an emergency, and I have to run. Goodbye, sir…and thanks again."

"Click."

My assistant and I stare at the phone and wait to see if the Chief is going to call back. After a Puerto Rican-minute with no return call, Don G. extends his hand to me for a handshake. I take his firm grip, as he breaks the silence, "Scott…."

"What? What is it, Don Gerardo?"

"Muchos juevous, mi amigo Americano!"

"And lots of scrambled eggs to you too, my friend," as I pump his arm up and down.

"No, no, what I said is translated more like—you have much balls, my friend."

"Damn, Don G., maybe I'd best stick to talking American."

IL:
Ivory-bill'o
Cubano

"LOSERS BUY PINAS COLADAS?"

"You're on," I agree and look to my doubles partner to make sure he's game.

On my fourth Columbus Day in the commonwealth of year-round green, I'm not sure tennis will ever taste the same as it does at Club Rio Mar. Spoiled here by easy-on-the-knees clay courts and ball-shagging ninos and ninas, I don't see how life could get much better.

One of my opponents is a Forest Service biologist friend from the Puerto Rican parrot recovery project. After he burns me with a passing shot fired down the line, he drops an exciting ornithological volley on me...not without under-spin.

"Scott, have you heard the latest about our long-thought-to-be-extinct ivory-billed woodpecker?"

"Oh, Lord, here we go again."

"Seriously. Verification pending, he is reportedly alive and well...in Cuba."

Thinking I hear the inevitable silently calling, I pretend to be shocked into submission by such a revelation as a resurrected woodpecker. Privately, I'm wondering if perhaps all of Granna's bird study with me, not to mention my training, was preparation for just this sort of thing.

The deuce courtside of my tennis team happens to be a friend who works for Alcohol, Tobacco, and Firearms. This ATF doubles partner knows me well beyond my looping cross-court, two-handed backhand with topspin. He looks at me with his stay-on-your-side-of-the-court expression.

"Don't even think about it, Scott," he warns.

"Come on…with all the rumors in birding circles flying amok, would I take gossipy grapevine talk like that seriously?"

"I see that glimmer in your eyes, and I'm here to tell you—this is no time to be caught in Cuba," he warns sincerely.

"Now why is that? Has ATF got Castro working on some secret cigars y'all don't want anybody to smoke out yet?"

He hits a lob that takes one of our opponents back to his baseline. We charge the net together.

"All I can say is—you could find yourself in a jail full of drug traffickers for a very long time."

"What's with you G-man wannabes and such smokescreens?"

"Scott, I'm serious as a heart attack." He easily puts away the overhead for a point.

"But it's not every day a birder gets an opportunity to witness a woodpecker doing the Lazarus number."

"Scott, you best take note and be advised—stay away from that idea. Now, concentrate on your tennis. We can come back if we get this point."

I drop the discussion, but I'm thinking my incentive to remain in the Caribbean may have just been re-birthed…as the final straw of weariness was about to rub through my backpack. I can't focus on my tennis. I sense that we are about to lose two piña coladas when a thunderboomer breaks loose and rains out the match.

———————

DURING MY FOUR YEARS of work at the Caribbean National Forest, I've had to deal with Washington and Atlanta by phone enough that I should have known better than to even ask. Both levels of my supervisors say "no" to my request for a Cuban detail. This means it's time to herd up my trusty bell cow for local counsel.

———————

"DON GERARDO, CAN YOU set me up with a trip to Cuba?"

"El estupido?"

"Probably—but I'm serious."

"So am I. Why would anybody in his right mind.... Scratch that. Why would *you* want to go to Cuba?"

When I explain about the ivory-bill being a worthy reason, Don G. doesn't let me down. He has a cousin who belongs to a clandestine environmentalist organization...and coincidentally runs a charter deep-sea fishing business.

Using my bi-annual home leave, no one will miss me from either of my worlds. Unauthorized arrangements are facilitated on the hush, so everyone here will think I've gone to Oxford, Mississippi, and everyone I know in Los Estados Unidos will be thinking I'm still in Puerto Rico.

Under the pretense of fishing for the mighty blue marlin and lesser sailfish, cousin Carlos and a deck hand meet me at a marina near Fort Cristobal. We'll fish during the day and make our run to Cuba during the cover of night.

Antillean tropicbirds and brown pelicans bid us adieu. At a surprisingly short two miles out, we hit blue water and start to troll for the big game fish in the rolling waves. Timidly, I remove my polo shirt and expose gringo-white skin to the sun's burning rays. My guide quickly and correctly determines that I have little to no experience deep-sea fishing.

"The first three fishing techniques you'll need to master are spitting on your bait, staring at your line, and holding your mouth right," he instructs.

"Wait a minute, that sounds like a wives' tale from stateside," I suggest. "Are you sure you're not really from the mainland?"

"Si, I grew up in New York City."

"Carlos, have you ever done this before?"

"Ha ha. So you think I'm just taking you for a boat ride, huh?" He motions for his deck hand to take the wheel.

"No, no, mi amigo, I'd trust you with my life."

"Yes, you have," he reassures me.

I can't help thinking my escort no longer stands with the ease of one who is at home with the sea.

"Snap! Zing...ing! The fishing line sings as it feeds out at a blurry pace.

"See what happens with good instruction? That, my friend, is how you demonstrate fishing technique," he brags...as if I had done the three things he joked about.

Carlos climbs the little ladder going up to the wheel and takes control of the boat again. Our deck hand attends to his prearranged duties, including helping me into a harness and then the fighting-chair. The rod is taken off a holder from the back of the boat and snapped into the swivel of my harness. My lap is now fastened through the rod, reel and line, to the fish. Not the chair. Not the boat. Not anything except one big fish, judging by the way he's taking line.

My right hand rolls the reel handle, as my left slides up the rod and searches for the most comfortable place from which to pull. Carlos keeps the boat steady, straight, and at a constant speed. I suppose he's trying to stay out and away from the fish in order to help me keep the line tight. Even reeling in as fast and hard as I can, the line zings out. As the reel continues to scream, the deckhand yells something in Spanish.

"En Ingles!" I yell back.

"He's telling you to pump and reel, pump and reel, pump and reel," Carlos offers, in translation from above.

I knew it was something three times—and pump and reel as hard and fast as I can. Surely the drag is set to give enough to prevent the line from breaking…or pulling me overboard and out to sea without a boat and never to be seen again.

My beautiful blue marlin surfaces and leaps through the air four times, one right after the other. He's eight feet long if he's an inch. Instead of jumping again, he dives deep and hard, taking about as much line as he wants. When I'm not pumping, I'm reeling. After thirty minutes, my fingers have blistered. Trying to shift the friction points to my palms is no good. My reeling doesn't work nearly as well…and my fish is still pulling like a Toccopola logging mule.

Our fight goes on for another thirty minutes. I manage to reel in about as much line as the marlin takes out. Recalling my reading of *The Old Man and the Sea*, I wish I had some gloves…and the grit of that old Cuban in the book. As my point of exhaustion is closing in, I think I can feel the pulse of the big blue beating right up through the line. I figure the tug-of-war is nearing a stalemate when Blue makes a deep run toward the boat and then quickly up toward the surface. I am unable to reel fast enough to keep our monofilament connection tight. Carlos doesn't detect it quickly enough to keep the boat as far away from the fish as it needs to be to help prevent the line from slacking.

Having reeled down and pumped back up several times, I can't find any tight line. The slack stays no matter how fast I reel or pull. Feeling no resistance, I realize my trophy of a lifetime must have worked the hook out of his monstrous mouth. As the empty hook comes up through the surface and finds my rod's tip, I know that is exactly what has happened. The old, worn-out saying about the big one getting away comes to mind as I realize just how tired and defeated I am.

Watching bottle-nosed dolphins below us and magnificent frigatebirds above us helps pass the time as I listen for another strike. I keep a sharp watch on my line, but the snap-zing doesn't come. Cloud formations are interesting as darkness slowly surrounds us. An overcast sky prevents star watching. I stretch out on a cot. The humming of the diesel soon lulls my tired, sunburned body into sawing sea-logs.

In the middle of the sea, in the middle of the night, we meet up with our Cuban connection. I'm awakened enough for introductions to be made and my transfer to a similar fishing boat. It is also captained by a Carlos. Carlos and Carlos share a rum and lime juice drink, along with their too-fast-paced Cuban Spanish. When they exchange briefcases, I try not to notice.

"Buena suerte y hasta luego," my original Carlos says to me upon leaving.

"Gracias," I respond.

"Hasta la vista." The new Carlos waves to the old Carlos.

As the Puerto Rican boat eases away along with my sense of security, I hear girls giggling below deck. My new captain gives me a short orientation and lays out my agenda. The Cuban fishing boat is to smuggle me to a laguna on the edge of the rainforest. It's close to the spot of an alleged ivory-bill sighting. In two days I'm to report back to a fishing cabin, ideally having verified and photographed the second coming of the woodpecker.

When we've run out of logistical questions and answers, Carlos speaks to his deck hand. I think I understand him to say, in his super-speedy Spanish, something to the effect of, "Show him below for the proper Caribbean welcome." The deck hand leads me to a small door and closes it behind me…without coming through himself.

All my previous best fantasies are history…big time. In identical yellow bikinis, identical twin sisters giggle as they step toward me to introduce themselves.

"I, Sonia."

"I, Maria."

"Uh, et tay...hi, I'm Scott."

Alternately gawking into two golden faces, each of no more than twenty-something years of ripe youth, I try to say something about the weather in my Spanish. Their response is twin laughter, so I guess I must have said something else. I stare at four beautifully browned, long legs and can't come up with anything clever to say. As the girls smile in the same fashion, I'm beginning to think they don't speak English.

"Hola, que pasa?" I try the simplest of my Spanish.

With more laughing as their answer to my simple Spanish, I suppose it's my accent.

"Hello, what's happening?" I translate...I think.

There is more laughter. "What you would like to happen?" Sonia answers in English understandable even to a dyslexic like me.

I think I know what she's getting at, and I'm absolutely sure I know what I'd like to get at. While I can't just come right out and say it, I'm hoping they'll understand that the way I'm looking at them indicates my desire to go along. Before I can think of what to say, Maria offers her hand. Sonia does the same as I begin to appreciate what might happen. They lead me to a small couch. "Good morning. How are you?" Maria finally demonstrates her command of my language.

Morning is long gone, but she's too delightful to start me worrying about her English...or the time of day that has the dim light of the cabin reflecting the copper tones of the girls' skin color. With one girl on each side of me, I sit in the irresistible glow of their sleek bodies. Maria puts her hand slightly above my knee. Sonia makes warm contact with her long bare leg pressing up against mine. The language of girl giggle now speaks in the universal tongue. As Maria strokes my new attempt at a beard, Sonia whispers soft Spanish love sounds in my ear. I think the translation of what they are saying has something to do with me becoming the center of a Cubano sandwich with the sisters as buns.

My new best fantasy is coming to life while Spanishly sexy Maria asks, "What purpose brings you to visit our island?"

As tempted as I am to say "you," I respond, "Et tay...tu Ivory-bill-o."

"Ivory...si, si. Maria y Sonia like ivory." She points to her sister's ivory bracelet and matching necklace. As if modeling for me, Maria stretches her long tan body to emphasize her incredibly inviting curves…with cleavage I'd crawl under her necklace to get to.

"No, no, an ivory-billed woodpecker," I explain.

"Pecker," Sonia giggles. "Si, si…we know pecker." She reaches down and starts unfastening my belt.

"Woh-oh-ho-Oh!" I gasp, unable to speak. "Ah…hh…y'all, uh…really, uh…we really need…to…woh-ohoo…y'all shouldn't…uh…. Never mind."

A gentle and soothing sea breeze comes through the open portholes of our boat…as Sonia's sensuous touches are like the sounds of salsa and Maria's music that of a steel band. Beyond any delights I've known, Sonia is coconut and Maria pineapple. Combined and concentrated they cause a stirring from my loins that's about to release 1,000 butterf……10,000 butterfli…100,000…a million butterfli…a-a-a-a-ah …iiiiies.

DAWN POPS IN THROUGH the portholes as waves slap the boat to wake me. The Latin ladies of my evening are nowhere to be seen. I hope they're not deck-side, giving my pleasures to the captain and deck hand.

I think about how these girls from the Caribbean have their own special attraction and unique expression of the culture. They are evolved by and for their island, just as I know Montana girls to have their own special cowgirl look. Just as I could spot a Mississippi girl in a whole room full of others, these awesome girls must be a sub-species of their own.

As I get up to test my rubbery sea legs, Sonia and Maria come below. They are smiling but no longer giggling. They have prepared for me a breakfast comprised of conch salad and a drink made from pure sugar cane. As the concoction tastes surprisingly good, I wonder if the Spanish language is any better than mine about having a word that means complimentary contrasts. What is it when a mild taste mixes with a tart tang to somehow work together? Mr. J. once told me about a French Canadian girl who liked to dip a dill pickle in fancy-grade maple syrup.

Once up on deck, I see we're about to make landfall. Wooden houses line hillside roads and share the haze in a pattern befitting a portrait. As if to greet us, the slopes of the rainforest come right down to the edge of the water. When our boat cuts into the coastal lagoon, Carlos points out our strategic fishing cabin. Young boys are cutting bamboo. Little girls are dancing up and down in a large vat-like container.

"Que pasa?" I ask.

"It keep de clumps out de cocoa beans for when they dry," one of the sisters answers in her best Cuban English.

"Oh…K."

"Did you find hospitality to your liking last night?" Carlos asks.

"Bien, bien, gracias, muchas gracias." I can't help my big grin, so I roll my eyes and admit, "I'm ready to move to Cuba."

The girls giggle again. We pull up to a little pier sticking out into the lagoon. Carlos makes sure I can identify the correct cabin and then reaffirms his promise to meet me there in two days. I hop off the boat and onto relatively solid footing. From the land's end of the pier, a trailhead becomes apparent.

The reddened sky gives cause to worry about the morning's weather. Triple checking in a pocket, I feel around to determine that I still have my write-in-the-rain notebook. Knowing the weather and my schedule are out of my hands, I dig through my backpack for my compass and altimeter. The compass points me straight up the mountain, and my altimeter reads one meter above sea level. I laugh at myself for having checked either.

Pico del Marcos is my initial destination. It's from there that I'll systematically start to man listening posts for fifteen-minute intervals as I zigzag back down the mountain toward the sea…in hopes of an ivorybill sighting.

The process of climbing-hiking about a hundred yards convinces me to take five for a sit down. I watch below until my life-support boat clears the breakwater and putters away. Another hundred yards up makes me realize that I really did need to check the altimeter at sea level…to calibrate it. Maybe there was some reason to point the compass uphill, too. Someday foresters will have instruments that triangulate off stars or satellites to tell them their locations. Not getting lost may take half the fun out of forestry work.

Up ahead of me is a man with a machete and a tow-sack. Since he hasn't seen me, I'm thinking it may be best to keep it that way. Hiding behind a large tabanuco tree, I decide to watch him for a few minutes.

Leaning my weight against the tree, I accidentally place my hand on a big glob of sap-like goo. Rubbing the sticky tabanuco sap between my fingers, I remember Don G. telling me about torches being made from it. Trying to wipe it off on my pants leg brings little success. I'll bet the stranger could tell me how to get torch-light sap off my hands and pants leg, but I can't risk that. After a few moments of observation, I determine he is harvesting orchids.

Without the orchid man seeing me, I ease on up the mountain. Negotiating the steep slope is the only part of my hike that's not pleasant. This place, like Puerto Rico's El Yunque, is a cool, shady, triple-canopied, jungle-like rainforest. Trees are so dense they seem to be clinging to each other for added strength. Strangler vines deceitfully appear to be anchoring the whole complex, but I know their real intention is choking everything. Heart-shaped leaves and purple flowers of what looks like a common morning glory twine their way up the first ten feet of the conglomeration. Maybe they'll win out over the strangler in the end.

The air is filled with spicy smells. I recognize the aroma of ginger flowers, strong-scented Caribbean grapefruit trees, and other citrus fruits. There is so much bird life present that the vegetation seems to be in motion. Calls range from those of loud parrots and parakeets in the high canopy above to those of the tiny birds that hop quietly from limb to limb near the ground. Some birds try to hide. Others seem to be showing themselves off.

The lower elevations are where I really expect to find the ivory-bill, if he's here at all. I only want to start high and work low for better hearing and quicker closing-in purposes. My feet sink into a spongy, sphagnum-like moss, and I cross a property line. I can identify it by a hedge of red boundary flowers. Along the planted fencerow, numerous bromeliad flowers also highlight the wet world full of strange frog sounds.

Next comes a brand new mahogany plantation of a little over an acre in size. This I'll have to inspect. I need to compare it to what we do and how we do it on the Caribbean National Forest. The seedlings are approximately eighteen inches tall, and each has a ribbon tying it to a stick. The sticks are stuck into the ground beside the seedlings for support, but the problem is obvious. This is a botanical world of such prolific sprouting that new leaves are appearing on the sticks. Rapid growth of the hibiscus sticks taking root will soon overtop and shade out the slower growing mahogany seedlings they are merely supposed to hold up.

Tucking my first Cuban forestry experience under my web belt, I check my map location with my allotted time. Hiking straight through lunch and making good progress during the afternoon, I still don't reach the summit before the darkness takes the lead and wins the race. Quickly stretching my jungle hammock between two dwarf palms, I'm asleep within moments of lying down.

After a not-surprisingly sound sleep, I awake and have only a short wait for the first light of day. When I have finished a can of tuna for breakfast and can see to walk, I break camp…which means nothing but rolling up my hammock and sticking it back in my pack. A socked-in cloud cover greets me when I reach the peak. Before the overcast has a chance to yield a view, I head back down.

I've just started when I hear the chatter of a woodpecker. It's the unmistakable rat-a-tat-tat sound of a large woodpecker. The call is very much like a pileated woodpecker but different enough to make me truly believe that it may just be the ivory-bill. I move cautiously and quietly toward the resounding drumbeat of the mystery. Within twenty minutes I have sighted him.

In the upper canopy of a yagrumo macho tree I see this incredible bird. Probably weighing between two and three pounds, he's most similar to our Mississippi hammerhead, who weighs half that. His swept-back crown is more noticeable than that of the Yocona bottom summer-hen. This woodpecker has a conspicuously elongated white band all the way down his body. I'd guess his bright ivory-white bill is designed by Mother Nature for flushing insects.

First there was Maria and Sonia…and now this…. The excitement of the moment and this thrill of discovery is so great I feel guilty for experiencing it. The echoing rat-a-tat-tat of the bird seems to keep pace with my heart rate. I wish Mr. J. could be here to see this with me. He told C.B. and me about the birds of old, the birds that no longer grace even the Mississippi delta. A flock of pigeons works its way through the Sierra palms, no doubt feeding on the little round palm seeds. With an eerie feeling and spooky sort of expectation, I look to see if the birds could be Mr. J.'s extinct passenger pigeons. They aren't…and I feel somewhat disappointed.

Having verified the ivory-bill's existence by sight, I manage to snap a few slides before the bird flies off. I hope one of my shots will come out clear enough to prove the identity of the bird. I can see it being circulated all over the birding world and bringing me avian accolades of the highest order.

On my trip back down the mountain, I'm ahead of my schedule. Upon re-crossing the little mahogany plantation, I have time to view the forestry dilemma in a different light. It's now a manageably small area having a big reforestation problem. Putting my tabanuco-sapped hands to work for somewhere between an hour and two, I pull the stick-sprouts out of the ground and drop them beside their mahogany seedlings.

I sit against a banana stalk to admire my release job and eat a banana. An unexpected thought ruins the moment that I assumed was victory. The hibiscus sticks I dropped beside each mahogany seedling may again root where they lie. If they do, they'll probably still catch up and overshadow their crop trees. After all this volunteer labor, if Mother Nature does that to me…the hibiscus can have the site.

Continuing downhill and into the more human-inhabited lower reaches of the rainforest, I stumble on an unnatural circle of rocks. Seeing what looks like chicken bones, I recall the herbwomen from around Taylor. They used to chant a cadenza about circles of bones and stones and how they don't lie. The forest gets suddenly darker. A gust of wind comes through, and something uneasy washes over me. I'm surrounded with a sense of foreboding. I do not believe in black magic, but this is a lot closer to the signs of it than I ever wanted to be. I sense something is going on here. I can feel a spirit moving.

I look at the circle of rocks again. Seeing such evidence of man's artificiality in the midst of Mother Nature's purity speaks loudly to me. In a voice just as if Mr. J. was talking, I hear his words about how carelessness could cause us to reap the bitter harvest of our transgressions. The voice is so clear I look around for him…and feel foolish for it. "Mother Nature usually does all right for herself," he would say, "if she's by herself and mankind is absent."

Staring at the voodoo circle, I think of how the circle of inefficiency surrounding my government is multiplied manifoldly by its various layers of checkers checking checkers until there are probably pecker checkers at the upper levels. I remember the red tape of a State Department with a bureaucracy that would not grant me a visa to be here. I can only imagine what they would do to screw up the odds of survival for probably the rarest of all birds in the world.

The flattest rock of the voodoo circle is calling out, "It's your serve." I'm suddenly fearing that my mere substantiation of Cuba's ivory-bill could result in mankind "protecting" it to death. Either of our governments could protect it, but the idea of both of them working together.... I fear it would result in their managing it right off the face of the earth.

Something sure to be spiritual guides my fingers as I open my camera's back. A force outside me knows what I have to do. I backhand the chicken bones off the stones and place my film of the ivory-bill on the smooth, hard surface of a single stone that's in the halo-like circle of voodoo. With a good hammering chunk of bedrock, I serve a smashing ace...for game, set, and match.

L:
Havana General

LEAVING THE BIRD AND frog sounds in the rainforest, I intrude on the lapping serenade of the surf. As I approach my planned rendezvous with Carlos and company, I suppose it'd be too much to expect the twins to be along again.

There seems to be a lot of activity around the Cuban fishing cabin. I'm thinking I'd best observe from a distance until I can figure out what's going on. Big trouble. Uniformed and heavily armed officers are swarming the site. Instead of Carlos II being docked alongside the pier, there's a boat with Policia Militar stenciled on its side.

Carlos and his deck hand are led out in handcuffs. Recalling my ATF tennis partner's comments about the real possibility of rotting in the Cuban prison system, I visualize my future going from whatever I choose to make of it to being in the hands of someone else. How in the name of Samuel El Hades am I going to get off this island?

Instinctively, I exercise my nearest option…retreating back into the mountain of unnamed shades of green. Important now for my safety are camouflage and the duller plain hues of my clothing. My mind churns at every steep step. In addition to the seclusion provided by the forest, I may have to depend on forest plants for sustenance in living off the land.

Thanks to the climate and the vegetation of the rainforest, my basic needs would be provided for. There are citrus trees and tropical vegetables, strange fruits and tubers, and other natural foods I might discover. I've noticed fresh-water shrimp and land crabs. The forest is full of pigeons. I'll just have to figure out how to catch them. My youth on the Yocona and Little Tallahatchie Rivers has prepared me for this kind of challenge.

I know I was naive to have come here the way I did, but I'm here now. Catching and killing whatever I could find while I was growing up has given me confidence in my ability to survive. There are two choices. I can spend the rest of my life being abandoned and alone or I can concentrate on turning my stupid lack of respect for fear into a solution to get me home.

Regardless of my pale complexion and slippery grasp of Spanish, an alternative may be going into the city and wandering the streets of Havana. If Cuba treats its mentally challenged with the same disregard Puerto Rico does, maybe I can blend in with the crazies. I could pretend to be a little more insane than I apparently am for real. By the time I've slept in these clothes another time or two and spent a week without a bath, I'll have kids picking on me...and dogs chasing me. I might even be able to take one of those boat rides to the U.S. that's the goal of so many Cuban rejects and dissidents.

As if reaching the clouds will hide everything and make me safe again, I trudge on toward El Pico. Flying close and low, a Cessna-sounding plane makes its presence known. For such socked-in weather and steep terrain, if he doesn't start climbing, he's going to—

"Cra...cac...boom...oom!"

With my instinct to help others, I head toward the crash site. I'm not sure I know enough first aid to help someone splattered all over the side of a mountain. The steepness of the terrain forces me to lean so far forward my nose is down in the floral perfumes and misty scents of the wet soil. Fog-like clouds shield me from seeing much of anything, but maybe the crash site won't be too hard to find. Surely there's going to be smoke. I've got to be getting close.

A full-fledged rain begins. It ends by the time I've climbed another hundred yards. Everything growing tries to trip me as I continue uphill. As the fog lifts and the clouds blow through, I smell aviation fuel. Now I can see a tangled mess of sheared-off tree tops. It's like giant barbers' clippers have cut a flattop through the mountain to expose its scalp.

Pieces of plane, clothing, and papers are scattered ahead of me. Bodies are strewn about...too many for this to have been a two-seater plane. An exposed leg bone is red instead of the white I always thought it was supposed to be.

Doubting that anyone is alive, I call out, "Hey! Can anyone hear me?"

466

Even the tree frogs are silent. As if Mother Nature were preparing for a funeral of her own, a petunia-looking plant with lavender flowers hides a boot with half a leg and a foot in it. Moving around clockwise, I systematically check for any signs of life. The closest face to me appears to be that of an American...and the second. I stumble on a Bible...and another. I'm suddenly thinking this may have been a planeload of U.S. missionaries.

Taking a people-inventory from among the pieces of bodies is gruesome and confusing, but I determine there are five casualties. It dawns on me that when the Cubans arrive, I can be a survivor. Surely they know there has been a plane crash, and they must be on the way to look for it. When they question me, I can play dumb...instead of stupid.

Picking out a crevice between two boulders, I drop my jungle hammock and non-missionary-like personal belongings down the hole. Unable to find the passenger manifest and add my name, I clutch a Bible to try to look authentic. There's nothing to do now but wait for a search party. Thunder rumbles, and the sky clouds over again. A chill consumes me. I know my wait could last anywhere from several hours until rainforest dark...if I'm even rescued today.

As I linger, I think of the families and loved ones of the dead missionaries lying about. They'll be mourning and remembering the victims of the plane crash with the heart-felt belief that they are now reaping the good harvest, but I'm the one who could use a good praying for right about now.

An amphibian of some sort crawls out from under a fig leaf. This rainforest is so wild I'll bet some of these critters have never been identified by man. A big lizard scurries up a tree like a squirrel would. The humidity here is so dense I'd guess he doesn't even have to drink to fulfill his daily water requirements. Just breathing such humid air probably does it for him.

As the sun breaks through and gives me an awesome view of bright, navy blue ocean, I mumble to an imaginary dog, "Toto, this ain't Taylor." The crash has created a vista. Two Motillo trees form the border like a natural picture frame. Evergreen vines with fragrant yellow flowers similar to those of Jessamine lace the tress. Beyond the forested foreground are banana plantations, sugar cane plots, and a pineapple field. I wish I hadn't dropped my camera down through the hole where my other belongings disappeared.

The sky over the big water seems to be below the top of the Cuban rainforest. A flock of parakeets comes screeching up a mountain ridge. They break my moment of serenity and make me think that they may not simply be closing in on a place to roost. They may have been flushed. In that case, their alarm could mean someone is coming. Expecting someone to be here soon to see if anyone has survived the crash, I cram my nose into the damp earth. I lie quietly, not moving but uttering a low moan from time to time.

"Aqui. El Captain, aqui, mira…Dios mio!" a potential rescuer yells.

As the area becomes saturated with searchers, the excited Spanish shouting is such that I catch only about my usual third. The search party is apparently celebrating being the first to find the crash site…so they think.

"Este Lt. Alejandro de Guardia Nacional, yo soy…."

As he goes on about overlaps and gaps in procedures, I understand enough to detect that there is some kind of tension between two groups. The arguing has to do with matters related to their authorities. For all my rescuers know, I could be lying here dying while they argue with each other over who's in charge. Seeing if someone might be barely living and needing first aid doesn't seem to be in anyone's priorities, as they fuss over who's to make what radio notifications to whom.

"Este Director Mercado," one of the men says into his radio, "helicoptero departamento de salud utilizaron para recoger los cadaveres…."

Hearing that, I want to jump up and yell that I'm not a cadaver but know it will be more prudent to stay in my fatal 'possum pose. Eventually, someone is bound to check.

Another boss breaks squelch and practically sings into his walkie-talkie. Accelerating his loud speech for emphasis, he cries out that he's the Jefe in complete control. "Este Command Post Chief Montalvo de Defensa Civil de Cuba, yo…."

El Sr. Rodriguez, of the Departamentos Estatales Policia, does not stand for it, and informs his own radio, "Aproximadamente a las 16:30…."

I peek through half-closed eyes to try to see if anyone is approaching any of the victims. Seeing a coordinator with his hand on his pistol, I try harder to appear unconscious.

"Este el Lider Hernandez, es una Avioneta Piper azul y blanca numeros Noviembre treinta y dos treinta y dos Franko…numeros Noviembre treinta y dos treinta y dos Franko…."

A Cuban Coast Guard helicopter now hovers over the crash site. Each boss who has a radio of his own tries to talk to the chopper…all at once. Without so much as a word of transmission that I could hear, the helicopter pulls away. When the noise and the wind from his rotor blades are out of range, the verbal battles and mucho macho matches on the ground continue anew. I wonder about the clash of policies concerning maritime versus aeronautical matters.

A shot is fired, in the air I hope…and apparently just to get everyone's attention. El Subdirector de Desastre explains the situation to one and all. With his emergency frequency overriding everyone else's, he has received direction that the rescuers have thirty minutes to get all the bodies put in body bags, pulled up to an opening, and ready to be air-lifted. Due to the fuel status of the chopper and the time left until dark, they must make that deadline. If they don't, they'll have to haul the deceased out by hand, on foot, and over the rough and steep terrain.

Quickest on the draw with his radio, a searcher from another agency informs the subdirector that they have no body bags.

"Quantos tiene?" the subdirector comes back.

Realizing they don't know how many body bags are needed, a mad scramble to find victims ensues…finally. As a man comes toward me, I give out a very slight moan, "Oh—hh."

"Jesus Cristo, Juan! Es Americano…alive!" he yells. "Senor, senor, como esta? Are you okay?"

"Oh—hh," I respond again, as the Cuban rescuer touches my shoulder.

Trying to talk my way out of this will be a last resort. If I can refrain from saying anything else until they get me to a hospital, maybe I'll have time to come up with a plan of what I must do. As Juan comes up on us, I'll listen to their assumptions and be better able to figure out what might work. Innovate, I tell myself, as I wonder if a deaf and mute missionary's chances of being sent home would be better.

"Don't try to talk, Amigo. Et tay, you'll be okay. Just hang in there. We'll get you some help."

Juan calls my rescuer by name…Carlos.

"Carlos?" I mumble in what I meant to be under my breath.

"What'd he say? Didn't he try to say something?" Juan asks.

I bite my lip and make a guttural noise from deep within my throat. Carlos takes my hand. He's not checking for anything but only doing what he knows best…trying to give me some comfort. It's working. I feel a real rapport with this one. I'll stay bad off and be on the good side of this Carlos.

When the helicopter comes back, there's still an argument going on as to how many body bags are needed. For some reason beyond my understanding, only the dead will be hoisted up and air-lifted out. I'll be toted off the mountain on a makeshift stretcher. Five body bags are dropped. Everyone is eager to help with that procedure, but only my new hero, Carlos, volunteers to grab a corner of my stretcher. As such, the assignments are made. I'm knowing that if these porters ever find out I'm faking, they will rightfully amputate my head.

My toters stop often for rest, setting me down hard each time. But by the time we reach the central highway, everyone is bragging about their humanitarian effort. Pride concerning the pecking orders seems to have worked itself out…at least to the point where the parties can co-exist in celebration. When I'm turned over to an ambulance driver, all dismiss each other as if they were in charge of one another.

A paramedic stays with me in the ambulance and monitors my vitals. From listening to radio talk, I understand I'm being taken to Havana General Hospital. The trip goes without a hitch. By doing nothing, I think I have convinced the paramedic I can't talk. Once I reach the hospital, I am treated like royalty but worry that it won't last.

As well as I can manage as a mute with nothing to express but a goofy smile, I befriend a nice nurse.

Aware of the lusting way I look at her, she makes jokes about Americano Baptist missionaries. As she comes by every hour or so, looking so soft and cuddly, it would be hard for her not to appear sexy in her starchy cotton-white hospital dress and white stockings.

On the other extreme, a couple of Catholic priests periodically visit me. From understanding what they ask and not answering their questions, it's hard for me to keep a straight face. They are obviously trying to determine if I know enough religion to be a missionary. Since I'm sure I don't, I figure my best response is to point my Bible at the questioner. As part of my loco act, I sometimes shake it but am careful not to let that stand for a yes or no answer. It breaks the monotony and seems to be suiting them better than my continual moaning.

Then, there is Inspector Gonzalez of G-2, a Cuban Criminal Investigation Bureau. I assume he's the Cuban equivalent to an American F.B.I. agent, and I'm extremely uncomfortable with him. He asks all kinds of trick questions ranging from those about hospital smells to visits from Puerto Rico. Clearly suspecting me of something, he professionally and proficiently grills me. In spite of him being my greatest challenge to silence, I begin almost to like him. If I ever started talking, I am sure there would be enough interrogation to trip me up and expose me for the fraud I am.

Over the next few days, I receive a few visits from others…and several more from Sr. Gonzalez. When he offers me coffee, I take a small sip and set the cup down. He stands for a moment without speaking and then pushes the cup toward me.

"Here, drink up. This will make you better."

I wonder if it has some kind of Cuban truth serum in it…or if the good inspector is merely trying to make Caribbean small talk in English. I drink but moan as if I am hurting, determined not to let him trick me into talking. As it gets tougher to continue making him think I don't understand his questions, I promise myself to be patient and persistent. While I can't tell if he's on to me, I do sense he's tiring.

Eventually I overhear Inspector Gonzalez tell someone outside my door that G-2 is through with me and they are going to send me on to Nassau. It must have been the original destination of the plane that went down. The only music that could be better to my ears would be to also hear that a couple of Red Cross nurses named Maria and Sonia will accompany me.

WITH MY BIBLE AND one small carry-on bag of Cuban mementos my nurse gave me, I am delivered to the airport terminal by a Havana General driver I have never seen. He tries to get me to talk but I don't. Since the authorities have searched my Bible for drugs or whatever three times, I search my carry-on bag to be sure I'm not being set up.

As I'm escorted to the door to board my plane, I am confronted by none other than Inspector Gonzalez. Holding some papers, he's standing in front of the door that I need to go through. A pair of handcuffs dangle from his belt. His face has what could very well be a G-2 "gotcha" look on it. When I try to walk by without noticing him, Sr. Gonzalez shuffle-steps to block my way.

Eye to eye and nose to nose, he asks, "Do you have any contraband in your luggage?"

I almost say no, but catch myself. Weak-kneed, I respond by pointing my Bible at him and shaking it in his face.

"Bien, bien, y buena suerte," he says…and steps aside.

As I ease around him, he whispers, "Good birding, my friend."

I hear the ripping of papers and feel both sides of my mouth curling up against my will. I want to look back for all I'm worth, but I know I can't. Stepping into the plane, I'm leaning toward thinking the inspector knew all along what was going on…and that Sr. Gonzalez represents a kindred spirit that not just every Americano knows to exist in Cuba.

What's more amazing is how can I be so privileged to see further than these governments. Can these countries be so different, yet both be destined to miss the final game of the match? It seems as if anyone would know how important it is to identify and cooperate with our foreign friends better. Sr. Gonzalez may just be in the same boat as was another friend of mine…the one who first introduced himself to me as Charlie Boy.

LI: *Epilogue*
Home's Coming

AS I COME TO the end of my four-year tour in the democratic Port of Riches, I am raring and ready for my *return'o* to Estados Unidos. Unless one considers skullduggery as another way to find adventure, I should probably feel a bit unworthy of taking the same exciting boat route Columbus once tried. Considering the nebulous circumstances under which I entered the agency in the first place, I am quick to agree to a short-term Forest Service face-saving reassignment.

By doing a stint at the Daniel Boone National Forest first, my placement at the Holly Springs won't have such obvious earmarks of blackmail…if someone out of the loop were to hear rumors of an aborted whistle-blowing. Ruffed grouse hunting with a Brittany spaniel and fly fishing for put-and-take trout help make the year go as fast as it was special.

The next year, I'm back home in Oxford, Mississippi. It's the early eighties, and I find things have fallen generally within the realm of my expectations. The town, the University, and the people have pretty much worked out their problems for better, with a few exceptions. Some people have changed. Others are still trying to tread water or swim upstream. In most cases, racial walls around my small hometown have shrunk, while societal fences have remained pretty much as they were.

In his fast-failing health and with neither of us having wives, Dad and I batch together. I had hoped to spend my spare time hunting and fishing, but there's something almost spiritual about a loved one's last years. Either that or it's a devil's due kind of payback when you have to reverse roles and be the caretaker of your parent.

By coming home, I also have a chance to resume periodic visits with

C.B. Still locked away in Golden Olden, he is bound to be having a tough time of it. It's my intention that Dad and C.B. face their respective problems of aging and illness with no more loneliness than necessary.

"HEY, C.B., HOW'VE YOU been doing? I brought you some goodies."

"Ah…ee…ee," he answers with his grunt-like groan, apparently still able to recognize me.

"Here, the next time you have a long night of fitful sleep, you can jump right in the middle of this basket. Pretend you're on one of our camp-outs, where you're always determined to eat everything we brought by nightfall. It wasn't often we had a breakfast that didn't have to come from the woods."

His eyes light up, and he grins, perhaps with a shade of understanding.

"You're not gonna believe this, buddy—I asked Dad what he would do differently if he had it all to do over again. Would you believe he said he'd get more involved with helping young people?"

"Ah…ee…ee."

"Yeah, he kept a straight face when he said it. I thought we were going to have our first emotional moment together in about fifty years. Wrong. I was assuming he meant he'd have taken a closer role in raising me, but he clarified what he meant. He said he'd have worked with church groups helping kids in general…not necessarily me."

"Ah…ee…ee."

"That's right, so much for our long-awaited tender moment, with Dad's stubborn pride stepping aside, huh? Fathers and sons should be closer than we were and create better bonds."

C.B. begins to doze and doesn't know when I pat his hand and leave. As I think how quickly he got over his excitement from my visit, it reminds me of Dad's showing so little appreciation for my coming home to take care of him…not that I wanted to return to Oxford.

I'M HOPING NATIONAL FORESTS across the entire southeastern United States now have their hardwood-to-pine conversion controversy nipped in the bud. Nevertheless, practicing stateside forestry is not up to the fervor or novelty of learning and practicing tropical forestry. In a matter of years, I come to the realization that life is not about me. I recognize the wisdom of Dad's comment about what he'd do differently if he had it all to do over.

Yearning for a greater cause and more inner peace than my once-beloved Forest Service can bring, I turn to what's perhaps a belated fulfillment from youth, if not a tribute to Little Scott. In spite of never having been in the Boy Scouts, I throw myself into becoming an active, adult scout leader. Developing along with the boys every step of the way, I help grow a group of boys from a Den of Tiger Cubs, through their Cub Pack, and into a questionable lair of Webelos, before transitioning with them into Boy Scouts.

I conclude that it would be hard to find a better way to learn about human nature than through scouting. I just hope the scouts haven't suffered too much as a result of my having so much to learn along the way. Although C.B. and I had each other and our revered Yocona and Little Tallahatchie bottoms, I now see how much we missed by hiding out in our own little world, growing up with entirely too much seclusion from other people. It's a startling revelation…and a little late to learn.

STUCK INDOORS AND MIRED down in computereze, I watch a forest inventory of wood fiber grow by images of bar graphs and pop-up pie charts. The numerous policy manuals and various handbooks stacked and racked around me might as well be a wall. While I'm longing to be in my favorite slough, my office looks more like what I would have expected from a PhD of the injustice system.

It's an ironic twist in the profession that the more years and pay raises one acquires, the further from the forest he is kept. Dealing directly with so much paper and only indirectly with the natural resource from which it comes is an indication of how much forestry has changed over the years. I'm close to feeling sorry for myself. When this happens, I think of how bad C.B. and Dad have it…and then feel sorry for feeling sorry.

Cynicism has become hard to guard against in my agency. It seems the years whittled corners that innovation could once smooth over. Drooping branches of the government tree challenge my optimism enough to make me continue to look elsewhere for satisfaction…where I find that square pegs and round holes also hamper cooperative work with other agencies and departments.

MY FATHER'S ABILITY TO care for himself ends. Golden Olden and C.B. make room for him. With Dad there, my visits to see my old buddy, C.B., naturally increase. In spite of the nursing home's exemplary efforts, Munford's years of hard work have taken their toll. Two years at Golden Olden do in the former Taxi-driver and grocery store owner. My family is now all memory.

"HEY, BUBBA, HOW ARE you doing?"

C.B. sees me and smiles. His upper body plunges forward. He appears about ready to burst trying to communicate, but I'm sure his bobbing back and forth will be the standard response.

"Pou…po…po…uh…oo…oot!"

"I hope you didn't save that just for me. Here we are at the turn of the century, and you're still greeting your visitors like that?"

At this stage, I don't know if he understands some of our conversations or not, but I'll keep talking and listening to his unintelligible garble. From one visit to the next, I should know to quit worrying about how much, if anything, he remembers. The visiting and remembering helps me, whether they do him or not.

DAYS PASS. WEEKS TURN into months, and my visits follow a familiar pattern.

"Hey, C.B., you holding up all right?"

"Umm."

"I kind of need to sit down here and share some peace and tranquility with you. Would that be all right?"

No response.

"I'm thinking that re-river proposal of yours for the Little Tallahatchie has about a fifty-fifty chance of becoming a project. It first has to trickle through all the government hoops so we may not see it in our lifetime. And that's all right, as long as it will be better for someone down the road...or river."

"Umm...mm."

ON A LATER VISIT, "What you know, partner?"

C.B. groans in response.

"I want you to know I've been eating crow casserole and humble pie over something. We've had ourselves so preoccupied with being agitated over the Corps and what a mess it made of our rivers, we haven't been tending our own garden."

"Umm."

"We've allowed a mean and tough weed to grow and grow and keep growing to the point it's about to defeat control. While we were preoccupied blaming other government workers as being witless, perhaps we might have been doing a little more worrying about a certain nasty green vegetative invader. Growing and preventing the reestablishment of everything except self, it's paralleled by nothing but the self-serving bureaucracy itself."

When an aide comes in with C.B.'s supper, I see it as a time for me to take leave.

"I'll get on now and leave you with your thoughts and your meal. Maybe I can make it back before our kudzu crop takes over the southeastern United States."

AS I AGE, THE years pass like months for me. I guess that time must drag for C.B. During another routine stop by Golden Olden, I walk in his room and catch him awake and relatively alert. "That cute little nurse been in here today?" I ask.

"Umm."

"I'm about to decide it's challenges that keep us going, so I'm going to tell you about a little something we can take some gratification over. It seems we have found us a U.S. Senator with your passion to live this particular life in a different and better world. Our bill has sailed through the House and the Senate and been passed into law. *Pueraria lobata* has been listed as a federal noxious weed. A kudzu control initiative is evolving, with kudzu-green dollar signs flashing for a half-dozen universities across the south."

An aide showing up to change sheets and give C.B. his bath is a good excuse for me to escape for the day. I don't know how long my old friend's body can keep up this kind of mere existence.

DAYS OFTEN PASS IN a blur now. Retirement is not all it's cracked up to be…but to be honest—I'm glad the Forest Service is a mere memory. Mixed memories crowd in about the agency, some good, some not so good.

No longer working out in the elements, I can now appreciate the blanket of December white covering the front lawn at Golden Olden. Somehow I manage to visit C.B. almost every day. Holly wreaths at various locations reflect the Season of Greetings.

Not wanting to leave wet tracks of snow across the lobby, I kick my heels together, glad I'm still able to. I look down to check the carpet and my shoes. Both are snowless. It's been eighty years that I have called C.B. my best friend. About thirty of them, I think, I've been visiting him here at Golden Olden.

I call it Go, not in abbreviation, but because everyone here is always wanting to go. I can't blame them for wanting to leave, to escape. Having witnessed three refurbishments and expansions of C.B.'s final home, I can tell them that things are not going to get much better.

My left leg trails with protest. Moving at my own slow pace, I shuffle down the long hallway with its faded shade of yellow wall covering toward C.B.'s room. I know I shouldn't complain. I don't recollect Dad griping about his polio-crippled leg, although he managed to do so about most everything else. More and more, things from my trials and tribulations remind me of the people who filled my life along the way. I realize now how I took folks for granted. With the exception of my mind being already full, I'm doing all right for an old man…for the shape I'm in.

Most of the folks here are not in touch with reality. There's something about old age that wears edges off the mind, but I guess numb is better than the sharpness that would bring sadness. It's sort of like sandpaper smoothing old wood. Thank God my mind is still clear. I know where I'm going.

Residents putter along holding to the handrails on the walls until they come to a wheelchair patient sitting in the way. Whether they're strolling or being rolled, they like to take the corners as if they had somewhere to go.

Sounds here are generally the same from day to day…and from year to year. In addition to some incoherent babbling, there is a lot of silence. There are occasional rages of cussing when irritability crests, but it's rare I hear a real conversation, except for mine with C.B.

Making my way to C.B.'s room, I think how clever I am for the way I remember his room number—seven come eleven and a half. The half comes from his latest room being partitioned off into two separate cubbyholes. I've dubbed that as the Golden Olden Rule—as dependence increases, one's space decreases. There's also what I call the Law of Relative-tivity…the less a person can do for himself, the more important family support is. I am C.B.'s family now. No one else visits him except for two nice black ladies who periodically come from their church.

The decline that comes with aging has not escaped me. Though my strength and endurance are failing, at least I can function independently. At night I toss and turn and catch about an hour's sleep on a given side before I have to wake for a pee break, which is better than the alternative. I can usually go back to sleep but sometimes wish I hadn't when dreams play their dirty tricks.

The caretakers here have C.B. sitting up today. He's patting the arm of his easy chair as if he were hearing a song off somewhere, but the intercom is turned off, I think. I don't hear so well any more.

"Hey, man, what are you trying to do to that chair?" I ask.

"Ah…ee…ee," he answers, looking glad to see me.

"Here, Bubba, let me straighten up your clothes and button your britches. What are you trying to do, perpetuate the legend of the Yocona Puff Adder? These lady nurses around here won't know if you've lost your modesty or you're trying to show off ."

I'm no longer sure what my friend understands. Even the most basic level of self-care has long since escaped his abilities. With a dull-eyed, vacant look about him, his once fat face is now long and sunken. He's almost bald, and his eyes are about all I can count on. It's nice the way his dark eyes still gleam at times. I think about how he could always spot a bird before me.

I slowly lower my long, curved body into a chair next to my old friend. Phlebitis, arthritis, and probably some other itis-es yet to be predicted are trying to make me into an old man. I'm glad I can still visit my friend. Remembering his good-humored nature, I'll talk to him whether I'm getting through to him or not.

"Your burpy breath stinks clear over here. I should have dropped by the Yocona bottom and got you some horse-sugar leaves to chew on."

Sitting atop C.B.'s chest of drawers, or Chester Drawers as he used to call it, is a pot of polyestered flowers that look like a sweetbay magnolia.

"C.B., do you remember some seventy-five years ago when we took the seeds out of a sweetbay cone? We took them to Granna to try to fool her. You told her that Auntay had sent them to her and they were a new cross between a pumpkin and a watermelon. She had us plant them where we could all watch over them. We thought we'd really pulled one over on her, until we discovered she'd outfoxed us by going back and replacing what we'd planted with some gourd seeds." I pause with a sigh. "They don't make Grannas like they used to—or Auntays either. I'd say we were blessed by some pretty good upbringing…if not motivated by it."

C.B.'s eyelids drop like a couple of fall leaves.

"Don't quit listening on me now. Where'd you learn your manners? Alongside a logging road somewhere?" I give his knee a shake. "Hey, if you're not going to say anything more than ah…ee…ee, you can at least stay awake long enough to hold up your end of my discussion by paying better attention."

A young nurse's aid with a blurry nametag comes in. "He's asleep," she says.

"No, no, he does a kind of playing 'possum," I inform her. "We call it selective listening. When I say something profound, he'll be there for me."

She ignores my witty wisdom and vast experience to go about her own business, waking C.B. enough to help him take a pill. I try again to make out her name but can't. It seems as if they would make nametags with large enough writing so people could read them. If Granna was right about there being some good in everything, I guess the good thing about old age eyesight is that dyslexia doesn't bother me as much as it used to. I'm still trying to figure out what could have been good about dyslexia.

"How you, Mr. Scott?" the aide asks, surprising me by calling me by name. "It's good you visitin' yo' friend so reg'lar. Most folks would find one of they own kind to spend so much time with. You know what I'm sayin'?"

"Well, there's a lot you could learn about friendship from us," I answer.

"Yeah, Mr. Scott. You right."

I move my left leg at a different angle to try to find some comfort.

She continues, "You somethin' else—a white man being such a good friend to a black man." She pats me on my shoulder and goes to the other bed in the room.

Loud enough for her to hear, I say, "C.B., you and I could pass on what we know to young folks like her if they had the patience to listen. All they'd have to do is take the time, but they won't. On the other hand, if they decided to listen to us, they probably wouldn't hear what we were really saying…not in a hundred years."

She walks out of the room smiling as if I'm an old fool.

"I guess it's a good thing we've got our memories to fall back on. If we can't share with others, we can always recall wily ways of long gone days for our own enjoyment. I'll bet nobody else around here has ever seen the river otters sliding down a Taylor Creek bank and climbing back up to the top just to do it again. I'd say no one here but you and me have sucked the wintergreen taste out of a north Alabama black birch twig to tame bad breath that was caused by eating a smoked mud-puppy supper out of Brushy Creek. People here probably haven't even heard a gray fox wailing its mating call in the spring of the year…or listened to the owls laughing at two in the morning on a Little Tallahatchie River bottom camp-out."

Everything about C.B. has mellowed since his early days here. As both physical and mental conditions have gradually worsened, even his old "ah…ee…ee" doesn't have the same "ee…ee" in it that it once had. A little more life has withered away every time I see him. Maybe he has learned to deal with the frustration. He always could adapt better than anyone I've ever known. He drops off to a snore that puts me into a doze of my own. I wake and find C.B. sitting there with his customary stare. I hope it's one of memory and not thoughtlessness.

"I wonder what's for lunch, buddy. A little Mississippi round steak would be all right, wouldn't it? Next time I come for a visit, I think I'll slip you another cold beer in here. How would you like that?"

For a moment I think I can almost see a smile in his eyes, but they cloud over. They could give him a beer like a daily vitamin if they really cared about his quality of life. I'm convinced it's the nothingness of nursing homes that finally kills folks to death. I think they just get tired of living like this. I shift my sitting position to try and find some comfort. There are too many aches and pains to come up with much more than temporary relief.

"You know, with the exception of that time Uncle Sam made such a stupid choice for you, I'd say you've used you own reasoning and made your own choices. That oughta count for something. It's good to have influenced your own life."

C.B. coughs and his breath becomes short and raspy.

"Look outside. A blizzard's coming through, right here in the middle of duck and goose season. What more could these young folks want? I guess you wish we were out there in it, huh? On the river, cold and miserable, our fingers so numb we'd be playing pocket pool just to keep everything warmed up...and all that intense waiting just to see something with cupped wings come gliding in from no telling where?"

"Ah...ee," comes a weak response.

"Yep, me too."

C.B. drools and coughs. I open the drawer of his nightstand to look for some Kleenex. Instead of tissue, a Gideon Bible finds my hand. Remembering how Papa and a certain Cuban inspector did to me, I hold up The Book and shake it at C.B.

"Look here, my old friend, you reckon somebody up there is trying to tell us something?" I wipe his mouth and chin with my handkerchief. "With time running shorter and shorter, we both might oughta try to appreciate the values of The Word. Think about it. Would you expect Papa and Granna and Dad and Auntay, all four to have been wrong in their believing?"

C.B. looks at me with an unusual awareness that I haven't seen from him in a long time. Before the moment passes, I feel the need to tell him my deep-down thoughts about a lifelong friendship.

"C.B.," I can't keep my voice from quavering, "If we do make it to heaven, you and I know it'll be by the skin of our teeth. If we don't get there, what I want to say is—to share life with such a good friend as you, I've already been blessed more than I deserved…up one side and down the other."

I watch him go from very still to having his body making little jerks. I call a nurse. When she gets him out of his chair and back to bed, he's quiet, but his eyes don't look right. She leaves to answer a call for help across the hall. C.B. begins taking short and fast shallow breaths. Then there are long intervals between them. I know he is letting go of life.

"Just imagine, C.B., how good things will be in that forever afterlife…with no messed up rivers and plenty of game and fish and wildlife to just watch."

He has a sudden, long drawn-out breath that almost stops my own. Then silence. Another gasp, a long shuddering breath, and no more. With a strange mix of grief and peace, I decide this is a time he needs only me to be with him. There is no reason for calling the nurse right now.

I take his hand in mine and whisper softly, "Goodbye, Charlie Boy, my old friend."

Tears fall down my cheeks. My throat has a dry ache. I can't breathe deep enough for myself, but reach for a prayer:

"Lord, please let him enter Your eternal forest. He believed You let Your Son, Jesus, die to be his Savior…even after You let his son, Scott, die too. Grant him this, God…please."

After a shaky moment, I push the call bell. A nurse I think I know comes in. She looks at C.B. and checks his pulse. I look at the large black woman and think of Auntay in her younger days.

Gently, she takes my hand away from C.B.'s and speaks in a soft voice, "Come on now, Mr. Scott. Yo' friend has passed. He's in a better place now."

"Thank you, ma'am." I'm trying hard to hold myself together.

"Let's go to your room, now."

"I'm just visiting here, Lady." I brush off her helping hand and wipe my tears on my sleeve. "Just visiting my friend. I don't live here, but I will be needing to get on home," I explain.

"That's right, and I knew that," she answers and pulls on my arm. "I'll just walk along with you." She's wide and strong and gives me a lift to help me stand.

"Thank you, Miss Belle."

"Miss Who?" she asks.

"Huh?"

"Never mind, Mr. Scott. You right. Now just come on and we'll walk down the hall together."

Arm in arm, we putter along and make our way around a corner. Her voice is soft and comforting. As we pass the large lobby, someone else I don't know calls my name. It doesn't surprise me that I'm known here. I've been visiting my friend at Go for more years than anyone here besides C.B. has been a resident.

"You gon' be all right, Mr. Scott," my escort assures me.

I'm hoping she's right about that because I'm trembly all over and have a deep hurting inside.

"You jus' need some rest." She leads me into a room.

"Let's set for a spell, Mr. Scott. I know you tired and here's a nice chair."

She eases me into a chair that fits like my old catcher's mitt. Seeing no incentive to be my usually rebellious self, I figure it won't hurt to sit for a minute.

"All right," I tell her. "I'll stay for a bit, but then I've got to go."

"Okay," she agrees.

"And I won't be coming back here, ma'am, not with my friend now standing with the tall cypress in wetland flowers. He's right in amongst their natural colors and good smells."

She pats my shoulder again.

"That's all right, Mr. Scott." She blows her nose. "Now, you jus' set here and rest."

I am tired. I think I'll close my eyes and rest for just a minute, if she'll go use the phone for me. I drift into sleep…and see a seven-year-old boy running across the gravel parking lot toward the Mansion restaurant. With his little black fists full of my marbles, he looks back over his shoulder. His grin goes from one of his big ears to the other.

"I'll be right back with something to help you relax," the nurse says, not realizing she was waking me.

"No, no, I've got to go," I remind her. "You'll need to call me a taxi, please…and be sure and ask for Munford."

— The End —

Give the Gift of

Yocona Puff Adder

to Your Friends and Colleagues

CHECK YOUR LEADING BOOKSTORE OR ORDER HERE

❑ **YES**, I want _____ copies of Yocona Puff Adder at $27.95 each, plus $3.95 shipping per book (Ohio residents please add $2.03 sales tax per book). Canadian orders must be accompanied by a postal money order in U.S. funds. Allow 15 days for delivery.

My check or money order for $_____ is enclosed.

Please charge my: ❑ Visa   ❑ MasterCard
                      ❑ Discover   ❑ American Express

Name _____

Organization _____

Address _____

City/State/Zip _____

Phone_____   Email _____

Card # _____

Exp. Date_____   Signature _____

Order online at www.yoconapuffadder.com

Or make your check payable and return to:
BookMasters, Inc.
30 Amberwood Parkway • Ashland, OH 44805

Call your credit card order to (800) 247-6553
Fax (419) 281-6883